MEIN GUSTAV

MEIN GUSTAV

Ira Campbell

To order additional copies of this book, contact:
Xlibris
1-888-795-4274
www.Xlibris.com
Orders@Xlibris.com
793481

ACKNOWLEDGEMENTS

Nothing is accomplished alone. In this case, yes, I did all the writing. But others were involved and they deserve mention. My wife, Paula, suggested the whole idea and encouraged me to continue with it, showing incredible support the whole way through. My parents planted the seeds of my WWI aviation interest with a tiny Fokker triplane model kit at age four, getting me to watch "The Blue Max" (arguably a horrible movie, but due to the flying scenes and accompanying soundtrack still my favorite) and read Captain Eddie Rickenbacker's serialized "autobiography" in my father's magazine. They included the Rhinebeck Aerodrome's Saturday WWI airshow in a family vacation. Numerous aviation authors and illustrators contributed to my accumulating knowledge and insatiable interest. Some of these folks have become friends. Another friend from high school, "lost" over time and rediscovered on a recent vacation, offered to read the nearly finished manuscript and then supplied glowing feedback and encouragement. (She can't wait for my next book!) Yet another friend took it upon himself to "fact check" my story, looking for terms that were not available during the time I was writing about. Whether this story becomes a blockbuster feature film or fizzles and goes away, I am in their debt. They have opened my eyes to a whole new avenue of expression. I have more stories to write.

ORIGIN

Life is wonderful and full of surprises. One night, out shopping with my wife, she stated, "You need to write a book. You know more about World War One aviation than anyone on the planet." (A gross exaggeration, but I have been reading and studying the topic for practically my entire life.) To continue: "You need to put that knowledge to work. Write a book. But not about a plane, pilot, unit, or air battle. That has been done. Make up some characters and put them into those circumstances. Write a World War One novel."

Ahh, she meant a historical fiction. I do not see myself as a novelist. I thought about it for a few days, saddled up the iMac, and wrote my opening scene. Then I wrote some more. And more. Hmm, it needed something. I started my German story. As I came up with ideas, I worked on the appropriate story until both were done to my satisfaction. I read each story, edited, and made adjustments. Then I wrestled the two beasts into one piece of literature. Several times.

About a year later, I told my wife I was done. "Done? Done with what?"

"My book."

"You gave up?" "I finished."

She was in disbelief.

This makes it seem fairly simple. But I have only been published previously in a historical context. There were hiccups. There were dry spells. There was frustration. There were days when my fingers could not keep up with the flow of ideas. There were tears, laughter, and a jump-in-the-air, fist pumping moment (once my fingers caught up with that idea racing through my head).

What follows is my book. I do hope you find some enjoyment in it. I tried to keep the technical information to the minimum I thought necessary to understand the story. If you, the reader, need further technical information, there are many sources. I would be happy to point to some. It is a fascinating topic, a "War to end all wars" fought a century ago, during which aviation, a diversion for the wealthy at the outset, flourished and became a practical form of transportation and showed signs of becoming a fearsome weapon.

Immediately following the story is a list of translations of German words and terms to English. If you are reading a physical book, find something to stick there. The entries are roughly in order of appearance in the text. If you are reading an ebook, perhaps you can print out the pages to refer to. Or maybe you can jam a digital thumb there and refer back to it. I merely wanted to add some "flavor" to the German story.

Thank you for choosing to enter my fictional world. There will be more.

CHAPTER I

British In the sky over France

"Shit."

I felt and heard that familiar zip-crack sound of bullets whizzing by my head and hitting my aeroplane. The port lower plane showed a few new holes. Geoff would not be happy with me. He was fortunate enough to patch the holes I collected, and swarms of Huns gave him plenty to do. Now, where did those bullets come from? I looked around.

It was a picture perfect day, a wonderful day to be up flying and cavorting among the clouds. The bright blue of the sky could not help but lift one's spirits as one took it all in, the blue getting deeper as one looked further up. There was a bank of clouds off to the east a bit and little puffs of cloud trailed off to the west-southwest, toward our aerodrome. Looking below, one saw the familiar brown-green patchwork of the landscape, increasingly brown after three years of war. There were no real landmarks any more, save roads and railroads and the doubled jagged line of trenches marking the front lines. Nonetheless, it was a great feeling to be up among the clouds in my SE. Strong V-8 engine, responsive controls, wouldn't it be fun to roll and loop among the— *there he goes!*

I spotted that Hun bugger who had just holed my wing, only just missing my head. The sun flashed off his wings as he banked around a cloud a thousand feet or so below and behind me. Odd, it looked smaller and different from anything I had seen before. Rather than the usual drab greens and mauves, it shone a silver or blue. No matter. The buggers were widely known for painting up their crates such that they really showed against the green-brown earth below. I supposed they were too good to fly simple camouflaged aeroplanes like our SEs and Nieuports. Well, okay then, whatever color it was, my opponent would look a little better with a flash of flame and a trail of smoke to mark it's path to destruction. I checked that my guns were ready, kicked

1

the rudder a little and pulled the stick back. The SE suddenly lurched upward, back, and dropped a wing as I settled into a dive after that flash of blue. Or silver. Or whatever it was. I was hungry and I wanted an early lunch of Boche.

I simply loved the SE. Officially the Royal Aircraft Factory Scout Experimental, fifth model modified, or SE5a, it was among the new Allied aeroplanes wresting the skies back from the Germans. Without hesitation it went into precisely the dive I wanted. Around the cloud we went, my head swiveling in search of my next victim. He was nowhere to be seen. Perhaps he continued earthward . . . .

"Shit!"

Gunfire. Close gunfire. Very close! The bullets pierced the lower wing closer to the fuselage and, in turn, me—after passing through the port upper plane! There came that nasty bugger again, vertically from above. It was like a dark cloud about to swallow me on the way down, the deep yellow nose within a hundred feet or so, and diving over me to port as I threw my stick to starboard to avoid a collision. Everything still in order, I pulled around in a tight diving turn to where he should have been, but nothing. He was nowhere to be found. I shan't soon forget that encounter, the flat, yellow nose over his rotary engine, so different from the shark-like Albatross fighters we had been looking at since before I arrived at the front several weeks ago as a new scout pilot. But it had markings on it—a face? It certainly looked like a mustache above the propeller boss. Odd. I wondered how that would look on my drab SE. No, never. It would never pass muster in the RFC. Little white geometric unit markings, a number or letter, and that's all they would allow. I supposed the blue. white, and red cockades showing our British identity were all the colors my SE would ever show.

"Where *is* this bloke?"

I was beneath the clouds, and there was nothing below me but the German held ground that was once France. My opponent was nowhere to be found. Indeed, this was exactly how *not* to collect a Boche before lunch.

Height is everything in aerial combat. The ideal is to be above your prey, dive down upon it, fire your guns into it, and keep going so they have no chance to fire back. Once out of range, one could climb above and set up another dive, if possible. So I had to get back up there in case this one was hiding among the clouds. I started back up among the clouds, my head constantly swiveling in an effort to catch a glimpse of my shiny, mustachioed, green nosed blue "friend". I was hungry, and a freshly killed Hun would sate my appetite. I had put a few rounds into enemy aircraft, yes. Even a "sausage"—that's what we called the German observation balloons. They floated these things above the back areas with men in a basket suspended beneath. The men looked over the lines for changes in our gun emplacements, ground troops, supply convoys, fresh troops. Or they monitored their own artillery fire, calling corrections by handset to the officers below to be forwarded to the gun unit. Anyway, though I had put a few rounds into German equipment here and there, as a pilot I had had no telling results. So I was very, very hungry for a good, clean kill. A mustache on it would make it all the better.

"SHIT!"

Erupting from the cloud to my right, here was my Boche, mustache and all! I ducked my head in an effort to avoid him, he was so close! I swear, his wheel nearly hit my head! He roared by, left hand extended in a wave or salute, I don't know which, and he snapped through a steep climb into a loop. At the top of the loop he effected a half roll, righting his craft and flying away to the east. He was obviously out of ammunition, or perhaps his guns had jammed, but I suppose he could not resist scaring me half to death by showing me how completely vulnerable I was in my efforts to look for him, much less fight him.

How does one sweat several thousand feet in the air? Though it was summer, the temperature at altitude was frigid. It was incongruous to watch pilots dressed in many layers of clothing climbing into their mounts in sweltering heat. But any time at all in the freezing temperatures invited frostbite. With all this in mind, I was mopping my brow. Or trying to, at any rate. My new German acquaintance had made quite the impression. Frankly, I was damned lucky to be alive. Vulnerable? Hell . . . .

It was my first good look at this new type of aeroplane. There were rumors. Always rumors. Some said there were captured Sopwith triplanes being flown against us. After my pre-lunch encounter, I could dispel those rumors. This was no Sopwith. It did, however, have three wings. Four, if one counted the tiny wing between the wheels. It was indeed blue, a vivid sky blue, with a deep green nose and "scratches" of deep green all over the top surfaces leaving much blue, and the standard black iron crosses stood out against squares of white. Oh, could it climb, though! I thought I had something with my SE, but that little bugger had out-climbed me handily. I figured attempting to scrap with one would be a bad idea. I made a note that diving from above and continuing past seemed the smart tactic should one have the opportunity to choose. Mine would be the interesting report.

But I needed to return to the aerodrome before I composed my report. Off to the west- southwest I flew, into the constant winds. No wonder we lost so many Brits in combat. If one was not mindful of the prevailing winds, one would be blown over Germany itself! It was always a struggle getting "home" through those winds. One often prayed to God to get home while climbing closer to Heaven. In the event one ran out of petrol or one's engine quit, that extra altitude could enable one to make it past the front lines. Fortunately I had enough fuel, and the Viper engine felt just fine. I merely had a dozen or so holes in the port wings, surely enough to put Geoff into a foul mood for the day. But if not for working on my SE, what would he do? Sit around staring at that photo of the young lass posing on the beach in the latest swimwear and daring to expose her ankle—and more? I was almost happy to have holed wings. Anything to give that rapscallion something worthwhile to occupy his mind.

With plenty of petrol, I had been climbing. As I saw it, there were two ways to cross the lines. One was to fly high and present a tiny target for the "Archie"—anti-aircraft guns. The other was to stay low to the ground and barrel through as quickly as the wide-open engine would pull in an effort to get by before anyone had time to train his gun on you. I found the high road preferable whenever possible. It would be one damn lucky shot that climbed to that great height and guessed your velocity. Besides, going in low and fast simply invited everyone to shoot at you— German *and* British. And the Yanks. There were more and more of the Americans arriving, some of whom were even trained to fight. But when something came buzzing above, it was only natural to pick up one's rifle and have a go at it. We had an American in the squadron. Oh, he was *it*. He was the one who was going to shoot down the entire German Air Service and make the skies over France safe once again. It must have been his name. Wellington. A century ago a Wellington liberated Europe from Napoleon, and this college lad was going to duplicate the effort. Oh, and he was confident. Cocky. There was no doubting him. We figured we would see how he felt in a week or two, once he learned the area and actually flew an offensive patrol. The ground crews had a betting pool on just when this Yank would fail to return. I so wanted to bet on his third patrol, but that one was taken. My money was on his fifteenth patrol, but he likely would not live long enough to fly it. We had a steady flow of replacement pilots. Mostly it was because so many men—lads, actually—failed to return from a patrol. The ones who did consistently return and accumulate experience were often transferred to other units as flight leaders or back to Home Establishment to train some of these replacements. Maybe, oh maybe they could pass along the benefits of their experience. This was not easy. Maybe, with these new SEs, we thought we could finally take the war to the Germans and their aging Albatross types, clear the skies of them, and make it back over the lines to celebrate our achievements. Especially Wellington. May he have a hundred kills. And may I have one hundred and twenty. Huh.

Having sighted my aerodrome, I began my descent. No Archie was close enough for concern, just as I had hoped. All looked quiet over the field and the windsock, as per usual, swelled moderately to the east, so I descended into the landing pattern and circled once before going in. I certainly hoped they had filled in the shell holes from last night. Especially that one near the center of the field. Avoiding that made the takeoff or landing run shorter and more treacherous. It was already a foolhardy proposition, dropping an aeroplane onto the perpetually muddy field at nearly one hundred miles per hour without brakes, letting it roll several hundred feet, and allowing several brave chaps to catch you and point you toward the line of sheds and tents so your ground crew could fuel, arm, and repair your crate for the next flight. Madness, I swear.

I lined up the SE, set it down, and it of course slid off toward the half-fixed shell hole in the middle of the field. I held my speed enough to kick the rudder a little, hoping to avoid crashing into the hole. I sloshed through the mud and missed the hole, but it was not a pretty sight. Not at all. I kicked right, and the SE leaned left. The port lower wingtip dipped, caught some mud, and that set me skidding back to the left. By that point, the hole was behind me. I gently corrected and headed toward my brave handlers. They took hold of my wingtips and swung me around in the proper direction, and I gunned the Viper, taxiing up to my hangar tent. First to come out, naturally, was Geoff, who let loose a burst of profanity upon seeing what I had done to his port wings. Engine running, I heard not a word, but I caught the scowl and watched his mouth form the usual sequence. Poor fellow. Time away from his tattering picture of ankle. And calf. Well, a little calf. Scandalous.

Ladders appeared on either side of the cockpit and a couple of lads climbed up to undo my seat harness and help me out of the crate. Other pilots and that Yank Wellington stood off a little and watched my hands. They wanted to see if I held up any fingers, indicating success in our field of battle. Sorry, mates, not this time. One of the lads steadied the ladder while I clambered down in my heavily lined flying suit. Though it was late summer, it did not feel the part in an open aeroplane at around ten thousand feet. Feeling the warmth, I tugged open the zipper of my suit. Just as I noticed it, the lad at my side puckered his face and asked, "What's that smell?" I tried to get away but there were simply too many bodies between me and my quarters. Oh, but I was desperate to get away and tend to the now urgent matter. The lad announced my misfortune to the squadron. And anyone else within earshot. "You shat yourself! Aye, 'e shat 'imself!" And I was surrounded by seeming hordes of blokes, one hand holding their nose and the other pounding me on the back. I felt so small. I almost wished I had hit that hole. It was going to be a while before I stopped hearing about that one.

The next few days saw no flying. Though I spent some time with my SE and ground crew, I did not have a good look at her. She was in the tent with engine panels off while the engine was being worked on. A motor-car racing enthusiast before the war, I always wanted to apply what I knew about motor-cars to my SE's engine. It seemed sensible to me that if the engine ran well I would stand a better chance of returning from a flight. In a similar line of thinking, I liked to check my gun cartridges. I found a template for the correct bullet diameter, and whenever I could I would place each round into the template. I rejected anything that was too large. If it would not fit the template easily, it would likely stick in the gun and cause a jam which would leave that gun useless against the enemy. Same for a round that was too small. I knew the circumstances surrounding my posting to a front line fighter unit. My odds for survival were not favorable, so I wanted to do everything I could to beat the odds. I wanted to fly home—or at least sail—rather than be shipped home in a box.

On two of the mornings I took a break from my SE and visited the lad who had announced my involuntary defecation to the aerodrome. Though I had been upset with him at the time, I realized any one of us would have done the very same given similar circumstances. We were all young lads, many of us away from home for the first time, and we were fighting a war. And while he was a simple lad from a farming village and meant no harm, he had offended a soldier of superior rank, something not tolerated in British military protocol. He had been instructed to fill in a latrine trench, using the dirt—well, mud—from digging a new latrine trench. I felt bad for him and took him tea. He appreciated the gesture and we conversed while he dug one trench to fill another. I told him I was unhappy with how he had been treated, but he responded that with no flying he had nothing better to do. It helped him pass the time. He was a fine lad with a solid positive attitude and I made sure the major was aware of it.

Finally we were scheduled for a morning offensive patrol. Morning patrols were very early morning. We were up before the sun, taking off into the mist at the very earliest light. Again, I did not have a good look at my SE even though I checked everything that could affect my flight. Propeller, control surfaces, control surface response to stick and rudder bar motion. If I was not in the air, I could make time to check my aeroplane.

We went up in pairs, six of us total, climbing to our assigned altitude. We did not cover much distance while climbing, but height was far more important than distance. The way things had been for the prior three years, the front lines were not likely to move much overnight. Anything short of a major offensive would not move them at all. We wanted to be above any German aircraft we might encounter. Ideally, we would be above and to the east of them. That way we could hide in the sun and be less visible to the pilots even as we initiated our attacks. We were happy to let our ammunition be our calling card, making the Germans aware of us for the last time. Hopefully.

Sunrises were wonderful, beautiful events. Combat flying did have it's privileges. The light slowly but perceptibly changed from nil to black to indigo to deep grey-violet to dark blue, and on until the sky was orange and then yellow in appearance. It took a good eye to spot enemy aerial activity in these conditions. Even with their gaudy colors, the aeroplanes did not stand out in the low light or glare. Sometimes we waited above a German aerodrome, watching for activity. Heavy squinting was sometimes rewarded by a little white puff of smoke as an engine sputtered to life. Maybe one pilot would see the motion of a takeoff. While we saw nothing, we sometimes switched off our engines to save petrol and extend the flight. It wasn't much, but it helped.

As the light almost imperceptibly increased, we spotted two aircraft rolling out for takeoff. We waited for the signal from our flight leader, but the two turned east and flew toward the German rear area. They were not worth the dive from nineteen thousand feet or so. We waited. It was bitterly cold despite the layers of clothing we wore. When dressed for flying, we looked like a collection of large, rotund creatures from who knows where. The Michelin Man was slim and trim next to us. I swear no two of us dressed alike. Everyone had their own ideas on how to stay warm. Surprisingly, the Royal Flying Corps had no objection, as long as our aeroplanes were green-brown with but small markings on them. At least they looked alike.

Alas our little band had no ragtime to play that morning. No German dance partners in our sector of the front, so after an hour or so of trying to stay warm we headed for home. After crossing the lines at altitude we descended toward our field. Thankfully somebody had found the time to fill in the shell holes and run lorries and equipment over the patches so we would not find a soft spot. Well, at least nothing softer than the surrounding terrain, for whatever that was worth. Everybody had arrived home safely and together. For once there had been no engine troubles with the geared Hisso SEs. The stronger Hispano Suiza engine was geared down to a proper propeller speed, and that gearbox was a constant headache for the ground crews. We learned that the French and British SPAD XIII units had the same problems—these units refused to turn in their older direct drive SPAD VIIs so they would have something to fly when the geared Hissos acted up, which was often. Fortunately some of our SEs had the more reliable direct drive Wolseley Viper engines.

I landed fifth. Everything went as it should have. I set it down, throttled back, let the tail touch down, and I rolled toward the next pair of handlers. As they caught me, first one and then the other lad began laughing. I thought that seriously odd. We had faced no Germans, so there was nothing wrong with my SE. What were they laughing about? I had no clue. They swung me around toward my tent and I gunned my engine to keep taxiing. Strange. As I progressed toward my spot, men began laughing and pointing at me. What was the matter? I dressed no differently than normal, just a large, filthy, oily Michelin Man barely fitting into my cockpit. No silly hat, nothing out of the ordinary. Could it be my SE? How? It was the usual green-brown with regulation blue-white-red national markings, the newly changed geometric squadron identification marking, and the letter "P" in white on the fuselage sides and port upper plane— and black on the starboard lower plane's linen undersurface.

Some of the men, apparently with nothing important to do, followed me to my spot. Others came from the opposite direction once they saw the chaos. As two ground crew chocked my wheels in place, two lads brought ladders and helped me out of the SE, just like always. But they, too, were laughing! What was so funny?

As I stepped onto the ground, I saw it. There was something different at the port front lower corner of the fuselage, something white. As quickly as the layers of clothing would permit, I waddled around the wingtip and approached the nose of my SE. There it was. Damn! Someone had painted the area underneath the exhaust manifold white . On it was a decent rendition of an avian wing, within which were the words, "DIRTY BIRD". Bastard! Someone had decided to memorialize my recent meeting with that little blue triplane with the mustache! Oh, how cold and cunning! How was I ever to live this down with a badge on the nose? I walked around to the starboard side, only to find a very similar moniker applied in almost the same position as the first. Did I need to check the "tail feathers" of my SE, just in case? The major was going to hear about this! There is no excuse for such behavior! I decided to seek him out right then and there so the responsible person could be—wait. There's the major. He is looking over the nose of my SE. And laughing. Laughing! Bugger! "Dirty Bird". Indeed. The indignity. I can see the papers. "Dirty Bird Gets Fifth Aerial Conquest." "Dirty Bird Awarded Distinguished Flying Cross." "Dirty Bird Downs Red Baron." For once I am pleased that if they even print anything about aerial victories it is in the back of the newspaper between ads for dry goods, sundry stores, and scores for American baseball! I must find a way to down another German airman in my SE. Short of dying, transferring out as another unit's flight leader will be the fastest way to leave "Dirty Bird" behind. Maybe.

For the next week or more, every time I was to fly, I was told to fly in the aft position, "bringing up the rear". I grew weary of any joke or comment about buttocks or fecal matter. At first I asked the men— men? children!—to put themselves in my position, an enemy aeroplane trained on their head at full throttle, coming out of nowhere. But they would only answer with guttural noises suggesting a bowel movement while flapping their bent arms, looking like big dodo birds. So I spent a lot of time alone or working on my SE. After an initial smirk the fitters had the decency to keep their distance, though I was certain one of them was the bugger with the artist's thumb.

To find something positive about my new moniker, I noted that it appeared to boost squadron morale. We had lost three pilots in the week or two after my encounter, a lef-tenant and two raw replacements. The lef-tenant didn't stand a chance. He found himself surrounded by what looked to be a complete German squadron. It looked like ants around a morsel of food, just endless attacks until his SE could no longer fly. Anyone trying to intervene only invited similar attention. I watched one replacement get killed. From my aft position, I saw that he was not paying enough attention to his surroundings. He didn't look around. He looked like he was pondering his next two dimensional chess move. They say it's the Hun you don't see that gets you. Poor bastard never saw it coming. Several Albatrosses dove out of the sun. The rest of us scattered, but he never wavered from straight and level. His SE continued flying roughly northeast for a while, then his starboard wings began to drop a little, and he gracefully descended to a vertical dive. Just before he hit the forest floor, his wings folded back on the fuselage. He probably caught a bullet in the head and never knew he was in a dive, never felt a thing upon hitting the ground. Probably a good way to go. I was not up when the other replacement bought it. I heard he became separated from the other five and never returned. He was considered as "missing" unless we somehow obtained word or evidence otherwise. Someone would gather his possessions into a box, and the major would write the letter no parent wanted to receive.

We often spent our rainy days talking about flying and posing "what if" questions to one another. One frequent topic of discussion was fire. "What would you do if your 'plane caught fire?" That was the situation no pilot wanted to find himself in. The discussion would inevitably boil down to two choices: stay or jump. If one stayed, maybe the fire would go out. Maybe the pilot could find a clever maneuver to keep the fire away from himself, all whilst trying to pass over the lines and make it to friendly territory. Sideslip or some fancy maneuver was unlikely to happen in the skies over France, however. So some pilots swore they would jump and endure the fall and impact rather than roast alive. There were no other options. Some of us had seen men jump out of their observation balloon baskets and float to earth under a parachute. That looked like a perfectly fine idea to us pilots. We asked the major about them and he told us the official policy: pilots with parachutes were more likely to jump out of their aeroplane at the first sign of trouble, thus wasting a perfectly good piece of His Majesty's property. Aeroplanes were not cheap. We couldn't abandon them merely because something "sounded funny". Imagine the chaos. Some of our pilots had never heard an internal combustion engine before they enlisted for military service. What did they know about an engine "sounding funny"? No parachutes. Carry on.

Stiff upper lip.

We flew as much as the weather would permit, and we worked on our aeroplanes when the weather had other ideas. I was still mostly assigned the aft position. I was often addressed as "Dirty Bird" or I would be greeted by boys with their thumbs under their arms, elbows flapping like pathetic flightless birds, and mouths emitting horrible squawking noises. I would mutter under my breath, "bugger off then", and keep about my business. Let the children play.

One morning started with fog. We dared not fly in fog. One could see nothing. Oh, there were pilots who could fly at night, but they had gone through special training involving extra instruments to compensate for lack of vision—and electric lights to illuminate them in the air as well as flares for landing. None of them were in our squadron. No training. No extra instruments. True, some pilots worked with a telescopic sight for their guns, but that did no good if the sky was too thick to see or fly through. With fog, we assumed we would not be flying that day, but the major changed all that. We were to have our SEs fueled, armed, and ready to fly as soon as the fog lifted. So we helped our fitters push the SEs out of the tents and onto the flight line. There, the ground crew saw to fuel, oil, and armament. We helped with inspecting the warplanes and making sure all was at the ready. Then we waited. More talk about "what if". More listening to records on the gramophone. More lying around looking at worn photos of sweethearts back home. Geoff sighed as he looked at all that leg his "special friend" was displaying in that torn out bathing suit picture. That Yank, Wellington, would talk to anyone who would listen about how he was going to score more than Hawker or Ball. He was going to be famous. He would be the talk of the town across Great Britain, France, and the United States. To note, he would never participate in those talks about fire in the air. He said it was defeatist talk and wanted no part of it. I suggested that maybe he had a way to put out fires or even prevent them in the first place. He ignored me, reciting the names of German airmen he intended to shoot down along that blazing path to glory. To wit, he had yet to make a claim, much less receive credit for an enemy machine downed. But he carried on, undeterred by the facts.

Somewhere in the middle of all that activity, or lack thereof, we thought we heard a gun firing at or near the downwind end of our aerodrome. Someone came running our way, screaming something. He nearly fell into our slit trench where we dove in the event we were attacked. Upon hearing what the man was screaming at us, many dove into the trench. "The Huns are here! We're being attacked!" Apparently the fog had burned off east of the front lines. We looked downwind and there they were, over a dozen of them. They looked like a swarm of insects about to attack. Black at first, as they drew near, we could see that particular shade of sky blue under the wings characteristic of Albatrosses. Anybody who could still see them any closer remembered seeing many other colors on the attacking aeroplanes. Stripes here, colored tail planes there, some with pictures or symbols along their sides, they looked like colorful dragonflies bent on destroying their prey. The SEs were in plain sight, out in the open, in an irregular line roughly paralleling the tents, fully fueled and armed. They were fat, helpless, and completely vulnerable to attack. As the second SE from the far end exploded, we heard a Viper roaring. I peeked out of the trench as the SE marked "W" cleared the flight line and turned upwind. It was Wellington! That foolhardy Yank! He didn't stand a chance! We cheered his nerve and watched his progress. His tail came up, he wove a little side to side, and he lifted off the soft earthen field. Seconds later, the SE almost stopped in the air. The nose jerked up just a little as the port wing dropped. We heard the engine rev hard as the nose dropped a little, but we all felt a little sick because we knew he had lost the airspeed necessary to create lift. It was over. To his credit, Wellington dropped his nose and tried to gather all the speed he could, keeping it pointed into the wind. The annoying lad did know what he was doing. But it wasn't enough. The port wing dropped again and contacted the ground, sending the SE into a fabulous cartwheel a little to the left and out of sight. We dared not chase after him while we were under fire.

The jewel-toned attackers set up their pattern around the field, firing on their upwind leg, circling about downwind, and lining up for another firing run. A few pilots dropped grenades, some of which blew up SEs. Others exploded harmlessly in the middle of the landing strip. Harmless, that is, until one had to roll around the craters on takeoff!

After a few short, intense moments it was all over. Some men remained at the field to put out fires and save what they could. Some of us with no specific responsibilities raced upwind to find Wellington's crashed SE. As I arrived at the crash site, they were laying him out near the remnants of the fuselage. It didn't look good. But he raised an arm to point at something and I heard some men talking to him. I didn't know how badly he had been beaten up, but he was alive to tell the tale. I could see his face was a mess, no doubt having hit the front of the cockpit opening. The stuffed leather padding was a thoughtful notion, but it was not very forgiving in a crash. As they pulled away his flight clothing, I could see his right shoulder was soaked in blood. He must have been hit as he climbed out from the field, the impact jerking his arm and pulling up his SE's nose. Despite his efforts, though, gravity took over. Wellington was taken away to a field hospital, where he would likely mend and fly again. The same could not be said for his SE. I did have to chuckle at an irony, however. That foolhardy, brave effort by Wellington amounted to his fourth offensive patrol, in a manner of speaking. Surprisingly, no one had picked that in the squadron pool. Not to worry, however, as the money would go toward keeping the unit stocked with "spirits".

As we turned to leave the scene, a mechanic appealed to us to help, even if just a little. So each of us carried some part of the 'plane back to the flight line. One never knew when a replacement aileron or something would be needed to keep another SE flying. The repair depot would never be able to rebuild this one, so we salvaged what we could.

We had already had a busy morning. We dodged the Huns' visit with but a few casualties. Surprisingly, nobody was killed. Several others joined Wellington, making the slow journey to hospital in the back of a lorry. We did not envy them. They had been shot or otherwise wounded, and then they had to endure the badly rutted roads in the anything-but-comfortable army transport which had hauled hogs before the war.

A few of us took a break from cleaning up after the Huns to join the major for a cup of coffee. Obviously, we wanted to know more about Wellington and his condition. The major told us what he knew, which was mostly what we saw. Wellington had caught a bullet in the shoulder and suffered at least one broken bone. He had lost a lot of blood. Smashing his face on impact with the ground did not help matters. His neck was sore from his head whipping about amidst the impromptu carousel, as were his arms. We did not expect to see him back at our squadron any time soon, if ever. We learnt that someone had shot down an Albatross, probably one of the many rifles, pistols, or machine guns pointing into the air since Wellington never got off a shot. No one knew who got the Albatross, but it was seen to crash, burn, and explode. The pilot was dead when the first men got to him. The major decided to claim the Albatross as Wellington's. It could be done. A lot of weapons shot the same round as the Lewis or Vickers guns carried on the SE. In all that confusion, who could say what flew past Wellington's nose during his brief flight? So the major "lost" the armorer's report and asked for a "new" one, which was included with his claim. Though no one particularly liked Wellington, he had found a way to fight back at the attackers when no one else could. He made the effort. He attempted. He bragged about shooting down the entire German air service, so we agreed to give him the first of those many. He deserved that. Besides, when he learned about his first victory, assuming it was approved, it would bring him some cheer and speed his recovery. He deserved at least that.

Well, there we were. We were a scout squadron without aeroplanes with which to scout. Using a few parts from Wellington's SE, the ground crew had one almost ready to fly. They promised another, maybe two, after lunch. I volunteered to take the one good SE on a lone patrol, but the major refused. He wanted to wait until he could send up several pilots together. He added that my "Dirty Bird" was not too bad off, so I could go with the patrol once it and any others were checked out by the ground personnel. I left to go help my mechanics prepare my 'plane. I was anxious to serve up some revenge.

I got my hands dirty working on my SE. There was much patching to be done, as the machine was riddled with bullet holes. Typically, once the patch of fabric was doped on, someone would follow up with a black cross painted on a white disk to show the damage. It was a badge of honor. It proclaimed, "Look at this—they hit me but could not stop me!" But on this day there was no time. The plain linen patches would just have to do. We were in a hurry to get in the air and mete out punishment and atone for the loss of Wellington. But by late afternoon we had but three SEs ready to fly. This would not do for the major, so he denied any requests to go up. We were ordered to help in any way we could in hopes of sending up an offensive patrol the next morning.

Someone wanted to paint the little black cross "badges" on the surviving and patched together aeroplanes. He said we had the time. But the rest of us all refused. It was more important to get more machines ready to fly. But since he wanted to paint, we got him a brush and some green dope in a bucket. We had a stock of PC 10 dope on hand for just such an occasion. Once he started to paint, he was surprised and a little put off that the dope did not match the dope already on the aeroplanes. It didn't surprise me, as no two SEs were the same color anyway. One or two were fairly new and looked dark green, but the others were varying shades of green, khaki, and brown. It was apparent that the PC 10 dope faded in the sunlight, and faded quickly. More correctly, some parts of the dope oxidized, resulting in a brown "shift" in its appearance. As our brush wielding mate got on with his job and the SEs sat in the afternoon sun, they all looked as though a pox had set upon them. The green dots looked black against the faded hues of khaki and brown. Some of the patches were large enough or close enough together that the dark green became a large area, and the SEs, normally doped PC 10 on all upper surfaces, started to look like SPADs. Most SPADs were doped in a disruptive paint scheme with five colors on the upper surfaces. I never understood all that effort going into painting the aeroplanes. After all, once the PC 10 started to fade, it blended in with the landscape of war below. Well, at least we could see the "archery target" cockades of blue, white, and red. Some pilots, though, even dirtied the whites of the cockades, making their aeroplanes even more difficult to see. Some pilots as well were alarmed by the dope's color discrepancy, but I knew it would work to our favor. Besides, the sun would fade the dope patches as well. It was not unlike getting a bad haircut—in a week or two, it would look okay and no one would notice.

Obviously, I was most interested in getting my "Dirty Bird" ready to fight. Patching done, I moved on to my usual routine of checking the engine's HT leads, the play in the controls, and the fit of the ammunition in my Vickers ammo belt and Lewis ammo drum. I was permitted to have my engine swung to life in order to listen to it and test it for problems, but I was not allowed so much as to taxi about the field. No flight wear was allowed to ensure I didn't do anything foolhardy. My controls, my ammunition, and my engine all checked out, so I was moved along to help the fitters with another SE. I made the quest into a challenge. Once all patching was finished, I looked over the machine as if they were mine and applied my standards. Again I checked the play in the controls, checked the sizes of the ammunition, and checked the HT leads. Once I had done all I could for that SE, I moved along to another. I hoped the pilots would get into their machines and notice the difference in performance and machine gun reliability. Maybe they would understand what I had done and ask about it. The better the performance of our machines, the better our chances for survival—and for shooting down a Boche who desperately deserved it.

To express his appreciation for all of us pitching in to help with repairs to the airstrip, the aeroplanes and other equipment, the major "liberated" a number of bottles of brandy, placing them at our mercy. We showed none. The major had hoped we would sample the brandy and maybe even turn in early in preparation for the next morning's activities. After an initial party starting with dinner in the mess and progressing to the briefing room, the men broke up into groups, roughly by job assignment: fitters with fitters, pilots together, administrative personnel, and so on. Most everyone saw their world through a little "haze". The fitters openly complained about the pilots who mistreated their aeroplanes. The paper pushers complained about the avalanche of reports they had to fill out and file for every action and/or reaction. The pilots were a little different. Oh, they talked about people they did not care for. Those still sober enough to string words into sentences turned toward a darker conversation. The pilots were the ones who flew into the air in the latest, most up to date aeroplanes, the best their country could mass produce and assemble for their use in destroying the enemy or the emery's will to fight. They flew cutting edge machines in what was still a fairly new technology. Man had been flying for little over a decade. For the first ten years there was notable but little real change from the earliest designs. Engines had become more powerful and arguably more reliable. The earliest wartime meetings between opposing pilots produced waves and salutes to one another. Then someone realized that though they were brothers in the fraternity of the air, they were still enemies and needed to do something to show that enmity. There were stories of bricks, rocks, handguns, rifles, and even an anchor, but soon enough someone took a machine gun into the air. After various experiments, it was found the machine gun could be mounted to the aeroplane such that the pilot merely pointed the aeroplane at the intended target and pulled the trigger. The gun was synchronized to the motion of the propeller. One could fire the bullets between the propeller blades as they swung past the muzzle of the gun. In fact, the SE's Lewis gun, mounted on the upper wing such that it fired over the arc of the turning propeller, was a holdover from some of the early experiments with machine guns. The SE's Vickers machine gun was synchronized to fire through the propeller arc. Some of the surviving veteran pilots preferred to keep the non-synchronized Lewis gun, so it was retained.

So aeroplanes were getting better and they were capable of firing automatic rifles through the moving propeller blades. But safety was still a problem for pilots. If anything happened to them in the air, their only choice was to land the aeroplane and see what could be done, if anything. But not all emergencies were alike. If a gun jammed, the aeroplane's performance was not affected. If the engine quit, one could glide the 'plane to the ground, at least if the enemy pilots and "archie" permitted. While other things could happen to these wood and fabric "powered kites," again the most fearful occurrence was fire. Fire was the nemesis of every pilot. Fire consumed the wood framework and highly flammable doped fabric of the aeroplane, possibly fueled by the oil and petrol carried on board. If enough airframe were consumed, it was no longer capable of sustaining flight. But more to the point, the flames could consume the pilot. None of this was seen in a positive light by any pilot on either side of the lines. The question was about what to do in the event of a fire on board. Though many pilots had seen observation balloon personnel jump overboard when attacked, these men were equipped with tethered parachutes. The parachutes were in packs attached to the balloon baskets, and the men on board wore harnesses that were attached to the parachutes. In the event of an attack, the men could simply grab any notes they had taken and dive over the side of the basket near their parachute pack. As they fell, their attached lines would pull the parachutes out of the packs and the parachutes would open so the men could float to the ground below. Usually.

Though the pilots had asked repeatedly for parachutes, their requests were denied. Some of the top brass believed that the men, equipped with parachutes, would jump out of their aeroplanes at the first sign of danger, thus wasting a "perfectly good" aeroplane for no reason. With no parachutes, the brass reasoned, the pilots would endeavor to save their aeroplanes and these examples of government property would be available to fight another day.

The awake pilots remaining sat or lay around, most clutching their bottle of brandy, and talked wide-eyed about the specter of fire in the air. "What would you do?" Oh, there were elaborate schemes hatched and discussed. Sideslip the 'plane to keep the flames outboard and away. Various other maneuvers were mentioned and debated as to whether they would be effective against a conflagration. There were rumors that a German pilot had climbed out of his flaming aeroplane and stood on the wing root and boarding step, reaching in to pilot the 'plane with the control stick alone, sideslipping the flames out the starboard wings. In fact, it was Austro/Hungarian pilot and eventual leading ace, Godwin von Brumowski, who did just that and then climbed back into the cockpit and landed the aeroplane with significant wing fabric burned away. Other pilots feared the very idea of fire in an aeroplane and claimed they would jump and get it over with. "No suffering for me. Over the side I go." Some pilots claimed they carried handguns for just such an occasion, preferring to end it right away rather than face consumption by flame, the horrifying, merciless, painful killer. The discussion went on into the night until the last pilot nodded off, his head at an unnatural angle due to being at least partially upright.

There was no early morning patrol. Although there were five SEs ready to fly and several close to readiness, only one had been pushed out to the flight line when the major entered his office. A good leader, he walked about the flight line, quarters, mess, and briefing room to determine the combat readiness of his brandy sodden men. He was short personnel in every department. There were very few men ready to push aeroplanes out of their tents, and even fewer ready to arm them and fuel them. And even if this did happen, there were not enough sober and aware pilots to make up a flight. So the major quietly told the few men on the line to relax. The unit had suffered a horrendous day and the men had quelled their frustrations with brandy. The Boche would be there. A few hours or a day really would not make much difference. He would merely report his unit as rebuilding after a vicious attack. Details be damned.

There was a bit of a stir after lunch. Actually, there were still very few men in the mess shed, such was the "bender" the night before. The stir came in the form of a lorry from the hospital in the nearby town. Specifically, it was the two nurses on board the lorry. They had asked permission to visit the squadron and report on the condition of their pilot, United States Army Signal Corps Corporal Wellington. The word spread very quickly that there were women on the aerodrome. The men arrived in twos and threes to visit with the nurses. Some men had tried desperately to fix themselves up for the women, mostly to no avail. They looked like they had passed out from brandy, slept too long in unpleasant conditions, and awakened but a few minutes before. Water and fingers were no substitute for bathing and a comb. No matter. It appeared their Yank, "Wellie", would be just fine. He had been tossed about at the expense of his neck muscles and several broken bones, but he would live to fight another day. The nurses were not able to tell the men how soon Wellie would be able to pursue his goal of scrubbing the skies clean of Huns, but he would be okay. As soon as they heard the initial news, the men tuned out what the nurses had to say. That is, until the nurses asked to see one of the fighting aeroplanes.

As luck would have it, there was one example of an SE5a on the flight line, the one that had been there since daybreak. Dozens of men led the two young nurses up the flight line to show off their state of the art fighting equipment. Oddly, Geoff, proud possessor of the picture of the woman showing "too much" leg in her swimwear, lagged behind, paying close attention to the nurses' progress up the line. With a furtive smile across his face. He was enjoying this, student of the feminine form that he was.

"Who is the man looking at the machinery? Is he a mechanic?"

"No, no," someone responded. "He is the pilot of the aeroplane."

I looked up to see the approaching entourage, scores of men surrounding two comely young lasses. One very thin, the other a little "sturdier" in form, both women were covered head to toe save their faces, which wore curious, contorted looks. I was elbow deep in ammunition belt. Having checked my cartridges for fit, I was carefully placing the belt of ammunition into its canister before feeding one end into the breech of the Vickers machine gun.

The women and their motley, disheveled escort party approached from the starboard rear of my SE. It was a fine looking bird in the midday sun, fresh dark patches looking surprisingly regular against the faded khaki of the rest of the visible fabric. The women took the lead in walking around the SE. This was obviously their first visit to an aerodrome and first closeup encounter with a fighting aeroplane, and they had many questions. My concern at this point was to keep an eye on them so they did not harm any part of my SE. It was, after all, doped fabric stretched over a wooden frame and not the most robust covering. It was certainly not immune to being poked by fingers. I did not want to miss any patrols due to more patching. Any questions the nurses had were answered many times over by the surrounding gaggle of authorities.

Then it happened. As the throng passed around the tail and then the port wing tip, one of the nurses squealed and pointed. "What is this?" Against my most fervent hopes, she had seen my SE's crude moniker, "Dirty Bird". Predictably, she asked why the aeroplane was painted with something like "Dirty Bird". The men were only too eager to retell the tale of my meeting with the little German triplane and the resultant soiling of clothing, resplendent with embellishments, hyperbole, and exaggeration. I was not sure any human could have excreted the amounts attributed to me for that event, but that was the story told, and the nurses' eyes grew wider with each sentence. Oh, how I wanted to duck into the cockpit and out of sight. The nurses insisted someone find a camera and make a photograph of them standing by the "cute name". And it was done. Once the photographic plates had been exposed, the nurses left information about their hospital so that they may receive copies of the resulting photographs and then hurried off to their lorry. It seems they had stayed too long and were concerned that they could be reprimanded for returning late. It was war, after all, and they would have work aplenty upon their return. Oddly enough, Geoff was the one with the information on how to contact the hospital and nurses. Oh, that bugger. Turned out it was his camera as well. How convenient.

Obviously enough, the nurses' visit, while welcomed and informative, delayed any offensive patrols. Who was going to pass up the chance to mingle with the fair gender, especially if they came onto one's airfield? Again, the major was very understanding. The men had been through a very trying morning the day before, and they had worked very hard to restore order to the chaos brought on by the German air attack. As they sobered up and became more aware of the day's events, the men were surprised and heartened by the major's actions. This kindness, even though it was against regulations and military protocol, made the men more fond of the major. They knew what he had done and what he had risked for them and they loved him for it. This squadron was ready to follow the major through the gates of Hell if it came to that.

Once the nurses had departed and their lorry disappeared from sight, the major asked the men if he could have an afternoon patrol. Every one redoubled his efforts to push other SEs to the flight line to join the "Dirty Bird". In short order, well another couple hours, the major decided there were enough aeroplanes to make up a decent patrol. We were ordered to check our 'planes and mount a patrol up and down the lines, staying over Allied territory. We protested, but the major was resolute. We were not to cross into German held territory on this patrol. We were just getting our wings back. He wanted us to fly a planned, uneventful patrol just to reestablish a routine after what we had been through. He was a good man and a good leader of men. We all wanted to exact revenge for the attack, the damage, even the downing of Wellington, but the major was not going to budge. We were to go up, maintain formation unless attacked, and make sure no Boche crossed the lines in either direction. With the prevailing westerly winds and the known fighting patterns of the Huns, we were not likely to encounter any of them, and that is just what the major wanted. He understood that having revenge as a motive could cloud one's judgement and he was not ready to lose another pilot or 'plane, especially to some foolish action initiated in haste.

While the ground crews finished their preparations for the patrol, we gathered in the briefing room for the major's final preflight talk. When the major joined us we were all surprised. He was in full flight gear. Some of the men had never seen him in his Sidcot, a one piece affair some of us wished we had rather than our "whatever works" contrivances. Funny how life worked. We had all joined the Royal Flying Corps to fly. Most of us had begun in our regional units of infantry, artillery, or even cavalry merely to go to war with the patriotic and romantic notion of fighting for our country. It was the British thing to do, after all. Some of us became disillusioned after some time in training and at the stalemated and stationary front lines. Shortly after the shooting war began, the front lines stabilized and neither side could make any headway. Once this was realized, both sides dug into the ground for protection from flying bullets and other ordnance. The series of foxholes was connected into trenches, which were often lined with sandbags and floored with wood in an effort to avoid the insufferable mud once rainwater had collected in the hole. And, of course, to prevent enemy incursions, some brave lads were sent up to install barbed wire barriers and other obstacles. The real estate between these barbed wire fences was referred to as "No Man's Land", what with machine gun emplacements set up to watch over the area. And if the machine guns and barbed wire weren't enough, the fields through which these trenches ran quickly deteriorated into a series of muddy and water-filled shell holes from the almost constant artillery barrages. If one had signed up with dashing notions of leading a cavalry charge against the enemy, he soon realized that this was no longer the case in modern warfare. Horses were used for pulling things or for rear area communications.

Surrounded by miserable, dirty men and not much to do other than look over a rifle at the enemy just in case somebody foolishly climbed out of their trench, men became bored very quickly. Aeroplanes became a distraction. Recently introduced as weapons of war, they would buzz or whine or sputter overhead patrolling the lines or crossing the lines to look in on or bomb the enemy. On a good day the German aeroplanes and British or French aeroplanes would approach one another and circle, maneuvering for position and the distant popping of gunfire could be heard. Mostly the popping would stop after a few moments and the aeroplanes would separate and go their ways, but every so often one would develop a trail of smoke and arc down to some point on the muddy earth. If its arc ended nearby, everyone wanted to dash off and see what it looked like, who was aboard, and what had become of it all after meeting with the earth. Many of these war weary men began to view the aeroplanes as did the upper brass. Aeroplanes and their pilots were the cavalry of the air. The men merely mounted a very different horse to perform the tasks of scouting enemy positions and movements and reporting any information to the military tacticians and strategists. This might have been the origin of the remark, "Take a picture—it lasts longer", for soon aeroplanes mounted cameras with which to photograph enemy positions. These photographs would be compared to older photographs to determine what the enemy was doing. Then came the realization that if "we" were photographing the Germans' positions, "they" were photographing ours. Something must be done to prevent the Germans from delivering their glass plate negatives to be developed, yielding valuable military information. This led to the escalation of aerial weapons related earlier.

All of this looked very exciting to someone mired in mud with little to look forward to other than letters from loved ones and maybe the lucky shot at an exposed enemy soldier or low flying enemy aeroplane. Many requested transfers to the Royal Flying Corps or Royal Naval Air Service just to get away from the mud, lice, disease, and boredom of trench warfare. Many such requests were simply ignored. One had to be an exemplary soldier to be considered for transfer to aviation. Or one had to be wounded in action. Some wounds were minor and the patient would merely recover and return to his unit. Other wounds were much more severe and required evacuation, often to Home Establishment (Great Britain) for proper treatment and recovery. Then there were the "in between" wounds, those that would render the soldier useless for further infantry duty but would still allow him to be an aerial observer or perhaps a pilot. Quite the number of soldiers made it into the air through this route. Perhaps they could no longer carry a rifle or machine gun, but they could still look at the enemy, take notes, and/or operate a camera while flying. And, perhaps, if they showed aptitude and ability, they could be trained to operate an aeroplane. Then they likely would take the other seat in an observation 'plane and fly over the lines while an observer looked about, taking notes and making photographs. Following that step, a good man, showing excellent flying ability and an aggressive spirit, could undergo further training and become a scout pilot.

* * * * *

Chapter 2

German Pilot quarters, airfield in captured French territory

"Scheisse."

No hot water? Again? After years of war, I could tolerate a lot. But shaving with cold water annoyed me to no end. I like a hot shave. I always have. Even on the hottest summer day. Hot water opens the facial skin pores and allows one to get a closer, smoother shave. After my time in the infantry, trying to breathe through gas attacks with a large, stylish waxed mustache which prevented the gas mask from fitting properly over my face, I have been clean shaven for a reason. The gas mask fits better over a clean shaven face and forms a better seal. Yes, gas attacks were that bad. Without a gas mask, they could be deadly. With a poorly fitting gas mask, one wished for death to alleviate the misery. I had been so, in complete and desperate agony, wishing for the pain to stop. No longer.

I was now a flyer, a *Kampfflieger*. The chances of being in a gas attack were remote. I was stationed with my *Schlachtstaffel* several miles behind the front lines. It was possible I could smell a gas attack due to the wind direction, normally west to east, but it could not affect my breathing at such a distance, maybe cause me to cough at most. Frankly, the damage was in my head, as the smell took me back to the dark days and endless nights struggling to breathe in one hospital or another. What were the *pickelhauben* thinking, launching a gas attack against the prevailing winds? How many German lives had been lost or ruined? But I kept a gas mask nearby when I was on the ground. Yes, the effects of the gas were so severe I could never allow myself to be vulnerable again. I could take the ribbing and name calling from the others in my unit. They thought I was overreacting and they were likely right. But still . . . one never knew. Let them laugh. It was good to have some levity, some relief from the routine of war. If my little obsession could provide that, perhaps it was not so bad.

I was with an infantry unit when the war began. We helped with the invasion of Belgium. We felt like we barely slowed down while taking the forts boasted about as impregnable. We dug in while our artillery units fired over our heads and into the forts. Some units took possession of these forts while mine was part of the "left turn" that took us south into France, mostly behind their extensive network of defensive forts. The attacks went too well, to be honest. Our troops went in fast and deep, exposing our flanks to our enemies, mostly the French with a few disorganized English to the north. We could not be assured the supply lines would hold. Though the French were very disorganized and the British were not even ready to join the fight, we were told to withdraw to the north in order to be assured of supplies, food, and ammunition. In a brilliant propaganda move, the Allies made up what they called the "Battle of the Marne", wherein we Germans were supposedly sent packing. Of course we showed them just how badly "beaten" we were in short order when we attacked again, took St Mihiel, and threatened the ring of forts surrounding Verdun. We were nearly unstoppable. We had a working battle plan. We dug in, let the artillery soften the enemy with "greetings" from very large and accurate modern guns, then sent in the infantry to raise our flag. This was our pattern until things stalled and both sides dug into the ground in a line of trenches that eventually reached from the North Sea to Switzerland. Then it looked like a war of attrition, at least from the Allied side. The French and English would send masses of men into the "No Man's Land" between the trenches, where they would be machine gunned, shelled, or subjected to a new weapon, the hand grenade. Sometimes they would manage to capture and hold a few feet of useless, heavily shelled ground. Sometimes we would put the artillery back on offense and take a little more land. Other than that, it was up to the generals and strategists to come up with new ideas that may or may not result in more territory gained. Aeroplanes were soon used to spot for artillery when our captive balloons could not be placed close enough to observe the shelling.

We used to watch the aeroplanes above while we were waiting for something to happen on the ground. We watched them fly back and forth overhead, some with black crosses for identification and some with red, blue, and white concentric rings. When we could make out the English or French "dartboards" we would train our weapons skyward and shoot. We never seriously thought we could bring one of them down, but as long as we fired our guns there was a chance, however remote. Some English types were easy to identify, so we were ready to shoot at them before they passed over. They had engines mounted behind the crew, which required the tail control surfaces to be suspended to the rear on lightweight booms. We called them *gitterrumpf.* I never got to see an Allied aeroplane brought down near me, I'm sorry to say, but a nearby unit managed to bring down one of our own aeroplanes. It crashed in "No Man's Land", overturned, and caught fire. Three daredevils ran out to try to rescue the crew, but the fuel tank exploded just as they arrived. The crew did not survive, and neither did two of the three would-be rescuers. The third man was burned badly, and we had to listen to him moan and sometimes scream until after dark, when several men went to retrieve him. I don't know if he survived. The war moved on and there was no time for pleasantries like concern over one man's plight. Someone did ask one day. He was told his job was to keep an eye on the "red pants" Frenchmen across the way and shoot any who dared to show themselves. *Der Kaiser* had other people to keep track of the wounded.

Things were markedly different at the *Schlachtstaffel.* Everybody mostly knew everyone else by name. The pilots tended to gather with other pilots, as did the rear gunners and other types of workers, because they had common interests and concerns about their assigned jobs. There was some co-mingling, to be sure. Several of the young men shared a common interest in horses, for example, not the least because they had served in various cavalry units before hostilities began. Some had tended to the horses on their family farms, and two had competed in equestrian events. In the infantry, one knew none of the men around him other than a close few. It didn't pay to form close attachments due to the nature of the ground war. One could make a good friend and find them gone after the next shelling. Was that their leg being carried away, covered by a tattered uniform remnant and countless bluebottle flies? Life in the trenches was not pleasant. War is not pleasant. Being transferred to the air service was a leap of a promotion. I was actually able to continue my recent practice of a complete, smooth, hot water shave, something I started while still in hospital after being gassed. The others made fun of me, asking why it was so important to look good. Who was I hoping to meet in a *Staffel* of men? They teased me over the only local female, the old French woman who took care of the cows on her farm adjacent to the airfield. Though we were the enemy, she sometimes brought us fresh milk. She said we reminded her of her son, who had been killed in October of 1914. She felt bad that we were fighting at such a young age over things none of us understood. There were tangled alliances between all the European nations, all of which fell in place like so many dominos when a Serb anarchist shot and killed an Austrian prince and his wife. All this over a prince? She assured us politicians were all crazed and unstable. And demanding. Her husband had been summoned by the French army. She said he could barely pull himself out of bed each morning. He would make a fine soldier, she chuckled. He had a fowling piece that had been in the family for well over one hundred years, but he probably couldn't lift it for all the cobwebs that held it to the walls in the corner. She had an aversion to firearms and would not even dust the corner. And he could barely bend over to dust anything. Yes, he would be a model soldier. Sometimes she bent forward, placed a hand on one hip, and let the other arm dangle while making grunting noises. Then we would share a short laugh, after which she would clap her hand over her mouth and mutter something about sharing military intelligence.

Strange things happened in war. Some of the men would actually go to the farm and help the old woman, Marie, with chores. Ah, the luxuries of free time. They brought back cheese she had made. Others would gather around, but the few men would fend them off, telling them they could help with chores if they wanted cheese. When a crew failed to return one day, someone took Marie the pilot's old unit cap. While she didn't much care for the cap, she appreciated the gesture.

Whenever she expected that man to visit, she would place the cap on a hook near the door.

Communication with Marie was easy. An Alsatian woman, she was conversant in French, German, and the dialect of German common in her region. I made a note of that in case we brought a captured Frenchman to the airfield and needed a translator. I suppose it would have been more appropriate to ask Marie how she felt about that. I imagined she would assist if we assured no harm would come to the Frenchman beyond typical prisoner of war confinement. I assumed she would liken such a young man to her own son.

At first I refused to go to the farm. When asked, I told them I detested the French after the gas attack that had nearly killed me. Then someone asked when and where it had happened and I told him. He laughed a little and I became indignant.

"No, no, please don't be offended. A cousin was there for that attack. It was an English attack. Not French, English. It's hard to tell the uniforms apart, especially with all the mud—even the red pants. And if you were gassed, you may have been unaware. And my cousin is well, thank you for asking."

"I was about to—"

That got me a slap on the back, a hearty laugh, and a compliment for my gas mask on the table next to me.

"That is a very nice mask. Still uneasy? I can't blame you. I, too, have been gassed. It is not pleasant. You wanted to die, as did I."

I learned that my new friend worked on the machine guns and synchronizers for our Hannover fighters. I made an excuse and went to the armorer area, where I introduced myself and learned his name was Rudolf. He said he had been going to help on the farm to be distracted from the war for a while. He knew he had an easy job, working on guns in the rear area, and appreciated that he was rarely shot at. But working on guns and gears and such, especially in the tight confines of a fighter aeroplane, could be tedious. He invited me to go with him to meet Marie some time when he went. He teased me that she might like my smooth babyface. Then he told me not to get excited. She was, after all, a married woman. Then came another backslap as he excused himself to get back to work.

The *Huaptmann* in charge of the *Stafffel* asked if I would care to join in a familiarization flight for a replacement pilot the next morning.

"But of course, *mein Herr,*" I replied as I saluted.

"*Nicht mit der 'mein Herr' scheisse!* We will take off after breakfast. *Danke!*"

We didn't fly much as a unit. We mostly flew strafing runs on the opposing British trenches to give our ground troops support and assistance . But the *Huaptmann,* Jakob, did not believe in routine patrols. If there were a reason or a mission, that was one thing. But he thought that the prevailing winds would deliver all the Allied flyers we would need in the event strafing was not enough to keep us occupied. No sense hunting for any day in and day out. Instead of constant patrols, he assigned crews to be dressed in flight gear with their Hannover nearby while strafing runs were in progress. If someone telephoned with information that any Allied aeroplanes were coming in our direction, he would call a nearby *Jagdstaffel* to intercept. We did patrols to show new pilots their way around our assigned area. Once they were comfortable with where they were, we would push them a little in order to see what they were made of. One pilot would challenge the new man to a mock dogfight and we would watch what transpired. Once they had landed, we would talk about the encounter and make suggestions in an effort to extend the crew's life at the front. We had to respect the Allied flyers' tenacity. Not only did they have to fight us over our own territory, but then they had to battle a headwind in order to get to their airfields. On the way, they had to be wary of our gunfire, whether organized antiaircraft fire or a lone gunman, one of many rifles in the trenches. And if they were wounded or their machines damaged, escape became yet more difficult. True, they were the enemy, but as pilots they deserved a measure of respect all the same.

The *Huaptmann* had specified after breakfast. I did not ask a specific time because I knew there was no specific time. We always took it to mean after *his* breakfast. So, with that in mind, those who were to meet after breakfast agreed to make sure all involved were aware of when he sat down to eat. Unless he had orders, he ran things somewhat like we flew, by the seat of his pants. We very much appreciated that, and we all knew that when the time came that he was strict about anything, we had to respect that as well. It was the only way to keep his relaxed ways intact.

Every pilot and gunner involved in the familiarization patrol was present when the *Huaptmann* entered for breakfast. We finished ahead of him but remained inside as a group, talking over coffee. After he finished, we all walked to the flight line where our Hannover two-seat fighters were ready to fly. We were all helped in and the pilots' harnesses pulled taught. The *Huaptmann* pointed at us one at a time and the pilots would respond with an upraised thumb, showing everything was okay. Then he made a sweeping underhand gesture that ended with his hand above the upper wing and we knew he was departing the line to take off. We followed him and we took off in ones and twos and fell into formation once we had climbed to his specified altitude. The replacement was in the midst of the formation, as if to insulate him from anything that might happen. Then we followed the *Huaptmann* wherever he went until he fired a red flare to direct us home.

Upon landing the *Huaptmann* would talk to the new pilot about the flight, answer any questions, and perhaps ask a few of him. After that, the pilot would return to us and we would discuss the flight again and offer what we could to help him know his way around. Had he seen the flight of Nieuports? No? Five Frenchmen above us. They could have been trouble had there been fewer of us, but they respected our superior numbers, speed, and firepower. We were happy he had seen the *gitterrumpf* spotting for British artillery. Another FE2 had been flying above in case we attacked. Next time, perhaps. The *Huaptmann* liked his familiarization flights kept simple unless something vital happened. I remember wanting to go after the artillery spotter, but the British artillery was more a nuisance than anything else, such were their weapons. They were much older and far inferior to our own.

* * * * *

CHAPTER 3

German

My time in the infantry was interesting and eye opening. The popular notion of infantry was men with rifles and bayonets, but we were learning different tactics with different equipment and weapons. We mostly did not carry rifles. We had shovels and grenades instead. Our role was to dig in and let the artillery do its job of clearing out the enemy. We had newly designed, state of the art guns. They were big, they fired big shells with great amounts of explosives, and they primarily sent out plunging fire which descended nearly vertically on the target. They had hydraulic carriages which absorbed the force of detonation, which meant the gun did not shift from the recoil of firing. This meant more shells could be fired in less time than in the old weapons like the French 75mm. The 75mm fired a lighter shell and could not elevate to fire over any significant obstacle or toward the top of a hill or ridge.

I was often asked to assist with artillery. Sometimes it was to help move a gun into position. I would sleep well after having moved such a large gun. Sometimes I had to help pass along ammunition and empty shell casings. Once in a while I would get to help aim and fire the gun. This was a feeling of power. There were observers, usually atop a nearby hill, who would help us "walk" the shells toward the target. One day the man firing the big gun hurt his hand on an empty casing and needed medical attention. I was closest to his position, so I was told to do what he did. I sent a shell skyward. We received a report moments later that my shell had landed next to an ammunition storage building and we needed to move less than one degree to the left. I asked if my shell had hit anything and I was told it landed next to a wagon carrying ammunition, destroying the wagon and probably killing everybody around it, as well as two horses. While it was actually a miss, I still felt good I had done some harm to the enemy. The man with the hurt hand returned as they were traversing the gun and I was relieved of my temporary position.

I tried to keep myself available for artillery duty, and I was beginning to be a regular with one local unit when the gas attack occurred, putting me out of action until my breathing was restored. I was assigned to a different unit which did not have the same opportunities with artillery. In fact, the unit was moving toward Verdun when I joined it. After about two weeks we were suddenly pulled from Verdun and sent to the Somme, where the English and French were both attacking. No one could believe they were attacking there. The Somme valley was already soft and militarily useless ground. Why would they attack there? There was no point. While I missed the spectacle, I learned that the Englishmen had simply climbed out of their trenches and marched toward our lines, almost in formation. They made no attempt to seek cover. Our machine guns took the men down faster than anyone could believe. They kept approaching, our men kept shooting, and the biggest worry had been that the machine guns would overheat. As my unit arrived, our men were actually retreating from our front line positions to more secure, drier, and higher positions. If the Englishmen wanted the swampy area that had no use, why contest it? Let them have it. We would be prepared in the event they tried to take more than we allowed them.

Even if we were going to higher ground, I was becoming disillusioned with the infantry. Being away from the artillery, I began to think of, and then apply for, a transfer to aviation. Circumstances smiled upon me as my application was accepted. Someone with the artillery unit I had helped earlier had been transferred to a position as a bureaucrat and remembered my name as my application crossed his desk. His recollection of my willingness to help in any way got me accepted into observer training.

* * * * *

CHAPTER 4

German

I never had a lot of interest in flying or aeroplanes. I was raised in a rural community surrounded by farmland. On occasion I would hear a faint drone and look to the sky to see an early aeroplane. I remember thinking they looked like kites without strings to tether them to anybody on the ground. They would approach from one horizon and proceed toward the other. They apparently paid me no heed, and I reacted in kind. I saw very few motorcars in my youth, and even fewer flying machines. There was the occasional dirigible. They were larger and, due to multiple engines, made a louder drone. But I had chores to do around the house and at my father's blacksmith shop and stable. At home I learned to cook and clean and perform basic repairs. At the stable I learned to shoe horses, make and adjust horseshoes, and fabricate parts for wagons to replace broken parts. I knew this would probably be my life, so I paid little attention to things in the sky beyond their value as curiosities. One day a man stopped at the stable with his motorcar. He had a broken shackle on his suspension and was very concerned. My father removed the part and handed it to me. He asked if I could duplicate it. I told him I could make him another one in a short while. Though the vehicle was unusual at the time, the part was very similar to a shackle on a wagon. He advised me to busy myself with it right away because the customer was waiting. In about an hour my replacement part was in place on the suspension and the customer was under way toward his destination. My father was proud and we had a good meal that evening. That was life before the war. I had just begun to attend meetings and drills of the local militia, such as it was, when the fragile political situation in Europe collapsed. The winds of war swelled enough to blow over the stacked cards. The mobilization effort swept me along like a leaf in the current and I was swiftly placed in an infantry unit. I was given a rifle and bayonet and shown how to use them, but it played a surprisingly small role in my service. The shovel was more important. In fact, I was issued a shovel to replace my rifle and bayonet. As we dug ourselves in at a given location, the artillery would soften the defenses and we would await our orders to move forward to take and hold ground. There was surprisingly little use for rifles. If we encountered any small arms fire, we were to return fire, of course, but with grenades, throwing them if we found groups of French soldiers or could not pick off a troublesome rifleman or machine gunner. While the rifles utilized a straight line trajectory, the grenades could be thrown so as to duplicate the plunging fire of artillery, though with a much lower apogee.

My experience with metal work gave me an interest in devices like artillery weapons and the vehicles that transported them. While I filled in operating the big guns I looked at their structure and how they were manufactured. I found myself fascinated with the things around me and how they worked. That led me to an eventual interest in aeroplanes. They were, after all, another device used by the military. And securing a transfer did get me out of living in a hole in the ground. I never minded the holes or trenches that much unless it was cold. Despite being sheltered from any wind, there was no real relief from the cold. I could not go inside. And the hole rarely had a roof, so any heat simply rose up and away. This led me to looking around for potential roofing for my hole wherever the war took me. Sometimes I would remove the outer heavy coat from a dead comrade. I was not interested in his valuables, just the coat. I could use it like a blanket and pull it over my head when I slept, thus trapping my body heat and keeping me warm. Once they understood my logic, others began to do the same. After all, the departed soldiers had no further use for the coats.

Upon my transfer to *die Fliegertruppe*, I held a quick auction for my extra overcoat. The others in my unit played along with me. At least some of them did. I "sold" my coat for a modest amount, which I used to purchase some schnapps for my unit. It wasn't much, but the gesture was appreciated.

I went on to my next assignment to an airfield outside Berlin. It was a large flat stretch of land surrounded by hangars, sheds, and other buildings. I was summarily dropped off at a big building with two moderately sized bags of clothing and personal effects. Thinking I was to enter the building where I was left off, I tried the door and found it locked. I walked around the building and saw for the first time the vast expanse of land before me. There was quite the assortment of flying machines. There were a few sputtering boxkites like what I had seen in my youth. They were a yellowish color, which I later learned was doped linen. They looked like they had flown off of pre-war posters for aviation gatherings. Then there were the latest aeroplanes painted in murky greens and mauves with sky blue painted bottoms. These had large numerals painted on the sides of their tails or near the iron cross markings on the fuselage sides. A few were fitted with guns. The old and the new were about a quarter of the aircraft present, at least near me. The rest looked like evolutionary steps between the box kites and the newest models. Some had reddish wood fuselages with doped linen wings. Others were painted greens and browns. All had the *eiserne kreuz* markings prominent from most angles.

I stood there for a few moments looking at all the activity on the airfield. There were men working on aeroplanes along the edges of the field near the hangars. There were aeroplanes taxiing back and forth. From my perspective they were daring one another to stand still and be chewed up by another's whirling propeller. Farther out aeroplanes were taking off into the wind. I could see other aeroplanes descending toward a point beyond the horizon. I was completely enthralled, especially with the men working on engines. I wondered if they would mind . . .

"You. You, with the bags!"

I turned on my heel. *"Ja?"*

I was face to face with what looked like a recent secondary school graduate. I dropped one bag and began to salute but realized he was of lower rank.

"What are you looking for, *mein Herr?*" He saluted.

I showed him my orders and inquired where I might find the specific building I was supposed to report to. He laughed a little, then apologized, though I thought nothing of it.

"*Mein Herr*, that is almost across the field from here. If you like, I can drive you and your bags over there."

"That would be great if you could. *Danke.*"

He gestured. "If you could wait over there for a moment, I will get a motorcar."

"*Danke.*"

As promised, he brought a car along the building and "hump-hump"ed me with the horn. I threw my bags on the open rear platform and climbed on next to my guide.

"I welcome you, *mein Herr*, to the next step in your military career! What are you training to be?"

"An observer. Or gunner."

"If you are one, you are also the other, *mein Herr*. You will observe, yes, and you will have a gun mounted next to you in the event an Englander gets too curious."

"I see. Thank you for clarifying."

"But of course, *mein Herr*. I wish I were joining you, going up in aeroplanes."

"You're not?"

"No. I am here to guard the field, keep order, help newcomers like you, and so on."

"I see. You could put in a transfer request."

"And I shall, as soon as I am able. I've not been here long enough."

"If it helps, you may use me as a character reference. I am Gustav Model. You will know where to find me, at least when on duty. Perhaps you could show me around sometime."

"I would be happy to, *mein Herr*."

"You may dispense with the '*mein Herr*'. At least when we are alone."

"*Danke, mein Herr*. Oh."

We shared a laugh and I asked his name.

"Hanstein. Hans-Joaquin Hanstein."

"Pleased to meet you, Hans. May I call you Hans?"

"*Javohl.*"

"And of course, please call me Gustav."

"Where are you transferring from?"

"Infantry. I've been in the trenches since the war's beginning."

"Over two years at the front? And you are still alive?"

"I did suffer a gas attack that put me out of action for a while. As a result, I no longer sport the latest in fashionable mustaches. I prefer to be clean shaven so the mask fits better."

"Mask?"

"Ja, die gasmaske. I keep one nearby all the time, just in case. It's packed in the larger bag in back. On top of the other contents."

"I see. That must have been some experience if you still carry one this far behind the lines."

"Ja, it could look silly, I suppose. But do have a laugh at my expense. I don't mind."

"Of course not. But I cannot promise for any others who learn of your mask."

"Trust me, Hans, I have had my share of ribbing. I don't mind. It takes their minds off of the war, however briefly."

"Gustav, you are the good natured sort."

"Thick skin, Hans. Thick skin."

"Well, *mein Herr,* this is where you are to report."

"I thank you for saving me a few steps! I do hope to see you again, once I've settled in. Would I find you in the area where we met?"

"Possibly, *mein Herr.* I watch the perimeter of the airfield."

"I shall try and find you. Feel free to look me up if you wish."

"I will."

"Auf wiedersehen. Pleased to meet you!"

"Javohl, mein Herr!"

That was a pleasant greeting to my next step in the military. What followed was drudgery. I attended classes where I learned the theory of flight, maps, weather, communications, machine guns, camera operation, and more. It just all ran together in my mind. Weather? I could just look outside for that. Did I not have enough to learn in a short time without weather? As an observer I would only be following orders, not planning strategy. Someone else could account for the weather. I could tell which way the wind was blowing, after all. The classes were far less pleasant. Besides, I was not able to apply anything they were telling me. I had grown up using what I had learned about metal and leather and whatever else I used at my father's shop. I could not form any cognitive associations until I went up in an aeroplane.

My next experience was just that, going up in an aeroplane. My first flight was nearly my last. This was not due to a crash or crazy daredevil pilot. It was me. More correctly, it was my reaction to the flight. I was one of a number of observer candidates scheduled to go up for our first flights. While the flights started in the morning, going up into calm, placid air, my flight took place during the heat of the day, with updrafts and increasing turbulence. My pilot, a fine fellow and excellent flyer, took off into wind which was changing direction. He had to "crab" the aeroplane somewhat to keep a more direct headwind and climb to altitude. As a result, I began to feel a bit queasy. Once we reached our altitude, he made circuits of the field, almost like in a large landing pattern with other aeroplanes flying similar missions. The legs of the circuit flown in a crosswind were my undoing. On the third circuit, when the pilot turned from crosswind to downwind, the need to disgorge the contents of my stomach overcame the desire to hold my lunch down and maintain dignity. I fought the lap belt and pulled myself towards the outside of the turn, and placed my head beyond the cockpit coaming. Just as soon as I was clear, I expelled my midday meal. And my stomach and intestines. Or so it felt. I thought it would never end, but it did. I withdrew my head, choking and trying to recover my equilibrium. The pilot looked over his shoulder to confirm that I was the reason for the weight shift he had felt, but made no further reaction to my misfortune. He completed the flight as scheduled. When he landed, I thanked him just as the ground crew brought a ladder to aid my exit from the aircraft so another student could take my place. I was pleased with myself that I was able to get my "product" over the edge and outside the cockpit. A quick walk around the tail revealed that I had not dirtied the side of the aeroplane. In fact, I never heard anything about my episode at all, though I did wonder from time to time just where it had landed. I hoped it had landed on a roof or field or something. I preferred not to consider the other possibilities.

Fortunately that never happened again. I don't know why it happened that day. Nerves. Food. Something entirely new. It could have been anything. But after that I had no troubles in the air. That was good for I had other things to learn and do. Direction was no real problem. Common sense and having an idea of the time was enough to discern direction. I made it a point to learn my assigned area and familiarize myself with the local landmarks. The camera was not hard to master, even if changing the glass plates was a little awkward.

Flying also helped me with my classes. As I had suspected, once I had something to apply this knowledge to, it fell in place. It did take me a while to remember the names of the various cloud formations, though "rain cloud" was the one that got the attention. That was easy.

I watched as the size of my classes diminished over time. Problems with flying, problems with discipline, problems with classroom material, there were all kinds of reasons. One student was summarily transferred after a local priest caught him in the storeroom for the wine and wafers. The priest had apparently entered the church and found an article of clothing draped over the arm of a pew. Then he spied another piece of clothing, and while retrieving that he heard a commotion. Upon entering the storeroom, he found the observer student with a *fräulein* from his own congregation, open wine, and more clothing on the floor. The student was reassigned to security around the airfield, said detail to last at least until the *fräulein* demonstrated the results, if any, of the ill-advised encounter. I never learned the punishment for the *fräulein* or whether there were any lasting consequences, shall we say. I had a war to fight and a homeland to defend, so I was too busy for such foolishness.

I did well in my classes, well enough to move on to the pool of trained observers. I did not languish there beyond a few days. I was sent to a unit on the eastern front. After a week or so I wondered why. I fell into their routine. There was a scheduled sequence of flights. I categorized them as looking for something to do, for there was nothing. There was the occasional Russian aeroplane in the distance. Not even daily. It seemed nothing changed. Of course, it was winter, and not much happened in winter. I wondered why we had to fly every day. I was told, "because we are flyers". Besides, "One never knows." Wishful thinking, I suppose.

I soon found myself bored. I went up with the same pilot every day at about the same time, weather permitting, in the same old Albatros, and looked at the same units in the same places. After a while, I thought I sensed a change. I asked my pilot to fly further over Russian territory so I could have a closer look. By his reaction, one would have thought I had asked him to paint the wings pink.

"But we never . . ."

"Please. Humor me. I could be wrong."

He reluctantly broke his routine. I was not wrong. There were more troops assembled behind the lines than I was accustomed to observing. I had to wonder what was going on. I expressed my concerns to the pilot, who suddenly appeared agitated.

"Let the *pickelhauben* worry about that. Take notes. Let them read and think about it. I fly. You look. They think."

"But this could be important, an enemy buildup!"

"*Ja, ja, ja. Kinder* . . . winning the war while still wet behind the ears."

I began to see why he no longer flew over the western front. No vision, no ambition. I know he was wounded on a flight, so I had to respect that. He wore his EK II on every flight. It was his badge proclaiming bravery and courage. Or so he thought. I learned what had happened. He had been on a flight over the lines, or at least flying with that intent. There were three aeroplanes on the mission. They took off at first light, or rather when there was enough light for the pilots to see where they were going. He thought it foolish to fly at night. He had had "difficulties" with his equipment, delaying the start time and making his piloting easier. Finally off the ground, the aeroplanes began their climb, intending to cross the lines at 20,000 feet or so, and he flew in the left rear position. The other flyers suddenly flung themselves into action. Pilots fired flares, gunners tested their guns. He flew on, paying no attention. He ignored the flares. He waved off his observer, even after the observer pounded on his shoulders and yelled at the side of his head to look at the Englanders. 'They are all crazy', he thought, and pulled a little more on the stick. 'The Englanders are having their breakfast, no doubt with tea.'

All three observers were firing almost vertically and toward the southeast. 'This testing of the guns has gone too far', he thought. Then a bullet burst into his foot, forcing the rudder hard to the right. Startled, he let go of the stick and the 'plane mushed to the outside, or left, in a negative bank. Something fell hard against his head and right shoulder, making it harder to grab at the stick and right the aeroplane. A moment later his neck began to feel warm and sticky-wet, and the weight would not lift off his shoulder and neck. He turned and looked over his shoulder to see what was the matter. He found himself face to face with his observer, the left lens of his goggles shattered and blood flowing through the opening. There was no response to his efforts to talk to, then scream at, the observer. The observer was gone and he was yelling at a corpse.

A skilled flyer, he managed to take his right foot off the rudder pedal and recover the aeroplane. He pulled into a climb so the dead observer could slide off him and down into his own cockpit. Then he found a nearby town with its distinctive church tower, and pushed his 'plane back to his airfield as quickly as it would carry him. The ground crew raced up to his aeroplane, having heard of the calls from front line units reporting the skirmish with the English. Seeing no observer, they clattered their ladders on either side of the rear cockpit to see how they could help him.

"Nein—me! He is *kaput!* Help *me!"*

One ladder was moved, then the other, and the pilot was lifted out and carried away. At the field hospital he had three toes of his right foot amputated. Once he had recovered from the loss of blood, he entertained all within earshot with tales of derring-do and how he had saved the day.

The official report varied somewhat. While the lead aeroplane had been shot down in flames, the other flight members had returned to the field with the observer carrying a bullet in his right arm. They reported the flight as it had happened and exposed the surviving pilot for the fraud he was. While the press praised him as a hero, risking his life for *der Kaiser*, the military felt otherwise. As soon as he was able to return to combat status, they assigned him to the slowest unit they had on the eastern front. They felt he could do no harm, and the constant state of ennui would give him a lot of time to think over what had really happened.

In my brief time with him on the eastern front I could see no indications of regret or change or devotion to *der Vaterland*. He was quite satisfied to do as he was asked and nothing more. I, on the other hand, was tired of the war and wanted to go home. The only way home was to kill the enemies and destroy their will to fight.

The day I forced my pilot over the lines into the Russian rear area, I turned in my notes and observations. And I made a verbal suggestion.

"We need to learn what the Russians are planning."

"*Ja*, we do." The *Oberleutnant* seemed a little disinterested in my verbal observation. "Tell me, what would you suggest? Shall we land someone to infiltrate the lines and spy on them? Share a round or few with the local cossacks, frisk them a little and see what shakes out?"

"*Ja, Herr Oberleutnant*. Just that."

"And when the clock strikes the hour in five minutes, will you be popping out of the clock to 'cuckoo'?"

"*Nein, Herr Oberleutnant.*"

"You are serious."

"*Ja, mein Herr.* We do have spies, do we not? Sympathetic locals who would help our cause, perhaps in hopes of their own homeland upon war's end?"

That got his attention. There were many civilians who worked on the airfield, as well as others who brought us food and supplies, who were interested in vanquishing the Russians. There was talk of a separate homeland after the war. My idea was taken seriously, and about a week later the mission took place. One pilot was to take the infiltrator to an area near the front lines, such as they were, land, and have her climb out. My pilot and I were to distract attention by firing on the Russians with a rifle a few miles away. Once we drew local attention, the other aeroplane would land and dispatch the passenger. Three days later we were to duplicate the mission, except the second 'plane would pick up the spy and return her.

The mission went as planned. I had my pilot fly a little low behind the lines while I shot at soldiers unloading a train. This brought an ad hoc gathering of men with rifles, shooting at the crazy Germans trying to win the war for themselves. They did nothing more than put a few holes in our wings, but they left quite the impression with my pilot, who was distinctly uncomfortable resuming his role as combat pilot. He complained the whole way back to the field. Not that I heard him. Or cared.

The problem came during the pickup mission. My pilot refused to cross the lines. I asked him politely. I told him to go. I yelled at him and called him a coward. Nothing. So I played my trump card and produced a Russian pistol. And I screamed into his ear.

"Listen, old man. We are to attack on the Russian side of the lines. You will fly me there, allow me to fire at the Russians, and then fly me safely back to the airfield."

"And if I don't?"

"You have plans for after the war, do you not? Follow the flight plan, and perhaps you will see the war's end. There could be another badge for you to wear. But remember, one Russian bullet looks like every other Russian bullet. You can die a hero. Today."

"Who will fly the aeroplane if you shoot me?"

"If I shoot you dead, you won't be here to worry. Besides, a crashed German 'plane would be a great distraction. Is that what you want? A posthumous badge?"

"*Schweinhund*!"

Over the lines we went. We played our part to perfection. The *fräulein* was picked up without incident but with plenty of information. Upon landing, the old pilot bolted out of the aeroplane faster than I had seen him move since my arrival at the *Staffel*. He told anyone who would listen what I had done, what I had said, and what I had threatened him with. When questioned, I praised his flying abilities and his devotion to the mission but had no idea what he was telling them. I suggested he be awarded a medal. Upon learning the *fräulein* had been picked up and found to be most useful, I requested a transfer to the western front. Since they had a need for observers in the west, I received my transfer immediately. The old man refused to fly with me anyway and continued to accuse me of threatening him with a Russian pistol. I denied everything. Even if they did find the pistol in the river beyond the airfield, there was no way to link it to me. If that makes me a *schweinhund*, so be it.

* * * * *

CHAPTER 5

British

I came to the RFC and, eventually, my scout squadron, as the result of being wounded at my ground assignment. I was in an infantry supply unit, bringing food and materiel from the rear areas to front line units. We started with lorries repurposed from civilian use, often with the commercial paint job intact. I remember my first lorry, which had been used to carry fresh fish from the docks to markets and restaurants near Liverpool. Though the paint was a bit distressed, it was still a vibrant yellow with red letters shadowed in dark green announcing to all what smell was about to follow. My job was to help unload whatever supplies were moved from the back of that horribly pungent lorry to wherever the supplies were to be stored at or near the front lines. We had the occasional artillery barrage to deal with, but it was routine work. But, like the fields of Flanders, scarred with the trench lines and shelled, bombed and rained into acres of mud, the roads soon became impossible for lorries to traverse. When they sank to the axles and beyond in mud, too many men were required to extract them. So we went from lorries to wagons pulled by horses. It varied, but typically there were two men aboard the wagon and two horses pulled the load. Allowing for road conditions, lighter vehicle weight, and the less frequent occasions mired in mud, it was seen as superior to lorries for transporting goods. And the horses smelled far better than the stale fish. One day we brought a load of ammunition to a forward artillery unit. Everything went well until we stopped to transfer the shells, one at a time, to the ammunition bunker. Of course, we stopped the wagon practically against the storage building to make transfer fast and easy. But once it stopped, the wagon began to sink into the ever-present mud. After the wagon was empty we set about freeing it for the return trip. The driver was pushing a wheel on the open side, the horses were pulling, several men were pushing the wagon from behind, and I was almost wedged between the wagon and the building while pushing a wheel. That was when the artillery attack began. I suppose we were seen delivering ammunition from a tethered observation balloon over the German lines, and that information was relayed to a German artillery unit. The unit fired a shell in our direction and awaited correction information from the balloon. They needed little correction. The shell landed off the port side of our wagon and exploded on impact. The driver and one horse were killed instantly. The other horse suffered significant injury and had to be put down. The men pushing sustained varying degrees of injuries depending on how close they were to the explosion. One lost part of his left arm as well as the use of his left eye, among other injuries. The two men farthest away from the explosion, though deaf from the concussion, covered with mud, and thoroughly tossed about, were the first to get to me. The exploding shell had propelled the empty wagon against the storage building, pinning me. I was blind, immobile, and in immense pain. Though the entire area as then in chaos the two men summoned others to help move the wagon and remove me from the area. It had to be lack of blood that caused me to pass out at that point, but I'm no doctor, so it could have been any number of things.

I woke up sometime the next day in a rear area hospital tent. I felt as though I had been loaded into an artillery piece, fired thousands of feet into the air, landed, and tumbled across the earth. Everything hurt. I could not see. I could not move my left arm. I was able to move my right arm, so I set about exploring. Under a blanket I found my right leg in a bandage. My torso was bandaged as well, making it a little difficult to draw a proper breath. Across my torso I found my left hand and forearm, apparently in some kind of splint or bandage. I found what must have been a sling angling down from my right shoulder toward the injured left arm. And past the stubble on my face, I found the upper half of my head tightly wrapped. My mouth was parched and dry.

"Shit. m-m-m-f-f . . ."

"A-ha! Well, private, I am happy to meet you also! Would you like some water?"

He sounded a fine chap, right cheerful in the middle of my misery. He helped tilt my head up so I could sip some water. That was a big help. He explained where I was and how I got there, as I remembered nothing beyond trying to free the wagon. I asked about my partner. He hesitated but did not tell me about my driver. That was okay. The hesitation told me what I wanted to know. Good man, that driver, and funny. In other circumstances we might have been the best of chums. My most recent acquaintance told me I had been pinned against the wall by the wagon after an artillery shell had exploded very close by. I had numerous injuries, most of them minor, though none of them felt so minor at the time. I immediately asked about my eyes and he told me I had taken a direct shot of mud all over, including in the eyes. He could promise me nothing at that moment, but he guessed the eyes would heal and I should see again in a week or two. Fortunately, he was correct on that matter, though it felt more like an eternity. He informed me that my left arm was the worst off. The wagon had hit my upper arm, breaking the bone in at least two places. The bone pieces had punctured my skin. I had caused quite the stir when I arrived at the field hospital. They had to clean the arm, remove pieces of uniform, wagon, and fragments from other clothing, and clean some more before they could assess the damage to my bones. They had aligned the bone pieces as best they could and bandaged me, knowing they would have to go back in later and look for bone fragments and foreign matter. He was as cheerful as he could be, but he was also straightforward. I was in great danger of losing my left arm to infection which could lead to gangrene.

The friendly chap then introduced me to another voice. This voice was much softer. The nurse who possessed the voice had been assisting me with my recovery, mostly keeping my left arm as clean as she could. She took my right hand and shook it in a proper introductory manner, though I barely felt her hand, just the motion and subsequent pain from having been jostled, if only a little. I felt a sharp prick in my right arm and shortly thereafter, in the middle of something the soft voice was saying, I passed back into unconsciousness.

That was the pattern for my next week or so, though I could not keep accurate track of time. I would wake up and receive an update from the friendly chap or the soft-voiced nurse, feel a prick, and drift off again. If anything else took place, I retain no memory of it. Part of my life was simply erased, or, I suppose, never recorded in the first place, at least by me.

One day I woke up feeling typically groggy. I had been feeling better and better. Well, I was feeling less and less pain over most of my body anyway. My left arm was still somehow anchored and immovable, but it was still there. My right hand reported fewer and fewer bandages about my leg and torso. I could breathe a little better overall. I was finally successful in opening my eyes. But what I saw was as if I were looking through the bottom of a very dirty glass. There was a little light but absolutely no focus. After a frustrating moment I closed my eyes again. My right hand worked its way up my torso and neck to my right eye, where it found a heavy layer of some salve or gook or something.

"What *is* this shit?!"

"Right. See here, Private, that is no way to talk. There are women present, after all!"

"Oh. Sorry. I didn't see."

"Of course not. Well now you know. Stiff upper lip, old boy."

This was a new voice, not the friendly chap or nurse I had been interacting with for the past however many days—and nights? I asked him where they were and he informed me they had not moved. I had. They were still in some field hospital tending to other injured soldiers. I had been moved to a hospital in Dover."

"Dover?"

"Yes, yes. Dover. White cliffs, Channel coast, all that. You are home. Well, at least you are no longer in France."

I was told that I was in a special hospital to treat the worst of my injuries, namely my eyes and arm. My eyes were steadily improving, this new voice was nearly happy to report. My eyes had been cleaned repeatedly, removing all the Flanders mud and any other foreign matter. They found I had scratched corneas which would heal if left alone. I would just have to wait it out.

"But . . . my arm?"

"You are one very lucky lad, I must say. No one gave your arm any chance of remaining attached. Twice they set up the operating table to remove it. But it seems you were the beneficiary of a nurse who took a real interest in your case. They say she rarely left the tent once she shook your hand. Every time they put you under she went into your arm and cleaned it of anything that did not belong there, replacing your bandages with fresh wrappings. The woman did a magnificent job. Thanks to her efforts on your behalf, you still have two arms. That's the good news. We still need to set the bones so they can mend. However, due to the nature of your break, we may not be able to set your arm properly. We are missing parts of your bone, so the resulting arm will be out of shape and of questionable use. It will likely be a little shorter than your right arm. And, I suppose, how useful it is depends on you and how you participate in your recovery.

"But I will not lose the arm?"

"No, likely not."

"And I have that one nurse to thank?"

"Correct."

"Who is she?"

"Name's not on your record."

"Can you get her name?"

"No. Too many other patients to see to."

"But how will I . . . ?"

"Sorry."

That was it, then. I had one woman to thank for not losing a very badly injured arm. One woman had actually stood in the way of amputation, at least twice. One woman had tirelessly cleaned my arm and cared for me in every way. And I had no way to contact her to thank her. Who was this woman? What moved her to pay such close attention to the fate of just another bloke in her tent?

I really had no time for that, no matter how it irked me. I could not even say thanks, never mind any attempt to repay the debt. The war, which had been predicted to be over by Christmas of 1914, raged on over a year later. I had to get past my personal injuries and get back to the war, fight for king and country and all that. I was told I would never see my old supply unit again, that my arm simply would never be strong enough to move all the weight required of my former position. I was told my military career was likely over, but I refused to settle for that.

My fellow countrymen were under assault by the ruthless Germans. I could not just give up and go home. There was yet fighting to be done and I needed to do my share. The bloody bastards had killed my wagon driver and nearly killed me. Somebody had to pay for that.

I applied for a transfer to the Royal Flying Corps. I was rejected out of hand. Rather, out of arm. They told me, sensibly enough, that my arm had not yet been set and I was of no use to them while I sat in hospital. If I could use my left arm following surgery, they told me, try again then. That did it. "If I could use my arm," they said. Indeed. I would show them. They would hear from me again. I now had scores to settle, both good and bad. The bad one was actually the easier score to settle. I would find a way to repay the Germans for what they had done to me. They would regret the day they shelled that artillery emplacement and killed my mate.

It was the good score that haunted me. How was I to thank the nurse who kept me whole and likely able to return to the field of battle? No name, no idea where she was, what unit, nothing. About all I had to go on was her voice. We hadn't talked much at all as I had spent that time mostly under heavy sedation. But I would know that voice if I ever heard it again.

My healing process was indeed long and difficult. The surgeons put my arm back together as best they could and the arm looked as promised. It was not quite straight. It was heavily scarred. And it was a wee bit shorter than my right arm. The muscles had atrophied from lack of use. I was kept in a cast for several weeks. Well, several casts, since they had to open up and check the progress of the arm and be sure there was no infection. Once I was no longer required to wear a cast, I was able to begin to rehabilitate the muscles of my arm and hand, which had seen little use as well.

My first order of business was simply to work the muscles. Clench a fist. Open the hand. Clench, open. Clench, open. Twist the arm. Flex the arm, straighten the arm. Lift the arm. Lower the arm. It was not easy. These simple tasks had not been performed in a long time. I longed to lift weights, but for what seemed like forever the weight of the arm alone was all I could manage. Ever so slowly I was able to perform these tasks with increasing ease, though not without pain. I remained undaunted, if impatient. I took the viewpoint that while the arm hurt very badly to move, at least I still had the arm. It was improving. It would continue to improve. I would attain normal status and get into the RFC and take the fight to the Germans. I would do it for my dead mate from the supply unit. I would do it for the nurse with the soft voice who had worked so hard to preserve my arm. King and country? Sure. But my mate and that nurse were my incentives. I would return and I would make a difference.

I became a nuisance around the hospital. I was always walking somewhere, flexing my arms, stretching, twisting, anything to restore mobility to my body, which had lain dormant for quite some time. The hospital administrator asked me to carry on outside whenever weather permitted. He understood what I wanted and how I would work to get it, but he also had a hospital to run. Besides, the sooner I got better and moved on, the sooner he had an open bed for another soldier or sailor. This grew into a small movement of sorts. Others who could would also come outside and walk and stretch and flex, if for no other reason than to break up the tedium. As their "leader", I was asked to keep an eye on them so no one fled the grounds. Seeing my "followers" gave me encouragement to continue my quest to get back into the service via the RFC and exact my revenge on the Germans. The responsibility of watching after the other patients helped me to work on leadership skills and nurturing others, which would become useful in time.

Recovery took several months. At least it took that long to get to the point where I felt I could again approach the Royal Flying Corps for admission into the observer program. My left arm was not as strong as my right. There was some minor nerve damage and mobility was less than one hundred percent. But I could lift light objects and perform simple tasks with my left arm and hand. I could lift enough weight to change the ammunition canister on a Lewis machine gun, the standard observer weapon. I could operate a camera and change glass plates. I could lift the equivalent of a grenade or light anti-personnel bomb. I could certainly read a map and navigate, though I would need to learn more about weather and how it affected flight.

I contacted the RFC and they agreed to have me in for physical testing. I was slightly deficient in a few areas, but they saw that what I lacked in physical ability I more than made up for in attitude and "fighting spirit". Assured that I was not done rehabilitating my arm, they allowed me into the observer program.

I easily passed the parts of the program that dealt with what I had already done in the army. I quickly adapted to the Lewis gun since I had learned about the Vickers machine gun in the infantry. The major difference was that the Vickers gun was belt fed and the Lewis was drum fed, so the rounds entered the firing chambers in different ways. I was aware of military protocol and the like. The most important courses to me were weather and navigation. I could navigate, but I lacked some of the proper terminology for military communications. Weather was a little bit of a problem. I learned which clouds portend what kind of weather. The other clouds were of no interest to me but I still had to know them to pass the testing. I learned about the prevailing west to east winds over France and Belgium, where I was most likely to be assigned. There were other things, like the cloud types, that I had to "know" to pass.

That led to my first flight in an aeroplane. I was helped into the front seat of a pre-war Farman pusher biplane and shown how to attach the lap strap that held me to the seat. While I thought I would be able to communicate with the pilot, any hope of that was dashed once the rotary engine mounted just behind the pilot sputtered, coughed, and grudgingly came to life. I was reduced to hoping he would understand whatever combination of hand signals I came up with. There was no ceremony. The pilot bounced the Farman down the field and turned around, facing into the wind. The sputtering, hesitant engine suddenly roared steadily and the biplane bounced harder and harder until it no longer bounced at all. We had left the ground, which was rapidly receding behind us. Well at least I hoped it wasn't yet another bounce. I grabbed the sides of the cockpit nacelle, surprisingly with no hesitation from the left arm or hand. I could see nothing but sky unless I looked over either side. It was an unsettling feeling, but not a bad one. The aeroplane rocked a bit side to side on the way up. Almost suddenly the pilot brought us to a level attitude and the horizon caught up to us. I could see almost all around the aeroplane and I looked at the ground below. The pilot tapped my shoulder and pointed to our port side and down. I looked and there was our airfield. It looked quite small. I looked around at the pilot, jerked my thumb upward, shrugged my shoulders, and mouthed the words, "How high?" He held up the five digits of his left hand, closed his hand, opened, closed, and opened his hand again. I asked, "Fifteen hundred feet?" He nodded. I saw water in the distance and asked, "Dover?" Again, he nodded. I pointed at him, me, and Dover and he responded by flying away from the field in the direction of Dover. He flew just offshore, then circled back toward the airfield. I saw my former hospital approaching, and the group I had supervised while there was outside at that moment. So I leaned over the side if the nacelle, shouted, and waved madly. No one noticed. No one even looked up. Then the hospital disappeared beneath the starboard wing.

The pilot made a routine landing and the bouncing returned as we alit and taxied back to the flight line. Once he shut down the engine, I am sure I squealed like a delighted child and asked for more. He said no, he had reports to fill out and I was to report to a certain officer for debriefing. "Debriefing?" I thought. "What was that?" Meanwhile, I thanked the pilot for the brief tour, hoping it would not add to the paperwork he was about to do. He managed a wan smile and walked off.

I soon learned what the debriefing was. I was asked a battery of questions about my flight and how I felt about having left the ground for the first time. Why did the pilot fly to Dover and back? I told him it was because I had asked him to, and please don't punish the pilot as it wasn't his idea. He found it curious that I asked about flying over Dover. I told him I would have asked to see Scotland if I had seen it from the cockpit, anything to extend the wondrous experience. Was I upset? No. Was I nervous? No. Was I queasy? No. How was my arm? Just fine, thank you. After a few more questions about altitude, distance, and weather conditions, I had a question.

"When can I go up again?"

* * * * *

CHAPTER 6

British

I had made it. I was an observer in the Royal Flying Corps. At least I would be once I was assigned a unit to observe for. Having passed through my first time up in a completely satisfactory manner, I was sent to classes on aerial photography, aerial reconnaissance, bombing, aerial gunnery, and contact patrols. I would be doing some or all of these tasks once I reached the front. None were at all difficult, and I was passed right along into a pool of observers waiting to get to the front lines. While there I continued to work on my left arm and hand, steadily improving mobility and strength. We also went on further training flights with specific tasks to accomplish while up. Fly from our "home" field to another field, then to yet another field, then return home. The observer was to tell the pilot where to go and the pilot was to follow instructions unless it would have put us in danger to do so. On one such flight our engine quit and we had to land in a fallow field. When the engine cooled down somewhat, the pilot stood on a crate and checked the engine spark plugs and HT leads for clean contacts, tight fit, and secure connections. Everything back in place, he carefully instructed me on how we were to restart the engine. I had seen it done a few times, but never participated. It was a sequence. He would say, "Switch off" and I would pull the propeller through a complete rotation, hopefully drawing fuel into the cylinders. The pilot would say, "Switch on" and I was to reach both arms through the lattice work booms that held the aft flying surfaces in place and pull the propeller as hard as I could, all while being careful not to fall. Contact with the moving prop could be deadly. Besides, as soon as the engine came to life I was to race to the front of the aeroplane and somehow climb into the cockpit for the flight to our next field.

It started like clockwork. He said, "Switch off" and I pulled the blades through a full rotation. "Switch on." I reached through the tail boom, pushed the prop away just a little bit, then pulled it as hard as I could, catching myself with my right hand on part of the boom. As the engine made its familiar coughing sound, I ducked under the port wing and jumped on the barely rolling port wheel, using it to spring upwards along the cockpit side. One foot caught the cutout step as both hands grasped the top of the nacelle side wall. With his free hand, the pilot grabbed the back of my jacket and helped me up and over the side of the nacelle. It was the boost I needed. I managed to fall sloppily into my front seat as the aeroplane taxied down the field. As the 'plane turned into the wind, I righted myself, fastened my lap strap and away we went.

We arrived considerably later than planned at the next field, and the officers in charge had numerous questions. The pilot and I were separated and questioned. Since our answers lined up with one another and the pilot's gloves and jacket were grimy from the engine oil and grease, we were released to our temporary quarters. We would eat and sleep there and return home in the morning.

Our arrival at our home field caused a minor stir the next morning, shortly before lunch. An officer at the other field had called the day before inquiring about our flight status, which caused a murmur among the men. As we left that morning, the officer called our home field again. He related our story about fixing the engine and completing the flight, albeit late, and commended us for our actions. We had saved one of His Majesty's aeroplanes, however outdated, and stayed the course to complete our assigned task. "Well done," he said. We were feted with a more special lunch than normal in observance of our accomplishment. The men, knowing the story of my left arm, were very impressed that I had mustered the strength to start a hesitant rotary engine and then climb on board a moving aeroplane. I gave all the credit to my pilot. After all, he had landed the aeroplane safely, performed the necessary repairs, and directed me just how to help get back in the air. I merely followed directions and had a lucky leap that enabled me to grab the nacelle side. The pilot had to help me in.

That was a lesson that helped me with my flying career. That pilot took my love of internal combustion engines and put it into action to solve a problem. He inspired me to learn more about these engines and how they worked so I could make them perform better. This would help me once I was assigned to a scout squadron. I was able to improve the performance of my Nieuport and then my SE by following simple rules of thumb. Make sure the cylinders were getting fuel and consistent spark. But I am getting ahead of myself.

* * * * *

CHAPTER 7

British

One morning I was called out and told to gather my things. I was assigned an FE2b to report to once I had my things in order. This would be my first time in a "Fee", as they were called. The FE2b was a front line observation machine, though rumors had that it was no longer an effective machine. It was another "pusher" with the engine behind the pilot, though this engine was a more powerful inline water cooled Beardmore. The inline engines did not cough like the rotaries. Where the inline engines had throttles like motor-cars, the rotary engines like in the Farman had cutout switches, commonly called "blip" switches. The pilot could use the switch and cut out some of the cylinders to reduce power. Release the switch and the engine went to full power. The pilot on my errant training flight used the "blip" switch to enable me to get into the cockpit. There was a "throttle", but it was an adjuster for the air to fuel mix in the engine to compensate for altitude more than anything else. Other than the type of engine, the Fee mostly resembled the Farman with the tail surfaces being held out back behind the propeller with booms mounted on the wings. This pusher design was going "out of style" in favor of the "tractor" designs which placed engine and propeller out in front. This made for a neater cruciform airframe. The fuselage was the "vertical" of the cross with engine in front and tail control surfaces out back. The wings formed the crosspiece. Simpler design, fewer wires, less drag, more efficient. But until someone came up with a more efficient tractor biplane for the RFC, the Fee was it. There were, of course, rumors, but one could not fight a war flying a rumor.

I was given a location in France and told to plot my course from my current home field to my destination. I had been selected to move up from a reserve field in England to a reserve field in France, one big step closer to a front line squadron. I could not have been more excited, and I set to work plotting my course to France.

This was to be my first flight crossing a significant body of water. The pilot called out the now familiar sequence for priming and starting the engine and the ground crew performed its tasks. Soon the engine was running and warming up for the flight. I showed the pilot our intended course to France. He approved, but I kept the paper handy in a pocket inside my flight suit.

One never knew. The takeoff was routine, and the Fee rose quickly to altitude. Well, quickly as compared to the underpowered Farman anyway. I found the aeroplane strong and reassuring. And there was a gun, a Lewis machine gun, mounted on a post in the front of the nacelle. There was also a post behind me in case I needed to move the gun and fire to the rear, over the wing and pilot's head. While we expected no opposition on this flight, the Lewis had a full drum of ammunition installed, and there was one spare drum in my cockpit.

After a few minutes' climb, we flew over the coast and above the Channel. I looked through the forest of struts and wires behind me to watch Dover disappear, and then I looked around me. There was nothing to see but sky and water. There was one ship below, steaming in the opposite direction, surrounded by several smaller ships. All of a sudden I felt very alone. No land in sight. I found it just a little unsettling. But almost as soon as that feeling came over me, France came into view. Very soon after flying over the French coast the pilot set the Fee down on a reasonably smooth airfield and proceeded to the flight line. After the Fee was secured and we were helped out of the aeroplane, the pilot asked me about the flight. What had I seen? I told him I had seen water and several ships. Any aeroplanes? No. Then he told me what he had seen upon approach to the French coast. There had been a flight of Fees forming a short distance to the south, two British flying boats below us to the northeast, and several Nieuport fighters had been above us to the east in pursuit of a German seaplane. My confidence was shaken. While the aircraft sighted were mostly British, I had not seen a one of them. In a hostile environment, this inability to see other aeroplanes in the air often turned deadly. I had some more work to do to develop the ability to see my surroundings while aloft. After all, I had to see the huns before I could shoot them down. I thanked the pilot for the disheartening news, as he only meant to help.

There likely would not be any aerial conquests for me. At least not for the moment. Once I was assigned, my duties would be to observe the enemy on the ground, take notes, make aerial photographs, and possibly hurl grenades or the like over the side of the cockpit to bomb German troops or transports. Or I could be watching an artillery barrage from the air, a new perspective for me, and correcting gun aim by communicating with the gun battery. But, while doing any of this I had to be aware of what was in the sky around me. There was no such thing as a dull mission. I would soon learn that scout aeroplanes were smaller, lighter, faster, and more maneuverable than anything I had flown in.

I then spent a lot of time outside, looking into the sky for aeroplanes and judging their distance. If a pilot was going up with no one on board I asked to go along so I could gain more experience watching the skies for "company". I wanted into the RFC, I got into the RFC, and I wanted to be very good at what I was doing. It was the only way I could pursue my revenge.

I soon got my chance. A front line FE2b unit had lost one aeroplane and one additional observer in a skirmish with the Germans. I was chosen, along with another fellow from my airfield, to replace the two observers lost. We were flown to the unit's aerodrome one sunny afternoon. It was a beautiful day. We started out over green vegetation, circled a few times as our Fees gained altitude, and proceeded toward the southeast and our new home. As we neared the front lines, the terrain went from lush and green to pockmarked and brown. Off the port wing we could see the scar of the trench lines in nearly parallel zig-zags. All the while I kept an eye toward the air, constantly checking for aeroplanes. There were a couple of Fees below and to the west, then several Nieuport scouts climbing out of their aerodrome, two silver and two dappled green and brown. Then I saw the sun briefly shine off something above and beyond my partner Fee. I yelled, pointed, and grabbed the Lewis gun to set it on the post to my rear. I located the dot above the other Fee and trained my gun on it, not knowing whether it was friend of foe. I squinted over the gun, straining to see what it was until my ears gave me the answer. I heard the popping of machine gun fire coming from the direction of the dot I was tracking. It was an "EA"—enemy aircraft. We were under attack! I trained my Lewis a little high and fired about fifteen rounds, followed by maybe ten more. I know I saw hits, but I will never know their effect. The EA abruptly broke off its attack and headed northeast, toward the lines and, presumably, its aerodrome. I was elated. My heart was pounding. I got one! I got one! My first kill! No German *flieger* was safe with me in the air!

When we set down I almost couldn't wait for the ground crew and boarding ladder. I had to hurry and file my claim for a victory, after all! I ran, still in full flight gear, toward the office of my new unit. Breaking into the office, I faced an adjutant and told him, "I need to claim my victory!"

"What victory?"

"On the way here, just moments ago, I shot a hun off the other Fee's tail!"

"Did you, then?" I could feel the sarcasm. The office was thick with it.

The paper pusher reached for a form and took my name, time, approximate location, 'plane number, pilot, and an endless list of other items, most of them nonessential. Then he asked me what I had shot down.

"I don't know."

"You don't know?"

"No."

"What did it look like?"

"Well, I didn't have a great look at it, but I saw pieces of it fall away."

"Pieces?"

"Yes. Well, bits."

"Bits."

"Yes, I thought I saw bits of it fall away after I fired at it."

"You thought?"

"Yes."

"What was your range?"

"Oh, maybe two hundred yards or more."

"Hmm."

"Hmm?"

"How many shots did you fire?"

"Two, maybe three dozen."

"Hmm."

"Hmm?"

"What did it look like?"

"Well, it looked rather like a Nieuport. But bigger. Wings brown and green, fuselage yellow brown, but pointy nose—rather like a shark."

"Hmm."

"Hmm? Could you stop the 'hmm' and just stamp it as a victory?"

"No."

"No? Why not? I answered all your questions. What more is there?"

"Well, I need to finish a few details on the report and submit it to the officer in charge of the unit. He will read it and send it to our regional headquarters. Once there, it will be compared with aerial observations from the ground and from the air. If someone else saw the action and can confirm the crash, then you have your victory. It did crash. Didn't it?"

"Well, no. I mean I did not see it crash."

"What did it do after you shot at it?"

"It flew away."

"Flew away."

"Yes, over the lines."

"Then it crashed."

"No. Then we landed."

"So you fired a few shots at a big Nieuport shark aeroplane and it flew away."

"Well, yes."

"The only reason I am forwarding this report is because I have spent so much time questioning you and filling it out. I can assure you this will not be a victory."

"Just why is that?"

"Well, you did not see it crash. You did not see it on fire or trailing smoke, right? Or did you?"

"Well, no, I didn't."

"So no crash, no fire, no smoke, just a few shots and a few bits falling away. Unless someone else saw your noble deed and excellent marksmanship and can confirm a crash—or at least some fire and smoke, you have done nothing more than waste my time! Try not to let this happen again. You need far more than this to claim a victory in the RFC. But . . ."

"But?"

"Yes. But you can continue to feel pretty good about having saved one of His Majesty's aeroplanes and the two men on board. Nice shooting. Sir."

With that the adjutant turned, walked away, paused to make a few marks on my report, and slipped it into a tray marked "OUT". Needless to say, I heard nothing further about my claim.

* * * * *

CHAPTER 8

British

That was my introduction to my new squadron. To some I had attained the status of glory hound before they even knew my name. Oh, but that was not my way, not at all. I was less interested in the glory than in vanquishing the huns responsible for this war in general and the death of my army mate in particular. It was less important that I received actual credit for killing Germans than the mere idea that there were fewer Germans left to fight. It was going to be difficult to overcome that first impression of me. Then again, this was not grammar school and I was not terribly interested in fitting in. It was war, I was in the RFC, and I was trying to end the war, one Hun at a time if need be.

Most of the pilots did not want to fly with me, thinking I would get them in trouble with my ways. I could neither say nor do anything to change their minds. But there was one pilot who seemed almost too anxious to fly with me, an old Scot named MacGregson. I say old and I mean old.

Why, he was easily the oldest pilot in the squadron, at twenty-six or -seven! The typical pilot was perhaps nineteen or twenty, and with that full red beard and mustache and faded old Scottish cap he wore everywhere, he could have passed for any pilot's father. Ebenezer MacGregson. The others called him "NeezMac" or just "Knees". I suppose it was a bit of a workout to pronounce the man's full hame. Besides, he went along with it. Encouraged it. Not much bothered him. Not much interested him. He would constantly pull a little from his sheep bladder, kept tucked discreetly under his old unit's tunic. Whiskey. Scotch whiskey. Those who didn't hate me told me I brought back the twinkle that was once a constant in his eyes. He took a fancy to me before I even set foot on his aerodrome. I was "thut cocky lad wit' nerve", what with the way I shot just over the other Fee landing to put rounds into the attacking Albatross. No, he knew I hadn't downed the machine, but he also knew I gave that Hun pilot new respect for British gunners. He had met me outside the adjutant's office and introduced himself.

"Lad, I'm Ebenezer MacGr-r-regson. You are the replacement for my observer, may God rest his inattentive young soul. If ye want, ye kin call me 'Knees'".

I began to salute—he was a lef-tenant—but he grabbed my hand on the way up. "Sir. My name is—"

"Balls!"

"Balls, sir?"

"Cease wi' the 'sir' shit, laddie! I'm nobody."

"But s—uh, Mr Knees, —"

"It's *Knees*, laddie! I'll 'ave none o' that 'mister' shit, too! Laddie, it took real balls to do what you did comin' in just now, shootin' at a bloody Hun over the field. Most children would have covered their heads. You, have balls!"

"Why, thank you, uh, Knees."

"I'm pickin' ye as me new observer, lad."

That was the positive side. I would be paired with an experienced pilot. I could learn a lot from him. Then there was the bad side of it all. Several of the men had heard our introductory conversation. From that they derived our name, and the name spread throughout the squadron. "Knees 'n' Balls". Never mind our given names or ranks. We were "Knees 'n' Balls". This was going to be interesting.

I met Knees the next morning. Morning. It wasn't even five o'clock yet. We got some of the typically thick coffee and he led me to our aeroplane. As it was pitch dark, I could see nothing of it other than it was a typical FE2b with a ladder leaning on the port side of the nacelle to help us enter our "office". At that moment a couple of the ground crew were loading extra ammunition drums for my Lewis machine gun. The Lewis was a curious weapon. The ammunition was carried in a round, flat drum that mounted to the top of the gun. Some drums carried forty-seven rounds, some ninety-seven rounds. Once one had expended the contents of a drum, one had to remove the empty drum, stow it on board for later reloading, and replace it with another drum. It was a bit to do in the heat of battle, being tossed about in a maneuvering aeroplane. It was good that I did not have to fly the aeroplane while doing this, but that would come later. Oh, did I forget to mention? There was no front seat. There was a safety strap to wear while doing nothing. If one was doing anything in the front cockpit the strap inhibited motion. And if one stood up to shoot the Lewis on its rear mounting post, everything above one's knees was above the level of the cockpit sides. Precarious was not an adequate description. My office was essentially a shallow bathtub.

Once the ammunition had been placed onboard, the ground crew started the engine to warm it up. A warm engine made for a better and more reliable takeoff. Since the engine was the sole source of motion through the air on takeoff, creating airflow and, therefore, lift, one wanted a warm engine. It was less likely to stall. In the event of an engine stall on takeoff, the aeroplane was in great danger of falling to the ground due to lack of lift. This made takeoff the most dangerous part of the flight.

I was given a set of map coordinates for our ArtObs, or artillery observation mission. We were to fly to those coordinates and wait. At five thirty, an artillery unit was to begin shooting at a German position just behind the lines. Our job was to observe the target and where the shells landed. If the shells were accurate, we had little to do. But if the shells were not precisely on target, we were to signal the unit how to correct their aim in order to hit the target using pre-arranged Morse codes on a wireless set. We would try to remain on our side of the lines, as it was safer over our own guns. Usually. Some on the ground were known to fire their rifle at nearly anything that was overhead. But we still had to watch the air around and above us. Though the Germans did not care to fight behind our lines, they were known to dive at ArtObs aeroplanes, usually out of the sun, firing as they approached, and zooming back up and over their own territory. If we flew too close to the front lines, the German troops would lift up their rifles and machine guns and give us a warm welcome. There were many things to keep track of.

Though we were not going to be very high above the ground, we were both bundled up with several layers of clothing. This made it difficult to clamber up the ladder and into the nacelle. The nacelle in a Fee was like a bathtub but with two tiers. I was in front, on the lower level, with my Lewis gun, ammo drums, and map case. The pilot sat behind me and slightly higher so he could see over me and fly. The radiator and engine were just behind the pilot and the propeller was behind the engine. The turning propeller drew a constant blast of cold air past the pilot and observer which made it feel even colder than it actually was. Our only protection from the frigid air came from the cockpit sides and the clothing we wore. Knees supplemented this with his bladder of scotch, which he claimed made him feel warmer. I was not inclined to agree with him. Not yet.

Thanks to the warm Beardmore engine, the Fee took off into the westerly breeze without incident and Knees circled it around to fly to our assigned coordinates. At the appointed time, the barrage began. We made a minor correction, which resulted in a hit on the ammunition supply for the German gun. This was a little personal, as I had been on the receiving end of just such an attack. I was thinking of my mate who was killed trying to push our wagon out of the mud when I was brought back to the moment by the "zip . . . zip-pock!" of a couple rifle rounds fired from the German side of the lines. One hit our upper wing just outboard of the nacelle within a few yards of Knees and me. Not bad for being at least three hundred yards away from us. I snapped around to look at the wing and heard Knees above the roar of the engine.

"Bah! 'e got looky!"

Knees did a quick job of triangulation, pointed at the lines and shouted, "Return the greetin' lad! Let Mister Lewis say 'allo!"

Now that was a great idea. While waiting for the next artillery round, I could be harassing the bloody Huns. Maybe even injure or kill a few. It was, after all, a gun. Why not put it to use? So I aimed across the trench line and no man's land, and emptied a drum at the German trench, five or ten rounds at a time.

"*Guten tag,* ye bloody Boche bastards!" Knees waved his bladder in the air over his head, then took a sip.

Shooting at the Germans made me feel good. I made a mental note to request larger capacity Lewis drums and maybe a few small antipersonnel bombs for future ArtObs missions. It would help pass the time.

That was the pattern for the next hour or more. We watched the shells fly and land, made corrections as needed, and shot at Germans on the ground while the sun rose to the east and filled in the voids of darkness. Knees watched the fuel gauge. When we got low on petrol, we returned to the aerodrome to get more of that thick coffee. We felt pretty good, aye, but we were cold. The early sunlight did nothing at all to warm us. Coffee would be very good along with whatever the cook had put out.

Once we landed and procured some more coffee, we filled out our reports. Since I had emptied several drums of ammunition, I had an armorer report to do. They would want to know what I had been shooting at. I mentioned it to Knees. As he squeezed a little scotch whiskey into his coffee he said, "Fritz wake up call. One of many services we provide." While I liked his response, I wrote, "Trench strafing."

We learned we were to go up again later in the morning, same mission but different coordinates. I went to the armorer and requested only the larger Lewis drums and maybe a few small anti- personnel bombs. He asked what I wanted all that for. I told him, "Dance lessons for Fritz."

When we climbed into our aeroplane for the next mission, I found someone had left me a present. I had requested some small bombs, but they could not just roll around on the cockpit floor. So someone had attached a rack to hold six of the little "calling cards" on the starboard side of the nacelle. I pointed to the rack and asked Knees, "Only six?" He nodded and shouted, "Aye, lad. We must watch our weight. The Beardmore can lift but so much." I looked about the nacelle to see if perhaps there was something we didn't need.

Our next flight went a lot like the earlier one. We took off and arrived at our coordinates in time to watch a fine show of artillery work. Between rounds we sometimes climbed a little and swooped at the German lines so Mister Lewis could greet Heinrich 'n' Fritz. I would add a bomb at the end for an exclamation point. The Germans would fire back with their rifles and pistols, mostly behind us but with the occasional hit on the tail surfaces. As we crossed the British trenches we saw our Tommies waving and cheering at our little assault. We returned the wave, happy to provide them with a distraction from their constant grind.

Following our third such visit I was waving at our troops below when Knees suddenly banked hard and dove. I looked up at him and he pointed straight up. In a hard turn to port, I saw past our starboard wing tip two or three dots growing larger very quickly. Each one had small flashes in the middle—machine gun fire! This was the "hun in the sun" I had been told about but never seen. I reached for the Lewis gun but Knees waved me off. He nosed down and headed west as fast as the Beardmore would push us. I saw why he was rushing to get out of the area. It looked like every gun that could be elevated was firing at the three Albatross scouts hurtling toward us. The fighters made one pass at us, putting several rounds through our wings, then zoomed for altitude and headed east. Though we made it out okay with nothing more than some patching to be done by the ground crew upon our return, it was a valuable lesson on why we had to watch the skies constantly. If my head was not constantly swiveling and looking up, down, and all around, I was placing myself in grave danger of being surprised and killed by a German airman. On the other hand, diving out of the sun looked like an excellent offensive maneuver. At least once I found myself in a scout squadron.

I knew I would get to my scout squadron. While I could see I was not going to do much to vanquish the German air service from the front of an outdated pusher, I could also see I had a fine opportunity to learn about my new "trade". Knees was a veteran flier. He had joined the Royal Flying Corps just before the first shots were fired in 1914. Like many, he had feared the war would be over before he could get over the front and make his mark. He had started from nil, learning about aerial fighting with the rest of the early war flyers. Though he hated to admit it, he had waved at German flyers. "Buck then we didn't know any better!" But two years into this war, with no end in sight and stagnant trench lines, he merely wanted to do his assigned tasks and kill Germans. The man knew a great deal about flying and fighting and I was in the unique position to pay attention and learn from his experience. He was more than happy to take me in and help me learn. He taught me what he could in the air, but we spent a lot of our down time together. As long as he had his scotch whiskey within reach, he was happy to tell me anything I wanted to know. And more. He had some stories to tell, and not just about flying. Most had common themes about them. All save one included drinking. All save one involved women and the pursuit thereof. (No, the exceptions were not the same story.) Being naked was a frequent occurrence, but that did not always involve having fun—even though that had been the original intent of the "mission". I did learn that small town French jails could be very cold. And women were not always the most reasonable of people. They, too, could be very cold if they were still interested in you but your interests had moved on. I learned that when you entered a building you should never lose track of how to exit said building. Once in a while I heard about his wife, whom he hadn't heard from in some time. I never did learn her name. He referred to her only as "me wife" or "coldest of wenches". He never spelled out how things got to be the way there were, but he didn't have to spell out that it would stay that way. I did learn that when he started talking about his wife, it was a sign that I had to find him more scotch. Once that was procured, more pleasant conversation could resume.

Lef-tenant MacGregson knew a lot about the Fee. I let him talk on about it, even though we both felt it was practically a relic in the current state of warfare. From his observations on the aeroplane, I learned how to look for the qualities of an airframe and determine its strengths and weaknesses. The FE2b, or Farman Experimental number two, second model, was an attempt to fire a machine gun forward without firing through the propeller arc. Though there was an existing patent for synchronizing machine-gun fire through a spinning propeller, it hadn't proven practical just yet. So rather than fire through the propeller arc, the designers moved the propeller and engine behind the aircrew. While it opened up a wide field of fire for the gunner, especially with a second gun mount between the crew members, it was a forest of struts and wires. There were extra booms to hold the tail surfaces out behind the rest of the aeroplane in addition to the regular struts and bracing wires between the biplane wings. All this drag made for a very slow aeroplane. This was the tradeoff for the open field of fire in front. Knees had done probably anything and everything that could be done in a Fee—yes, even that—and I was convinced there was no better source on how it flew and fought. I knew that if I kept the scotch handy I could absorb what this veteran flyer was willing to share. I also knew that if I were patient, he would allow me to fly the aeroplane. I was confident that he would show me how to work the controls, what to look for, what to do, and how to do it. I just had to bide my time. And keep a supply of scotch as an "instructor fee", in case his stock ran dry. I considered it an investment in my future.

After almost every flight we would sit somewhere quiet and discuss what had happened, just Knees, his bladder of scotch, and me. I learned a lot from him indeed, mostly about flying. No matter what the others said, no mission was routine. Each mission was different. Some of the differences were minute, but the flight could be affected by such little things as wind speed, wind direction, overall weather conditions, what artillery crew one was spotting for, and so on. Many missions were similar, but no two were quite alike.

* * * * *

CHAPTER 9

British

Knees did a little cajoling and got us a different assignment. One morning we were to load a second Lewis gun onto our "bus" as we were to fly escort for another Fee while the crew did ArtObs. The Germans had become a little more protective of territory of late and more watchful for spotter aircraft, stepping up their patrols along the lines. Knees and I were assigned to fly higher than the observing crew and keep a watch for German fighters. Upon sighting a German patrol we were to warn the other Fee by firing a red flare and then prepare to defend them. The second Lewis gun was to save the the time and effort of moving one gun between mounts. Because of the extra weight of the second Lewis gun, I was unable to bring along any grenades.

Our day began like a normal flying day. We were up early and had coffee. We met with the other crew and discussed the mission, and then went to our waiting Fees to get underway. Since we had more climbing to do, we took off first and started toward our assigned coordinates. This part of the mission was the most pleasant. I had nothing to do, so I could look around. Darkness was yielding to light. I watched campfires going out with little wisps of smoke. The few remaining lights also went out with the daylight reaching westward with increasing intensity. The colors were constantly changing, even on the drab earth, mostly brown with little spots and patches of green. The green areas were the surviving areas where plants had refused to die despite the horrendous growing conditions. Looking at the green gave me a sense of hope. This war would not last forever. The green areas would grow again, perhaps as a field. Or flowers. Or foodstuffs. Life would go on. Perhaps I could pursue my dream of being an artist, painting the burgeoning landscapes as war receded and nature and agriculture rightfully took over. Of course I shared Monet's fascination with light and how it was constantly changing. I could spend hours sipping tea in a garden, letting light and color change around me. I would look for pleasing combinations of color in just the right grouping and light conditions. Charged with all this information, I could go later and put brush to canvas. I could easily do two or more paintings just to demonstrate how light changed one's perception of color, perhaps even adjusting the grouping for aesthetics. Change was and is a constant in the world around us. This fighting from stagnant, immovable trenches went in the face of nature. Nature was always changing. I felt that if I did my part to win the war, then I could pursue my art when the fighting came to an end.

I was thinking of where I would establish my painting studio when I felt the wings rocking the Fee from side to side. Coming back to my current situation, I looked over my shoulder. Knees put the end of his clenched fist onto the opposite palm. We had arrived. I had to concentrate on the skies around me in order to protect myself and the other crew members around me. I set my head to rotating and looking up and down, focusing far and near, and squinting into the sun. Flying in our antiquated barge, I wanted all the warning I could give the pilots. The German Albatross flew and fought very well, at least compared with the FE2b. It was a completely new generation of aeroplane. Gone were the "expedients" of large field of fire at the expense of rear mounted engine and masses of wood and wire dragging in the wind. The Albatros was smaller, sleeker, more powerful, more aerodynamic, more maneuverable, and better armed than the Fee. The Germans had every advantage and were not ashamed to exploit it. War was not meant to be fair. Each side worked for an advantage over their opponent with the intent of using it.

There were no huns in that morning's sun. I checked and checked but found none. Nothing entered our vicinity save the artillery shells just passing through on their way to their German targets. Other than the strain of looking, it was a very easy mission. Our petrol situation dictated that we return to our field, refuel, and wait for orders. I fired a blue flare, our signal to break off and go home. The other Fee turned toward the aerodrome and we followed behind and above. I continued to search for surprises but none were to be found. The Boche were either sleeping in that morning or just not interested.

That afternoon we were ordered to fly another escort mission. We flew with the same crew as in the morning. They worked with the same artillery unit, but the target was a short distance from that of the morning assignment. The flight was very similar to the morning effort except we were flying in full sunlight with only a few light clouds. The light did not vary as much as earlier. The other aircrew got similar results on their new target and we found no enemy aeroplanes in the sky. How was I to deplete the supply of German aeroplanes and aircrew with no targets to shoot at? I began to think more about pilot training and a scout squadron assignment.

When we returned we were dismissed for the day. Knees and I went off to a nearby garden to talk a while. I shared my frustrations about having no aeroplanes to shoot at and my desire to join a scout squadron. Shooting down Germans was the sole reason for scout units, wasn't it?

Knees appreciated my desire to cut a wider swath, but he also wanted to keep his gunner. He told me about the attrition rate of scout pilots in front line units, who lasted but several weeks on average. I asked him the difference between that and being in an antiquated FE2b. It was only a matter of time before some Hun in a sleek new Albatross got the right combination to send us down. In a one-on-one confrontation, there was no possibility that the Fee could defeat an Albatross. It was a matter of seeing them before they saw us and then having time to prepare, whether to run or to fight. Knees took in a bit of scotch and said he would try to get me more opportunities to kill Germans. After all, did it matter whether they were in aeroplanes or on the ground? He did have a point. While aerial combat was arguably more glamorous than ground strafing, dead Germans were dead Germans. He then pointed out that the shell that had put me in hospital was from a German artillery unit, not an aeroplane. Besides, he added, whether he meant it or not, our squadron was to get the new Bristol two-seater. It was rumored to be faster than some single seat scouts and quite maneuverable. Now that was an interesting bit to know.

I told Knees I wanted to know more about flying. I asked him to show me more about the controls and how they worked the aeroplane. He found that line of questioning much more agreeable, so we walked back to the flight line and to our Fee. I got a ladder and climbed into the cockpit where Knees normally held court. He stood on the ladder and guided me throughout the cockpit. Due to other aeroplanes landing and taking off, we were not able to taxi about the field. But I'm sure I asked about every gauge and handle in the cockpit. In response to his answers I told him that the more I knew the safer we both would be. In the event he was wounded on a flight, I could take over and fly us home. He chuckled at me, if only a little. "How cute, huh?", I volunteered, "Just like that".

"Aye, lad. Joos' lack thut."

Lef-tenant MacGregson was a curious individual. Indeed, he had a lot to say, when prompted, but little of it was about himself. He would talk about life experience but not necessarily his life experience. I knew about the "wife that wasn't" but little else. Little bits may have come out here and there, but nothing of consequence. He appeared consumed by the war to the point that little else mattered. I took the constant nips of scotch as attempts to numb his perception of the world around him. Was it the war and all the horrors he had seen? Was it his wife? Whatever was troubling him, it truly did not affect how he conducted himself in the air. When piloting the old FE, he was as good as the RFC had to offer. He knew the aeroplane and its characteristics from general performance to the little quirks of our particular machine. He used that information, tempered with his prior experiences, and seemed always to know what to do to get out of a situation. One would think he would be impaired by the scotch, but he never showed any hesitation in the air. It was always comforting to have such a skilled and experienced pilot behind me. He helped me work with my inexperience and inadequacies and shaped me into a confident spotter, gunner, bomber, photographer, and whatever else my assignment required me to be. I had asked him once or twice about his wife, his family, his home. Each time he had just taken a nip of scotch from his little bladder and looked over my shoulder. Far over my shoulder. I decided that if he wanted me to know anything about his personal life he would tell me, but on his terms and not merely because I had asked. So I kept conversations mostly about the war and flying.

The next morning delivered us just that, war and flying. Knees and I were to fly escort again. After slugging down coffee with the mistaken notion that its warmth would help us stay warm in the frigid air at altitude, we went out to the line and our Fee. The ground crew helped us into our idling aeroplane and then Knees surprised me. Flying escort, we were to fly as light as we could so as to help the FE's rather lame "maneuverability". I felt a tap on my shoulder and I turned to see Knees with his hand inside his flight coat. When he withdrew it, his hand was holding not his bladder, but two small grenades, which he handed to me. Then he produced several more. I was touched. He left his bladder behind so he could give me something with which to harass the Germans in their trenches.

I soon discovered just what he had in mind for that flight. Once the ArtObs Fee was established and we had searched the sky for German aeroplanes, Knees flew straight toward the German trenches. He tapped me on the shoulder and gave me a hand gesture associated with "after you". I was tickled. I opened up with the Lewis, sending a hail of "*guten tag*" into the trenches, followed by a grenade. I saw a machine gun emplacement being set up out of sight of our trenches, pointed it out, and Knees flew right at it. I dropped a grenade. We circled back on the spot to see the gun blown several yards from where it had been and the area littered with German soldiers in unnatural positions. We heard what sounded a lot like machine gun fire and felt a couple zip by, so we headed back toward the ArtObs Fee. Craning around to look, I saw the source of the bullets. The grenade had started a fire that was consuming a few crates of ammunition. That had to be delightful on the ground. I felt bad for them and smiled.

The rest of the flight was routine. As we packed up and headed home, I thought I saw a few specks above. They approached us, but seeing we were going behind the lines they held off. It was a good flight. The other Fee had directed fire which led to the destruction of an artillery battery, I got to vent some of my frustrations on the German trenches and machine gun crew, and we brought our bus home with but one bullet patch needing done on the port lower wing. I told the lad how the holes had come to be there, and he didn't seem to mind the task at all. In fact, when we returned to our Fee for the afternoon escort mission we saw the patches had the oft added white disc with black cross. Forward of the discs, however, there were white marks resembling narrow pie slices, the effect being that of an exclamation point. How novel!

The afternoon flight was similar to the morning flight. Making sure the other Fee was safe to work, we again headed for the trenches to get rid of the few grenades I hadn't used earlier due to the excitement caused by the detonating ammunition below. I saw plenty of winking rifles and pistols and no lack of clenched fists being raised toward us. This time, however, we had company. Once again, from out of the midday sun dove two Albatrosses, their bullets announcing their presence. I fired a red flare ahead of the other Fee and checked that the Lewis to my rear was cocked. Knees did a little bit of a dive and then pulled the Fee into a tight left turn in order to evade the fighters. We watched as both 'planes streaked past us and flew directly at the other Fee, which was flying in a straight line in the direction of our aerodrome. Knees pulled out of his left turn to give chase, but it was for naught. The Fee could not catch up to a diving Albatross on the best of days. It only gave us a better view of the destruction of the other FE. The gunner, in the unit maybe a week, stood up to shoot his rear Lewis over the wing. He hadn't even grasped the grip when his head snapped down onto the gun butt, the result of several bullets knocking him away from the gun and against the front rim of the cockpit. There he lay, head and one arm dangling over the side. Mere seconds later we were sickened to watch a fire break out under the port upper wing. The petrol tank had been hit and set ablaze. The pilot never had a chance to make a decision, if indeed he was even alive. The fire spread rapidly across the doped fabric covered wooden airframe. The port wing, losing its lift, began to dip and the flaming mass went to the ground in a short, slowly twisting dive. We were certain neither man survived. The German pilots, quickly drawing the attention of anybody on the ground holding a gun, used the momentum of their dive to climb quickly and turn in the direction of their lines. Their zooming turn took them roughly around us. First one, then the other pilot waved at us as they departed. We returned their waves with the ancient gesture of the bowmen. Bugger off!

Back at the aerodrome, we reported the loss of the other aeroplane and crew, but word had already arrived via telephone. We were ordered into the mess, where we were questioned sharply at length. How had this happened? Where had we been that we did not see the enemy aeroplanes above? Why had we abandoned our charge just to harass a German trench? What had we hoped to accomplish? Where had the grenades come from? Did we not know we were to fly with reduced weight for escort missions? The questions just kept coming. I wanted to go get Knees his bladder. I'm sure he would have welcomed a nip of scotch right about then.

Knees answered the first few questions, and then he shut up. After a few more, I slipped a little in my answer, stammering a bit from all the intense scrutiny. He sat still. Then the questions went directly to him. After a few head shakes and a roll of the eyes, he finally drew a breath and, starting softly and building a long crescendo that composer Richard Wagner would have appreciated, gave a general answer. "We did set up the other crew to do their job. We did check the sky and made sure it was clear of any Hun bastards. We flew the shortest distance we could to overfly the German trenches so we could *kill* them. Is that not our job, *killing* Germans?! The lad kept looking up and saw no German aeroplanes. The ruddy buggers came out of the sun! The *sun*! We did not see them until it was *too late!* Allow me to take *you* up so *you* can stare into the sun from the front porch of a patched up old barge. Do ye think *you* can do any better, ye paper shufflin' desk bound daredevils?! We were and are very distraught over the loss of our lads. It could have been *us*. We did the best we could, flyin' these ancient box kites! Tell me when we are getting modern aeroplanes to fly! We canna' be expected to win a war while flying these ridiculous, outdated contrivances against the latest German killing machines! These old things are beyond wishful thinking! Give us some *weapons!*" By now he was leaning forward at the interrogators, screaming, deep red in the face, and holding the seat of his chair to keep from hitting somebody. I sheepishly pointed at him—his words—and nodded.

That rebuke bought us cancellation of any activity off the aerodrome unless we were flying in an old FE2b. No visits to town, no leave, nothing. Fly missions, stay on the grounds. It could have been far worse, but they knew Knees was completely correct. His record was impeccable and they knew it. After a few days we were told that the rumors were true. We were to get the new Bristol F.2b, a brand spankin' new two-seater tractor design with guns front and rear and about a hundred more horsepower. The rumors said it would make the FE look like someone's bad dream. That was the good news. The bad news was that they did not know when we were to begin receiving this wondrous new machine. The factories were hard at work building as many as they could, and ours would arrive as soon as they were ready. While we were heartened by the news, nothing changed for that moment. We were still flying our tired old buses.

Poor visibility cancelled our first mission the next day. I went back to sleep. Knees woke me up from a serene dream, slapping my boot as I lay on a back table in the mess.

"C'mon, laddie! I've got a surprise fer ye."

"m-m-m. Wha - - ? Surprise? More grenades?"

"No, laddie. C'mon! We're goin' up in an 'F2B'!"

"F2B? Shit! You're pullin' my leg! An F2B . . . "

"Laddie, let's *go!*"

I leapt from the table and ran out the door to the flight line, where I saw nothing but Fees, several of them warming up to be flown. I slowed my pace to follow Knees, who was walking at a much brisker pace than was his norm, as he approached our old barge. Then I started to laugh out loud.

"*This* is the F2B?!?"

"Right ye are, laddie. Aye, this is the F2B. Would ye luck a hund into your office?"

I thought I had smelled fresh paint among the exhaust fumes and raw petrol as I approached the line. Now I knew why. Knees had gone 'round the bend. He had obtained a pot of white paint and a smallish brush, and on each side of the nacelle he had painted in large, thick characters, "F2B".

"What the bloody *hell!* Sir."

"Laddie, we have the first F2B in the squadron. Now, then, let's go kill some Hun bastards, shall we?" With that, he spanked my bottom as to spur me to climb the ladder. I shook my head and obliged.

"Permission to board, Lef-tenant?"

"Aye, lad, granted. Now, outta me way so's I kin tind to me business."

Knees handed me the map for the mission. We were to fly escort yet again. We both knew we had to bring the other crew back safely, so no straying away for personal gratification. So away we went on our escort mission, strictly by the book.

We had been socked in that morning, but by the time we lifted away the clouds had lifted as well. There were still some higher clouds, and I found that Knees had a plan to use them. We climbed out and kept climbing as we approached the area we were to watch. The other crew flew with us but decidedly lower. They looked a little lower with each passing minute, but they were at altitude. Knees was still climbing, though at a slower rate. I saw his plan. He was going to check the sky for Germans and then fly among the clouds, creating the impression that the other Fee was up with no escort. Then he and I were going to watch the sky constantly for any other activity in the vicinity. The delay in takeoff pushed our time back to about midday. We soon discovered that the Germans didn't necessarily take certain times off to eat. I caught a tiny flash above me and pointed it out to Knees. He had seen it, too. He held up two fingers, then his fist. There were two huns above, maneuvering to get into the sun. We watched them to the point of blinding ourselves. They assembled, circled a few times, then dove, one a little behind and to the starboard of the other. Apparently they had not seen us in the fringe of the clouds, as they looked to be diving at the Fee we were protecting. Knees let his experience show again, lifting the starboard wing sooner than I thought was appropriate. But he knew his sluggish old barge. The timing was perfect. We emerged from the clouds as the Boche were about four hundred feet above us, too late to maneuver out of the way. I trained my Lewis on the front scout and opened fire, leading him perfectly. I was admiring my work, watching bullets hit the engine and penetrate the fuselage just aft, forming a dotted line toward the pilot. Then I nearly leapt out of the cockpit. There was an indescribably loud noise immediately behind my head. Just as the lead Albatross exploded about fifty yards dead ahead of us, I realized that Knees had reached over to the rear Lewis gun and fired it at the upper Albatross.

"SHIT!" I dove down into the cockpit.

"Wot, lad? I was merely tryin' ta hep ye!"

I peeked over the edge of the cockpit to see the upper Albatross on fire and trailing thick, black smoke. The pilot wasted no time in climbing out of the cockpit and hanging onto the port side of the fuselage. It did him no good. He reached back into the cockpit for the control stick, but must have hit it with his bulky gloved hand. The starboard wing suddenly dipped. The pilot lost his grip and appeared to lean backward, toward port, and fall free of the rolling bird. As the tail surfaces went close over him, the turbulence caused him to rotate backwards in an awkward backflip. We watched the pilot tumble as far as we could make him out. As fellow flyers, we were sick to our stomachs. The mere fact that he was the enemy allowed us to get over our momentary horror. The burning Albatross bored through the more slowly falling debris from the disintegrated Albatross,, and it all appeared to be heading for the German trenches. An explosion on the ground confirmed the point of impact immediately in front of a trench, probably on some of that inevitable barbed wire.

We finished looking at our handiwork and started to laugh. We were surrounded by flares of several colors. We followed the path of the most recent red arrival and realized that the other Fee had been trying to get our attention. We waved and I shot a blue flare between the other Fee and our aerodrome. Let's go home.

When we landed, we saw there was a huge throng gathered around the aerodrome. We landed shortly after the other Fee and found that everybody was pointing at us. I smirked and thought about the fresh "F2B" painted on the nacelle sides and finished stowing my equipment.

As we pulled up to the flight line, the ground crew grabbed our wing tips and pushed our barge to its spot. Then they waved and smiled as they placed the wooden chocks by the wheels. We saw the crowd converging on our aeroplane and wondered what was wrong. What had we done to draw such a crowd? This did not look good. The throng closed in and began beating on our nacelle. Scary though it was, I had to laugh a little as a few of them withdrew hands with white marks on them from the fresh paint. Eventually some soldiers and gendarme arrived to pull the people back somewhat and attempt to restore order.

"What the hell!"

A few people broke past the gendarme and jumped at me.

"What is the meaning of this?"

Someone yelled in French something about "deux boche". One of our recent interrogators arrived below us, this time all smiles.

"Everyone is excited about your two kills."

"Two kills?"

"Why, yes! Ground observers saw the whole thing and telephoned us."

"I got one, but—how did they know it was us?"

"We had no idea until you landed. But the witnesses said it was an FE with 'F28' painted on the sides. And here you are! Great shooting, lad!"

"But I got one."

"Two were confirmed as shot down."

"Oh! That was Knees—uh, Lef-tenant Mac—"

"I bloody know who Knees is! But how the—"

I explained how Knees had nearly frightened me to death with a Lewis gun next to my head and . . . .

"Save it for the reports. That was a marvelous show. Well done."

Well done. That was it. Hell, I thought we would get more grief over the painted fuselage. Regulations, you know. But Knees' little prank had worked in our favor. Two confirmed kills, both landing in the enemy trenches, and we were local heroes. Needless to say, all prior transgressions were forgiven. We were free to go as we wished, and the others wished we would go more than we did. We had a stream of visitors from surrounding squadrons, the nearby towns and villages, virtually every unattached female from nuns to nurses and widows to farm girls. We had our photograph made for the local newspaper. We were actually kept from flying in order to satisfy all the local curious. Eventually, some of the upper brass arrived to shake hands and make promises. Among the promises was one that we would get the very first Bristol F2B to arrive at our squadron, though the much-anticipated arrival date was still murky at best. I asked for that promise in writing and felt Knees' boot hit my shin.

The rest of the squadron personnel did appreciate one aspect of our newfound fame. We did not want for fresh food. People brought us eggs, vegetables, grains, freshly killed game, chocolates, wine, bread, nearly anything one could imagine. And flowers. There were flowers everywhere, freshly picked from local gardens. I found the array of colors wonderful and fascinating. Who knew they still had gardens? Sometimes, while waiting to entertain more locals, I would arrange the flowers on a sunlit table and gaze upon my creation as the sun played its light on and around them. Something made me think of my unseen heroine and benefactor, the nurse who seemingly dedicated herself to healing me and keeping me whole. Thanks to her devotion to my care, I had overcome my injuries, kept my arm, and returned to the war bent on revenge. Perhaps I should make an effort to find her. She deserved, at the very least, the thanks I was unable to give her at the time due to my heavily sedated state. But how would I "look for" her when all I had was a voice. One doesn't look for a voice. Nor does one "listen for" anyone. "Excuse me, but could you say something soothing so I can listen to your voice? No, that's not it. Thank you all the same." Folly. It was all folly. Finding a voice in some anonymous field hospital was not likely to happen then, was it? But part of me had to look—listen—search for her.

All the local food brought to the unit inspired our mess cooks. Suddenly they all thought they were French chefs. Believe me, French cooking takes on a whole new life when interpreted by men from around the British Empire. If any of them had any kind of training I was not aware of it. I believe one had been a waiter while going to school for his law degree before the war intervened. Sometimes he would step into the kitchen when a cook overslept—or slept one off. But none of that mattered. The cooks thought anything good could be made better with wine and *fromage*. Add wine while cooking, then pile on the *fromage* to serve. This was their rendering of French cooking. No one seemed to care after a long day. If someone didn't like it, there was food aplenty to choose from. Bread and wine was a popular meal when the cooks got a little too creative. We were never lacking for something to talk about at mealtime.

* * * *

CHAPTER 10

British

We finally got a reprieve with a flight assignment. We were to join another FE and escort a third FE over the lines as it photographed a near back area. The brass hats apparently thought something was happening back there and we were to provide the proof. I looked over the mission plan and asked if we could get one of our nearby scout units to contribute a few Nieuports. I just thought that a few scouts flying higher up would help put the odds in our favor, what with us all flying the ancient, outmoded FEs. We were more likely to encounter German scouts over their own lines, so having scouts of our own simply made sense to me. Surprisingly, someone making decisions favored my point and lined up two Nieuports to rendezvous with us. I had hoped for more, but two Nieuports were certainly better than none.

The French Nieuport was an interesting design. Nieuports were known as racing aeroplanes before the war, competing for the Schneider Cup, among other events. Their latest design was an expansion of their trim little scout from 1915. That design, the Nieuport 11, had a Lewis gun mounted atop the upper wing, firing in line with the aeroplane's flightpath and above the arc of the propeller. The lower wing looked almost like an afterthought, it was so narrow. The reason was to allow the pilot downward visibility. With the upper wing in the pilot's line of sight and the narrow lower wing, the pilot had a large field of view. The Nieuport 17s that accompanied us that afternoon were very similar but slightly larger and more powerful than the earlier 11.

When the three of us met up with the two Nieuports I saw that both had synchronized Vickers machine guns mounted atop the fuselage and one had a Lewis gun on the upper wing. Both were in a bright greyish silver finish with the usual British cockades, identifying letters, and a very small amount of red trim. They looked very sleek when compared to our old buses and added an air of confidence to our mission.

The pilot of the camera 'plane fired a green flare and we started for our assigned area while continuing to climb. The Nieuports climbed almost like balloons released underwater compared to our FEs. They circled as they climbed since they were significantly faster than our 'crates as well.

It was near midday when we approached the area to be photographed. The rains which had delayed the mission from its originally scheduled time were over with, but there remained splotches of cloud over the region, slowly drifting to the east. I looked below at the lad setting up his camera for the photo run. I looked off to port at the second escorting Fee, and I looked above for the Nieuports. I could not see them for the clouds, but my gaze was met by first one, then another red flare fired from almost directly above. EA. The Nieuports had apparently spotted enemy aircraft. Two red flares were the signal to abort the mission and head home.

Quickly I waved at the other escort FE and pointed at the flares falling just to starboard. Then I repeated the two flare signal so the camera crew could see.

The next sight I shall never forget. Following a loud clatter from above, I saw a Nieuport emerge from a cloud above and ahead of us. At first glance it looked like too much Nieuport, but I quickly realized that it was both Nieuports with a black cross in the wreckage—an Albatross! Though I will never know for sure, it appeared the Albatross had miscalculated it's dive and hit one or both Nieuports. There was a huge mass of flame and debris falling together toward the ground, a cross here, cockades there, struts and smoke. We were fortunate that it passed at least a few hundred feet away as Knees had no time to react. After the odd flaming collection of aeroplane parts dropped, I saw one grass green and pale blue Albatross lower wing fluttering slowly down not much faster than a falling leaf.

But there was no time to ponder what had happened above. The other players in the tragedy we had just witnessed were entering our stage now as two Albatross scouts dove practically across our nose. They appeared to be trying to get to the camera 'plane below, as their tracers reached out for it. The Germans never saw the escorting FEs. Knees and the other pilot exchanged glances and down we went after the huns, hoping to save the camera crew and its valuable information. Knees nosed us over close behind the second Albatross and I sent several bursts in that direction with no immediate effect. Knees took us a little to the right so as to avoid the other diving FE, but I corrected my fire to the left. I watched holes appear in the fuselage and approach the cockpit, and I saw some hesitation in my prey. Did I get him? The Albatross dropped a wing and spun about a rotation and a half, but then the pilot righted it and continued after the camera 'plane. I fired the last few rounds in my drum and had to replace it with a full drum. Just then our FE pulled up suddenly and seemed to pause in mid-air. Then it leveled out but felt unsteady. I looked back and saw that Knees was in trouble. He had arched his back and extended one arm to the side. I saw blood around his mouth—he had been shot and did not look good. With his other hand he struggled to keep the Fee straight and level, even if it was not a good combat tactic.

I looked quickly about as another Albatross hurtled past us toward the skirmish below. We did not look to be a threat for the moment and he could always come back up for us. Oh, but if he did, . . . there was no time to think like that. Knees was in trouble and he was flying the aeroplane. Or trying to. The FE must have looked like a drunk at closing time, such was its flight path. I had to do something or the war would be over for us both. Using the rear gun mount for stability, such as it was, I hopped up and flopped my belly on the nacelle between the two cockpits. Between the mounting post and its support wires there wasn't much room to be had. I poked at Knees and got no response. I lifted his head and looked into his eyes. Nothing. I punched him but he was inert. Damn. He was gone. No, not just yet. His head moved a little and he blew little bubbles in the blood coming out of his mouth. He reached into his flight jacket, pulled out his bladder, and put it in my hand. Then he attempted a salute, raising his hand toward his head. From about jaw level, it simply dropped to his side. That was it. Knees had passed along his prized possession to me, then departed. He was no more.

Shit. Now what to do? I was about ten thousand feet up in a woozy aeroplane with a dead pilot and no way to control the 'plane or my fate. If I couldn't do something and fast, I was done for. If the old bus didn't dive and crash, it would surely be shot up by an Albatross or few. I had but one choice if I was to survive. I had to get to the controls. I pulled myself a little further aft and pushed Knees back in his seat. Figuring I lacked the arm strength to hold him, I put the top of my head in his chest. I unbuckled his lap strap and tried to pull him up out of his seat. That being unsuccessful, I pulled myself alongside him, putting my feet to starboard of the seat. From there I was able to lift him off the seat and forward. I planned on getting him into the front cockpit so I could attempt to take him back to the aerodrome for proper disposition. Somehow, with pauses to adjust the control stick to maintain level flight, I managed to get him mostly out of the rear cockpit. I got behind him, braced myself, and gave one shove toward the front. I shoved him out of the rear cockpit, but he did not quite clear the rear gun mount. He started slipping off toward port. I briefly held onto him but realized he was more likely to take me out of the cockpit than I was to move him forward. So I did the only thing I could do to save myself.

I . . . let . . . go.

Knees, or at least his physical remains, slipped off the cowl and off the nacelle into open air. He briefly paused as if lying on his back. His right arm appeared to swing toward his head, as if he were saluting me or waving goodbye, but his body continued to fall slowly backward as he disappeared from view. I swear he nearly hit one of the Albatross scouts below, but by then I had moved on to other things. I had to get back to the aerodrome.

First I attached the lap strap so I would stay put. Then I realized that the strap could barely contain me. Knees had been a larger man. I had to tighten the strap a bit so I could reach what I needed without tumbling loose into the busy sky. I thought back on the time spent right there in the cockpit with Knees showing me the features and telling me what they did. My first move was to rock the stick gently from side to side and gauge its sensitivity. Response was a bit sluggish, I imagined, but that was preferable in those circumstances. I wasn't likely to throw the old kite on its back.

Control established, at least somewhat, I then determined that I was flying nearly due north over the trenches. I had to turn left at least one hundred degrees and head toward the west/southwest in order to get to the aerodrome. Fuel was not an immediate concern, but I could not waste a lot of time. I began a tentative turn to port, dipping the port wing tip and nudging the rudder bar. It was a slow, flat turn, but I was not worried about my form at that moment. I had performed the maneuver and I was headed home.

I had lost track of the battle over the camera 'plane and its crew. I did not know who had survived or what had happened. But I learned in a hurry that at least one Albatross pilot was still about and hungry for more blood. I pushed the throttle forward to hasten my exit but there was no escaping the Hun with his superior Albatross scout. I watched as he climbed toward me in a broad circle. It was maddening. Here I was in this damned old bus with no gun in reach, watching the latest in German scouts, a smaller, sleeker, lighter, more maneuverable, more powerful, faster, and better armed machine, as it circled to get above me. I recognized the tactic. He was going to dive on me from the left rear in case there were a gunner, which, obviously, there wasn't. Being a sitting duck would have been preferable at that moment. What could I do? Stir the soup with the stick? I rocked the 'plane violently out of frustration. Wait. Did I hear something? What just rolled along my foot? I looked down and could not believe my luck—a grenade! There was a grenade along the port side of the nacelle, near my foot. Aha! I may have been in the German pilot's sights, but at least I was not completely without means to fight back. I dragged the grenade back along the side of the nacelle and loosened the lap strap so I could lean over and pick it up. I then looked hard at the controls in order to figure out how to get the barge to do what I needed it to do.

I pulled the stick up a little and looked over my shoulder. There was the Albatross above me and to the port side a little, resplendent in the midday sun. It had what looked to be dark green wings and a deep yellow nose. And it was entering its dive. I started into a shallow dive of my own, feigning escape. Then I waited. He was diving hard at me, guns blazing away. I saw holes appear near the Fee's port wingtips. Then they "walked" across the wing toward me. Just another moment, I waited. Sensing just how close he must have been, I suddenly gunned my engine and entered a hard roll, raising my starboard wing tip. The faster Albatross was just behind me and below. As I rolled up and to the right, I flipped the grenade into the air with my left hand, grabbed it with my right, and threw it hard at the middle of the 'plane's mass. I had hoped to put it into the cockpit, but I missed. Instead, it hit between the gun butts in front of the cockpit. Close enough. The grenade exploded and took out a large chunk of the middle of the aeroplane. It was no longer a threat.

The blast, however, forced the Fee to complete its roll and begin to tumble a bit. I managed to put it back to straight and level while I regained my composure. So that was what a roll felt like. It was my first. Again I found my direction and pointed the bus toward the aerodrome. I was alone in the sky. Or, at least, no one else was bothering with me for the moment.

I managed to arrive at the aerodrome, still in one piece. I circled it once and then attempted my first landing. Nothing looked right. I seemed to be too low, so I climbed. There, that was better, but—wait! Someone else was landing. I had not seen them, and I caused them to land in an awkward manner so as to avoid me. I climbed some more and circled around to try again. I aimed at the near end of the field and pushed the stick forward. This caused me to dive, so I yanked the stick back, overcorrected and found myself hanging nearly still in the air. I pushed the stick forward again and closed my eyes. That was it. I had done what I could and created a most ungainly flight path. There was nothing more I could do than let gravity take over.

* * * * *

CHAPTER 11

British

When I opened my eyes again I was lying on my back on a table in the mess. I was surrounded by flowers. Lillies. "Oh, no," I thought. As my eyes opened the room broke into a very loud and long cheer. Oh, and did my head hurt! I asked what happened and how I came to be on the table. They told me about my go-around and subsequent landing attempt, the dive, the stall, the next dive, and the splat! I had hit the ground with such force that I wiped the landing gear off the bottom of the bus, no mean feat. The poor old thing skidded a few yards and started to come around a little. They said it appeared I hit my head on the edge of the rear cockpit cowl. They also said it looked like there was more blood on me than the minor flesh wound warranted. I started feeling about myself, checking things over, when I came upon the bladder. I just stopped. After a moment to recall what I had just gone through, I pulled out the bladder, raised my head off the table a little, and had a nip. At that point, I deserved it. I had made it back to the aerodrome.

I asked about filling out the reports, but the men insisted I rest a while. The bloody reports would be there, they said. Though they had many questions, they thought I needed time to rest and reconstitute myself first. I just closed my eyes and lay on the table.

Knees was gone. I no longer had the older lef-tenant to go to for guidance. He had done all he could for me. I was now on my own. But, oh, what an education. He took some brash lad silly enough to attempt shooting down an Albatross in order to defend a fellow countryman, saw it as guts, and helped mold him into some kind of fighting animal. I had had the anger in me when I arrived. Knees gave me the tools to enable my mission. That was it. I had managed to fly myself back to the airfield, even if poorly executed. The way I saw it, I came out of the landing alive, so just how bad had it been? The battered old Fee needed replacing anyway, so no real harm done there. Perhaps my—*our*—old "F2B" would be replaced at last by a Bristol F.2b.

So I could fly. Yes, I needed work, but I could fly. And so I put in my request for pilot training. I was reminded I had reports to fill out, but I told them it could wait until I had finished my formal request. After making everyone wait for those few minutes, I got to the reports. One of my former interrogators came in to talk me through the ordeal. He was much more sympathetic than he had been the day Knees had ended up shouting at him. He knew it had been a bad mission when the observer landed the 'plane with no pilot on board. He did tell me that the camera crew had made it back ahead of me but the other escort had yet to be heard from. Unless they had landed at another field, they were assumed to be dead or missing. I held my opinion since I had not actually seen them go down. But their circumstances were fairly desperate the last I saw of them.

I began to recount my story of that flight. As I got started, another squadron member entered the room and sat down. Then another. And so it went, more and more people stopping in to hear what had happened that cost the life of a veteran squadron pilot. Though no one knew about the grenade, they had heard about the telephone calls crediting me— us—with victories over two enemy scouts, possibly Albatrosses.

I was given two weeks off flying, in part because I had no pilot. I was told I could do whatever I wanted within reason. So I borrowed a lorry and set about "listening for" my nurse. I gathered a list of field hospitals to visit, but I soon found this to be futile. So many hospitals had changed locations to suit local fighting and casualty conditions. Personnel had transferred between units. Some had finished their service and gone back home or been reassigned to home duty. There were, after all, a great many hospitals back in the UK where service personnel were being treated. While "listening", I had kept an eye open for the doctor who had treated me. No news there, either.

After the first week I gave up trying to find my former nurse. It was past time to contact Knees' family about his loss. I was given permission to go through his effects in hopes of finding a relative or someone to contact regarding his demise. There was nothing. No pictures, no clues, never mind names and addresses. Just another dead end. The dead end seemed to represent my fate in the war. One assignment ended with the death of my mate on the supply wagon. After recovering from that, I found a new mission. This one, too, ended with the death of a friend. I could only hope to get my flight training in that I might get a hold of a scout and go kill Germans. If having friends meant that the friends had to die, maybe I no longer needed friends. Maybe I needed to concentrate on killing Germans and let friendship wait till after the war. There was a simplicity to the notion that I liked. Pay attention to the job at hand and never mind the distractions.

Though I was still to be away from flying, I could not stay away from the flight line. I found myself going back to see if I could be of assistance to the fitters. Sometimes they had me patch bullet holes while they tended to the more intricate systems, namely the engines. I knew that they had done nothing with the wreckage of our FE, "F2B", since it was not in the way of daily operations. They called me a "good chap" and thanked me for bringing it to rest where I did. Then they asked me if I would be willing to help with salvage operations. Since the RFC did not plan to repair it, some of the parts could be useful in repairing other FEs Having nothing better to do, I was happy to help. The engine, radiator, some of the control parts, and miscellaneous bits like struts and fittings could be removed and stored in the event they could be used elsewhere.

A good lot of blokes, they offered to cut away the badly smudged "F2B" from either side or both for me as a memento. Though it was damned thoughtful of them, I had all the mementos I needed. I had Knees' bladder and his scotch whiskey, an appropriate reminder. And I had the memories of our time together in my head. I offered my warmest thanks and suggested they could put one or both in the mess if they wished. Or anywhere they wanted. They would be nice to see, yes, but I did not need to have any of them with me.

I had put in a full day on my former FE. As we broke at midday on the second day, I was summoned to see the CO. When I arrived he told me I had been approved for pilot training.

"The brass were most impressed with your performance, piloting the 'plane to the field and putting 'er down like you did."

"I had to, sir. My only other option was to die, and I was not ready to accept that. I merely found a way to live another day. I intend to kill many more Germans."

"They admired your fighting spirit and were very quick to confirm your two victories."

"Thank you, sir."

"They will likely recommend you for the DFC."

"I will be sufficiently happy merely learning to fly, sir."

"You obviously can fly. It's your landings they want to work on!"

"Uh, yes, sir."

* * * * *

CHAPTER 12

German

I very nearly did not make it to the western front. Often personnel were transferred by aeroplane as part of transporting that aeroplane to another location. However, most of the aeroplanes in use on the eastern front were outdated models no longer effective on the more active western front. Fighting was more aggressive and required the newest and best technology in order to compete. So I was taken by horse-drawn wagon to the railway depot, where I continued my transfer by rail. My train approached a junction in western Germany just as it was being bombed. The engineer applied the brakes to keep us out of the attack, and we slowed to a stop on the outer limits of the yard. We found that not all the bombs landed in the center of the target area. One errant piece of ordinance found its way into a nearby ammunition storage building, resulting in a massive explosion, hurling much shrapnel at our train. Many windows were broken, including the one I was looking through. As a result, I was hit full in the face with glass and whatever had penetrated the window.

I woke up a short while later in a large wooden shed, surrounded by other German soldiers and civilians, some apparently medical personnel. I was assured I would be fine. I had come out on the losing end of the encounter with glass and a sharp metal object.

"*Gott im Himmel*! What hit me, a cannonball?"

"No. A window, *mein Herr*. And this . . .'

A most pleasant round face with brown eyes and framed by short auburn hair smiled down at me. She was wearing white under her dark overcoat. The woman took my hand and placed in it an object, which I raised so I could see it.

"It seems you stopped a pipe, or at least this part of it. The pipe entered your compartment through the window. It hit you full on your cheek, leaving a nasty gash, knocked you to the floor, and remained on your chest."

"And you found it necessary to save it for me."

"I thought you would want to be better acquainted with the little miscreant. After all, it left a big impression on you."

"How is that?"

"Well, there are numerous glass cuts, mostly minor in nature. I don't know how all that debris missed your eyes. But the pipe did the most damage, cutting deep into your cheek. I'm surprised it didn't break your cheekbone or knock out any teeth. We cleaned the wound thoroughly and I stitched it the best I could, but I'm afraid it might not heal as well as you might like."

"These things happen in a war. I'm pleased I am still alive to discuss what happened."

"I like your attitude. *Das ist gut.* We are going to be together, at least for a short while."

"How is that?"

"I'm taking you with me. You need rest and you need to be monitored after what happened to you."

"Nonsense. I have a war to fight. This wound is nothing." I sat up and began to swing my legs off the bench or table I was on . . . and sagged back to horizontal.

"Go ahead and fight your war. Tomorrow, maybe. You were hit very hard and you lost more than a little blood. Consider this. Even if you were well enough to continue, there is no good way to get to your destination. Nothing will depart or pass through this junction for at least a day or two. Damned Englishmen did a through job. Our men need to clear the debris off the tracks and determine what repairs need to be made. You do not want to be on a horse cart in your condition. Not on these roads."

"So you are my assigned nurse."

"Not exactly. But yes."

"Not exactly? What do you mean, 'not exactly'?"

"I'm not a nurse. And nobody assigned you to me. I work near here. I was walking to work when the attack happened, and I saw the explosion that hit your train. I could not help with the building that was on fire, but I thought I could help with people on the train. I saw you lying there with your pipe. You were bleeding badly and needed a compress on your wound. I raised you and held a rag to your face. Once the bleeding subsided I got some others to help get you off the carriage and over here with the other victims."

"*Danke.* Wait. You are not a nurse. But you stitched my face."

"*Ja.* A student nurse helped me clean your wounds, but he was afraid to do stitches. There were more seriously wounded people about, so I took the needle and thread from him and sent him to help with others."

"But you are not a nurse."

"I helped in a hospital while I was in school. I've seen doctors stitch patients. How hard could it be?"

"And that is why my wound may not heal well?"

"No. The pipe tore out a bit of your cheek. I fixed it the best I could, but the wound needed to be closed to keep out infection. Look. You lie still. I am going to see if I can get you anything for the pain. I'll be back soon. I will not leave you. You are going to need someone nearby in the morning."

With that she was gone. I drifted off to sleep. Well, I passed out from lack of blood.

"Come on, come on. Let's sit you up and see how you feel. We need to get you out of here."

She was back. I found myself helping to get me into a sitting position. I was a little dizzy yet, but I wanted to stand and get my bearings.

"Let's go. I'll get some food for us and take you home to rest until tomorrow."

"I cannot let you buy me food," I protested.

"I'll just get it. You needn't worry."

"How is that?"

"I run the tavern."

"Fine. We can eat there."

"*Ja, ja.* Okay, okay. We will eat there. Pay for it if you must."

"Of course. I have money."

"I'm sure. But we need to get you home to rest. Let's go."

With that I stood next to the table where I had lain. I kept a hand on it for stability.

"How are you?"

"Okay. With help, I can walk. But I may need to stop now and again."

"Great. I will help. Take my arm. I will make it look as if I am taking yours, in case you are concerned with appearances."

"I do not need the approval of others. As long as we accomplish our task."

"Even better. Tell me if you need to stop. Are you ready?"

With that we left the storage shed where I had been tended to and walked to the tavern, a short distance away. I paused once before crossing a street, but I was feeling better with movement.

We entered a tavern near the center of town. The workers called out to my ersatz nurse, and I learned her name was Käti. They teased her about sewing up a relationship with a handsome young soldier and she waved at them, shaking her head.

"Sit here. I will get you some tea and some soup." She was gone before I could respond.

Before long we were both seated at a table with food and tea in front of us. The soup was rich and very good. Everything was good, rich, and flavorful, but my face hurt when I attempted to chew. I mostly had soup and tea.

"Why is it I am going to your home? Is there nowhere else for me to stay?"

"No, there is nowhere else. The inn is full. We have no hospital, and there are no military installations, just camps of soldiers. They would have to transport you by cart to their nearest aid station, and I feel you need to be stronger before you attempt that."

"But people will talk. I do not wish . . ."

"Let them talk. Like you, I do not live for others' approval. I am merely being practical, helping a German soldier."

"Airman."

"*Ja*, airman. I did see your observer badge. Someone from town went off to be an observer but did not last long. How long have you been flying?"

"Almost two months. I am transferring to the western front."

"I see."

"I was in the army before the war started, and I was in the infantry until recently."

"Do you fly the aeroplane?"

"No, not yet. I feel I need to learn more about what I am doing and what the pilot does before I request pilot training. I want to know I can do it before I try. So far it looks appealing, but more so in a single seat *Jagdstaffel*. Nobody to share the aeroplane with, smaller, lighter, more guns at my disposal."

"It appears you have a plan of action."

"*Ja*. My plan is to do what I can to kill the enemy and win this war."

"That would be nice. Three years now I have been hearing about being home by Christmas. It has yet to happen. Germany is losing so many fine men. This nonsense needs to stop."

"*Ja*. I have other things to do with my life."

"Have you eaten enough?"

"I have, thank you. Please tell me what I owe."

"You owe nothing."

"That is not acceptable. Tell me what I owe or I will just guess."

"Guess, then. I will cover cost with it and give the rest to the *frau* who served us. Will that make you happy?"

"It will. *Danke*."

Money having changed hands, my new friend Käti led me to the door. Once outside, she again took my arm and guided me to her home, not far from the restaurant. Once inside, she took me to her bed. There I protested.

"This is your bed."

"*Ja*, it is. But you need to be comfortable so you can sleep and heal. I have a large chair where I love to read and drift off to sleep. It is there where I shall spend the night. No more protest from the patient. I will take a short walk while you get ready to sleep. Once you are asleep, I shall get ready. I will be back in a few moments."

With that she walked out the door. I rinsed the best I could, removed my coat and shoes, and lay down on top of the bed. I really was worn out from the day. In no time I . . . was . . .

I awoke at some point, likely soon after I drifted off. It was the door. I half opened my eyes as Käti came into view. She was getting ready to go to sleep. She added some wood to the fire, then began to undress. Käti was an average woman with a "little extra," as they say. I mostly saw her from behind as she removed most of her clothing and put on a nightshirt, then a robe. She washed her face, brushed her hair for a while, then picked up a book and sat in a large chair near the fireplace. She looked complacent as she read, turned a page, settled in, turned another page, and . . . .

I woke up again. I was warmer than I had remembered being when I went to sleep. It felt great. My back was warmer than my front. My hand, near my chin, felt a cover that hadn't been there before. Moving my hand down my front, I encountered another arm. That definitely wasn't there before. I opened my eyes and looked toward the fire. The chair was empty. Things were adding up. About then I lost track of my arithmetic due to the throbbing under my left eye. No wonder that eye wouldn't quite open. I decided my best course was to close my eyes and wait for morning. Käti and I would work on the face then.

Yet again I stirred and became aware of my surroundings. I was still warm, but not as warm as earlier. I was still covered but alone. I smelled coffee. I opened my eyes to see light coming into the room as well as a few electric lights. Käti was sitting by the fire with her book and a cup of coffee.

"*Guten tag, mein Herr!*"

"*Guten tag, mein fräulein.*"

"There is coffee for you when you are ready for it. Take a moment in private. I'm sure you need it." She smiled, a big, bright, radiant and inviting smile.

"*Danke.* I shall."

I felt pretty good standing up and walking across the room. My face still throbbed, but I had expected it would. And I was stiff. I supposed bouncing about the inside of a rail carriage had something to do with that. Overall I felt fortunate. Very fortunate.

"Thank you for putting me up for the night. I very much appreciate your concern, your assistance, and your putting yourself out like you did. You are very kind."

"I am very happy to have served a purpose. You have been no trouble at all."

"You lie very well, dear lady."

"No lie. I enjoyed having company."

"Company? You put up a sore soldier."

"Airman."

"*Ja*. Airman. I was no company. But I should like to make it up."

"You needn't worry. You made one *frau* very happy last night."

"I did? I do not recall."

"*Ja*. The money you put down on the table at the tavern—I gave it all to the woman who served us."

"*Wunderbar*. But who paid for the meal?"

"The owner. Or he will. He is like that. *Für das Vaterland*."

"Very kind of him. Oh, and did I have company last night?"

"I have no idea what you are talking about."

"I could explain."

"No need. You were shivering to the point where your teeth were chattering. I did what I thought best. You should have been under the covers in the first place."

"It felt very nice."

"Yes, I thought so. I hope you have the chance to 'make it up'. Under better circumstances it could be quite enjoyable."

"Agreed. But we must find a way to get me to my destination. Or at least in touch with someone military. I need to report what happened and request new orders, though I suspect they will be the same orders but adjusted for time."

"We also have to get to a doctor and verify that you are fit to serve. I suspect you would be grounded for a few days until the swelling goes down. First, however, let us go break bread at the tavern. I would like the owner to meet the soldier he is feeding."

"Airman."

"Airman. *Ja*."

The chilly morning air felt so fresh after a night spent near a wood fire. Walking was markedly easier than the prior day's efforts, even with the throbbing face. We entered the tavern, Käti sat me at a table, and went to get more coffee. She brought us several pumpernickel rolls as well. An older man followed her to our table.

"*Guten tag*, Käti. It is good to see you. Is this your excuse for missing work?"

"*Javohl*. He was injured in the attack yesterday. And I . . ."

"You were the only one who could save him from the Englanders. Right?"

"Well, I was right there when it happened. And I remembered my training as a . . ."

"I understand." He chuckled. "It seems you made quite the catch, a fine, proud, German soldier."

"Airman." Käti and I said it together.

"My apologies. What can I bring the airman to eat?"

We ordered a big breakfast and the owner, Ernst, referred us to his doctor, who was just walking in the door.

"I'm sure Ralf will look at you while he is waiting for his food. Perhaps then I can obtain the services of my manager." He smiled.

Käti and I approached the doctor, who had heard the conversation. He was happy to look at my face and ask a few questions.

"The stitching does appear a little crude, if I must say. The face is somewhat contorted, odd for a straight line laceration."

"*Mein lieber Herr*, I did the best I could. There was flesh missing. The appearance of a straight wound is deceiving." Käti was a little offended.

"*Ja, ja*, that does change the nature of the wound and influence treatment, as well as my opinion of the stitches. This was well done, considering what was there to work with."

"What about the throbbing and swelling?"

"Cold compresses will help with that. Are there any other residual injuries?"

"No, *mein Herr*, just the minor cuts you see, and overall soreness from having been bounced about the rail carriage."

"And your vision. Do you have any trouble seeing? Headaches?"

"No, sir. As long as the swelling stays down I have no trouble seeing."

"Are you dizzy at all? How well do you stand and walk?"

"It was difficult yesterday, but he had lost blood. Today he appears much better."

"*Ja*, I am fine except the swelling and throbbing."

"Then you should be well enough to continue with your service. Just pay attention the next time you go up in an aeroplane, in case there are aftereffects. Have anything unusual looked at."

"Good advice. *Danke*. I should be fine."

We left the doctor as his food arrived, and returned to our table.

"I suppose our next step is to put you in touch with the military. I will not do you much more good."

"Don't sell yourself short. You have been wonderful and quite possibly life saving. You have gone out of your way for a stranger. That will not be forgotten."

"I only did what anyone would have done."

"Run out in the open during a bombing raid? Hardly. Without a doubt most people were running away from the bombed area."

"Okay, you have me there. But most people have no medical training."

"And yours was how long ago?"

"Does it matter? It worked. And it is impolite to ask a woman's age."

Just then a delivery wagon approached, full of soldiers. We went outside and waved, they waved, and then Käti motioned for it to stop. She explained my situation and asked where they were going. It turned out they were going nowhere near my destination, but they agreed to pass along my situation later that day and have someone telephone instructions at the tavern. Käti had them wait while she went inside and got them some fresh bread. We all waved as they departed.

"That gives us a little longer together."

"Except the owner is expecting his manager at work."

"*Ja*, he is. But I will need to freshen up and dress for work, so he will have to wait just a little longer. Besides, we took very little time to solve the military problem. He will have his manager."

"If you would like, I could cook a meal for us to eat when you come back."

"You cook?"

"*Javohl.*"

"*Wunderbar.* So you shall."

We entered her cottage and she immediately began to undress.

"I can take a short walk while you are getting ready."

"That is up to you. I am only getting ready for work."

She turned toward me, bare from the waist up, and walked toward me. When she reached me she wrapped her arms around me and pulled me close. She touched her nose to mine.

"I am in no hurry to get to work."

"But the owner is waiting for you."

"Let him wait. I can cook there after I've finished cooking here."

"Don't you think some things are better without the constraints of time?"

"I do. Usually. Why? Are you afraid?"

"*Mein lieber fräulein*, I have been shot at and gassed and, most recently, bombed. I have lived through all these events. Believe me, I am not afraid of a half-naked woman."

She then backed away and continued changing her clothing. "I think I know. Okay, I can wait. I'm sure you are worried about getting the right ingredients. For your meal."

"No worries. Are you ready to go? I need to find the market and get started. I shall make you a delicious but simple stew. The key ingredient is time. It needs time to cook and allow the flavors to blend. Some things in life just require time."

"While I cannot argue with your contention, I say some things are perfectly acceptable when done in short order. If I cook for myself, it is quick and simple, over with in no time. Often times it is very tasty with very little time invested."

"I have no doubt."

"Let us along. I can point you toward the market, though he may not have everything you want."

"I will work with what he has. One must make do with what is on hand."

With that we walked to the tavern. On the way she pointed out the market, and I returned there to buy what I needed. The market was better stocked than I had anticipated. I returned to Käti's cottage and started on my stew.

Once I had the stew where I wanted it, I went back to the site of the explosion, or, more specifically, the rail carriage I had been on. I explained to the officials supervising that I had been on that carriage when the building exploded. I pointed to my face as proof. I asked if my bags had been recovered. They said nothing had been removed. I could look, but only with an official at my side. That being no problem, I was able to access the carriage and take my bags. I proved they were mine, then thanked the men and took my bags back to Käti's.

I stirred my stew, tasted it, and added some more spices. I decided to walk back to the tavern to drink coffee and watch people. Sometimes it is fun to watch as people go through their lives. It would be nice to see Käti again, especially since I would be leaving soon. I had never met such a special person before. She was kind to a fault and I was the fortunate beneficiary of her kindness. I had met nice people before, but Käti was a standout in any crowd. She would certainly be one to look up once the war had been won.

Ernst greeted me as I walked in the door and found me a corner table. I asked him for coffee and a roll of some kind, and he said someone would bring it out to me. It was midday and the tavern was busy, both for food and for drinks. There were no seats available at the bar, and the men holding it down with their elbows were discussing the war. It was a lively discussion, to be sure. Everyone had a strategy and put it forth. Some thought it would be a good idea to cut back on troops in the east, build up troops on the western front, overrun France, and then go back to vanquish Russia. Others felt just the opposite, preferring to vanquish Russia first and then send everything west. That idea was scoffed at, citing disorganization and disorder in Russia. They said Russia would no longer be a factor in six months because the government was about to collapse. The young woman tending bar seemed bored other than filling orders and taking money. She was doing the best she could, but she obviously had other things on her mind.

"Does Elsa strike your fancy, soldier? Would you like to meet her?"

"Airman. And . . . " It was Käti with my coffee and a generous piece of bread. "I am sure Elsa is a lovely woman, thank you, but I am perfectly happy with my current company. Perfectly. Some other time, perhaps, as she appears to be occupied this moment."

"*Ja, ja, der pickelhauben.* They will win the war for Germany. They have all the answers. Right and wrong. They are regulars. Some of them were wounded in this war, some of them in Africa before the war, and some work in town."

"*Der pickelhauben?*"

"*Ja, der pickelhauben.* That is my name for them. Everyone else calls them *der Fritzen.*"

"Why *der Fritzen?*"

"That is what the Englishmen call us Germans. So it has been bestowed on the brain trust seated daily at the bar."

"*Der Fritzen.* I like that."

Käti sat down. "There was a call for you this morning. They must need you badly."

"Who needs me?"

"The *Staffel* you are to report to."

"Why do you characterize it like that?"

"Because they are sending an aeroplane for you tomorrow. The road out of town passes to the south and bends toward the west. They will pick you up there at about this time and fly you to your new *Staffel.*"

"Most impressive! I will need to be there, of course."

"You will be. The owner will drive us both there so we can see you away."

"You are going as well? Why?"

She kicked me under the table.

"Okay! I am pleased, actually, but did not think you could leave work."

"Do not worry about that. "Ernst is happy to assist you."

"He must like you as well. But then I am confident you do your job very well."

"He knows he does not need to be here when I am working. He treats me well."

"No doubt. I should get back to my stew."

"Do you need help cutting the vegetables?"

"Done. it is simmering. I need to stir and taste it."

"You already have it over heat? I am impressed."

"I told you, it's simple. It just needs time."

"Not much time, I hope. I do not expect to be here all day. There are things to be done."

"Such as?"

"Your bags from the railway carriage. You cannot report in my clothes."

"Done."

"Impressive."

"It had to be done, and I had the time. And proof of ownership."

"*Ja.* No questioning you were there. Great, then. More time together before you depart."

"I will look forward to you joining me."

"Käti, why are you still here?" It was Ernst. "Don't you have things to do?"

"But the tavern."

"The tavern will be okay without you. At the moment it could run itself. As long as Elsa keeps *der Fritzen* in drink, at least. Lubrication for the brains behind our mighty war machine. We need to expedite your airman to the front before the war is over and all the medals are won!"

We shared a good laugh.

"Just leave. I will stop to pick you up in the morning. It should be a good day for flying."

"*Ja.* It has been too long on the ground."

"You don't enjoy my company? I am offended."

"Be offended, if you wish. But I cannot help win the war eating stew with you. I have my duty."

"It appears, my fine airman, that you have more duty than that to *der Kaiser*. Go."

We made the brief walk to Käti's cottage. Upon entering, she took off her apron and began to draw a bath.

"Would you like some of my stew?"

"*Ja*, I would. But you said it needed time." As she spoke she removed another garment. "I will give it more time. Come wash my back."

"Wash your back?"

"*Javohl*. Start with my back. Formal attire not required."

* * * * *

CHAPTER 13

German

Suffice to say I proved my point about cooking with time. By the time we got to my stew it was perfect. The potatoes were soft, the meat was falling apart, and everything felt like it would stick to my ribs and keep me warm in the air the next day.

"This is quite good!"

"*Danke*. It is, isn't it?"

"Do you cook more than stew? You could have a job waiting for you after the war."

"I had not thought of after the war. I still have the war to attend. *Der Kaiser* would appreciate it."

"There is more to life than *der Kaiser* and his war. Once he is finished awarding you his medals, you could come back here to me. You do nice work on my back."

"Your back."

"*Ja*, my back. It was a very good start. You just do nice work."

"*Danke schön*. I'm pleased that there are no complaints."

"None. In fact, I may request further service."

"Now?"

"Well when the stew settles in a little. For now, come sit by the fire. Unless there is someplace you need to visit . . ."

"No place."

* * * * *

CHAPTER 14

German

"Do you need all that clothing?"

"I do. It will be very cold."

"There is a bit of a chill in the air, *ja*, but . . ."

"You do not understand. Once we lift off the ground, the air above gets very cold very soon."

"I didn't know. How cold?"

"Without clothing and a salve to protect my skin, it could freeze. Sometimes it still does."

"Frostbite?"

"Happens very often, *ja*."

"That is cold."

"*Javohl*. Now that I know it is all here, I can put it back in the large bag for the drive. I can dress while we wait for the aeroplane."

"The large bag? I thought the small bag was your equipment."

"No, the large bag is my military equipment. I have very few personal possessions with me. Mostly my shave kit, *gasmaske,* and some off duty clothing."

"I see. *Gasmaske?*" I explained about the gas attack that nearly killed me.

"There will be no room for bags on the 'plane. Besides, we have to mind our weight. The engine can only move so much."

"So many restrictions . . ."

"*Ja*, but so much freedom once aloft in the sky! I am sorry you have never flown. It is a thrill. Every moment."

"You mean accomplishing your mission."

"Well, that is part of it, true. But just being in the air is a thrill. I cannot wait to go up today. It has been too long."

"I sense your excitement."

"It is wonderful, especially after living in the trenches for so long. But it will get better."

"Better? How?"

"Soon I intend to be the pilot and not just the passenger who goes along."

"That could make a difference, I suppose."

"Yes. I will control the machine and not suffer the idiosyncrasies of another flyer. Some of them are so mechanical. No sense of balance or flow. To them a turn is just a turn."

"It is just a turn, though, isn't it?"

"In a practical sense, I suppose it is. But I look at the approach, the bank, the actual turn, and then pulling out to the desired course. It is *how* one turns that makes a difference."

"I am not sure just what you mean, but I have never flown."

"Here. Let me demonstrate. Hold your arms out to your sides, making yourself a letter T."

"Okay."

I stood behind her and matched her arm position, lightly grasping her hands. "We will walk toward the table, then turn to port—the left. Ready?"

"*Ja.*"

"Now. Follow my motion." I nudged her left leg, then right, and we walked toward the table. Abruptly I pulled her left arm back, pushed her right arm forward, and pushed her to the left.

"How was that?"

"We turned left."

"*Ja.* Now back to where we were."

The second time I tilted her gently toward the left, raising her right arm. I caused us to begin moving toward the left sooner with a broader turning radius, and restoring us to upright gradually as we straightened out facing left.

"How was that?"

"Compared to the other turn, it was almost poetry. It was very graceful, a little like ballet."

"There. Now you understand. One cannot always execute such turns, but it is fulfilling when one can do so."

"Okay, I see. But we must get outside. Ernst should be here in a moment."

"*Ja*. We cannot keep your owner or *der Kaiser* waiting."

We walked outside just as the saloon squealed to a stop. Ernst told his driver to leave the engine running and he exited the vehicle to help with my bags. Then he held the door for Käti and myself before climbing in with us. He asked the driver to proceed.

The talk was about what I did in the air. There was some small talk about nothing in particular, and the two of them talked about the tavern. The ride was shorter than I thought it would be, but it would have been quite the walk while carrying my bags. We were waved to a halt by a soldier standing on the road. He approached the driver to explain what was happening. As he did, he saw me in the passenger compartment and saluted. I returned the salute and he asked me to get ready to meet the aeroplane. The pilot would put it down from behind us onto the road, into the prevailing wind, taxi westward, turn around, taxi to about where we were, turn into the wind, then take off. I hopped out of the motorcar, helped Käti step down, and helped pull my bags from the vehicle. From the large bag I removed my heavy fleece lined pants, lined boots, overcoat, helmet, lined gloves, goggles, and heavy scarf.

"How can you do anything once you get all this on?" Ernst was incredulous.

"I manage. If I do not dress for the exposure to the cold, blowing air, I will freeze. First rule of warfare—personal survival. Frozen airmen do *der Kaiser* no good."

"You have a point."

"See what the pilot is wearing when he arrives."

Just then I heard a somewhat familiar drone approaching. I looked up and picked it out before the others, a blue-grey smudge against the western sky. As it approached it took shape, growing wings, tail surfaces, and landing gear. It was a newer type than I had flown in operationally, but I had seen it while training. The pilot circled the area once, then set up to the east for a westward landing. He came down low over our saloon, causing Käti and the owner to duck, which made me laugh. The aeroplane was easily thirty feet above us. The pilot set it down beautifully and let it slow. Once he was clear of any persons or obstructions, he revved the engine and kicked the rudder first right, then hard left to turn around. As he approached us, several infantrymen "caught" the wingtips and guided the aeroplane around facing westward. Two other men produced a ladder, which they placed against the left side of the fuselage so I could climb into the rear cockpit. I awkwardly stepped up the ladder, tossed in my helmet, gloves, boots, and smaller bag, then climbed and stepped into the cockpit. I sat on the fuselage behind the cockpit and pulled on my boots, then slipped back into the cockpit. Käti, looking a little miffed, approached. Hair and clothing being blown by the propeller slipstream, she said, loudly, "I wanted a kiss!" Then she held up her hand, which I took and held for a long moment.

"And you shall have one—and more—when I return. You have been beyond wonderful. But I have a war to fight and win. Soon you will hear of me and read about me in the papers. And I shall return for you. *Danke, danke schön*, for everything. You have saved my life and touched my heart. I will carry you with me aloft in spirit until I can take you up to share the thrill of flight."

Käti removed a delicate chain from around her neck and put it in my hand. "For luck!"

I slipped it over my head. "For luck!" Then I tapped the pilot's shoulder. He waved his arms apart and everyone stood back from the aeroplane while he revved the engine and proceeded down the road and up into the sky. I twisted around and lifted my arm as the crowd receded into the brown and green landscape.

As I pulled on my helmet, goggles, and gloves, then adjusted my scarf, I looked around. The aeroplane swiftly climbed into the midday sky. It was a beautiful day to be aloft. I looked about at the green and brown fields of the surrounding farmland, largely untouched by the war. We were in a delightfully streamlined "*Walfisch*", built by the LFG firm known as Roland, after the great Teutonic knight. The fuselage was roomy due to a different way of being made. A lighter framework of wood was encased in two half shells made with glued strips of wood, forming a hard shell and assuming some of the stresses of flight. This also allowed for a more aerodynamic shape than a square wooden structure covered with stretched linen could allow. Fewer struts, fewer rigging wires, it was a beautiful aeroplane. This one had its upper surfaces painted in dull greens and browns. One wing, a replacement, was a muddy mauve color with a little darker green toward the tip. While it was still an open cockpit aeroplane, the oval shape of the fuselage allowed me to sit deeper into it and protected me somewhat from the cold. And I had windows to let in light, one on each side. Someone had taken a greasepaint marker and drawn suggestions of tied back curtains on the windows, a humorous touch I was sure women would appreciate. Women are so funny. They want a house with windows to let in light, and the first thing they do is cover the windows.

* * * * *

CHAPTER 15

German

I did not have much time for musing. The pilot soon landed on an airfield. After the usual turnaround and taxi, the machine was parked near a large wooden hangar and the engine shut down. Ladders appeared and we clambered out, the pilot being first. Once on the ground, the pilot removed his headgear and awaited my descent to the ground. As I removed my own headgear, I thanked the pilot for a perfectly wonderful flight and complimented his obvious flying skills.

"Danke schön, mein Herr! Vizefeldwebel Model, welcome to your new home! I, your humble pilot, am *Huaptmann* Jakob Einhorn, *kommandeur der Schlactstaffel.* I run the stable. And from what I hear, you will be a fine addition. I am told you are very good at what you do. And I am told you are perhaps a little impatient and show a tendency toward boldness. I feel that is a little misplaced on the eastern front, but it will be welcomed here. I share your impatience. I want this war to end. Thus far the English and French have shown themselves to be better meat grinders than military opponents, foolishly feeding their young men to our war machine. At this rate, they will soon run out of soldiers and we will win by attrition. I intend to help the Allied generals kill off their men. I have my own life to live once this war nonsense is behind me. You will know what to do. I will see to it you learn the area. Once you are settled in, your ideas will be welcomed. As long as your ideas aim to shorten the war and get us all out of uniform. There is still time today if you wish to have a look around your new area of operations."

The *Huaptmann* finally returned my salute. "I would enjoy touring our area, *mein Herr.*"

"I understand you had a head wound, *ja?* How do you feel after our flight? I hope I did not cause you any pain." He smiled warmly.

"*Nein, mein Herr.* I hadn't even thought about it before you mentioned it. I am a little sore, but it should not affect my ability to perform my duties."

"*Wunderbar.* Your time off apparently did you some good." A knowing smile.

"But, sir, . . ."

He waved me off. "I am not worried about the time away. There is a war going on. Sometimes it gets in the way. It even gets in the way of fighting the war. Amusing, no? As you are not feeling any ill effects from your flight, I will send you back up with your assigned pilot. See if you can make him laugh. He has been a little lonely since his last observer got shot and had to leave. He's a good man. Like me, he wants to finish the war and go home. He has a young son he would like to help raise. Maybe he wants more, I don't know. But you will need to take good care of him. He is married to one of my cousins. I'll go get him. Good to meet you, Model."

"*Javohl, mein Herr!* The pleasure is, of course . . ."

"*Nicht mit der mein Herr scheisse!* Model, I am not interested in all the '*mein Herr*' formalities. We are all together here, fighting a war. Common courtesy will be quite enough, maybe a salute now and again. The only times we need '*mein Herr*' are during an official visit and if one finds oneself in trouble. Can you remember that?"

"*Ja,* . . . " I forced myself not to call him '*mein Herr*'. He noticed.

"Wait here. I will find you a pilot." With that he slapped the fuselage and called, "Men? Please set her up again, this time with both guns." Then he walked away.

I watched as several men swarmed around the Roland. Between them they tugged at all the wires, examined the control surfaces and wings, checked the hot engine oil level, added *benzin*, hoisted a Parabellum machine gun and mounted it outside the rear cockpit, then armed it with a belt of ammunition fed from a drum mounted on its side. Finally they turned the machine around so it faced the airfield. Once done with the *Walfisch*, they came over to me, extending hands and greetings and making small talk. I did not hear a bad word from any of them, indicating good unit morale. I knew then I had taken a step upward from the eastern front unit.

"Ah! *Der Walfisch!* Jakob, when will you put this old relic out of our way? It needs to be sent back for training pilots! It doesn't fly—it hobbles through the air, it is so old! Why not show the new man one of our Hannas? Now that is a fighting machine!"

"You complain like an old woman! You are not flying a mission, *Frau* Kittenger, you are going sightseeing. Tomorrow he will meet Hanna. Today he can look at them as he takes off and lands. Be nice and do not aggravate his wound. He has had a rough week, thanks to the English. But I understand he has met a new *fräulein* . . . maybe he will tell you about her? Oh, and take care of my *fräulein*. If you are good to her, she is good to you."

"I will treat your *alte Frau* well, the old hack!"

"I certainly hope so. She means more to me than you do!", he joked.

The pilot waved him off with a laugh and turned to address me. "So! You are the new man, the one who will soon have the good fortune to follow me everywhere I go—at least in the air! My name is Jure and I will be your pilot today—and tomorrow! Would you please have a seat, once I have shaken your hand?"

"*Javohl, Herr Leutnant!*" I snapped to attention and saluted. "I am Gustav Model."

"*Ja, ja . . . nicht mit der 'Herr Leutnant'.* We are friends here. He shook my hand firmly. "Please, after you. Oh, look! You get a gun! I hope you can use it. If the Englanders are up, they will shoot each other down to have a crack at this relic! We could be busy."

"I wouldn't mind having an Englishman for lunch. Let's see what we can find." Wearing flying boots made it difficult to climb the ladder, and I porpoised into the cockpit. Taking my place once again I kicked my personal bag under the fold down seat. I checked the gun to be sure it was loaded correctly. Meanwhile Jure climbed into the front seat, complaining the whole time.

"I see that since you have a gun, I no longer have a meter. So this taxi ride will be on *der Kaiser*. Ah, this old bird. Jakob loves her. Must be sentiment. She shows well—for her age— but she doesn't go so well. Time and technology have marched on. Next time we will go up in my Hanna. She will entice you with her looks, and deliver in the air on every promise she makes on the ground. She is big and she is beautiful—but no longer *einer schöne jungfrau.*"

"No longer a maiden?"

"No. She has taken two Englishmen. Maybe more, if our claims are approved. We will see. I caught one blighter daydreaming about teatime, not paying full attention. And my most recent gunner shot one off our tail. We have sent a few others down, apparently out of control, but they could have been play-acting to escape. Good man, very good shot. He took three bullets from the Sopwith he then shot down in flames. We had to lift him out of the Hanna and on to the tender. He lost a lot of blood, but I understand he is stable and will live. Perhaps he will return and the two of you can swap tales about how wonderful your pilot is."

"Perhaps."

"Ready for your tour?"

"*Ja*, the gun is loaded."

"Aha, we think alike!" To the ground crew, "Switch is on!" The men stood clear and the propeller turned. The engine came back to life, the turning propeller became a blurred disc, and we moved out from the hangar area and down the field. The sun was high overhead as we rolled into the wind and took to the air. The *Walfisch* rose gracefully above the browns and greens below. I looked around and took everything in. There was the steeple of the church with the damaged corner I had seen coming in, a few men apparently working to repair it. I spied a familiar sight, a building with a fenced in yard with horses. Smoke rose from the chimney, telling me the blacksmith was at work on horseshoes or a part for a wagon or . . . .

Something caught my eye from above. I looked up and thought I saw something move, though the sky appeared to be empty. I tapped Jure's shoulder and motioned upward. He leaned back and looked up. After a long moment, he nodded his head in an exaggerated manner and held up two fingers. Then he advanced the throttle and began to climb.

As the *Walfisch* clawed its way toward the unidentified specs, I kept watch on the suspicious area. I saw one, then two, then one speck in the sky. I decided there were likely two of them trying to hide in the sun. Maybe more. Though I knew it was in order, I checked the gun again. I could not do much until the specs came closer. And come closer they did. As they came into view, I saw there were three of them in a triangular formation of sorts. One was well ahead of the others, which caused me to wonder. I thought it looked like two following one. Their path was ahead of us, well above, and angling toward the east. Coming into focus, I saw what was happening. A German aeroplane, possibly an Albatros or another Roland, was being pursued by two English Sopwiths. Jure obviously saw the same thing and aimed our bird ahead of the other German. He waved his arm and pointed at the two Englishmen, looking over his shoulder at me. I nodded and pulled the gun forward in case I had an opportunity to shoot.

The action drew closer, though I could see we would not play much of a role in the outcome. The lead aeroplane was a two seat Albatros, and the two behind were English Sopwiths with square noses, possibly of the SE type. Though we were at least three hundred yards distant, Jure and I both shot at the Sopwiths. I observed a little smoke coming from one of them, but they both seemed under control and intent on their prey.

Jure followed in the direction of the chase which had passed us by, but they were quickly fading against the patchwork below and soon disappeared. We lingered in the area for a short while in case we saw the Sopwiths returning toward their lines, but nothing materialized. Jure took us back to the airfield.

"Damn this old hack! Damn it!"

"What's the matter?"

"We were up there in this quaint old buggy, completely unable to help our fellow German flyers. Had we been in a Hannover, we could have shot the Sopwiths down! But this damned old thing! A rowboat would have been faster! Jakob needs to put this thing in a museum!"

"Oh, well. Nothing more we could have done. Next time?"

"*Ja*, next time. I'll drink to that. Let's go eat. Then I will write my report."

Jure and I entered the mess hut. Some of the men began to point. Someone asked the question. "Is this the new guy from the eastern front?"

"*Ja.*"

"The one who held a gun on his pilot?"

"That is what the pilot said." I responded. "I merely insisted he perform his assigned duty."

"But a pistol? That is crazy!"

"He was lazy and refused to fly his mission. I simply reminded him of his duty to *der Kaiser und das Vaterland*. He was not happy."

I smiled and everyone cheered. "*Danke schön, danke.* I am Gustav Model. Please call me Gustav. I am happy to be here, and I hope to live up to your expectations. Let's do our part to win this war so we can all go home!"

Everybody cheered and suddenly there were several beers in front of me. And schnapps. I motioned for Jure to share, which he readily did. Lunch was wonderful and then I accompanied Jure as he wrote his report on our flight.

"I hate this paperwork. Nothing really happened, so why do I need to report on nothing?"

"I understand. But it gives the paper pushers something to do while they are piloting their desks."

"*Ja*, we must keep the paper pushers busy."

"It was such a paper pusher who got me into *die Fliegertruppe*. He remembered me helping his artillery unit while I was in the infantry. So I have a certain fondness."

"Okay, okay. But I will never believe that a report about nothing can help win the war."

"Fair enough." Jure scrawled at the form for a few minutes, then put it in a box for collection. "Now that I have fulfilled that duty, would you like to meet Gwendolyn?"

"Gwendolyn?"

"Yes. My lovely Hanna. I have named her for *mein Frau*."

"Yes. I would be delighted to meet your Gwendolyn."

We walked back out to the flight line, all large, generously proportioned aeroplanes with a sense of purpose. They were not beautiful so much as handsome. The inline engine was cowled in an efficient manner, flowing into a large but sensible fuselage profile. This profile tapered toward the rear, where a curious biplane tail section replaced the typical left and right horizontal stabilizer. The pilot had a stationary machine gun built into the fuselage and the rear cockpit had a Parabellum gun mounted on a ring. There were brackets that held grenades and flares and bombs, all designed to make life more difficult for trench occupants, artillerymen, and anyone else who got in the way of a German victory.

"Gustav, meet Gwendolyn. She's a beauty, isn't she?"

"Yes, she is. Very different from what I expected, to be honest. I thought they were sending me to another observation or artillery spotting unit. This is a pleasant surprise."

"Oh, she will allow observation, spotting, or photographing trench works. But she does so much more. She will hold her own against single seat scouts. She can attack as well as defend. No need to sit up there and wait for the war to happen. She can take the war to the enemy."

I looked her over. The fuselage was painted in irregular dots or splotches which were sprayed over with a dull, dark translucent color. The wings and tail surfaces were covered with the new preprinted camouflage fabric, darker tones above and lighter below. Beneath the front cockpit there was a white rectangle with 'GWEN' painted on it. Beneath the rear cockpit was a similar rectangle bearing the name 'STEF'. I thought 'Käti' would look better, but I was too new to make that request.

"You may have the 'STEF' painted over or removed if you like—unless your *fräulein* shares that name."

"How funny. I just pictured 'Käti' painted there instead."

"I will see that you get your 'Käti'."

"Do you mean someone else will paint it instead of me?"

"*Ja*, unless you want to paint it yourself."

"*Nein!* My paintwork leaves something to be desired."

"I understand. So does mine. I will have someone on the ground crew take care of it. But it could cost you beer or schnapps."

"Tell them to name their price. It would be worth it."

"I see you two are getting on well—spoiling for a fight?" It was *Huaptmann* Einhorn.

"He is much more interesting to talk to!" Jure chided. "We were just talking about paint."

Ah, paint. Fascinating topic, yes. You want to paint her, but he hasn't even been in her? I think not. Besides, paint adds weight which diminishes performance."

"No, we like her paint—and the bad curtains covering he wings. I offered to have 'STEF' painted out and another name added."

"I say leave the 'STEF' and take him into town so maybe he can meet a *fräulein* who shares the name!"

"Is that permission to slip away for a few drinks, *Herr Huaptmann*?"

"Certainly not. But if you took the tender and picked up some supplies, it could take you a little longer to get back, depending on road conditions or enemy activity. We are not scheduled to fly again today. Would you like to go for supplies?"

Jure snapped to attention. *"Javohl, mein Herr!"* He slapped me in the chest. I also snapped to and barked, *"Javohl, mein Herr!"*

Huaptmann Einhorn laughed and gave us a halfhearted salute. "Dismissed. Tomorrow we shall do some damage to the Englanders. Tonight, well, don't do too much damage in town."

The rest of the day went well. Jure and I picked up the items the *Staffel* needed and stopped for a few beers. While there were several lovely young women paying us close attention as soldiers—airmen—in uniform, Jure was married and I was more interested in getting to know Hanna that I might kill some Englishmen and shorten the war. Besides, none of them were named Stef. It was not a late night.

* * * * *

CHAPTER 16

German

The next day was one of those cloudy days with no sunshine but a lot of glare. Jure and I were not scheduled until midmorning. We ate and downed some coffee and walked over to visit our aeroplane. Jure did not point it out, but I noticed it: a fresh white banner below the rear cockpit bearing the inscription, 'Käti'.

"Fresh paint. Nice touch."

"*Kamerad*, once you climb in and go up, you will forget all about the fresh paint. Still, try not to touch it for the next day or two."

"I look forward to my first flight in her. She appears to be a very efficient killing machine. Like the woman who saved me from the bombing attack, she is generous of proportion and intent."

"So Käti is not a long term affair?"

"No, at least not so far. I never knew her before she found me in the train. On her way to work, she saw the explosion that damaged a nearby rail carriage. She ran in to help if she could, and she found me bleeding on the floor. She helped, indeed, and may have saved me from bleeding to death."

"You are a fortunate man."

"Very fortunate. I am deeply in her debt"

"Touching. You may forget the fresh paint, but I understand if you do not forget her."

I took a nearby ladder over to the Hanna and climbed along the engine.

"What are you doing?"

"Don't worry. Hanna will be safe. I am merely looking. I'm fascinated by machinery and how it works. I used to look at the engines on the Albatros type I flew in on the eastern front and others while training. Before the war I worked in my father's stable and blacksmith shop."

"I see. Maybe one of the mechanics will give you a tour of the inner workings of one of these beauties. But they might want you to help. Especially if you don't mind dirty hands and grease under your nails."

"That would be a fair trade."

"So you are here already! Can't wait to get in the air?"

"The new guy says he smells fresh Englander and would like a trophy for his quarters." Jure winked at me.

"Would you like to go hunting now? The next patrol will be okay without you. Besides, a lone Hanna with bombs and guns would be something different for the blighters. We don't want them to feel neglected, do we? You are at liberty to go up as soon as you like, with my blessings."

I looked at Jure. "Thirty minutes?"

"Or sooner. Go get ready. I'll have her readied immediately."

I returned presently, carrying my lined boots and headgear. Jure started the engine as I approached. There was a ladder by my cockpit to help me get in. I tossed my boots and gloves into the cockpit, donned my helmet and scarf, and climbed the ladder. I sat on the rear of the cockpit and pulled my boots on, then slipped in and checked my gun. Jure looked over his shoulder, held up a fist, and extended his thumb upward. I returned the gesture, and he waved at the crew to remove the wheel chocks. We were away.

The taxi was nothing special, but it never is. Once the Hanna was turned into the wind, Jure pushed the throttle forward and I had to sit down awkwardly, having been caught unaware by the strong acceleration. This machine seemed as anxious as we were to get up and go kill someone. We were going to make a wonderful team, the three of us.

Once we reached altitude, I stood up to look around. I had a sweeping view and a clear field of fire for my gun, which was already situated above the upper wing. The biplane tail was unusual, but it gave a pursuer less room to hide from my fire. I had liked the *Walfisch*, but the Hanna completely outclassed it. And the old Albatros from the eastern front should have been a training machine. A few Hannas out east would make a big difference, especially with aggressive crewmen.

Since I had such a magnificent view, I put it to work. There were numerous German aircraft up, most of them behind the lines, but a few very high up, heading west to look in on the English back areas. Over the lines I saw mostly English going about their patrols. I was sure Jure had in mind to wait until a flight went toward the end of their patrol area and then dive low over the English trenches, do some damage and fly for home.

That was his plan. He shadowed a flight of Nieuports for a while. Then he held up his hand, then bent it forward and lowered it, suggesting a dive. I smiled and checked my gun. Things were about to become interesting. Jure pushed the throttle forward, went into a shallow dive, and pulled back hard on the stick. The Hanna stood on her tail and fell off to the right. Jure adjusted it into a hard dive on the English trenches. He flew just behind the front trenches, kicking his tail back and forth a little as he sprayed the troops with his machine gun. I had the ride of my life. I laughed out loud as I was tossed gently from side to side. I pointed my Parabellum down into the trenches and squeezed the trigger. The stricken Englishmen often leaped up before falling into their muddy trench. A part of me felt bad, having done my share of time in the trenches, but that was the nature of war. Someone had to die. And from my perspective, it was better that the English did the dying. To that end, I threw a few grenades into the mix. There were many fists shaken at us, and not a few rifles, pistols, and machine guns pointed at our rapidly passing aeroplane. There was no time for them to aim, and later we found but two places where their bullets had found our machine.

Jure turned to the northeast and crossed over our lines, where many of our soldiers waved and cheered at us. We were the closest support they had, and we were greatly appreciated. We stayed low for a short while, then climbed to about 200 feet for the rest of the way home. I could not erase my smile as I watched the skies for any possible threats. In no time we were on our airfield. A crewman placed a ladder under my cockpit and I climbed onto the back to remove my boots before coming down the ladder. Jure approached and offered to shake my hand, but withdrew suddenly.

"I see from your smile that you had a good time—I am pleased! You sounded busy back there. But I see you did not heed my advice to let the paint dry!"

I looked at my outstretched right hand. "Oh, 'Käti' is on both sides? How thoughtful! I had not noticed." Jure clapped me on the back and laughed. "Let's get some coffee and take care of paperwork."

"*Javohl*. Then maybe we can go up again."

"Perhaps, yes."

There was no "perhaps". We took the paperwork to the mess and filled it out over coffee and whatever food was there. We dropped it off with the adjutant, then sought permission to go up again.

"It seems the three of you have really hit it off, then."

"As you know, Hanna puts your *Walfisch* to shame."

"Now, now, no need for that. My baby is back in her crib and you need not worry about her. I know how you like your Hanna, and I'm pleased you are so happy with her. I'm trying to get your Hanna a present so perhaps you'll love her even more."

"A present? For Hanna?"

"Yes. I think Hanna will better serve you if we could procure a Daimler-Mercedes engine. I used to serve with someone who now works in salvage operations. He owes me a favor, and I have asked him to get a few Mercedes engines from wrecked Albatrosen. I understand Hawa is working on mounting a Mercedes in a new model, so let's assist them in their research, shall we?"

"Well, if it's in the name of research, and it manages to facilitate killing more Englanders, I am happy to participate."

"*Wunderbar*. I'll keep you abreast of developments. In the meantime, feel free to go back up and get to know one another better—with my approval."

That was all we needed. We treated that like we had just been given free reign to fly and kill as we desired. We agreed to pick up our gear and meet at the flight line. Surely the ground crew had patched that wing panel. If not, I could help. How hard could it be?

Assured both holes had been patched, we had the Hanna topped off and checked over for flight. One crewman said the patches might not be completely dry, but we told him the slipstream would help. We pulled on our gear and got in, and while I pulled on my heavy boots Jure started the engine.

Takeoff went as always, without incident, and we chose another gathering of Englishmen to look in on. We commenced firing on a front line trench, and I shot up a machine gun emplacement. As I looked back toward the trench something above caught my eye. I clapped Jure on his right shoulder twice. When he looked I pointed upward. The "something" was growing larger and sprouting wings. It could only be an English *jäger*, coming down in an effort to spoil our day. Jure began to climb and I threw out the last few small bombs I had left in order to lighten the aeroplane. As it approached, I noted the dihedral in the wings and identified it as a Sopwith of the SE type, more than capable of ruining our day. I saw two more "somethings" in the glare above and decided I did not want to face those odds, so I clapped Jure on the shoulder, pointed forward, and in his ear yelled, "*Schnell! Schnell! Drei!*" He got it right away, pushed the nose back down, pushed the throttle forward, and sped away. The Englander was not about to give up. He adjusted his flight path to keep us in his sights. When he was about three hundred yards away I loosed a thirty round volley to show him I knew he was there. He did not respond, but drew nearer. The other two specks were getting larger as well, but I was relieved. The Englander was about to receive unwelcome company in the form of two Albatros *jägern*. One, then the other started shooting, as evidenced by the flashing I saw atop their engine cowlings. A few seconds after that the SE snapped into a roll. It went around almost twice, looked a bit unstable for a few seconds, then settled into an inverted spin. As it fell, I noted the wing gun was still shooting, tracers firing outward and creating the impression of a snowflake or starburst. The Englishman was likely dead already. His SE settled abruptly behind a second line trench. Many English infantrymen climbed out of the trenches like so many ants from a mound, hoping to help their countryman. But they scattered almost right away as the two pursuing *Albatrosen* strafed the site. Passing the stricken SE's resting place, the two *jägern* pulled up alongside our Hanna. They were beautiful. One had an orange-yellow nose back to the cockpit, the other a cobalt blue nose, and both had black rear fuselages with tailplanes banded in red, white. and black. The blue nose had printed fabric wings, and the other had printed fabric lower wings and an upper wing painted dull green and mauve. We waved our *unseren dank*, they each swept their arm toward us as if bowing, and Jure made a motion like hoisting a stein to his mouth.

Both pilots made a similar motion, waved, and pulled away.

We landed soon after that. After guiding our Hanna into position and chocking the wheels, one of the crew looked it over and exclaimed, "Were you napping? Only one hit!" We laughed as we climbed down, then told the gathering men what had happened.

"I think Jure just made a date."

"With whom?" It was the *Huaptmann*. "He is a married man. Happily married, I trust?"

"With the two *jäger* pilots, of course! I don't know that they saved us, but they did save us the work of fending off the English 'plane. Certainly that is worth a beer or few."

"*Ja, ist es.* It never hurts to stay on good footing with the neighbors. See that they are made to feel most welcome."

Our conversations was interrupted by the sound of two aeroplanes landing. I turned about to see two Albatros *jäger* types taxiing toward us. One had a blue nose, the other orange-yellow. I took one of the ladders from the side of the Hanna and carried it to the blue nose Albatros, then helped the pilot out of the cockpit and onto the ground.

"*Guten Tag*! Welcome to our humble home! While we have 'met' before, I should like to shake your hand. I am Gustav Model, gunner in the Hanna you saw moments ago."

"The Hanna I saved from the Englishman coming out of the sun?" he laughed.

"Saved? Hardly. We were playing with him like a toy. I left him a few calling cards from my gun." I shook his hand. "But we are always happy to see friends like you. And we do not mind sharing our toys."

"Ha! *Danke! Ich bin* Wilhelm Maier. Call me Willi."

"Good to meet you, Willi! What can we do for you?"

"Your pilot offered us a beer."

"*Ja*, he did."

"We would like to take him up on his offer another time. But hot coffee would be good for now. Do you have any near here?"

"*Javohl!* Come with me! Jure! Come meet the men who stole away the Englishman we were playing with!" Jure broke away from his conversation with a wave and followed us to the mess where we each poured ourselves a cup of coffee.

"So, Model—uh, Gustav—this is your pilot?"

"*Javohl*. Willi Maier, meet Jure Kittenger, my pilot. Jure, Willi flies that blue Albatros."

Willi spoke up, "Jure, I am pleased to meet you, having saved your skin from that Sopwith! Gentlemen, please meet my partner, Josef Engblom. Call him Swiss."

"My skin was just fine, *danke schön*, but you are welcome to our Englander any time. We were distracting him, setting up your kill. We are not selfish. As long as they go down, we don't care who sends them. The result is the same."

"Ah! You two are good sports." Swiss joined in. "Maybe we need to meet more often."

"You don't mean set up an ambush, do you?" Jure asked.

"*Ja*, I do. We coordinate our efforts. You choose an area you would like to shoot at and we fly above and cover for you. If any Englanders try to ruin your fun, we dive on them and send them down."

"Well, Swiss, it's certainly not original, but I like it. We get to strafe and bomb with a higher degree of safety, and you get to play with the smaller English scouts. That can work. After all, we get to kill more of them on the ground while you send them down in ones and twos."

I had to ask, "Does this mean I can no longer shoot the ones in the sky?"

Willi answered, "Of course not! Just be careful as we make our entrance. You do not get credit for shooting down one of your own!" We all laughed.

Jure inquired, "Does your *Jastaführer* allow others to make appointments with you?"

"As long as we make our scheduled patrols he doesn't care."

"What about your *Schlastaführer*?" It was Jakob.

Jure laughed. "I don't think he cares, as long as we are killing Englishmen and bringing the Hanna back in one piece."

"Jure, you know me all too well. Permission granted."

"Who was asking?" Again we all laughed.

"What do we call ourselves?" asked Swiss.

"Nothing for the moment. We need to see if it continues to work. Then we can name our little group and paint our aeroplanes in pretty colors. Just not red."

Jure asked, "Why not red, Willi?"

"It's been done." Another good laugh ensued.

Willi stood up. "We need to get back to our unit and claim our kill. Thank you for being so understanding. I appreciate your thoughts on working as a team. Like me, I am sure you just want to finish this nonsense and go home."

We all agreed to that, toasted the notion, and downed the rest of our coffee so we could get back to the flightline. We asked if they needed more fuel or anything, but they said no.

Jure shouted, "Same time tomorrow, if the weather is good?"

Willi responded, "I looked. It will be like today. Where will you be?"

"About a mile to the south. Maybe we will see you?"

"Perhaps, if you get any uninvited interruptions."

"Fair enough! *Auf Wiedersehen!*"

"*Wiedersehen!*" With that, the pilots climbed into their *Albatrosen*. We helped turn them around, then they started their engines and departed.

* * * * *

CHAPTER 17

German

The next day found us diving out of the midmorning sun on the promised section of trenches. Jure announced our arrival with his machine gun. I had brought two bombs too many, making our Hanna slightly overweight, but I handed them off to the Englishmen below. I doubt they appreciated my generosity. I dropped another bomb before taking up my machine gun, always keeping an eye open in the event of any visitors from the RFC. On our third pass over the area I caught something moving several thousand feet above, and I stopped shooting in order to watch. There were four, maybe five, flecks moving around one another, too far away to be of consequence. I tossed over another bomb, which landed near a machine gun emplacement. Jure kicked us around for one last pass and I saw one speck growing larger as it approached. It did not have the pronounced wing dihedral of the SE type, but I still watched, gun at the ready. Then I saw the orange-yellow nose and relaxed. It was Swiss. He dropped almost to our height, wagged his wings, then banked away to the northeast.

A short while later we landed and found Swiss' Albatros on our flight line. I was a little concerned that he was visiting alone. But he arrived at our side, carrying a ladder to Jure's cockpit. We exchanged greetings and I asked why he was alone.

"What, you are not happy with only me?" he smiled. "I am, after all, the better looking one!"

"But of course! Come have coffee with us, handsome!"

"Well, okay, but I was only bringing regards from Willi. On a later patrol yesterday Willi stopped a few bullets from a Sopwith."

"That is not how to win the war. You can tell him I said that."

"Ha! He will consider your advice, I'm sure. He took a hit in the shoulder, one in the right arm, and another in his bottom. Of course we tease him without mercy as he stands to eat, but he did a good job landing his crate. He needed to use both hands on the stick, but we could not tell by the way he dusted it onto the grass. He is a very good flyer."

"Is he a good shot? We can put him to work here. He can stand the whole time in the back position and shoot with his left hand. He only has to sit during takeoff and landing."

Jure asked, "But what are we to do with you, Gustav? Can you fly Willi's blue crate?"

"No, not yet. I would like to, however."

"You are not happy with your current driver? I'm hurt. I bring you back safely each time."

"You are a wonderful driver, Jure, almost as good as Jakob. I have no complaints. I merely have curiosity at work. Flying would be a new skill to me, and I enjoy learning new things. I learned about fixing wagons and motorcars while working in my father's stable. I learned about artillery while in the infantry. And now I am surrounded by pilots. You understand."

"So my Gustav is the ambitious man. He wants to know about everything, including flying. I would hate to get in the way of that. I can show you how the controls work. I can have you sit in my seat and feel the controls work, even if they feel different while moving through the air. But I need to find a training crate with controls in both cockpits. To bad Jakob's old *Walfisch* does not have rear controls. On the other hand, imagine the look on his face when I tell him an observer is flying his treasured baby! His eyes so big, his face so pale!" We all had a good laugh and made mocking facial expressions.

Swiss stood up to leave. "I will pass along your advice and your offer to take him on aeroplane rides. You would offer him a discount, wouldn't you? He is, after all, serving *der Kaiser!*"

Jure quipped, "I will even come to his door and pick him up, no extra charge!"

"Ha! He will expect you to be flying a blue bus!"

"I will watch as he paints it."

"He didn't even paint his own. He gave one of the boys a bottle of schnapps and said, 'Blue to here, then black' and showed how he wanted the tailplane painted. I gave him another bottle and said, '*Ja*, but yellow.' Boy wants to be an artist, so he took license with the actual blue and yellow, but we don't care."

I told him, "It was enough this morning to keep me from shooting at you. I know your color."

"*Ja*, I saw you, thumb in the air, admiring the boy's work. You are a connoisseur of fine art. I am curious to see what the boy does with Willi's crate after the wings are patched. Willi does not care for just any patch with the English cockade. He will complain. But that's Willi. I will ask him about a trainer crate. Maybe he knows of one. *Wiedersehen!*"

Swiss walked out and we considered the conversation. "Gustav, you are in a hurry, aren't you?"

"To finish this stupidity and go home to continue my life? *Javohl*. I am. This is no life. Yes, I am in the service of Kaiser Wilhelm. But for what? A cart load of fragile alliances that fell together after some royal got killed? It makes no sense. I am to kill Englishmen and Frenchmen. I understand. But why? Are they not just like you and me but for the language? We shoot at men who could be our friends if not for the war. We could be performing at air meets with some of the pilots we exchange shots with."

"All true. But did you fly before the war? I recall that you did not. So, because of the war—"

"*Ja, ja*, I know. There are good and bad in everything. War has brought me the freedom of flight as a military expedient to kill the enemy. The flying part is simple delight. The killing is bothersome. But it is my job. So I swallow hard and pull the trigger. I sometimes think it would all go better were I swallowing liquor to numb the senses. But one needs one's senses in order to survive. I just want to finish this job and put it behind me, one way or another."

"You don't think Germany can win the war?"

"I think we can win the war. I read what I can and try to get through the propaganda to the truth. On this front, we stand a good chance. The French and English seem intent on sending their nineteenth century style soldiers with bayonets and rifles into the modern German onslaught of accurate heavy artillery. As long as the Americans stay out of the war, we can win this front. While the eastern front is quiet—almost a vacation, from what I saw—Russia is on the other side. Russia is tremendously large. Germany could never win a war of attrition against Russia. But the Russians appear to be in the midst of some internal turmoil. If that continues and even increases, perhaps Russia would sign a treaty with Germany. That would allow troops to go elsewhere. There are fronts to the south, in Africa, and in Persia. It seems the entire world is at war. But I can see a way for Germany to win the war. We simply must do so before the Americans send troops to back the English and the French."

"You are probably right, Gustav. I have seen the advantage in technology change hands between Germany and her adversaries. So it is a matter of chance as far as that goes. I believe it is the man who makes the difference, but a good machine is always nice to have."

"*Ja*, I agree. But even if Germany loses the war, how does it affect our lives? I grew up in a family with modest means. Once the immediate postwar turmoil settles, life will go on much as it did before the war. Oh, there will be punitive measures. Some land will be taken, restrictions placed upon the loser, perhaps a military presence. I could shoe horses, farm, even fly, and never think of the restrictions. But I suppose this conversation need not take place here and today. Agreed?"

"Agreed. But how am I supposed to go shoot at Englishmen now, thinking they could be my friends if not for the war and different uniforms?"

"We could go help the mechanics look over our Hanna. There must be something we can do to make her a better flyer. There is always something."

"Good idea, Gustav. Even if the improvements are defensive—they can save our skins and improve our chances of surviving this war."

"And there you have it, Jure. I am not finished with my life. And from what I hear, neither are you."

"I am marking time until the shooting ends. After that I intend to enlarge my family."

"I see. I have no such plans, at least not so far. We will see what happens with—Jure! There! I just had a thought. I don't know why it didn't occur to me earlier. Do you think Jakob would permit us to go over the lines?"

"We do it all the time."

"No. Beyond the lines. Into the enemy rear area."

"I don't see why he wouldn't. Why?"

"I met my friend Käti after having been bombed on a train while at a railway junction. She stopped the bleeding on my face and stitched it back together. Anyway—why couldn't we go over the lines and return the favor? Even if we do not bomb a train, we could destroy bridges or just ruin track. Maybe shoot up a junction or ammunition storage. On days when we have a conscience, we could even do it with little or no loss of life. Just a lot of cleanup and rebuilding so we can go back. What do you think?"

"I like it. The Hanna is not the fastest crate, but at low level it will appear and disappear before most can raise their guns."

"Just as I thought. Take one route out and another one back. Do you think Jakob will approve?"

"Approve? He might send a flight over. He might even go along. I'm surprised he hasn't sent us on similar missions. We need to go find him."

"No need to go looking. I have found the two of you. And just how are you plotting to win the war?"

"Fast, low level attacks on enemy rear areas. Bomb and shoot up railway junctions, ammunition and supply areas, bridges, roads. Designate a target area, fly in fast and low by one route, then return by another route. It could slow their ability to supply and rearm their front line troops."

"Would this be a solo run?"

"Jakob, you are the commanding officer. That is your call. I could see multiple targets with perhaps flights of two or three Hannas on each target. Enough to do damage, not enough to get in each other's way."

"Well, as commanding officer, I am grounding you two."

"Why is that?"

"I have received two engines from my *kamerad* at the salvage depot. One, a high compression Daimler-Mercedes, is going into your Hanna this afternoon. Once it is installed, I will require you to test it in the air. If it is satisfactory, consider your restrictions lifted. But while you are grounded, you might want to look over a map and some photos in order to plan your attack. Your idea, of course, is a good one. I should like to go over with you, once I choose a gunner."

"We could help with that. The pilot of that blue nose Albatros is available. He took a bullet in the bottom and cannot sit down much. But he is a good shot. We could telephone his *Staffel*."

"*Nein*, I have people here whom *der Kaiser* pays to perform such tasks. We shall see. Don't stray too far, in case your crate is ready."

"*Javohl*."

I told Jure I could not resist watching or even assisting with the engine replacement. Such was my fascination with things mechanical. I arrived to witness what seemed like a swarm of men working on our Hanna. There were men who had just leveled the aeroplane by placing a padded trestle under the rear fuselage. More men were removing the propeller. Others were disconnecting the engine controls, electrical parts, exhaust, fuel and water lines. There was a large tripod nearby. I watched men moving the tripod over the engine. Chains had been attached to lifting eyes, and these were in turn connected to a larger chain suspended under the tripod. They lifted the Argus engine out, pushed the tripod away so the Argus engine could be placed on a workbench, pushed the tripod over the Daimler-Mercedes engine, lifted it, positioned it over the Hanna, then lowered it into the engine bay. One man hurt his hand when it was caught between the engine and an engine support beam. At that point I stepped in to help secure the new engine and attach the various functional pieces. There were minor difficulties like variations in the methods of attachment for the throttle linkage, but these weren't difficult to fix.

Once everything had been reattached and all the fluids filled, the engine was primed, the propeller pulled around, and the magneto cranked to start the engine. After only a little coaxing the Daimler-Mercedes coughed and came to life. I remarked that it did not sound much different from the Argus, but I was assured I would feel the extra horsepower on takeoff and ascent.

The engine was allowed to run for a short while so the mechanics could check for leaks. Any leaks found were taken care of and the Hanna was cleared for flight testing. I searched for Jure, woke him from his nap, and we dressed for the flight. Jure was excited about the new engine. He liked the idea of testing something new, as did I. He had hopes it would make a difference in the Hanna's flight performance. I knew that ten to eleven percent more power would make a difference, but not a lot. However, every little bit helped.

Takeoff did feel just a little stronger. Everything about the aeroplane was a little more responsive, even if it did not feel like a completely new machine. We appreciated the improvement. I knew Jure was watching his gauges. When he pointed toward the front I was wary, but he was the pilot. To the front it was, though I had no bombs or grenades to toss and any ammunition there might have been was what was left from the last flight. No matter. There was no real point to the flight beyond checking out the new engine installation. I kept an eye open to my surroundings, and it was fortunate I did. The twinkles I saw well above us took the forms of SE type Sopwith *jägern* as they approached. I had my gun ready, even if I did not have a full load to shoot. Jure signaled for me to sit, which I did. As the scouts started to fire at us, Jure suddenly pulled up and did a snap roll. The scouts flew past us. Jure opened fire on the scout to the right. I undid my lap strap and brought my Parabellum around to fire at the other. I did not see any telling result of our fire. Jure banked hard and dove for speed as he turned toward our aerodrome. The scouts recovered and followed closely, shooting short bursts at us as Jure's maneuvers permitted. He could not shake them or fool them with further fancy maneuvers. My bursts only kept them at a distance, but I could sense they were waiting for a mistake on our part.

It was not unusual for the Englanders to pursue us behind our own lines. Most air fighting took place above German held ground. But these two must have been experienced. They showed no hurry to break off. It was like they were sharks sensing blood in the water. But they failed to look around beyond their intended prey. They did not see what I saw rapidly approaching from above us. There were two Albatros *jägern* diving hard and fast, angled to intercept the English scouts. I recognized Swiss' orange-yellow nose, and the other one was a bright turquoise. Swiss did a half roll and swooped in on the scout to the left as if coming out of a loop. He led the scout with a perfect burst which peppered the fuselage about the engine and pilot, resulting in wisps of black smoke that steadily increased. While the scout was arcing toward the ground, the other Albatros closed in on the tail of the remaining Limey. He fired a succession of short bursts which caused splinters of wood to flake off the fuselage. Suddenly the 'plane seemed to stagger. The nose came up and the right wing dipped sharply, causing the scout to tumble like a falling leaf in a gentle breeze. The scout was out of control, the pilot likely dead, and it kept tumbling until it fell through a few trees and disappeared beneath the barren branches. A plume of black smoke marked its resting place.

Though it was quite cold several hundred feet up, we were both sweating. We were lucky Swiss and his *kamerad* saw us and were able to assist. Though we had about the same horsepower as the English scouts, they were a bit lighter and therefore a little faster and more maneuverable. We flew directly to our aerodrome and set down. I checked to find I had fewer than ten bullets left in my gun. Jure had more, but he could not bring his gun to aim at either attacker. Lady Luck had indeed smiled on us that day.

Our saviors landed not long after we did. Swiss was the first out of his Albatros. He motioned for the other pilot to get out and join us. Swiss was very happy, having downed another English crate, but he was insufferable as well, insisting he had saved us again.

"You two know just when to get into trouble, do you not? How did you know I was up? You are, of course, quite welcome!"

"*Gott im Himmel!* We were toying with them! You spoiled our fun!"

"*Scheisse!* What fun was that? Counting English bullets? I hope you count quickly! Walzer, meet Jure *und* Gustav. They are getting to be old friends—and now they owe us more beer! Jure, Gustav, this is Heinrich Strauss. We call him Walzer, even if he has no musical rhythm."

"No rhythm! *Scheisse!* Ask *der fräuleinen*— they love my rhythm, on the dance floor and off!"

"Hah! You are no *walzerkönig*!"

"No need to be. My good looks serve me well!"

"You two put on a great show. We would like to book you to appear in our Officers' Club. And you shoot well—which I find more important. *Danke schön!*"

"Ah, Gustav, for you it was nothing. See, Walzer? Gustav is more gracious. Maybe next time we should save only Gustav!"

We all had a good laugh. I invited them to have some coffee.

I asked, "How is Willi?"

"Willi is angry. He cannot fly his blue bird. But he is practicing sitting down. He should be ready soon. Why? Do you not like Walzer?"

"No. He is too good looking." We had another good laugh. Jakob joined us to ask about the new Daimler-Mercedes. We reported our observations and told him about our flight.

"I thought as much when the *jagdfliegern* followed you home."

"They only follow us because they get lost and cannot find their own home!"

"*Danke schön*. We appreciate that you keep an eye on us. You are always welcome here. No need to follow anyone, just stop in for coffee or whatever we have on hand."

"*Danke, Herr Huaptmann*. It is good to see you again. I hope you are well." Swiss and Walzer stood to salute, but Jakob waved at them to sit and relax. "We are all friends here. No salutes unless there is an official visit going on."

Turning to Jure, Jakob asked, "Is the Hanna better with the new engine? I should think it is an improvement, however slight."

"It is, Jakob. I suspect the engine will make more of a difference at higher altitudes. But it does help us down low. We appreciate your getting it. Unless there is truth to the rumor of the even more powerful engine about to become available . . ."

"Ah, the rumors. Pay no attention. If something better comes out I will do my best to get some here." Addressing the rest of us, "I should like to offer our guests some schnapps as a thanks for returning our troublesome sheep."

After yet another good laugh, everyone present had a round of schnapps. Jure and I walked Swiss and Walzer out to their fancy birds, shook their hands and saw them off.

"Jure, don't you wish you had one of those to fly?"

"*Javohl.* I like the Hanna. It is a wonderful weapon, but I dream of flying a *jäger* with a *Jagdstaffel*. Lighter, faster, more maneuverable, all the better to bring the twin machine guns to bear on the enemy."

"I understand, but at this point I would love to learn to fly anything. Then maybe I can dream of an *einsitzer*."

"Gustav, I can show you how the controls work. It is not all so different from driving a motorcar. There are three dimensions to control rather than two, but the controls are simple. Then there is the throttle, not unlike a motorcar again. Add air/fuel mixture control, a hand pump or two and that is flying. Once one knows what the controls do, the rest is coordination. Oh, and having some sense of what to do when something goes wrong. It can be more involved than coasting to a stop just off the road!"

"You know I love anything mechanical. When can you show me?"

"I'll go ask Jakob if I may show you on his *Walfisch*. It has more room inside so I can see what you are asking about or doing. You don't have any pressing plans just now, do you?" He smiled.

We found Jakob where we had left him, doing paperwork in the mess with coffee nearby. Jure approached him with his question. "Jakob, do you think we could use your treasured *Walfisch* for something productive?"

"Productive? What is it you have in mind?"

"Our new gunner would like to pretend to be a pilot, and your old bird is the only one big enough for him and *die gasmaske*." I punched his shoulder, knocking him briefly askew. "Okay, okay. Gustav is curious about being a pilot and I told him I could show him around the 'office'. It would be easier in your old girl."

"*Was ist?* It is not enough, shooting at the Englanders from the back seat? Maybe he needs a more daring pilot—one who has no family to worry about!"

"Maybe he wants to take my place so I can shoot at Englanders from the back seat."

"Now there is a thought. Please. Do show him anything he wants to know. You may use my pretty old girl. She is so gentle, she may even be the first to have him . . . in the air, that is."

"We like how you think, Jakob. You are a good sport."

"*Ja, ja,* now go. This is not helping me get through these papers."

"Just do not let me fall into that trap. Command is not for me."

"Don't worry, Jure. No one is setting a trap for you. Consider yourself safe."

We opened the hangar doors so we would have more light looking into the cockpit. Jure placed a ladder against the fuselage side and I climbed into the front cockpit. "First, grab the stick and push it away, then pull toward you. Away causes the tail to rise, putting the aeroplane into a dive. Toward you lowers the tail, coming out of a dive or climbing. Now side to side, which would cause the wings to rock left or right. Put your feet on the rudder bar in front of you. Push the left end forward to move the tail to the left, causing the 'plane to turn left. Do you get the idea?"

"*Ja.*"

"Feel the travel of the controls. Just remember, they feel completely different with air rushing against the control surfaces as you try to move them."

"I see."

"You see the throttle and mixture control to your left, and the hand pump to your right."

"*Ja.*"

He continued, pointing out the gauges and magneto switch, explaining how each worked. In all, it did not seem very difficult. I would have to see about taxiing so I could start to feel the controls with some resistance. This could be fun.

We closed the hangar doors and saw Jakob entering his office. We followed him in.

"Jakob, we thank you for allowing the tour. We came to help with your papers."

"*Schwein!* You know I just finished that drudgery. But you can stay and help me file it."

"Uh, don't we have another patrol to fly?"

"You do. But in the morning. I have decided to send you and three other Hannas to cause a little havoc in the English rear areas. Jure, here is a map showing several targets. There are two ammunition storage facilities and one rail line. If you destroy a train, that would be great, but ruining the track is the objective. The trains are useless without track. You choose your other aircrews and brief them. You lead the flight."

Jure slapped my back as he exclaimed, "*Javohl!* Gustav—care to join me?"

"*Scheisskopf!* I will consider your offer. Jakob, how can I help you now?"

I helped Jakob with filing his paperwork. Jure grudgingly joined in.

* * * * *

CHAPTER 18

British

The major held his preflight briefing. It was the same plan he had put forth previously, but with a few added specifics. We were given our limits of travel. Unless attacked, we were told to turn around here, turn around there, and stay on our side of the lines. We objected openly but he didn't care. He knew we were just venting and would do as told. That was a part of his leadership style. He would be very lenient with us and allow us the room we needed, but only as long as his orders were followed. He was very fair and understanding of his young charges. Unlike so many in leadership positions, he remembered what it was like to be young, indestructible, and headstrong. He encouraged us to come up with alternate ideas and express them to him rather than merely complain. Sometimes—rarely—he would accept an idea someone had put forth. Then he would invite the man or men responsible to help work out details so the plan could be put to action. That was a tremendous boost to morale, the idea that any of the men could influence a part of the war, however small. That told the men that their major was not interested in ordering them around or pulling rank. He was interested in their safety first, but also willing to listen to any concerns or ideas his men may have. Unit morale was quite high as a result.

The briefing was indeed short. The major was coming along, as we surmised from his Sidcot. The ground crew had made another SE available, so the major would fly behind us and above. I knew he did not think he had to ride herd on us. It was just an excuse to get up in the air on what should be a routine patrol and help with numbers. He, too, had joined the RFC to fly but being a squadron commander kept him from flying as much as he wanted. The upper brass discouraged such experienced officers from flying so as to preserve their acquired expertise.

And the major had experience aplenty. Word was he was born in 1885 but he never confirmed or denied this. He just smiled and waited for the topic to change. Born Rogers Paul Campbell, he was the second son of four. His father ran a small commercial fishing fleet that was quite successful. Though certainly not royalty, the family still did not want for much. His childhood was comfortable. His parents allowed him to explore what interested him, and flying interested him. Paul (he did not care for Rogers) was looking into higher education when word reached Great Britain that the Wright brothers had been the first to achieve powered flight. That helped him choose his schooling. He signed up for his local cavalry unit and sought schooling through the military. He could see the writing on the wall. The horse was doomed as a dashing military mount. Once the flying machines were strong enough and reliable enough, they would replace horses. Young Campbell would be ready. As soon as His Majesty had any kind of air arm, he would volunteer and be with it from the ground up, so to speak.

And so it went. While Paul very much enjoyed riding around on horses while wearing a dashing uniform, he kept an ear open for anything about aviation. He kept careful track of those Americans, Orville and Wilbur Wright, and any developments they put forth. This would translate into a recurring story within the Royal Flying Corps that Campbell had learned to fly from the Wrights themselves. But early on he had his pilot ticket, license number with but two digits. He was flying the very latest in modern technology. He was familiar with the products of Bleriot, Farman, Deperdussin, Bristol, Blackburn, A. V. Roe, and more. He had done test work with the Nieuport seaplane racers for a Schneider Cup team. If it could be flown, chances were he had flown it. Nothing else mattered. He had no romantic interests, only flying and, of course, the military.

Campbell was with the first RFC unit to get to France in 1914. Unlike his later SE5a squadron, that early unit had one or two each of a number of types. He was able to fly any of them he needed in order to carry out any mission he was ordered to do. The top brass loved him, thinking he was almost too good to be a regular soldier, much less an aviator.

This all came to an end one afternoon over France. Campbell had been ordered to take up a lef-tenant to do some rear area reconnaissance. They were in a BE2a, or Bleriot Experimental, second design, early model. The BE was a "modern" tractor biplane with the engine in front. The observer sat in the front cockpit, between the wings amidst a forest of struts and wires. Campbell took off and all seemed normal as the BE climbed to altitude over Allied territory in order to cross the lines at a pre-determined altitude. They flew over their assigned area and the lef-tenant made his notes. After being directed over the assigned area for a while, Campbell spotted a German observation balloon in the distance and made sure the lef-tenant saw it. The lef-tenant produced a rifle and waved Campbell toward the large, hydrogen filled "sausage". Campbell was more than willing, and away they went toward the balloon. The lef-tenant demonstrated that he wanted to be flown along the length of the balloon so he could fire more shots into it. That seemed reasonable enough, so Campbell set up and executed the run. What they did not know at that point was that there were numerous machine gun emplacements around the balloon, and flying a straight and level course along the length of the balloon was signing one's own death warrant. The gunners were quickly able to discern the height of the offending aeroplane, roughly the height of the balloon, and open fire. At that low altitude it was difficult to miss. Holes began appearing all over the airframe. Without waiting for orders, Campbell abruptly turned the BE toward home and pushed open the throttle. It was not quite in time. Suddenly, all Campbell could see was flame ahead of him. A bullet or piece of shrapnel had hit the petrol tank, which erupted in a ball of fire, engulfing the lef-tenant. Campbell immediately sideslipped the BE to port, which had the effect of moving the flames out along the starboard lower wing. He determined the shortest route to the Allied lines and pushed the throttle to its stop. He knew he had little fuel left and intended to use it to make good his escape before the flames got to him. It was close. Campbell came in low over the Allied trenches and looked for a flat area. He found a plowed field and planted his BE there. While he would have preferred landing with the plowed furrows, he had no time to correct. The engine quit just over the trenches and he set the powerless aeroplane in the plowed field "against the grain" or nearly perpendicular to the raised furrows. The next thing to happen was the landing gear separating from the rest of the airframe. The gear stayed mostly in the first furrow. A few furrows further in, the heavy nose dipped into a furrow, causing the whole aeroplane to flip over on its back. One hand on the harness release, Campbell hit the soft ground as soon as he felt everything stop. While he was quite pink from the heat of the fire, he suffered no injuries beyond a little singed hair and he would be stiff and sore for about a week or so.

The crash landing was easy compared to what came next. Expecting to be taken to a field hospital to be checked over, Campbell was taken instead to the nearest air field and placed under arrest while his immediate superiors came to collect him and get to the bottom of this tragedy, the loss of a Royal Flying Corps officer. Campbell was on his own: the lef-tenant had been burned to something stiff, black, grey, and smaller, more resembling a crude chimpanzee sculpture than an officer in His Majesty's Royal Flying Corps.

While he waited he consumed an inordinate quantity of water, thinking of the intense heat and wishing the water were something more potent. It had been a horrific dash over the lines, the lef-tenant screaming like nothing he had ever heard while being consumed by flames. He had watched the lef-tenant lift the rifle toward his own chin in an effort to end the suffering, but the gun never made it. The rifle slipped back into the front cockpit as the lef-tenant changed in appearance from red face in brown flight gear to a black and grey cinder, not unlike a log that was about to burn out. The screaming had at last stopped and the world seemed silent despite the coughing engine and rapid gunfire and zipping bullets. He didn't remember setting the BE down or releasing himself to fall from the half burnt aeroplane onto a plowed furrow. He remembered the screaming man, the silent corpse, and the men who pulled him out from under the 'plane. Then he had been hurried to the air-field to wait. He desperately wanted the burning image to depart his conscious thoughts.

"Corporal!"

Campbell snapped out of the chair to attention, facing the door. The salute was a reflex.

"Aye. Sir."

"You left on a flight over the lines with a lef-tenant, but came back alone and crashed one of His Majesty's aeroplanes. Would you care to tell us how this all came about?"

There were five of them, all officers, all in neat uniforms with polished boots and buttons, only slightly dusty from the drive in the open lorry. Pasty faces all, he knew right away he was in for a rough time with these veteran desk pilots who had never been farther off the ground than flights of stairs could lead them. They had no more than a passing knowledge of what he did as a pilot, never mind the procedures he followed or the missions he flew or the risks he faced. For all they knew, he might just go up a thousand feet or so and joyride about with a cigar in one hand and cognac in the other. This was not going to be pleasant at all.

"Certainly, sir." He stretched and moaned just a little, hoping they would not hear.

"What was that, corporal?"

"Begging your pardon, sir. I am a little stiff after having crash landed and inverted my BE, then falling head first to the ground from the elevated fuselage."

"Are we to feel sorry for you? Take pity, perhaps?"

"Oh, no. Sir. I will be okay. I am quite happy to be alive and able to tell you what you want to know. As you likely know, the lef-tenant and I were to fly over the German rear area so the lef- tenant could observe the enemy's movements and take notes regarding any changes."

"Go on?"

"Well, we performed that task without any trouble. Then I pointed out a Hun sausage—German observation balloon—to the southeast and the lef-tenant ordered me to fly to it."

"Ordered you? Do you intend to blame all of this on the dead lef-tenant?"

"Sir, you asked me what happened. That is what I am telling you. I dared to question the lef- tenant, and then he showed me he had brought along a rifle. Again, he ordered me to fly to the balloon and fly the length of it so he could shoot at it. As I approached the sausage, every Fritz 'n' Jerry on the ground opened up with whatever weapon they had. I turned for home, but it was too late. Something hit the petrol tank and it burst open all over the lef-tenant and the engine or something that ignited it. I sideslipped the BE but there was no saving the lef-tenant, sir. It was horrible. My engine quit over the lines and I had to put 'er down. I found the field but had to land crossways to the ditches from the plow. That wiped off the landing gear, then the nose dipped into a ditch and the whole thing went arsy-tarsy on me. I think."

"You think, corporal?"

"Yes, sir. It has been a bit of a day, sir. Looking at the wreckage and not able to get the screaming, burning lef-tenant out of my head, that is how I piece it together. Sir, I flew the aeroplane according to plan and then followed my orders from the lef-tenant. I did as I was told. You can probably verify my story through ground observers. Someone had to see our BE go after that sausage. The BE is nearby, on its back. You can probably find what's left of the lef- tenant's rifle and maybe his notes, I don't know. It's not my job to blame anybody. I just answered your question. Sir."

"Do I hear a bit of attitude, corporal?"

"Perhaps. Sir. I flew my mission, but the lef-tenant apparently wanted to be a hero and it went badly. It was not my idea. I tried to save the lef-tenant but I'm afraid I just couldn't shit a miracle right then. Sir. Now he's gone and you want someone to crucify. I'm the only bloke left, true, but all I did was follow orders and did my best when it all went to Hell. I am sorry, truly sorry for the lef-tenant—he will be with me for quite some time. I am sorry you were inconvenienced by venturing so close to actual fighting. I'm even sorry about your soiled uniforms, but—unlike the burning lef-tenant still shrieking in my mind—they can be cleaned. Now, unless you have something more you would like to ask me, I request permission to seek medical attention. Crash landings are not daily fare in the RFC. I am a bit sore in places. Perhaps you can understand. Sir."

Campbell then saluted the five astonished faces and walked out of the room to find whatever medic was nearby. His body was tightening up from having been tossed about and then dropped upside down to the earth. Perhaps the medic had some cognac. For medicinal purposes, to be sure. But he knew cognac would not remove the image of the charred lef- tenant from his mind. That lef-tenant would be with him from then on.

* * * * *

CHAPTER 19

German

About an hour before sunrise the crews flying the rear area mission met in the mess where Jure passed out maps. Well, six of us were there. Two of the gunners were late, but we were not worried since they mostly went where the pilots took them. The pilots were told about the separate routes approaching the target area and returning. They were advised to fly fast and low, especially over the lines. The maps had likely military targets marked on them, as well as the railway lines. Everyone drank hot coffee as they listened. There were very few questions.

There was not much discussion as we approached the Hannas, which had already been started by the ground crews. As the sun began to peer over the horizon we lifted off and quickly sped to the southwest toward the front lines. Jure and I were in the lead, flying very low to the ground, especially over the trenches. The other three Hannovers followed us quite closely, but over the trenches one trailed a bit behind the others. It rapidly departed the mission when it began to trail a little smoke, started into a roll to the right, and dove to the ground from an inverted position. It apparently crashed into an ammunition supply point, for the blast was far too great for one aeroplane alone. We were thankful the end came very quickly for the crew. Watching its path, I surmised the pilot had been hit by ground fire. We would have time to observe the loss after we returned.

With my commanding view I watched the terrain as we flew on. I spotted the railway off to the right, its path to intersect ours a short distance ahead. There was a train on it. I tapped Jure on his shoulder and pointed at the train moving slowly in a direction similar to our own. No further explanation was needed. Jure adjusted our course and we flew up on the rear of the train as he began firing. I waited a moment and began to drop small bombs and grenades. Jure put several bullets through the locomotive boiler, releasing pressurized steam and causing the train to lose what little speed it had. I saw one other Hanna fly over the train with both guns firing. I did not see the third Hanna at that time. We busied ourselves shooting at and bombing several military supply points and what looked to be some kind of headquarter tent complex. We saw no red crosses anywhere on them so we shot them up.

The rest of our raid was very much like this. Jure broke away to fly the alternate route back to our airfield with the other Hanna close behind and to the side. Still no sign of the third Hanna. We took some bullets on the way back over the lines, a few in the wings and tail surfaces.

That was when it became interesting. As we passed over the German trenches I heard the zip- zip of bullets going past us from the rear. I saw three Sopwiths closing in from behind and above, all guns firing. I beat Jure on the shoulder and yelled in his ear, "*Schnell!*" Then I fired a red flare across the path of the other Hanna. Turning to face the Englishmen, I held my fire until they came closer. I glanced at the other Hanna and watched the gunner standing upright and pounding his fist on the breech, likely indicating a jammed bullet. I knew I did not have much ammunition left in the gun. The situation did not look good for us.

The SEs suddenly climbed away, leaving us alone. I looked about and saw what must have distracted them. There were five *Albatros jägern* diving on them. We recognized three of them as our friends with the orange-yellow, blue, and turquoise noses. The other two had green and red-orange noses but were similarly painted on the aft fuselages and tails. Low on ammunition and possibly *benzin*, we raced back to our airfield. Surprisingly we had no visitors afterward.

When we arrived at our field we saw the third Hanna. Once we were down we learned it had had engine problems as it crossed the lines. The pilot managed to turn around and fly to the field. We were happy we had but two to mourn. We sat down to a somber lunch, the two empty seats all too conspicuous. Jure and the others knew the men well. On the other hand, having recently joined the unit, I did not know them beyond their names. I was saddened by their loss, of course, as they seemed to be good men, but I was less involved in the reminiscences. The gunner had recently acquired a dachshund pup and named it Sopwith. Jure agreed to care for Sopwith, intending to take it home on leave and give it to his son. Jakob brought out some brandy and made it available to all. I drank a toast to each of the fallen, as did Jakob, and after that he asked me to step outside.

"Well, Gustav, how did the raid go? Were you able to make a difference over there?"

"*Ja*, we left evidence of our visit."

"You do, of course, know how to operate a camera."

"*Javohl.*"

"*Wunderbar.* Would you like to accompany me on a flight? I should like to have pictures of what you did and just how inconvenienced you left the Englanders."

"I would be honored, *mein Herr.*"

"Good. Gather your gear and meet me at your Hanna in fifteen or twenty minutes. I will have a camera mounted in addition to *benzin* and ammunition."

"*Javohl*—I will be there." I resisted the urge to salute.

I arrived just as Jakob was being helped up and into the Hanna. I could hear the celebration mounting in the mess, though it was anything but a drunken brawl. Once Jakob was strapped in, I was assisted into my "office". Once I got into my boots, I checked the camera and plates and of course found all in order. The Parabellum was loaded as well. I was ready.

I found Jakob to be a superb flyer. He did nothing flashy or showy. He merely did what was required to take off and climb to altitude in the most efficient manner. He did look over his shoulder and wave at me. As I looked at him he pointed at the engine and gave me a firm "thumbs up" and a smile. He approved of the new engine.

Jakob followed the route on the map. Spotting the site where the Hanna had gone down, he held up his hands forming a frame with his thumbs and index fingers, indicating he wanted a photograph made. He swerved to fly above it and I exposed a plate. As he drifted back to our approximate route, I replaced the exposed plate with a new one. I tapped his shoulder and pointed at the railway line off to the right. I traced a line following the rails ahead of us, and he saw in the distance where the train had been strafed and bombed and was stalled on the track. There were numerous soldiers at work around the train. From ten thousand feet they looked like ants congregating around a morsel of food. As Jakob held up his hands forming the frame I tapped his shoulder and gave him the "thumbs up". I knew he would want a photograph.

And so the flight went. We retraced the earlier route and I made photographs of significant damage. I kept watch around us in case any Englishmen became curious. Nearing the end of our tour of battle damage my vigilance was rewarded. I tapped Jakob on the shoulder to show him we had company. I had spotted at least four English scouts over the lines, potentially blocking our return. Jakob nodded, pushed the throttle forward, and began to climb for altitude while circling where we were. I kept looking around and above, spotting at least four more specks above, nationality unknown. As we came around to face them, I tapped Jakob's shoulder and pointed above. He nodded and continued to circle and climb. I noticed two of the original scouts had apparently spotted us and begun their climb to intercept us. While I was not necessarily in fear, the Hanna being quite the capable warplane, the apparent odds were not very good. I would have to shoot while Jakob maneuvered and shot when he could.

Initial contact was made by two SE types, approaching from slightly above us and hoping to keep us from crossing the lines. One started a shallow dive from several hundred yards away. I was familiar with the tactic. He wanted to dive below us and then zoom up at us in our blind spot behind and below, where I could not shoot at him. I watched his descent, and as he approached our altitude I loosed about ten or fifteen rounds ahead of him. Incredibly, he did not zoom up under our tail. Instead he continued his dive, trailing a stream of white mist behind him. I must have hit a *benzin* tank and possibly disrupted the fuel supply to the engine. I was not able to follow him down, as his partner above us pulled up and fell into a direct dive. He was anticipating our path. I tapped Jakob on the shoulder and then punched his upper arm. He responded with a sudden snap roll which he pushed into a dive. The SE adjusted his dive and followed. When his distance was about two hundred yards I began to pepper him with ten round bursts from the Parabellum. He pressed his attack. I watched both guns flash and heard zipping and snapping as bullets whipped past near my head. Jakob jinked the Hanna in an irregular manner in an effort to avoid the gunfire. I caught a glance of two SE types approaching from below. Suddenly I did not feel so frozen at altitude. I started to sweat a little under all the clothing.

In a moment our Hanna appeared to have flown into a spider web. There were tracers lacing past us from three directions. I fired bursts as I could, trying to disrupt the Englanders' aim. There were at least two more aeroplanes diving at us from above, as well as more from the east. Before I could count them all the Hanna jerked in a manner very uncharacteristic of Jakob's flying. I looked at him and was surprised to see one side of his head covered with frozen blood. I could not make out any details, but I knew he was flying hurt. I did see a hole in the shoulder of his overcoat. His right hand was red as well. He worked the control stick with both hands. The bullet count zipping past us was climbing and I could hear the airframe taking hits.

Suddenly things became relatively quiet. There were fewer zips in the air. I looked around and cheered out loud. Never had I been so happy to see bright colors at altitude. I realized some of the specks I had seen earlier were *Albatrosen*. There were familiar colors coming toward our swarm of Englishmen, as well as colors I had not seen. It felt good to be no longer alone with all the blighters shooting at us. I put a hand on Jakob's good shoulder and he raised a thumb a little above the stick. I pointed at the throttle and then the lines and he understood. He pushed the throttle forward and flew directly at our airfield, leaving the SEs to fight with a flight of *Albatrosen*.

Jakob's landing was surprisingly smooth, considering his apparent condition. He put the Hanna right where it had been when he climbed into it, shutting down the engine several yards away. I yelled for help to remove our stricken leader. He was obviously losing blood and had to have assistance immediately. Several ground crew came running with ladders while two ran to the mess to sober up the men with news of Jakob being wounded. Everyone streamed out the door to help. In no time Jakob was out of the Hanna and placed on a nearby wooden table. Several men came back to help me clamber down. One of them pointed out that I, too, had been shot. With all that was happening around me, I had never noticed. I caught a bullet in my left shoulder. Another had passed through my heavy boot and left calf. They lowered me and carried me to a bench near Jakob. Someone ran back to the mess and returned with two partial bottles of brandy. Jakob refused, but I was not so strong. I appreciated the warmth and strong note of the intoxicant. After a few hits from the bottle my head began to swim. I suppose I had also lost . . . some . . . .

* * * * *

Chapter 20

German

I felt warm. As I woke up I realized I was on a cot and under a blanket. There was a great deal of orange light. Late afternoon sun. The dark ceiling was far above me. This caused some concern and I looked around me. All of a sudden things were more familiar. My cot was just inside an open hangar door, the hangar which housed Jakob's *Walfisch*. There was normally much extra room, for though the hangar could accommodate several aeroplanes and workbenches, the *Walfisch* was the only regular occupant. Sometimes one would find a *benzin* cart, used for refueling, or a toolbox. There was another cot nearby, with disheveled blankets on it and medical bags around it. I heard voices in casual conversation approaching, but I could not immediately identify them as they were silhouettes in the direct light of the soon to be setting sun. I felt Sopwith, all ten pounds of him, hop onto the cot and lick my face.

"Ah! Our gunner has decided to remain among the living! How are you, *mein Herr*?" They were two of the men who regularly helped flight crews into their aeroplanes.

"Rested, *danke*. I hope I have not been much trouble."

"Not at all. You have been sleeping like a baby—just not as crabby. Your surgery went well."

"Surgery?"

"*Ja*. Right where you are. Medics removed a bullet that had lodged between two ribs near your shoulder and they dressed the wounds where another bullet had passed through. You had lost a little blood. Once you glugged down some brandy you were out, so they moved you onto the cot and got to work. You looked so peaceful afterward they did not want to move you. They said the sunshine would do you good. Sopwith checked on you regularly, but this was your first reaction to his licking."

"Ja, my pillow is moist. I was wondering. And Jakob—how is he?"

"They worked on him over there. A bullet grazed his head. Lots of blood, no real harm. Another bullet apparently just missed you, passed through the fuselage decking and hit his shoulder. Stopped against his shoulder blade. Minor wound. His right hand was hit as he was holding the stick. That made a mess. His hand is bandaged but he could still lose a finger or two. He is resting in his quarters with a medic nearby."

"Good to know. He put up a good fight and then brought the crate back. Set her down like nothing was wrong. He is a wonderful flyer."

"They have not talked with him as he is still out. He did lose a lot of blood. What happened?"

I told them about the flight, the Sopwiths, and the escape. I asked if they got my plates.

"*Ja,* they took out the camera and turned it over to the intelligence types We should have some photographs soon."

"You remember the pilots with the brightly painted *Albatrosen.* That was the *staffel* which allowed us to escape the English. There were some we have seen before and a few new to me. I'm surprised they didn't stop here. Or did they? I hope they are all well."

"One did stop. The pilot thought it was you and Jure, but Jure met him and told him about you and Jakob. He stopped to see you, but you were not taking visitors at that time. He asked me to tell you Swiss left his regards. I don't know if any of them were injured."

"I'm fortunate they seem to know where I or we go. We do owe them a debt."

"It does appear you have a system worked out. You go out in a Hanna, cause the English some trouble, and when their *jägern* come to chase you away, our *jägern* meet them and do battle."

"That is indeed what we worked out. But today's incident wasn't planned. We were lucky."

"Well, maybe if somehow we could arrange for that *Jagdstaffel* to occupy the same field as our *Schlachtstaffel* we could work in closer cooperation."

"I would like that. I like to think we can take care of ourselves, but having increased strength from above can't hurt. This is not a fair fight. It's war. And we intend to win, whatever is required."

Just then Jure joined us. "Well, Gustav, you have returned to the world of the living! I'm happy to see you have enjoyed your nap in the sunshine. Sopwith has been anxious, waiting for you to come play!"

"I'm touched—well, licked. And you, my friend, back to sobriety? Greetings!"

"Jakob has also awakened. Would you care to see him?"

"*Javohl*—but only if I can stand up."

"Take my hand and try. I know you have a sore hoof. Perhaps we can take you to the village blacksmith and you can make yourself a new shoe?"

I attempted to punch Jure in the arm, but he dodged it and I stumbled a bit due to the throbbing pain in my leg. Sopwith yelped at the sudden excitement. But Jure caught me and held me steady. "Careful, there, backseat boy. Let's go visit Jakob."

After what felt like a lengthy walk, we entered Jakob's quarters and found him to be awake but groggy. We exchanged greetings and assessed each other's wounds. "Gustav, it's good to see you up. I wish I could join you."

"And you will, soon enough. It's good to see you."

"It's good to be here. Just don't ask me to play piano."

"Don't worry. I never cared for your stylings anyway."

"No? I am hurt." Fake pout.

"It's a good time to pursue another hobby."

"I could cook. I would like to, but I'll wait until after the war."

"As will I with my track and field aspirations." We all chuckled a little at our feeble attempts at humor.

"Seriously, Gustav, you did well this morning. I am fortunate you were my gunner. And your friends with the Easter egg *jägern*—they were wonderful. They are welcome here anytime for anything they desire."

"Agreed. They saved *unseren arsch*. But you surprised me, Jakob, with your flying skill. You are a wonderful pilot—Jure could learn from you—but you brought our Hanna in for a flawless landing in spite of your wounds."

"It was by rote. I have landed more than a few times. And Jure, I would be happy to help you once I can get back into a cockpit."

"I'm beginning to feel under-appreciated. Maybe the English pilots should have done a better job of shooting!"

"Somebody give Jure a towel for his tears. Apparently the dog is not enough for his self- esteem. So, Gustav, are you fit to fly?"

"I'm an airman, not a doctor. I would love to go up. But I think I need to let my body heal for a little while. I would hate to bleed all over Jure's pretty Gwendolyn again." Jure held up his hand as if he were going to slap me.

"Would you like to take a few days away? I can easily arrange that."

"I had not thought of it, but that would be good."

"Where would you like to go?"

"I will have to telephone my friend and see if she would like a visit."

"Use my office. Make your arrangements and I will approve it. Take a week."

"*Javohl!*" I snapped to and started to salute but caught myself. "*Danke.* I will."

"While you are away I will look into teaching you to fly. If Jure should be hurt, I will need a replacement while he goes away."

"Do I have to be hurt? I can't just go away?"

"We should be so lucky!" Jure gave me a shove but had to grab me to keep me from falling on Jakob. He apologized but we all laughed a little. Sopwith yipped and wagged his tail.

I went to Jakob's office to telephone the tavern. Käti answered. When she heard my voice she almost came through the handset to visit me. She was very excited. And she wondered what was wrong.

"Does anything have to be wrong? I can't just call?"

"No, you cannot just call. Something has happened to you."

"Alright, alright. I was shot today, . . ."

"*Shot?* Who shot you?"

"*Liebchen*, there is a war. I was shot by an Englander. I was shooting at him, he was shooting at me. We were doing our jobs. It wasn't personal. Besides, I may have shot him as well. I have shot many Englishmen."

"Were you hurt?"

"Of course. I was shot. One bullet stuck between two ribs. The medic pulled it out and gave it to me. The other passed through my flying boot and my calf. Someone found it on the floor of my crate and gave it to me also. I lost some blood and slept most of the afternoon, but I will be alright."

"I am so happy you are well . . . or will be."

"*Ja,* so am I. I need to heal before I go up again. Would you like some company?"

"*Javohl!* You know I will heal you."

"*Ja,* I know. You can do that with your smile. But you may have to change a bandage or two."

"I will, I will. When will you be here?"

"I will be on the train as soon as my *schlastaführer* approves my arrangements. He will approve anything I present. He was my pilot this morning and was shot worse than I was. He, too, will be alright. I will tell you more, but for now I will say *Wiedersehen* and reserve my place on the railway. I will telephone to tell you when I will be there. Or maybe I will just knock on your door."

"My door will be open for you. Always."

"I will see you. Soon."

I telephoned the railway depot just beyond the aerodrome and made my arrangements to travel. I made a note of my itinerary and presented it to Jakob for approval.

"*Ja, ist gut,*" he said and set it aside.

"You didn't look at it."

"I don't need to look at it. You have shown me you intend to end this war as soon as you can. You cannot win a war while recovering from bullet wounds or spending time with your *liebchen*. You will be back as soon as you are able to fight. I trust you. If you need more time than you have presented me, take it. Telephone me so I know. Is there anything else?"

"No, *mein Herr*—Jakob! Well, I do wish you a speedy recovery."

"*Danke. Wiedersehen.*"

When Jakob told me I could use the telephone in his office he did not put any restrictions on the offer. With that in mind, I went back to his office and telephoned the railway depot again. The agent told me he had a train leaving in just under two hours. Assuming no delays, it would put me at my intended destination by mid-evening. I changed my reservation, thanked him, and put down the handset. I packed hurriedly, grabbed a quick bite to eat in the mess, accepted a number of handshakes and well wishes, and limped out. It happened that Jure was about to enter.

"Sneaking out, are you? Without a word?"

"Of course not. What word would you like?"

"Give me your word you will have a good time and heal rapidly."

"It's not like you will be lacking company."

"No, but I will be lacking the rear half of a good team."

"You will, this is true." Jure knocked my hat askew.

"I am sorry you were wounded, but I'm happy you will see your *liebchen*. Perhaps you will make a photograph to bring here when you return."

"I like that idea. I shall look into it. But I must go now."

"Are you walking? To where?"

"The rail depot."

"Don't be silly. I will take you there and wait with you until your train arrives."

"Now you are being silly. I will be fine."

"You were shot but a few hours ago. Walking will not heal your wounds. It could cause the wounds to open and bleed. I will drive you."

"You talk like you care. I promise, I will tell no one."

"Care? Me? Ha! I merely hate to break in new gunners. Now sit here while I get a tender."

The tender pulled up very soon and Jure tossed my bag in the back. Then he made sure I was steady climbing into the cab. I thought it was a lot of fuss for the short distance we were to drive, but it was nice to know he cared. Despite the gruff manner he put on, he was a good man. I knew why Jakob liked him and was pleased to have him in the family. For now, it was my job to protect him in the air so he would have a chance to add to and raise his family after the war.

Though Sopwith had established himself on my lap, I had not yet settled in my seat when we arrived at the depot. I started to climb down from the cab but Jure scolded me to wait.

"Jure! I am not with child! I can do this myself."

"*Dummkopf!* You were shot. Twice. Be easy on your body!"

"I will tell everybody how caring you are."

"No one will believe you."

I checked in with the agent and then we sat in the waiting room. While Jure held Sopwith, we talked about the war, the Hanna, the new engine, his wife and son, letters he received from Gwendolyn, Jakob, and more. It was a very pleasant conversation with a fine man. No one would believe me if I did tell them.

The train arrived a few minutes ahead of schedule, which I took to be a good sign. Jure carried my bag to the carriage door, shook my hand, and handed me my bag.

"Come back soon—but not too soon!"

"We have a war to win. The sooner I return, the sooner we win the war, and the sooner we get on with our lives. Käti will take care of me. She will not let me return until I am ready. *Danke schön,* Jure. *Auf Wiedersehen!*"

"*Wiedersehen!*"

* * * * *

CHAPTER 21

German

I sat in my compartment, placed my injured leg on the seat opposite me, and watched Jure lift Sopwith into the tender and drive back to the other end of the airfield. While I wanted to sleep a little, I knew I would not be able to. Käti was going to be very surprised. It was going to be wonderful seeing her friendly face and the smile that could brighten the darkest day. They were but outward harbingers of the vast kindness, decency, and camaraderie that were within. She was simply a wonderful human being to be with. I found that no matter how much time I spent with her I wanted more. I had never met someone with that capacity. She had a way of making me feel wonderful simply being in her presence. She was worth any amount of effort, even fighting a war and facing the possibility of dying. This fabulous person was at the other end of a fairly brief journey. I would soon have her in my sight and in my arms. With those thoughts and anticipation of basking in her warm personality, I knew sleep was out of the question.

There was another minor complication. While it distracted me from warm thoughts of again being with Käti, it also put sleep far out of mind. I was slapped back to reality by the unmistakable sound of bullets whizzing by and hitting things around me. The train was the object of a strafing run. I pulled open the window and looked forward and up, only to see three SE type Sopwiths bearing down. I withdrew and fell to the floor between the facing seats for what little protection they might provide. My thought was that a flight of Englanders must be returning from an aerial engagement behind our lines, burning up ammunition on targets of opportunity. The train passing below them must have looked harmless enough, but it was anyone's guess what it was transporting, be it military supplies, civilians, or an aspiring *jagdflieger*. I did not enjoy being shot at, but I understood why they were doing it.

One thought was to advance that air fighting opportunity and see that they pay for my inconvenience.

It was inconvenient and not a little painful, struggling to get back into my seat from my huddled position on the floor. The leg and shoulder were yet sore, and the areas around the wounds were inflamed because of the disturbed tissue. While my left arm was suspended in a sling, it was more a reminder to go easy on it. I managed to attain a seated position. I held that position for a few moments in order to allow my body to recover from the ordeal. Then I stood up and left my compartment to see if I could be of assistance to anyone else who may have been hurt. Fortunately there were no major injuries, mostly property damage and bullet holes in the carriages. Everything seemed to be in order, so I returned to my compartment, passing the stares of a few children and at least one admiring woman. I did not like to stand out like that, but I understood that having a wounded soldier—airman— on board made me an object of some interest.

I was able to rest a little longer before my stop was called. My heart pounded a cadence of anticipation as I picked up my bag and waited for the train to slow to a stop. I returned a few waves from other passengers as I departed the carriage and stepped onto the platform. From there it was a short walk to the tavern. I decided to stop there since it was on the way to Käti's cottage. Besides, it was a pretty safe bet she would be working.

As I stepped in, Ernst called out, "Gustav! What a surprise! Welcome!"

"*Danke, mein Herr!*"

"What can I get for you?"

"Oh, nothing. I am looking for Käti."

"Oh, but she has gone for the evening. I'm surprised you didn't see her. Are you sure you don't want anything? Name it, and it is on me."

"You are too kind. I will go to Käti's. Maybe we will return."

"I wouldn't bet on it. Good to see you!"

After another brief walk I turned the corner to see Käti's cottage. A light came on inside just as I looked. It seemed to take hours to close the several yards to her door. I knocked.

From inside I heard a familiar voice. "No visitors. I am tired. Come again another time."

"You said your door was always open to me!"

And indeed it was. There stood the most beautiful sight I could imagine. Her hair was disheveled, her face smudged with something from the kitchen, her blouse open and hanging off one shoulder. She grabbed me out of the air and pulled me in very close. I winced a little from the pressure on my shoulder. At some point she noticed I was in pain and stopped kissing my face.

"I am so sorry! I'm simply excited!"

"So I see! I'm excited as well."

"Oh—your arm—your shoulder!"

"It's all right. I will heal."

She grabbed me around the waist and pulled me close again. "Better?"

"Better. But I was not complaining before."

"Oh, Gustav—you could have telephoned!"

"And miss this greeting?"

"The greeting would have been the same. Trust me. I have missed you. You have to be hungry."

"Oh, I—"

"Give me a moment. I'll change and we'll go get you a meal."

"No, you're tired."

"I *was* tired. No longer. Just a moment. We will go."

"May I use your chair?"

Yes, you may. Consider it your chair as well."

"*Danke.*"

I sat down and watched as she partially undressed and freshened herself. She made no effort to do anything with her hair beyond tying it back. It made no difference. She was simply beautiful to behold.

"Ready? Here, I'll give you a hand."

"No need." I probably resembled a turtle trying to right itself, reeling fore and aft, struggling to get my weight above my feet.

"Give me your good hand." The words were icy and firm. I complied and she anchored my next attempt.

"Danke schön. Ready."

We left the cottage and walked to the tavern. My leg was beginning to throb a bit, but I was not going to tell her.

"Your leg hurts."

"It should hurt. How can you tell? I'm walking properly, no limp."

"No, you are not limping. But you're trying too hard to hide it and your gait is almost studied and formal."

"You read a lot into my gait."

"I know people. You are a proud airman. You have been shot and seriously wounded, yet you act like you cut yourself shaving. I understand that, but you are with me. No need to put on appearances. You have already impressed me. Now simply be with me."

This was one remarkable woman.

I opened the door for Käti and she entered, holding my hand in the air. "Look what arrived at my door!"

Cheers rang out from everyone in the tavern. Ernst sat us down, brought us two beers, and said he would have us food shortly. We did not care. In ones and twos, seemingly everyone in the tavern stopped to greet us, hug Käti, and shake my hand. Ernst came back with two plates of hot food. We attacked the food with knife and fork. The food didn't stand a chance. The beers kept arriving. When he saw I was finished eating, Ernst asked me to stand.

"Everyone, this is Käti's friend, Gustav. He is a gunner in a *Schlachtstaffel.* He was wounded this morning over enemy territory and has come to visit our Käti and recuperate. He has discovered how wonderful our Käti is. Gustav, you are a lucky man. We are very happy you and Käti are together. You make her very happy." Cheers erupted once again. Someone asked what had happened. Someone else called them rude.

I spoke up. "No, I don't mind the question. This morning my pilot led a raid over English territory. We bombed and strafed military targets, did much damage, and lost two of our *Staffel* members when their aeroplane crashed into an ammunition depot. The *Schlastaführer* later asked me to accompany him to photograph the damage our raid caused. Returning from that mission we were attacked by English *jägern*. We were both shot, but we were saved by our own *jägern* and were able to return to our airfield. *Der Huaptmann* suffered more severe injuries. He is resting well, but could lose two fingers. Next to his injuries, mine are as if I had cut myself shaving." Käti hit me. "You are all too kind. Please know that I will take care of your —our—Käti. *Danke schön!*"

We were gluttons. The food was excellent and the drinks never stopped coming. We just kept eating. Käti decided she wanted dessert and left me to go to the kitchen to find something. As she disappeared from view Elsa left the bar and walked over to me. I stood up to greet her.

"Elsa—is it?—I am Gustav. I finally have the pleasure of meeting you." I extended my hand. She took my hand and pulled herself to me, wrapping her free arm around the small of my back. Placing her lips practically against my ear, she whispered breathily, "*Ja*, Gustav, I am Elsa. I have heard much about you. Käti often speaks of you. I almost feel I know you." She gently kissed me by the ear, then a little more toward my mouth and a little more, each kiss getting more intense, until her lips were at mine. She flicked her tongue against my upper lip and then clamped her lips over mine. Her tongue slipped into my mouth just a little, then trailed off my upper lip to the opposite cheek, the kisses becoming softer again. Into my other ear she whispered.

"It has been a pleasure getting to know you, Gustav. I will buy you a drink any time, just stop and say hello. But do remember to take care of my dear Käti. She likes you very much. You make her very happy And she is precious to each of us. You are very fortunate to have her."

With that Elsa loosed her grip and returned to the bar. Once in place, she wiped around her lips and reapplied her red lipstick. Just as I realized what she had done, Käti returned with dessert for us both. She took one look at my face and her eyes widened, then narrowed. Setting down the plates, she fairly bellowed.

"Elsa—*No!* Hands off—this one is mine!"

Käti took a big bite of chocolate cake and walked to the bar. Slipping behind the bar, she grabbed the more slender Elsa in a bear hug and began to kiss her lips and cheeks repeatedly. When she finished, she backed away to admire her work. Elsa was out of breath and there were chocolate smudges all over her face. "You are the sister I never had. I love you. But hands off!" Käti picked up Elsa's rag from the bar, wiped her own face clean, and handed the rag to Elsa. As Elsa turned away Käti slapped her on the rear and then returned to me.

"Gustav, you must have some of this cake—it's delicious!" I barely heard her over all the clamor as the patrons showed their appreciation for the women. Käti wiped the lipstick off my face and put my hair back in place. "I hope Elsa did not offend you. She can be an animal."

"Offended? I should say not. It was good to meet your animal—uh, friend."

"I'll bet. I will deal with you later."

"I certainly hope so."

The chocolate cake was indeed delicious. After a few bites Käti asked me, "Did you like it?"

"The cake? *Ja*, it's delicious."

"It is, but that is not what I am asking about. I think you know it."

"I did like it. Very much. It was unexpected, it was exciting—and it was terrifying."

"You liked it?"

"It was a great moment. I would not make a habit of it. I would never expect anything like it to happen again. Ever. It was unique among my experiences and worth treasuring. You need not worry. I cannot get enough of you. I want to get back to the war so I can win it and then be with you. What else can I say to convince you?" I leaned close and began kissing her on and around her lips.

"Gustav, if there is any chocolate cake on my . . ."

"You worry too much." More kissing. "Are you ready to go home?"

"Are you expecting a welcome home celebration?"

"Just had one. I expect nothing. Being alone with you will be simple and pleasant, even if we but go to sleep for the night. I will enjoy holding you or just being with you."

We stood up to leave. Elsa blew a kiss to me. Käti shook her fist at Elsa, who smiled.

After a short walk in the chilling night air we entered Käti's cottage. I put wood on the fire and she asked to see my wounds. I demurred.

"Gustav, we need to change the dressing anyway to prevent infection. I will wash them and tend to the dressings."

"You need not worry, *liebchen.*"

"I am not worried. I'm only being sensible."

I undressed near the fire so Käti could have a look. As the wounds were recent, there was bruising and swelling. "Gustav, this looks terrible. But you will heal soon. We will keep the tissue clean and you will be well in no time."

"You are in a hurry to send me back?"

"No, I would like to keep you here with me. But it makes sense to send you back so you can do your part in the war. Then you can return to me and we can begin our lives together."

"That sounds like something worth fighting for."

"I hope that idea appeals to you. But make no mistake. I will not allow you to return to your *Staffel* until you are healed. You must no longer be susceptible to infection at the very least. You must fight, but I must see to it that you are healthy enough to fight well. Now, this is going to hurt."

It did. She thoroughly cleaned the wounds and applied fresh dressings I had brought with me.

"Now, my Gustav, you have had a very long day. Lie down and rest. I shall join you once I have washed myself."

"I can watch?"

"I am flattered. If you wish."

I lay down and positioned myself to watch Käti get ready to come to bed. I do not remember anything beyond the first few stays she undid. It had indeed been a long and trying day, capped by more than a fair share of food and celebration. I awakened to relieve myself of some of that celebration. Käti looked so peaceful in the light of the fire. I dared not disturb her. While I wanted very much to show my appreciation, I felt that sometimes one needed to defer and enjoy the moment. Before my lay a perfectly beautiful woman. Generously proportioned, perhaps more so than the regarded norm, with a face one would have thought found only on angels. She was a perfectly beautiful woman, immensely capable, caring without bounds, and drawn to me. From the beginning I was flawed physically and a burden on her. Helping someone in need I could understand. But taking them into her home and life was more than anyone could have asked for, much less expected. And then romantic attachments? I was truly dreaming. I lay there to take in the serene face, reflections of the firelight frolicking across its features. No, this was a moment to be cherished, not disturbed by lustful actions. There would be time for that. Besides, my capability for such lustful deeds was in question. My body was very stiff and sore as a result of the air battle earlier in the day. One would think being hit by a tiny bullet would not hurt so much, but it was the shock to the body from the force behind the bullet in addition to the round's destruction of tissue. The entire upper left quadrant of my body was resistant to movement. When I had finally wrestled myself to an upright sitting position, the next shock hit me: my leg did not want to support my weight. I found my gait was almost a hop. I would swing the wounded leg in front and hop over it as it touched down. The short walk to the toilet was such an ordeal that I sat down to perform the necessary evacuation. I would never have admitted to it at the time. Standing up again, I found the leg to be a little more accepting of the weight. A little. My hop became a heavy limp. But it was an improvement and I was willing to accept that. However, donning heavy clothing, mounting a ladder, and climbing onto and then into the rear "office" of a Hannover was among the last things I envisioned that moment. It appeared I would need that week to recover. I half fell onto the bed and managed not to awaken my cherubic friend. I struggled back under the bedclothes and lay on my right side. I wanted to put an arm around Käti, but I feared I lacked the grace to do so without clubbing her in the process. Like the more aggressive actions I had considered—briefly—there would be time for that. It was more important to sleep. And to heal.

* * * * *

CHAPTER 22

British

Major Campbell took full advantage of his time away in an aeroplane. He sat in the cockpit of the SE just brought to the line, still cold. He would go through the starting sequence himself rather than task a ground crewman. Having already checked the externals of the SE, found the control surfaces were free to move and no obvious insect infestation anywhere, he checked that the magneto switch was off.

"Switch is off," he called to the crewman out front. The man then walked the propeller in the proper direction to draw petrol into the cylinders. He held up his hands to show he was done.

"Switch is on." The major adjusted the air/fuel mixture lever to "choke" the engine, making it easier to start. The crewman gave the propeller a brisk pull and stepped away to the side in one swift and sure motion. The engine whirred a bit, then began to cough. The coughs combined into a sputter, the sputters evened out and became a roar. Now the major could play with the air/fuel mixture while the engine was warming up to gauge the response of these controls.

Once his SE was up to operating temperature and the wheel chocks removed, he taxied downwind to where they would all turn around and take off into the wind. He stayed a bit to the side so he could watch the others taxi and then take off. He waved them on as they approached him. Even though he had the farthest to climb, he was in no hurry. He watched with pride as every other pilot took off without incident, and then he followed. Nothing special or flashy, he merely sped up, lifted first his tail, then the whole airframe off the ground. As the rumbling of the ground roll ceased, he smiled. He really missed that feeling of initiating powered flight. It felt good in any aeroplane: it felt better in an SE. Compared to other types, the SE5a was almost overpowered. It was quite responsive to its controls and the big water-cooled V-eight out front just pulled without effort.

It was always good to take off in an SE. It simply exuded confidence. Tell the engine what you wanted it to do, through the controls, and it did just so.

There was ample power and ample maneuverability, but the 'plane was still stable enough to shoot from.

Major Campbell was thrilled beyond belief at going on patrol. The sky looked better up there than it did from the ground. Everything felt better in the air. Cold? No matter. One would have thought he would have done a barrel roll or something to show his joy, but he kept his "stiff upper lip" and just took off and climbed to altitude. That was plenty. There would be a time for aerobatics. This was not that time.

The major saw this as merely a joyride in the sky. His "lads" had been through a harrowing day, what with the early morning air raid, the loss of a squadron mate and a lot of equipment, and then the cleanup and attempt at normalcy. Though it was never a bad idea to have aeroplanes in the air, he expected no encounters with German flyers today. This was a tour of the front, a look around, a display of defiance in the wake of a devastating raid. One could not keep a good Brit down, especially in the Royal Flying Corps. The squadron was thumbing its nose at those clever Huns. They got us, yes, but we're back. Would ye like to 'ave a go now?

The SEs were gorgeous in the afternoon sun on its slow descent toward the western horizon. Though the airframes, generally khaki-brown but with irregular dark green spots from fresh patches, blended in with the battlefield below, the blue-white-red cockades stood out like dartboards, especially in the sun. Perhaps they should do something to tone down the colors, particularly the bright white, in the interest of blending in a little better. But the cockades did something more, whether out on the wingtips or closer in toward the center. They brought out a sense of pride in one's mates and the Royal Flying Corps. April— "Bloody April," they called it— had been a bad month with many men and machines lost to fine German airmen and their better machines. But the growing numbers of SE5as, along with the new "Camel" scout from Sopwith, had brought things closer to even again. They needed more of these superb aeroplanes and well trained pilots before they could think of clearing the skies of Germans. From his own experience, he knew the SE would outfly anything Fritz could put up against it. With more of them, perhaps the Boche could have a "bloody" month of their own. That sleek Albatross was no longer a dominant force in the skies, even in its newer, sleeker form. And the newer Pfalz scout, which resembled the Albatross at a distance, was nothing exceptional. An experienced pilot could still be a problem in these fading designs, but one could tell the Germans had their share of fresh young pilots, still wet behind the ears, as it were. They were easy to spot. They were the ones who looked mostly straight ahead. Experience had a way of teaching a pilot to look around constantly. Or killing the ones who did not adapt. Kill or be killed. That was the game. Small wonder they referred to an aerial skirmish as a "dog fight". The way things often worked into a circle certainly looked like—

"What the *hell!*"

Campbell snapped out of his little reverie to the "zip-zip-zip-pock-zip-pock" of bullets passing and hitting his SE. It was the last thing he expected, a "hun in the sun" on his own side of the lines. Pretty good shooting, too, within a few feet of the cockpit. The major instinctively advanced the throttle and shoved the stick hard right and back, throwing the SE into a snap roll, in hopes that the still unseen hun would overrun him and become the victim.

I was below the major and off to port. When I heard the gunfire from above and behind, I dove a bit to the left to zoom upward and see what was up there. I saw one Albatross diving at the major as he snap rolled away. I also saw four other scouts above the Albatross. Knowing the major's abilities, I banked and flew farther behind our lines so I could climb and meet the other scouts above. As I gained altitude I surveyed the situation. Major Campbell had hoped to have a shot at his Albatross, but the pilot was ready for his snap roll and pulled up to retain height advantage. I watched the major fire off a red flare to alert the others. Then he appeared to slow a bit and fly straight and level. Why would he commit such an error, especially in the midst of an attack? Then I saw it. Fire. The major had been hit, and his petrol had caught fire. I desperately wished for fifty more horsepower as my SE strained to get above the major and protect him from the other specks about to arrive. After several eternal seconds, the major's SE dropped its starboard wing and sideslipped, pulling the flames out toward the port wingtip. Then the SE began to tumble, not unlike a falling leaf. I climbed past the major's attacker, expecting the upper scouts to dive at any time. My squadron mates were coming around to engage the Hun who had set the major's SE ablaze. First checking above, I then looked for the major below but could not find him. I felt a little sick for a moment. Major Campbell was a good man.

Looking above, I saw one of the scouts fall out from the others and come in my direction, the sun exposing the deep blue of his upper wing. I entered into a shallow dive, then pulled the stick back to begin a loop. Going just past vertical, I rolled to right myself and found the blue Albatross ahead and above me. He had compensated for my move and was approaching in a shallow dive. I reached up and unlocked the Lewis gun so I could pull it back and elevate the barrel. Then I fired two bursts of about twenty rounds at the blue spinner. Just after I began to fire, I saw the flashes of his guns and heard the "zip-zip" as his bullets passed me to the side. I hadn't missed, as I saw some bits flying away from the fuselage. He then began to smoke a little and broke off his attack to head for the lines.

At this point I didn't care to pursue the blue Albatross. I was more concerned with my mates and the major. I looked about and found them not too far away. One had started toward me to help with the scouts above, which had abandoned any further offensive action and followed their stricken blue comrade toward the lines. The other SEs were in loose formation below. I fired a blue flare to suggest we return to our aerodrome and find out what had happened to Major Campbell.

A short while later we landed. We were elated to see an SE had returned ahead of us. There it sat on the line. We could see the lower port wing was badly burned and might have to be replaced. The upper port wing was singed a bit as well.

Once we had clambered out of our SEs we went to the mess where we found the major with a healthy dose of cognac. We were all hollering at once with our various inquiries, and the major raised his empty hand to call for quiet. Someone persisted.

"We saw you, sir, on fire!"

We all knew what had happened before with the lef-tenant in the BE.

"Yes, yes, lad. The bastard shot my fuel line and I caught fire. I slipped to starboard and the flames climbed my other wing and went out. At that point I played dead and fell away. Since I wasn't too far from here, I glided in and put down on my own field. The lads on ground crew have some work to do on that SE, unfortunately."

"But sir, the fire . . . weren't you afraid?"

"Bloody right, I was. But I had to try something. I am not one to call it quits and clutch a lily to my chest."

"But . . ."

The major stood up, tossed down the remaining cognac, and set down his glass.

"Enough of this. I am and shall be alright, thanks. Let's get our reports done so we can eat. Thanks, lads. Well done."

* * * * *

CHAPTER 23

British

The ground crew worked into the night to repair the SE the major had borrowed. The next morning found it on the line, ready to be flown, but with dark green port wings and khaki brown starboard wings. While it wasn't a red nose or anything similar, it was unique and made the aeroplane easy to spot in the air, at least from above.

Major Campbell had ordered an early patrol similar to that of the prior afternoon. Point A, turn around, point B, turn around, and stay on the Allied side of the lines. The major wanted us in the air, but not fully engaged until we had something approaching unit strength. To be sure, no one was happy with the order. I still had my desire to rid the skies of German aircraft and/or kill Germans. I went to the major.

"Sir. Permission to fly a solo patrol."

"Denied."

"But Major, I have experi—"

"No. Out of the question. Yes, you have experience. I want to preserve your experience to be passed along to lesser experienced pilots as we receive them. Do not cross the lines. The only air combat you may engage in is defensive, on our side of the lines. Do you understand?"

"Aye, Major. Sir."

I joined the others preparing to take off. I would be looking for huns in the sun or anywhere else they might be hiding. While I had shot at and hit the blue Albatros the day before, I had not claimed it due to the other things going on. It likely did not crash, at least not from the damage I had caused. I would pursue any such action harder today should it occur. It wasn't the number of kills that concerned me. I didn't care for any decorations. I just wanted my revenge for my mate killed practically at my side. And for Knees. I only wanted to kill Huns. I was happy with knowing that the ones I had killed would no longer be a threat to anyone. More would be better, but I need not keep score.

With a little help from a crewman, I found my way up the ladder and into my "Dirty Bird", already warming up. Getting strapped in, I developed a smile. The lads looked at me funny but I didn't care. I could kill Germans without violating the major's order and I intended to do just that.

Takeoff went without a hitch, everyone lifting off and ascending to our assigned altitude. As we approached the lines, I allowed my SE to get just a little ahead of the others, the first step in my scheme. We followed our prescribed patrol route with the predictable results. When we finished the patrol, the rest turned to head home but I stayed the course until I thought the others were far enough away. Then I made my move. Carefully staying behind the lines, I eased into a shallow dive. Now and again I would allow my nose to drift in the direction of the enemy trenches and I would fire bursts from both guns. Even if it was over a thousand feet away, I had to be doing some damage or disruption to the Germans.

Using up most of my ammunition, I decided to head for the aerodrome. I had followed the letter of the law, so to speak, and was just a little behind the rest in landing. No foul committed, no harm done.

But I was wrong.

Once I taxied to the line and shut down my Viper, I was approached by a pair of soldiers who waited while I exited my "Dirty Bird". Once I was firmly on the ground, they ordered me to follow them to the squadron office.

"I must ask, what is this about?"

No answer.

"Is it against regulations to be late for a meal?"

No response.

When I entered the office, there were several more soldiers inside, as well as Major Campbell. The major looked quite upset. I saluted and asked what this was about.

"Did you not count the SEs on the flight line when you taxied in?"

"No, sir. Why?"

"One of them is missing. Or, at least, not where it is supposed to be."

"I'm afraid I didn't notice, sir."

"Pity. I always regarded you as more observant than that."

"Sir, is there a point to this?"

"Why, yes, there definitely is a point. You are responsible for the missing SE and its pilot."

"I am? How so, sir?"

"When you executed your little stunt to exact further revenge on the Germans, recent arrival Corporal Wade followed you. He apparently thought it better to get closer to the German trenches before firing, and—"

"Oh, no . . . ."

"—the Germans obliged by shooting him down into No Man's Land. Before poor Wade could even get out of his SE the bloody bastards shelled the wreckage. So, because of your inability to follow orders and control your personal vendetta, your squadron is short another aeroplane and Corporal Wade is dead."

"But sir, I thought he had . . . shit—sir! No one was supposed to see. I never meant to take anyone in with me. Hell, I didn't even go over the lines. This is bloody awful. I can but accept sole responsibility for my actions and their consequences. I cannot bring back Corporal Wade, sir. Oh, hell, sir, I would take his place if I could. This was *not* supposed to happen. I apologize, sir. I am sorry that my actions cost an innocent life. You have to under—"

"I knew as much. I can tolerate little stunts like yours from time to time. We are not all cast in the same mold, so I understand we each have our own quirks. But I cannot allow these quirks to cost us British lives. I know of your, uh, 'disdain' for the enemy and I expect you to lash out at them. So you step out of line a bit. I don't care. That is part of who you are. But you are a good man and a good pilot I am proud to have in my squadron."

"Thank you, sir."

"But this cannot go without punishment. I am sending you to HE as an instructor. You will help to shape young men—much like our departed master Wade—into good pilots. You know how to fly. You know how to attain that 'edge' that can make a difference in a fight. You need to take classes of lads and turn out competent pilots. I am fully aware you would rather have your SE with which to kill Germans. But think of it as sending over as many Wades as you can, as many Hun killers as you can program. Give them the tools they will need to fly, fight, and survive the front line combat they will face once they are assigned over here. Teach them your skills and your knowledge. Let them acquire your hatred for the enemy. Send squadrons of yourself over here so that we can prosecute this war and maybe be home by this coming Christmas."

"HE, sir?"

"Yes, Home Establishment. You will take your "Dirty Bird" and fly the Channel as soon as the weather permits. Until then, you will remain here, on the ground. Find something useful to do in maintenance."

"But my SE."

"You will take it with you to HE. We need aeroplanes, yes. But no one will fly yours. The "Dirty Bird" is for you alone." "Yes, sir."

"Lad, I know you are unhappy with this assignment. But take it seriously and do a good job with it. You will be back in France and soon. But until then, train as many of you as you can. I hate being in France to fight a bloody war. When I think of France, I want to think of food, wine, women, art, music, and enjoyment. Being in France to kill just seems incongruous. Let's put an end to this unpleasantness so France can recover and I can come back and enjoy what she has to offer. Cheerio, then, eh?"

"Yes, sir."

I saluted, he dismissed me, the army personnel melted away, and I went to the mess to eat. One of the cooks had kept some food warm for me and found me a little scotch for later. No one in the squadron thought for a minute that I had led Wade away, even though it appeared that way. They knew I had intended to squeeze off a few bursts out of frustration more than anything else. While I ate, men stopped by to make small talk. I could feel what they did not say. They did not blame Wade's death on me. They wanted the "Dirty Bird" and me to stay.

One would have thought I was back at HE already, what with the weather the way it was. Birds hardly flew. I helped a lot in the hangar tents between the engines and the guns and ammunition. Some of the pilots came in to learn some of what I knew. They envied me for having no engine failures or jams. I showed them how easy it was once one knew his way around the aeroplane. It was not exciting information, to be sure, but it could be mighty exciting to survive a scrap and get back to the aerodrome today and perhaps home soon thereafter. That little bit now could mean a lot later. Suffer through a little tedium now and have stories to tell about the war in the future. If one chose to share.

The fitters took full advantage of having an extra body around for several days but I didn't mind. What else did I have to do other than watch the weather? My "Dirty Bird" was ready to go whenever the weather lifted. I could not even volunteer to fly with patrols as there were no patrols. On either side. It was just as well. The major would never have allowed me to fly patrol. Geoff even asked me if I wanted "Dirty Bird" changed to "Flightless Bird". I told him I would rather have someone paint that picture he carried around on the nose. He asked why I didn't paint it myself. I told him I didn't find it inspiring. He was incredulous. I shrugged.

* * * *

CHAPTER 24

British

One morning I woke up feeling a little different. I could not say for sure what it was, but the light was not the same light I had seen the prior morning or the morning before. This was going to be the day I fly the Channel to HE and begin my new assignment. I took my time about everything. Oh, there still was no flying, not right away. Major Campbell had received word that there were several new and repaired SEs at the repair depot. I was not considered for ferrying any to the squadron. If I were to fly at all, it would be in my own SE en route to HE.

Fog and mist are wonderful events to behold. Fog is considered to be a large monolith that simply fills in all the places where light tends to reach. Stifling. Still. Dead. Lifeless. I beg to differ. I watched fog any time I could. If one did not understand that it was a collection of water droplets, essentially a low cloud, one would swear it to be a living being. As the sun rose, the penetrating light revealed constant motion among the droplets, some unknown competition between varying groups, perhaps for some ethereal purpose. To us with our schedules and duties to fulfill, it was simply an obstacle, putting us off from achieving our goals. But if we were unable to pursue our goals and chose instead to look at the fog and mist, we would see a completely different world. There was constant interplay between factions of mist and vapor, vying for a goal we could never discern, much less understand. As light increased, the activity became more frantic among fewer and fewer contenders until it was gone. Fog often arrived in darkness, so unless there were a bright moon, one assumed it had simply shown up. But as the sun shone brighter, we could sense its departure, though we could not pinpoint just when it went away. It was like striking a low note on a piano while holding the sustain pedal down. The note constantly diminishes in volume, but who can say just when the sound disappears?

I was watching the swirling mists with a cup of hot tea when I received the word. Pack and go. It was time. There was not much packing to do. What would I take beyond my issued uniforms and such? In fact, I had found a small trunk. I packed my dress uniform, never worn, dress shoes, and little else into the trunk to be shipped to my newly assigned base of operations. I discovered later that since I hadn't locked said trunk, several squadron mates had added scotch, wine, and cognac. Bloody thoughtful of them! Ripping! For the flight I took a spare duty uniform, a few personal hygiene items, and Knees' bladder, filled appropriately. Once I cleared the coast I figured it would be a brief sightseeing tour, and a nip or two of scotch seemed appropriate. So I "packed" the bladder under my heavy flight coat. I would toast my late friend as I journeyed to my next step in the war, which appeared to be approaching its fourth Christmas. I smirked. "We'll be home by Christmas", they had said. I thought, "Yes, we will—

but in what year?"

I walked out to the flight line, where the "Dirty Bird" sat alone, separate from the other SEs. The engine was idling as temperatures climbed to spec. The ladder was in place for me to enter my "office". Once I reached the top, I found on the seat another bottle of scotch. Wow. These blokes were apparently going to miss me. I had no idea. I wanted to promise I would be back, but that decision was beyond my control. It was a good unit. I was going to miss it. And I was not likely to find another squadron commander like Major Campbell. He was one bloody decent and fine chap, worthy of maintaining contact with.

* * * * *

CHAPTER 25

British

Quite the number of men came out to see me away. It was touching, really. I was no one special, just another pilot doing his part to win the war and go home. I had a few aerial victories to my credit, yes, but I knew not how many. Didn't matter. I was satisfied that I had killed a number of enemy combatants and likely wounded many more. It wasn't something I dwelled on, but I sincerely hoped their recoveries would be long and painful, not unlike mine. No, my name would never be uttered along with names like Ball, McCudden, or Mannock. I didn't care. As soon as I was able, I intended to continue killing huns and help win the war. In the meantime, I hoped to teach others to fly, fly well, become good shots, watch for the enemy, and know how to take care of their assigned mounts. If they picked up my hatred of the enemy, all the better. I would perform this task to the best of my abilities.

Assured my SE was fueled to the gunwales, I made my flight plan. By the time I was strapped in and anything carried along was secured, the engine had reached operating temperature. I waved the wheel chocks away and taxied out downwind. Reaching the end of the field, I turned round and saw the complex of sheds and tents had been swallowed into the remaining mist.

The sun shone into the myriad droplets to form a phantasmic, iridescent sea of sparkles that caressed the ground. Fifty feet up the air was completely clear. This made the takeoff almost magical if not for the dull thud of artillery in the distance. I climbed out like any other takeoff, this time looking about at little pockets of mist and one larger patch of fog. I climbed to about twenty thousand feet and looked about for Boche two seaters. Their Rumplers were known for flying so high that we simply could not reach them. By the time we climbed to their height, they were back over their own territory and out of practical reach.

I circled a bit in hopes of catching a stray or something, but there was nothing to be had. Since I had been admonished against it, I flew over to the lines and slightly behind. I wanted a "souvenir" of my flight to HE. But the Germans were not going to facilitate it. There was nothing for me to shoot at. I took my time, flying lazy S turns in the general direction of the coast, following the line of trenches. There were a few explosions behind me a short way. I looked back behind me and found white puffs of smoke, indicating the "Archie" was Allied! I could not be upset, though. At that height, one could not distinguish nationality, and the Rumplers were known to ply this route while heading over our rear areas to look for changes. I did make a mental note to pass along, "Advise anti-aircraft artillery to lead their targets more."

Friendly fire being the extent of the attention paid me that midmorning, I straightened my path and flew roughly north to the coast. There were still pockets of mist shrinking below, some most certainly hiding a military secret, at least for a few minutes more.

At a mile or so off shore I reduced my altitude to get back to air with higher oxygen content. That made things a bit easier. Though I continued looking about for any signs of danger, I knew I was quite safe from enemy activity at that time of day. Any raiding bombers or zeppelins had likely returned by sunrise at the latest. They flew their raids at night in an attempt to avoid combat with lighter, more maneuverable scouts. I looked at the surface as well. There was light sea traffic, mostly things and/or personnel moving between Great Britain and France. I did spot a surfaced U-boat, but I had nothing to drop at it. Machine gun fire from my height would certainly be ineffectual, and by the time I dove to attack, it would be gone beneath the surface. I shook my fist at it. Sure, nobody saw it. But it made me feel better.

In a very short time I saw the cliffs of Dover approaching. I used Dover as a navigation point and adjusted course to get to my next assignment. In mere moments I knew where that was. From a distance I had seen a black column of smoke. As I neared my new "home", I saw the column was just upwind from the airfield maybe half a mile. That told me what had most likely happened. Some lad had taken off, only to lose power while climbing out. He foolishly thought he could make it back to the airfield, but as soon as he dipped his port wing to turn, everything "fell off the shelf". The aeroplane, with no lift, stalled and fell to the left, out of control. With no air flowing over the wings and control surfaces, there was nothing that could save the young pilot. Or any other pilot who made that mistake. He had might as well been piloting a brick. This was a primary lesson I intended to hammer into my students. "If your engine quits on takeoff, *do not turn back*. Put your nose down in an effort to recover airflow over the wing and re-establish lift. And look ahead for a place to park. A dead stick landing straight ahead will be the only hope to survive." A stall at that point in the flight was deadly as there was not enough altitude to recover. Too many had perished after engine failure on takeoff. I knew I could help. Events like this fueled my contention that if one paid more attention to one's engine, one could likely prevent the engine problem in the first place.

I circled the field once, set down, and taxied to the flight line. Once the lads had helped me out I found the office and entered. I was led into the major's office, where I saluted, surely a sight in all that flight gear.

"Good morning, sir. Corporal No—"

"Ah! 'Dirty Bird'! Right."

"uh, sir, . . ."

"Not to worry. I've seen your record and I have looked forward to meeting you and working with you. You have the fighting spirit we need to win this bloody war. I understand you have been a naughty lad."

"I certainly hope Fritz thinks so, sir."

"Hah! Bloody good! Too bad about that lad who followed you last week. It appears your fighting spirit got the better of him."

"Well, sir, I didn't—"

"No, no, no. I am not chastising you. No one believes for a moment that you intended to take him or anyone else with you on your little vendetta. Wade was probably in a blind spot. Bloody good thing he wasn't a German scout."

"Yes, sir."

"Major Campbell had been looking into getting you transferred out of the squadron for a while. At the same time he didn't want to lose you. But he sees more potential in you as an instructor than as a scout pilot."

"But, sir, I—"

"You want to fight the war and win it all by yourself. Yes, yes, I understand that and I understand why. You have lost at least two close mates to the Germans and you are very upset. I don't blame you. Nobody blames you. But that isn't the way to win a war, dashing off in a scout with bullets and grenades and such. I know you feel better having killed a few sorry Fritzes in the trenches and your revenge motive is sated for a while. But that is not how the war will be won. It must be a team effort with much coordination. The top brass chooses the site for attack, softens it up with artillery barrages, then sends the infantry toward the enemy trenches with scouts flying cover. That is the tactical picture. Then there is the strategic picture. Send light bombers to destroy the enemy rear areas and disrupt supply lines. Send heavy bombers to destroy enemy factories and rail junctions. Tell me, just where in that picture do you see a lone lad tossing grenades over the side?"

"I don't, sir."

"Precisely. I knew you would understand."

"But sir, I understood that coming here was punishment."

"Oh, right. It was framed that way, yes. Bloody Campbell found his excuse to transfer you out. Though it may look and feel like punishment, I assure you it is an opportunity."

"Opportunity? Sir?"

"Yes, lad. This is your opportunity to pass along what you have learned over the front. We have many young pilots coming through the system. You will take these pilots, once they have learned to fly the aeroplanes, and teach them how to fight with them. I see in your record you turned back from a mission once—"

"Sir, that was water in the petrol."

"Yes. Right. That is noted in your record. Nothing you could have done would have prevented that. But the point is that you have never had an engine failure. Having a Viper rather than one of those damned geared Hissos helped, but even so, never once has your engine let you down."

"No, sir. I have an interest in engines from motor-cars before the war."

"Precisely. You can show the lads how you help take care of your engine. And your ammunition. You also have never had a jammed gun. Why? Because you care enough to make sure everything is right before you leave the ground. You can help us change the concept of going to war."

"Change, sir?"

"Yes. So many lads think they can fly a mission, shoot down a squadron of Germans, then go drink all night with the local *mademoiselles*. You need to show them that fighting a war demands more than merely buzzing about the sky for an hour or two at a time. They need to take an interest in their machines when they are on the ground. They—and you—need to grasp the big picture of how to win a war. They need to understand cooperation and coordination of forces, aerial, ground, even naval. Maybe you are not killing huns here, but you will be training a number of pilots in your image to go fight the war and win. Call it your own aerial force, if you like."

"I see."

"I had hoped you would. Right. I'll have someone show you your quarters, Lef-tenant."

"But sir. I am—"

"You *were*, lad. You have been promoted for your excellent record and to give your student pilots someone of authority to look up to. Well done."

"Sir, it seems you have had a crash this morning."

"Oh. Right. That. The lad took off, and—"

"Engine quit. Thought he could make the field, so he turned back, stalled, and spun in."

"Oh, you saw it?"

"No, sir. But I've seen many just like it. Can't turn back. Nose down, look for somewhere to put it. Only option unless the engine restarts. And even that will not guarantee enough airflow over the wing to regain flight."

"And there you are. That is why we want you teaching our future scout pilots. I am hopeful you will help reduce my load of paperwork. Every time some lad thinks he can turn back and gets killed trying

I get a pile of reports to fill out. And a letter to write. I don't mind correspondence, but telling parents their son is coming home in a box is a bloody bugger. Perhaps they will listen to you."

"Will I be getting a new machine, sir?"

"Certainly not."

"But sir, that old SE—"

"—is a combat aeroplane. That is your calling card, your resume, your aerial experience. Who hasn't heard of the 'Dirty Bird'? That machine has killed any number of enemy troops in the air and on the ground. That old SE—like you—has achieved a degree of notoriety. Believe me, having that old SE on hand will only boost your popularity and confirm your experience among the trainees."

"I suppose, then that someone should divine my actual number of kills and paint little iron crosses on the bonnet to keep track."

"How silly, Lef-tenant. You know better. That's something I would expect from the bloody Germans or French. Besides, they already know. They have read about your exploits in the newspapers. They know about your trying to shoot down an Albatross upon arrival at your corps squadron. They know about you tossing your pilot out of the FE and flying it home yourself. You are something of a legend."

"But sir—I was trying to put Knees—the pilot—into the front cockpit to take back with me for—"

"No matter. Come here and look for yourself."

The major beckoned me to join him at a window. I was surprised by what I saw. Or didn't see. All I could see of the "Dirty Bird" was its upper wing. It was surrounded by at least a score of young men, moving in a slow counterclockwise circle and pointing at this and that on the SE, particularly the bullet patches, some of which had the typical white disc with black iron cross painted over the slapped-on PC10 dope.

"Now, Lef-tenant, go out there and introduce yourself to your admiring public. And allow me to warn you, they will see you as old and probably give you a name denoting father figure. Don't let it bother you. It's a sign of respect and admiration. You can start with them tomorrow. That is, unless you care to put on a demonstration today."

"Sir, I am not much at aerobatics. I do what I need to do to survive combat and kill Germans, nothing fancy. I don't see much point to flying pretty like that."

"Nothing wrong with that at all. You can show your pragmatic approach to flying by doing only basic rolls and a loop or something. Maybe buzz them low and see who dives into the ground or something. I love watching buzzed cadets getting up, spitting grass and dusting off their clothes. Just—please—just don't shoot them!"

With that I saluted and left to meet my first class of young lads whom I hoped would survive more than a few days of life at the front. This was serious. What I told these lads could save their lives and bring them home to their families and friends. I would be scrutinized from below, so to speak, as well as from above. My behavior in front of my men would be important, as well as what I said and did and how I flew. I had to reinforce the basics they already should have been shown as well as "tricks" gained from combat experience. I had to tell them things about the various German aeroplanes I had faced that could give them an edge in combat. The Pfalz, usually a dull silver, was overall just a little sluggish. The Albatross types did not dive well for fear of losing their lower wings, which were built about a single spar.

I walked out of the office—waddled, actually, still in full flight gear—and approached the throng gathered about the "Dirty Bird". Several of the budding pilots saw me and met me on the way, shaking hands and just being excited in general. It was flattering and embarrassing, to be honest. I had done nothing extraordinary, after all.

Some of them asked me about specific bullet patches. I told them I had no idea of when they were done, what opponent, whether it was a kill, none of that. The patches had been done by the ground personnel, along with patches on numerous other machines on any given day. Taking a hit was a fairly common occurrence, and it didn't mean there was a victory involved. The patches had to be done to maintain the strength of the fabric and, on the wing surfaces, maintain proper airflow for lift and the ability to fly. When I inspected my aeroplane before a flight, I was concerned with functional items like control surfaces, engine, and guns. I could care less if they had painted my wings blue, as long as my SE was functional.

Somebody asked me the story of "Dirty Bird". The others all scolded him, saying it was from my epic dogfight with Werner Voss—didn't they read the papers? I humbly had to correct that notion. Though it seemed so long ago, it was actually a fairly recent event. I told them it was less a dogfight than a lesson in aerial combat. I had been taken by surprise, been eluded, and surprised again by an excellent pilot in a remarkable machine. I was also most fortunate that he either had jams in his guns or was out of ammunition and/or petrol or I might not be there to recount events. Frankly, I had been young and afraid and that encounter turned me around. Turning my experience into a lesson, I implored each of them to remember my every word. My purpose was to teach them lessons that would enable them to survive most aerial combat, kill the enemy, and come home when all this utter nonsense was over with.

"These patches I remember. This is where Voss hit me." I pointed at the port wing root.

"But you eluded him—"

"No, he missed. I was lucky." There was a murmur among the lads.

"I am not here to show off or feed an ego. To be honest, I would rather be in the air over France killing Germans. But I have been ordered here to share with you my experience. So please pay attention and don't waste time. I am here to help you and give you an idea of what you will see upon assignment to your squadrons."

Some of the lads expressed an interest in flying the "Dirty Bird". I told them no. At least not now. I would need to get to know each pilot and how well they flew and understood how to get out of a mess. (Truth be told, once one understood the controls and a few basic procedures, the rest of learning to fly was what to do when something went wrong.) I told them that if they proved to me they were competent enough, they could take a turn in my SE. After all, it was nothing special, just another Wolseley Viper powered SE5a off the line. But I did see that the major had been correct. My worn battle 'plane was indeed a source of interest and fascination I could use to get to these lads. Hopefully all, but definitely some of them.

I asked to be excused so I could find my quarters, get some food, and prepare for some more formal training. We agreed to meet right there in a couple of hours.

* * * *

Chapter 26

British

I was most pleased with my quarters. Oh, I was in a sparsely decorated room, to be sure, but it was more than adequate. The pleasure lay behind the curtain. I opened it to reveal a lovely little garden just outside my rather generous window. There were various plants which bloomed at different times of the year, so each morning I would have something to look at to take my mind off the war, if only for a moment. The window faced roughly southeast, so I would benefit from the rising sun and changing light playing off the flowers and leaves. If this assignment lasted any length of time, perhaps I could set up an easel and capture a still life. How wonderful it would be to get reacquainted with my artistic side! I could explore the interplay of color and light and how this all changed. But no, I should not have such thoughts. I needed to concentrate on my task of training these lads to go to their units and prosecute the war. As much as I loved my art, it would simply have to wait. Such are the cruel realities of war.

I didn't need much time to move in, at least not just then. My things, such as they were, were on the way and would arrive presently. I had my SE and a change of clothes. My newfound lef-tenant rank would probably net some new uniforms and maybe more. This was new territory for me. I had never even thought of being an officer. I had pictured myself working with horses until the aeroplane helped make them obsolete in the cavalry role. Even the cavalry role had become obsolete as I found myself driving horses pulling a supply wagon. I then considered myself a pilot, a flyer, with no mind toward rank. Once I had become a flyer, my sole concern was killing the enemy. Rank was not a factor in killing. Anyone could kill. Rank and/or insignia made no difference in one's abilities, though I suppose rank could come with experience. At any rate, it made no difference to me unless there were trappings to go along with rank, preferably something to assist my desire to kill Germans and take my revenge for friends lost by their hand.

Once I had "freshened up" a bit I returned to the flight line to meet my students. The lads hailed from all over His Majesty's realm. There were Brits, Scots, Welsh, Irish, AnZacs, Aussies, and more. There were Canadians. And there were Americans who had gone north to Canada rather than wait for their President Wilson to enter the war. We had some things in common.

We loved flying and we shared a desire to kill our German enemies. Some wanted to help win the war. Others wanted glory and fame from their abilities to kill enemy flyers. We were of a common thread in that we all wanted to be there. We had applied in various ways to get out of former duties and into the air. Some, like myself, had been wounded to some degree. Some were disillusioned at how they were supposed to win a war sitting in a stagnant trench, fodder for machine guns and artillery, not to mention aerial assault. Some had actually thought the cavalry would play a significant role in this new, modern war. They, too, were soon disillusioned.

No matter. They had all made it off the ground. Most had been through observer school and duty. A very few went straight into the pilot program. But they had all made it here to learn from me. There I stood before them with no syllabus and very few standard requirements. While I imagined there were actual written standards somewhere, they had yet to find me. I made a note to inquire about these standards. In the meantime, I decided to do as had been done with me. There were several SEs handy, as well as a couple Sopwith Camels, but I decided to eschew the Camels until I had a chance to take one up and shake it out for myself. One cannot teach what one does not know. I assumed it would be like a Nieuport, what with the rotary engine, but I felt it was improper to work from assumptions. We had time. The SEs would be just fine for now. They were likely more stable than the Camels, so I thought that would be an advantage for the moment.

Going by the seat of my pants, so to speak, I devised a "schedule" of maneuvers for the pilots to follow and sent them up one at a time to fly the maneuvers for me. I thought that might give me a better idea of what I had to work with. I told the pilots to take off, get the feel of their SE, and wag their wings before beginning the schedule. I got what had to be typical results. Most flew their maneuvers well, a few were exceptional, a few were sloppy, and one had to return to the airfield with engine trouble. I made a note to look into the engine problems with my pilots along as part of their instruction. I feel a pilot should have a basic working knowledge of his machine in order to perform his duties.

My impromptu "schedule" gave me the desired results. I now knew who was competent, who needed help, and those who could improve themselves by helping others. My plan, in addition to visiting the maintenance hangars, was to work on the majority of good flyers, get into practice fights with the best flyers, and share instruction time with the best in working on those needing the most help. The goal was to get the least talented to perform better or drop out of the program while honing the skills of the majority. The best students could be marked for leadership roles such as flight commander, or at least considered once they had acquired front line experience.

In addition to air time, there would be ground classes on weather, prevailing conditions on the western front, German tactics, clearing jams, and just staying alive in the hostile skies over France and Belgium. Not knowing what conditions were like along the far south, where Italy was facing the Austro/Hungarian Luftfartruppen, or the Middle East, where British units faced Turkey, that was the best I could offer His Majesty.

My first stop was the maintenance hangars. I took the pilots along to observe or contribute, if they were able. I inquired about the machine which had to return earlier that day. Why did it not work properly? Internal combustion engines are basically simple devices which move air. They take air in, mix it with combustible petrol, add an electric spark to detonate the pressurized mixture, and expel the burnt exhaust product. Each detonation propelled a piston which, through a cranked connection, turned the propeller shaft. So generally any failure to operate has to do with air flow, fuel flow, or electrical connections unless there is a mechanical breakdown. I stepped in with the mechanics to aid the diagnosis. In that case, we found that the petrol had a significant quantity of water in it that prevented the mixture from burning in the combustion chamber. This caused significant misfire with the result that the engine could not climb or, indeed, sustain flight. The pilot was able to get the machine back to the airfield and do a safe "dead stick" landing with no harm done. The fix was simple. Drain the fuel tank, let it air dry, and do not use any more of the contaminated petrol. I suggested pulling the spark plugs and check for fouling, which was done by my students under the mechanics' watchful eyes. This lesson had little to do with actual flying, but it was a valuable lesson to learn moving forward. Know your machine and what goes into it.

While we were there, I came up with an idea for ground target practice. This was, of course, inspired by my countless dives on enemy positions. Germans did not have to be piloting aeroplanes to be killed. My idea, while certainly not original, was approved and an area designated for practice. Since I had approval, I had the men get their ammunition and check the size of the rounds while loading their own belts and drums. It was tedious work, to be sure, but it was an important part of being a successful scout pilot. What better did a man have to do when not flying than tilt the odds of survival in his favor? Know your machine and what goes into it.

I felt the lads staring daggers into me for all the tedium of loading ammunition. I didn't care. It was part of the job, as I saw it. Once everyone had loaded their rounds, we went to the flight line. We had three SEs at our disposal plus my "Dirty Bird". I picked the first three men to accompany me, they loaded their ammunition into their SEs, and away we went. We met, as arranged, off one end of the target area. "Target area" may have been overstating the grounds allowed us. There were four athletic fields that had fallen into disuse after the start of the war, roughly end to end. There were old bed sheets and blankets that were to be discarded, laid end to end along the middle of the two center fields, allowing over one hundred yards to each end for safety purposes. The idea was to line up with the sheets, dive to about three hundred feet, and shoot at least one gun the length of the sheets and blankets, preferably in twenty to twenty- five round bursts. Once one pilot had made one pass, all were to wait above while I dove down to see the results of that pass. It was inexact to be sure, but one had to start somewhere. After that the next pilot would have a go and I would check and so on.

I pointed at the first student and wagged my wings. He wagged his wings, then dove on the target. I watched as bursts of machine gun fire stirred up dust below, mostly on the sheets. He climbed out and I followed, seeing most of his shots had registered on target. I signaled the second student and watch as he dove entirely too low. I thought he was close enough to land on the sheets. His guns raised no dust on the target area. Worse, almost at the end, his propeller threw a sheet in the air. At first it resembled a one blade windmill, but that vision was very brief as the fabric "blade" got tangled in another propeller blade and the engine choked to a stop. Somehow the lad kept his wits about him and he set the SE down dead stick to the right of the sheets, drifting farther away in the tall yellow grass. He was lucky.

I fired a red flare, indicating the other students should fly back to the aerodrome. I could not take the chance of someone firing at the ground with a student stranded so close by. Once I knew the other two lads were headed in the correct direction, I checked for hits on the ground and then circled the still SE. Nothing moved until my second revolution, when I saw a hand reach up out of the cockpit and wave. He appeared to be okay. I returned to the aerodrome.

When I landed I was greeted with good news. I saw the other two SEs had made it back and landed safely. Once I had climbed out I learned the other students had made the CO aware of the situation.. A medic would be sent to look over the pilot and bring him back. I arranged for a lorry to fetch the SE so it could be evaluated and fixed as needed. I was calm with the other lads. After all, nobody appeared to be hurt and the SE likely had minor damage, if any. There would be disruptions. That was part of the learning curve. I pointed out to the lads who were there what had gone wrong. I told them they needed to fire into the trenches and/or down on an emplacement from a dive to get a good angle. Flying as our errant student had just done, too low and level placed the bullets' trajectory above the heads of those in the trenches, making the pass essentially useless. I also reported that I doubted the Germans would mark their positions with bed sheets. At least I had not seen any in my experience. This brought back a little chuckle.

After I debriefed the men, I was able to obtain another SE to use, so I took the student who had not fired on the target and two others for another go at the "Bedsheet Boche". This round went mostly as planned other than one man consistently shooting to the left of target. I made a note of it, figuring if the next pilot flying that SE did the same thing the gunsights needed adjusted. If not, it was the first student.

I felt we could get one more flight in that day, so I chose the students to accompany me, watched as they loaded their ammunition, and prepared to take off. Once over the target area, we used the same signals and the students dove, one at a time, at the line of rapidly disintegrating bedclothes. The first student did well and the second laid down a perfect barrage. After checking, I wagged my wings and sent the third student down. From the next moment I saw it was not going to plan. His nose pointed down to initiate the dive, but it kept rotating downward until just past vertical, when it hit the ground just to the left of the sheets.

"Oh, *shit!*"

Knowing the grass was entirely too long, I landed anyway, figuring to come to a rest to the right of the sheets as close to the wrecked SE as I could get. On the way down I fired a red flare to dispatch the others back to the aerodrome. I put it down as planned and rolled up just a little short of my mark. No matter. Unrestricted by the heavy flying gear, I was able to bound out of my cockpit and run toward the inverted SE. It had hit nose first and the nose had dug in a little. All the energy of the descent carried the SE further past vertical and pushed the tail onto the ground, breaking the fin and rudder. Surprisingly, there was no fire. I was at a dead run, the kind where one felt one's body was moving faster than one's legs could propel it and the impending feeling of falling forward occupied part of the mind.

"Get out! *Get out!!*", I screamed as I came upon the scene.

I was greeted by some guttural noises and moaning and groaning, punctuated by irregular gasps. He was alive! I dove under the cockpit area to help the lad out before the whole affair caught fire. I reached up to undo the seat harness and realized the source of the noises. This SE had an experimental harness. It had five anchor points as opposed to the standard four point Sutton harness or two piece lap belt. The fifth point was at the front of the seat, in the center, between the pilot's legs. It was this fifth harness point that had caused the guttural emanations. Poor lad had had his "bells rung".

I positioned myself best I could, then reached up and undid the harness. I tried to keep his head from spearing the ground, easing him awkwardly onto the grass. I saw no blood or limbs pointing askew. Except for the obvious indignities, it appeared he would survive the incident. I cradled his head and pulled him out from under the SE. It appeared we would not have a fire, which was a big relief. I checked the lad over and kept him talking while we awaited the arrival of other personnel.

"Damn lucky," I muttered to myself. "This one was damn lucky."

When I finally got back to the field, I approached the CO with a theory. I told him I suspected mechanical failure had caused the crash.

"Why is that?"

"The lad flying the 'plane is too good to have done something that stupid."

"We both know what nerves can do."

"Yes, sir, but not this kid. Somebody needs to look over the SE for problems."

"We haven't the time for that. Once he recovers, I'll just wash him out."

"No, sir. I'll go over the SE myself if I have to, but this lad needs to stay, learn, and go across to France to help win the war. He has what it requires. I assure you he will leave his mark."

"Good enough. You will go over the SE with whomever volunteers from the fitters. You had better find something very convincing or your lad is gone."

Both the stricken SE and my "Dirty Bird" arrived soon after the conversation. The pilot was in hospital in overall good condition. He wanted a good stiff drink and ice. He got the ice. I would help with the other request once he was out of hospital and back in my care. The nurses shrugged off his discomfort, muttering something about childbirth, but we guys all knew what he was going through. Several of us made plans to go harangue him later. Nothing takes one's mind off cracked nuts like a bunch of guys making fun of you when you're down. Though we all felt his obvious pain, we would not let that get in the way of a good ribbing.

As expected, the "Dirty Bird" arrived safely. I was more interested in getting to the other SE. I knew I would be able to clear my student of any wrongdoing or nervous reaction. A local boy, he was the son of a local city councilman. He excelled at anything he took an interest in, whether sports or academics or flying. He was a cocky kid, but he backed it up by being the best flyer in the class. He could do more things with an SE than I could, and he did them flawlessly. Having gone through my little list of maneuvers at the outset, he added in a few moves of his own. I had to chide him for technically disobeying orders, but I also pounded him on the back, congratulating him on his prowess. There was no possibility of this lad succumbing to nerves. Not in a routine training flight. I would find out what really happened, even if it took me all night.

It didn't take long. In the fading light I looked over the wreckage. Sitting on its landing gear, the SE was open for inspection. I removed the few pieces of the vertical tail that sat on the stabilizer so the elevator could go through its arc of motion. When I got to it, it was positioned down, as in a dive. I grabbed both port and starboard elevators and pulled them upward. They stopped just shy of the neutral middle position, not quite parallel to the stabilizer. I tugged and tugged, but I could not get the elevators to the neutral position, never mind past it. There was the problem. The controls stuck. But why? Everything looked normal on the outside of the aeroplane. The hinges were not blocked and the control wires cleanly entered the fuselage. The problem, then, was internal. I climbed into the cockpit, sat down, gripped the stick, and pulled it toward me. Just like the elevators, the stick stopped about halfway through its arc and would go no further. But why? I could neither see nor feel anything unusual inside the cockpit. I climbed out, got a ladder, and looked again. Nothing. Then I got a hunch.

I climbed down off the ladder, moved it, and then began to undo the lacing that held the forward end of the fuselage fabric in place. It took a little while, but I finally exposed the part I was looking for. There it was! It had to be a one in a thousand combination of events, but I found it. I sent a mechanic, working nearby, to bring the CO. I was right and the CO had to see it so he could believe it.

Several long minutes later the CO arrived.

"There it is, sir!"

"There what is?"

"The mechanical failure that caused the SE to crash. Do you see it?" I pointed.

"Bugger." The CO mused. "Bugger, bugger, bugger!" He saw it.

"You were right, by Jove!" The CO reached in under the floorboard and pulled out a hip flask. It almost had to have been put there during construction of the aeroplane, possibly to avoid being caught drinking on the job at the factory. The flask had been there throughout the service life of the SE. Somehow, in the sequence of movements, the flask had become trapped between the bottom of the control column and the crossmember just forward of it, preventing the stick from being pulled back. It had essentially locked the SE into its dive.

"Your lad will be welcomed back once he is discharged from hospital and is ready to fly. You were correct about him when I jumped conclusions. And you saved me a lot of paperwork and bother trying to tell the lad's parents why he could no longer fly. That would have been most unpleasant. I thank you."

"I only knew the boy was a better flyer than would nose one in like that. We are most fortunate it didn't turn out any worse. Talk about paperwork."

"Right you are. Well done. Carry on. Well done."

At that point I left the SE for the mechanics to work on, whether they were going to repair it, scavenge it for parts, or send it out to a repair depot. I had proved my point and I was hungry.

* * * * *

CHAPTER 27

British

The next day was similar, ground target practice and moderate aerobatics. Everyone seemed to get the knack of strafing, and the one incident of consistent fire to the left of target was a sighting problem with the SE's Vickers gun. This was easily fixed. The aerobatics, such as they were, had not changed much from the first day, except that my star student was absent. Most were adequate, but I urged them to work on their flying. I didn't even expect uniform maneuvers, only the ability to perform them in a competent manner. The Germans did not award points for form. They were too busy shooting to kill to be bothered. I wanted good evasive maneuvers, that's all. Slopping about the sky would most likely get one killed. It was a brutally simple point. I feared a couple of the men would be better served leaving the scout program in favor of bombers or a corps unit.

During a midday break telephoned the hospital to check on my wounded student. I was relieved that he was merely sore in the obvious places from the harness, as well as a strained neck from having had his head tossed about. He was still too sore to fly, quite understandably, but he had been asking to get out. I was surprised when somebody took the phone to ask where my airfield was, but I told them. Then I went back to my quarters to work on reports. The file clerks needed something to do, and part of my job was to supply things to file. Or so it seemed. While finishing up my reports I decided on the next tactic to use on my students.

We assembled for our afternoon session in the air, and I unfurled my little scheme. I told the lads I was going up with one of them. Actually, I would be leaving first and the student would take off three minutes later. I gave them the biggest hint they needed; where I would be attacking from. I would have blank rounds in my Vickers gun and they would have none. This way I could simulate the sounds of an attack for them. I chose a promising lad from the upper half of the "bell curve" as my first "victim". The instructions were simple. I would attack by diving out of the sun. They would elude me and turn the tables on me if they could. Whenever one pilot had a kill shot, they would fire a red flare to signal as such.

I lifted the "Dirty Bird" off the field and climbed out quickly so as to have maximum altitude from which to pounce. I took advantage of the moderate cloud cover the sky afforded me for the day and climbed among them, confident I could not be seen by my students. I arrived at my altitude and looked below, spotting my "prey" immediately. I watched him turning his head and looking up and down while flying straight and level. Oh my, this was going to be too easy. He kept looking up at me over his upper wing. I could see the sun glint off his goggles. I was sure he had seen me, but his flight path varied not a bit. As he approached the end of our predetermined area, I watched him float into an easy turn. At that moment, I cut my engine, dropped a wing, and entered into a dive. I aimed it at a point ahead of his expected path. He did not disappoint me as far as "prey" goes. He did disappoint me as far as teacher's lessons and their value went. I knew right where I would find him and there he was. At about eighty-five yards I opened fire off to his starboard a bit. Seeing his reaction, I was most pleased he had his harness on or he might have leapt out of his aeroplane. His SE mushed about for a few seconds while he decided on a plan of action and throttled up his engine. Just as he appeared to regain composure my red flare arced in front of him. In different circumstances he would have been victory number . . . oh, whatever was next, I didn't know. I would have seen a likely dead enemy pilot and that was all that mattered. I could only hope the next student was paying more attention.

He wasn't. I did the same thing while he entered his second turnaround. He showed a bit more composure and better reaction time, but he dove in the same direction I was headed. I was afraid I might need more red flares at this rate.

When I set the "Dirty Bird" down, I was summoned to the CO's office. When I entered I noticed a man and woman standing near the CO's desk. I soon learned through introduction that the man, a Mr Trafford, was a local city councilman as well as the owner of a millinery.

His wife, beautifully dressed from her hat to her shoes and parasol, was president of the local women's club. I thought it a little odd she was not standing closer to her husband.

"Good day, Mr and Mrs Trafford. I am Lef-tenant Noble-Brown, your son's flight instructor." This seemed to cause them much joy.

"Oh, thank you, thank you, thank you for saving our son! He told us you landed at his side the moment his aeroplane hit the ground and pried him from the wreckage, saving his life!"

"Oh, no, sir," I replied, having my arm nearly pulled from its socket by the father's grateful handshake. "I did land as close as I could to your son, true. I did undo his harness and ease him out from under the SE—his 'plane— and make sure he was okay. He was lucky, to be sure, but it wasn't as bad as it should have been. I think his harness saved his life, in addition to his 'plane's robust construction."

"Oh, you are nothing short of a *hero!*", Mrs Trafford practically sang. Her husband hushed her in an almost scolding manner.

"No, madam, I am merely in the business of preparing lads like your son to go to France, kill Germans, and, most importantly, return home when this nonsense is over with. Your son is a damn—uh, excuse me, very good flyer. I see a fine future for him if he survives his first two weeks over France."

"Yes, that was another thing," the father said. "I understand they were going to dismiss our son but you made it possible for him to continue."

"Sir, again, your son is an excellent flyer. I knew he would not have run his SE into the ground like that on his own, even if he had been nervous. I knew it had to be something mechanical and I found it. Your son is free to continue the program unless he wishes to do otherwise."

"Oh, no no no! This is his dream. Jeremy has wanted to fly since he was able to make sputtering engine noises as a toddler! Quit? Out of the question. He would be flying today if they would only let him out of the hospital."

"I am familiar with the story, believe me. I will do all I can to help your son follow his dream. You can bet on that."

Mrs Trafford spoke again through her husband's disapproving look. "We brought you a small token of our appreciation. This man said it would be all right." She stepped to the side, pulling her husband with her, to reveal two bulbous baskets on the table behind them. One was full of flowers, an incredible array of colors and types, some of which I had never seen. The other basket was full of fresh fruit. Gold could not have been better in my eyes.

"We are forever in your debt for taking care of our son," she continued, shushing her husband's protest. "Please accept this gift, paltry as it is. And here is the card for my husband's shop. You may reach us through the shop. Do not hesitate to ask if you need or want anything. If you need a hat for that special someone . . ."

"Lef-tenant, please forgive my wife and her emotions. She is normally more obed—"

"Not at all. She is perfectly delightful, if perhaps a bit overenthusiastic. I merely did my job. But she shows wonderful spirit, something I admire in a woman. If I may say, sir, you need never apologize for your wife at all." I watched as she stifled a small grin. "You needn't have gone out of your way like this. Between the flowers and the fruit, I feel I am in your debt. You are most kind. Thank you." I took the card with my left hand, took her right hand in mine, and kissed it.

"We have taken too much of your time. Do keep the card. And please call upon me should you need anything. Anything. Thank you very much. Thank you!"

With that Mr Trafford took his wife by the elbow and led her out of the office to a waiting motor- car. As she was being guided toward the door, his wife looked over her shoulder at me with the prettiest smile, a tear starting out of one eye. I know Geoff, back at the scout squadron, would have loved a picture of her. Maybe, if I happened upon one, I would do him the favor, exposed ankle or no.

Before leaving, I offered the CO some fruit. He took some and offered his thanks.

"It appears you have made some new friends. I can tell you they are excellent friends to have around here. He is a councilman, as you know, as well as a leading manufacturer of hats in the region. She is very active in social circles. If there is anyone worth knowing in the area, one or both of them are likely on a first name basis with them."

"Sir, they are just grateful parents. I really didn't do much. The lad was very lucky. I had nothing to do with that. True, I found the problem with his SE, but had he been killed in the crash, that would have mattered very little."

"All the same, they are good people to know. If you are near his hat shop, do pay a visit and offer your greetings. It will serve you well."

"Aye, sir, I shall. One never knows."

That afternoon saw me playing "hun in the sun", attacking my fellow Englishmen. Mostly it was the earlier flights all over, but there were a few with better reflexes and powers of observation. One surprised me. While he did not appear to be paying a lot of attention, I did see his head bobbing around a bit. When I cut my engine and dove on him, he pulled up into a stall before I even fired my gun. With my engine cut, I had to continue to fall until the engine caught. My student recovered from his stall by pushing the stick all the way forward, causing the nose to rotate downward, almost on my tail. As soon as my engine came to power, I tried something I had heard Lef-tenant Werner Voss used to do in his triplane. I kicked the rudder hard to starboard without using the ailerons, which caused my SE to rotate on its vertical axis. As soon as I was pivoting to the right, I kicked hard left rudder and rotated the other way, coming out on my student's tail again. I shot a few blanks in his direction and fired yet another red flare. This lad was pretty good.

And so it went. For the next week or so I led the students in classes and discussions about aerial fighting and did flight demonstrations and devised exercises to try and simulate what they would find over France. I only wished I had an observation balloon to attack. Downing these things was treacherous work. It was hard to talk about how to fight them without an example to work with. But even if I had one to shoot at, I did not have a way to simulate everyone on the ground firing every kind of weapon at the attackers. Or the balloon being winched in at the first sign of trouble. Or the escort of scout aeroplanes dedicated to protecting it. Balloon busting, as some called it, would have to be observed over France. I could tell them all about it, but this one would have to be learnt in the field.

* * * * *

CHAPTER 28

British

About a week after I met his parents, my student who nosed in his SE returned. He was changed. I pulled him aside to see what the problem was. I found his confidence had been rattled. I had told him the crash was not at all his fault. The control column had been jammed by some assembly worker's careless action. No one could have recovered from that dive. I told him he should have been killed but that newer harness had saved him, even if it didn't feel like he had been saved at the time.

He started asking me questions about things that had happened to me over the front, how I had dealt with them, and it dawned on me. Part of my experience at the front was just outside the building. It was worth a try and he needed to get back in the air, so I offered to let him fly the "Dirty Bird". His eyes grew incredibly large.

"*Your* SE, sir?"

"Certainly."

"But . . . the last one I touched I broke, damn near destroyed. Sir."

"Aye, it met its demise at your hand. But you didn't cause it. Someone else did."

"But what if I manage to break yours, too?"

"Laddie, I'll get another. They are mass produced and all the same, at least in theory. One is like the next."

"Well, okay, sir."

"How's this? You take the 'Dirty Bird' and I'll take another SE off the flight line. You take off first with no live ammunition. Just blanks. I will have the same blank rounds and we will both have flares. When one knows he has a kill shot, he will fire his flare. You, going first, have the controlling circumstances. You may want to be higher. You may want to hide among the clouds. You may want to hide in the sun. You decide how you want to attack me. But, at the same time, I will be looking for you. When I find you, I will attack. Just remember, we are on the same side and this is but an exercise. Think you can do this?"

"Aye, sir. It was my pleasure to know ye."

Cocky kid. I could feel his confidence coming in already, like the tide. He would be fine. If he could work his way past me. And just like the front lines, I would show no mercy. It was kill or get killed Over There. No sense building a false confidence. He would learn nothing if shown special treatment.

This quickly escalated into a big deal. Word spread that the experienced instructor was lending out his personal machine to a leading student and would meet him in the air for mock combat. They all knew I had survived at the front for over a year when most perished in a few weeks. They also knew that the young lad was an exceptional flyer and very talented at aerobatics. This show should be worth witnessing.

As the SEs warmed up, I noticed a bit of a crowd near a maintenance shed, men joining, looking excited, and then leaving to find a place to watch from. They weren't placing wagers, were they? I looked around and found the CO, not too far away and within easy view of the sideshow. He really was looking the other way. He was with a smartly dressed couple whom I recognized immediately. It was the lad's parents. His mother wore a beautiful hat festooned with ribbons and fresh flowers and carried a fashionable parasol which complimented the hat. Both were white, purple, and yellow, perfect accessories to her cool lavender skirt and jacket and white ruffled blouse. She also wore her best accessory, that smile. Her smile was plainly visible beneath her large hat. Were it a competition between the two, the hat stood no chance. Though her hair had been gathered atop her head, there were still tresses flowing out from under the hat and making the transition from ribbons and flowers to large brown eyes that seemed at once to laugh and cry. Slight crow's feet, nay, laugh lines gave her unmistakable character. Her slightly pouty lips were spread thin to reveal a large and happy smile. She was thrilled to be there to watch her son return to the air. She was very proud of him and what he had done. Then her gaze shifted from her son to me. As our eyes met, I watched her smile change, though I would be at a loss to say just how. I mostly saw intense beauty. And not a little bit of trouble.

Fuel pressure. Must check fuel pressure. And oil pressure and temperatures. Gauges. Yes, look at the gauges. Lots of information here. Right, then. I needed to focus on the matters at hand. I could not count on my experience alone to get me through this cocky lad. I had to participate. Concentrate. This young man could make an SE twirl and dance across the sky with an array of moves I couldn't fathom. I did not have that ability. I flew according to the prevailing circumstances. If I could kill of a hun with a simple dive and a couple of bursts on the way to escaping on the deck, that was plenty good enough for me. Stalking, whirling, and twirling were fine for some, but I was more the type to get in, do what had to be done, and get out. Unless there were more vermin to kill.

I heard a familiar sound, though from an unfamiliar vantage point. My Viper engine gunned as the young student departed the flight line and prepared to lift the "Dirty Bird" into the air. I've seen takeoffs. I was watching his mother as she was watching her son, full of pride but with a little trepidation. She knew that this flying business was dangerous enough without maneuvers and guns. Anything that moved presented risks, and these SEs could move. When I entered the Royal Flying Corps I could not have pictured the SE5a or anything like it, though similar machines formed images in the backs of our minds as we crewed the Farman, Voisin, Bleriot, and Royal Aircraft Factory designs of the day. The SE was far above and beyond the abilities of anything in the air in 1916. Ah, the progress mankind made when he felt the need to kill a foe. Such progress would take a generation or two without the war. This was a sad assessment of the human race, the notion that killing fellow men propelled us so much more than the betterment of the world around us.

A cheer arose from the assembled crowd as my self-confident young student took my "Dirty Bird" into the air. At one hundred fifty feet he wagged his wings to acknowledge the crowd, as if he had heard them. Not the brightest idea while one's aeroplane was struggling to fly, climb, and just stay aloft, but I'd seen worse. He made it, continuing to rise and grow smaller until he was swallowed into the distant clouds.

Though my temps and pressures were all good, we had agreed to a five minute delay for my takeoff in order to allow him to attain altitude and choose his tactics. I knew I would have an uphill battle, figuratively and literally. I had chosen a faded SE, figuring it would not stand out over the brown soil of early autumn. In that regard, the "Dirty Bird" was similar in appearance, but with bullet patches in colors ranging from a darkish green to the same chocolate brown as the SE I was in. Experience would give me the advantage. I was accustomed to picking out the form of an aeroplane from the earth below. I could find a German aeroplane despite their best efforts. Earlier in the year they had changed from green and brown camouflage to green and a muddy purplish color. Then they started to cover their aeroplanes with fabric already splotched with colors at the factory. What they didn't understand was that it was the motion of the aeroplane, at least in my case, that gave them away. Colors were similar to the ground, true, but I saw the moving airframe against a stationary ground. A little like the motion of the lavender skirt shifting in the breeze against the fading wood of the building behind it. That caught my eye, which followed the line of the parasol to the arm, on up to those eyes, those lips . . .

Had it been five minutes? Already? Right! Time to go reset that lad's clock, give 'im a bit o' me mind, an' show 'im how the game was played.

My red flare was already in the pistol. This would be one short flight.

I taxied out, kicked the tail around, and pushed the throttle forward. Just as I had expected, the Viper engine revved like the Viper I was used to. I had checked it over before like I had always checked my aeroplanes. It pulled me along, all the lift points coming as they should have. At about a hundred and fifty feet off the ground, I lifted my left arm above my head and waved. A moment later I suddenly dove for the ground and pulled into a climbing left turn. My sixth sense had paid off. As I came around a near full circle, I found myself on the tail of the "Dirty Bird", though it was moving much faster from the dive. I put my nose slightly "downhill" again in order to build some speed which I hoped to trade for altitude. I watched my student pull up into a beautiful half loop and roll out at the top, pointing in the opposite direction of my path. Fine. I started a slow, steady climb, reaching for the cloud cover ahead. I planned to hide among the clouds and watch for him. No hurry here. I had at least an hour of petrol and nowhere in particular to go other than the tail of my usual aeroplane in order to teach a lesson.

I leveled out at about six thousand feet to have a look around. I could see the sun above the clouds. I could see the pattern of the clouds traversing the countryside. I could see some distant showers to the northwest. I could not see the other SE in the sky around me. I continued to "hop" from cloud to cloud as I kept my eye toward the sun. I blocked the sun itself with a gloved finger. Nothing. Then I caught something in my peripheral vision, something off to the right and a little higher. I trusted my vision, so I added power to climb and went to see what had caught my eye.

There I was, or at least my aeroplane. It was skirting a cloud at about my height. I pushed the throttle forward and pulled the stick back and to the side, intending to roll above my student into a dive, from which I would finish him. Beautifully executed, I prepared to fire my blanks . . . into an empty sky. Huh. In the moment when the wings blocked my view, he had apparently dived into the cloud. He was again out of sight. I played a hunch. I pulled up a bit, turned about two hundred seventy degrees to port, executing a three quarter turn back into the clouds. I raced the engine and aimed at what should have been the outside edge of the cloud. When I emerged it looked like I was going to land on the other SE's wings, it was that close. I had him completely by surprise. But I was too close to use it to advantage. The only gun I could have fired at him was the flare pistol, which I would have done in combat over France. But torching a student was not the best approach to teaching, so I released my grip on the pistol. Some reflexes. The SE entered a shallow dive to port, away from the cloud. I pulled my SE into a vertical stall and kicked the rudder to starboard. This put me behind him, but again he had the speed advantage. I pushed over into a dive of my own, hoping to pull out aimed at his belly. It worked. Just as I was about to pull the trigger, he did something I had never seen. It appeared the SE had just tripped over something. The nose suddenly pointed down, the tail rotated up, and the starboard wings dipped. All this snapped at once, the result being I could no longer draw a bead on my intended prey. Then I heard it.

There was a loud crack. It sounded "structural". It wasn't my SE—I would have felt it. I strained to look over the tumbling SE ahead of me and I saw the source. The starboard stabilizer was at an incorrect angle. Something had broken. It did not look good. The flight of the "Dirty Bird" looked like a piece of paper that had been wadded up and thrown across the room at the waste can. It tumbled every which way, increasingly down. My star lad had dug himself a hole and I doubted he could pull out of it. But he surprised me yet again. The SE began to tumble less, though it hardly appeared to be under control. A moment later it was mostly horizontal and slowly rotating on its vertical axis, clockwise, as I saw from above. The rotations slowed but the SE continued downward. Then it settled into a shallow dive, turning broadly to the right. Apparently looking for somewhere to put it down, the student settled, ironically, on the very field where he had crashed not long before. He landed downwind, but there was a lot of room for it to roll out, especially with the tall yellow grass.

I waited for him to come to a stop, then I landed in the opposite direction, stopping nearby. Running over from behind him, I noted the stabilizer was about forty degrees above normal. How did this boy hold it together? I had never flown a 'plane in such a state.

"You all right?" I hollered as I approached the 'plane. As I arrived at his side, he responded.

"Shit! Sir!" That had a familiar ring to it.

"Lad, that was one fine bit o' flying there! How'd you do that?"

"Well, sir, first I need to tell you I understand why this crate is called "Dirty Bird".

"You didn't."

"Aye, but I did!"

"When I nearly landed on ye, lad?"

"No, sir, but that really scared the bejesus out of me! It was when I pushed over to escape you."

"That tumble? That looked quite nasty."

"Oh, no, sir. That I meant."

"You *meant* that?!"

"Aye, sir."

"Then when—"

"When the tail snapped, sir. 'Holy shit', I thought, 'how am I going to fix this?'"

"How *did* you fix it?"

"I merely reduced the rotations on the various axes by nudging the controls."

"Merely? Holy shit indeed! That was an incredible bit of flying, lad. Ho-ly shit!"

"Did what needed done, sir. Too soon to die, things yet to do."

"Aye. Let's get you out of there."

"I am a bit, uh, soiled, sir. 'Dirty,' if you prefer."

"I've been where you are right now, lad. Don't worry. A breath or two later will draw clean air."

I helped him down out of the SE and he led me around to the tail.

"I'm very sorry, sir. I'm afraid I broke your bird."

"Don't worry. I'll get another. Or have this one fixed."

"Perhaps a new seat, sir?" I saw a twinkle in his eye.

"Bah! That's funny! Won't be necessary. That is the original seat, nothing wrong with it."

About then the first lorry arrived, a couple of mechanics and the CO on board. I assured them we were okay. Just one aeroplane to fix, that's all.

"How's your—"

"I'm fine, sir."

"Sir, you need to get him back to his mother, uh, parents. I'm sure they are concerned."

"I cannot see them like this! I need to, uh—clean up!"

By now the CO realized the problem and smiled.

"With no offense, son, I will say your mother changed a number of your diapers at one point. I don't think she will mind. You survived what should have killed you. Again. I doubt she notices. Get in the lorry."

That left me with the two SEs and mechanics. There would be more vehicles there soon enough. I pulled out that old bladder and had a nip of scotch.

After a crazy morning over the aerodrome, more or less, I kept a low profile. We were short two SEs. While the one would only get a good once over in the maintenance hangar, my "Dirty Bird" needed more attention, likely in the form of new tail surfaces. I did not see much wrong with it, the lad did such a good job bringing it in, but there could have been damage caused by the stress of the tailplane being broken and out of place. I was not worried. The Royal Flying Corps would see to it that I had aeroplanes a-plenty for training. Technically, I shouldn't have had my SE from the scout squadron anyway, so I just had more time with a good friend that always brought me home no matter what.

I brought the students together to discuss the flights we had had of late. I was less interested in putting any of the young men on the spot than having the group learn from some of the mistakes made up there. This was a team effort, after all. The days of the "lone wolf" mission were over for the most part. Flying was more and more a unit endeavor. Like swimming, there was safety in numbers. One rarely found a lone German pilot out testing the air either. They flew in formations, whether flight or unit size. Flying alone into a large formation or a lone pilot playing "bait" for the larger formation above would all but guarantee an empty seat at mess that evening.

That discussion led into my next task, formation flying. I warned them. It was going to be boring, but it was of vital importance to be able to create and maintain a formation throughout a mission's duration. Each formation member had his part, and the others would depend on them to be in their proper position. We would begin the next day with whatever SEs we had on hand and build from there.

* * * * *

CHAPTER 29

German

I had had a wonderful time with Käti and her friends and coworkers at the tavern. Elsa had dallied with me a little, but it was only to get Käti riled. I imagined Käti had felt threatened by the tall, slender red-haired woman, but she had no need to fear. Elsa was a little wild and playful, but Käti had won me over with her character and conviction. It didn't hurt that she had a positively addictive smile. I would have strafed Hell for the promise of that smile at the end.

I had been reflecting on my two weeks away when the train slowed into the station at the end of the aerodrome. I collected my three bags—three!—and stepped off the carriage onto the platform. I had insisted nobody drive me back across the aerodrome, but I knew Jure would be waiting. He was not. I reached the end of the platform and looked for any sign of him with a tender or motorcar. Nothing. Satisfied that perhaps they had listened to and respected my requests, I walked along the outside of the hangars, then slipped between the last two in order to access Jakob's office.

Jakob stood up from his desk to greet me. He gently shook my hand, as his was still bandaged. "It is so good to see you, Gustav! I trust you are well?"

"*Danke, mein Herr.* I am well enough to get into my 'office' and kill Englanders. I see Jure respected my wish to walk here from the station."

"No, he would have been there for you. But he is in hospital."

"*Mein Gott, nein!* How is he? What happened?"

"Ah, Gustav, he became a bullet-stopper like us. He took a new gunner up for a strafing run. *Das kind* was more like a puppy on a joyride, looking at all the sights. I think he hit his head on the gun. He certainly didn't shoot anything with it. A flight of Limey Sopwiths attacked. Before the *Albatrosen* could help, Jure took a number of hits and had to crash his Hanna. He is pretty bad but will live and perhaps fly eventually. So yes, Jure would certainly have picked you up if he could have. He misses you."

"*Und das kind?*"

"*Tot.*"

"Too bad. Never fired a shot?"

"Not a one. No spent rounds at all. I wonder what they teach gunners these days. It should be more about guns."

"And you have a patrol out?"

"*Nein.* No one to send out. I have one crate left and your crate is being salvaged for the engine and what parts we can use."

"All this because I went away?"

"Hah! Gustav—*ja*, it is all because of you!"

"Have you seen any of the boys with the pretty *Albatrosen?*"

"They have also had an interesting week. You will need to talk with them, but I can tell you they brought down an Englishman."

"*Einen Engländer?*"

"There were more, I am sure, but this one said some interesting things."

"It must have been interesting for you to mention it."

"The English think there is some kind of super *Staffel* called *der Fritzen* whose job is to roam the front and clear any trouble spots."

"That is the whole point of our *Jagdgruppen und Jagdgeschwadern.*"

"*Ja.* Funny, isn't it? It used to be *Jagdstaffel* 11 with Richthofen, at least in their minds."

"Is there a particular unit they think is doing all this?"

"There is. They say the unit flies pretty or pastel *Albatrosen.* Your friends."

"Interesting. I am sure they are amused."

"I would think so."

"Jakob, if they think they are flying against some kind of super *Staffel,* why don't we give them one?"

"How do you propose to do that?"

"Look at what you did for the Hanna with the new engine. Great? Perhaps not, but certainly an improvement. *Albatros* has replaced their D.III with the D.V, which is no better. It might not be as good. And the problem with the lower wing falling apart in a dive is no better. Our local friends are still flying the D.III."

"Good point."

"The Austrians are flying their version of the D.III without troubles. Why is that?"

"Another good point."

"Jakob, could you arrange to work with your salvage friend for improved engines for the D.IIIs?"

"I can ask."

"Can we learn the differences between the Austrian *Albatros* and our own? Perhaps we could alter the structure of ours to replicate theirs. Or just get some replacement wings. With more power and stronger wings, we would be ahead of the units flying the D.V or the sluggish Pfalz D.III."

"Gustav, I see you did not spend your time away alone with your *fräulein!*"

"Oh, we came up for a breath now and then," I winked. "We had to eat."

"What else would you do to create this super *Staffel?*"

"I would use a few Hannas with stronger engines along with the *Albatrosen*. Jure and I were bait to draw the English over so the *jägern* could dive on them. And one more thing."

"*Ja*, Gustav?"

"Teach me to fly!"

"Gustav, you have presented an interesting plan. I shall have to work on that and forward it to the proper eyes. You want a hybrid unit flying modified aeroplanes utilizing baiting tactics to draw in the English. It could be crazy enough to get approval."

"You agree, then?"

"It makes sense to me. As you point out, the Entente have the advantage in the air. Our manufacturers give us the D.V Albatros and the D.III Pfalz, which are no better than the old D.III Albatros. They give us Fokker's little triplane. Well, once they forced the cheap bastard to spend a little money and build proper wings for it. Richthofen loves the little thing, but how good is it? No speed, all stunts, the English just dive at it, shoot, and keep going. It's better suited to an air meet—a 'flying circus'. So if we cannot get them to make us better aeroplanes, we can make our own. It cannot be worse than what we are provided. And just maybe somebody will be watching our results. I will prepare the proposals, probably in the morning, as I have some papers left to fill out and file."

"You fill, Jakob, I will file."

"*Danke,* Gustav. Oh. I will teach you to fly myself. Be ready tomorrow."

"*Javohl!*"

* * * * *

CHAPTER 30

German

After my conversation with Jakob I walked around the aerodrome with Sopwith as my shadow, and talked to the men who were there, mostly mechanics and various technicians and ground crew. Ours was a defunct unit with but one operational Hannover. In order to be an effective *Staffel* we needed at least another five to seven aeroplanes and crews to man them. My thoughts on a super *Staffel* actually began to make sense. We could use two or three Hannas total and a full compliment of modified *Albatros* D.III airframes. Presumably our nearby friends were at or near full strength, even if not modified. I'm I was afraid we would have to perform the modifications one or two aeroplanes at a time. After checking over the airframes, we would have to install new lower wings built to Austrian Oeffag standards. My research into the Albatros types revealed that during the second production series Oeffag did away with the propeller spinner in favor of a rounded nose with propeller mounted out in front. This reduced drag and added to the airplane's top speed. This would improve the performance of aircraft equipped with standard engines. Again, the engine replacements would have to be performed as engines became available.

The other *Staffel* sharing our aerodrome had been transferred out, so we had room for the local *Albatros Jagdstaffel* and room for modifications and fabrication as needed. Jakob was going to request that our friends be permitted to fly out of our aerodrome. It would aid the formation of the super *Staffel*.

I had intended to stay away from Jakob in the early morning so he could do what was needed. However, I was drawn in.

"Is there anything I can do, Jakob?"

"You could start with a ban on all paperwork!"

"Done. Is there anything else?"

"No. Between the usual mundane reports in triplicate I managed to formulate your ideas into a formal proposal. I can send it with a currier or I can fly it over. Care to go up for a short while?"

"*Javohl!*"

"Meet me at the *Walfisch* in ten minutes or so."

* * * * *

CHAPTER 31

German

The *Walfisch* was indeed a wonderful design. I did not understand Jure's disdain for the machine, though it was admittedly dated as far as its fighting abilities were concerned. It was not a terrible machine; time had simply moved on. Its lines were arguably more aesthetically pleasing than the Hannover's, which were more purposeful and businesslike. Even the coloration was dated. The red-brown camouflage color was banned from production machines because it had been mistaken for red Allied national markings, such were the tricks of the eye at a distance. The color was replaced by a lilac or mauve. This was evidenced on Jakob's machine on one wing. Then came the pre-printed fabric, designed to skip camouflage painting altogether. One could find a little of that on Jakob's machine as well. These bits of newer development enhanced the appearance of aging but did nothing to mar the classic design. The fuselage faired most everything over with a smooth molded wood design, even to the point of eliminating the usual wing center struts. The wings were simply faired into the four corners of the fuselage at that point. The fuselage was rounded everywhere else. The simple "I" struts between the wings helped the streamlined appearance. There was far less rigging than on a typical Albatros two-seater like the one I had flown in on the eastern front. It was a clean, simple, inviting design. I was walking around it while the crew was checking it over prior to flight. Jakob joined me.

"Admiring the old girl, are we? Care to heap more insults on Jure's pile?"

"No, sir, not at all. She is beautiful. Like a woman, she is not less attractive merely because she is not young. She may have been replaced by newer, faster designs, but she still has her grace, character, and purpose. Obviously she has found favor with you, for here she is. And others like her have served on as training machines. I only hope some of the students appreciate her for what she is, a beautiful woman."

"I'm impressed. You have a good eye. Or at least you can appreciate an evolutionary step and not simply eschew it because it is not the newest, latest design available."

"Well, she may be out of her place here at the *Staffel*, but you do not expect us to fly her in combat. She is not hurting anyone by being here. As *Staffelführer* you deserve something that brings you some joy."

"I enjoy flying her. I hope you do as well."

"Oh?'

"*Ja*, Gustav, she will be your first."

"It will be my pleasure."

"Watch me as best you can while we fly. Feel the results of my motions on the controls. Flying is an exercise in subtlety, gently blending movements to produce smooth transitions in the air. Of course, if you have some Blighter on your tail trying to kill you, some of that smoothness will be left out in favor of elusive, evasive maneuvering. But generally a smooth flight is a good flight."

"*Javohl*."

With that we climbed into the Roland, and Jakob went through the starting procedure. After a swerving taxi so Jakob could demonstrate the rudder bar, he kicked the tail around and began his takeoff run. As I was accustomed to, the bouncing increased in frequency until it went away completely. I watched how Jakob brought the tail skid off the ground, then lifted the entire airframe away from the grass. It was all smoothly effected, very subtle and refined. The climb was nothing spectacular, but we were not going very high, at least not for the purpose of delivering a proposal to an IdFlieg official visiting a nearby aerodrome. I had to remember the older, less powerful engine pulling us. But it was all so pleasant to experience. It felt special and not like a quick hop to get somewhere. Jakob had what felt almost like magic in his touch on the controls.

In addition to watching Jakob on the controls and enjoying the flight, I kept watch around me. Ours was but a brief flight behind our own lines, true, but there was a war going on. The Englanders were always open for business between predawn hours and late evening, not to mention the overnight bomb runs. That day was no exception. Several faint dots appeared to the southwest, over the lines. Two were coming toward us. As they drew nearer I could see the sun reflect a little off the wings and their dihedral. The English were curious. Just after I identified them, however, they were distracted by the other dots which turned out to be *Albatrosen*. I made Jakob aware of the skirmish and watched as the aeroplanes circled each other in three dimensions. Writhing, twisting, rolling, half-looping, firing, all with no real effect showing at that distance. There was the occasional zip as a stray bullet passed us by. A pop I heard turned out to be a bullet passing through our lower left wing. Our flight took us away from the action, so I saw no results.

We arrived at our destination but had to circle the aerodrome for a short while due to a flight of *Albatrosen* landing. They were the sleeker looking D.V model with the more rounded fuselage. Unfortunately, the performance did not measure up to the appearance. Pilots complained that they were no better than the D.III they were meant to replace. Pilots from Richthofen on down expressed bitter disappointment over the state of the German aircraft industry. The SE, the SPAD, and the Camel were all better aeroplanes than anything we put up against them. Something had to be done. Fokker's triplane was not much more than a distraction. Pilots reluctantly kept their D.III *Albatrosen*.

Jakob brought the *Walfisch* down smoothly on the grass field and taxied toward the hangars. A ground crewman gestured toward an open space and Jakob obliged. The usual swarm of men caught the wingtips, chocked the wheels, and brought ladders in order to assist us out of the elegant old machine. We were offered assistance getting to our destination, but Jakob knew where he was to go. I followed him into an office where he struck up a conversation with an *Oberst*. He handed over his proposal and introduced me as its inspiration. I saluted the *Oberst*, then shook his hand.

"You, a gunner in a *Schlachtstaffel,* think you have a better idea then the German aircraft industry?"

"No, *mein Herr*, I do not. However, it appears the pilots are not receiving any benefit from them against Entente machines that are steadily improving. Frankly, it appears the factories have been resting on their laurels since April. Everything they have made is no improvement over the D.III *Albatros*. I have noticed that the Austrians have tinkered with the D.III design and built a better aeroplane. My idea is merely to follow the Austrian lead and improve the existing D.III with stronger engines and wings. With more power and no fear of diving, our pilots stand a better chance until the factories give them an improved product. My proposal is to supply one *Staffel* with these improved machines and keep track of their results. I add a few attack aircraft to expand tactical scenarios."

"And what military training do you have that qualifies you to challenge the entire aircraft industry?"

"*Mein Herr,* I am but a humble peasant, trained in my father's stable and blacksmith business. I began this war during the first week while in the infantry. I have been with the *Luftstreitkräfte* for almost a year. I tend to be practical and pragmatic. I merely want to win this war and put it behind me while I get on with my future. I certainly mean no offense to you or the industry. In the infantry I observed the superior German artillery guns and the tactics they helped develop. I would simply like to have the same advantage in the air. With the overall advantage in equipment and the increasing numbers of troops arriving in the west from the former eastern front, we should be able to win this war before the Americans flood Europe with fresh soldiers. Is that not what we all want?"

"I have seen your record. You are no stranger to, shall we say, innovative means of persuasion. This proposal is not without merit. Frankly, we all tire of Richthofen telling us what we already know. Your idea makes use of existing machines with sensible modifications and low expenditure of funds. While mixing aeroplane types appears on the surface to be a step back, I'm sure you have interesting ideas there as well."

"Perhaps. I only suggest using the Cl types as bait to lure the English while the *Albatrosen* wait above. Only it's one *Staffel* rather than coordinating between multiple units."

"And what would you call this mixed *staffel?*"

"*Der Fritzen.*"

"That is not what—*der Fritzen?*"

"*Javohl, mein Herr.* The English like to call us 'Fritz' in a derogatory manner. I say we give them an entire *Staffel* of them out of defiance. Besides, the name is already being used by the English. A captured pilot told us the English already suspect a super *Staffel* with that name. We can make their wish come true."

"Well, it is an experiment. As long as we don't have to name every unit, I don't see the problem. Let me look over the proposal and I will talk to you then. Oh, and I appreciate your sense of irony."

"*Javohl, mein Herr. Danke schön!*"

Jakob pulled me aside and asked me to wait for him in the mess. A short while later he joined me.

"Gustav, you have made quite the impression. Your idea has gone over well."

"It was you, Jakob, who typed it up into military coherence or whatever you did."

"But the idea was yours. Anyway, this is what will happen. Our *Schlachtstaffel* will join your friends' *Albatros Jagdstaffel* and be based at our current aerodrome, at least for now. My friend's salvage facility will procure for me the over-compressed Daimler-Mercedes engines like the one I had installed in your Hanna. In the morning the Oeffag firm will be contacted and we should have whatever technical drawings we need in several days. Meanwhile a hangar will be converted to a shop where replacement lower wings will be built and fuselage modifications will be performed. You, Gustav, will be given several days of leave before you report for pilot training. Assuming you do well there, you will then proceed to *Jastaschule* where you will learn to fly the *Albatros*. You should return soon to your own aeroplane. How does that make you feel?"

"A bit overwhelmed. That was easy enough. I wonder what other great ideas I can conjure in order to end this damned war."

"Please do. You may leave as soon as you like, once we return to our airfield. The next few days are yours. Any questions?"

"Why are we still here?"

* * * * *

CHAPTER 32

German

Jakob provided another splendid flight. All I had to do was keep watch around the sky for enemy activity while enjoying the view. Once he set us down I followed him into his office to arrange my transportation to Käti. I hoped those surprises were more frequent. Truth told, I wanted them to go away altogether so I could live my life with this most wonderful person.

I thanked Jakob, gently shook his hand, and set about preparing to leave. I knew I could ask someone to drive me to the depot, but I hated to put someone out if I could take care of it myself. Besides, the walk would be good for healing my leg. I arrived with plenty of time before the train was scheduled to arrive. I sat down and thought about Käti and my last visit. I thought of Elsa and her clever little ploy to make Käti jealous. Though Käti returned the favor, I had a score of my own to settle. The short time I spent waiting was not wasted.

This time the train was unmolested by Englanders and the ride was mundane, not unlike how it would be after the war. Hmm . . . after the war. That was something to look forward to. I had been at it for over three years and I had had enough.

The train pulled up to the depot and I was the only one leaving it. I carried my light bag to the tavern, where I knew Käti would be found. I walked in the entrance near the bar, where I found Elsa providing beers for members of *der pickelhauben* as they debated how to end the war. I didn't see Käti. I set down my bag as I slipped behind the bar, finger over my lips, and approached Elsa from behind. Just after she set down a beer stein, I hooked her elbow, spun her around, took her into my arms, and planted a big, wet kiss on her lips. After the initial shock, she met my lips with hers. With both arms I pulled her tight to me and allowed one hand to drop a little low and grab her bottom. By now *der pickelhauben* had forgotten the war and started yelling and hooting at the skirmish going on before them. Elsa put her arms around me and pulled my hips close. I responded with my tongue, which bypassed her defenses and conquered her tongue. About this time a hand firmly grasped my shoulder and broke my grasp.

"My turn, *flieger!*" It was Käti. She took over where I had been and did about what I had done. After what seemed like an interminable few seconds she let Elsa go and cast her against the bar, where I steadied her. Käti whispered directly into Elsa's ear, "If you enjoy being played with like a toy, come to my home when you are done. Bring sandwiches and chocolate cake. For three." Then she looked at me. "I see you are feeling better. Come with me. You'd better hope Elsa shows up with food. You are going to need it." She caught my elbow, I managed to grab my bag, and we left the tavern.

"You, my dear Gustav, are terrible! And I love it! That was so much fun! Poor Elsa didn't know what hit her."

"And if she comes over later?"

"We will think of something. You will need the food if she does."

"Is that a promise?"

"Javohl!"

It was indeed a promise. We took a few moments to clean up and then spent a good deal longer creating a need for more cleaning up. Things started by the fire. As the fire made more heat from the wood I had added, we made some heat of our own. When things became too warm by the fire, we relocated elsewhere. I was still tender from my recent wounds, but she was careful. Once we were satisfied we sat together in her oversized chair by the fire and caressed. We were about to retire when there was a gentle knock on the door. Käti went to the door. With me just behind, she asked who was there.

"It's Elsa. With food."

Käti looked at me. "Do you want food?" I nodded my head. I was hungry. She continued, "Do you want a toy?"

"Okay, but I'm more interested in the food."

"Thank you for bringing food, Elsa, but did you bring a toy?"

"Perhaps. See how you feel once you've eaten."

"Fair enough." Käti opened the door and took the box Elsa offered her. While Käti put the box on the table, Elsa sidled up to me and placed her head on my good shoulder. Käti returned and hugged me with Elsa in the middle. We held that position for a short while.

"Well, you wanted food and I brought food. Are you as hungry as I am?"

With that we sat at the table and opened the box of food. There were sandwiches and salads and vegetables. Käti opened two bottles of wine for us and we ate, drank, and talked. Elsa asked if we wanted any chocolate cake. As my eyes grew large, Käti said, "No. Maybe later. Now, you stand up." Elsa stood up. Käti told her to turn, slowly.

"What are you looking at?" Elsa asked.

Käti asked me, "Do you like her?"

"Of course I like Elsa."

"Elsa, take off your clothes."

"You take them off." Elsa was defiant.

"Gustav, take off Elsa's clothes."

"Better yet." Elsa smiled. I smiled. I began by pulling her blouse off over her upraised arms and progressed through her skirt, shoes, hose, bodice, and on and on. As the last garment came off she traced her hands up the opposite arms to cover her modest breast.

"Very nice, Gustav. Care to hug your toy?" She did not have to ask me a second time. I caressed Elsa around her crossed arms. She was a little chilly, being away from the fire.

"Hold her arms behind her." As I undid her crossed arms and moved them, Käti removed the belt from her robe. She looped the belt several times around Elsa's wrists, then cinched the loops together before tying the ends. Elsa quietly gasped, gulped, then remained quiet.

"Please hand me a scarf, Gustav." I complied and Käti blindfolded Elsa.

"Elsa has had a long day. We must bathe her." She led Elsa by an elbow to where we both washed her and then each other. Knowing she would be cold, I pulled down the bedclothes. Käti disrobed and lay down and helped guide Elsa onto the bed. Then I lay down and pulled the covers over us with Elsa in the middle.

"Elsa, how are you?"

"I'm cold."

"I know. We will warm you, don't worry." And we recreated our earlier hug, best we could.

"Gustav, would you be so kind?"

"What would you like?"

"I would like some chocolate cake. Please bring it here." She nodded toward the nightstand. "Cut a few pieces. Elsa gets the first piece."

"But my hands . . ."

"Don't worry, my dear Elsa, we will help you."

I set the sliced cake on the nightstand and offered a slice to Käti. "No, Gustav, you may feed Elsa." I lowered he slice to Elsa's mouth and she opened to accept a bite. She chewed, swallowed, and opened her mouth for more. As she closed her mouth over the last bite, Käti motioned for me to give her a slice.

"Follow my lead, *liebchen.*" She rubbed the slice on Elsa's chest and upper torso. I took my slice and rubbed it on down the rest of her torso. Elsa cried out loud and then laughed.

"What have you done?!?"

Käti took a little more of the cake and rubbed it around Elsa's mouth. While Elsa sputtered, Käti exclaimed, "Why, Gustav, our toy is dirty! Would you please clean her? Start here." She kissed Elsa lightly on the lips.

I took the cue and kissed Elsa on the lips and started to lick the chocolate from around her mouth. Elsa's tongue met mine. From that point I'm not sure if we were cleaning anything or just spreading the mess. Käti followed me and took over kissing Elsa as I moved to Elsa's neck and chest. Käti allowed me to linger a while, then pushed me further down Elsa's lean torso. Elsa had long since ceased her protest and seemed to be enjoying her role as our toy.

Soon, Elsa was very content. Käti was about to drift off to sleep. Elsa turned her head and whispered to me over her shoulder, "Do I need to be blindfolded at this point? It's mostly dark."

"I don't see why." I removed the scarf from her head and she thanked me.

"What about your hands?"

"*Danke,* but I like them as they are. What do you think?" With that she began to play with what was near her bound hands.

"I think you are trouble."

"What are you going to do? Tie me up?" I put an arm around Elsa and our night went on a bit longer while Käti slept.

I woke up a little chilled. At least my face was chilly. The fire had gone down considerably. I sat up, then added wood to the fire and poked it a bit to stir up more flame. Then I slipped in next to Elsa, hands still bound, and pulled the covers back up. I could smell chocolate. It was everywhere. I knew then what I would be doing for my first full day away from the front. I put an arm around Elsa and found her to be thoroughly sticky. A protrusion on her chest told me she was also cold. Then she moved her hands. She was not cold. I moved my hand down her torso and caused some quiet murmurs on her part. Käti rolled a little and began to snore lightly. "Must be the chocolate," I thought. Elsa shuddered, then tugged on me, guiding me to where she wanted me. I obliged. After a moment she pushed on me and I stopped. She pushed me away, then guided me again as she forced her face into the pillow. Once again I obliged, but as I resumed my rhythm it all came to a sudden halt, ending in spasms, Elsa whimpering into the pillow, and me opening my mouth to keep my breathing quiet. Käti snored on peacefully.

I stood up and helped Elsa stand so she could take care of her needs. I lightly washed up and started to cook breakfast, for I assumed the women had to get back to the tavern. Käti awakened, stretched, and pulled her robe on to take care of her morning needs. She appeared a little at a loss when she attempted to tie her robe but found no belt. She spotted a still bound Elsa sitting on the arm of the big chair next to the fire. Then she showed a knowing smile. Holding her robe closed, she approached me at the stove.

"*Guten tag, liebchen.* How was your sleep?"

"I was very relaxed, so I slept well. Apparently you did also." She nodded.

"That is sweet of you to cook breakfast. I have a few things to take care of this morning, but then I am yours. I do hope you don't mind."

"No, of course not. You were not expecting me, after all."

"Sweet man. I shall compensate you." She reached around me, untied my robe belt, and removed it. Then she approached Elsa, whose eyes grew larger. "Come here, my lovely toy." Elsa stood and Käti kissed her lightly on the forehead while guiding her to the bed. She lay Elsa down and tied her ankles in a like manner to her wrists. Then she pulled the chocolate covers over her once again.

"What are you doing?" Elsa asked.

"I am eating and getting ready to go to the tavern. You do not go in till later, if you work at all today. I don't remember. But you can wait for now and eat later."

"And I have to be tied like this?"

"For now. Once I leave, Gustav can work out details. If he wants you tied or blindfolded or whatever, that is up to him. He can free you if he wants. You, my dear, are the toy. You do as we wish."

"All that and I get fed? I can get used to such a role. As long as I don't have to—" suddenly Elsa squealed. I looked over my shoulder to see Käti recovering the blindfold scarf and using it to gag Elsa. "You talk a lot for a toy."

"*Liebchen,* come eat. I will tend to Elsa the toy once you leave for work."

"I'm sure you will."

Elsa remained quiet while Käti ate and finished dressing. Käti pulled on a coat for the walk to the tavern. On her way to the door, she lifted the cover off Elsa. She caressed Elsa's face, looked her lovingly in the eye, then loudly smacked one of her buttocks. She dropped the cover and opened the door to leave."

"*Wiedersehen, liebchen!*"

"*Wiedersehen!*"

I waited but a few seconds to go to Elsa, who had had a long night. I lifted the cover. The first thing I saw was the red handprint on her pale cheek. I put a knee past Elsa on the bed so I could untie her gag, but Elsa would have no part of it. She shook her head violently. Her hand had found my "handle", and she proceeded to play with it. Obviously Elsa was not done being the toy. She drew her knees underneath her and pushed against me. There was no resisting that. Her breakfast would just have to wait a little longer.

* * * * *

CHAPTER 33

German

"The eggs are a little overcooked."

"What, and you blame me?"

"Well, you cooked them, so yes . . . and no. Okay, I had a hand in it, too, I suppose."

"On it, anyway."

Elsa snorted a little as she giggled with a mouthful of food. A few bits fell back on the plate.

"I very much enjoyed the night. Thank you."

"You liked being tied up and used like that?"

"You joke with me. I was in charge of everything."

"But you were—"

"My hands were tied and I was blindfolded, mostly in a dark room. But I was the center of attention. I received all I could have asked for. And you two were very careful that I would not be harmed. It was beyond any fantasy. But Käti has always loved me. She changed my life."

"She saved mine."

"Yes, and she saved a good man—a very good man. Käti is one very special woman. I meant what I said before. You had better treat her like the extraordinary woman she is or you will face my wrath."

"You need not worry. I know special when I see it. I intend to spend the rest of my life making sure she never forgets how special she is."

"I certainly hope so."

"And last night? That was Käti's idea. I had no idea she would invite you. I thought she was joking with you. When you knocked on the—"

"I also thought she was joking. But I thought I would play along and bring food. I was going to eat anyway. Yes, I was surprised by her actions after we ate, but I know her. She would never lead me into harm's way. And she didn't. You both were wonderful. I hope she wants to do this again. I don't want my first time bound to be my last."

'Your first?"

"Ja."

"And you would allow it again?"

Elsa picked up one of the robe belts from the table. She offered me her free arm, palm up and relaxed. She extended the other arm above the first, belt in hand, crossing at the wrist. Her hazel eyes stared into mine as she very slowly nodded her head.

* * * * *

CHAPTER 34

German

Käti returned home early in the afternoon, apologizing as she walked through the door.

"No need to apologize, *liebchen*. You were not expecting me to be here, remember?"

"But you are here, and I want it to be special."

"Just seeing you is special. You have succeeded."

"You have been busy. I smell stew. And I do not smell chocolate."

"There is cake, if you want any."

"Perhaps later. Are you going to smear it all over someone before I can have any?"

"That is up to you. I know where we could find a willing subject."

"You think so? When did Elsa leave?"

"Not long ago. She helped me clean the bedclothes, but I'm afraid they're not dry. Do you have others?"

"Of course. Did Elsa say whether she had a good time?"

"Elsa had a wonderful time. She was very excited over the whole adventure. She hopes you will want to do it again."

"She does?"

"*Ja.*"

"I had no idea. I made it up as I went. And she enjoyed it?"

"Immensely. She loves you and trusts you implicitly."

"What about you? She trusts you as well?"

"She does. Because you chose me and she trusts your judgement. She says you changed her life."

"I never looked at it that way, but I suppose I may have."

Käti retrieved the fresh bed clothes and set them on the table.

"How did you know she would enjoy being bound?"

"I didn't. She enjoyed it? Really enjoyed it?"

"*Javohl.*"

"I told you. I made it up as it happened."

"Have you ever been bound?"

"Never."

"Then I want you to hold your hands behind you."

"Why . . . ?"

"You are going to feel a little of what Elsa felt."

"Oh, Gustav, I . . ."

"Liebchen, do you trust me?" I turned her around, hooking both elbows with my arm and bringing her hands behind her.

"But of course . . ." As she had done to Elsa, I looped a robe belt around her wrists several times, then cinched the loops several times and tied the ends. I reached my arm around her collarbone and gently pulled her back on my chest. "Oh, I don't know . . . this is very . . . uh"

"You did not allow the toy to talk, did you?" I placed my hand lightly over her mouth.

"Nein." I used a fresh scarf to gag her. I then leaned her forward onto the bed, lifted her skirt and moved any other garments out of the way so I could pleasure her. At first she struggled, but eventually she gave in and allowed the waves of pleasure to overtake her body. I lifted her upright, led her to the chair by the fire, and sat her across it, her legs dangling over the arm closer to the hearth, and bound her ankles. She briefly resisted.

"Just a little longer, *mein liebchen.*"

I left her like that while I made up the bed. That chore complete, I returned to Käti, predictably right where I had left her, and untied her gag.

"This is what dear Elsa went through?"

I shook my head no.

"But my hands, my feet bound. The gag. *Ja,* this is what Elsa experienced."

"Elsa was bound all night, helpless against our whims and assaults, and on into the morning. You have been tied but a quarter of an hour, not much more." As I spoke I untied her ankles and turned her facing forward in the chair.

"My hands—are you going to untie them as well? This is not comfortable in the least."

"Elsa enjoyed it and hopes we can do it again."

"Then Elsa is someone very special." I reached around Käti and untied her wrists. I could feel the tension leave her body. "Gustav, did you enjoy it?"

"Do you have to ask?"

"Good point. I also had a wonderful time, even if I did not keep up with the two of you."

"It's not a competition, *liebchen*. It is pleasure. You got what you wanted and went to sleep. There is nothing wrong with that. Besides, we can do more. With or without Elsa."

"You like going around restraining women, do you?"

"You started it." She frowned. "But no, no need. I do think, however, that we have both seen it can be fun on occasion."

"Okay, we all had a good time last night. That I will admit. But I cannot say I enjoyed being bound at all. However, if you must."

"Pleasure should be mutual, not forced. I do not expect you to do something you don't like to do. Not just for me. Perhaps we save that for Elsa."

"Perhaps. I shall see how Elsa feels. Now, about that stew you have been working on. Is it ready to warm me from the inside?"

"It is, *liebchen*. Please, sit down."

"You are not going to tie me?"

"Only if you ask."

* * * * *

CHAPTER 35

British

Predictably enough, it rained the next morning. I decided to go into town, just for a break. The light into my room was perfectly miserable, so much so that I could draw no inspiration from the flowers, indoors or outdoors, or the remaining fruit. The day was completely dreary. I thought the change in scenery would be good for me. I didn't need anything. I merely decided to get away for a bit. It seemed the other pilots were all sleeping in. No one cared to accompany me on my little trek. So I borrowed a unit motor-car and went in myself.

There were few people walking the streets, and their faces expressed the desire for even fewer. They were out because they had to be. Who in their right mind would be out on such a dreary, chilly, wet morning? I just wanted a change of scenery, a quaint notion considering I flew an aeroplane and saw the region most every day. Call it a fresh perspective. It turned into an artist's excursion, I suppose, watching the muted light of the sun trying unsuccessfully to burn through the low clouds and undo the rain's mischief. I never understood why people so detested rain. It could be an inconvenience, true, but without it we would have nothing. Perhaps it was the timing of rain. If people could schedule rain to suit their needs and fit their travels and obligations would it be more appreciated? Yes, rain, please, while I sleep and in the morning be dry so I can show the lads how to kill Germans. Can that be arranged? Maybe pray to God with that specific request. We pray to God to win the war, right? Then again, so do the Germans. Hmm. Trouble, that. God would have to play favorites, and playing favorites among one's children is not viewed favorably. "Whom would God choose?", I wondered.

Right about then I spotted a gent opening a cafe for the day's business. I noted that he did not set out the chairs around the outdoor tables. Not yet, maybe not today. I thought some fresh coffee and maybe a pastry would sit well, so I stopped the motor-car and went in. The proprietor and I were the only ones there and we struck up a conversation. Oddly enough, we started with the weather, which would keep his business down until midday unless the rain quit sooner. Then he noticed my uniform and inquired about what I did. I told him I worked at the aerodrome outside of town.

"Oh, a flyboy, eh? I see where your goggles cover your face."

"Well, I get up when I can. Lovely view."

"Then you must know that dashing lef-tenant."

"Oh?"

"The bloke that saved the local lad after a crash. I heard he risked his life pulling the severely injured lad out from under a burning 'plane!"

"I didn't think it was burning, but—"

"Aye! We're lucky the whole town didn't catch fire, what with all that long, dead grass in the old ball fields! That was one brave man. I hope they give him a chest full of medals!"

"We shall see. He was just another of His Majesty's aviators, doing his job for king and country."

"You aviator chaps. You're quite the modest bunch. We back here at home do appreciate what you do. Tell ya what. Your coffee and cake are on the house. Do come again."

"That's hardly necessary, but I appreciate it."

"Well, we appreciate you and what you do for us." I heard an oddly familiar voice from behind. I lifted up off my elbows and looked over my shoulder. A clear sunrise over a field of flowers could not have been much brighter. There stood the mother of my star student. She was the vision of an ideal spring morning in a yellow jacket, deep green skirt, and yellow floral blouse, topped with another fine hat in yellow and green. Only the business-like umbrella at her side, dripping onto the floor, spoiled the vision, but that was understandable.

"Well good morning, madam! What an unexpected surprise!"

"I, too, am pleased to see you! Could you use some company? I don't care to have breakfast alone if I can avoid it."

"But I should think—"

"Yes, you would think. My husband is at work early, as usual, the cook is off today, and I hate to cook breakfast, especially for just me.

I love a good breakfast, but it's such a chore to cook it. I always get a good breakfast here. Please stay and keep me company. I'd be happy to buy you breakfast as well. I feel I owe you for—"

"That would be delightful, madam, thank you. Perhaps that table back there?" I gestured toward a darker, more intimate corner, hopefully out of earshot.

"Perfect! I love to watch the people go by as I eat. I wonder where they are going, even if it is just to work. I find the various facial expressions fascinating, the irritated, the happy, the blank, all of them. And what they wear—aren't people interesting?"

"Aye, they are that. I hadn't thought of people in quite the way you do, though it is worthy of consideration. I have more of a fascination for light."

"Light?"

"Why, yes. If you look at it, it always changes. Change is a constant, as discombobulated as that sounds. I love to watch as the light interacts with color. Plants and flowers in light. Still life. Landscapes, constantly changing as the light changes with the angle of the sun, clouds, mist, so many variables."

"Well, I had never thought of that aspect. I just see flowers. Sometimes it's bright, sometimes less so."

"But that's it! Monet sometimes used to paint the same subject several times over, attempting to show the change of light over a constant object. He probably still does. It is usually quite subtle, and most don't see it, but it is there nonetheless."

"Why, Lieutenant, you have opened my eyes. I shall have to consider that when we have more light upon us."

"But you don't necessarily need more light. Perhaps there is a garden nearby. We could visit after we eat and I could show you what I mean."

"That sounds perfectly charming. Let's."

Breakfast was most interesting. Having already had coffee and a pastry, I ate entirely too much. I kept thinking how hard the SE's engine would have to work just getting me off the ground, never mind combat maneuvers. I was in the company of a very witty and charming woman who felt free to express herself to me with no one present to stifle her. I watched her as her shoulders relaxed and looked less formal. I watched as she smiled, took a bite, and smiled some more. She was beautiful to behold, even with food in her teeth, such was the power of her smile. Normally kept silent by her husband, she was like a pot boiling over, but with ideas, observations and opinions about anything and everything, or so it seemed. I learned how she felt about the war and how it was being fought. I found she shared her son's—and my— fascination for aeroplanes and flying. She had been scared to death when he went in nose first, but she was thrilled when he returned to his love, flying. What more could a mother want for her son than for him to do what he loved most? She told me about her husband's millinery and how he ran it. Then she told me how she could run it better and more successfully by sampling women's opinions rather than the same stuffy old men who had been making fashion decisions forever. Who knew better what women wanted to wear, after all? Though I had already seen it, she got around to telling me how she felt like one of her husband's accessories, not his partner in marriage. She was to be seen and not heard. And don't worry, he'll do her thinking for her. Yes, he had been a wonderful provider. She wanted for nothing material. But there was no relationship. They occasionally had a morning or evening meal together and that was most of their time together. That and special occasions, when he was "required" to have his wife along for appearances.

"He dresses me spectacularly and hangs me on his arm for all to see. Huh!" "Do you mean to say he doesn't talk to you?"

"No more than it takes to run the household. I run the household, but the way he wants it run. I have no say in any matters unless they relate to my health or ability to carry on running things at home."

"That is such a waste!"

"Why? I am only a woman. Nothing more. He would not have me except for running his home and accompanying him to mixed social gatherings."

"Why are you still with him?"

"Where else would I have all that I have? I have the best of things and a wonderful son, thanks recently to you."

"Oh, I jus—"

"You just saved his life! You can put it off all you want, but you preserved the most precious thing in my life, my Jeremy! I am pleased you are enjoying the flowers and fruit, but they are nothing. I shall see to it that you are most handsomely rewarded for what you did."

"But madam—"

"Pauline! Call me Pauline!"

"And you may call me—"

"I rather like 'Lieutenant.'"

"You do . . . ."

"Yes. I do."

"Not Lef-tenant, like everyone else?"

"No. I was born in France. The word is French. Lieu-tenn-annt. I like the way it feels."

"Feels?"

"Yes. I like the way I have to move my mouth to say it. It's almost sexual."

I dropped my spoon.

"Lieutenant? Sexual?"

"Lee-ewe-tenn-annnt. Yes, sexual. It feels like my mouth is doing something naughty. But fun!"

"Naughty. Like . . . ?"

"Oh, I don't know! Just naughty. I'm afraid I would have to read a book about sex before I could do it again! They do write them, don't they?"

"You don't mean . . . ! Oh, I do apologize! Pauline, this is none of my concern."

I was having trouble controlling my spoon. It wanted to toss sugar cubes about the table.

"Twice."

"Twice? Twice what?"

"Twice since we found I was carrying Jeremy. One of those resulted in another child which I miscarried. Of course it was my fault, me, the mere incompetent woman. The other was when he became so drunk with his 'gentleman friends' that he staggered into the wrong bedroom. He said horrible things to another woman, some 'Rachel', and was very coarse, but it was the most attention he had paid me—or my body—in a long time so I just let it happen. It didn't much hurt. Not physically, anyway."

"Madam, I—"

"Pauline!"

"Pauline, this is highly irregular. I have no—"

"Lieutenant. I saw the way you looked at me. I heard you defend me as a person of value. I appreciate that. You are the first person to see me for who I am and not merely somebody's wife. Is this not the case?"

"Well, I . . ."

I was dispatching the coffee about the table to be sweetened by the scattered sugar cubes.

"I need somebody to talk to. Somebody who appreciates who I am. What I think. How I feel. Someone who will treat me as a person, not just a big shiny thing to hang on his arm. Someone who will converse with me and challenge me, not just say 'yes, ma'am', pivot, and carry out a household chore. Someone who will help me feel alive and have something to live for, not just a functionary fulfilling a list. You, Lieutenant, have done that. You can do that. And more."

"Pauline, it is obvious to me you are a vibrant woman full of ideas and questions, thoughts and opinions. It boggles the mind that no one else sees any of that. I cannot—"

"You can. And you do. Nobody else has cared enough about me to share anything like you just did about light and how it moves and changes. You actually think I can understand that."

"Aye. You can. It's not a matter of intelligence. It's a matter of observation."

"Yes, I understand. And I cannot wait for you to show me more. But it is bigger than that. Oh, I get a little respect here, a little small talk there, but you are the one who puts all those little pieces into the big picture. You treat me as a woman, a complete woman. I treasure that beyond what you would likely believe."

I was trying to catch up and sort this all out. I didn't know what to say.

"Lieutenant, have you had quite enough to eat?"

"Aye, m—Pauline. And then some."

"Would you still wish to show me about the light in the park? There is one not so far from here if you would."

"But it's—"

"Raining. I should care. Are you game?"

"Why, yes! I have a motor-car here. I would be most honored to take you where you wish. Here, I'll go and—"

"You will not. I said I would pay for breakfast and I shall. I shall join you outside presently."

In a moment, Pauline joined me, offering her business-like umbrella against the light rain. I refused until she grabbed my elbow and pulled me hard against her. In a few steps we were at the motor-car. I opened her door and she climbed up and in. I walked around, cranked the engine, sat at the wheel, and asked for directions. In a moment I found myself driving among fabulous houses—or estates—as I would never have imagined existed anywhere I knew.

"When do we get to yours?"

"Soon enough. We have already passed it by."

"And the park?"

"Patience, Lieutenant. I am trying to remember. I have seen mostly athletic fields with my son, remember, for the past ten years or more. Parks are altogether different. Wait—there is an arboretum not—turn here—left!"

I turned left as directed and was rewarded with a sweet aroma of flowers, a bit late in the year for my recollections. It seemed I could not inhale enough. So I continued to inhale while I awaited her next direction.

"Turn right, then your first left. That's it."

Just as promised, there was a smallish arboretum. I had seen larger in France, but alas, we were not in France. On the bright side, we were neither carrying guns nor expecting an attack. So smallish would do nicely.

The rain was tapering off some, but we still shared her business-like umbrella. I could get used to her firm but gentle grip on my arm. It was most charming and appealing. We looked upon some flowers planted about the sign, then entered the building to see the grounds. Everywhere we looked there were sprouts, some with buds. Ahh, the promise of beauty yet to come. A little farther along we found some more seasonal plants with appropriate blossoms.

"Here. Pauline, look at these white ones. There is not much light, but look for ten, fifteen seconds, then look away for a bit."

Pauline looked for ten seconds or so, then looked away for a few.

"Now what?"

"Close your eyes, look back at the white ones, and open your eyes again. What do you see?"

"White flowers."

"Same white flowers?"

"Yes."

"Look harder. Look at the shadows upon the petals."

"Shadows? There isn't much—"

"Look away again, wait, and look at the flowers. Tell me what you see."

"Wait."

"What do—"

"I get it. I get it!"

"You get what?"

"The change! The shadows have moved. They have moved! The entire flower looks different—but it's still the same flower!"

"I think you do get it! There. That is what I look for. I love the interplay of light and objects. A flower at nine o'clock will look one way, but at noon that same flower will look altogether different, mostly if one takes the time to look beyond merely a white flower."

"But it doesn't wait three hours to change. It's changing now. It's different again! Oh, Lieutenant! How incredibly fascinating? That was wonderful of you to share that with me!"

It took a moment to catch my breath after her firm and unexpected hug. But she understood. Most people would just shrug and walk away.

We continued about the grounds despite the indecisive rain. A little harder. A little less. A shower over there, just wet grass for us. There were many wonderful exhibits, including a "butterfly garden". I didn't see any butterflies, but I also did not see any flowers. One needed one to lure the other. Give it time. Maybe we could come again.

We at long last returned to the motor-car, where I once again got her door and assisted her entry, cranked the engine, and got into the other side.

"Lieutenant, I am a bit chilly. Would you care to take some tea with me?"

"Certainly I could. Where would you like to—"

"Just drive and I shall direct you."

A turn or two, a short drive, and another turn and she pointed.

"In there, Lieutenant."

It looked like a coach house.

"In here?"

"Yes."

I drove in and stopped. She exited the automobile herself, then pulled the coach house door to.

"This way, Lieutenant."

The way she said "lieutenant". It was a little sultry. At times.

She pulled open a door before I could get to it. Leaving her business-like umbrella outside, she took my elbow and led me in. She removed her exquisite hat and set it on a small table by the door. Removing her waist coat, she offered to take mine and draped both over separate chairs to air out a bit, perchance to dry, if only a little.

Opening another door, she invited me to follow her.

It was a kitchen. She drew some water to boil. I offered to help, but she refused.

"Lieutenant, you are a guest in my house. You need not bother with tea. I shall get it. If you prefer, I can handle the sugar this time."

I blushed. All of a sudden it was quite warm where I was standing.

Pauline boiled the water beautifully. Or, rather, she looked beautiful doing so. Her deep brown hair which had been gathered to the top of her head had begun to break free. More than a little had cascaded onto her shoulders. All the moisture in the air had caused a bit of a curl to form here and there. The dark tresses were a wonderful contrast to her pale skin and the perfect compliment to her brown eyes.

We carried on a conversation about her son, who was doing very well in training. He could outfly anyone in his class and his instructor, but he had yet to top said instructor in tactics and get that "victory". No one had, so it was not a point of shame. He was young and still new to the challenge. I had full confidence in his abilities to fly over France and kill Germans. Soon. I wanted him to best me in the air, but I was not going to give it to him. This was serious business, a matter of life and death, not something harmless like a music lesson. If he was not the best, he would return home in a box. If he returned at all. So many had not. It was unrealistic of me, but I did not want any of my students dying in the air over France.

I was boring her with my commentary on how her son could clean up the tops of his loops when the kettle whistled. We would be sipping hot tea in a moment. Things were definitely heating up.

Pauline poured the water over the tea balls and asked me to follow her, which I did, into something of a sun room. Well, on that day it was an overcast room, but it did overlook a charming little garden.

"Ah. You have been holding out on me."

"How so?"

"You have a garden of your own."

"Hardly, Lieutenant."

"Why it's perfectly delightful. It need not be big to be appreciated."

"Thank you, Lieutenant. I shall tell the gardener of your admiration for his work."

"Yes. Do. I could make a lovely painting of this. With the right light, of course."

"Of course. Lieutenant, where do you find the time to paint? Training young men like my son must occupy a lot of your time."

"Aye, it does." I paused. "Truth is, I have not held a brush with intent for several years. When the war broke out I was in my local cavalry unit."

"Cavalry? With horses? I love horses."

"Aye, magnificent creatures. But it was my love of aeroplanes."

"Aeroplanes in a cavalry unit?"

"Aye. I had a sense that if a war should occur the military would find horses a distant second to aeroplanes for gathering intelligence. As you know, war was likely, and I wanted to be ready to make that change. When we went to war, we were made a supply unit with lorries. Then the lorries bogged in the mud and we were back to horses. And wagons. I managed to get into the RFC after I was badly wounded and then recovered."

"So you are a man of vision. You sense things beyond changing light."

"I dunno 'bout vision. It just seemed like common sense to me. The horse must remain on the ground and get through enemy lines to view the rear areas. In an aeroplane one can merely rise above it all and look down."

"It's that simple, then? Go up and have a look?"

"Well, the idea is simple. In practice, there are many people who do not want you looking at what they are doing. So we attract "Archie" and face other blokes in their aeroplanes, all intended to stop us from looking at their rear areas."

"'Archie'? What is that?"

"Oh, sorry. Anti-aircraft fire. Big guns pointed up. We call it 'Archie' from that song—"

"You mean 'Archibald! Certainly Not!'? I love that song! It's so much fun to play on the piano!"

"You play piano? Wonderful! I used to play cornet, but I got away from it. Painting, horses, aeroplanes, war . . . "

"Cornet? Oh, how funny!"

"How so?"

"My Jeremy plays cornet! Or he did. He put it down and walked away from it. I was sick over it. He was pretty good, and not merely because he was my son. He could carry a tune. But he simply lost interest. I used to play along with him. He would do popular tunes, American 'ragtime', and exotic arrangements by some Frenchman. Urban? Arbuckle? I don't remember."

"Arban!"

"Yes! That's it—him!"

"You don't mean the theme and variations. He could play them?! How marvelous! I would try and try. I prefer the pretty melodies. I could play the themes, but the variations tied my tongue and fingers into knots!"

"Oh, the theme and variations were easy. For the pianist. Room-pa-pa, room-pa-pa. Nothing to it." Then she smiled.

"Not for me. I'll take the popular melodies, maybe ornament a little here, a little there. I love Scott Joplin's tunes. I could play them all day. I simply love to play rags and jass." "Would you like to?"

"I wish I could. Father pawned my cornet when he saw I was no longer playing it. Said it took up room we didn't have. That never made sense to me be—"

"I'll give you a cornet."

"You will do no such thing!"

"I will if I wish to. My son has three of them, two of them very nice instruments. I shall give one to you. He'll never miss it. Probably never even notice it's gone. I don't think he knows where they are. When you are not flying or filling out reports, you can play. Work on your scales and lip slips or whatever it is you do to get in shape. Then come back and play with me. Pick your tunes, your rags, anything you want from my pile of music. Or I can play while you make something up. I don't care. Just let's play."

"Oh, I don't know . . ."

"Look at it like this. It would be awkward to paint right now. You could transfer anywhere at any time. It's war. All the paints, brushes, easel, you don't have room. Then there's the little cornet. It fits into a little box with a handle on it. Easy. If you cannot take it with you, I will keep it for you. Come back and claim it. It's yours."

"You make a good point. It is so wonderful to have music in one's life. Well, mine. I love it."

"And you have an accompanist sitting right here, eager to make music with you."

"Okay, let's. But I shall consider it a loan."

"Consider it any way you wish to. Please give me a moment. I will get one now for you to take with you. I know the light is poor, but try to enjoy the garden for a bit."

"I shall. Not everything requires bright light."

While the garden was modest, it served its purpose. The plant selection assured that there would always be something in bloom and always foliage. The garden did bear some resemblance to the one outside my window at the aerodrome, but it was better cared for. This was not unexpected, for this was a well-to-do residence, able to afford constant care for such things. My garden, as I called it, was on a government property during wartime. There were more important things to spend funds on. I had thought of tending to it myself, being the primary beneficiary, but I had yet to get to it. And now, getting reacquainted with a cornet, I doubted I would find the time for a garden. Pauline had indeed made a good point about the cornet taking very little room. And was it fun to play! Every day a challenge, it was an exciting avocation. And I could lose myself from time to time in beautiful melodies, popular songs, ragtime, and jass. It was a wonderful creative outlet I should look forward to. Who knows? I could even be invited to play with the aerodrome orchestra, such as it was. I had heard them, mostly culled from various staff members, mechanics, and pilots as they transferred in and out, and they were decent. Especially with a glass of wine or a little scotch from the bladder.

I was studying the blooms on one of the flowering bushes when I heard a slight rustle behind me. I thought nothing of it until I heard Pauline's voice.

"Is there enough light for this?"

I turned and was instantly grateful I had set down my cup of tea. There, on a chaise, lay Pauline. She had changed. Her elaborate garb of a few moments ago was replaced by a simple pink full length robe. Her dark hair, fully released, was cascading upon her right shoulder. Lying on her right side, her left leg was drawn up a bit, revealing her bare right leg about halfway up her calf. Instantly I thought of Geoff, back at the scout squadron, and his well worn photo of an ankle—that was his focus, anyway. That lass looked nothing like this. Pauline was certainly

not Rubenesque, but neither was she skin and bones. She looked . . .
very pleasing. Her legs swelled to her hips, then a gentle slope down to
a slightly generous waist and then disappeared beneath her arm. Her
ample bosom was not overly large, but it was a wonderful compliment
to her waist. She was very well proportioned. She was an incredible sight
to behold. And very unexpected.

"I, . . . uh . . ."

"Here's the cornet."

I hadn't seen it until she moved it a little. It was at her waist,
a beautiful instrument, bright silver, heavily engraved, and with a
"shepherd's crook" bend at the rear. It certainly caught what light there
was. As Pauline lifted it a bit with her left hand, the upper part of her
robe opened a little, exposing a nipple. I about fainted.

"Isn't it beautiful?"

"Y-ye-*yes!* It is! I've never seen one like it. Anywhere."

"But I though you used to play one."

"*Oh!* The horn! Uh, I've never seen a silver cornet before. Uh,
anywhere." That was an awkward and unconvincing recovery. I had
been taken completely by surprise by the first female nipple I had ever
seen. Imagine. I had been shelled and then shot at by half the German
Luftstreitkräfte, including Werner Voss and any number of their ace
pilots, and I nearly fainted at the sight of a nipple. It was a lovely areola,
to be sure, but still, it wasn't going to kill me.

"Well, Lieutenant, come take what's yours."

"The cornet, of course . . ."

"Well, . . . of course."

Still taking it all in, I approached slowly. This was quite the sight.
A woman, beautiful in every way, in repose with barely a cover, missing
only—wait, there it was, her all-conquering smile. As I neared her, she
lifted the horn toward me and her robe fell back into place. The vision
was spoilt not a bit. I reached for the gleaming horn, and it was then
that she surprised me. She extended her right arm to the inside of my
left leg and gently traced upward. I was most relieved to find she still
had a grip on the cornet, for surely I would have dropped it. Oh my! I

had never had such a sensation! I recovered enough to take possession of the horn. I fumbled to remember the proper grip.

"Care to play a little? Lieutenant?"

"The horn?"

"Uh, sure. The horn."

"Well, even if I could, I wouldn't last very long."

"I'm sure it would be plenty long enough. I am confident you will last longer with practice. But since you're up, why don't you put that little thing in its box."

"What?"

"The cornet. The case is at the foot of the chaise."

"Oh, of course."

She wasn't done. I bent down at the foot of the chaise and placed the cornet in it's tidy little box. As I fastened the latches, Pauline lifted her left leg just a bit, revealing more of her lovely self.

"I sure hope it is nice enough for you."

"Oh, Pauline, it's more beautiful than I could have imagined. I can't thank you enough for your kind gesture."

"There is more where that came from. And you are welcome to—"

"Oh, one cornet will be more than enough! I shan't take advantage."

Pauline sat up and slapped the chaise.

"Lieutenant. Sit down."

I complied. Before I had a chance to settle in, she attacked like the Hun in the sun. One hand behind my head, the other across my waist, and her lips against mine, it was a devastating opening volley. I couldn't escape if I wanted to. I did not want to. I reached across to her side and helped her to a position straddling me with her arms atop my shoulders. The robe was completely open and hanging from her shoulders. There were no longer any secrets. Our lips had never parted and would not for a while. They were slick and firmly attached. I briefly hoped the rain would hold up and make it easy to explain my unkempt appearance. Thankfully the rain did cooperate and help cover my trail.

* * * * *

CHAPTER 36

British

No one at the aerodrome even missed me. The rain had remained hard enough to scrub any flying for the day and my lads all appreciated that I had gone into town for the day. They got to sleep as much as they wanted or gather together in small groups to talk about flying, the war, sports, automobiles, even women and the prospects of being with one. I did receive a few comments on what sounded like a medium sized animal being tortured and killed in my quarters, but mention of a cornet I had picked up in town satisfied my inquisitors. I assured them I would improve with practice. And even last longer. Huh.

Needless to say, I couldn't wait for it to rain again. The rain was a signal to go have breakfast at a particular cafe in town. I would meet a certain someone, eat, and visit a local garden. When we exhausted the supply of gardens, we found other ways to occupy our time. The hired help appreciated the time off—with pay—and never asked any questions. And with practice I came to last longer, as we both knew would happen. Pauline was most satisfied with my progress. She suggested I look through her music for any old favorites or anything that looked interesting, for next time I was not to forget "my" cornet.

I was thrilled to find she had a number of Joplin tunes and even some of the better Irving Berlin tunes, including "Alexander's Ragtime Band". I could return to my jass. I stayed away from the Arban theme and variations. Not knowing if and when I might be transferred out, I wanted to play things that did not require a lot of work and preparation. She also gave me some of her favorites to work on. These became special tunes to me, obviously enough. Oh, to please her with thoughtful renditions of songs she loved.

There were days when I simply did not want to think about flying or killing Germans. Occupational hazard? Simply tired of the war? Something more interesting in my life? Certainly the latter, possibly the two former. I had never had feelings like those taking me over. It was a completely new and different set of feelings. It was far removed from a childhood crush, or so I thought. Everything from intimacy to eating to conversation to simply being in the company of felt better than anything I had ever experienced. Add to it the easy availability of music and artistic expression and life was nearly complete.

How did I make this life complete? I suppose the threat of discovery going away would be an improvement, but that was mostly covered. Mostly. No guarantee there, merely predicting the future actions of a certain spouse based on his past behavior. Learning about this alleged "Rachel" might have been handy, but how did one find out about that without revealing one's own secret?

Painting. Oh, how I missed painting. Mixing the colors, tinting just so to achieve the perfect color for the occasion, feeling the brush as it scratched, then glided across the canvas, smelling the pigments and thinners and solvents . . . it was more than holding up one's thumb while holding the brush aloft with the other hand. Did anyone really do that? The French? I never saw the point. While I retained my passion for still life painting, I now wanted to paint Pauline. And Pauline. Pauline in a white smock. Pauline in her green and yellow floral ensemble. Pauline nude but discreetly hidden. Pauline nude and exposed. Pauline on her chaise.Pauline in her garden. Pauline with aviator's leather helmet and goggles and scarf. I could add the SE cockpit surround later. Pauline with hair wildly out of place, in low light, as viewed by her lover. But to share the paintings was to expose the truth. Painting simply needed to wait. I loved painting, the planning, the exercise, the product, but it would have to come later. For now, there were too many things demanding my attention, high among them the welfare of Pauline's son. There was also the possibility of transfer, however slim.

Transfer. Where would I go? The only place I could think of was back to the front. Kill and be killed. Well, kill *or* be killed. There were foot soldiers who would fire at anything above them, seemingly without even looking to see what national symbol was painted on it. They were that bored or that afflicted, I was never able to cipher which. Then there was the "where". I knew I was being considered for flight leader or even squadron commander. But if I kept sending capable hun killers, maybe I could stay where I was and enjoy, shall we say, the local culture?

Stay and enjoy? Our lads, those of the French, the Italians, and even the Americans were being killed daily. Dare I think of staying in Blighty at a posh training position? Well, if I sent good flyers and hun killers, I could justify remaining a Home Establishment instructor. But what about my vendetta? Was this forgetting my infantry mate who was conked? My friend and mentor Knees, who taught me so much and then was taken away by the Germans? There were so many decisions that had to be made. I was happy I did not have to make them now. I was still a new instructor. The brass hats needed to see what I could do with a typical class to make their decision. But, hell, even if they did decide to send me back to the front, it would take a while to filter down through the bureaucratic red tape. I was safe for now and the foreseeable future. I would be staying for a while, at least. I needed to show them what I could do for king and country if I wanted to enjoy the fruits of Home Establishment.

There were so many possibilities before me. I decided I needed to stop my worrying and let things happen. I was not in a position to decide my own destiny, so there was really nothing to worry about. First I had to prove my ability to send capable pilots to the front or to other training facilities if I felt they were not the type for scout work. I hated to deny anyone the scouting role if that was what they wanted, but some men were simply not the proper material to be molded into scout pilots. Some men were better suited to a machine that reacted more slowly and an officer who directed them from place to place There was no shame. His Majesty needed all types, not just scouting types. All the various flying roles available were important or the opening would not be filled. Even instructor. While I wanted to kill Germans, it was perhaps more injurious to send heinie killers by the dozens. Many pilots to stand where I had been, ready and willing to kill Germans for whatever reason.

I kept up my practice on the cornet because it was something I could control. Or try to, once I had built up my lip's endurance and remembered how to finger all the notes. Like so many things in life, there were patterns to the notes and their fingerings. Or partial patterns, at least, because of the physics that went into how the lip vibrated to produce the sound. Oh, the patterns remained, but there were overlaps and redundancies in the fingerings that could get complicated. The cornet was not an instrument to be approached casually. If one were to be proficient at cornet, one must be willing to dedicate time to learning it, then time to maintain what one has learnt and developed. It was an exercise in dedication, to be sure. It fit in with my nature, however. I was one to do something completely if at all. If I could not be very good at something, I would let it fall out of favor so I could move on to something else. I was quite good on the cornet at one time, but it lost out to painting and then flying. And no matter how badly I wanted to paint, Pauline's advice rang true. The cornet would provide me with an artistic outlet with less bother than painting demanded. I hoped that once the war passed into peace I would have the good sense to keep at the cornet while getting back into painting. There could be room for both, after all. And Pauline could be an active participant in both as well.

Work went on at the airfield. I was honing the skills of most of the young men I had acquired upon arrival. All had managed to survive thus far, though a few had been deemed better suited for other kinds of flying. By happy coincidence they were all to be assigned to long range bomber duty after completing training elsewhere, so we were able to see them off properly with a party in the mess. We generously augmented the RFC supplied food and drink with locally obtained delicacies. And more alcohol. I doubt any of them remembered how they got to their next assignment.

There was word of an impending German attack, but that was nothing new. Rumors were rampant, many involving an impending German attack. Apparently the brass hats had acquired some knowledge or information they deemed trustworthy. How did this affect me? My lads were being taken from me and assigned to the pilot pool in France. From there they would be assigned to front line units to replace those who could not carry on the fight for whatever reason, killed, wounded, accident, taken prisoner, taken ill, shot nerves, or failed to return. I protested that not all were ready but no one would hear any of that.

They were all going. Orders. Carry on. Stiff upper lip. I was to receive a new lot of students as soon as these lads were gone.

This news put me in a bit of a funk. I suppose it was the newness of my position. I had become attached to my lads and perhaps I needed to amend this in the future. It was war. There were demands to be met and the demands did not always seek to satisfy all persons involved. I had to take what was given me and whip it into shape quickly to make room for more. That was part of the job. Not everyone would come home happy. Not everyone would come home.

I channeled this funk into the cornet. I explored the blues, a distinctly American style of music, not unlike jass. There were differences, though, and I felt my way through them both, learning as I went. I decided I would triumph over the funk and use it to fuel my passions. I would take something bad and put it to good use.

There were times I simply craved Pauline. Bright, sunny days with great light for enjoying all the beauty about me went for naught without my most treasured friend, her wit, her music, and her smile. While the smile was a ray of sunshine on the overcast days when we met, I had but once seen it in bright light. At a distance. That was a funk I had to put behind me. I had to look at the positive side. It rained over Britain. A lot. Many were the mornings when I could go share a wonderful breakfast with great company, then go work off the excess food. Cornet, after all, was very physically demanding and could leave one drained once it was over with.

One rainy morning we followed our little ritual of meeting at the cafe, but I could see Pauline was in a bit of a mood. Oh, she was fine company, but the smile just wasn't the same. I had to push her a bit, but I finally got her to talk about what was on her mind.

"Jeremy is leaving for France. I know, that is what he signed up to do. He will be flying, doing something he loves to do and is very good at, thanks in no small part to your expert instruction. But he could be going to his death. No mother wants to see that."

"I understand. Perfectly. Of course you don't. I almost feel he is my son as well, but with a score of so of brothers. I am losing an entire class of students to the front, and not all are as capable as your son. Though I hope I am wrong, I fear some will not return home."

"Could we go? I am very anxious to get to our music."

"Excellent release, music. Let's."

We made the brief drive to Pauline's carriage house and entered the house in uncharacteristic silence. Pauline asked if I would mind it if she took a moment and changed into more comfortable clothing. I had no objections, so she departed the room while I "blew the dust off" the cornet with a few gentle notes and passages. I was musing a bit with some blues riffs when she returned. She still had a distant look to her, but it was understandable. She traced a finger up my arm and across my shoulders as she crossed the room behind me toward the piano. She sat down and played a dominant chord with a few added notes in her right hand, answering the last blues line I had played.

"Good ear," I said.

"Good key," she responded, "one of my favorites. Shall we continue . . . "She played a four bar intro and nodded at me. I took her cue and started into a soft, sad blues, befitting her mood. No song in particular, just a mood. She was right there, meeting every probing line with one of her own. Back and forth we went for several choruses of twelve bar blues. I pointed at her and she took the lead going into the next chorus while I kept up a soft countermelody. I would push her from below and force a reaction from her. Then she would return the thrust with another invention. I shouted a note several times then went down with a spiraling phrase. She took the spiral and brought it back up again. On and on we went, one pushing the other, until we reached a thrilling and satisfying climax, then found a way to end it.

"Wow," she exclaimed, "you have been playing, haven't you?"

"Aye, indeed I have. You approve, I trust?"

"I approve, yes. That was quite the exchange. Most impressive, Lieutenant. Would you care for some tea? I have water on."

"Delighted."

We took our tea looking out at her garden. Though I thought our bluesy interplay had chased out her funk, she appeared withdrawn again. I prodded with a few queries, which she mostly ignored. After a few quiet sips, she finally spoke.

"Lieutenant, I have a request I wish to make of you."

"Yes? What is it?"

"I want you to make me yours."

Being all too aware of her sham marriage, I asked, "How so?"

"Well, Lieutenant, I think it obvious that you find me appealing."

"Why, yes. I'm sorry if I am too—"

"Sorry? Don't be silly. Your affection has given me something to live for. I find myself craving rainy days just so I can see you, hear you, smell your breath, feel you looking me up and down and wishing I were naked."

"Uh, well, . . ."

"I'm not finished. I want you to take me. Just have me, any way you wish. The next room, as you know, is a guest room. In there you will find plenty of rope, scarves, more than what you should need. I have donned old clothes about ready to be thrown out. I want you to attack me, render me helpless, and take me any way you wish."

"Attack you? But I might—"

"Lieutenant, you would never hurt me. I see that. If I did not trust you completely, I would not put myself in this position. There are but three rules. Nothing shall bind my neck. Nothing shall obstruct or pinch my nose. If I hum 'Alexander's Ragtime Band', you will stop immediately and remove all bonds. Will you observe those three rules?"

"Yes, but of course."

"I was certain you would. Anything else said from this point can be considered part of our game. Cries of protest or help are part of the game. Only my humming is a sign that I need to stop. Do you understand?"

I nodded. I was a bit unsure of things, but I thought it could be fun.

"Then why haven't you taken me? Are you a man or a pipsqueak?" She poked my shoulder, hard. "You're a pipsqueak, letting a woman push you around!"

That was it. She wanted to play, I would play. I grabbed the points of her shoulders, spun her around, gathered her arms at the elbow with my left arm, and clamped my right hand over her mouth. I pushed her into the next room, off balance, then pushed her face first onto the bed. I grabbed a small bundle of rope and used part of it to lash her elbows nearly together. I knotted that and left the rest loose for the moment. Holding her down with my weight, I picked up a scarf and put the center in her mouth, wrapped it a few times around her head and in her mouth and knotted it beneath one ear. I returned to the rope and bound her wrists together. Another small bundle of rope served to bind her ankles. I lifted her onto the bed completely and tethered her ankles to the footboard. With Pauline bound, gagged, and helpless I left to finish my tea. Let her wait and anticipate what was next.

I sat near the window over the garden. My tea had come down to the perfect temperature. I watched the roses in the rain, petals defiant against the relentless pelting by water droplets. Roses were such sturdy plants, beautiful to gaze upon but with strong defenses. I heard a little scuffling from the next room. I heard muffled cries of protest. I did not hear any Irving Berlin tunes.

Having finished my tea, I went back to the guest room to see how my "guest" was doing. She looked a bit disheveled, but otherwise okay. I saw she was a bit flushed and breathing a little heavily, so I thought I would give her a reason to be excited. Her eyes grew large as I pushed her onto one side, facing me. While her clothing was disposable, I knew I could not tear that heavy skirt so I unfastened several buttons before pulling the waste to about her knees. That was far enough for the moment, and the skirt still restricted her knees. I saw she had done me the service of leaving her undergarments behind when she changed. Thoughtful. Next, I pushed her onto her back She was squirming and trying to scream or something, but she wasn't humming. I yanked the skirt the rest of the way off her legs. It was caught in the tether but it didn't matter. I had other things on my mind. I grabbed her blouse a few inches below her neck, just above her breasts, and pulled it open. Buttons scattered across the wooden floor. At this point her eyes were very large, and the surprise registered on other parts newly visible. Once again she had saved me the trouble of fussing with undergarments. She had obviously planned in advance, and I intended to give her everything she had planned for and maybe more. After sampling her wares, shall we say, I rolled her over face down and straddled her, still clothed, and leaned forward. She released her breath with a groan. When I reached my hand around her hip, she squealed and began to buck.

I noticed that outside the rain had intensified. Good. No flying that day. I could devote more time to roughing up my captive wench. I rolled her on her side, facing me again, and slowly undressed and placed my clothes neatly on the chair. Then I approached, rolled her over, and used another scarf to blindfold her. She moaned and groaned and umffed a little, but I didn't pay any attention. I put her where I wanted, fondled what I wanted, made her do as I wanted, and generally had a wonderful time. When I felt I had had enough and perhaps she had had a little too much, I started to remove her trusses. I freed her feet. Next I removed her gag, but I replaced it with my hand. I pulled her head back onto my shoulder, then her face to mine, and planted a firm kiss on her so she couldn't talk. I pulled my lips away and repositioned her across the bed, on her back, head hanging off the side. Presently I sat her up on the edge of the bed and sat next to her. Once again I kissed her as I removed her blindfold. I reached behind her with both hands to untie her wrists and elbows. She curled herself up and lay her head on my chest as I lay back. I held her and stroked her hair as she fell asleep. She did indeed trust me. I worked my way out and covered her with a shawl, letting her sleep for a while. I went for the hot water and made some more tea to sip while looking at the garden and considering my new experience.

I stayed as long as I dared, then woke her up so I could help her with any cleanup before I left. The rain was tapering off, but no one had ever asked about my trips into town so I had nothing to worry about. They were happy to know I had found a friend to play cornet with. It kept things quiet around the airfield. Well, except for the aeroplanes and their engines. Oh, and the gun range. I was happy I contributed to the peace, if only in a little way.

* * * * *

CHAPTER 37

British

The next day was the last for my first students. If the weather cooperated, there was to be a ceremony of sorts to see them off. The plan was to gather together, along with guests from town and/or family members, have the instructors fly in formation over the flight line, and have dinner and drinks. The weather did not cooperate. I awoke to rain once again and had breakfast in town. Pauline and I went to our usual table. She was morose.

"Are you alright?"

"Yes. It's my son."

"Aye. I understand. I must ask. Other than your son, are you alright?"

"Perfectly. I cannot remember the last time I slept so well. That was a magnificent experience to be removed from any and all control, just relax and go along with whatever happened. I suppose it was a little like being with my husband but he could not imagine that much fun, much less share it with me, that old stick in the muck. I am just to look good and hang on his arm. Thank you for playing along. You may be called upon to play that game from time to time. I hope you don't mind."

"Don't mind? I simply love to be with you. If you want to play a little rough, okay. If you want to see a garden or have tea, all right by me. It's your company I seek."

"You are so kind."

I wanted to kiss her right then and there, but we had public decorum to consider, an RFC officer and a woman married to a local merchant and councilman. We dared not start any rumors beyond being friends and having her son as a common thread.

She continued. "Of course you know I intend to be at my son's reception. My husband will likely pull himself away from his work or whatever he is doing, however grudgingly, to attend. I shall likely ignore you completely unless we speak. Please, please do understand."

"Think nothing of it, Pauline. I shall be pleased to share a room with you. I consider it an honor to host you in my home."

She smiled. "You are so funny! Your home. His Majesty's flying school. So cute. I shall look forward to war's end and your having your art studio. I should hope you would have time for me. I could pose. I know you like still life, but do you think you could paint a woman?"

"Why, certainly, madam! What color would you like to be? And where to paint the bowl of fruit?"

"Hah!" she laughed. "Put the bowl of fruit beneath the hanging fruit, of course. I shall have to consider the overall color, though . . . . "She giggled a while. "I'll bet the brush would tickle, wouldn't it?"

"We'll see next time you're trussed up—okay?"

"That, Lieutenant, is up to you. When bound, I do not make decisions."

"I see."

"In any case, I was suggesting that I pose to have my picture painted."

I lowered my voice. "Would I have to tie you down to hold you still?"

She started to laugh, then coughed, her mouth full of coffee. "I suppose, if that's the kind of picture you want to paint. You are the artist."

"That's good of you. I shall keep that in mind. What about nudes?"

"Any one in particular?"

"Only one in particular."

She sighed. "That's good of you."

We went to Pauline's house afterward, had tea, and played some music together. We started with some pieces from Bizet's "Carmen" and moved on to similar flirtatious songs. Sometimes when our eyes met we started to laugh, never a good idea while playing a wind instrument. We kept our interaction to our music and cut things a little short in case the weather cleared up enough for flying that afternoon. It was good just to see her and share a musical moment or few.

I returned to the airfield to prepare for the occasion. I made sure my uniform was clean and pressed. Then I polished my shoes for the evening. Obviously I was not concerned with my flight gear. No one could tell what I was wearing in the cockpit, or indeed if it was even me. Hell, I wouldn't even be in the "Dirty Bird"—it had been sent out for repairs because of suspicions about the fuselage longerons and whether they had been strained or even broken by the deformed tailplane. If the longerons needed replacing, they would salvage what they could and scrap the rest. I might receive the "Dirty Bird" panels or maybe the serial panel from the rear of the fuselage as souvenirs, but it didn't much matter to me. I had my memories. I might be assigned a new SE, but I didn't know if I would get one as an instructor when new SEs were needed at the front. That, too, was understandable. Again, no matter. As long as I was able to lift off the ground, do my job, and land, I was satisfied. Come to think of it, though, perhaps Pauline would appreciate one of the big "P"s painted on the wing? I could ask.

Well, the rain did let up, though it appeared the field would be very soft and a little muddy in places. There was talk of placing duck walks over the area closest to where the reception area would be so as to keep the guests separate from the mud. How considerate. Huh.

At the appointed time, the ceremony began. There were a few short speeches by the CO and two of the instructors. I was preparing to fly, so I missed all that. Then they read the names of the students leaving for France and had them rise to be recognized. There arose a round of applause for the lot of them, and all came outside to view the flying instructors' parade. Though it seemed pointless to me, it got me off the ground for a short while. We flew by the assembled throng in order, from the instructor there the longest to me, the most recent arrival. The instructor there the longest decided to fly past the crowd again, this time looping. Brother. Then another flew by inverted. I saw where this was going, so I thought of what I would do, just a plain old flyer. I watched the instructor ahead of me do a beautiful, sweeping barrel roll the length of the line of buildings. Could he fly! I was gaining altitude for my maneuver. As I was the newest instructor, mine would be last. Of course, Pauline was my inspiration. I approached the field up high, entered into about a forty-five degree dive. Following that, I pulled up into a loop, rolling at the top and going into a forty-five degree dive in the opposite direction. Once again, I pulled into a loop and rolled at the top, facing my original direction, and continued out of sight. I then circled to enter the landing pattern, set down, and went to change for dinner.

The first instructor, the one who looped, walked with me.

"Just what the bloody hell do you call that maneuver you did? I couldn't decide if you were drawing a lazy eight of some sort or a pair of breasts! Beautiful symmetry, whatever it was, very nicely done. I thought you weren't much for aerobatics."

"I'm not. I guess I was just moved by the moment. Let's *call it* a lazy eight, shall we?" I winked. "Right, mate!" He smiled and slapped me on the back, and we parted.

I took my time changing and arrived a little late for cocktails, so I went right to dinner. After eating, I was passing the time with some of my students. Last minute reminders and advice, things like that. Then there was a voice behind me.

"Excuse me, Lef-tenant?"

I turned around to see my star pupil standing there with his parents.

"Sir, I just wanted to thank you once again for all you have done. I trust you remember my parents?"

"Why, yes I do! How are you, sir? How is the millinery? All is well, I trust?" I shook his hand warmly.

"Yes, yes, couldn't be better, my lad. His Majesty just approved an extension of several contracts—but you don't want to hear about all that. Mrs Trafford and I are eternally grateful for what you have done for our Jeremy. Please stop by the shop some time and I will see to it you have the hat of your choice. Several. You need only ask."

"Sir, you needn't."

"But I insist. No need to call ahead. Just stop by when you are in town."

"Yes, sir. I shall."

"You may remember my wife . . ."

"I do! Certainly. You look just as lovely as last I saw you, madam! I am pleased and honored."

I saw her lips purse as if she were going to correct me, then she relaxed and smiled warmly, almost seductively. I took her hand as she extended it. When I bowed my head to kiss it, she slipped a finger into my palm and did a brief massage.

"Why, Lieuu-tenn-annt, you flatter me. I echo my husband's sentiments. We thank you."

"Why, yes, madam."

Her eyes were very stern as she squeezed my hand hard.

"Wasn't your figure eight a bit . . . lazy, Lieutenant?"

"Was it? I thought I got 'em—uh, the maneuver—just about right."

"Pauline, come with me. The lieutenant has more important things to do than to listen to you babble on about what you know nothing of."

How wrong he was.

"My good lef-tenant, that was a fine exhibition. Come, darling, let's not bother the lef-tenant any longer."

The unit orchestra, such as it was, started to play for dancing. Having no one there I could dance with, I was standing along the edge of the dance floor taking flak from the instructor I was talking with earlier.

". . . a lazy eight. Who ever heard of such a thing? You and I both know what you were doing up there. Come on, out with it—who is she?"

As he took a sip of his wine, I got walloped from behind, propelling me into my fellow instructor, spilling his drink all down the front of his uniform.

"Pauline! Did you forget how to dance?!" I should have known.

"Oh, I'm sorry dear. My heel slipped." Turning to me, she inquired, "Lieutenant, are you all right? I'm deeply sorry!"

"I am fine, madam. It was my pleasure, I assure you. Too bad about the captain's uniform, though. That will have to be cleaned, I'm afraid."

"Oh, Lieutenant, you are always so good natured. I apologize for my clumsiness. Do have the captain drop the cleaning bill by the hat shop. Maybe you could take it there when you get your hat?"

"I shall pass that along to the captain later. Feel free to drop in on me any time, madam." I smiled as she blushed and smiled back before being pulled away by her less than understanding husband. I was sure he was missing his Rachel. Too bad. Fool. My good fortune.

"Lef-tenant, please do forgive my wife. That must have been embarrassing."

"No, sir, not at all. Your lovely wife probably found a wet spot on the floor and slipped. These things happen. I'm pleased I was able to keep her from falling to the floor. *That* would have been embarrassing."

"Right you are, Lef-tenant. Thank you for being so understanding. I shall see you at my shop. Good evening, Lef-tenant."

"Good evening, sir. Madam . . ." She glowered at me over her shoulder. "Go ahead," I thought, "correct me."

I strolled about, looking for the wet captain. Passing between two groups of people, I heard a very familiar voice. I knew the voice. Unmistakable. But how did I know the voice? Who was she? I caught a glance of the captain, leaving the room in the direction of his quarters. I would deliver the message later.

I picked up another glass of wine at the bar and circled back toward that voice. Lingering a while, I at last heard it again. The woman with the voice was talking enthusiastically to one of my departing students. There were several others in the loose group, some bearing a resemblance to my student. I inserted myself into the conversation.

"Well, lad, it appears you have the largest gathering of any of my fine students. Good for you. Everyone, William here has done a fine job of learning his craft. Once he gets his aeroplane in France, the kaiser himself should be quaking in his boots!"

There was some polite laughter as William introduced me briefly to his parents, an uncle and aunt, two brothers, and his sister. As she uttered the usual pleasantries, I knew I had found the voice I had been listening for since that stay in the field hospital in France. William's sister was named Clara.

"Please forgive my saying so, madam, but I know we have met before."

She looked at me with a blank expression. "No, I do not believe we have met. But in my work, I meet a lot of men. Forgive me if I do not remember you. It's nothing personal."

"You are forgiven, of course, but I am positive we have met. May I inquire as to what you do?"

"Certainly, Lef-tenant. I am an instructor at the school of nursing on the other side of town."

"Oh, near the arboretum?"

"Yes, that's it."

"Have you been there long?"

"Well, six weeks or so. Is that long?"

"I suppose that depends on one's perspective, doesn't it? Where did you teach before?"

"Before being sent here, I was a nurse outside London. And before that I was in various field hospitals in France."

"In France? A-ha! That is it! You and I met in France. I was a Tommie with a transport unit.

My wagon was shelled, my mate killed, and I was taken to a field hospital in pretty bad shape. I was blinded and nearly lost my arm."

"Yes! I remember that patient! That was you?! But I was certain they would amputate that arm. And you fly now? That is most remarkable!"

"Yes, I am an instructor here. After I 'met' you, I was transferred to a hospital near Dover. After surgeries and therapy I applied to the RFC. They took me, made me an observer, and eventually a pilot. And now, here I am. As I understand it, I owe it all to you. I am told you spent countless hours cleaning my arm and checking my eyes. Unfortunately, I remember almost none of it for all the narcotics I had in me."

"You were not at all well when they brought you in. Others gave you up as beyond saving, but I could not just let you go. You were a man with a life, after all. It meant something to you, if to no one else. I had nothing to do beyond the hospital, so I stayed there as much as I could stand to, what with all the death and injuries, and tried to do what good I could."

"From my perspective, you did a lot of good. I am eternally grateful. I must find a way to repay you."

"Oh, no, Lef-tenant. I only did what was right and proper. I am most pleased you are well."

"But I shall insist. If I am not imposing, would you care to dance?"

"That sounds wonderful. Thank you, Lef-tenant. Shall we?"

The band leader was just counting off the next number, so we took our place and started with the crowd. I learned that Clara was actually my age, a month older, in fact. She had the same enthusiasm for medicine that I had for flying. While she wanted to be a doctor, maybe even a surgeon, she said that there were innumerable roadblocks because she was "only a woman". I told her I simply did not understand the logic behind such thinking. We are all functioning humans, aren't we? How is it that possessing female parts is so different from having male parts? In any case, Clara had been preparing for a medical career as long as she could remember, starting with bandaging up her brothers and the neighborhood children when they had minor accidents while playing. She had worked her way through the school system and gone into nursing as the best alternative available to her. Now a nursing instructor, she felt she had little more to do other than fight to be a doctor, for now, and then a surgeon. Fascinated with her story, I asked her how I could help. She insisted there was nothing I could do. It would take someone in government or someone on the board of directors at the nursing school, at the very least. She did not know anyone with influence, so she saw little hope for moving on with her desired career. I told her I did not know if I could help her, but that I would certainly look into it. It was the very least I could do for her after she saved my arm, if not my very life.

I asked if I could contact her, but she said she could not see me socially. She was engaged to be married. She allowed that I could contact her through the nursing school in the unlikely event I came up with an idea. I should have to settle for that, I thought.

I thanked her for the dance and told her some nice things about her brother, his flying, and his chances for survival. We were both of the opinion that something had to happen to end this silly war and soon. Too many lives were on hold, indeed being snuffed out, for the transgressions of politicians. Why is it that young and innocent men have to go away and die when politicians don't get along? Can't the politicians go have a fistfight on a hill somewhere? Pistols at dawn? There had to be a better way.

No sooner had we parted than I felt a hand clamp firmly on my right buttock. Startled, I turned around and found myself face to face with Pauline, who took me in a dance position and asked me who my friend was. My, she was a bit forceful. Could she be a little jealous? I told her it was the nurse who had saved me in France after I had been conked by a German shell. It was the first I had seen her ever, since my eyes did not function at the time I was in her care. It was sheer chance that I had heard her voice and recognized it. And to pad the story a bit, I told Pauline she was promised to another soldier and awaiting his return so they could marry.

Just as Pauline found it in herself to relax and maybe even enjoy the dance, her husband cut in. I yielded, of course, and he proceeded to walk her out of the room.

I stood there a moment, in the way of several couples who were trying to dance. I apologized and excused myself from the floor. While there was wine to be had at the bar, I returned to my quarters for a nip of scotch. It had been some evening. I owed practically everything to Clara for her diligence as a nurse, going above and beyond on my behalf even when told I was not expected to live. She then saved my arm from amputation. I could see she was genuinely happy for me, but I so wanted to do something for her. There had to be a way to repay her.

Then it struck me. I couldn't wait for another rainy day.

* * * * *

CHAPTER 38

British

The next day we received several SE5as from the repair depot. The "Dirty Bird" was not among them. I did receive a package from one of the ferry pilots, however. It contained the well worn panels onto which my impromptu "Dirty Bird" logo had been painted and the two fabric strips from the rear of the fuselage with the aeroplane's military number painted in black on a white panel. I didn't particularly want them, but I kept them for the moment. Maybe I would find a use for them at some point.

Anyway, I was told that I could have first pick from the SEs and choose my personal machine. None of the other instructors had lost theirs, so they were mine to choose from. I looked them over. I had hoped for another Viper powered SE, but these were all "Hisso"s, powered by the Hispano-Suiza engine with gear reduction. It was the gear reduction unit that caused all the problems. Oh, well, I had to settle for now. Maybe I could salvage a Viper or swap for one or something. I had to choose now, however.

"If I may, I should like to choose this one." It was overall greenish chocolate brown, but the upper wing was deep green, indicating the fabric, if not the entire upper wing, had been replaced. I just liked the contrast of the green against the brown machine.

"Right, then. It's yours, Lef-tenant. Care to take 'er up?"

"That would be splendid! I'll get my gear."

I returned to find they were just pulling the propeller through to draw petrol into the cylinders, about ready to restart the engine. The prop was interesting, being four bladed instead of the two bladed props in use at my old squadron. The blades were quite wide and had quite a pitch to them, indicating it was a geared engine meant to slow down the revolutions per minute (RPMs) of the prop so the engine would run at its best power setting. The blades would really take a bite out of the air, a necessity at slower propeller speeds. I helped the mechanic coming down the ladder to the ground, and he in turn, assisted me with getting my harness attached.

The basic controls were the same as the Viper SE, and the layout of the gauges was similar enough in case I needed to look at them. In general, if I was looking at a gauge, it was because of a problem and could well be too late for the gauge to help anything. In combat or, to a lesser extent, in instructing, there was simply too much going on outside the cockpit to pay much attention to the gauges. As long as there was petrol, we would keep going, so we watched the fuel gauge and the clock. The rest of the gauges sure looked nice, though, and made pilots appear smarter. There was, after all, a whole lot of information to manage and utilize. I merely preferred flying to managing.

Takeoff went well. I thought the Hisso SE performed about like the Viper SE. Engine speed was a touch higher, but the prop was geared to turn more slowly. The large paddle blades, however, pushed a lot of air. So on takeoff and climb out I felt no real difference. The rest of the airframe was the same, so I did not anticipate any surprises.

This flight was a joy ride. I had no adversaries waiting to shoot at me. I had no students to mind. I had nothing to prove to anyone. I could fly for the sake of flying. I had clearance to go anywhere I wanted to fly. I could put down at any RFC or RNAS airfield and get anything from petrol to a bite to eat because I was a brother in arms. I knew what I wanted to do. I flew toward town. I overflew Pauline's house. I found the arboretum, and from there spied the nursing school. Having done that, I flew toward the coast. I had not seen the white cliffs of Dover in a while, and it seemed like a nice enough day to have a look.

Well, there they were. Still cliffs, still white. I think the real fascination was that I was closer to France and the real fighting than I had been in a while. And though I had the petrol to make it, I had not the permission to do so. Nor did I have any ammunition. My Vickers gun was useless without ammunition, so it just was not a good idea.

I looked about and found myself alone in the air. Must have been tea time, I smirked. What true Brit flew during tea time? No matter. Since I was so alone, I decided to fly my little maneuver again. I really liked that move, the lazy eight. I had not seen it done, only parts of it. I doubted it had any real value in combat, but it never hurt to have something ready just in case. I was not enthralled by the name. It was certainly not what I had been thinking of when I flew it, but it was something the press could report on. If they ever had a need to.

I flew it. Down, up, back, down, up, back. Okay, not bad. Once more to get a feel for it. That felt better. I saw a distant formation ahead which would roughly cross my intended flight path so I flew no more fancy stuff. Straight and level, head for home.

I set her down without incident and taxied to the flight line feeling quite pleased with my choice. The machine had responded to my every command without hesitation. What more could I want? The lads at the repair depot had done a nice job and I was happy.

* * * *

CHAPTER 39

British

The next few days gave me a lot of free time. No student pilots. All reports caught up, I had no paperwork. I had plenty of time to practice the cornet. I took a few more joyrides in the new SE.

As the weather was beautiful, I saw nothing of Pauline. Perfectly delightful weather. How depressing. I did go into town one morning, just in case. I stopped at the cafe and ordered somewhat lighter fare than my usual when I had company. The proprietor did not miss a beat. He must have known something was going on, but he never so much as mentioned my usual breakfast partner, much less asked anything about her or us.

It turned out that he had a nephew who had just left for France after studying with another instructor and he had been at the event. He had been taken in by the impromptu aerial demonstration, especially the aerobatics, brief as they were. He understood what the first pilots did and especially liked the long, graceful barrel roll that had preceded me. Then a quizzical look clouded his face as he mentioned the maneuver I had done.

"What did that last bloke do? It looked like a figure eight being drawn in the air on its side, but it looked somewhat, I don't know, droopy. What I saw was a pair of breasts, but that couldn't have been his intent."

"I was working on an engine and missed the demonstration. I didn't know they were going to do any stunts."

"You missed a fine demonstration by all five pilots. I would hate to have any of them shooting at my tail!"

"I can only agree with you, good sir." I paid for my breakfast, leaving extra for a tip, and drove back to the airfield.

When I dropped off the motor-car, the CO saw me.

"Say, Lef-tenant, were you stunting over the Channel earlier this week?"

"Yes, sir, I was, just briefly. Did I somehow disturb somebody?"

"Oh, no, nothing of the sort. One of the other fellows was in Dover for the day and happened to see someone doing that maneuver you flew at the ceremony. He's never seen anyone do that, and neither have I. He thought it might be you, that's all. No harm done."

"T'was me, sir. I did it twice before I saw a crossing formation. Then I flew straight and level."

"Ah. Good show. Say, what do you call that maneuver? It could be some kind of figure eight, I suppose, that needs cleaning up. Or it could be a woman's bosom."

"Your choice, sir. I call it a lazy eight, but I'll see if I can clean it up a bit."

"Right. Carry on."

I was to the point where I wanted to look at Arban's Theme and Variation pieces. With no students, I had that much time on my hands. How bad could they be if I was that bored? Waking up the next morning with strains from "Carnival of Venice" lilting through my head, it took a moment to register that it was raining. Raining! I could not get myself together fast enough. I packed my cornet away, grabbed the box, and fairly ran to check out a motor-car. I raced to the cafe, where I had a coffee at the counter with the proprietor. Again, he was fretting over business lost to the morning rain.

As I was being served my second cup of coffee I heard a muffled curse behind me. I turned and saw the most beautiful vision. There stood Pauline in a light trench coat pulled taught over a black ensemble. The hat, which looked to be red and black, was crestfallen and probably ruined. She was without her black business-like umbrella, and her usually perfectly coiffed hair was matted to her head. In fact, everything was pretty well stuck to her and in dryer circumstances might have appeared a bit scandalous. Anyone else would have kept going, passing her over, but when our eyes met, she smiled. That smile was the most beautiful vision.

"Good lord, my friend," I shouted, "where is your business-like umbrella? I thought you knew better!"

"My umbrella is jammed into a trash can a block from here. A wind gust hit it just the wrong way, and it is no more."

"Maybe I could fix—"

"No! After what I did to it, it is no more. I can get another one, at another time. It would do me no good at this point anyway."

"I cannot argue with that. Coffee?"

The proprietor set us up at our usual table. Pauline did not feel much like eating, what with her disheveled appearance and all, but we still ordered something small. I thought it best to get her home soon and out of those wet clothes. Maybe into some dry ones. We would have to see.

In the meantime, we talked about the recent event at the airfield. She had had a miserable time except for seeing her son and our curtailed dance. "That bastard husband of mine is such a curmudgeon. He refuses to allow me any opinion of my own. He doesn't care what I think, what any woman thinks. He must think breasts are badges of stupidity." "Aye, he must. I hope some day he realizes his mistake."

"And speaking of breasts," Pauline said in an aggravated tone, "just what the hell was that maneuver you did during the aerobatics portion? I know what I saw!"

"Well, some have posited that it looked like a figure eight on its side, but it needs work."

"Bullshit. I saw a pair of breasts. MY breasts!"

"Okay, okay . . . did I do them justice?"

"The lines you traced were damn near perfect. You have an excellent memory and complete mastery of your machine. If my Jeremy can fly anything like you, I have complete faith he will be in my arms in no time, having defeated anything the huns put up against him."

"He's better, actually. But his moves must be reflexive when he is under attack, executed without thought. He's a wonderful flyer. He just needs to have a stronger survival instinct. One close scrap will teach him that. It did me, and I was an observer."

"What could you do as an observer? Point your gun?"

"Aye, for starters. But I had my pilot teach me how to fly, though I never got the chance to do more than taxi. But one day he was hit and killed. I had no choice but to fly the 'plane back."

"Oh, that was *you?!* You threw your pilot overboard and brought the 'plane back to your field and crash-landed?"

"Yes, but I didn't—"

"I read about that. My God! I had no idea!"

"Wait. Pauline, this is important for you to know. That pilot was my friend and my mentor. I never would have thrown him overboard. I was trying to get him into the front cockpit when he slipped from my grip and fell off the side. He was already dead. His last act was to give me this." I showed her the bladder. "He carried it everywhere. It was his scotch."

"That is so sweet. I knew you had a sweet side, but sentimental as well?"

"I owed him. Still do."

"You, Lieutenant, are a wonderful man. Would you mind taking me home so I can change out of these drenched clothes? If you're nice, maybe I'll refresh your memory a little for your next aerial stunt." Her smile was all the brighter with that evil gleam in her eye. It didn't necessarily bode well, but it generally turned into a lot of fun.

Music took a back seat that morning. In fact, the cornet could have stayed in the motor-car. Pauline was simply cold from all the wet clothing. We spent our time looking for various ways to warm her and keep her warm. She appeared quite content when I left her, sound asleep under her robe and a shawl. My memory had indeed been refreshed.

Back at the airfield I put in my practice time. Though I played a lot, I stopped short of the theme and variation pieces. Perhaps it was because of the theme and variations I had performed earlier with Pauline. I hoped the cold front would stall long enough for another morning of rain.

The front was indeed stationary. I got my desired rain and met Pauline at the cafe.

"There was something I wanted to bring up to you yesterday, but didn't get to it. I'm so sorry I fell asleep. I meant no—"

"None taken. I had something to discuss as well, but it wasn't urgent. What's on your mind?"

"Well, okay, I wanted to ask about the fair haired woman you were dancing with after dinner. If you were trying to incite a spot of jealousy, it worked."

"So noted. I felt the wrath. More than once."

"I'm sure you did. How is the captain, by the way?"

"He is well. I did pass along your apology and your offer to clean his uniform, which he appreciated. If he presents me with a bill, I shall bring it to you. Or the hat shop."

"But who was she?"

"Ah. Jealous, are we?"

"I don't know what you're talking about. I am merely, . . . curious."

"Uh-huh. I see. You need not worry. To your concern, I am pleased to inform you once again that she is engaged to be married once her intended returns from the war. So you see, she poses no threat to you."

"Threat? I don't know what—"

"I'm sure you don't. Anyway, I wanted to bring her up to you."

"Oh? Coming clean, are we?"

"Nothing to 'come clean' about. It was due to her efforts that I got into the RFC."

"How did a mere woman help you into the RFC? Women are no more than decorations to men. Most men."

"Perhaps you didn't hear me while we were dancing. I told you, I was injured by a shell blast while serving with a supply unit. My mate was killed outright, several others were injured, my arm was shattered, and I was blinded. She was the nurse who cared for me in the field hospital."

"But if you were blind, how did you recognize her? You never saw her, did you?"

"Quite correct. I heard her voice. I was heavily sedated the whole time in her care. My eyes were useless, so I never did see her, but I heard her voice. She talked to me though I was unable to answer. She talked to others around her. I have been listening for her ever since. She informed me the other night just how bad off I was. The doctors wanted to leave me for dead, a hopeless case, a waste of their time. She felt I could be saved, so she dedicated herself to keeping me alive. The doctors said my arm was too far gone to be saved—you've seen it, the scars—but she felt it could be saved. She spent endless hours cleaning my arm and preparing it for the later surgery and therapy I had to go through. So you see, I owe her my life and my ability to function as a normal, complete man. If not for her, I would never have met you."

"Well, you are complete. 'Normal', however . . . ." She smiled.

I smiled. "I never claimed to be normal."

"Right. It was my assumption. I shall have to reconsider it. However, that is quite the tale. I know you expressed to her your desire to pay her back. That is your nature. But how does one repay such a monumental debt?"

"That is what I wanted to bring up with you."

"What, you want me to repay—"

"No. Of course not. But again, maybe you could help me to help her. You well know the dedication your son and I have to aviation, right? Clara—my former nurse—has that same dedication to medicine and healing. She has been working in the medical field her entire life. She wants nothing more than to be a doctor—a surgeon—but cannot get past men who see her as only a woman. Certainly you can sympathize with her plight."

"I can."

"Getting Clara into school to be a doctor will require some political influence and a social movement. If my research is correct, your husband is on the board of directors at the nursing school over by the arboretum."

"He is."

"Your husband is also a politician and moving up in that world."

"Yes."

"And you are president of the local women's club, among other things, are you not?"

"I am."

"I wonder if first you, then your husband could help this woman to realize her dream and become a surgeon. I know, it is asking a lot. But this woman saved my life and enabled me to continue along the path to my dream. In my view, no one is more deserving than this selfless woman who wants no more than to be able to help people."

"Lieutenant, you make a most convincing case. I should like to meet her, of course, but I see no reason why I cannot help your cause. As you know, I face similar circumstances at home. So I fully understand her situation. I would enjoy helping her through the senseless barriers holding her back. My husband will be a hard one to convince, but I can give it a go. It could be wonderful publicity for his hat shop. And maybe he will take my advice and finally hire some women to help his business."

"I am eternally grateful for your efforts. I shall never be able to repay you."

"No, likely not. But I shall give you the chance to try once you drive me home."

"Fair enough."

We got up to leave. As usual, Pauline insisted on paying. But when I went back to retrieve the cap I had "forgotten", I left a bit more for our friend the proprietor. Perhaps it would help his slow day.

"You know, Lieutenant, I shall have to think a bit about this idea for your nurse. So I cannot be bothered making decisions. Will this put you in a bind?"

"Me? Why no, not at all. Think all you want. If you're not too distracted."

"Why, Lieutenant, you are so agreeable. I appreciate your flexibility."

"I just hope I don't hear any Irving Berlin."

Once we arrived in our little tea area, Pauline removed her clothing in something of a burlesque routine, complete with teasing and overly large stage smiles. Luckily for me, she went beyond the tease. Once she had bared all, I took her into the guest bedroom, sat her on the bed, and obtained a handkerchief, a scarf, and three small bundles of rope from the sideboard.

I gagged her with the handkerchief and scarf. I pulled her hands high in front of her, about the level of her face, and used part of a bundle of rope to secure her wrists. Then I went to the other side of the bed and pulled her to about the center. I lay her back and secured her hands to the headboard with a tether. I tied each ankle and tethered them to opposite posts at the footboard, leaving her very exposed. In lieu of a blindfold, I pulled the door to, eliminating most of the ambient light. I undressed and climbed onto the bed to examine my prize. I played and teased and then went about pleasing her. I listened to her severely muffled screams and stopped pleasing when I sensed she had had enough. Play continued. Her muffled sounds told me the pleasures were mutual.

Eventually her "ordeal" ended. I undid her bonds, left her lying face down, and put water on for tea. About the time I poured the water, Pauline rejoined me overlooking her garden, which was being prepared for winter.

"You are right about helping your friend Clara. There is no reason to hold back such dedication because of different body parts. She deserves the chance she has fought for her entire life. I truly know how she feels, living my life as arm jewelry when needed and little else. I am so happy you and I have become acquainted. You don't tolerate me, you talk to me. That is the best thing about being with you. You have many things going for you, Lieutenant, but my favorite is that you treat women like people, not decorations. We have something to say beyond 'yes, dear'. We need more people—more men—to hear our demands for respect. We do more than make babies and run households. We deserve to be recognized."

"Hear, hear."

"We can start with your Clara. Once she is on her way, we can find another and another."

"We can."

"Lieutenant, you are brilliant."

"No, I . . ."

"Come with me, Lieutenant. Such brilliance deserves its reward."

Who would have thought that such an ordinary weather term as "stationary front" could have erotic connotations?

* * * * *

CHAPTER 40

British

Arriving at the airfield, I followed several lorries onto the property. They were full of young men, no doubt students. I dropped off the motor-car and cleaned up in case I was needed. I was otherwise organized and ready. At this point I could talk to them and get an idea of who they were and what they had done. The stationary front . . . m-m-m-m . . . uh, had to go away before any flying evaluations could be done.

I decided to stay close in case I was called upon to help with the new arrivals. I pulled out my cornet, warmed the lip a little, and fussed around with a tune from "Carmen". Music is such a wonderful medium. It can be manipulated in time, in tone, in feeling, in volume, in so many ways to express oneself. One can play the very same tune any number of times and play it differently every time. Feelings can and do affect performance. Oh, there are those who feel every performance should be like every other performance. I can understand that for large ensembles like orchestras. Everyone play the same, every time. But again, an orchestra follows a conductor, and how that conductor feels affects how he manipulates the orchestra. So even there, there is room for interpretation. I certainly appreciate orchestral music. Mozart was a genius, to say nothing of Bach or Beethoven, Haydn or Handel. Even more recent composers like Tchaikovski or Stravinsky certainly elicit emotions. There is nothing like a good brass band when one is in the mood for one. I prefer soloists with minimal accompaniment. Ragtime, blues, jass. Give 'em a rhythm section and give 'em room. That is music. Loose scripting with maximum flexibility. Ah, music. Making music is like painting for the ears.

After playing a while, I made some tea and looked out the window at the rain falling on my garden. I was happy I had found time to do some weeding while the weather was too good to go have breakfast. It looked wonderful. The droplets formed on flowers were always special

to me because they did not last. They might disappear with the next
well placed rain drop. Or they might linger long enough to evaporate
and thus disappear slowly. A breeze could move the plant and the
droplet could be moved or combined with another droplet. So many
possibilities. As I watched the water play upon the plants, I wondered
just how long this stationary front would remain so. I had duties to
perform, especially with the new student pilots arriving, but it seemed
I could never get enough of Pauline's company. She was wonderful.
Intimacy was incredible, what with all the feelings between us. But
intimacy was not how we defined our relationship. What defined us
was how we felt when we were together. We complimented one another
very well. Being with Pauline simply felt good. Was that not the basis
for a successful relationship? We both hated the limiting factor, namely
her marriage. Even if it was a sham, it was still legal and binding. It was
not a contract easily broken. And even if her husband had no regard for
her as a person, he understood the value of having such a person to hang
on his arm. Everywhere he went, people were envious of that chap with
the younger woman and her endearing smile. He would not give her
up. Nor would I ask her to leave. I was not in a position to provide for
her in such a lavish manner. And she deserved nothing less than what
she had. So it was, without doubt, a flawed and doomed relationship.
But I would enjoy her while I could. On my side, I could be transferred
out at any time, whether to another school or to a front line unit. It was
war. I had to live today and hope for tomorrow. And I had to work to
reward Clara, for without her efforts I would not be there to fly or be
with Pauline or anything else.

The front which had made its home over my head for the past few
days finally moved on. I woke up next morning to light rain, but I could
see in the distance that it would not last past midday. I picked up the
cornet and headed into town for breakfast and, hopefully, a little music.
Sure enough, I arrived just ahead of Pauline. It was a delight to watch
her walking through the rain, so feminine, but with that business-like
umbrella. In the miserable light I could not tell whether it was black or
dark blue. As the light was not likely to change while we were together

that morning, I might have to ask. If we ran out of things to talk about, that is.

Just as we sat down with our coffee, Pauline reported that she was making progress on Clara's behalf. She had visited the nursing school and met with Clara as president of the women's club. She had felt Clara's zeal for learning and healing and remarked on her enthusiasm. Then she had called upon some of her social contacts and made them aware of Clara. These contacts were married to some important people around town, as well as at least one member of the school's board of directors.

"It's not a lot, I'm afraid, but Clara is now more visible within the community. I hope she doesn't mind, but she will be in the spotlight. If she is as dedicated as you say and I feel, she will catch the attention of people who need to know. While I have several more contacts to visit, that is likely all I can do for the moment, make her visible so they can observe her at work and look up her record. That was easy. The hard part is yet to come. I need to make my husband aware of a woman with a brain, a woman who can do immense good despite having female parts. Unfortunately, he is interested mostly in the body parts, though I'm not sure just whose at the moment. Certainly not mine."

"His loss," I said, rolling my eyes. She laughed so loud she squealed. I continued, "Madam president, your efforts are most sincerely appreciated. I shall thank you on behalf of Clara and myself and the medical profession at large." Holding up my coffee, "May the community of doctors soon welcome a new member to their ranks."

"Hear, hear."

We enjoyed a light breakfast and retired to Pauline's garden room to play some music before I had to be back at the airfield. We kept it to light popular fare, but for some reason neither of us could make it all the way through "Alexander's Ragtime Band" without laughing. We would have to find a way, though, since it was such a marvelous tune.

After a wonderful morning of company and music, I drove back to the airfield to meet my new students. I tried the same thing as before, having each student fly a pattern of turns and mild maneuvers so I could observe their technique. After about the first dozen I saw the familiar bell curve forming. Then one went up and just did not look good from the takeoff run. He looked shaky on the climb out, and the first left turn was no better. Then, with no airspeed to speak of, he pulled into a loop without a preparatory shallow dive. There was no possibility of completing that loop. None. The SE, one of the new rebuilds, simply pointed almost straight up, stopped, and slid backward. I could see the student stirring the stick frantically, but with no airflow over them the control surfaces were useless. The port wing dropped and the SE entered into a spin from which there would be no recovery. It fell straight down, crashing in the area used for sighting the guns. Luckily the area was wet from all the rain of late so there was no fire. Upon arrival we found the student was dead, nearly decapitated by the windscreen. It appeared he had undone his harness and was thrown up, out, and down by the force of the crash and his feet sticking on the rudder bar stirrups.

"A-w-w-w *shit!*", I exclaimed upon seeing the lifeless body. The two students who were with me froze, eyes wide and mouths agape. I waved the others off. It was not an inspirational scene for budding scout pilots, even if it did happen. I cancelled the rest of the flights for the day.

I suspected something might have been wrong with the SE, so I got the CO's permission to look it over on the scene. I suspected the gearbox for the propeller and the control wires. There was no way to inspect the gearbox, as it had been destroyed by the weight and force of the crash. The control wires were a little loose for my taste, but I could not prove they were what caused the crash. My newly rebuilt SE had none of the problems I suspected there. I decided to look over the other new arrival SEs before they were flown again by anyone.

I did my inspection that afternoon. One had what I considered a suspect gearbox, in that the prop had less resistance in a pull than the other new Hissos. I suspected worn gears or something loose in the linkage. The same SE had what I deemed a sloppy control stick. Too much play in the stick before control surfaces began to react, indicating loose wires to the control surfaces. I called that one SE unfit for flight pending further investigation by the CO with representatives from the repair depot and RFC present. I was later congratulated for my decision, but I told them it was just a gut reaction. I could not prove the crashed SE was defective, but I did find another from the same depot that was suspect. The offending depot was put on notice and inspections were tightened. But it was too late for the dead lad from Kent.

After I inspected the SEs we continued our initial flying program without further incident. As a result I recommended two of the students be transferred to another program. I felt they lacked the finesse to handle a scout. It had almost appeared that the SE was flying them and they were having a difficult time keeping up. I put several more on notice that they could be transferred out if they did not show immediate improvement. My recommendations were not to chastise anyone. It was a simple matter that we are not all cut out the same. Some are better suited to high performance aeroplanes while some are a better fit in something that is more stable or docile. I was looking to put the right peg in the right hole and save lives at the same time. The SE, while a wonderful aeroplane, could be a real handful to some.

As a Home Establishment flight instructor, I was allowed certain privileges not afforded combat pilots. While the RFC was strict about how their aeroplanes appeared at the front, this was somewhat relaxed at the training schools. It was not unusual to find an instructor with a heavily decorated aeroplane. There were starburst patterns painted on wings, overall red/white/blue schemes, playing card representations, animals, and more. Some of it was personal whimsy, some of it was for quick recognition by students in the air, the list of reasons went on. I had decided I wanted to have my SE painted up as I wanted it before some wag did it for me. I took my idea to the CO and he approved it right away, even before I presented what I wanted. He didn't care what I did as long as I kept up my performance as instructor and ad hoc airframe inspector. His only qualification was that I not take anyone away from a more important task in order to decorate my aeroplane. Fair enough.

As a painter, I could come up with an infinite number of ideas for painting an aeroplane. My idea, however, was less about art and more about recognition by students. I wanted my fuselage, fin, and upper tailplane painted white, the fuselage bottom and that of the tailplane black. They could leave the military serial, B'708, and cockade or they could paint them over, I didn't care. And I wanted a motif painted on the top surface of my upper wing which I would paint myself. I wanted to trace the path of the maneuver I flew in a bold white stripe across the wing from cockade to cockade. They could call it "Lazy Eight". I didn't care.

I surveyed the lads in the maintenance area and found one who had the time and was happy to help. He painted the fuselage and tailplane right away, while I had an indoor class with my remaining pilots. I looked in on him after the class to find he was nearly finished. He had left the cockades in place under and behind the cockpit and left a khaki panel behind the B'708. I thanked him for a job well done and for making the time right away.

"It was my pleasure, Lef-tenant. Happy to be of service. But it will be tough keeping that white clean, sir."

"That's okay, laddie. I know where to find you!" I clapped him on the back and made a mental note to pick him up some pastries or maybe some cognac next time I was in town. If I take care of these lads, they will take care of me. They already appreciated that I did a lot of my own upkeep on my SE and spent time with them.

I spent the afternoon with the new students, going over their flying skills. We talked about each pilot's performance so the class as a whole could gain some knowledge about flying in general. Then we had a discussion about flying at the front. Mainly, I related my experiences and they asked questions, but again it was an opportunity for them to learn. I could not stress enough the need to look around constantly. It was the Hun you did not see that would get you. Again I stressed the importance of good equipment. Check your machine, learn how things work, check your ammunition, do everything you can to survive in the air over the front. They had to understand there were many people over there who wanted to kill them.

Once I thought they had enough to think about and discuss among themselves, I excused myself and went out to the maintenance area, where I had arranged for several ladders and a board to form a scaffold along the rear edge of the upper wing. With paint and brush in hand, I stepped onto the scaffold and began to paint. First I painted a stripe between the cockades, from the inside edge of one to the inside edge of the other, on the line of the forward spar. Then I used the edge of the brush to trace the path of my "lazy eight" maneuver. Satisfied with the rough centerline, I fleshed it out to the width of the spanwise stripe. Done. Easy enough. What was a "lazy eight" to many was a reminder of nonflying fun for me. Anything to keep up morale, if only my own. Another boost for my morale would have been to bring Pauline to the airfield and show her my SE, but that would have been wholly inappropriate. It would have to wait or maybe never happen.

* * * *

CHAPTER 41

German

Jakob was busily coordinating efforts to create the new *Staffel*. The necessary drawings were being sent from Austria, the appropriate craftsmen were traveling to the airfield in order to modify the *Albatrosen*. The *Jagdstaffel* was now flying from the airfield and several more Hannas were on requisition. Jakob was busy enough that he had no time to inquire about the health of his recently wounded pilot, Jure. Then there was the matter of combining the personnel from the two units and transferring out the ones not selected. More rumors and reports were circulating about the impending collapse of the Russian government. Perhaps enough German ground troops and air units would make the journey west in time to secure a victory before the Americans arrived in earnest. It was Germany's only hope.

Part of Jakob's job was looking over the records of the various men in the *Jagdstaffel*. He found the pilot records particularly interesting. Each pilot had tallied a fair number of confirmed victories. If the unit had acquired a pilot who did not score, he was transferred out. The *Jastaführer* was ruthless and seemingly without patience. As a result, the average number of aerial conquests across the unit was better than in any other unit, even Richthofen's vaunted *Jasta* 11. There probably was not a better unit with which to establish an elite *Staffel*. Another factor was the *Jastaführer's* decision to keep only the *Albatros* D.III and pass along the D.V and D.Va models, as well as the Pfalz D.III and Fokker's triplane. The D.III was simply a better aeroplane, unsurpassed even by the firm's "improved" D.V or D.Va. The latter models looked sleeker, but offered no improvement in performance or, more importantly, safety. The lower wings were no better than those of the D.III, and looks would not win the war. It just made sense that giving a talented group of veteran pilots an improved aeroplane would add up to a better unit.

* * * * *

CHAPTER 42

German

Jakob found he was still sore and tired from recently having been shot. Oh, the soreness was beginning to fade, but did that mean the wounds were healing? Or was he adjusting to the pain? Probably both, but he felt a little better each day. He had lost a lot of blood, however, and as a result he tired more easily. He had not flown combat missions much over the past few months anyway. A *Hauptmann* was not expected to fly much. His job as *Schlachtstaffelführer* was more one of management than participation. He was to tend to his men and make sure they were doing their assigned duties. He accepted reports from maintenance, spare parts inventory, flight leaders, other *Staffeln* in the vicinity, and from the hierarchy of command above. He read a lot. And filed a lot. He found himself gaining a "little something extra" around the middle from his lack of physical activity. But he needed to read, and he could not read in a ninety mile per hour slipstream. Filing reports was a chore, especially in the lower drawers. His lower back was beginning to hurt. He knew he needed more movement in his routine in order to feel better. And he would. But it simply sounded like a lot of work.

He found himself weary from all the reading, filing, and extra paperwork involved in setting up this "super" *Jagdstaffel*. Apparently *IdFlieg* wanted to go with a split command for the *Staffel*, keeping Jakob to do primarily the administrative work of, yes, reports, requisitions, and filing. Oh, *wunderbar*. The actual flying leadership would be carried out by the current *Jagdstaffelführer,* which made perfect sense to Jakob. And grated on his nerves. He admired the record the *führer* had amassed, both as a *Jastaführer* and as a flyer. With twenty-three confirmed victories, he had been awarded the *Pour le Merite* and would soon receive it. But he detested the man himself. Though their *Staffeln* often worked hand-in-glove, they kept communications terse and only about military matters. If they were both required to be in attendance at an event, whether social or military, they each sought to get the obligatory handshake out of the way so they could withdraw to different areas of the room, if not separate rooms. It was a terrible situation, for though they had been acquainted for some time, they knew they could not spend any time in close contact without a shouting match or even a fistfight breaking out.

Barely able to keep his head up, Jakob lay down to nap. Reluctantly, his mind wandered back to his first meeting with the current *Jagdstaffelführer*. Jakob was born and raised on the outskirts of Berlin, where his father was an administrator in the city government. A hairdresser before she married, Jakob's mother still did hair in her time away from raising her family for a little extra income. Theirs was a modest, cosmopolitan home. After attending public schools, Jakob joined with a local militia group. Shortly after the war's outbreak his group was assigned to care for horses and equipment of a neighboring cavalry unit. Once the lines stabilized, the cavalry unit was no longer needed, and the cavalry horses were to be removed from the front lines back toward Berlin. While wrangling horses Jakob fell and was trampled by two frightened steeds. He suffered a concussion, several broken ribs, and a broken arm. HIs hospital was not far from an airfield, and he heard aeroplanes flying nearby each day. Like many others, he found the idea of flying more appealing than living in a muddy hole, and he decided to apply for transfer to *die F*liegertruppe. To his surprise, he was accepted for observer training. He found himself with a roommate from eastern Prussia who also had a background in horses, as well as farming. Emil Strasser zealously talked about Aryan racial purity and how people should be more interested in an agrarian lifestyle and less concerned with greed and capitalism. Jakob mostly let Strasser talk and instead concerned himself with learning the duties of an observer. They got along, but Strasser always seemed irritated that more people did not see things his way. When Jakob invited Strasser to attend his wedding, that led to the major schism between them. Jakob married a woman who he viewed, naturally enough, as wonderful in every way. Strasser became extremely upset when he learned the woman was Jewish. He railed on and on that the Jews were a major component of capitalism and accused them of causing essentially anything negative—or, in his words, corruptive or evil. He denounced all Jews and vehemently opposed Jakob's marriage as further dilution of the Aryan race. Fortunately Jakob was soon assigned to a unit and took his leave of Strasser and his rants.

Less than two years later Jakob found himself looking admiringly at Strasser's record as a pilot and *Jastaführer* while detesting the man for his unyielding far right views. He could see that commanding the *Stafffel* with Strasser at his side was not going to be easy. He knew that he, Jakob, could prosecute the war and keep conversation brief and focused on the war effort. But Strasser was not focused strictly on the war. He refused to allow any Jewish flyers in his unit and thought nothing of going on a rant against Jews as the problem with anything and everything. Jakob made it a point to assign Strasser an office in another building. The less contact or conversation, the better. There had been discussion about *Staffel* mobility, and Jakob hoped it would come to fruition, since Strasser would travel with the *Staffel*. Having Strasser based, even temporarily, at another aerodrome would be a relief for Jakob's blood pressure. Unfortunately, anything dealing with airframe modification would require the participation and approval of both men. Jakob would have to keep any conversation to the topic at hand and ignore the inevitable rants about Jews in general and his *frau* in particular.

Jakob's adjutant did him the service of waking him up with, yes, more paperwork to be reviewed and filed. But the news was not all bad, as the adjutant handed him a tube containing the technical drawings from the Oeffag factory in Austria. Work on the airframes could begin in earnest now that the last of the craftsmen had arrived as well. Jakob took advantage of the opportunity to get out of his office and away from the paperwork for a short while and walked the drawings to the conversion hangar. There he found most of the workers who would be performing the modifications to the *Albatrosen*. He handed the wing drawings to the carpenters. There was a list of components needed to build the Oeffag wings, the specifications of which were to be compared to the factory drawings on hand for the German D.III. The carpenters would determine whether it was more feasible to modify existing wings or build new ones. Of course they would compile a report which Jakob would read and use to make his decision. Jakob already knew it was likely more practical to build new wings rather than "unglue" existing wings, but the idea merited looking into. Briefly. He did ask the carpenters to create jigs for building wing ribs, as there were so many needed for each wing. He also mentioned that the existing wings could be made available to other *Staffeln* as replacements.

Another matter was the elevator. The Oeffag drawings showed a slightly larger elevator in the fore to aft measurement. Jakob asked that one Oeffag elevator be built and tested against the standard *Albatros* elevator.

Jakob's salvage friend was searching for more powerful engines, namely the over-compressed Daimler-Mercedes, for use in the modified airframes. In any case, the engine cowling would be modified to eliminate the spinner found on virtually all German *Albatrosen*. There would be a very slight weight reduction in the airframe, and a rounded nose behind the propeller would give the aeroplane a marginally higher top speed regardless.

While he was in the hangar a fabric shipment arrived. He had ordered fabric with which to cover the new and/or modified wings. The limited remaining supply of plain linen would be used to patch bullet holes and the like. The new pre-printed fabric would be used on wings and elevators, though the elevators would be painted black as part of the tricolor *jasta* marking.

Everything was on hand to begin the conversion process. More engines would arrive as his friend was able to procure them. As was his style, Jakob walked over to the mess to ask who wanted to be the first to have their aeroplane modified to the new standard. He advised the men that their aeroplane would receive the stronger Oeffag lower wings and rounded nose. It would also be fitted with the Oeffag elevator, which would be tested by several pilots. The 'plane would retain its current engine unless a more powerful engine could be procured. Of course, every pilot wanted to be the first. The men loudly discussed the proposition and decided that since Walzer had downed a French

SPAD the day before he should have his 'plane modified first. As the decision was being announced, Strasser entered the mess and asked what the commotion was about. Willi spoke up and informed Strasser that Walzer would be the first to have his 'plane modified. As was his nature, Strasser objected.

"I am the *Jastaführer*, so my *Albatros* will be the first."

The men were outraged that Walzer was to be denied their award. Willi spoke up. "*Mein Herr*, with due respect, we thought Walzer should be rewarded for the SPAD he brought down yesterday. The red pants flyer was a wonderful dinner guest last night and told some interesting stories. Do you not agree?"

Strasser stroked his beard while he considered the comment. "Walzer, I know you like to play billiards. Would you care to place a friendly wager? Stroke the cue ball against the opposite cushion. The man who leaves his ball closest to the near cushion without touching it wins."

"*Javohl, mein Herr!* Tell the men to roll my pretty girl into the hangar now. This will take but a moment."

"Hmm. Amusing. You may be first."

Walzer placed the ball next to the breaking dot and practiced his stroke with the cue stick. Satisfied, he moved behind the ball, set up, ran the stick between his fingers a few times, then extended his stroke to include tapping the ball. The ball rolled straight and true to the far cushion, bumped it, and returned, slowing to within four inches of the cushion where he stood. Another pilot marked his results with a chalk cube on the side of the table.

"Very nice, Walzer. Very nice. But not close enough. There will be no charge for the lesson." With no preparation, Strasser placed the ball next to the breaking dot, felt the stick in the air, lowered it, and stroked the ball just right of center. The ball went to the opposite cushion and banked to the right, striking the side cushion very near the side pocket, and stopped near where it had started. The men cheered for Walzer.

"Wait. Did I not mention this was to be best of three?" The men, well aware of Strasser's temper and distinct lack of patience, briefly murmured and then went silent.

"*Mein Herr,* you may have mentioned that. It was a little loud, though, and I may have missed it. Would you care to go first this time?"

"*Danke.* I will." Strasser again placed the ball, again ran the stick through his fingers in the air above the table, set up, and stroked the ball. The ball rolled true, bumped the far cushion, and returned to within five inches of the near cushion. This was marked to the side. Walzer took a deep breath and stretched, holding the cue stick across his shoulders and behind his neck. "That was nice, *Herr Leutnant.*" He then chalked his left hand, waved off the excess, and slid the cue a few times in his fingers off to the side. Satisfied with the feel, he set up behind the ball, slid the stick a few more times, and stroked the ball. The ball took the transfer of energy, rolled straight and true once again, and began to slow on the return roll. It passed the marker on the side, and stopped about two inches shy of the near cushion. The room was silent.

"*Herr Leutnant,* that was two. Do you wish to shoot a third time? Or shall I have my *Albatros* rolled in so they can get to work?"

Strasser looked briefly at Walzer, then glared at the ball on the table. He briefly turned red in the face, then returned to normal. Strasser drew a deep breath, exhaled, and responded. "Walzer, please have the men roll your crate into the hangar. Let them experiment on yours so they can get it right with mine."

"*Danke schön, mein Herr!* I am happy to offer my 'plane for experimentation. You are welcome to fly it, of course, so you can decide if you want yours modified as well." Walzer saluted smartly.

"That will be all." Strasser poured himself a cup of coffee and returned to his office, passing Jakob as he went through the door without acknowledging him. Jakob stood still a moment, rolled his eyes at all the unnecessary drama, and congratulated Walzer on being the first with an improved aeroplane.

* * * * *

CHAPTER 43

British

While taking my evening meal in the mess I witnessed the latest scuffle between two of my students. These two simply did not get along and no one really knew why. They had just been playing football out past the landing strip, and one had apparently tripped the other, leading to a fistfight. The others had separated them, but in the mess the fistfight resumed. I pulled rank on them and made them quit. I told them they could solve their differences the next morning. I ordered them to choose from the pool of SEs which one they would fly the next morning and spend the evening going over their choices, checking the spark plugs, wiring, controls, and ammunition. They were to have blank ammunition with tracers every tenth round. They were to meet me at sunrise and toss a coin to see who took off first. Then one would take off to seek whatever advantage they wanted, followed five minutes later by the other. I would take off and circle the area of the old athletic fields, where the mock combat was to take place. The two would fight it out as I watched. Once I felt there was a winner, I would fire a red flare and we would all return to the airfield. Call it an updated "pistols at dawn". I accompanied them as they chose their mounts and had them set up in separate areas to perform their checks.

Naturally enough, by sunrise everyone was up and awaiting the two contestants. The "dogfight at dawn" had been the only topic of conversation the prior evening, and someone had even gone to the trouble of fixing ten foot long streamers to the tailskids, red on one and blue on the other, so they could keep track from the ground. The duelists approached me, fittingly enough, from opposite sides of the airfield. I met them, shook hands with each, and advised them that they were to shoot "at" one another, but not to hit one another, the idea being to show me who was better at getting into position to deliver a killing volley. I then tossed a coin in the air as one lad called it. He won.

The other protested, "Two of three! Sir!" I acceded and tossed the coin again while the other lad called it. He lost. So, winning the toss, the lad with the blue streamer elected to take off first. I wished them luck and dismissed them to their SEs.

Blue took off, circled the field, shook his fist at Red, still on the ground, and climbed into the dark western sky. Red retaliated with the sign of the bowmen. I had my "Lazy Eight" started and got strapped in while we counted down the five minutes. Everyone who could be spared piled into lorries and headed for the old athletic fields to view the event.

Five minutes after Blue took off I waved my arm over my head and signaled Red to take off. Once he had cleared the boundary I followed. Red struggled, pushing his SE to climb as fast as it could. I climbed at a more leisurely pace to about five thousand feet and circled the old athletic fields. Looking about me, mostly above, I could see Red still climbing off to the east. I could not see Blue, but I did not have to wait long for him to arrive. He screamed past me, about three hundred feet to port. He had dived hard in order to come up beneath Red and fire at him from below and behind, a classic maneuver which allowed Red no defensive fire. Red never saw him coming. I watched Blue's tracers fire just past Red in what would have been a clear kill shot. It was over that quickly. Reaching for my flare pistol to end the contest, I was stunned by what happened next. Following through his maneuver, Blue zoomed up past Red, twirling about his longitudinal axis to rub in the quick "kill". Just as they were at the same altitude, I saw Red extend his arm out of the cockpit. I saw a flash of pink light as Red fired his flare pistol directly at Blue. The flare hit the SE and ignited the fabric and soon Blue was ablaze. I watched as Blue stalled and fell into a spin. He managed to recover after an agonizing thousand feet and circled back over the athletic fields, cutting his speed. He then climbed out of the cockpit, which was about to be engulfed by flame. As he shimmied toward the tail atop the fuselage, his weight pushed the tail down. Just as he reached the tailplane, the SE stalled again and the lad appeared to dive off the tailplane. He slowly tumbled in the air, falling into the trees bordering the fields. The SE, now mostly afire, spun in about a hundred yards away and set the long, dead grass afire as well.

On the ground, the spectators raced on foot and by lorry toward the point of impact, but as the grass fire grew they had to keep their distance. They were helpless to get to their fallen mate, much less attempt any assistance, which would likely have been futile. The fire approached the point where the pilot had hit. What I saw next stunned me yet again. Red flew low over the fire, shaking his fist at his fallen victim. What gall! I was half surprised he didn't strafe the wreckage. This young man had really dug himself a hole. I fired a red flare such that he could see it and I returned to the field. I could do nothing from above in my SE, though shooting him down did briefly cross my mind.

I landed, jumped out of my SE, and alerted everyone in earshot what had happened. Firefighters had to be sent to the scene to control the blaze. I held out no hope for the downed pilot. I expected the remaining pilot to land at any moment, and I arranged for him to be placed under arrest. But he did not show. I remained along the flight line with several armed officers and, eventually, some local bobbies. There were no calls about the missing SE. We had but to wait him out.

The firefighters were able to push the flames back enough to recover the crumpled and badly burned body of the victim. Putting out the grassfire would take a little longer. We were fortunate that it had rained so much recently or it would have been worse. But things were bad enough. We had a dead student on our hands and his killer was still aloft, at least as far as we knew.

But our day was not over.

The telephone started to ring an hour or so later. Word had reached the town and people were reporting that the SE with the red streamer had been seen heading toward the airfield. Sure enough, we soon heard him approaching. He dove low over the airstrip, pulled up, circled downwind, dove low again, then turned back into the wind and set down, engine still running strong. This was highly irregular. He set down at a speed much faster than he should have and then aimed his SE at the line of SEs parked near the maintenance buildings. There was nothing anyone could do. He crashed his SE into the end aeroplane, pushing it into the next one. As the men converged on this chaotic scene, the pilot stood up and waved his flare pistol in one hand and a revolver in the other.

The enraged pilot yelled, "Everybody back away!" The crowd stopped in a loose circle.

"Put the guns down, get out of the aeroplane, and present yourself for arrest!" It was the CO.

The lad pointed his flare pistol at the SE he had plowed into.

"I said get away! I meant it! Back away or I will set this whole place afire!"

I stepped closer, within the circle of men. My student, my responsibility.

"You killed a man. Anything you do now will only make it worse for you. Get out of the 'plane."

"That bastard had to die—he needed to die. He assaulted my sister! Ravaged her, cut her, left her for dead! But his father, a barrister, kept him from trial, bribed a few officials, and made it all go away!"

"And you thought killing him would make things better? Save that shit for the Germans! Look, you are in a mess. But stop now, get out of the 'plane, and we will see what we can do."

"The filthy bugger ruined my sister's life! She is disfigured and nobody will go near her, much less marry her! He did this to her! He had to die!"

"I understand that. But you must stop this now before you ruin your life completely!"

"You don't understand. No one does." He pointed the flare gun at the next SE. Then he lowered the revolver and pointed it at me.

There were two shots in quick succession from the other side of the airfield. I watched as the student's body recoiled from the force of being hit. The revolver dropped onto the top of the fuselage and then slid off and fell to the ground. The lifeless body fell backward out of the cockpit, caught momentarily at the knees, then tumbled to the ground next to the revolver. Overhead a red flare added a strange light to the bizarre scene. Men rushed in and picked up the guns, then the pilot, dead from two gunshot wounds to the chest and neck.

The immediate danger was over. The CO congratulated the man who had climbed onto a hangar roof with a rifle and ended the matter. He was much celebrated about the town and he was recommended for an award. But we had two dead pilots and three SEs to fix, not to mention pilot training to be resumed so that we could continue the war on the Germans. Flying was cancelled for the day and we instructors were posted to the mess in the event any of the other students wanted to discuss the day's events.

A number of students came to the mess, but they didn't feel much like talking. Though there was a low buzz of halting conversation, it was mostly quiet. Some of the townspeople stopped by and left flowers or food. Neither of the dead had lived nearby, so there were no family members to console, at least not yet. It had certainly been a surreal morning. I excused myself from the mess to visit the CO.

"Yes, Lef-tenant?"

"Sir, I came to face up to my responsibility."

"What responsibility is that?"

"Well, sir, the idea was mine to send the lads up and have them fight it out."

"And the idea was not a bad one. With such enmity between them, it could have been something for the other students to watch. The one lad's technique was fast and to the point. The fight, as you planned it, was over in seconds. You had no way of knowing the other would use his flare pistol as a weapon. You are in no way responsible for what happened. And I admire the way you confronted the armed student and tried to talk him into surrendering. Good man. Well done. I am pleased to have you on staff. Now unless you have another matter to discuss, get back to the mess and do whatever needs done there. Rough day."

"Aye, sir. Thank you. I owe it to you to help out with the mountain of reports and such you will have to do because of my idea and what precipitated. Please let me know if and when you would like me here to do so."

"I may take you up on that. After all, you know how it all started and ended. That could help simplify things for me. Thank you, Lef-tenant. I'll let you know."

"Aye, sir, please do."

When I returned to the mess I loudly offered to go get my cornet and liven the place up a bit with music. My offer was impolitely rebuffed by all. I did offer. Another instructor asked if I wanted to play in the orchestra. That was an interesting idea. I made a note of rehearsal times. Seeing I was really not needed, I announced that I would be in my quarters with my cornet. If anyone needed to see me, they could just follow their ears and I would be happy to see them. Some of them threw rags at me as I left the mess. Ragtime. Wonderful suggestion.

I was as upset over the morning's events as anyone there. Probably more so, as it was my idea that led to two deaths. But somebody had to try to lift spirits around the place. Life is for the living, as they say. So while I grieved the losses, I chose to express my grief through my music. It was a release. We people are wired differently, so we do not all express feelings in the same manner.

* * * * *

CHAPTER 44

British

Flying was cancelled the next morning. I decided to go into town and visit the cafe for coffee and cake. It was a nice enough day, partly cloudy with the sun trying hard to prevail, and the cafe had more customers than usual. More than I saw on rainy mornings, at any rate. The proprietor poured my coffee and asked about what had happened at the airfield the day before. He had heard about the rifle shots that killed the student pilot holding pistols.

"But I heard there was somebody trying to talk sense to the boy before he was shot dead. Is it true the boy had his guns pointed at that guy?"

"Well, he had a revolver pointed at him, yes. The other gun was a flare pistol which was pointed at the next aeroplane."

"You saw it?!"

"Aye. I was right there."

"What nerve! Talking to some crazy with two loaded guns? I could never!"

"No, not the safest place to be. Not at all."

"I guess he didn't get through to the boy, did he?"

"I suppose not."

"I heard he wrecked a whole line of aeroplanes."

"Three, actually. He crashed his SE into the first one in line, and that one got pushed into the next one. They will all be looked over, but I think they can all be fixed."

"Just what makes people do things like that? He was completely around the bend, wasn't he?"

"It appears that way. We will never know."

Someone sat next to me and I heard a familiar voice asking, "Could I have what he's having?"

"Pauline! What a surprise! What brings you here?"

"I just had a hunch they would not be doing much work at the airfield today, so I came over for coffee."

"I'm so glad you did!"

The proprietor brought Pauline her coffee and cake. We ordered some more food and went to a table near our usual one. I was simply elated. I knew I would start feeling better and soon, just being able to spend time with Pauline. She had that effect on me.

Once we settled in, Pauline started the conversation. "I received a letter from Jeremy yesterday."

"You did? How is the lad?"

"He seemed fine." He has been assigned a squadron. He recently reported to a Major Campbell."

"Paul Campbell!"

"Yes—do you know him?"

"Yes! That's my old squadron! Major Campbell will be very good for Jeremy. He's an excellent commander. He follows the book, but not very strictly. He allows the men to be individuals, to a point, but in return he expects them to listen and obey when he puts his foot down. I hated to leave, but they wanted to bring me back here to instruct."

"Yes. I'm so glad." She smiled and grasped my hand under the table. "You would go back, then."

"Yes. If ordered, I would. Nowhere else I would rather be assigned— if I have to go back to the front. Your son is in good hands with Major Campbell."

"I'm being perfectly selfish, I suppose, but I hope you stay here and instruct until this dreadful war is behind us. I have a vested interest in your survival."

"You have?"

"Why, yes. With you I have someone to talk to. I do not get that unless you are around. I have my social circles, of course, but they are so stale. They trade off talk of their children's achievements, husbands' work accomplishments, and trivial gossip. I get so bored. Conversing with you stimulates my mind—I actually use my mind when talking with you."

"You flatter me, madam."

"Jeremy does write of some strife at your old unit, however."

"Oh?"

"Yes. It seems the Germans have put together some kind of elite squadron."

"You mean *Jagdstaffel* 11? With Richthofen—the Red Baron?"

"He didn't mention that mouthful, no. Something about the Fritz. Yes—the Fritzes! That's it!"

"This is news to me. The Fritzes?"

"Yes. They have no assigned area, no specific responsibilities. They roam freely based on reports and advice gathered from the various air units. If one area is having trouble with Allied air units, the Fritzes go in and cover the top—I think—"

"Fly top cover?"

"Yes! They fly top cover and swoop down in specially modified scouts to rid the sky of Allied airmen. What did he write . . . Albatross?"

"Ah, interesting. But Albatross scouts? They cannot hold their own against the SEs we fly. You've seen our SEs—they and the French SPADs are the cream of the crop. The Albatros has a problem with wings falling off in a hard dive."

"According to Jeremy, word is that these are more powerful, faster, and stronger than the usual Albatross. Rumor has it they will be the first to get the new German super fighter at any time." "Super fighter? Maybe I have been away for too long."

"Away from me, for sure!"

"No, the front. This is all news to me. I shall have to take this up with the CO and find out what I can. *Der Fritzen* . . . ."

"*Derfritzen?*"

"*Ja*—yes—The Fritzes in German."

"German now? Speaking German? The only German I know is "kaiser" and that funny word some say after someone sneezes!"

"How cute you are! I do wish we could go see your garden."

"I'm afraid not, Lieutenant. Not today. We could go to the arboretum and see how the light shines on what is left of the blossoms there, though."

"Well, okay, but I don't think we will find a piano at the arboretum!"

Between us we overpaid for our light breakfast, which the proprietor appreciated. Then we motored over to the arboretum to pass some time there. It was pleasant enough. It always was with Pauline. But her news from the front stuck in my mind. *Der Fritzen*. I would have to find out more, if I could, from the CO when I returned the automobile.

While I wanted to drop Pauline at her door, that would have been far less than discreet. So I left her off near the cafe, which was a very short walk away. She made me promise I would not watch her walk away, saying it made her self-conscious. Women can be so funny.

* * * * *

CHAPTER 45

British

When I dropped off the motor-car, I went straight into the CO's office. Of course, he was eating. It was midday, after all. I asked him what he knew about *der Fritzen*, but he had little more than Pauline had. He was able to clarify that it was believed the "super Albatross" was the latest version of the Austrian Oeffag Albatross. It dispensed with the spinner for the propeller and sported a rounded nose, as well as a slightly larger elevator. And it had a more powerful engine, over two hundred horsepower according to some, as opposed to the one hundred eighty horsepower Mercedes engines in the German Albatross type I had fought. And it was stronger. It could dive like a rock and pull out at will. The German models would lose their lower wings and compromise the entire wing structure if they dove too hard or pulled out suddenly. This was interesting to know. The CO added that it appeared the Albatross firm had made a deal with the Austrians to build the Oeffag machines in their OAW factory. Nice to know, I suppose, but where they came from mattered less to me than to some bomber unit. I wanted to know how to shoot one out of the sky.

I moved on to the "super fighter", but the CO had less information on that. He talked about the little Fokker triplane, the one I had seen in September. The Germans seemingly all thought it was the greatest little thing, the way it could maneuver in close combat. While that was undoubtedly true, the answer was to avoid close combat with them. Attack from above, shoot, and dive away, using that energy to climb back above if another pass was needed or desired. There was no sense trying to scrap with the little buggers on their terms, though the Sopwith Camel could hold its own with them. The SE and SPADs were better off using their superior speed in a dive.

The CO said that according to rumors Fokker had a new fighter in development that should outshine the Albatross and Pfalz scouts currently in use and eclipse Fokker's own triplane. But rumors were all he had. No word on the engine or anything that would make it stand out. For this one we would have to wait and see.

That was certainly food for thought. A German attack squadron, tasked with clearing the air of Allied scouts and, presumably, whatever else they encountered. Knowing how the British structured their air campaign, I knew that would be trouble. A squadron of "super Albatross" scouts would be a handful, never mind the rumored "super fighter". I was not aware of anything coming up that could handle the "super Albatross". The Hisso and Viper engines were very good overall, but I wondered if they could be tweaked for more power. I would have to look into it with the maintenance department. Certainly one of them, if not more, had a talent for engine development. It would win the war now and could be very lucrative after the war had been won. I began to wonder whether I could do any good against the Fritzes if I were to go back to the front. If I could help find a development for the SE and then team up with Jeremy . . . . But first I had my reduced class to teach how to fly, fight, and survive at the front.

I decided to go easy on my remaining students the next morning, and have them strafe bedsheets over by the athletic fields. But when I arrived with the first group, I found they were still working at the crash scene. So I went to my next idea, something I had not wanted to do just yet. I fired a red flare so they would all know to fly back to the airfield. When we arrived, I had everyone meet me inside where I told them we would work on formation flying. I stressed the importance of looking around and maintaining one's position in the formation. I got six volunteers for the first go. I assigned positions, and we headed for the flight line.

Takeoff was pretty good, just one climbing a little more slowly than the others, but he soon caught up. I fired a green flare to have them form up as assigned, which they did. I maintained a position behind and above. I watched some jostling around which should not have happened, but it settled out. They were new to this. After a short while I fired a white flare to signal a turn to port. Five of six made a proper turn, but the one at the starboard rear position turned too abruptly and nearly hit the port rear SE. I flew alongside the offender and used hand signals to try to tell him, then returned to my position. I fired another white flare for another turn to port, and it looked about like the first one. I again flew along the offender and indicated a wider turn. He nodded and I returned to my position. I did not have a good feeling about him, but he did acknowledge my direction. The next turn to port actually looked better. I fired a blue flare to indicate a turn to starboard, and the starboard rear pilot went completely out of formation, again turning too abruptly. Fortunately, his error did not threaten the others, and I signaled for the men to return to base.

When I arrived on the flight line, I pulled the offending pilot aside to talk to him.

"I have seen you do better turns than what just happened up there. Is there a problem? Is the SE responding properly?"

"Yes, sir, the SE is working well." "What is the matter?"

"Well, sir, seeing the place where the other bloke went in . . . it just gave me chills, sir. He was a lot like me, and now he's dead. It doesn't seem fair, sir."

"I understand. But he didn't die through any problems with his flying. He was murdered."

"I know. Sir. But it's just not right."

"I agree. But there was nothing anybody could have done. It was beyond your control and mine. We must move on."

"I'm sorry, sir. I found it difficult to concentrate on my position."

"And that lack of concentration could cause an accident and maybe a death, possibly your own. Formation flying is vitally important. I know you are upset, but your performance must improve and quickly. I cannot turn you loose into a unit if you cannot fly formation. Do you understand?"

"Yes, sir, I do."

"Okay. Take the rest of the day off from flying. Go see if you can help in maintenance. If you need to talk further, I will be available later. Or you could visit with the chaplain if you prefer. Just remember my criticism is to improve your performance, not to tear you down. We will try again tomorrow. Okay?"

"Yes, sir. Thank you, sir."

I went inside and congratulated the rest of the flight members on their skills. Then I chose six others to go and practice. This group was better, that is to say all six did a pretty good job of holding position. It was a little sloppy in places, but that is to be expected of someone learning a new skill. We returned, I did a little critique, and then I chose more students. When I was finished with the formation work, I returned by way of the athletic fields to confirm they were finished with any work there. I could easily understand how the young men could be affected by the events of the prior morning. It was a complete shock to us all. I was only trying to reestablish routine. On the other hand, this could be an indicator of how one might react in war. But that was not necessarily bad. How does one prepare for war? How does one react to the carnage that is war. War is not a chess match. Nobody bleeds playing chess. Nobody dies playing chess. War is fought with weapons that injure, maim, and kill. I knew from personal experience, both on the receiving end and giving end. I watched friends die and I caused enemies to die. How has it affected me? I could not give an answer, but it has. Funny how the perception of war changes within one. When war breaks out, the first notion is to sign up and fight. Enlist. Go forth and eradicate the enemy. There was a certain romantic notion about dashing off to war, saving king and country, protecting the folks at home, the future generations, and so on. But often when one attempts to talk to a veteran of war, they do not want to discuss it. War is certainly not pretty. War causes people to do things they have to do, things they are not proud of after the fact. This happens on both sides of any war. Another common theme one hears from combat veterans is forgiveness of their former enemies. They were "doing as they were ordered, just like we were". There are also those who hold a grudge, but forgiveness seems to be more common. That is just how people are wired, not all alike. What jars one may not affect the next person. Who is to say?

The next day I decided to stick with formation flying, though I hated it as much as the men did. I chose groups of men different from the groups of the day before. In actual practice, any man should be able to fly any position in formation, so I intentionally mixed things up. The first group did well, so we returned and I commended them. The second group did not start off so well. One pilot took off too soon and almost got caught in the prop wash of the prior SE. He was fortunate he did not stall or get thrown out of control. Once they formed up, I realized who the pilot was. So I watched him carefully.

He held position well through the first turn to port. Then I mixed it up a bit and signaled a turn to starboard. The pilot I was watching was in the forward starboard position. As the rest of the men turned starboard, he turned port. He immediately realized his mistake and pushed the stick forward in an attempt to dive under the forward port SE. He almost made it. His propeller tore into the starboard lower wing of the other SE, causing it to buckle and collapse around the nose of the errant SE. The two were locked together for what seemed like forever, then the errant SE broke loose and dove away. With no propeller, the pilot had to find somewhere to put down, which he did. He found a stretch of road next to a field. With no vehicular traffic, he landed on the road, but turned off toward the field as soon as he had slowed. The SE that had been hit posed a major concern. It now had two port wings and one starboard wing. The pilot had to handle it delicately, and eased the stick toward port to compensate for the unequal lift. Satisfied he had achieved level flight, he then nudged the rudder in order to fly back to the airfield. He still had power and a propeller, so it was a matter of keeping balance. While it seemed longer, he actually arrived in about a quarter hour. Escorted by other SEs, he landed first without further incident. I wondered to myself if we had another "Dirty Bird" on our hands.

Once I landed, I went to the CO right away to report the events of the flight. As soon as he had dispatched personnel to retrieve the stricken SE, I told him I had decided to take the offending pilot out of the scout program, if not the entire flying program.

"Lef-tenant, you may wish to reconsider. This lad has 'well placed' parents who will be displeased with your decision."

"Sir, I would far rather displease one set of parents than an endless number of them. This lad cannot maintain his concentration long enough to hold formation. We are lucky you are not starting another pile of 'we regret to inform you' letters right now. The lad flying the stricken SE has a gift, the knack to fly something when it is no longer able to be flown. He stays. The one who hit him? Finished. I will risk no more students. If you want to keep him in the RFC, that is up to you. I say no more piloting for him. Put him in a backseat or make him a bomb unit navigator. He's no good as a pilot unless they start giving credit for downing British flyers."

"Perhaps you are being a bit hasty, Lef-tenant?"

"Sir, yesterday I watched him wobble the whole time he was in the air. In addition, he had a near miss with the adjacent SE on a turn. Twice. Today he turned the wrong way and hit the next SE. Fortunately they were not both killed. They were tangled briefly before the offending SE fell away mostly unharmed. The one that was hit should have fallen apart, but that pilot recognized the danger he was in, coddled his stricken machine and brought it home. That was a fine bit of flying."

"You make a good case, Lef-tenant. Please put that in your reports and I shall see you no longer have to work with that pilot for the moment. I will submit your recommendations and—"

"Sir, if need be, I will talk to the pilot's parents. I am speaking the truth, so I am not afraid to face them. This lad is also risking his own life."

"I will keep that in mind."

* * * * *

CHAPTER 46

British

Fortunately it rained overnight and into the morning. Of course, I was drawn to the cafe and departed the airfield as soon as I could secure a motor-car. Almost there, I saw a familiar business-like umbrella and stopped to offer Pauline a ride. She was happy to take advantage of the offer since the winds were picking up. We sat at our table, ordered, and got busy catchingup on conversation. I was complaining about the sorry performance of the pilot who could not follow formation. It turned out she knew one of his parents from school.

"Troubled child from way back."

"Shame."

"He has never been able to apply himself to anything for any length of time."

"That is unfortunate. However, I must look at it through my perspective. How would you feel getting a letter informing you that Jeremy has been killed because a problem flyer was given just one more chance? Not so good, I would suppose."

"No, you are right. It is too bad. But maybe he can find something elsewhere in the RFC."

"Speaking of Jeremy, have you heard any further from him?"

"Why, yes I have. He is getting along famously with Major Campbell, who sends along his regards. I get the impression the brass hats, as you call them, like what you are doing with your trainees. Good for you! And, . . . good for me!"

"It's funny you would say that. I am always happy to be with you. But, . . ."

"But?"

"I have been wondering about *der Fritzen*. Is there any further word on them from Jeremy?"

"No, no mention. Why?"

"You know why. If there is a problem, I want to go solve it."

"I'm happy to hear that, Lieutenant. I've a bit of a problem of my own. Care to—"

"Love to. I could spend a lifetime solving that problem, yet it never seems to get any better."

"Such a shame, isn't it? Just keep working on it, Lieuu-tenn-annt."

"Yes, madam, I shall." I watched her nostrils flare. "But at the moment I am intrigued with *der Fritzen*. I was merely hoping for more information."

"I'm sorry, Lieutenant, nothing further on that front. Would you care to discuss my problem a little more?"

"But of course. Have you had enough to eat?"

"I've had enough breakfast . . . ."

I left the cornet in the motor-car.

It seemed I could get no further information on the Fritzes. Certainly they existed, but information was scant. It seemed my recent student had about as much information on the unit as anybody, though I was confident he had never faced them. Major Campbell would have seen to that. In talking with my CO about the unit, I learned he would not release me to go hunt for the Fritzes. While disappointed, I did understand he had a training base to run. Keeping me there only made sense.

"However, Lef-tenant, I will offer a small consolation."

"That is . . . ?"

"If Major Campbell or any unit commander in the area has solid proof your Fritzes are operating at the far north end of the front, I shall release you to go investigate. In the interest of keeping you up to date on the latest combat flying conditions, of course," he winked. "But you mustn't go it alone. You will need flying help."

"I would? I mean yes, I would. Perhaps Jeremy from my first class. I would have to look up that yank Wellington and see how he is coming along. I'll start organizing my help, sir. Just in case."

"Just in case. No promises."

"Aye, sir."

I had to consider the other side of the coin, so to speak, in my quest for information about the Fritzes. It was going into winter. Historically, warfare slowed down over winter. One wonders why they wouldn't set up markers and agree to resume fighting on a certain date. But if they could agree on that, then they could agree on whatever started the war in the first place and just stop the bloody thing. Ah, politicians. Best not to dwell on that topic. It could be a book. But the slowed fighting over the winter could explain the lack of information I kept coming up with on the Fritzes. Perhaps they weren't actively flying just then. Imagine that, "Take the winter off." "*Javohl!*"

* * * * *

CHAPTER 47

German

I became aware of the late afternoon sun streaming into Käti's cottage. I felt warm. Quite warm. Almost stifled. The fire still looked robust. I was under a blanket. I had my arm around a still somnambulant and lightly snoring Käti, who held my hand with both of hers. Too warm, yes, but I was not about to trade places with anyone. I was with a superbly wonderful woman, generous to a fault and possessed of a smile like no other. And she enjoyed my company. I moved my legs a little, about as much as I could, and stretched my free arm past my head.

"I love a nap in the afternoon. I find them so refreshing. Don't you?" Käti yawned and stretched.

"In my line of work, if you could call it that, naps are necessary whenever one can fall asleep. Buzzing about in the frigid cold with a constant blast of air going by while shooting and being shot at takes its toll on a man. The higher we go, the less oxygen is in the air—which makes the same tasks more difficult to perform. It is not unusual to find flyers passed out anywhere in the mess or in their quarters, even in the hangars or in the sun next to their aeroplanes. We all know that when we are needed no one will be shy about waking us up. But I can appreciate how you find naps refreshing. Thank you for sharing yours with me. I have enjoyed it."

"How long have you been awake?"

"Long enough to take in my situation, being a little too warm with a woman too good to be true, listening to the crackling fire and the gentle snoring of a very—"

"I was snoring? Why didn't you wake me?"

"Why should I? I don't think you would sleep unless you needed it. You were sleeping, so you must have needed it."

"But my snoring!"

"Your snoring poses no threat to the sawmill on the edge of town. Don't worry. If it gets too annoying I will let you know. But remember, I live on an aerodrome. Besides, what if I snore? Would you wake me?"

"Of course I wouldn't. And you do snore. Sometimes, when you are very tired."

"There you are."

"Okay. But if I ever—"

"I will."

"All right."

"Would you like to eat?"

"I would. Have you made some of your stew?"

"Hardly. I've been trapped back here behind you. And I was afraid of the growling bear outside the cave."

"Growling bear? You said my snoring wasn't bad! Gustav!" I blocked the pillow she swung at me, then wrapped my arms around her. No more pillows.

"Relax, *liebchen*. Can't I have a little fun?"

"At my expense?"

"I'm sorry. Would you like to go to the tavern and eat? Maybe say hello to Elsa?"

"Aha! You *do* want to have a little fun!"

"*Nein*, I did not mean it like that. Just hello.

"Oh, okay. I must hand it to you, though."

"What's that?"

"You do not mind sharing your toys."

"Please. If Elsa makes you uncomfortable, I would be happy to see what is at the market. I'll cook you something here."

"No. You need to relax and heal so you can go learn to fly. I know you want to take the aeroplane where you want to take it, not just go along for a ride. We can go to the tavern. You may say hello to Elsa."

"I don't want to upset you."

"Elsa does not upset me. I love Elsa. And that whole idea was mine. How can I blame you for liking my idea? You may be my *liebchen,* but you're still a man. I understand why you would like Elsa. Don't worry. I know where your heart is."

"As long as you're not holding a knife when you say that . . . "The pillow nearly knocked my head off.

A short while later we entered the tavern and sat down at a table. Käti made sure I could easily see Elsa behind the bar.

"Gustav, would you get us each a beer?"

"*Javohl, mein liebchen!* You want to make sure I say hello?"

"Elsa would enjoy seeing you. And I would like a beer."

"I will not be long."

"Good. I like my beer cold. Remember. Cold beer." I was relieved she had not brought a pillow.

I walked to the bar and waited until Elsa had a moment. When she saw me she stepped out from behind the bar and approached me. She kissed my cheek, placed her head against my shoulder, and stood there for a long moment while I lifted my arms around her. She lightly whispered, "I miss you, Gustav. I would like to see you again. You and Käti. I cannot get that night out of my mind."

"I am sure we can have another time together. Käti is just a little insecure."

"About what? Me?"

"She loves you. Never question that. Käti is insecure about herself."

"She is the most beautiful person I know. She doesn't need to—"

"I agree. She is beautiful. She is insecure because she doesn't look like you."

"She is silly. She is beautiful, especially on the inside. Her appearance is not important. Besides, my looks could change. You would never choose me over Käti."

"You need not be so hard on yourself, but I am very happy with Käti, yes."

"I can see that."

"Give her time. When she no longer fears she has created a monster, she will be all right. We cannot push her. Why don't we get together some time and keep it friendly and sociable? We can simply enjoy being together. Would that be all right?"

"It would. I can still miss you, though. You are good for me." I held her just a little tighter for a moment, then eased my arms away.

"Could I trouble you for two cold beers?"

"*Javohl!* I will bring them to your table."

"*Danke, mein schönes fräulein.*" Elsa held my head in her hands, kissed my cheek, and went behind the bar to tend to her customers. I returned to Käti.

"Did you forget something, *liebchen?*"

"*Nein.* Elsa will bring them in a moment."

"She wants to say hello?"

"To you."

"But we—"

"Work together, *ja.* Remember, she loves you, too."

"She does. I know. I'm sorry, I am simply . . ."

"I understand. You have nothing to worry about. Elsa is lovely, but I am yours."

"But she is so, so . . ."

"What? Slender? She is, *ja,* but looks do not make the person, at least not to me. What matters to me is what kind of person they are. You have shown me your mettle, and I very much like who you are—in addition to your good looks. *Liebchen,* there is no competition here. I am yours."

"You two make the best couple! I am envious." Elsa set two steins of cold beer on the table before us. "Just wave at me and I'll bring you more." Then she leaned over, put an arm around Käti, and kissed her cheek before returning to the bar.

"What did she say?"

"Nothing. She kissed my cheek, paused there, then went back to work. What was she supposed to say?"

"Anything she wanted, I suppose. She is not my puppet."

"She is sweet. You're right. I need to stop worrying. I'll go see if our food is ready."

"Someone will bring us our food, will they not?"

"*Ja,* they will."

"Let them. Relax. You are not at work."

"You're right. But it's so difficult."

"I know. Maybe we need to go to the tavern near the sawmill."

"We could, but the food is not as good."

"We will find somewhere else then. Or I will cook for you in your kitchen."

"Now I like that idea. When can you start?" I reached out my hand and Käti took it.

As if waiting for a signal, the food arrived. It was excellent and perhaps a little more than we needed. Despite that, I waved at Elsa for two more beers. A short while later Elsa arrived with two more steins. This time she sat toward my bench, nudging me over to make room. She reached for my hand and positioned my arm behind her with my hand on her hip. Then she rested her head on my shoulder, prompting Käti to ask, "Elsa, what is the matter? Do you want to come over after you are finished with work? If you do, we will welcome you. You are always welcome in my home."

"It's not fair to you two. Gustav is only here for a short time, so you two need the time together."

"Elsa, we both love you. You are not in the way. We enjoy your company. Besides, I could use your help keeping Gustav away from me so I can get some sleep." Elsa looked a little too happy upon hearing that remark. Käti pretended not to notice.

"I love you both. I will see how I feel when I finish here. Don't wait up for me."

"Just knock. I will send Gustav to let you in. Unless he's cooking for me, of course."

"I could still answer the door if I'm cooking."

"Liebchen, you are so helpful. Is there no end to your many talents?"

"You two make the perfect couple. You're so funny!"

"We're pleased you are so entertained. Back to the bar with you. Perhaps we will entertain you later as well."

Elsa kissed Käti on the cheek, then tripped as she turned to kiss me. I caught her and brought her over and mostly onto my shoulder. I winced a little as she squeezed me just beneath my sore left shoulder, then smiled as she kissed my cheek and righted herself before returning to the bar. I had no doubt she would visit us later.

Käti and I dared to talk a little about after the war. I told her how happy I was to have met her despite the circumstances. She joked that it was a new tactic she had tried to "meet that special someone" and I told her she should have picked another carriage to assist. I felt her thanks on my shin. I told her how delightful her cottage was, but she said she wanted something a little larger.

"Children?" I asked.

"*Nein*, well, I don't know. I have never had someone like you before, so children were never a consideration. I suppose I have been 'married' to work. It has served me well, but now things are different. If it happens, I will adjust. Right now, I am not making plans for any. I just want a little more room, nothing grandiose.

"You want Elsa to have her own room? Or at least her own bed?" I smiled.

"Ha! It would be more comfortable come summer."

"She would miss us." Again Käti thanked me via my shin.

"We would need another bath. Three people cleaning and grooming in one?"

"Three? With the two of you working, why would I have to?"

"You make a good point, Gustav. You could stay home to clean, launder, obtain food and supplies, cook, and tend to all our domestic needs. Perhaps I will keep my cottage and you could build a new bed and bath for us. Elsa would be happy with the current accommodations and I do not need such a large yard. Wait. You could raise vegetables. Do you sew? We women like our clothes."

"I can make shoes, but I don't think you or Elsa would wear them."

"You make shoes? Perfect!"

"My father taught me."

"You learned to make shoes from your father? Is it a family business?"

"*Ja*. He has a blacksmith shop and small stable." At least Käti chose to thank me via my *other* shin.

"Gustav! *Scheissekopf!*"

"*Danke schön, mein liebchen!*"

We decided we had had more than enough food for two people. As we stood up Käti asked if I wanted to go near the bar so Elsa could say her goodbyes. I told her it was not necessary since we would see Elsa soon enough.

"Oh, Gustav? When will we see Elsa next?"

"When will she finish here? She will knock on your door within an hour afterward."

"You sound confident."

"I find it helpful in my current line of work to know what people will do before they do it. Elsa will finish here, make herself more presentable, and come to your door tonight."

"If you are so sure, would you care to wager on it?"

"*Ja.* Loser makes dinner for tomorrow?"

"*Javohl!* I would like ham."

"I will eat ham, especially after *you* cook it. Make enough for three."

Käti stomped on my boot.

* * * * *

CHAPTER 48

German

"Gustav—someone is at the door."

"*Ja*. I will let her in."

"Her? How do you know it is a female?"

"It's Elsa. The knock is the same as the other time she visited, soft, timid, almost apologetic. If you object, I shall send her away."

"You will do no such thing!"

"I thought not."

I opened the door and there stood Elsa. She had changed clothes and she emanated a floral scent which I found very pleasant. "Elsa, it is so wonderful to see you. Please come in."

"I am interrupting. I should go."

"We were talking about after the war." "The lights are out."

"Our ears need no light to hear. Come in, you are always welcome."

Elsa stepped in and I closed the door. By the firelight I could see she carried a small basket.

"I brought something."

"Not chocolate cake!" Käti almost screamed, laughing out loud. Elsa and I had to laugh as well.

"*Nein*. Next time. I brought a bottle of my favorite wine. Would you like some?" "Elsa, you are wonderful," Käti said. "We would be delighted to share. *Danke*."

Käti opened the wine, I poured, and we talked quietly. Well, mostly they talked, largely about work and some of the people they worked with. I mostly looked at them as they talked, sipped the wine, and occasionally nodded my head. I could see the bond between them. I could feel it. They were outwardly discussing work, but there was an unspoken feeling. Immense love and respect. It was increasingly obvious that the two of them had shared an event, large and meaningful. There was an understanding. Elsa had said Käti had changed her life, and I was beginning to believe it was a literal statement, not merely a toss-off phrase. I would probably learn of it eventually, but perhaps I would ask Käti if the time were right.

We finished the bottle, a wonderfully sweet riesling. The conversation trailed off somewhat. Elsa looked a little sad and suggested that she should probably leave us alone. Käti and I both told her there was no hurry. While I wanted to say it, I waited for Käti to voice for the both of us, "Elsa, you need not leave. If you would like to stay,—"

"Käti, I have already been a nuisance. It's not fair to you. Either of you. I should go."

I approached Elsa from behind, rubbed the tops of her shoulders, then gently held her upper arms. "Elsa, did you not hear Käti? You are welcome to stay. Please stay. We enjoy your company." My hands slipped down to her forearms, pulling them slightly behind her. She clasped her hands.

"Are you going to tie me?"

"I had not planned to." Elsa looked sad. "Why, Elsa? Did you want to be tied?"

"The night I spent here, tied between you, was the most wonderful night I can remember. I felt warm, I felt safe, I felt free, I felt loved. I knew I could trust you both to keep me safe. I don't know how else to describe how I felt. I was secure, protected, and relaxed. I have not drawn a breath since without thinking of that night and the warmth and security I felt with you."

"Elsa, go to the water closet. Leave your clothes there. Return as you intend to sleep."

"I will be but a moment." Elsa loosed a few buttons, dropped her simple dress off her shoulders stepped out of it, nude, and entered the closet. She returned and stood before Käti, who removed the belt from her robe and handed it to me.

"Gustav, I gather you like this part. Please bind your toy." I did so as Käti removed her robe and went to bed. Elsa let go a sigh as I cinched the knot. I led her to the bed where Käti assisted her. I extinguished the candles and joined them.

"Elsa, are your hands—"

"I am fine. *Danke.*"

I went to sleep. Or tried to. It took Elsa a few moments to settle in. Against me. I slid my arm over her onto Käti.

* * * *

CHAPTER 49

British

"Damn, it's cold!", Jeremy exclaimed to no one in particular. While he was thankful for the building he got to sleep in, he was not fond of the constant draught. It always felt like someone had a window open, a silly notion with on and off snow flurries throughout the region. Hot water for washing up would have been nice, he thought, but he was grateful water still flowed at all. He had heard the stories of the frozen pipes, no washing up, and wet floors when the pipes burst. This was nothing like his comfortable, warm home just outside the business district where he had grown up. He remembered his father always telling him about the cold, hard realities of life, but he had thought that was figurative, not literal. But cold and hard seemed an apt description. "Thank you, Father."

France thus far had left a less than favorable impression on the fledgling scout pilot. Away from the "island" effect on the weather of being surrounded by water, it was indeed cold and not just a little miserable. That was on the ground. Bundled in every sweater his mother had sent him and another wrapped around his head and face, he was still incredibly cold aloft, even with all the heat thrown off the Hisso engine and radiator he sat behind. There were days when he wondered whether holding his hand next to one of the long exhaust pipes along the cockpit would give him any relief from the numbing cold, but he never felt any heat in his face when he looked over the side. He decided against it, preferring to retain what little warmth he might have had by keeping his heavy gloves on. Besides, after one of the first missions he had flown, he removed a glove after landing and felt the long pipe, finding it only marginally warm. It made sense, being at least six feet removed from the engine and surrounded by cold 100 mph slipstream most of the time aloft.

Like his instructor, he wanted to fly and kill Germans so he could return to Britain and proceed with his life. He was uncertain just how he wanted to proceed, but most anything would be better than taking off into the frigid atmosphere in an open cockpit aeroplane. While his father thought it would be good for him to carry on the millinery, Jeremy thought there might be more appealing options, something more glamorous. Then again, he had succeeded in becoming a scout pilot, fighting the enemy and making the world safe for Britons and their friends and allies, only to find there were not enough clothes in Britain or France to protect him from the damned cold. Maybe glamor wasn't all it was cracked up to be. Perhaps a career in law? Medicine? His mother had loved it when he played the cornet. She had bought him three of the wretched things—three! One was plenty enough, to be sure, so any additional must have been punishment. Some days he had really loved it. Other days he wanted to investigate its aerodynamic properties and launch it toward a wall. On some of the longer passages he thought he might pass out from lack of oxygen. And those tunes with variations by that French bloke—Urban? Arbuckle? They were enough to increase one's vocabulary. Of profanities. No, music was not a career option. Music could be fun, for sure, but not on cornet. Perhaps piano, like Mum, or some rhythm instrument—something that allowed one to breath more regularly than on a cornet.

"Well, here I am," he thought as he pulled his SE5a into the bitterly cold morning overcast, "the latest hot shit scout pilot, out to hunt down and kill any and all Germans who had the nerve to come aloft and face me. Anyone? Come take your medicine!" For the next ninety minutes or so every aeroplane he saw had blue, white, and red markings. Not an iron cross to be found anywhere. Well, perhaps twenty thousand feet up one might find a Rumpler traversing the lines, but that was not his mission that morning. He was a subscriber to the theory that Germans were indeed more intelligent people, what with the complete lack of opposition in the air. They must have the good sense to keep their air force on the ground except for the poor Rumpler crews doing reconnaissance over the Allied rear areas. With the prevailing winds, the Allies could drift over at any time, and it was easy to send up a few of

Fokker's triplanes. No sense flying if they did not have to. So the British were the de facto masters of the skies that morning. Yes, the bitterly cold skies, with snow. And sleet. At least keeping that "stiff upper lip"

wasn't a problem. The problem was keeping "stiff" from becoming "frostbite".

Setting down, Jeremy sought some hot cocoa to thaw his face. Oh, he would drink it eventually, but he first set it on the table and hovered his face over it to catch the heat. While the nerve endings in his skin regained their functions, he bemoaned his lack of air fighting. That was his purpose, fighting the enemy. Why could the Brits not do as the Germans? See any Germans in the air? Telephone us, we'll go up 'n' at 'em! Good God, the birds stayed in on days like this!

Jeremy ached for another shot at that bugger in the triplane with the vivid blue upper wing and tailplane. Flying the highest position, aft of the others on patrol, he had been surprised when the triplane had come out of a cloud behind him and walked a stream of bullets across his starboard upper wing. He was lucky the stream stopped just short of the cockpit. Was the heinie teasing him? The triplane dropped just in front of him and to the left. The pilot sprayed a quick burst at the others in the flight without effect, climbed without effort, performed a quick snap roll and disappeared into the cloud. Watching that level of dexterity in the air, Jeremy suddenly felt like he was flying a lorry. Oh, to have something like that to stunt about in! He would have to inquire. Hmm. Surely they had brought one of the little buggers down. Perhaps they could patch it up, and swap in a couple of Vickers guns and a Clerget engine? He had heard of a Hun chap who preferred the more powerful—and apparently more reliable—Clerget in his black triplane. Food for thought. In the meantime, he would have to fly a little higher and hope for the chance to dive down on one with both guns firing. That had to be the best way to combat one, for the SE would never hold one in a turn. Climbing with one was not possible. Maybe a quick burst at its tail feathers with the Lewis as it climbed away. That was probably the best of a set of poor options. The SE was more than a match for any other German scout, but the Fokker could fly rings around it, given the chance, other than all out speed. The best way to handle the aerobatic little Fokker was the way they dispatched that Voss bloke back in September: surround it with a squadron of ace pilots. They got him, but some of them were lucky to get back to their aerodromes. Voss' shooting had been good enough to cause several SEs to be rebuilt or scrapped.

With the cocoa cooling enough to drink, Jeremy took it along while he filled out his morning report. It didn't take long. Name, time, sector, aeroplane number, no activity. Maybe next time. Maybe. For the moment, more hot cocoa.

Jeremy followed Major Campbell into the mess. Since the major did not appear to be in a hurry, Jeremy approached him with his notion.

"Excuse me, Major? I have a silly question to ask."

"Son, I apologize for the poor quality quarters. Feel free to raid anywhere on the aerodrome for materials to slow down that draught."

"Why, thank you sir, but that was not the question."

"What's on your mind, son?"

"Well, I was recently attacked while on patrol by a Fokker triplane diving out of a cloud. I'm sure you have seen the reports."

"Yes, I remember that incident."

"Well, sir, I am a pretty good aerobatic pilot, and—"

"Yes, your last instructor was very enthusiastic about your ability to stunt about."

"Yes, sir. I am just curious about that triplane. I have heard a lot about its ability to fight in close."

"It is a remarkable machine. Quite the elusive crate at that."

"Well, sir, have we brought any down in serviceable condition?"

"We have brought down two. One has been sent to HE for evaluation. It was from Richthofen's unit, if I'm not mistaken."

"And the other, sir?"

"That one is down the road, so to speak, a mile or two, being stored at the unit where it landed. As I understand it, the engine was damaged and the pilot had to bring it in deadstick."

"What will become of it, sir?"

"Hard to say. They already have the one being evaluated. I doubt they need another unless that first one crashes or something. Why? Do you want to see it?"

"More than that sir. I want to fly it."

"Oh, a little stunting, son? The engine is bad and they need to—"

"No, sir. I want to fly it operationally. I believe the rumors have one of the Hun aces putting captured Le Rhones and Clergets in his triplane."

"Oh, yes, the chap with the black triplanes. He will supposedly pay a bounty to anyone who procures him an operational Clerget. More horsepower than the Oberursel that typically powers the triplane. And probably more reliable."

"Well, sir, I thought we could fix it, install a Clerget engine and two Vickers guns, and paint over the iron crosses—"

"And give it to you to fly!"

"Uh, yes, sir. I was thinking about that bloke Voss who flew the triplane so well. It took a squadron of aces to bring him down, and he still shot up a number of our 'planes. Since the Huns are flying a number of them, I thought having one on strength might be a feasible idea. The SEs cannot keep up with a triplane in close combat. If they can't dive on them, shoot, and keep going, there's not much they can do with them."

"You are correct. And your idea is not the worst one I've heard this week. But how do I justify giving a captured scout aeroplane to, uh . . ."

"To an inexperienced pilot, sir? Good point, of course, sir, but remember who trained me and sent me here—uh, to the front."

"Good point. Even if you never bested him in mock combat."

"True, sir. The old bird still has some good flying in him. Maybe you should bring him back here. I am the better flyer but he is the better combatant. He and I would make a good—"

"A good team, son?"

"Yes, sir."

"You would, at that. You with the little Fokker, him in a Viper powered SE . . . that would be interesting. I cannot deny that."

"Something to think about. Sir."

"Son, you intrigue me. Let me see if I can arrange to get that triplane brought here. Just don't be too disappointed if the brass hats don't buy it."

"Oh, no, sir. I think it's wonderful you are even trying. Thank you, sir." "And as far as getting your instructor reassigned,—"

"Oh, no, sir. I understand. Orders are orders, sir. As long as he is not working with out of date information. It has been a while since he was fighting at the front. Sir."

"Son, what are you planning to do after the war? Law? Politics? You have an uncanny way about you."

"Oh, I hadn't thought much about it, sir. I am engaged right now in surviving the war. Assuming I do that, I will think of something then. But thank you, sir. My father would be proud to hear that. He is in politics on a local level with an eye toward regional."

"I'm not surprised. If I make any progress on the triplane, I'll let you know. Just don't—"

"No, sir, I shan't. Thank you, sir."

With that, Jeremy got some more hot cocoa and went to sit by the fire and await further flight orders. He drifted off to sleep thinking about how he would have his triplane painted.

* * * * *

CHAPTER 50

British

The front that caused snow over France that morning extended over southern England and brought rain. That inspired me to take my cornet and go into town in hopes of running into my accompanist. Pauline was actually at the cafe ahead of me, sipping coffee at our usual table.

"My, but you are looking eager this morning."

"Oh? Does it show?"

"I can see it. What brings you out so early? A letter from Jeremy?"

"Well, he did write, but there is nothing of interest to you. Wait, I didn't mean anything by that. He is just frustrated, that's all. He says it is so cold they no longer get any of that 'white shit'! He also thinks the Germans are on holiday. He has not seen any in the air of late."

"No, I suppose not. They don't fly any more than they have to when it gets that cold. They keep watch to the west and roust out a few if we get blown over their lines."

"And there we have covered Jeremy's letter. I wanted to ask you about the American blues music. I was poking the keys yesterday and I have a number of questions."

"I'm sorry, ma'am, but I am not the one to ask. But if I should run across an authentic American blues musician, I shall bring them along to your parlor, where we both could stand to learn something."

"My, but you are the funny one!"

"Well, as I understand it, there aren't so much rules as there are feelings. While there are notes that imply the blues, they do not necessarily create the blues. There are different ways to approach the blues. Some say that a given solo should contain all twelve notes. Others say the blues can be expressed in a single note, if it's played right. Most interpretations fall somewhere in between. I think it comes down to how one feels and how one expresses those feelings when they play. Does that explain it?"

"Certainly. Now I have no idea what to play. This merits further study."

"No, this merits more playing. We learn by doing. We learn by making mistakes. Playing jass and blues is like flying. One needs to know what to do when something goes wrong. The way I see it, if a musician makes a mistake in jass or blues and no one notices, then he is a good player. The best just play and cover their tracks as they go. Is that any clearer?"

"Like a glass of prune juice, Lieutenant. I think you are correct. We need to go play. But I would like to eat first. Care to join me?"

That turned into a wonderfully challenging morning. First there was trying to be inventive and spontaneous on a full stomach, never easy on a wind instrument. And second, trying to keep a straight face when one of us would make a colossal blunder from which there was no recovery. Oh, and third, laughing uncontrollably on a full stomach. But we learn from our mistakes. Even if we sometimes repeat them.

Pauline made us some tea and we sat together on the chaise making small talk. She had been making some progress with her contacts, but nothing notable regarding Clara. She had skirted the issue with her husband once or twice but he either didn't notice or didn't care enough to respond.

"I need to go visit your husband."

"You *what?*"

"Well, several times you have told me I need a hat for that special someone. I cannot buy you a hat because you already have a garden of them in your voluminous hat box collection. So I suppose I am that special someone. I should like a spiffy hat, and your husband can take care of that."

"Well, yes, that is all true. You don't mean to bring up Clara, do you?"

"I don't know. I should like to, yes, but only if the conversation lends itself. I could ask him about Jeremy and somehow use that as a bridge. He does know about Jeremy's letters and how things are at the front, doesn't he?"

"Why, yes, he is Jeremy's father. Jeremy is important to him, of course. I am less important, naturally, being but a woman."

"Quite the woman, I must add."

"Why, thank you, Lieutenant. I'm pleased you think so. But women are not so important to him. Not even his customers, apparently, since he still employs a staff of men to design hats for women. So Clara will likely be of no interest to him. So try if you wish, but I would advise you not push the point."

"You are no doubt correct. But a little reconnaissance won't hurt. And it will be good to see the old bean. He has always treated me well."

"Agreed. Do reconnaissance on him. With me, you'd better be ready for an attack."

"An attack? An attack on you? Or from you?"

"I don't know. It depends on how that dog-fight goes." With that, she did her best "hun in the sun" and the skirmish began.

* * * *

CHAPTER 51

British

Back at the airfield, I dropped off the motor-car and the CO called me into his office.

"Lef-tenant, I just heard from Major Campbell. He sends his regards."

"Oh, jolly good, sir. How is the major?"

"He is rather cold at the moment. Snow flurries, a little sleet. He feels simply terrible that his pilots have to go up in the stuff. That is brutal. He keeps his patrols to a minimum and keeps a few pilots on standby at the field in the event the huns are up and showing signs of activity. You need to know he is rather taken with your star pupil."

"He is? Has the lad downed the entire *Luftstreitkräfte?*"

"No, hardly. But there is no lack of fighting spirit in the boy. He wants to take the war to the Germans every day. Campbell says the lad reminds him a lot of you."

"I'm touched, sir. Good to know. I'll be curious how he does come springtime when the Germans come out of hibernation."

"Well, I am told he has big plans."

"Oh? Do tell."

"Do you remember that triplane you saw back in September?"

"I shall never forget, that large face coming directly at me like he was going to land on my wing!"

"Right. Voss. Well, there are a number of the little devils at the front in addition to the Albatross and Pfalz types you have seen. They're all the rage. I cannot fathom why. They maneuver very nicely, from all accounts, but are very slow."

"I suppose, sir, it depends on how one prefers to fight. With the triplane, one can fight in close and low to the ground, circling until one gets a good shot. With something like the SE, one is better suited to diving on an opponent while shooting at them."

"Right you are. Well, it seems that your aerobatic student has taken a liking to the little Fokker. Apparently a nearby unit has one that landed on their aerodrome with a damaged engine. No one has any use for it since one is already being studied here. So your lad wants it. He wants to put a Camel engine in it and paint out the black crosses. Isn't that a treat?"

"Well, he is a natural at aerobatics. But he lacks combat experience. I can see him in Voss' mold, so to speak, with that squirrelly little triplane. I don't know if he is able to grow that mustache, though."

"Funny. He feels he should have the triplane and fly patrols with the SEs. I imagine he thinks he can save the day in the event of a close-in dogfight."

"Well, sir, I've heard worse ideas. But I don't know. I would have to see the triplane in question as well as the modifications he wants to do to it."

"Once they get the triplane to your old squadron, I will see if I can get you there for a day or two, in an advisory capacity. You could discuss the triplane and see what you can learn about combat conditions, such as they are. If you think the idea is feasible, I know we can scare up a Clerget and a couple of Vickers guns, whether here or over there."

"That would be jolly good, sir. I would enjoy seeing the major again. And maybe my student and I can come up with a way to end the war, eh?"

"Yes, see that you do. I shall keep you up to date."

* * * * *

Chapter 52

German

The Fokker triplane arrived by lorry while Jeremy was on patrol. When he returned he nearly forgot the cold, such was his excitement over the triplane. At a distance, on the back of the lorry, the Fokker looked great. He hoped it would look so good on the ground and assembled. As he walked around the lorry he made mental notes about the 'plane. The damaged engine was still dripping oil on the bed of the lorry. That barely registered to Jeremy since he already knew it needed to be replaced. He wondered why it was even brought along if it was no good. Beyond the engine, he noted a bullet hole needing patched. Some of the finish work was not as good as what he saw regularly on British machines. And the way it was painted struck him as odd. Accustomed to the PC-10 green/brown on upper surfaces and clear doped linen on bottom surfaces, he noted that the Fokker was painted a light blue on the under surfaces that had almost a turquoise look to it due to the yellowish clear dope applied over the blue as a sealant. The rest of the airframe was painted in irregular streaks. Some areas looked like the brush had been dipped in light blue and green-brown at the same time, then dragged in regular strokes in one direction on one part while other parts were similarly painted, but in different directions. Among the blue/green-brown areas were other areas doped with green-brown and grass green. At a distance the camouflage was effective, looking almost like splinters of color but blending in with the ground below. The only marking of any distinction was a white cowl over the damaged rotary engine, and that may have been a squadron marking.

The CO had seen Jeremy looking over his "prize" and bundled up to join him.

"Well? What do you think of 'er?"

"Sir, she's a beauty! She will need some work, but nothing too terribly taxing."

"Bear in mind, lad, that the maintenance personnel are already taxed with keeping SEs in the air. They can only help you if their squadron work is completed and they wish to help you. I know you have plans for it. I frankly cannot wait to see what you do with 'er."

"Well, sir, the first order of business will be to paint over the crosses with cockades and stripes of blue, white, and red. I don't want to be shot down in a heinie bucket before I shoot down any Huns with it!"

"Wise choice."

"Then there's the engine, sir."

"I am trying to get a 130 horsepower Clerget dropped off for it."

"Oh, ripping! Sir, you are the best!"

"I told you. I want to see this happen. I will help you any way I can, but we have a war to fight through proper channels first."

"Oh, if only my last instructor could see this!"

"He will. I'm working on getting him over here for a few days, in an 'advisory' capacity. He must stay current on front line doings, as you know. Even if any doings are few. He will just have more time to help with your project. Shame, isn't it?"

"You dab hand! Sir! How could this get better? He'll bring dope and brushes, won't he?"

"Hardly. We already have that here. It's getting a bit nippy out here. I think I'll get in. Carry on, lad."

"Thank you, sir!"

* * * * *

CHAPTER 53

British

It appeared we were under another stationary front. The ongoing rain kept me from flying and limited me to group discussions of various aspects of flying and fighting the war. These were helpful to the students and often rather lively in nature. Those left in the class were very enthusiastic. I only wish I had the "Dirty Bird" to offer them. Not that there was anything wrong with my Hisso SE. It received excellent care and it performed well. I rather enjoyed it, in no small part because I chose my own markings for it.

The good side to the stationary front was time spent with the inspiration for at least part of my SE's markings, not to mention musical and artistic ventures. We would sometimes overeat at the cafe and then go work it off, whether with music or exercise. Even indoors one could work up a jolly good sweat. I asked her one day about progress for Clara. She had little to report. So I proposed a scheme to jumpstart things for her.

"Lieutenant, have you been thinking? I think I smell the wood burning."

"Cute. But yes, I have been giving Clara a good deal of thought. Rather, her situation. And I have an idea that could possibly expedite matters. Possibly." "What do you have in mind? Taking her to meet my husband?"

"Why, yes." Thankfully she was already sitting, for her jaw only fell into her lap.

"I wasn't serious!"

"I am."

"Do you actually think that is a good idea? You know—"

"Of course I know how he is. But he has extended an offer and I feel it would be good to take him up on it."

"Yes, I remember, you were going to go pick out a hat."

"Think of it. His Majesty the king provides my wardrobe. I don't need a hat. But perhaps Clara does."

"No."

"Yes. Think, darling. There are other benefits as well."

"Such as . . . ."

"I arrange to take Clara to the millinery. She agrees not to mention her fiancé. She and I put on the appearance of a couple. A casual couple, not entirely serious, but enjoying one another's company. If there is any suspicion on your husband's part, that would throw him off the scent."

"I fear no suspicion—he barely even notices me—but I get your point."

"Anyway, we talk hats and work in how Clara is a nursing instructor and the rest of the story. Maybe she can even help design her own hat? I would imagine he would be open to some minor variation on one of his themes, right?"

"Well, for you, certainly. He is very grateful for what you have done for Jeremy."

"Speaking of, have you heard anything from your son?"

"Yes, I have been receiving regular letters. They don't say much. Due to the weather and a slowdown in fighting, he has a lot of time on his hands for writing his mum. I'm just happy he thinks enough of me to keep writing."

"Yes, I'm sure he does."

"Oh, he did mention some special project or aeroplane or something."

"Yes, I'm sure he did. He had a scrape with a German triplane similar to my September incident. The little bugger danced all amongst Jeremy's flight, shot around at them, then zoomed out of sight. Jeremy got the worst of it, but no one was hurt."

"Thank God for that! He didn't mention that in his letters."

"No, I'm sure he didn't. He likely didn't want to worry you. He is in a war, after all, and will get shot at."

"You are so very reassuring . . . ."

"Anyway, he has taken a real interest in the little Fokker—"

"What?! Oh, Fokker, the aeroplane fellow!"

"Yes. Jeremy has been interested in Fokker's triplane. He asked if Major Campbell knew of any triplanes not needed by the brass hats and the major found him one."

"He did? What is Jeremy going to do with a German triplane?"

"At the moment we're not sure."

"We? We're not sure? Are you part of this?"

"Not yet. But I likely will be, and soon."

"What are you—"

"Major Campbell knows the 'bond' between Jeremy and myself. He has arranged for me to visit the squadron for a day or two in an 'advisory' capacity. I will be talking with the pilots about conditions and tactics on the front so I am up to date on what is going on there. And I will help look over the triplane and advise the Major and Jeremy on what good it could be, if any."

"So you will see my son and maybe even fly with him again? How exciting!"

"I will see him and spend time with him, but I don't know about any flying. The brass hats are rather protective of their instructors. My experience is valuable for instructing new pilots, as you know."

"But how will Jeremy use this little triplane?"

"We don't know just yet. He has talked about flying patrols in it with the SEs of his unit. He thinks he could be useful in close-in combat, where the triplane excels. That could give the others in their SEs time to gain altitude and dive on the Germans Jeremy is occupying and distracting. The latter tactic is better suited to the SE."

"But won't his German aeroplane become a target for British gunners?"

"That is a possibility, to be honest, but we are looking into how to make everyone aware that he is on our side. I feel it's all in how the little bugger is painted. I think that once the black cross markings are eliminated, there should be no straight lines, no Union Jacks, or anything suggesting a cross. I think things should be kept round and blue, white, and red so it is painfully obvious that Jeremy is British. Once operational, I feel that the triplane should be escorted to various Allied units in the area so they know it is ours and no longer German."

"Sounds good thus far."

"I cannot guarantee you anything, but I can assure you the emphasis is in numbers. The idea is to mount larger patrols rather than let everyone flit about as they please. This increases safety and accountability. There are actually rumors about that a leading 'ace' is inflating his score with his lone wolf flights. Very few of his victories have been seen by anyone. Though he is a known liar and cheat, for some reason his claims are not questioned. Anyway, the Germans are almost always in swarms of half a dozen up to a score or more aeroplanes. Those are long odds for someone out on his own."

"I shall have to take your word on that, Lieutenant. You are, after all, an instructor. And I'll bet you know all the latest tactics, tricks, and deviations, don't you? Are you up for a lone wolf mission? Or do you prefer the safety numbers provide? Well, . . . what will it be, Lieuu-tenn- annt?"

That turned out to be a vicious encounter, but I am happy to report there were no casualties. I could only hope the stationary front remained so. I had some tactical considerations to work out for the next morning in the event it did.

* * * * *

Chapter 54

British

Jeremy pulled the wrench tightening the bolts holding the Camel propeller in place while one of the mechanics threaded the wire holding the cowl in place around the newly refurbished Clerget engine. Another mechanic was busy painting out the iron cross markings with white dope.

"It's been a long day, mates, but we've accomplished much. Many thanks for your efforts!"

"Aye, can't wait to see how she flies for you. Let's hope we have visibility between patrols."

"I'll likely taxi 'er tomorrow in order to get a feel for it. I don't want to fly 'er until I have the major's blessings. It *is* still a German aeroplane, and I do not want any confusion."

"Not willin' ta take a chance, eh? You know you'll want to pull on the stick once she's moving. She's no penguin! Show some respect, mate, an' take 'er into the air where she belongs!"

"Huh. What will it be, mates? Ale or cognac?"

"No schnapps?"

"Hah! I could ask Major Campbell if he has any captured stock."

* * * * *

CHAPTER 55

British

When I left Pauline's I drove to the nursing school to see if I could catch Clara free. I was told she was busy teaching class, but she would be available the following day at about that time. I left my name and a request the she meet with me at about that time.

The weather obliged the following day with a rainy morning. Eager to take advantage of the opportunity, I again visited the cafe and saw Pauline. We ate light fare and busied ourselves with music and then I told her I intended to meet with Clara that morning. Pauline asked to go along for encouragement and I agreed to the idea.

Clara came right down when I had her summoned, and the three of us sat down in a parlor. I told her of my idea to visit the millinery together and obtain for her a hat. At first she objected, but when I told her it would not cost me anything she slowly came around. I added that the underlying reason for the visit was to have her meet Mr Trafford and possibly approach the subject of her wanting to be a doctor. Pauline and I made her aware of our efforts on her behalf, which left Clara a bit stunned. I told her of the connection between myself and Jeremy, how I had assisted him, and how grateful his parents were. This was made possible by Clara's efforts on my behalf in that French field hospital. Jeremy's mum had already marshaled the forces she had, namely her social contacts. It was time to approach Jeremy's father, a member of the board of directors of the nursing school with other connections. I thought it would help to have Clara along when I approached the subject with him. While Clara was still a bit skeptical she agreed to come along. No harm could come of it, and she could always use another hat.

Departing Clara, Pauline insisted I come in with her for tea. Having worked out tactics in advance, I was the aggressor that day. As she finished her tea, I attacked, detained, and interrogated a "prisoner". When the scenario was over, Pauline complimented my on my plan of action. She also warned me that I would have to be on my guard in the future, as she would not soon forget what had befallen her. She followed her threat with a sly half smile, but couldn't help letting it blossom into a full smile as she pulled me in to a tight embrace.

* * * * *

Chapter 56

British

The next day dawned bright, clear, and cold. It was a perfect day to engage the lads in mock combat. I gathered my students, paired them off, and reminded them of the rules of engagement. I knew everyone wanted to win their combat, but I reminded them that we were all on the same side. They were to save the actual killing for the Germans. We broke off to get bundled up for flying in the cold. I had the maintenance crew roll out my SE and six others, and warm up mine and two others for the first flight.

I climbed out to about ten thousand feet. The cold was just as brutal as any winter morning. There were no clouds to speak of, so there was no hiding or surprise attack. I watched the first two students approach from roughly opposite directions in the vicinity of the old athletic fields. One rolled on his back and the other drove right at him. They did pretty decent rolls, a loop, and an excellent maneuver involving a stall and free fall. After a short while they ended up in the typical circle, each looking for an advantage over the other. After about five minutes of looking at each other across their merry-go-round, I fired a red flare, sending them back to the airfield in a draw.

The next pair were similar in nature, but tried a number of decidedly awkward maneuvers in an attempt at breaking the circle. They returned to the circle again and again, and I sent them back as well.

The third pair just looked a little more spirited. They were more aggressive and a bit more accomplished at their attempted maneuvers. They were up and down and all around the sky, but neither could get a clear shot at the other. As they settled into that horizontal circle, one pilot decided he would not stand for that. He pulled his SE up, as if to loop, but cut power, forcing a stall. That's when things went wrong. As he was sliding backwards, his opponent continued his path around the circle and saw the problem too late to do anything about it. The stalled

SE slid tail first on top of the circling SE, the tail section hitting the port upper wing and collapsing it. The two were now entangled and tumbling out of control. Though ten thousand feet seemed like a long distance, they covered it quickly and met the ground with an audible crunch. They fell near the edge of one of the old athletic fields and I set up to land. I had to be careful, as the grounds were a bit soft from the recent rain. I flew along the ground as long as I dared, losing speed, then stalling it down the last few feet so as to avoid nosing over while rolling. By that time, the whole mass of interlocked SEs was burning, probably from a ruptured petrol tank or severed fuel line. I tried to get to the pilots, but the flames kept me away. Neither was moving. There was nothing I could do but await the personnel from the airfield once word reached them. I ran back to my SE and pulled out my flare pistol. When one of the next two students appeared above, I fired a red flare to get his attention. He dove, waved as he flew over, and raced off toward the airfield.

I stood in the bright sun in order to get what warmth I could and cursed the situation. One pilot had tried something new and was to be commended. But the timing was just wrong and the other student didn't catch on quickly enough to avoid him. Fine lads both, we were now short two more pilots. They would never fire a shot in anger. I was furious with myself, even though there was nothing I could have done. I was furious with the British authorities for not allowing parachutes, even if it was questionable whether parachutes would have saved either lad in this case. It was just one of those things. Flying is dangerous. There are bound to be casualties. But in my mind the casualties should all be Germans. It was not realistic, but then again no one wants to see their favorite sports team lose. It was bound to happen.

In addition to the firemen and unnecessary medical personnel, the CO came out to pick me up so he could ask me about what had happened. He could see I was exasperated and did what he could to calm me. I knew what to expect. Carry on. Stiff upper lip. Work with the remaining students.

Ah, the remaining students. My class kept getting smaller. There was not much spirit in the room that afternoon as we went over the events of the morning. We discussed the various pairings and I made suggestions on how the pilots could have improved their tactical situations. I talked through the final dogfight, commending the pilot who had stalled his SE and using the other unfortunate chap as an example of why we needed to be alert at all times. One student wondered whether I was being a little cold and indifferent toward the latter pilot. I had to stop for a moment, gather myself, and tell them that I had to be somewhat dispassionate in my position. My job was to prepare these lads for something about which they had no knowledge, aerial combat. The simple fact was that the one pilot had tried something and the other was slow to react. I cared very much for all my students regardless of how they were progressing toward being scout pilots. Each was a human being and each had their own "gifts". If I sent a pilot out of the scout program, it was not because I didn't like them or care for them. It was because I felt they were not proper material for the scout program. They were better suited as bomber pilots or observers or mechanics or cooks. If I transferred someone out, it was likely because I did like them and did not want to feed them into the grinder of being a scout pilot in combat if they did not possess the requisite skills for it. Though I was but a few years older than the students, I looked on them almost as a father would his sons. I could not go into the whole parachute subject for fear of appearing insubordinate. There were limits to what I could voice opinions on, after all.

* * * * *

CHAPTER 57

British

The next day did not dawn. It couldn't. There were too many clouds, not to mention the steady rain. Before I left for the cafe, I called the nursing school and made arrangements to pick up Clara after lunch and visit the millinery. It was a certainty Mr Trafford would be there, at the helm of his empire. Pauline was already at our table in the cafe, thus confirming her husband was indeed at work. Not that there was any doubt. While looking pretty as always, I noticed she was looking a little worn, for lack of a better term. She had a little bit of a cough, but we both felt it was just a cold or something minor. There were far bigger things to discuss. She was both excited and apprehensive about my taking Clara to the hat shop. In her opinion a lot could go wrong. I knew it would be a little tricky, perhaps. I knew he would like Clara as my friend, a decorative woman to adorn my arm. I didn't know how he would react to her desire to be a doctor and not just a nurse. But if we made no effort on her behalf she would certainly remain a nurse. In life one must take chances in order to make any headway. How could he not be touched by the story of Clara's devotion to my wounds and my treatment in that field hospital in France when the doctors wanted to leave me for dead more than once. If not for her efforts, his son might have had a different course through his training. Because of Clara's devotion to her medical craft I was able to please him very much with how I treated Jeremy.

Ah, yes, Jeremy. Pauline had along Jeremy's latest letter. She informed me that they had painted over the German national markings and replaced the engine on the triplane. Jeremy had taxied up and down his aerodrome, but never left the ground more than a little, certainly no more than a few feet. I reminded her that once my class moved on I would be visiting Jeremy at his squadron. I was also curious about the Triplane. With more horsepower from the Clerget engine, it should be quite the animal to tame. I looked forward to taking her about the sky myself!

Other than the triplane there was no real news from the front. Fighting was very slow due to the winter and the attendant disagreeable weather. I hoped I could get there before the weather broke into spring, for the Germans were certain to launch an attack once they felt the winter was over with. I wanted to help my old squadron in any way I could. I liked the idea of the Fokker flying with the SEs on patrol. Unorthodox, yes, but like my upcoming bid with Clara's medical career, one had to try new ideas. Maybe they would work, maybe not. But one had to try, evaluate the results, and move on.

Pauline's cough was irritating her to the point where she did not want to play any music that morning. We kept a more low key tone to our time together. We spent more time than usual in the cafe, ordering some tea in hopes of soothing her cough. When the appointed time drew near, I dropped Pauline at her home and continued on to pick up Clara at the nursing school.

Clara looked resplendent and business-like. She had a build similar to Pauline's but was not quite so tall. She was ash blonde and had a mesmerizing pair of pale green eyes. While not the most attractive woman in a room, she was the most captivating with her distinctive eyes. This day found her wearing a black skirt, white blouse, and pale pink overcoat to fend off the mood of the weather. I complimented her on her looks and outfit before recapping our plan. I knew it was not necessary, but I suppose I was a little wary going in. It would be an uphill conversation to convince this board member that a woman could be an effective doctor, nay surgeon. Our cause would be well served by the points we had come up with, and I thought I could include his own experience running his business over the years to help illustrate the lifelong commitment Clara had to her medical career. It would not be easy, and it would likely not happen that day. It was, after all, a different idea, and people are so resistant to change. A woman could be a doctor. Just because it was very rare did not mean it could not happen again, here and now. Different had to yield to practical. We all have our "gifts", and Clara's was her dedication to healing people and taking care of their ailments.

I assisted Clara into the motor-car and drove to the millinery. Knowing Clara to be the independent type, I reminded her I wanted to open her door and assist her out for appearances. She readily agreed, and so it went. As it turned out, this happened under the watchful eyes we had hoped for, as the owner was just inside the door checking a display he had just had erected. Everything had to be just so, and so it was, with every hat showing to maximum advantage. He even opened the door for us as we approached. He looked most pleased to see my companion.

"Lef-tenant! Good afternoon! And good afternoon to you, madam! Welcome to my hat shop."

We bade him a good afternoon as well and entered the storefront.

"Lef-tenant, I was just thinking of you. I have received letters from Jeremy in France."

"Oh? How is the lad?"

"He is quite bored. It seems he cannot find any Germans who will come out and play with him."

"Perhaps it's the machine guns Jeremy takes everywhere he goes over there. They can put a body off."

"Clever! Perhaps that is it. Jeremy reports that due to the severe cold—too cold to snow— there is very little activity on the front. Do they wait for the spring thaw in order to prosecute the war?"

"Well, in effect they do. I would imagine one side or the other will initiate an offensive after the last frost. I'm pleased that Jeremy is well and keeps in touch. Please do convey my kind regards."

"I shall, thank you. Now, what can I get for you? I have some dashing hats that would look great on you, my fine lef-tenant."

"Well, actually, it's not for me. No offense, but I already wear some of your fine wares, courtesy His Majesty's Royal Flying Corps." "Ah, yes, and so you do."

"I had hoped my companion, Clara, could choose something for an upcoming occasion. Would that be possible?"

"Why, certainly it would. I am more than happy to assist. Madam, please do have a look around. If you don't see anything you like, talk to me and I shall have it made to order, ready within a week. May I ask the nature of the occasion, if that is not being too personal?"

"Yes, sir, it is for a graduation ceremony at the school of nursing."

"Oh, you are graduating? Why, congratulations!"

"No, sir, I will be presiding over the ceremony as one of the instructors."

"Dear madam, I do apologize. Please forgive my assumption, it was my mistake. I certainly meant no offense."

"All is forgiven. Indeed, how were you to know?"

"Mister Trafford, Clara here has devoted her life to the medical profession. In fact, I met her through her work in France."

"Oh? Dare I ask?"

I went through the story. Badly injured, left to die. Clara worked above and beyond to save my life and then my arm. If not for her selfless dedication, . . . and so on.

"Ahh. So, Clara, if I may, you have reached the pinnacle of your profession—unless you become headmistress at the school, of course."

"No, sir, I do not believe so."

"Well, what more could a woman want?"

"If you will forgive my saying so, what does my gender have to do with my career? I am hopeful that I can further my studies, become a doctor, and then move on to be a practicing surgeon."

"My, but you are quite the ambitious one. But it is not standard practice to put women in those positions. You have quite the battle ahead of you."

"But Mister Trafford, why does it have to be that way? There are few men who know as much as I do about the medical field. My work has been published in medical journals. I refuse to accept that my body parts can keep me from progressing in my chosen field. I am very good at what I do, and, no offense, but I have proof standing next to me. You think the world of the lef- tenant because of what he has done for your son. The lef-tenant is a good man. And though I hate to be so forward, my efforts kept this good man alive and enabled him to become what he is. Do you feel I should be denied the opportunity to achieve my dream merely because of my gender? It may be unusual, but as more women come along with my abilities, they, too, could advance in the same way. Then it would not be quite so unusual, would it?"

"Madam drives a good point. I cannot refute your argument, though I must say I have never heard such an argument coming from a woman. This is remarkable. Madam, you are likely not aware, but I sit on the board of directors at the very nursing school where you instruct. I shall have to bring you up to the other board members. Perhaps we can open a door for you. I cannot promise you anything more, but you deserve the opportunity at least to try. You make a very good case for yourself, and it helps that I have witnessed just how good a man your former patient has grown to be."

"Thank you, sir."

"And Lef-tenant, this sheds some light on you as well. I had no idea of what you had gone through to get where you are. I see it has been more than buzzing about the sky, to say the very least. My son is far the better for having crossed your path."

"Sir, you are too kind."

"Madam, have you found a hat to suit your taste? I swear, the two of you make for one smashing couple."

"Well, . . . thank you, sir, but we are not quite that couple. At least not at this moment."

"No?"

"To be honest, we only recently became reacquainted. I am most thankful for the opportunity to know this incredibly dedicated medical professional. I find she is also quite charming and, as you just heard, quite resolute. I am happy to count her among my friends."

That went far better than I could have ever hoped for. It appeared that the one board member was convinced immediately. What a surprise. That made me wonder what it was that he saw in Pauline, easily the most fascinating woman I had ever met. So many questions.

I dropped Clara off at the nursing school, only a little late. I made her promise to contact me when her hat was ready so I could take her to pick it up. Though she did promise, I also knew how she was. She might let me know, or she might not.

From Clara's, I returned to Pauline's to report on the meeting. I entered through the carriage house as she had asked me, but she was nowhere near. As there was no activity in the house, I decided to look around a bit. I did not have far to go. I found Pauline in the guest room, sound asleep on the bed. There was a sound, but it was not snoring. It was more like a rattle in her air passages. I had heard similar noises in the field hospital, among other places, the result of a gas attack. I would have to make note of it to her.

I did hate to awaken her, but she did want me to come report about the meeting. So I tried to make it as pleasant as I could. As she was facing away from me, lying on her side, I knelt on the bed and began to nuzzle her neck and ear very lightly. At the same time, I caressed the curve of her hip and dropped down to massage the small of her back. She loved these actions, and I knew fussing with her ear would do it.

"M-m-m-m-m . . . huh . . . ?"

"Pauline, it's your lieutenant, here to report."

She slowly sat up out of her slumber, accompanied by an amplified rattle of a cough. I did not like the sound of that.

"Oh. Did you see the old—"

"Yes, we did. In fact, he let us into the shop."

"How did it go? Did he like Clara? Did you ask about—"

"It went surprisingly well, I must say. There was no holding Clara back. She went right at him, making excellent points. While I thought he might throw us out of the shop, he was actually quite receptive. While he admonished her that hers was a most unusual quest, he did say he would bring it up to other board members. The whole key was the chain."

"The chain?"

"Yes, the chain of events. Clara used her not inconsiderable skills to save my life and limb. This enabled me to go through my flying experiences and use said experiences to instruct Jeremy. I didn't tell him what I do for you, ..."

That got me a pillow in the face.

"I should think you did *not!*"

Then some more coughing.

"Pauline, my dear, do you think you should have that cough looked at? Listened to? Checked?"

"No. I'm fine."

"You have a sort of 'rattle' when you sleep. I've heard it before. There is something wrong with your bronchial tubes, and it is affecting your breathing."

"I said I'm fine. You needn't worry."

"I shall show concern if I wish. I care for you deeply and wish to spend as much time with you as I can. Please take care of yourself. Forgive me, but I must return to the airfield now."

"Wait!"

"What is it, my dear?"

"The hat. Tell me about her new hat!"

"I can't."

"You can't? Why? You were there."

"Yes, quite obviously I was. But after looking at what was on display, she decided to take his offer and order something to be made."

"Bitch!"

"I beg your pardon?"

"She will have something unique then. Damn!"

"So?"

"You've seen my hats—you *know* hats are important to me! Do you not see the problem?"

"Oh. That. Well, now that you point it out, yes, I do understand. How thoughtless of me. Can you forgive me?"

I sidestepped to avoid the pillow hurtling at my head, then left the room before the missiles became more destructive.

* * * * *

CHAPTER 58

British

As the airstrip was too muddy for any operations, I met with my diminished class for a general discussion of flying, tactics, my experiences, ammunition and engine maintenance, and wherever else the talk took us in the realm of fighting and winning the war. There weren't many of them, but they were a good lot.

The following day was a continuation of the overnight rain showers. Naturally enough, I took my cornet and went to the cafe. I had the usual talk with the proprietor about goings on in the war and the airfield while I had coffee and cake. The person I was waiting for did not show up. Now that was odd. Hmm. But apparently something more pressing had come up. I lingered over more coffee and another cake, but it was obvious she was not going to meet me that day. Oh well. It will rain again, I thought, and I returned to the airfield.

The next several days were abysmal. The weather was nearly perfect for flying, and we got a lot of flying in. Mock combat was popular, formation flying less so. But I must say that the remaining lads were exemplary. They understood everything I showed them and caught on very quickly. A class of flyers like Jeremy? Well, no. But they were not far from that mark. Having a group like that to work with almost took my mind off Pauline. I was a little rattled, so to speak, that she did not show the last rainy day. I knew she was not truly upset over the hat exchange. We had been much crueler to one another on prior occasions with no repercussions. So that was not it. I kept thinking back to the cough. I found that disturbing and worthy of attention. Perhaps she had come around and gone to have it looked into. Her health was far more important than the two of us having breakfast and cavorting about.

But I was a little anxious for another rainy day.

Between activities, I sometimes stopped in to visit with the CO. We were in communication about the triplane at my old squadron, as well as any further information on der Fritzen. I had the impression they had taken the winter off as well, but that stood to reason. If there were not hot spots to tend to, then they were not needed. If they were an elite unit, they would not be wasted on mundane patrols. Let the silly Englishmen fly in the bitter cold. Let them check on the front line trenches, as if they were going to move or slip away during the night.

Apparently Jeremy had yet to go up in his "repossessed" triplane. I knew he was concerned that there was no confusion over the "strange" aeroplane, so he must not have finished his repaint. I was looking forward to my visit to France. I, too, wanted to go up in that Clerget powered Fokker. Thinking about flying that creation was one of few things that kept me up at night. Hmm. The Clerget was a rotary engine, meaning the entire engine spun about a stationary crankshaft and the propeller was bolted to the whirling engine. I mostly had flown the stationary engined SE5a since arriving at my scout unit in July, and only briefly flew rotary powered Nieuports in scout training and my first week or so at the front. This was probably an excuse to go up in a Camel, some of which were also powered by a Clerget rotary. Call it planning ahead. Or call it catching up. It depends on one's viewpoint, I imagine.

It happened that among the Camels on hand at the airfield there were two Clerget powered examples. One was being used by an instructor, and the other mostly sat in a hangar. The powers that be generally felt it was wiser to attempt to indoctrinate scout pilot candidates on the slightly less powerful Le Rhone engined Camels. The Camel was a tricky mount to control. The problem dealt with engine torque. Fighter aeroplanes were as light as they could be made so as to achieve maximum performance and maneuverability. This quest for light airframes had lead to some unfortunate results on both sides, as pilots would almost routinely exceed the airframe's capacity for maneuverability, resulting in collapsed airframes at altitude and the likely death of the overly exuberant pilot. But the Camel was a robust design. All of its heavy elements—engine, guns, ammunition, fuel, and pilot—were concentrated at the front of the fuselage. This, along with the spinning engine, promoted a strong gyroscopic effect which affected performance. Camel pilots liked to say that when all else failed, just "right turn them to death". Nothing could keep up with a Camel in a right turn, which "went with" the engine's rotation. It stood to reason that a less powerful engine would cause less rotational torque. The Camel was a handful to fly because of that torque, so training pilots mostly learned on the "tamest" Camels available.

I put in a request with the CO to fly a Camel. Naturally, I wanted to go up in a "tame" Le Rhone Camel first. Of course, the CO readily approved my request. I told him I intended to fly the unused Clerget Camel as soon as I could. Knowing what I was up to, the CO had the Clerget Camel looked over and put at my disposal.

After the day's flying was over with, I borrowed a Le Rhone Camel. After having her refueled, I got some of the men to swing the prop and down the runway I went. My first sensation was that I was not alone in the cockpit. No ghosts or anything supernatural. But she wanted to dip the right wing, ever so slightly as I worked the "blip switch" while taxiing. Reaching the end of the downwind taxi, I released the switch for increased power to turn left and get into takeoff position. The left was almost difficult, and the right wing nearly dug into the ground. As the engine went to maximum power, the 'plane quickly accelerated into the wind. And the right wing kept reaching for the ground. I had to push the control stick to the left and apply left rudder to counteract the torque. I continued pushing to the left a bit as the tail quite leapt off the ground and the entire airframe ceased rolling and commenced flying. Suddenly, like the SE, the Camel just seemed happier. After all, the wheels were only a necessity for its time on the ground. The machine was designed to fly. And fly it did. The sound and feel were very dissimilar to the stationary engine SE. I could not take my mind off the feeling that she wanted to turn right. Oh, she would most certainly turn in any direction with minimal effort, but she "wanted" to turn right.

I took her to about four thousand feet so I would have some recovery room, and then I started to play with her. She was quite unstable and heavy in the tail. Knowing she wanted to turn right, I started with left turns. Gentle left, hard left, climbing left, diving left, stall . . . to the right. Ahh, she was fighting me, trying to impose her will. It seemed any time I stalled her, she dropped her right wing. Almost as a challenge. "Control *me*, will you?" She was feisty and coy. Not demanding, but often pushing. Not annoying, but always on the mind. She was definitely a hands-on girl, this one.

After a few more left turns, (after all, I held the stick, didn't I?), I teased her with a wide right turn and then a modest dive to gain speed for a loop. She was right with me. It was so easy, like she wanted to do it again. "C'mon . . . "After another loop, I rewarded her with a gentle, sweeping right turn. "There you are . . . ready?" She was. I went from a sweeping right to a sweeping roll, slowly, the right wing leading the way. I could feel her. She was furious. But she was right there with me the whole time. So I rewarded her with a complete turn to the right. All the way around. She sang. Gentle dive, quick, hard loop, extend the exit a bit and then a snap roll to the left. Oh, she screamed and dropped that right wing and around we went, twice, thrice. I swear she thanked me, though she was certainly not breathless. I gave her yet more, dropping her right wing and executing a series of right turns. They were not unlike the left turns that initiated the sequence, but she was no longer fighting me. I used the last diving right to go into another loop. That led into another, slower loop, and then we gently descended in a long, slow spiral to the right to return to the airfield and land. She had been magnificent.

On my final approach, I saw I had attracted a crowd. As I touched down, the throng dispersed to the sides of the runway. Several lads caught her wingtips and pointed me to her slot in the flight line. I shut her down and someone chocked the wheels, and a ladder appeared at my side. The CO himself climbed the ladder to help me undo the lap strap.

"I thought you didn't care for aerobatics."

"I don't."

"Then who was with you up there?"

"I don't know, but she was quite the partner."

"I'll say she was. That was a fine display. Not perfect, but well executed. I'll bet that with the Clerget engine, some of your tweaks, and more time in the air, you will outfly your star pupil from your first class."

"Jeremy? I already outfly him."

"No, Lef-tenant, he handily outflew you. But with your combat experience and that extra sense you have developed, you always defeated him. There is a difference."

"Why, thank you, sir. I think."

"I would wager that the two of you, together in matched high performance aeroplanes, would be quite a show to watch."

"You think so, sir?"

"Certainly. Perhaps you two should investigate that after the war?"

"Perhaps, sir. But first we have to *win* the war."

"True enough. Lef-tenant, do you want to take up the Clerget Camel"

"Oh, no, sir. I need to savor this moment and rest up a bit. Tomorrow should be another day. Perhaps then?"

"Certainly. We will all look forward to it. I will consider selling tickets!"

"Quite humorous. Sir, if you will kindly give me a hand out of here, I should gladly buy you a drink."

"I had hoped you would offer."

Once I finished eating, I went to the hangar where the Clerget Camel was waiting. I could smell the petrol and castor oil—the two were mixed for rotary engines, a curious mixture that lubricated the engine as well as provided combustible material for detonation. The lads had looked her over. That was all well and good, but I intended to fly her and soon. I wanted to look her over myself. I took my time with her. I had nowhere else to be, no reports to fill out, and no chance for rain. Looking over spark plugs, control wires, flying wires, landing wires, and whatever else I could think of took up my evening. Then I returned to my quarters to relive the afternoon flight.

I had found the flight in the Camel a moving, satisfying and liberating experience. I had always enjoyed the power, maneuverability, and stability of the SE. The SE was an extremely dependable mount, other than the geared Hisso engine, which could quit, foul, or even fall off the aeroplane at any time. While most of my SE time was with the direct drive Wolseley Viper, my experience instructing with the geared

Hisso had also been good. But the Camel, even with another 'spirit' on board, had allowed a freedom in the air I had never felt. I was not going from a lorry to a touring car. But it was perhaps going from a touring car to a racing car. Things happened more readily. I would imagine that more time in a Camel in order to grow more accustomed to the strong gyroscopic effect would result in increased freedom of flight.

Then I mused about fighting in a Camel. While the SE had a synchronized Vickers gun in front and a Lewis gun overhead, the Camel had two Vickers guns mounted immediately in front of the pilot. How would the Camel respond to guns and maneuvering?

So many aspects to consider. I would most certainly fly the Clerget Camel on the morrow.

* * * * *

CHAPTER 59

German

A strange pattern was developing. It seems most men find a woman, one woman, and are very happy with that one woman. I had found Käti. Well, actually she had found me in less than perfect circumstances. Fabulous woman. Oh, I was grateful for her having helped me, possibly saving me from bleeding to death. But beyond the medical assistance I found she was incomparable for companionship. We had fun merely being together, whatever we were doing. Then there was Elsa. Elsa had found her way into my life with what appeared to be a tease and a warning not to hurt Käti. But, through furtive looks and more teasing between the three of us, she had become a part of the "perfect couple". Käti seemed to have no objections, and Käti was not shy with her opinions. I was sure any other woman would have drawn daggers. But she could care less about Elsa. Typically I would arise with Käti, make her coffee and breakfast, and she would go open the tavern while Elsa, usually nude and often bound, slept in and then spent time with me before going home to change clothes for work. I began to wonder whether Käti was serious about adding on to the cottage so Elsa could live with us. I was a little uneasy with the foreign concept of two women. I decided not to worry about it. I had a war to fight before I could move on to domestic matters.

There was a slight delay before I could get to *die fliegerschule,* but the day arrived when Käti and Elsa accompanied me to the railway station. Standing on the platform with bags in hand, I had two remarkable women kissing me goodbye, one on each cheek. Sitting down in the carriage and waving through the window, I wondered if the two of them would be living together when I returned.

* * * * *

CHAPTER 60

German

Arriving at *die fliegerschule,* I was asked whether I minded rooming alone. I saw no difference, as I was there to learn to fly, not necessarily to socialize, and I told them so. I dropped my things in my room and sought out my classroom, where I was to be told again about weather. *Ja, ja,* there were reasons for the clouds and how they looked. I was not there to hold my head in the clouds. I was more interested in the stick and rudder. But bureaucrats need something to do, and structuring flight training was one of those things. I would learn more about the sky and the clouds *für das Vaterland.*

The next class more than made up for the weather class. We were to learn the basics of the engine and how it worked. This was more for me, even if a lot of the material was not new to me. I paid attention just in the event there was something to learn. I was something of a thorn in the instructor's side with the questions I asked, most of which were beyond the scope of the class.

From there I went to learn about the theory of flight. It was all about Bernoulli's Principle and how the shape of the wing aerofoil caused the wing to lift the aeroplane and allow flight. All this technical information was rather exciting, so I enjoyed my time there.

Finally I attended the gathering I was there for. The setting was less formal, in a hangar, but the information was critical. We were shown on a mockup of a cockpit what the controls were and what they did. I had been shown the basics, so I knew something of the content, but this more thorough demonstration filled in some answers to questions I had had before. We were told that the next day would find us taxiing and beginning to get the feel of the controls. I, for one, could not wait. I was free the rest of the afternoon, why not start right away?

This became my routine, clouds, mechanical matters, theory of flight, and aeroplane. I was pleased in that I seemed to grasp it all better than many of the others. I was there to learn. I wanted to get back to my *Staffel* and help win the war. Sometimes I mused over what color I wanted my *Albatros* to be. Then I snapped back to the reality of the situation. The color did not matter. What mattered was that it flew and delivered bullets where I aimed them, namely at the English and French flying before me. The bullets were all the same color.

My instructor kept insisting I was clumsy with the controls. My basic taxi had been fine, but as soon as I did anything that brought the control surfaces into the picture, I did nothing to his liking.

"Model, you perform the functions I ask you to perform, but your form is poor. I cannot fail you, for you complete every assignment and have not crashed an aeroplane. In some cases you have been lucky. I will pass you, but hear me say: You need work."

"Javohl, Herr Leutnant! Danke."

Having passed through *die Fliegerschule,* I learned I was to be assigned to an artillery observation *Abteilung,* flying older *Albatros* C Types. That would not do. I telephoned Jakob and complained. Was there something he could do? I was anxious to get back to *my Staffel.*

"Gustav, I am touched that you miss me. But Jure has returned and I do not need another Hanna pilot right now. However, I will talk to friends on your behalf. Remember, Gustav, walk, then run. Fly the *alte frau* for a few weeks, then go to *die Jastaschule.* By then I will be able to have you back. Don't worry. I will not let them end the war without you!"

"Danke, mein Herr! Your advice makes sense."

"A-ha! I see you forget already. *Nicht mit der 'mein Herr'!"*

"I apologize, Jakob. But on my first day here I was in all kinds of trouble for *not* saluting!"

"That is funny. It is I who should apologize. I will make it up to you, Gustav. The *Albatros* conversions are going well. We achieve more successes because the English don't think we can dive with them. Imagine their surprise! Willi shot down a SPAD the other day—in a dive! And SPADs dive like bricks! I will have your Albatros waiting for you with your very own color in front. Unless you wish to choose your color, of course."

"No, *mein—uh, Jakob!* I will be proud to fly for you whatever the color. *Danke schön!*"

So I went to my assigned unit and flew the old *Albatrosen.* I must say that Jakob's advice was good. While I tried to emulate his wonderfully smooth flying style, I found it was not so easy as it felt. Everything he did seemed without effort, but my efforts seemed to be a series of overcorrections. During my first week I had three observers complain about my flying. One had become airsick. For the first time. The *Führer* suggested I take up another, more experienced pilot and fly behind the lines, which I did. This was enlightening. After a brief time in the air, he indicated I should land. I returned to our aerodrome and bounced the old bird down to something of a landing. We both clambered out of our cockpits and onto the ground.

"*Vicefeldwebel* Model, the solution to your problem is simple. Relax. Go with the aeroplane. This *alte Albatros* is a very docile and forgiving machine. Work with it. You are too stiff and controlling. You fly like you are conducting a marching band in a parade. You need to think more like a waltz, something smooth and relaxing. The American, Joplin, and his ragtime. If you want a smooth flight, you must work the controls in a smooth manner. May I show you?"

"*Javohl, Herr Leutnant!*"

"*Ja,* spoken like you fly. So military. Fly the aeroplane like you are talking with your woman. Be soft, be gentle, show respect, don't be so controlling. Please step into the rear office."

I could have sworn Jakob had stepped into the front cockpit, the flying was so incredibly smooth. Same aeroplane, same day, same prevailing weather conditions, completely different flight. After a few moments the *Leutnant* set down like he was rolling down a ramp. Only the rough texture of the field got in the way of his perfect landing. He turned around to face me.

"Now you fly again."

We exchanged places and I took off again while aping his moves. I allowed the machine a little leeway as we traversed the sky, as if we were conversing. After a brief flight, I brought us in and set down, mostly gently, on the field. As the ground crew caught the crate yet again, the *Leutnant* stood and placed his hands on my shoulders.

"Now that was much better, *Herr* Model. If you continue to fly like that, I will go up with you anytime. Were you thinking of your woman?"

"Ja, I was."

"See? Treat your aeroplane like a lady and she will be good to you."

"Danke schön, Herr Leutnant!"

"My pleasure."

* * * * *

CHAPTER 61

German

I had the scare of my life the next day. I was assigned a *Leutnant* who briefed me on the mission at hand, yet another artillery observation run. He had me fly a slightly newer bus than I was used to. Slightly. That bus had a wireless set installed, so the *Leutnant* could lower an aerial and signal his unit in Morse code. He told me where our sector was and that he would guide me as we neared the area. Fair enough. We climbed into the aeroplane and got strapped in while the engine warmed up. Satisfied all was ready, I waved off the chocks and we were pointed downwind. At the end of the field I kicked the rudder to turn around and proceeded to take off. All went well until I got a little over five hundred feet in the air, when the engine sound changed from a roar to a sputter. This was the very worst time for an engine to quit, as the engine-driven propeller created all of the airflow over the wings on takeoff. To put it in terms of Bernoulli's Principle, the wing airfoil lacked the requisite airflow to create lift. The big biplane promptly stalled, slid backwards a little, then dropped its left wing. I heard the *Leutnant* behind me screaming, "Turn around! Turn around!" But I knew that was the very thing *not* to do. I put my nose down and looked for a place large and flat enough to land on while fussing with the air/fuel mixture control and magneto switch. Nothing would bring back the roar we so desperately needed. I could find nothing in the way of open fields or empty roads. Worse yet, there were utility wires ahead and I was too low to fly over them. On a positive note, there was a big fallow field beyond the wires if I could get past them. The *Leutnant* managed to notice the wires as well. I heard him back there cursing and pleading with Mother Mary to get him out of his mess.

I didn't think I had enough room between the two poles to squeeze the big barge through, but I had a plan. So did the *Leutnant*. I heard kicking and scuffling behind me. I glanced over my shoulder and found he was climbing onto the edge of the cockpit. "To each his own," I thought, "I'm staying with the bus." I heard a scream, then nothing beyond the sputtering engine. But my tail suddenly felt about one hundred and forty-five pounds lighter, give or take. I stuck to my plan. With nothing to lose, I kicked the rudder a little to the right as I approached the wires above me. The crate turned on its vertical axis, effectively reducing the wingspan passing between the poles. I also cleared the wires. The problem was that I hit the field beyond the wires at an odd angle thanks to the crabbing move. My wheels hit the ground and the tail kept coming around. Now unencumbered by the landing gear, the crate was free to spin around as it pleased, and it pleased approximately one and one quarter rotations before coming to a rest. I was strapped in tight, but my arms and head flopped freely around. I was alive, I was okay for the moment, and I knew I was going to be sore later.

I sat there while the world stopped spinning, both externally and internally. My neck was tender, as were the backs of my hands. After a few moments I started to undo the harness so I could try and climb out. I could smell no *benzin,* so I was not worried about fire. It just seemed a smart thing to do, get out of the crate. As I started over the cockpit side I glanced behind me to see a group of people gathering around the *Leutnant.* I started to walk in that direction, and a few of the people came to meet me. They told me the *Leutnant* was *kaput.* What a shame. If only he had trusted me. Even if I was only lucky. One of the men, a tender driver, offered me schnapps and I accepted. I tossed a little down of offered it back to him. He just waved it off.

"You need it far more than I do. I will get more."

Of course I was not done with the episode just yet. There was a mound of paperwork to be filled out and processed. And I was brought before several officers to explain what had happened. I told them. I got to five hundred feet and the engine quit. I looked ahead, found somewhere to put down, and did so.

"Why did you not restart the engine?"

"I tried. It must have had some contaminant in the *benzin.*"

"The poles were too close to fit through."

"I had no choice, so I crabbed it around to fit."

"You ground looped. And you destroyed an aeroplane."

"Hitting the poles would have done at least as much damage. There was no saving it for tomorrow."

"What about the *Leutnant?*"

"Ask him. I was trying to land the crate, so I was more than a little busy. He apparently did what he thought best."

"If you will pardon me, . . . " It was the *Leutnant* who had been up with me the day before.

"What is it?"

"I was circling the field when it happened. I saw the whole incident. The engine apparently quit. The aeroplane stalled, and *Vicefeldwebel* Model found somewhere to land. His passenger was throwing a tantrum from the moment they stalled. He jumped rather than trust Model, who performed a pretty remarkable feat. He lost the crate, but he did his damnedest trying to save it. I doubt I would have done any better. I give him credit for not trying to turn back. Then we would be without the aeroplane, both crew members, and who knows what else on the ground? Don't punish him. He will learn from this. That is his nature."

The officers talked among themselves for a while and then faced me.

"That is all. You may go."

It was fortunate the *Leutnant* happened to see the stall and subsequent crash. I knew I had done nothing wrong, but it helped to have someone of superior rank witness the sequence of events. I thanked him for taking the interest and speaking on my behalf. Without his statement it would have taken longer to exonerate myself.

"I merely reported what I had seen. There was nothing you could have done to improve the situation. You didn't tell the observer to jump. And it was unusually wise of you to put your nose down and continue flying straight ahead. Most pilots would have tried to return to the airfield and land."

"But with no lift . . ."

"Precisely. You pay attention to what you are told. And trying to crab the machine between the poles? Very creative at a time when most simply would have panicked."

"I tried to save the aeroplane, *mein Herr*. I failed."

"You made the best of a very bad situation. You have nothing to be ashamed of."

"Danke, mein Herr."

"You are the one marked to go to *die Jastaschule.*"

"Javohl, mein Herr."

"Come with me. I have just the thing for you."

We talked about flying while he led me to the end hangar. We pulled open one of the doors and he gestured for me to enter.

"Vicefeldwebel Model, would you care to fly a *jäger*? By current standards this is an *alte frau,* but you will get the general feeling of a smaller, lighter, more maneuverable aircraft."

"Ja, mein Herr." We were standing by an *Albatros,* but one with square, equal wings. He told me it was a D.II model.

"With a more powerful engine this would fly with most anything in the air. It is less maneuverable than the D.III, perhaps, but it won't fall apart in a dive. Like everything in life, there is a compromise. Funny, *Albatros* tried to fix the D.III but they only made a slightly prettier 'plane. It's heavier than the D.III, no better, and the wings still depart pulling out of a dive. And the headrest? When I go hunting for Frenchmen or Englishmen, I am not relaxing by the fire. The damned thing succeeds only as a blindspot."

"The *Jastaführer* of the unit I will likely join has refused the D.V models and kept only D.IIIs."

"Ja, and I hear rumors that the D.IIIs are to be modified so they are stronger in a dive."

"Ja, mein Herr, and given stronger engines and a rounded nose. They will also be faster. We should be able to hold our own with the newer Sopwith types and the SPAD. Maybe better."

"Well, we need something. I like Fokker's little triplane, but I don't see much use for it. Maybe for home defense. They climb well and could be used to intercept bombers and observation aeroplanes. No matter. You and I will not solve all the problems talking here. Would you like to take this old bird up and have a look around?"

"Javohl, mein Herr!"

It was my first time looking at an *Albatros jäger* so closely. I had seen *Albatrosen* before, but that was not in the context of flying one. They were being flown by others. This time I was to take one up, so I was looking at it closely. Compared with the two seat two bay biplane *Albatros* I was then flying, the D.II was miniature. It was a single seat single bay biplane and just smaller in every dimension. I could only imagine the difference in performance. We summoned a few of the ground crew to assist pushing it out into the light and onto the flight line, where it was checked over, fueled, and armed. I was assisted into the cockpit and strapped in before going through the starting sequence of pulling the propeller through to fuel the cylinders and then cranking the magneto. The engine came to life more quickly than I had anticipated. When the temps were nearly where they needed to be, I waved the chocks away and started my taxi down the runway. While I knew it was underpowered by *jäger* standards, it was quite lively to me. Same engine, smaller airframe. I kicked the tail around and pushed the throttle forward, allowing the engine to push me back against my seat. This was going to be a wild ride, at least for me. "Smooth," I thought, "keep it smooth." I brought the tail up and soon thereafter lifted the little *Albatros* off the ground. The additional power gave me confidence and I pulled the stick a little farther back than usual, increasing my rate of climb. This was fun! I loved the little thing and I had yet to turn it, never mind any kind of aerobatics. Aerobatics. I was thinking ahead of myself. No aerobatics. Yet. I was content to turn this way and that, dive and zoom into a climb. More turns, climbs, and dives into more turns. I was having the time of my life, but at the same time realizing how much more I had to learn. I had watched the *jäger* pilots and the English scout pilots fly. I would need my time in *die Jastaschule*. Then I wondered if I would have to learn even more about the weather.

Though I felt like I had only just climbed out, I set the *Albatros* down and rolled it up to where I had climbed into it. The *Leutnant* assisted me out of the straps and guided me down to *terra firma* and asked why I wasn't more excited. "You did not like the little *Albatros?*"

"I did like the *Albatros, mein Herr*. It's a fabulous aeroplane. It climbs and turns very easily as opposed to the barge I usually fly. But as I flew it, I realized I did not know all the things I needed to know to be a *jäger* pilot. I must get to *die Jastaschule* if I expect to survive flying at the front, much less maneuver my way behind the English scouts so I can shoot at them. It's a completely different style of flying."

"Do not feel inferior. You simply need more training. That flying is not all that difficult once one has the chance to learn and practice it. There are no secrets. There are good tactics to employ and there are favorite situations to maneuver into, if you can. But you must be spontaneous, flexible, nimble, and alert. You should already know to keep looking around at your surroundings. Never stop moving your head. That is the best advice I can give you, always know what is around you. The greatest aerobatic abilities will not save you if an enemy catches you by surprise."

"*Javohl, mein Herr!*"

When do you want to begin *die Jastaschule?*"

"Tomorrow."

"Ha! I like it! Let me see what I can do. I will talk to some friends and check your flying record here. Unfortunately, I think you will need more time to prove yourself a better flyer. But I will keep a close eye on you. I know you have had certain 'assurances'. But I cannot let you get ahead of yourself. It could be deadly to you and the others in your *Staffel*. You do understand."

"*Javohl, mein Herr*. I understand, but I am still impatient. *Danke schön.*"

The *Leutnant* departed and I assisted the ground crew as they pushed the *Albatros* back into the hangar. While frustrating, the flight was wonderful in and of itself. It helped whet my appetite. I knew that I must keep improving my flying so I could advance myself. It was good incentive.

I found the *Abteilungführer* and asked if he needed me to fly any more that day.

"I will see, just a moment. Was that you in the D.II earlier?"

"*Javohl, mein Herr.*"

"*Wunderbar*. How was it?"

"Different. Very different."

"I know it was. Did you like it?"

"*Javohl! Mein Herr,* compared to our usual *Albatrosen,* it was like an infantryman shedding all his equipment and running."

"*Ja . . . .*"

"At the same time, I realized I'm not ready to utilize it fully. I have much to learn."

"If you can maintain your current level of flying, you will be at *die Jastaschule* before you know it."

"*Danke, mein Herr.* But I will not get ahead of myself. I am still here and I will serve you well."

"You have served me well, Model. But now you understand flow and style. You are a whole new man in the air. The observers talk. They say nothing but good about you. Even after your recent crash landing, you receive praise for your flying. It was a shame about the *Leutnant,* but we all know he caused his own death by leaving the aeroplane. Had he stayed with you he would have lived."

"*Danke, mein Herr.*"

"Model, you may relax today. If someone takes ill I will find you, but I have you next flying tomorrow at eight. Go dream about your flight. The newer *Albatrosen* are better flyers than that old crate. That will give you something to look forward to."

"*Javohl! Danke, mein Herr.*"

That afternoon set the tone for my flying thereafter in that unit. It seemed I was the preferred pilot, or at least one of them. There were some veterans there who flew like they were on rails. They looked like Jakob in the air, so smooth and so effortless in appearance. That was my goal, to fly like them. My flying in that unit was not complicated, so I strove to do it as smoothly as I could. I felt there was always room for improvement in anything one did.

One afternoon, after a routine flight, the *Abteilungführer* approached me with a question.

"Model, I know you are looking forward to *die Jastachule.* I wonder, would you consider another school?"

"Another school, *mein Herr?* What school is that?"

"Observer school."

"I have been through that training, *mein Herr.*"

"I know. But they could use a flyer with your skill to fly new observer candidates. A refined pilot like yourself will not startle them going up in the air for the first time, which will allow them to concentrate on what they need to learn. Do you think you could do that?"

"To be honest, I know I could. But my goal is to learn more and rejoin my *Staffel.*"

"I understand and I will not stand in the way of that. But you have options. I know, shuttling around new observers is not at all exciting, but at the same time it is not as dangerous."

"Very true, *mein Herr,* on both counts. But how can I win the war in a rear area *Fliegerschule?*"

"Indirectly. *Jagdfliegern* mostly kill the enemy one at a time, often with much time between aerial victories. And they are subject to being killed by the enemy, whether scout pilots, antiaircraft fire, or some lucky shot from an anonymous rifle. Everyone wants to bring down *eine flugzeug.* But if you are flying observers, you are helping on a strategic level. The students you help train will direct artillery fire, killing more enemy soldiers in less time while reducing incidents where our gunners fire on our own soldiers. Your students could go on to fly reconnaissance flights, take notes, and make photographs that help shape the course of the war as *der pickelhauben* discover weaknesses on the opposing side. Whole armies could move because of something an observer sees and photographs, which could shorten the war. *Herr* Model, do you have *eine fräulein?*"

"*Ja, mein Herr,* I do."

"Your odds of surviving the war and spending time with her improve if you work with student observers. That is worth thinking about. Easy flying. Nobody shoots at you. Another thing to consider is a routine schedule. You know when you will fly, no surprises. Can you come with me to my office?"

"*Javohl, mein Herr.*"

In his office he showed me a map and where two observer schools were located.

"By chance, does your *fräulein* live near one of these locations?"

"Ja, mein Herr." I placed a finger on the map.

"Let me give you something else to think about. Your *fräulein* is but a short train ride from this location. I could have you assigned here and you could see her on days when you are not flying. If she is so inclined, she could sometimes visit you at the school. You could take her up when you are not on duty, as long as it does not interfere with the routine. Is this worth considering?"

"Mein Herr, you drive a hard bargain. Jakob—*Huaptmann* Einhorn—is expecting me to—"

"Jakob Einhorn? I know him. We attended *fliegerschule* together. His flying was exquisite."

"It still is. He was my pilot when I was shot recently. He was wounded worse than I, but he set that Hanna down like butter on a griddle. I knew he was badly wounded, but no one else knew until I called them over to him. From his flying they could not tell he was hurt."

"Ja, das ist Jakob. He is a very good man and a superb pilot. Piss poor soldier though. I should clarify. He does everything asked of him without complaint. But he hates all the military pomp and circumstance. He always used to say, *'Nicht mit der mein Herr scheisse!'"*

"Ja, ja, ja! 'Nicht mit der mein Herr scheisse!' Das ist Jakob!" We shared a good laugh.

"Model, I will telephone Jakob. It will be good to talk with him. I am going to see if we cannot share you."

"Share me, *mein Herr?"* That struck an oddly familiar chord.

"Ja. You want to fly with Jakob's *Staffel. Die Fliegerschule* could use a pilot like you for new observers. I am confident Jakob and I could work something out. Maybe you could break in the first time flyers, and once they have the idea that flying is not necessarily deadly, you could join Jakob's *Jagdstaffel* until the next class forms. If you are willing, he and I will work out the details. And you could spend time with your . . . "

"Käti?"

"Käti? *Ja,* Käti. Remember, that *Jagdstaffel* is to be used as needed up and down the front. When the need slackens, and you are not needed at the *Fliegerschule,* you could see Käti. Would that be worth considering?"

"*Javohl!* uh,—*mein Herr!*"

"*Nicht mit der,*" (together), "*mein . . . Herr . . . scheisse!*" Another good laugh.

"I will talk with *'Herr Huaptmann'* and talk with you again soon. It's going to be a good war, *mein Vicefeldwebel.*"

That was a lot to juggle. *Jagdstaffel, Fliegerschule, und* Käti. That could indeed be a good war. I could see potential drawbacks, but overall it seemed like an idea that was too good to be true.

I decided right away not to mention it to Käti or Elsa. I simply loved to surprise Käti. Anything to get her excited and see her smile. It could be fun to greet Elsa as well. Plenty of flying to keep me busy and in the air. Varied locations so I would rarely, if ever, be bored. Flying some of the most up to date aeroplanes on the front. And the possibility of taking Käti flying! If they could work out the details, I simply could not say no.

Several routine days later the *Abteilungführer* greeted me after I landed and invited me to his office.

"Model, I have talked with Jakob about sharing you with *die Fliegerschule.* Jakob is more than willing to work with the arrangement you and I discussed. He only wanted the ability to pull you in to his *Staffel* should circumstances dictate. As we are fighting a war, that is not unreasonable, so I agreed. I assume you have thought about it—what do you think?"

"I like it. I am willing to participate and be flexible, as Jakob requests. But are we forgetting *die Jastaschule?*"

"*Ja und nein.* Jakob tells me your friends Willi and Swiss are happy to teach you aerobatics. You will be available to fly a Hanna while you learn. I hope this will be acceptable."

"*Javohl!*"

"*Wunderbar!* Your first assignment will be at *die Fliegerschule.* Jakob does not have an aeroplane for you right now. He will advise you directly when he does and you two can work out details. When you finish your obligations here on Friday morning, you have leave for about two days.

You will report to *die Fliegerschule* airfield Sunday evening and begin work there Monday morning as needed. How you spend the time is up to you.

"Javohl, mein Herr!"

I made arrangements to go to Käti's village by rail Friday afternoon and to the airfield Sunday afternoon. *Die Abteilungführer* arranged my accommodations at the airfield and made sure I knew them. Suddenly I could not wait till Friday.

* * * * *

CHAPTER 62

German

After a decent railway ride, I stepped onto the platform and walked over towards the tavern. I knew Käti would be there on a Friday afternoon. When I entered, Elsa was nearby, staring off into nowhere. I placed my bag on the floor and approached her from behind. Gently I put my hands over her eyes. She leaned back and placed her head on my shoulder. After playfully nibbling on my earlobe, she whispered, "So, Gustav, are you going to tie me?"

"Perhaps."

"Perhaps? You don't care to?"

"I love to. But you spoil me."

"No, my dear Gustav, it is *you* who spoils *me*."

"Is there room in this mutual admiration society for a third person?"

"That depends on the third person."

Käti hooked my elbow and spun me around into a tight bear hug. "Gustav, it is so good to see you! I love when you surprise me like this! Unfortunately, I need to stay here. Dinner will be busy, what with payday and all."

"Not to worry, *mein liebchen*. By happy coincidence I am hungry."

"And thirsty? And I hope you are—"

"Elsa, *mein* Elsa, you are getting ahead of things. Relax. I am all of those things. Once this lovely hostess seats me, would you be kind enough to bring me a beer?"

"*Javohl, mein* Gustav! Käti, show the man where to sit."

"And so I shall. Please follow me."

"With pleasure. It is good to see you as well. We have some things to talk about later."

"Oh? Good things?"

"*Ja,* I think so."

Elsa brought me a stein of cold beer as I was settling into my seat. As if I needed the incentive, she bent over just a little too far for propriety's sake.

"Elsa, are you working for tips?"

"I want more than tips."

"Elsa . . . ." She was incorrigible. And I enjoyed it.

I ate and had too much beer. After I finished, I told Käti I wanted to go lie down. She of course agreed, telling me she would be home as soon as she could get away. I told her to wake me if I didn't wake on my own. Elsa was busy when I left, so I figured I would apologize later for not saying goodbye.

I woke up later that evening when Käti returned home from work. She apologized for not coming sooner, but she took the time to eat after a busy day. I reminded her she need never apologize to me. Eating only made sense. She didn't need my permission for that.

"Gustav, you are so wonderful to me. I am the luckiest woman there is."

"I am only being practical. You are a sensible, reasonable person. I appreciate your ability to think for yourself. If that makes you feel lucky I am all the happier for you."

"But Gustav, not all men are so reasonable. From my experience, you are the exception, not the rule. Take, for example, Elsa's husband."

"Elsa is married?"

"Not any more."

"Do you care to explain?"

"Oh, anything about Elsa?"

"You were making a point. It just happens to concern Elsa. But I do like her."

"That is quite apparent." I smiled, but she continued before I could say anything. "I first met Elsa at the tavern. She was an occasional customer. She used to come in, never looking up, sit down, order, eat, pay, and leave. I didn't want to intrude, but I could see something was wrong. One day she came in wearing a black eye. Big, dark bruise. I could no longer hold back. I asked if she was all right, if she needed to see a doctor. She said it was nothing, mumbled something about falling while hanging out the wash. I could tell by looking at her that she was making it up. I told her it was a shame that someone so beautiful as she never smiled. Again she demurred. As I pushed her harder, she became more agitated until she left. I knew I was onto something. I watched for her, both in the tavern and around town. She always looked sullen, never made eye contact with anyone. I saw her one day with a very young girl, newly walking, and a man about her age, perhaps a little older. She recognized me and quickly shook her head, then looked down again. I noticed the man looked angry and the girl was bruised. I certainly did not like what I saw.

"The next time she came to the tavern I pressed my questioning. Something was not right and I was determined to find out what. She told me she was not permitted to talk to anyone. I asked her who had given such a ludicrous command and she told me I had seen him. I pressed again, asking if the older man was her husband, and tears began to form in her eyes. I guessed that the little girl was their daughter. She nodded and began to cry. I continued despite her tears. I accused him of hitting her and her daughter, and she began to bawl. I took her into the store room so she didn't draw any attention. I held her, hugged her, and told her nobody deserved such treatment.

"In the room, alone, she opened up. 'He beats me, he beats us both. He says it's my fault every man looks at me, they all want to take me from him. He beats our little girl because she looks so much like me. He goes out, drinks, comes home angry, and beats us because we are female. He hits me if I cannot get a stain out of a shirt or if his meat is overcooked. He expects me to do everything at home and it must all be perfect. No one can live up to his expectations. I have no opinion, I'm too stupid. I'd better not let his little girl grow up to be such an evil witch. We need to improve our ways or he's going to do something drastic. He is going to kill me! I know he will! He has no control!'

"I left her in the store room to calm down. I took her more food to eat and more to take home to her daughter. When she finally regained her composure, she became agitated again that she had been gone so long. She was worried it would upset him. I tried to calm her, but she left at almost a dead run. She left her daughter's food behind, so I followed her with the basket.

"Sure enough, he was angry. She went in the front door of their cottage and the screaming and yelling started right away. He bellowed at her in such a way that no one should have to put up with. I heard things breaking and banging against the walls, I heard her screaming in pain, the noise kept building. Then I heard their daughter squealing, shrieking at the top of her lungs followed by a loud thump on the wall next to the front door where I stood. There was no more squealing. Then I heard loud but unintelligible screaming from Elsa and more bellowing from him. She said something about dead and he yelled something about having it coming. I put down the basket of food and burst into the house. I found them in the kitchen. He had her arm behind her and was pushing her hand toward the back of her head. She was bent over the table. With his free hand he was reaching for something, but I got to it first. I grabbed the large knife off the counter by the sink and plunged it into him just below his ribs and up into his heart. He let go of Elsa and reached for the knife with both hands, but there was too much blood. He fell forward onto the handle, gasped a few times, and lay still.

"Elsa had been beaten, to be sure, but had no serious injuries, just many deep bruises and a few cuts. Her daughter was not so fortunate. She had indeed hit the wall by the front door, and collapsed to the floor, unconscious. When I stooped at her side I could see blood and the flat spot on her tiny skull. She was dead."

I could not believe what I had just heard. "When Elsa said you saved her life, she was not exaggerating. It was the truth!"

"I'm afraid so."

"What happened then?"

"About that time a constable entered the cottage, having heard the commotion, and accused me of killing the two of them. He placed me under arrest and took me to the jail. Elsa followed us, cut, bruised, in torn clothing, and gave her testimony which convinced the authorities I had acted trying to save Elsa and her daughter from being killed. I was released immediately. I took Elsa back to her cottage but she could not stay. I insisted she gather what she needed and come with me and stay at least for the night."

"So I was not the first stray you took in."

"I would not put it in those terms, but no, you weren't. Elsa stayed with me for a while. I showed her how to tend to the bar and she began to work with me at the tavern. She has blossomed into a beautiful woman that everyone loves. But she refuses to form any attachments with men."

"So when Elsa says she loves you, she truly means it."

"We have a bond."

"And it seems I owe you an apology."

"About what?"

"You recently said you knew where my heart was and I made a remark about being happy you weren't holding a knife. I had no idea. I am very sorry."

"What?! It was funny at the time. I was teasing when I hit you in reaction. There was no way you would have known. I was not upset with you. We were just teasing."

"So I don't have to lock away the knives, *liebchen?*"

"Only if you become a narrow-minded, overbearing, insufferable ogre of a man. I for one, don't think you have it in your character, or you would not be where you are, in my home or in my heart."

"Life is too short to try to control others. I love that you have thoughts, opinions, and viewpoints. Even if they don't always agree with mine. Not yet, anyway."

"What?"

"Nein, liebchen. Only teasing."

"Let's hope so."

"This explains something else I have wondered about."

"What is that?"

"Elsa has become very close to me, in more ways than one. Yet it doesn't seem to bother you. Now I think I know why."

"You are perceptive. I trust you and her both. I know you love me. Elsa loves me also. Neither of you would intentionally hurt me. You are the first man with whom Elsa has initiated any kind of relationship beyond patrons at the tavern. She is great as long as they keep their distance. She cannot get enough of you. Spending time with you shows Elsa that not all men are like that one. I don't know how this all works out. It is not normal, I know, but there seems to be some kind of love going all three ways. I'm pleased we all get along so well."

"Käti, *liebchen,* you are one remarkable woman."

"I am only me, but if you think I am remarkable, I am happy with that."

We sat by the fire and talked quietly. I remember Käti falling asleep in my arms.

There was a light knock on the door.

"Moment mal!" I slipped out from holding Käti and opened the door, knowing who I would find. There stood Elsa. She had stopped to change her clothes after work and stood there in the dim light with a basket in her hand. I invited her in and she accepted, stepping into my arms and placing her head on my shoulder.

A sleepy voice behind me asked, "Elsa, what is in the basket?"

"Chocolate cake!"

We had a great laugh and the three of us enjoyed a wonderful night.

* * * * *

CHAPTER 63

British

As predicted, the next morning dawned bright and uncharacteristically sunny. Any other day I might have been depressed over such weather, but today I had something to look forward to. After the day's flying, I would go up in the Clerget Camel in order to see just how temperamental she would be. Her "sister" had been quite the partner.

Well, it's funny how things change. One of the mechanics reported to me with apologies that when they pushed my SE in for the night, they managed to bung up a wingtip. He said it was a minor fix but they had not repaired it just yet due to an engine change they had to finish. He did, however, offer a consolation of sorts. They rolled out the Camel I had worked on the night before and placed it on the flight line. I could fly that if I wished.

"Well, mate, she will have to do, I suppose. No harm done. Please tend to my SE as you can get to it, will you?"

"Aye, sir." He saluted and left in the direction of the flight line.

So it turned out I would spend more time with my new acquaintance today. I was anxious to see how we got along. Then I thought I could throw a wrinkle at my students. I called for a day of mock combat. We could start off with the lads fighting me one on one. I called an order and instructed then that when their turn came, they were to approach the athletic fields from the north and I would approach from the south. As always, no live ammunition. Red flare signaled an apparent kill. Then we set about loading blank ammunition into our guns. Truly, the best part was yet to come.

The first student rolled out in his SE, took off, and climbed into the northern sky. A few clouds would have provided some depth and effective framing, but the sky was nearly devoid of clouds. So much for nature catering to my artist's eye. After three minutes or so I took off in the Clerget Camel. Leapt into the air would be a more apt description.

She was more of an animal than her "sister" had been. She only had a stated amount of twenty horsepower more, but it felt like far more than that. It could have been the propeller design also, I suppose. In any event, she lifted her tail almost immediately and was off the grass a blink of an eye later. The climb rate was remarkable, like nothing I had ever been in. I climbed off to the south. I thought I would try the "hun in the sun" maneuver. Not that it was original, but one had to start somewhere.

I kept climbing, all the while watching for my student. He was out there, likely to the north, concocting his own scheme to be the first to best this instructor in combat. I honestly wished him well, but he would have to earn it. I was not one to lie down and accept defeat. At around thirteen thousand feet I leveled out and looked around. Ha! Out to the northeast I spied my young student, flying straight and level, and heading roughly in my direction. It could not have been prettier on a silver serving tray. I anticipated his speed and initiated my gliding dive for the kill. I nosed her down and shut down the ignition, correcting my lead as I dropped. He did not appear to have seen me, as he maintained straight and level. Things were about to happen, things the lad would not like . . . .

Just as I was about to fire my guns, the student surprised me by pulling up short, falling off to the right, and diving away. Good move, lad! But something did not sound right. I heard him go to full power, but there was another engine to be heard. As I reached for the magneto to restart my Clerget, I looked up and to the northwest, where another SE was hurtling straight at me. This was not right! No matter, it was mock combat, so I decided to see what our interloper had to offer.

With a little flare of flame from the cowl, the Clerget woke up with an urgency, and I went straight to the Camel's advantage. I turned right. Hard to the right. Looking straight up to where my new adversary should have been, I just did catch him slipping out of his dive toward his left. I decided to bait him. I flew in his general direction but in a slight dive. Once I was sure he had seen me, I started into a slight diving right turn, hoping he would follow me. And follow me he did. I knew the SE would close on me quickly and I was ready. When I sensed he would pull the trigger on me, I executed a very hard snap roll to the left, throwing his aim off. I heard his guns, but he had anticipated another right turn and his rounds were way off the mark. Out of my roll, I went into a left turn and he followed me, setting up a "Lufbery Circle". That was when I got my dose of surprise. My new adversary was flying *my SE!* I immediately recognized the shapely—uh, lazy eight!—on the upper wing! Now that rattled me for a moment, but I was sure that was part of his scheme. I had to think and fast, so I dove slightly, then pulled up to climb vertically. He had anticipated that, and he was climbing as he came around. I let her stall and fall off to the right, and I continued to the right as she recovered. This put me into a fast spiraling dive with him on my tail. I traded speed for climb again and pulled up hard. He had anticipated that as well, for I heard shots from his Lewis gun. He had elevated the Lewis on its mount and fired where he thought I would be. But this time I got her to fall off to the left with a hard kick on the rudder bar and his shots passed harmlessly by, to the right and behind me. I had to get the upper hand in this match and make him react to me. He had the speed advantage, but I could climb better. I finished my recovery to the left with a shallow dive which I redirected into a wide, climbing right turn. As he started to anticipate my moves again, I threw in a few "stutters" to throw off his senses and slow him down while he decided what I was going to do.

The Camel was not slow. But the SE was faster. That speed demanded respect. This fight had to frustrate my opponent. His best tactic in the SE was to dive from above and either keep going or climb back to a height advantage. It didn't matter who flew it, those were the best options. I had to bait him so I could use my maneuverability to best him. So I watched intently while I climbed, looking for a clue as to his next move.

Suddenly I heard another engine. It was my student, hoping to catch me unawares. Poor lad didn't get up early enough. I saw his dive just in time. I snap rolled left to an inverted state, brought the controls to neutral save the rudder, which I kicked hard right. The result was that the Camel turned on her vertical axis and I was able to keep my guns on him as he dove.

Allowing for the safety factor of mock combat, it would have damaged or killed him. I righted the Camel and fired a red flare at him, all the while looking for the other SE, *my* SE. I didn't have to look for long. My SE was at my altitude, hurtling directly at me from roughly astern. I executed a shallow dive, which he followed, and then I pulled into a hard right turn. Again he followed. He had to know he could not stay with a Camel in a right turn, but he appeared to try just that. A moment later I heard his Lewis gun. He had pulled it down so the gun was pointing vertically, or across the circle, but the shots were nowhere near me. I pulled into a sudden loop—or at least vertical, pushed hard on the stick, and managed to fall forward just as he passed under me. As my nose fell I fired my guns and followed up with a red flare. I had managed to "down" him as well.

I had to pat my gal on the cowl. She had been astounding. I was drenched in sweat despite the cold at altitude. I followed my latest "victim" down toward the airfield, taking my time so he could land at his own pace. I could not help but wonder who was at the controls of my SE. He had put up quite the fight. Could it be Jeremy, home on a slow winter day? No, doubt it. Hmm.

Once again, the landing strip was quite the sight when I approached it. It was a sea of men, filling in after my SE had brought its mystery pilot down intact. Oh, hell! I could not resist it. I fussed with the throttle for more power, overflew the field while initiating a slight climb. I went around, and when I was again into the wind I started into about a forty-five degree dive, half loop, roll, dive, half loop, roll, and continued on around again. The next time around I brought her in for a landing, the men darting out of the way to make room. Several men ran out and caught the Camel, pulling her to a stop. I slid my goggles up and looked toward my SE, where the pilot was sitting on the cockpit edge. He removed his leather helmet and revealed himself as . . . the CO! Bloody Hell!

I peeled off the wide lap strap and fairly jumped to the ground as I ran over to my SE.

"Just what the hell was that?! Sir!"

"Lef-tenant, you may call it what you will."

"Just what is the meaning?"

"Call it a test. I don't care. You passed!"

"But at the least it was irregular, sir!"

"Aye, it was at that. But you made the best of it. Damn fine flying! Let me ask you: Are you done with your class of pilots?"

"Why, no, sir, I am not."

"What more could you possibly teach them? Take a toothbrush? Write your Mum?"

"Well, sir, I could work on—"

"Lef-tenant, you are going to France! You need to let go."

"France, sir?"

"Aye, France."

"But—"

"You *do* want to go, don't you?"

"Bloody right, sir, but—"

"How is that Camel? You two seemed to get along very well."

"She's a beauty, sir. Just a few more minor tweaks, and—"

"She's going to France with you."

"Beg pardon, sir?"

"Would you please give me a hand down from here? We'll go talk."

So that was the major's way of sending me off to France. Jump me high in the sky and try to "kill" me. I have to hand it to him, it was effective. I could not wait for the details.

I told the CO I had to keep it brief so I could get back to my students and more mock combat, but he assured me they would continue amongst themselves with other instructors looking in on them.

I had to ask, "But sir, is there a problem with my instructing?"

"Heavens no, my lad! This is the plan you and I had talked about."

"Yes, sir, but that was to be after this class left."

"Consider them gone. You have done a bang-up job with them. They are ready. I do hope that you are here for the ceremony to send them off. I'm sure there are those who would want to meet you."

"Oh, sir, I don't know. Maybe I could sit in with the orchestra with my cornet."

"Splendid idea. We will know where to find you then. Say, why don't you take the rest of the day to start getting your affairs in order. Take one of the motor-cars if you need to go into town for anything. Relax for a while. I cannot promise France will be quiet when you get there."

"Speaking of France, sir. Any late word? Anything on *der Fritzen?*"

"No, nothing new. I would imagine you will be working with Jeremy on that triplane of his, as well as visiting with Campbell. You know he will send you up on patrols whether there are any Germans to look at or not. And, of course, knowing you, you will find your own trouble to get into over the trenches."

"Guilty, sir, as charged. Will they throw me in a brig somewhere?"

"Hah! I have my doubts. Now why don't you get going so you are ready to go."

"When am I to go, sir?"

"Why, any time you are ready. Do drag your feet a bit, so you can see your students off, however."

"I shall, sir. Say, do you know about tomorrow's weather? I haven't checked."

"Pretty good chance of rain, I believe. No matter. You are grounded unless you get permission from me."

"Grounded?!?"

"No, of course not! Bugger off, would you?!"

Well, that was a surprise. Just like that, off to France. Hmm. I couldn't help but wonder what the CO knew about my goings-on, if anything. After all, the military wasn't exactly known for letting one get their affairs in order. They order, you obey. On the other hand, if nothing was going on in France, there was no hurry to get me over there. So I suppose it made sense.

From the office I placed a call to the nursing school in hopes of catching Clara free. Oddly enough, she answered the phone. Hers was the one voice I would know anywhere.

"Lef-tenant, how good of you to call! My hat is ready to be picked up, and I know you wanted to be along."

"Why, yes. Are you free tomorrow?"

"I can make some time around mid-day. Would that be acceptable?"

"Certainly it would. I shall have you paged when I arrive."

"Splendid. I shall see you then. Thank you!"

That would work well, especially if it rains in the morning.

With arrangements made to visit town the next day, I decided to stay around the airfield for the rest of the day. I could start to organize things and tidy up my quarters. I could play the cornet for a while, just in case I ran into an accompanist in town. That would be pleasant.

After working with the cornet, I put it down to rest the lips. I thought about that morning's flight, my first in a Clerget Camel. She was indeed quite the animal. Where the Le Rhone attacked, the Clerget devoured. She was a wonderful partner. Okay, the SE was faster. But the SE was faster than anything the Germans were flying. Only the SPAD XIII could fly with the SE, at least when the Hisso gear drive unit wasn't broken—in either case. I know I had been lucky with my geared Hisso, but mine was the exception.

* * * * *

CHAPTER 64

British

As desired, it rained the next morning. Of course, I checked out a motor-car and went to the cafe in town. The proprietor was pleased to see me and had a hot cup of coffee waiting for me at the counter.

"Top o' the mornin', Lef-tenant!"

"Aye, good mornin' to you as well!

"Say, did you see that dogfight over the airfield yesterday?"

"Dogfight?"

"Aye. I'm told one of the instructors was pounced upon by his commanding officer and they went all over the sky after one another. Wonder what the devil that was about! They say it was a helluva show!"

"Oh, that. Yes, I heard about that. I had my hands full and only saw part of it. I don't know what it was for, either, but it had everyone talking at the airfield. They say the chap never saw it coming. I can only imagine."

"Oh, but I wish they would bring some of those antics over here so maybe I could see part of it one day!"

"I don't know that the other folks in town would want aeroplanes cavorting about the sky overhead. If something comes loose or quits or worse, that could be a big problem."

"I suppose you're right. But any time they hold a ceremony at the airfield I close up early and go, just in case they're gonna fly. Seeing the rolls and loops and whatever that last fellow did at the most recent ceremony is certainly exciting."

"I'm glad you enjoy it."

"I just put myself up there. I come back and picture myself in one of those machines, going up against the kaiser's best flyers."

"You would like to do that, would you?"

"Good God, no. One has to be so much younger than I and not a little crazy to do what those lads do up there. While I picture myself clearing the sky of German aeroplanes, I wouldn't know the first thing to do in their shoes. The first time some Fritz would shoot in my direction, I would likely cry and go home. That won't win a war."

"I'm afraid it won't."

"But I put in my time. There was no war at the time, but I was a sailor on the HMS Dreadnought."

"The Dreadnought? Wasn't she the one with all the big guns?"

"Aye. First of her kind with all the main guns in that same large calibre. She could make other ships pee in shame. Not that anyone could tell, mind you! Ha-ha!"

"Now I couldn't imagine being on board when they let loose with all those big guns. I would look for something sturdy to hide under!"

"There ye are, then, eh? We are all different, aren't we?"

"Can anyone join in the discussion? Or must one be a soldier or sailor to participate?"

Now there was a familiar voice. I looked over my shoulder at Pauline as she approached the counter. I saw right away that she was not herself. We continued with small talk for a bit, then we sat at our usual table off and away.

"How have you been? I have been worried about you since you did not show the last rainy day."

"I have not been well, I'm afraid. My cough simply got worse, making breathing miserable. It has subsided somewhat, but I still don't feel well. I had to come see if you were here today. I've missed you so."

"And I you."

We held hands under the table. From her clammy hand, I could tell she wasn't well.

"Are you sure you should be here?"

"I did not want to miss seeing you. It's been too long."

"Yes, but you must—"

"I will be okay. I want to continue seeing you when we can, and I have a beautiful son who will one day come home from France. I have too much to live for, don't you see?

"Speaking of Jeremy, I will be going to join him soon."

"You will?! When?"

"As soon as I am ready to go. The CO has asked that I remain here until they have the ceremony for the latest scout pilots moving along to the pilot pools here and in France."

"How long will you be gone?"

"I have no idea, but I doubt it will be very long. I am, after all, an instructor, and I am only going there to catch up on doings at the front and help Jeremy with his triplane project. In the meantime, you need to take care of your health."

"Please don't worry about me."

"Also, I am to pick up Clara today. Her hat is ready and she has graciously allowed me to accompany her to the millinery. Your husband thought we made a fine couple, by the way."

"He did. Jolly good. You do make a fine couple. Clara has beautiful eyes, and you . . . . But don't make any plans. She is spoken for, and from my perspective, so are you."

"Duly noted, no objections."

"Good to hear, Lieuu-tenn-annt. Carry on, then."

"Aye, madam."

I watched her eyes focus hard as her nostrils flared.

"Say, Lieutenant, is not part of your job maintaining order and quelling public disobedience?"

"I do suppose that it is, somewhere down there in the regulations. Why do you ask? Where is it I need to restore order?"

"It could be right here, if you are fortunate enough."

I felt her hand depart mine. It traced down the outside of my thigh, around my knee, and back up the inside until it came to rest on my "unmentionable" parts. Then she pet the area as if it were a small animal. I was afraid she might "awaken a beast" if she persisted.

"Madam, . . . " my voice cracked.

"Yes, Lieutenant? Having difficulties, Lieuu-tenn-annt?"

"I must warn you. If you do not stop such a rude public display, I shall be forced to remove you from the premises, detain—"

". . . and interrogate me? I hope?"

"Yes, madam, that is a likely possibility."

"I will go pay the good man for breakfast. You stand up and cover yourself . . . against the cold."

"It is a bit brisk today."

And so it went. I transported the rebellious prisoner to a nearby parlor, where she was tightly detained and interrogated without mercy. Frankly, I did not get much information—she was still tough to crack—but we both thoroughly enjoyed the effort. I had kept the public safe from her malicious attempts at disobedience, after all.

Once I was assured that public morals would not be corrupted, at least that morning, we took some tea.

"Could you take some things with you for Jeremy?"

"I would love to, but I have nearly no room to carry anything and weight is a factor."

"I wasn't asking to go along!"

"Of course not. Have you ever seen a scout aeroplane up close? If it were a piece of clothing, it would be considered snug, a tight fit. I could probably take a sweater or two if they were packed flat, and very little more. Perhaps a tin of biscuits? If I pick them up early in the morning, he would have them by mid-day."

"Now that is a good idea—Mum's biscuits. Something personal. I like that. I shall provide the telephone number for here. Please keep me informed as to your date of departure. If you would, telephone in the morning between eight and nine o'clock so I would be the one to pick up the telephone."

"Certainly I shall."

I stowed the phone number safely and took my leave of Pauline. She was most enjoyable, but one could see she was worn. And that cough only seemed a little worse. But I had to assume she would take care of herself. She was, after all, a grown woman. And a mother.

I arrived at the nursing school and found Clara waiting inside the front door, out of the winter weather. I apologized for keeping her standing, but she insisted she had not been there long enough to shift from one foot to the other. After seeing her into the motor-car, we made small talk en route to the shop. Upon arrival I helped Clara step out of the car and into the shop, where we were promptly greeted by Mr Trafford himself.

"Ahh, good day to you both! Please make yourselves comfortable while I bring out the hat."

Moments later he returned with a large hatbox. He held it in front with both hands and had to strain to see over the top.

"I should say I am most pleased I drove a saloon today or we should have to tie it atop the roof!"

Clara smiled and thrust an elbow into my ribs.

"Madam, here you are. I do hope it is to your satisfaction."

I assumed it was. When he produced the hat Clara's jaw dropped.

"Ohh, . . . my . . . ! That is without a doubt the most beautiful hat I have ever seen! It looks as if it had been made with my pink overcoat in mind. It is perfect!"

Said hat was pink silk with a wide brim, matching broad pink ribbon and bow, large white feathers, and one large black feather high and to the rear. Clara could not stop looking at it, first in her hands, and then in the mirror once she donned it. She trembled a bit as she replaced the hat in its box. Then she hugged me and placed a warm kiss on my cheek.

"Thank you, Lef-tenant, for bringing me here and for arranging for such a spectacular hat! And thank you, good sir, for a hat like I have never seen! Certainly there is a balance due . . . ?"

"No, madam, there is nothing due. It is the very least I could do for you and especially the good lef-tenant after he took such good care of my son. I would happily make another or a dozen and still feel indebted."

"Have you heard from your son?"

"Why, yes, I have. No news, I'm afraid. It seems the war is on hold pending spring."

"We should not have long to wait, then. I will be visiting Jeremy's squadron, by the way."

"You will?"

"Yes, sir. Within a week. I need to wait until the current class has its departure ceremony, and then I need a clear morning for the flight."

"Could you take him a gift from his father?"

"Only if it is a new tie—but I don't know where he would wear it, France being what it is at the moment. Scout aeroplanes are a tight fit, after all."

"Ah, yes. If I should think of anything, may I call upon you?"

"You certainly may."

"Madam, do you still wish to become a surgeon?"

"Most certainly, sir, I do."

"You realize, of course, that it will not be easy for you. I understand you have the requisite knowledge and abilities, but you will be fighting staid social norms the entire time."

"Mr Trafford, I am most aware, believe me. I have been a fish swimming upstream for most of my medical career. This is nothing new. I remain undeterred."

"Noble of you, to be sure. I ask because I have had occasion to speak with some fellow board members at the school. I can report that you are held in very high esteem for a woman in your position. One of those I have spoken to was aware of your goal. The others showed various degrees of surprise. One of the gentlemen is still against your advancement, but I see his position shifting slightly. The others show signs of approval. There are yet more members with whom to broach the subject, I'm afraid, so I cannot give you a complete report just yet."

"I am moved, sir, that you have done so much in such a short period of time. Thank you. Is there anything I can do?"

"No. Not just yet. But I think it will come down to you facing the board of directors. You may need to present a case before them. You will likely have to answer questions and justify why they should allow a woman to advance beyond where you are. It is unusual, after all."

"Yes, sir, I admit that it is unusual. But if it happened more often, then it wouldn't be quite so unusual. Dare I say that women and men exhibit similar lines of thought. There are differences, of course, but these differences may actually favor women over men in certain circumstances. I mean no offense, of course. It is merely scientific observation that has been tallied and reported in medical journals."

"You read medical journals?"

"Of course. I read as much as I can on illnesses, epidemics, treatments, medical procedures, medicines, and medical research. I have had articles published in some of them. How can one advance without keeping abreast of ongoing developments in the field? I am confident you keep up with style trends, materials, techniques, and the like as you run your millinery."

"Wonderful answer. Marvelous. Lef-tenant, your companion could be on the way to her career advancement. But I cannot promise it yet."

"Good sir, we certainly appreciate what you have done thus far."

"Aye. Thank you, sir."

"Now, please forgive me, but I must take my leave. I have deliveries to inventory as well as other pressing needs. Madam, I am most pleased you like your new hat. Kindly tell everyone who made it—but not its cost to you!"

Clara smiled as I carried her hat to the motor-car and deposited it in the rear. At the school two young men came out to the car to offer to help carry the large parcel, then smiled when they learned it was but a hat. They took the box anyway. Clara thanked me once again and went inside to resume her day.

I did stop by to report to Pauline, but found her again in the guest room, sound asleep. Her rasp sounded a bit worse yet. I added another light blanket to stave off what little draught there was. She did not stir so I returned to the airfield.

* * * * *

Chapter 65

British

"Well, 'allo, sir! Do you like it?"

"Aye, laddie, I do. Other than the simple fact that it is a German design, there is nothing visible that says 'German' in any way. I would say it is probably safe to take it up if you wish. When you do I will contact the local units and alert them not to shoot at the blue triplane with British cockades."

"Wise of you sir. And very kind."

"Of course. But I came to tell you your instructor will be visiting and very soon."

"Ripping, sir! I shall be happy to see him. When is he to arrive?"

"I am unsure of the exact date. He is waiting for his current class to depart, and then he will need clear weather to make the flight."

"Well, that is good news, sir! I shall be happy to watch him set down his SE alongside ours."

"Except, lad, that he will be bringing a Camel."

"Sir?"

"Yes. He thought about your Clerget triplane and decided to brush up his rotary skills in a Le Rhone Camel. The next day found him in a Clerget Camel and he quickly grew to like it. We could call it a 'forced marriage', but have *him* tell you the tale. I will tell you, though, that he has another surprise coming before he crosses the channel."

"Do tell, sir, do tell!"

"No, lad, I shall let him tell you. I shall make you aware when he is to arrive. Carry on, then. Be sure to file with me when you are going up in this schnitzel-burner."

"This wha—aye, sir!"

This was all news to Jeremy. He had known his instructor would visit, but not just when. Jeremy had hoped to engage him in mock combat with his triplane. But now he was to fly a Clerget Camel. This meant that Jeremy had that much more work ahead of him if he wished to best his instructor at last.

"Sir! Excuse me, sir?"

"Yes?"

"May I be excused from the early patrol tomorrow?"

"No. But you may take 'er up after the early patrol if you wish. And I will make your second patrol optional if you feel you need more practice—I mean more time with the triplane."

"Thank you, sir. Bright and early it is, then!"

Jeremy once again realized why Major Campbell was such a well loved leader. The major did not always give in, but he did a lot of give and take. That made him seem fair to all but the most unreasonable.

Jeremy wanted to take the triplane up right then, but he knew it was not a good idea. While he could gain clearance for the flight, the light was beginning to fade. Less light made identification less positive, even for a thoroughly repainted triplane. The trigger-happy sorts would go crazy aiming at an obvious German design. Jeremy was taking risk enough in broad daylight. And broad daylight would be the element for his first real flight in what he hoped would be a new weapon against the Germans.

* * * * *

CHAPTER 66

British

The day after Clara received her splendid new hat dawned like many. It was overcast, even foggy, but it was not raining. I visited with the CO.

"Just how is the weather over the channel, sir?"

"I suppose it is not unlike what you saw outside on the way to my office. Why?"

"Oh, just curious, I suppose."

"Or anxious. In a hurry?"

"Oh, no! Of course not, sir!"

"Right. You will be participating in the flying part of the upcoming ceremony, won't you?"

"Yes, sir, I had assumed so."

"Good. We will be happy to have you. Would you care to practice your routine?"

"It's hardly a routine, sir. It's merely a spot of aerobatics. I think the SE could do it without me, frankly."

"The SE? You won't be flying the Camel?"

"Honestly, sir, I hadn't much thought about it. I suppose . . . ."

"Since you will be taking it to France, I should think you would want every minute of flying time to get acquainted."

"You would think, sir. But she flies as though she knows what I want to do. Like an extension of my body—or mind."

"I could have her readied for you to fly as soon as the fog lifts." The major reached for the telephone.

"She is ready sir, save maybe a little petrol and oil. I've been keeping up on her."

"Okay, son, your choice. Did you want to borrow a car and go into town?"

"That will not be . . . no, wait . . . a fresh biscuit and coffee would be great. Thank you, sir. Could I bring you something?"

"Mighty thoughtful, son. If something turns up on my desk later, ..."

"Say no more . . . !"

I indeed had no business in town, but getting away for the morning sounded good to me. Coffee with that naval chap at the cafe was always pleasant, even if I did deflect some of his questions. I merely didn't want special attention. I was no better than the many thousands of other men in the various services. Like them, I was trying to win the war by killing Germans. Flying a scout aeroplane did make me somewhat exceptional, I suppose, but I preferred to think of myself as a soldier who rode a different steed, that's all. Otherwise my mission was the same.

The fog was unusually thick. And I have seen more than my share of fog by virtue of being British. So thick was the fog that I actually pulled off the road, but it wasn't fear of driving in limited visibility. I had flown in fog at nearly one hundred miles an hour, but there are fewer obstructions at altitude. It was the fog itself. I wanted to watch the fog as the sun arose and illuminated it. I enjoyed the way the sun slowly entered the fog, gradually achieving penetration. And I was always fascinated to watch the excitement within the moving cloud as the sun penetrated further and droplets moved faster and faster. While one could reasonably anticipate some sort of climactic event, the climax, as it were, was the disappearance of the fog once light had penetrated completely. And while it was a bit of an anticlimax, it was well worth watching for inspiration. Besides, I had little else to do. I could not call upon Pauline. Or Clara, for that matter. I could not fly just yet. I had the time, so I spent it observing nature. It was most satisfying. I never understood why people didn't stop to take in beauty. We are surrounded by beauty in one form or another everywhere we go. Yet, busy schedules allow no time for that. But one need not come to a complete cessation of all activities. One need only be open to beauty and be aware of one's surroundings. If I were to have three enemy scouts diving on me out of the sun, I couldn't pause to inspect the cloud formations. But I know they are there, and perhaps I will get a chance to see them in a few moments. Or perhaps not. Life can be like that. But to wear blinders and never enjoy the surrounding beauty is such a shame. One must be better to oneself than that.

I looked around as I entered my favorite cafe, but the only familiar face I spied was that of the proprietor. As I sat at the counter, he was pouring me coffee and offering his newest cake.

"'ere ya go, sir. This one is on me. I hope you like it enough to buy some more."

"Why thank you, sir. I'm certain I shall. In fact, I will buy two right now. Please take them to the couple at my usual table with my compliments."

It appeared the couple could use something to smile over, so it seemed a good gesture.

When he returned, the proprietor asked how things were at the airfield. I told him things were winding down toward the latest class of pilots departing to the scout pilot pool. Thankfully there had been no significant bloodshed of late, at least nothing beyond a skinned knuckle or the like.

"I will be away on an assignment soon, but I shan't be gone long. I will fill you in when I return."

"Going off to clear the skies over France of Heinrich and Fritz, are ye? Godspeed, good sir!"

"Oh, no, nothing so glamorous. I doubt I even get a shot at one, though I will be on the lookout for the opportunity."

"Take along a few grenades if you are flying the Channel. Drop them on any U-boats you might see with my kind regards. If you cannot get grenades, I will get you some of the day old biscuits the bloke down the street is selling! That should dent the hull, maybe hurt someone!"

"Great idea! I shall keep you posted on my departure!"

And so it went. I could see my retired naval friend was anxious that he could not do more for the war effort than buy government bonds and give cakes to servicemen when they stopped in. He was envious of me, though he would not consider going up in an aeroplane. "Nothing higher'n a crow's nest" for him.

He was becoming busier than I was accustomed to seeing. The fog had mostly lifted and the townspeople were coming out. I was happy he would have a good day. It also gave me time to lose myself in thought. My friend would not want to fly, but I could not imagine not flying. I had been looking forward to cessation of all this nonsense that I could get back into my painting. Thanks to Pauline, I also had music to play. But if I could no longer fly, life simply would not be the same. I knew not how many times I had been up in the sky, but I was forever spoilt. Flying would have to be available to me at the very least, if not my job after the war. If I even survived the war, that is. I was doing everything in my power to ensure I would still be standing once the war stopped. Would it be enough? The SEs and my newfound Camels were wonderful against anything the Germans sent up to fight, true, but the Germans were not stupid people. Stubborn, perhaps, but not stupid. They were certainly developing something new with which to take over the skies. What would that be? When would they put it to use? Would we be able to fight it on at least equal terms? The last thing we needed was another Bloody April. That was a key part of the training I was now doing, avoiding another "bloody" month. I had to do what I could to find out more about the 'super' Albatross supposedly flown by the *Fritzen* squadron. What sort of technology made it so 'super'? Were the Fritzes flying advance copies of the latest German fighter? Would they fill the skies with their new 'super' Albatross? What more could I do to learn more?

"Excuse me, Lef-tenant, but is this seat taken?"

It was the most unmistakable voice in my world. I bolted to attention out of respect.

"Clara, what a pleasant surprise! There is a table nearby. Would you like to sit there?"

"That would be delightful."

I waved at the proprietor, held up my coffee cup and signaled for two. He was there just as we settled in.

"Thank you. When you get a chance, could we get a few of your cakes, including the new one?"

"I think I may have one or two left. If not, I'll take back the two you sent to that couple. They have hardly touched their coffee, never mind the cakes—but they did appreciate the gesture."

"So, dear Clara, how are you?"

"Well, classes are going well. I am still in shock over that hat—thank you!"

"You are most welcome, of course, but how are you?"

"Does it show?"

"I do not know you all that well, unfortunately and understandably, but I have the feeling something is amiss."

"It does show. Okay, I feel I can trust you."

"With?"

"I have a funny feeling about my fiancé. I haven't heard from him in some time and I am concerned as to his whereabouts."

"I understand. But you need to give him the benefit of—"

"Oh, it's nothing like that, not at all. He was sent to the Middle East not so long ago, and the last I heard from him was a letter saying he had arrived after an unpleasant voyage in a transport ship. I know him. He writes regularly, even if there is not much to say. He loves me and writes to tell me he misses me. He is not one to let his habits go."

"It could be the Post. Or U-boats could have—"

"Yes, yes, I have thought of those things also. I think it's him. Something must be amiss with him. If he is able to write me, he will write me. But what if he can't?"

"Oh, my dear. I understand. I know I cannot give you a good answer. But all you can do is wait. Wait—could you give me his name, unit, and location as best you know it? I can ask my CO to look into it. With things slowing up at the airfield, he will have the time to inquire. I'm afraid that is the most I can offer."

"That is kind of you. Of course I will give you what I can."

"Certainly. I would be happy to help in any way. Meanwhile, can you stay? I am happy to be in your company."

"But don't you have things to tend to? I cannot think of keeping you."

"No, I have the day to myself, or at least the morning. My class is finished. I am waiting for their ceremony. After that, I go to France for a short spell."

"Squadron assignment?"

"No. They feel I'm more valuable as an instructor. I will be visiting my old unit in order to glean the latest information about fighting the Germans in the air. Perhaps I can be of assistance as they are expecting an offensive after the last frost."

"But I would assume you will be flying combat patrols."

"I don't know. Fact is, the war is at a near standstill until spring. I may find no Germans up to shoot at."

"You cannot learn about fighting Germans if there are no Germans to fight."

"I see you have a firm grasp of the situation, dear Clara."

I decided we needed to lighten the conversation to something other than war. I decided to bring up my old saw about light and color. Maybe Clara would appreciate the arboretum. Clara caught onto the concept right away, but she still liked the idea of visiting the arboretum, if only briefly. There were few blooms to be seen outdoors, but there were indoor plants to appreciate. All in all, it was a very pleasant time. I found Clara was very likable beyond her skill and dedication to her chosen field. She had a quick wit and a very easy laugh. She would be quite the catch for her fiance.

Suddenly Clara remembered an appointment and feared she could be late. But she was relieved to know the arboretum was very near the nursing school. I dropped her there, saw her inside, and returned to the airfield.

I returned the motor-car and stopped in to see the CO.

"What a beautiful day it has turned into, sir!"

"Aye, 'tis. Makes one want to fly, doesn't it?"

"As a matter of fact, ..."

The major picked up his telephone, rang someone over in maintenance, spoke briefly, and put down the telephone.

"Your Camel will be ready when you are. Was there anything else?"

"Only if you have an update from the front on Jeremy or the Fritzes."

"Sorry, no further word in the few hours you have been gone."

"You're keeping an eye on me, then, sir?"

"Oh, certainly not. But you generally walk past me to pick up or drop off your motor-car, so I often see you. Especially when you come in here on either side of your morning away."

". . . which is fairly often. You will miss me when I'm away, sir! Especially if no one is bringing you anything like this." I placed two boxes of fresh cakes on his desk.

"Why, Lef-tenant! How sweet of you!" Pun intended, I'm sure.

I went to my quarters to change into my flying gear. It might have blossomed into a sunny day, but it was still winter, so keeping warm at altitude could be difficult. Once I resembled the Michelin Man, I made my way toward the flight line. I stepped out the door and the sight of my Camel stopped me cold. My jaw dropped. Then I saw the CO standing next to the boarding ladder, so I waddled at maximum pace to have a word.

"I see somebody has been busy, sir."

"Oh, Lef-tenant? How so?"

"You know damn well how so! Sir."

"Well, okay then. Do you like it?"

"I should say so. Very nicely executed, sir."

"We had the original nearby, so it was not that difficult. We just wanted you to think of us while you are in France. Hurry home, all that."

What took me aback was the upper wing of the Clerget Camel. It now told everyone she was mine and mine alone. The CO had had it painted identically to my SE wing over a fresh coat of PC10 dope so the white 'lazy eight' would show full contrast. I was touched.

"Why, sir, you are very thoughtful. If you continue to exhibit such behavior, you will never get a command in France."

"That will suit me fine. I no longer want one. I'm quite happy here. And I will miss you while you are gone. You do bang-up work and manage to keep the place interesting while turning out fine candidates for scout work. Now, I'm going to cease with the compliments while your head gear still fits. So go study the blues, look for cloud animals, or count cloud sheep or whatever it is you do when not shooting at Germans. We can talk when you get back if you like."

I clambered into the cockpit of the Camel and a mechanic helped strap me in. We went through the normal procedure, pulling the prop to draw the fuel/oil mixture into the cylinders, switching on the magneto, and pulling the prop to start the engine. The Clerget played its part well, progressing from pop to cough to sputter to stutter to roar. Once it settled into a normal running speed, the mechanics pulled away the wheel chocks and I slowly rolled toward the far end of the field. I was on and off the "blip" switch to keep the taxi speed low. There was no hurry. I was switching my head to flight mode. If the largest part of flying is knowing what to do when something goes wrong, one needs to pay attention to what is going on. I found it necessary to put other things to the back of my mind. I could not worry about things like Clara's fiance, Pauline's cough, or my upcoming visit to the front. I had to listen to the engine and feel the controls. I had to look to the field and sky in front of me. I had to keep an eye on the weather. I saw what the CO was talking about with the cloud animals. There were herds of cumulus clouds all about the sky. I was about the enter a zoo in the air, as it were.

I checked that the field was clear of traffic. I looked around above and found nothing in the landing pattern. All was clear. I checked the windsock, then released the "blip" switch. The Clerget was anxious to reach full power and pull the little aeroplane along. The tail quickly came up and the Camel fairly leaped into the air. All that power just fueled my confidence. This was some machine. I resisted the urge to do something showy on the way up and away from the airfield. The engine wanted to. I could hear it taunting me. The Camel wanted to. I could feel her forces on the stick and rudder bar. Everything about the machine was saying, "Let's *do* something!" But I insisted on a safe takeoff and standard climb-out. After all, I was in control. I had many eyes on me, so stiff upper lip it was. This time.

I had a feeling of obligation to my students, to the CO, to His Majesty, to Pauline, and even to Clara and the proprietor of the cafe. My role was that of military aviator. Stiff upper lip indeed. I represented the kingdom and all its far-flung subjects. I was in His Majesty's aeroplane and dressed in His Majesty's clothing. There were expectations. Just as all His Majesty's aeroplanes were painted basically the same, drab with essential minimal markings, all His Majesty's pilots were to act basically the same. As much so as circumstances permit, at any rate. Takeoff and climb-out? The engine pulled everything along, so no reason to deviate from the norm. Had the engine failed, all bets were off and I had to do whatever would bring me safely to the ground and hopefully not damage His Majesty's aeroplane.

Right, then. With that bit of show out of the way, I could get on with my flight. Truth be told, I had no destination, nowhere I needed or wanted to go. I just wanted to be in the air and to explore, a little more formally, just what this girl would do. I had to throw her into some wild and unexpected maneuvers against the CO. I didn't think an SE would do a lot of the things we had done that day. But that flight, like meeting a new love interest, had intrigued me. I thought we could steal off somewhere, alone, and get to know one another better.

I flew over the athletic fields. There were no student flyers about, and no one was working on the grounds. It was perfect. Just my Camel and me in a 'herd' of cloud animals. We could take each other places we hadn't been together. We could work on timing and coordination. We could bask in the sun and each other's company, forming a stronger bond through being together.

Naturally enough, I began with dives. I started with shallow dives, separated by climbs back to altitude. I tried steeper dives. I tried various ways to enter into a dive, as well as exit them. She was right with me, surprising me with her ability to pay close attention to my commands. She never hesitated. This one was quite the partner.

I moved on to turns, beginning with left turns. She wanted to push back at that point, but I led her on, putting her where I wanted her. She resisted but never complained, taking commands and making them deeds. Level turns, diving turns, climbing turns, we did them all. Then the pace picked up when we explored right turns. Here was her specialty. She was truly in her element. It was I who hesitated a little, such was her enthusiasm. Once again, level turns, and so on, through the gamut.

Rolls were next. Now at this point I was less analytical and I flew by feel. Let the artist out to play. Up and down the fields we went, rolling one way, then another. Snap rolls, long, open barrel rolls, turn around, and return.

I had never had much use for aerobatics unless they would get me out of a tight spot. What I had flown up to that point had not inspired aerobatics. The various aeroplanes had all been either too stable or underpowered. Or both. I could not deny the SE was a fairly nimble machine. We had gone through a lot. But it could not stay alongside the Camel, especially the Clerget. This partner made me want to do more. She obeyed every command yet taunted me to push limits, both hers and mine. She was tempting, naughty, promising she would do as she had teased, so long as I could stay with her.

Loops. We did loops. I started her slowly, diving slightly then taking that speed and trading it for upward momentum. We drew a great vertical circle in the air, then repeated it a few times to clean up some lines that didn't feel just right. We were new at this. We soon moved on to more complex things. Half loop with a half roll at the top. Tight loops. Endless variations. I wondered about an outside loop. Start with a dive, then continue past vertical into inverted flight and back up. Could I stand the pressure of the blood flowing to my head? It was difficult enough doing a normal loop. I decided to try after climbing to a higher altitude. I wanted time and room to recover. I initiated a shallow dive and kept the stick forward, picturing the circle I was drawing from the top, not the bottom. I went past vertical. That is where I started to feel the pressure in my head. After just a few degrees I had had enough. I half-rolled her and pulled back until we came about to level. Maybe next time.

We had yet to do stalls, so waiting only long enough for my head to clear, we moved on. I wanted to feel just what she did when stalled. If she recovered a certain way, I could use that information in a fight. She repeatedly showed me she would follow her engine if there were no control input and 'drop' her right wing, slowly rotating clockwise from my perspective. Of course, I could manipulate that via the controls, but I wanted to know what she would do, left on her own. I did several more stalls, varying my control input to gauge her responses. I took note of what she did for future reference. This was a new and feisty partner, replete with a bag of tricks, and I needed to know that I could keep up with her.

An experienced scout pilot, I kept looking around for any activity as I went through my 'routine'. I found plenty of activity, but not in the air. Oh, there were other aircraft about, but nothing that interfered with my doings. The activity I spotted was on the ground. There were people gathering on the athletic fields. No huge throng, but there were maybe one hundred to one hundred fifty people, especially close to the passing road. I saw them slowly migrating away from the road and the vehicles parked almost carelessly about. Most had a curious posture about them, one hand held over their eyes, the other pointing in the air. At me! It appeared I had inadvertently made a spectacle of myself as I tested my new partner's mettle, along with my own.

Feeling flattered and a little embarrassed, I felt I could not just leave them. Even if I was done for the moment, I thought I should give them a little more, perhaps a bit more organized from their perspective. They had, after all, taken time from their day to watch me, so it was only fair. I did a broad turn and flew the length of the fields, toward the road, rocking my stick and wagging the wings as if to wave "hello". Passing the end of the fields, I turned about and flew the opposite way, this time performing two slow rolls. Another turn, then three rolls. One loop.

Two loops. Then a half loop with a half roll at the top to gain some altitude and a circling climb. Happy with my height, I dove slightly and climbed vertically as far as she would go. She decelerated steadily until she stopped in the air. I released the controls and she started to rotate with the engine as she slid backward on her tail. The right wing started down and we were spinning to the right. I quickly opened the spin into a right turn, dove, and half looped again with a half roll at the top. Another climbing turn, then a dive followed by another climb to her stall point. This time I held her steady, and when she started to slide I pushed her nose over forward. She tumbled twice, then I brought her into an inverted spin. This I held briefly, then countered the spin and pulled the stick back so she would recover as if finishing a loop. I knew I was running out of sky, so I finished this over the far field with very few people nearby. For a little drama, I let the diving recovery go to the tops of the high yellow grass. This put me out of sight of most of the people and likely caused a gasp from an uneasy few. I turned around at the far end and powered over them all in another long roll. Again reversing just past the road, I rocked the stick again to wave goodbye and started to climb out in a broad turn. I could see some of the people waving, so I held out my left arm to return the gesture.

But I was not quite done. Once more facing toward the road, I started into a forty-five degree dive, half loop, half roll and did the same in the other direction. This faced me toward the road again, completing my 'signature' maneuver which was depicted on my upper wing.

That was enough for this day. All the tossing about the sky had me almost out of breath and definitely in a sweat. A check of the clock revealed I was low on petrol. I took her home so we could both recover. It had been a wonderful hour and then some, and I looked forward to more.

When I lined up my final approach to land, I noted more than the usual number of blokes on and about the airfield. I imagined someone had telephoned about the imbecile who was trying to separate the wings from the rest of his airframe. I set her down and rolled into the waiting grasp of several smiling lads who slowed our progress and pointed us where we needed to be. There were two ladders astride the cockpit and not a little pounding on my shoulders as the lads helped me out of the grasp of my partner. I rolled out of the cockpit and felt my way down the ladder to the ground as the CO approached.

"Are you marketing your other job?"

"Sir?"

"Training lads to kill Germans isn't enough for you, eh?"

"Why, certainly it is, sir!"

"And in your spare time you entertain civilians?"

"Well, I did not invite them, sir. They just showed up as I was wringing out my new . . . uh, Camel, sir. They had watched my droll testing and getting acquainted, so I thought their attention deserved something perhaps a little better arranged."

"'A little better arranged'? From all accounts telephoned in, it was simply brilliant!"

"Oh, sir, I don't know. Most of them don't fly, they don't know."

"There were a number of student pilots in attendance, returning from town. They had all wanted to engage you in mock combat—until they witnessed you moments ago. Now they're asking for time in the air to engage each other and work on aerobatic maneuvers. Lef-tenant, you keep finding ways to amaze me. That was absolutely brilliant, inspiring students—not just yours—to utilize their remaining time here to better themselves and improve their odds of survival at the front rather than just wander about town. Good show! Well done."

"But sir, I was only—"

"That is the ironic part, Lef-tenant. I thought you had no real use for aerobatics in and of itself, just something to use as needed. But now it appears you could teach it."

"But sir,—"

"Perhaps we should really paint up that Camel and send you about demonstrating your maneuvers. You could draw new recruits and raise money for the War Bond program."

"Sir?"

"We could recall Trafford from the front with his triplane, put the crosses back on it, and the two of you could fly mock combat together. Of course, you would always win . . . ."

"Well I rather like the sound of that, sir. But do you think the brass hats would—"

"I'm going to telephone some *dramatis personae* right now and get a feel for what the brass hats would think. Hell, we could send the two of you to Canada—the United States, for that matter. You could push our War Bond program as well as theirs."

"Shouldn't we be working to end the war first, sir?"

"Of course. But we need money in order to prosecute the war. You could help raise more of it."

"I should be happy to oblige, of course."

"I've got to go. Good man!"

* * * * *

CHAPTER 67

British

The flight had just landed after yet another uneventful patrol. Any Germans sighted were far behind the lines and obviously not interested in contesting the skies over the front lines. While the ground temperature was warmer than it had been of late, it was still frigid at altitude. The sun was just coming up when the flight landed, so it was no source of heat at all. Not that it helped much anyway, tracking over the southern hemisphere.

Jeremy closed his eyes and sat still for a moment once he shut down his SE. Oh, how he hated those patrols where they only went aloft to look at one another. What a waste of resources. There was nothing to be gained by flying through an empty sky. Maybe he needed to follow his instructor's example and shoot at the German trenches. If nothing else it would roust out the vermin. It could ruin someone's day, as being shot is apt to do.

One of the ground crew undid Jeremy's lap strap and the other steadied him as he climbed up to step over the side of the cockpit, down the ladder and onto the ground below. Hot cocoa would be wonderful right about now. Or coffee. Tea, even, as long as it was very hot. Going up in his repainted triplane did not look so appealing at the moment, but he knew that would change. There was a bright side to the inactivity in the air. It gave the mechanics more time to spend on Jeremy's captured triplane. They had something to do. That it was not normal routine was all the better. He knew they would line the landing strip in order to watch their work take flight. This one was personal.

Jeremy walked into the mess just as someone was refusing a hot cocoa, so Jeremy took it instead. He could care less what it was. He had no immediate plans to drink it, so taste was less important than temperature. The heat felt great on his hands and face. At least they would when his hands and face could feel anything at all. He thought of the time the major had spent with him, going over the rotary engine and how it worked. While he had worked with the Bleriot 'Penguin' in preflight training, he really had not worked much with rotary engines, Obviously, he had finished his scout training in the V-eight powered SE5a. The rotary seemed to work just fine while taxiing the triplane, so how different could it be in the air? He had spent a lot of time working the 'blip' switch just to keep the contraption on the ground. He could tell it would be a lot happier in the air. That would happen shortly, once he had the feeling back in his toes.

He hated the prospect of untying and then retying his boots, but removing them and putting his feet up near the fire was the fastest way to warm them. If he wanted to get up in that Fokker anytime that day, he had to do it. So began the ordeal. While the cocoa had helped his hands, proximity to the fire helped more. Undoing the boots was indeed a good idea, well worth the time and effort.

Somebody bumped into Jeremy, waking him up.

"Are you going to drink that cocoa?"

It was the major.

"Uh, I, uh . . . ."

"Unless you are thirsty, I would advise against it. Your triplane is out and ready to start. Are you coming? Or do I have to fly the little bugger and report back to you?"

The major walked away, his mission accomplished. Jeremy got to work pulling on his boots.

Moments later Jeremy emerged from the mess dressed in full flight gear, gloves and headgear in hand. It would not be any warmer, even with a bright sun out, but the sunlight would lend a little warmth on areas exposed to it. Small tradeoff. The major was standing by the boarding ladder.

"Well, son, let's get going. That is, unless you are having second thoughts. But somebody is going to take this thing into the air and now."

"Is that an order? Sir?"

The major smiled. He helped steady Jeremy and his heavy flight gear up the ladder. He would have smacked Jeremy on the bottom, but he knew it would never be felt beneath all those layers. After Jeremy was settled in, Major Campbell helped him with his harness.

"Any questions, son?"

"No, sir, I've thought this through and I'm ready. Thank you for the wakeup call, by the way. You can buy me another cocoa when I come back down."

"Only if you have earned it. Is the switch off?"

"Switch is off!"

Two men teamed up to push the propeller around to draw the petrol mix into the cylinders. Then they stood clear.

"Switch is on!"

One man leaned in from the port side and took hold of the propeller while the other man held the free hand of the first one. They nodded their heads simultaneously, and on the third nod both pulled hard to port, swinging the prop and getting well out of the way. The Clerget coughed for a few seconds until Jeremy adjusted the throttle to more of a choke position. That did it. As he fussed with the fuel/air mixture, the coughing yielded to a strong drone. After a few seconds Jeremy waved his hands outward, the signal to remove the chocks. That was done, and the prop pullers grasped the port wing tip so the diminutive Fokker could pivot toward the far end of the flight line. Jeremy utilized the 'blip' switch to hold back the powerful rotary engine as he taxied. His head swam in information, all necessary to wrangle the rotary in a strange airframe. His heart had never beat so fast or hard. This was going to be fun. He hoped.

At the end of the field he kicked the rudder to turn the Fokker around. In the same motion he allowed it to roll out for takeoff down the field, now lined with curious men, and into a moderate wind. The tail came up almost right away and he had to nudge the rudder a bit to starboard to keep the triplane in the middle of the field. It was not a direct headwind, and the machine seemed to have its own thoughts on where it wanted to go . By the time he felt he had the roll under control, adding left rudder to counter the engine torque, he was in the air. "That was easy," he thought as he eased the stick back gently to climb above the gathered men. He was easily seventy-five feet off the ground before he got to the largest assemblage. He had never felt such a strong climb. This was indeed going to be fun.

The little tripe buoyed to fifteen hundred feet in no time. Small wonder, between the more powerful engine and all the lifting surfaces. Jeremy tipped it a little to port and pulled the stick back to go into a fairly tight left turn. Without hesitation the triplane obliged. Same with a right turn, but the response was even more eager. Then he flew straight and level. Or tried to. He found he had to stay on the controls constantly or the 'plane would wander off course. No matter which direction Jeremy pointed it, into the wind, with the wind, crosswind, he had to fly it hands-on the whole time. Crosswinds were the worst. There was no flying straight in a crosswind. Jeremy made a note of this and wondered what a landing or takeoff would be like in a crosswind. Maybe he could meet with a captured triplane pilot and get some helpful information. Huh. Right. Okay, maybe more experimentation was in order.

Jeremy continued to work with his new triplane. He found it would turn like nothing he had ever experienced. It would climb like air bubbles through water. It would dive, but not very quickly. He imagined it was all the frontal wing area creating drag. Straight and level speed, or at least an attempt at straight and level, was also quite slow, even with a powerful Clerget in front. He kept it below three thousand feet for this, his first flight, but wanted to look into performance at altitude. Next time. It was a good introductory flight, one which provided plenty of things to consider.

Jeremy brought the triplane in normally, cutting the engine with the 'blip' switch. It seemed hesitant to set down, so he guided it down almost to the ground and gently stalled it down the last few feet or so.

Major Campbell was waiting when he reached the ground.

"Well, son, how was she? A little wild?"

"Major, sir, you have no idea. I can tell you about her—or you could take her up yourself and see."

"I would love to, but not today. I shall be happy to learn from you for the moment. Come on, I'll buy you a drink."

"As long as it's hot, sir."

Over hot tea the two continued their debriefing, as it were.

"What was easy?"

"Climbing and turning."

"I see. What was difficult?"

.Flying straight and level."

"Straight and level?"

"Yessir. It was like a small child at a carnival. It could not decide which direction it wanted to go next. I had to fuss with the controls constantly or away we would go."

"Hmm. Must be that short fuselage. Not enough tail."

"I'll take your word for that, sir. I only fly them. I don't know how they go together other than what part does what to keep it in the air."

"Of course."

"Sir, the thing is very unstable and quite slow. It is completely useless for tactics the SE uses, dive and shoot. It should outmaneuver anything in the sky. Anything wanting to dogfight it should finish in second place."

"I see."

"It could be a useful learning tool for our pilots. I could fly it and they could try to outfly it. It should validate what we know, dive and shoot and keep going. No SE is going to stay with it in a dogfight. Do consider, sir, that this is only my initial impression. I have yet to fly stunts in it and I have yet to fly it above three thousand feet."

"That is quite the initial impression. What about your instructor? Could you outfly him in it?"

"Oh, handily, sir. He is not one for aerobatics and this triplane is built for aerobatics. He could never dogfight one."

"But could you shoot him down in it?"

"I would not want to say. He could never stay with it in a dogfight, but the old bird—begging your pardon, sir!—is very resourceful. I would not carve his headstone just yet."

"Fair enough. Son, your instructor will be here in a matter of days. If you want to outfly him, I suggest you log some more hours in your new toy!"

"Aye, sir. I shall."

"And do keep me abreast of whatever you find out about the thing."

"Yes, sir."

Major Campbell got up to leave. Jeremy made himself comfortable so he could relive his flight. He knew that if anyone wanted him they would wake him up. If no one woke him up, he would go up again in the triplane when he awoke on his own.

* * * *

CHAPTER 68

British

From the mess I could see the crowd around my Camel. I wasn't sure what they expected her to do. I hoped no one was holding their breath, at any rate. It was just a Clerget powered Sopwith Camel, not unlike any number of other Clerget Camels. Well, I had gone over her from stem to stern in an effort to work out any minor imperfections, just like I had done my SEs. Every system in the machine was at its peak. To me it meant a world of difference, but in fact it only improved performance slightly. I was more interested in reliability. Improved performance was an unintended, but welcome, consequence.

I finished eating and went to my quarters to play my cornet. "This should make them want to leave," I thought, as I warmed up after a few days away from it. Cornet is something that must be done every day in order to maintain any kind of proficiency. Oh, sure, one can miss a day here and there, but the point is keeping the lip in shape. If the lip is not kept in practice, one's endurance goes away, followed by one's tone. Well, my endurance was on the decline, and my tone probably had a few of them begging to be sent directly to the front. It was not pretty. Nor was it at all tuneful. That said, I tend to be pretty easy on myself, being a flight instructor and all. So it was bad. I finally put it away and hoped no one was about to do a strafing run on my quarters.

Playing at the cornet—it was too bad to be considered *playing* the cornet—made me think of Pauline. It had been quite some time since I had heard from her. Yes, the circumstances made regular contact difficult, but we had missed a few opportunities to get together and I was growing concerned. Was it her cough? She had not sounded at all well the past couple of times I had seen, well, heard her. I felt it was indicative of some serious malady, and I have never been one to dwell on such things. I found myself wishing for rain.

The lip worn out, I walked to the CO's office and placed a telephone call to the nursing school in town. Clara was not available, so I left a quizzical message, "How is your new hat?" She would know who called. As I replaced the receiver, the CO walked in, so I passed some time with him.

"Sir, have you had any time to look into that soldier whose information I left with you recently?"

"No, son. Well, that is, I have placed a few inquiries but none have come back with anything.

I'm sure something will turn up. Remember, there is a war going on. That does tend to slow communications somewhat."

"Cursed war. But you are right, sir. Of course. I appreciate your looking into it."

"Certainly. Say, you do know, don't you, that everyone wants to fly your Camel?"

"I had that impression, yes."

"Well?"

"Well, what? You did say it's *my* Camel."

"Aye."

"There are other Camels. Let them sow their oats in those. I have gone over mine completely and improved every aspect of her performance, starting with reliability. There are no secrets. I have shown them again and again what it takes to be a scout pilot, including time spent working on one's machine when not flying it. Let them spend that time on their machines rather than chasing the local females on their off hours."

"You are being perhaps a little harsh, aren't you?"

"No, sir, not at all. I see it as being consistent. I have taught every one of my students the advantages of caring for one's own machine. Let them care for theirs—or all of them— and reap the benefits. It will help them at the front. Let them start here. I do not see it as harsh at all, merely realistic. Besides, I have to fly that Camel to the front soon. It needs to cross the Channel without difficulties."

"Good point. You and your Camel will likely fly against the Germans as well. I don't blame you."

"Thank you, sir. I trust the lads will put her away when the sideshow is over with? Or do I need to check up on it?"

"Well, it's not like you have a lot of other options. Go on and help the lads bed her down. Unless you want to go start another impromptu air show, of course."

"Tomorrow will be another day, sir."

* * * *

CHAPTER 69

British

'Twas another day indeed. A rainy day at that. As was custom, I borrowed a motor-car from the pool and went into town for coffee. As I approached I could see business was predictably slow. Upon entry, the proprietor poured a cup of coffee and led me to "our" table. And there she was.

Pauline looked just a little disheveled, even for a rainy day. Her hair looked, well, half-hearted, and she just seemed to sag a little as opposed to what I was accustomed to seeing. There was no polish. Something was indeed wrong. She coughed and took a sip of her coffee.

"Good morning, Lieutenant. Shall I order for you?"

"Certainly. I trust you."

As our friend left with the order, conversation continued.

"Pauline, why are you here? You look the devil. And I can see you are not well."

"But it's been entirely too long since we have been together."

"Well, yes, it has. I certainly have missed our time together, but your health must come first."

After another fit of a cough, "Yes, yes, but I can't seem to shake this cough. I have lost my appetite and my clothes are beginning to hang on me. What's left of me. I just know I wanted to see you. You always make me feel special. I love being with you. I know it will help me to feel better."

"I know not what will help your ailment. I am not a doctor."

"No, but you bring the right medicine."

"I am pleased that I give you something."

"I am hopeful you will give me that something. It always helps. I feel a bit like a victim today."

"A victim? A victim of what?"

"A victim of your aggression, of course. Or shall I draw you a diagram?"

"Hardly," I smiled. "I can take it from there."

Our food arrived presently, along with more coffee. Pauline had not ordered much for herself, but at least she was eating something, a good sign. The body needs fuel, after all, in order to fight off an infection. Or just to sustain.

"Lieutenant, I trust you heard about the aerobatics demonstration?"

"Oh?"

"Yesterday. Over the old athletic fields. I saw some of it at a distance but had to go back inside and lie down. I missed the ending. If there was an actual ending, that is. It could have been one of your students keeping in practice."

"If you missed the end, then you missed the best part."

"So you did hear about it."

"No. I flew it."

"That was you? I didn't think you had much use for such flying."

"That was before this Sopwith. The bloody thing just demands to be flown, not just guided across the sky. She is quite the demanding partner. Straight and level she will do, but grudgingly."

"Doesn't care for missionary? I can understand. But *she*? What is she, a ship?"

"Well, in a sense, yes. But before her, they were just aeroplanes. This machine has a soul. She reminds me of you."

"Me?"

"But of course. As you noted, she doesn't care for missionary or mundane things. She prefers a sally into new territory and the quest for adventure. While straight lines are acceptable, she prefers to embellish the ordinary. How am I doing?"

"I can't wait to feel you taming the wild beast. Or trying to."

"Oh, I'll take the situation and make the best of it. It's worked thus far."

"That it has."

Pauline put her empty cup down and left to pay for breakfast. I paused and then went to say goodbye and shake the proprietor's hand.

Once in the motor-car, she continued the conversation.

"While my clothes do hang on me, these clothes in particular are hanging on me for a reason. They are to be torn off, if you wish. Once we arrive, you are to make me yours in any and every way. You of course have my trust, and I am most confident you will take matters into your own hands. And arms."

"But are you up to—"

"Lieuu-tenn-annt, I am a victim. Your . . . victim."

Helping her down and out of the car, "Yes, madam. As you wish."

I caught the arm she swung at me and used it to turn her around and propel her into the house and the guest room. I clamped my hand over her mouth and undid her coat while keeping her off balance. I forced her facedown on the bed, her knees a bit above the floor, removed her coat, and secured her wrists behind her. I removed a few other items, bound her ankles, and positioned her on her side, open for my manifestations. She was calling me names, so I muffled that fusillade. That did it. She was mine. She was about to be a victim, and she struggled to put up what fight she could.

I took a moment to sit down and admire my work and remove my boots. She was clad in some manner of hosiery and an open blouse. Anything else was my doing. She was the picture of temptation. She struggled, but to no avail. She would be mine. My second boot came off and joined the first next to the chair. I stood up and undressed slowly to let her anticipate the treatment she was about to undergo. I approached her and watched her eyes grow while I traced my hands over her warm body. This had been a long time coming. If this was how she wanted to rekindle things, who was I to complain? I have been happy to show her physical love any way she wanted short of actual harm. There were tender moments, there were attacks, there were detentions and interrogations and sometimes silly games. All were avenues to similar conclusions. Even missionary. It's good to be flexible.

Pauline coughed. At first I thought little of it. But it persisted and she was turning red to purple in the face and upper chest. I dove for my uniform and pulled out my pocketknife. Sitting her upright, I cut away her gag so she could do what she needed to do to breathe. While her episode subsided I undid her other restraints. Then I pulled down the bedclothes and helped her to a sitting position under the covers I have to say she looked magnificent, what with her wild looking hair and bare breasts partially exposed beneath the open blouse. But to the matter at hand . . . .

"Can I get you anything? Water?"

"Yes, water. Please."

Getting up to leave the room, "But of course."

I returned as quickly as I could, whereupon she started to laugh.

"What is the matter, my dear?"

"Oh . . . nothing!" she lied.

Then it dawned on me. There I stood, naked but for a pair of socks, with a glass of water. That had to be quite the sight. I could not blame her for laughing. A I handed her the glass, I joined her in a good laugh. She tentatively sipped at the water.

"Do you still feel like a victim?"

She sprayed water everywhere, but mostly on me, as she laughed through the mouthful.

"Maybe another time."

There it was. I saw a glimmer of that smile. It was the first I had seen of it in quite some time. She could lose weight, she could gain weight, it didn't matter if she still had that smile.

I shared my concerns for her health. I suggested she visit her physician, but she resisted. After pursuing that line nowhere, I changed course a bit.

"What about Clara?"

"Clara?"

"Yes, of course."

"But she's a nurse."

"But she wants to be a doctor. She has been studying her entire life to be a doctor. Even without accreditation, she knows what doctors know. She could help you."

"Why, yes, I would think she could. And it could further her cause."

"Now you are beginning to understand. You need to call the nursing school and get her over here."

"You could go get her."

"No, I cannot. No one knows I have ever been here but you."

"Oh, of course."

"If she called me for a ride, that would be one thing. But she would have no reason for that. She would have to find her own way here unless you sent a driver or your husband."

"You are correct. I apologize."

"No apology needed. You are not feeling well. You need to get help and take care of yourself."

"Yes, yes. I know."

Her proper color restored, we said our goodbyes and I left her where she was. I could only hope she would telephone for Clara.

* * * *

CHAPTER 70

British

I returned the automobile and walked past the CO's office, where I heard him call for me. "Yes, sir?"

"Come in, please."

"What is the matter, sir?"

"I have word on that soldier you asked about."

"What is it, sir?"

"Deceased."

"Deceased? What happened?"

"I have nothing on how it happened. But he is deceased. I verified it with a second source. It is certain. I can inquire further, but it could take time."

"Yes, sir, of course. Please do, if you do not mind."

"Who was the lad? A friend?"

"No, sir. Never met him."

"Then why did you ask—"

"Do you remember the last dinner, sending off the pilots to their assignments? One of them had a sister there, and she was the nurse who cared for me after a German shell nearly killed me."

"Ahh, yes, I remember, the blonde you danced with once?"

"Yes, sir. That was Clara. The soldier in question is—was—her fiancé."

"Oh, I see."

"She had not heard from him since he transferred to the Middle East, and I offered to ask about him."

"Apparently the notice has not reached the lad's parents yet. Are you going to break the news?"

"I suppose I shall have to, sir. She works in town. May I use your telephone to place a call to her?"

"But of course. I shall leave so—"

463

"No, sir. I will just leave word for her to contact me. She is most likely busy and cannot be disturbed."

I left word for Clara and then thanked the CO for his efforts. I knew I would be going to my quarters to spend some time with the cornet, but the sound from the day before was still echoing in my head. So I stopped by the hangar to look over my Camel. I reflexively checked the tension in the control wires but held off pulling the plugs. I could do that later or in the morning. I was merely anxious about getting to the front. I did not care to wait out the class ceremony, but my group, numerically diminished though it was, were a good group of lads and deserved having their instructor present as they left for their assignments. I could not begrudge them that. It would happen soon enough.

I retraced my steps past the CO's office so as to stay inside while going to my quarters.

"Lef-tenant?"

It was a corporal from the CO's office.

"Yes?"

"I have a message for you, sir."

I walked back toward the lad and took the note he presented to me.

"Thank you, Corporal."

The note was brief. Clara would be free the next morning. I could borrow a motor-car and go face her while I told her the very last item of news she would ever want to hear. I could tell it was going to be a wonderful day.

I whiled away the day on the cornet, then lying on my cot, watching the light play on the meager winter garden outside my window. The cornet was actually starting to sound a bit musical. I had heard far fewer guttural noises being made outside my door than a few days earlier. "Sorry!" I would shout, "the piano usually covers the bad bits."

Came the reply, "Only if someone were jumping on it!"

Right, then. We had no lack of critics on the airfield. I'd wager they all play a mean gramophone.

I spent a perfectly restless night. I might have slept an hour or slightly more, but only due to boredom from trying to sleep. It takes a lot of effort trying to force oneself to sleep. So, due to boredom or herculean effort, I did achieve minimal sleep. I hoped it would be enough to carry on a coherent conversation with perhaps the most intelligent person I had ever known, but I had my doubts. Indeed this was going to be a wonderful day.

I awoke entirely too early. I could not watch the light play on the garden unless I switched on an electric light. It would not be the same. On the bright side, there was plenty of hot water for a shower and shave. The messenger would certainly be clean.

I waited around until I thought maybe my naval friend in town would be opening for business. As I approached in the motor-car I watched his lights begin to illuminate the cafe. I was at the door when he unlocked it. We shook hands and exchanged greetings, and he apologized the coffee was only just beginning to brew.

"Oh, nonsense. What twit is out at this hour looking for coffee? I can wait."

"Lef-tenant, you are so kind. Tell me, what brings you out this early?—if you do not mind my asking, of course."

"No, not at all. I'm afraid I need to deliver some very bad news to a friend."

"The pretty one who often meets you here?"

"Oh, no. You see, I met a woman some time ago when I was wounded in France."

"You were wounded?"

"Aye. An artillery shell exploded next to a wagon I was unloading. I was trapped between the wagon and the munitions building."

"You were lucky you didn't go up with the bomb and all the munitions!"

"Lucky does not begin to describe it. I was saved by the wagon that crushed me, at least one horse, and my wagon mate."

"Wow. And you were mostly okay, then?"

"Hardly. I was blinded by foreign objects in my eyes, and my left arm was very badly crushed. The field doctors wanted to leave me for dead. That was when I met this woman. Well, she met me. I was unconscious. She made me her mission. She insisted the doctors look at me. She made every effort to care for me. Because of her, I not only survived, but I kept my badly crushed left arm. I have no idea how many hours she put into cleaning my wounds and my eyes. She certainly saved my arm from amputation." "Sounds like an extremely fine woman."

"Aye. I lost track of her when they moved me to Dover for recovery and therapy. I never had her name, I never saw her. I only heard her voice."

"And you have somehow met and you want to thank her?"

"Well, no. We have already met. She was in here one day, but you were busy and probably don't remember. She had a brother in the first class I was connected with at the airfield. I managed to recognize her voice in the crowd at the reception. Unmistakable voice."

"And you are beginning a relationship?"

"No, I'm afraid not. She was engaged to marry an army officer but had not heard from him in a while. I told her I could look into it, and I did. I'm afraid she will not be marrying any time soon."

"You don't mean . . . ."

"But I do. He was on assignment to the Middle East and was somehow killed. I am on the way to tell her."

"Aww, mate, that is bloody awful. I'm happy to send you along with some fresh cakes if you think it will help at all."

"Maybe a few couldn't hurt. Thank you kindly for the suggestion."

"If she is here in town, they will still be warm when she gets them."

"You're a good man."

"No, mate, you're the good man. I would prefer a room full of angry customers to what you are about to do."

"I owe my life, all that I am, and everything I have to this woman. I will tell her the truth and help her get through it. It's the very least I can do."

"Coffee's ready, Lef-tenant. What else can I get you?"

I had a good breakfast as others came in for coffee and socializing. I joined in conversation about the war, speculations on when the bloody thing would end, and so on. It was a pleasant enough way to pass the time. I managed to look over some shoulders to watch the light grow along the street, illuminating the buildings and the increasing number of people up and about. I love the way light modulates and changes one's perception of the world. Simple dark goes to indistinct dark shapes to browns and greys of buildings, streets, and sidewalks. Bits of motion slowly take the shape of people walking past. Drab clothing assumes colors indistinguishable but a moment before, sometimes topped by women's colorful and/or floral hats. The closer faces transform from light shapes to features and expressions of emotion or lack thereof. One can then tell, for the most part, who is walking to work or the market, as opposed to who is simply out for fresh air or perhaps a visit to the cafe for coffee and conversation. Another couple enter the cafe as I turn to add my two farthings worth on the next German offensive.

The time worked its way toward normal business hours, so to speak, and I thought it was time to go face Clara with news of her deceased fiancé. I paid the proprietor, took the fresh cakes, and walked to the motor-car. Maybe I could detour past . . . no, that would not be appropriate on this, a bright morning blossoming into a gorgeous winter day. Perhaps I could detour a little and go past the—no, that only delayed the inevitable. Best to get there early and have the time available to begin healing her emotional wounds. I had obviously assumed the worst. She would certainly be upset. That was to be expected. But I did not know her constitution in such circumstances. Maybe she almost expected that would be the case. All the speculation was causing my temples to knot with tension. I needed to get there and begin the process in order to see what would happen next. I eased the throttle forward.

I parked the motor-car and entered the nursing school. After asking for Clara I took a seat in the lobby. Half an eternity passed, or so it seemed. Clara approached me after a few minutes. I suggested she get some coffee or tea and join me in a nearby room and held up the box from the cafe. She smiled and said she would bring us coffee.

"So, Lef-tenant, how are you of late? Are you packing to go to the front?"

"I am well, thank you, and I will be departing for my old squadron soon, but there is hardly any room in the aeroplane for luggage, so there will be no packing. But that's not why I am here."

"Well, it's always a pleasure to see you, but what brings you this morning? The note I received from the telephone operator did not say much."

"I did not tell her much, I'm afraid. I wanted to deliver the news to you in person."

"News?"

"Yes. I have received word on your fiancé."

"You have?! How is he? When will he—"

"The news is not good."

Her bright, excited smile began to melt like wax in bright sunlight.

"He's not coming back, is he?"

"I apologize for the lack of detail, but no, he is not coming back. Word comes back that he is deceased. I'm afraid that is all I have. I know nothing of the circumstances, only that he is no longer with us. I am deeply, deeply sorry."

I watched as her green eyes began to water. It was stunningly beautiful save the tragic circumstances.

"Well, there is a war going on, seemingly the world over. They call it the war to end all wars, and his war is over. Pity. He was a wonderful man."

"I am sorry to bring you such news."

"Don't be silly. I asked you to look into his welfare, and you did. I am grateful. It's no fault of yours that things have taken this course. You didn't even know him. I cannot be angry with you."

"But, Clara, what can I do for you? There must be something."

"Stay awhile. If you have the time, of course. I do not want to keep you."

"No, I have nothing needing attention. I am waiting for the students to have their departure ceremony and ship out. Then I leave for the front. I am yours. Tell me what I can do for you."

"Ahh, I don't know. Just having your company is wonderful. The news needs to sink in before I better know. It's been so long since I've seen him. Maybe the transition will be smoother not having seen him. I don't know. This is a new experience to me."

"I fully understand. I shall remain available to you as long as I'm still here, if that will help."

"It will help to know that. You are most kind."

"No, I am forever in your debt."

"In my debt? Don't be silly. France? I was just doing what I do, what I have always done. But if you feel in debt, you can start with whatever is in that box. It certainly smells wonderful. And I am hungry."

She could be so disarming.

"Certainly, dear Clara. Here you are. Fresh this morning. If you want more, I can take you there. Anything."

Through a mouthful, "Oh. This is delectable!"

"They are all yours. If you want more to eat or more to share, I am happy to facilitate."

"That could happen—you are a good man. Thank you for being so wonderful to me."

"Not to worry. In addition to being in your debt, I happen to enjoy your company and appreciate your skills and dedication. Would that more women were like you."

"Would that more women *could* be like me. Women are an untapped resource, if I dare say so."

"I very much agree. And women who are involved in a cause have an additional dimension to appreciate. Pardon my saying so, but I find it quite exciting."

"And well you should. Sitting around the house all day does nothing to inspire thought, creativity, and conversation. Talk devolves to whispers about what the neighbors allegedly do. Rumormongering is simply not interesting, at least to me. Give me something of substance, something to stimulate thought, something to challenge, something to chew on, so to speak. I see no reason why men should be the only interesting ones. Women have much to offer as well."

I sipped coffee as I watched her devour her cake in a decidedly unladylike manner. As she reached for another, I could see how she was dealing with the sad news, at least for the moment. Food. Relieve the stress through food. Reflecting on her position and ambitions, I could see why she carried a few extra pounds. Oh, she was not at all unattractive. I always preferred women with that little something extra. Something to have and to hold, if you will.

"These really are very good. Do you think he still has some? I would love to get some for the other faculty members."

"I could go inquire. Would you care to accompany me?"

"Yes. I'll get my coat."

I brought the car to the door while she donned her coat. In no time we were at the cafe. There were no more cakes to be had, but the proprietor offered to make more. Clara objected, but he insisted it was no trouble at all. I knew he was doing it because of our conversation earlier that morning.

"I'll tell you what. You make more and I will buy the entire batch."

"You don't need to."

"No, but I shall. I can distribute some to friends and tell them where they came from."

"That would be wonderful, sir."

Clara and I took some tea at the counter while the proprietor set about baking. She had become quiet and a bit withdrawn, perfectly understandable considering the news I had brought. The war had taken from her a part of her life she obviously had looked forward to. She was not alone on that count, but that did little if anything to console her. She had met someone she was perfectly content with, enough so that she was willing to share her life with him. Then comes the war and that is taken away. It causes one to question just what the purpose of the war was. King and country? Why? Did it matter that much? Some archduke gets shot by an anarchist in the far end of Europe and next thing everybody gets excited and lines up to form sides the world over. Losing any life is tragic on some level, but does it have to cause so many consequent deaths and tragedies? That archduke meant nothing to me. I had never heard of him. But here I am, serving king and country, dedicated to killing bloody Huns. Why? Okay, granted, they had assaulted me in any number of ways and killed friends, so I felt justified. It was personal. And I know I had caused similar personal animosity with bullets and grenades of my own. But had the world not lined up to shoot at one another, conceivably I could be taking tea in some German cafe. Or

French. Or Austrian. I could be painting in a studio in Paris or in the Alps or on the Mediterranean. But no, these were not viable options unless one wanted to be shot at or bombed or subjected to any number of unpleasantries. What was the point of this war? King and country? Was it to make better aeroplanes, better guns? The aeroplanes we had depended on at the war's outset were hopelessly obsolete but three years later, such had been the progress in the field of aviation. The FE type I flew in with Knees had been withdrawn from the front, at least from the missions I flew them for, and replaced by much improved RE8s and the promised F2b. The latter was on a par with the SEs I flew, but with a second crew member manning a rearward firing machine gun. All this progress in order to kill the enemies of king and country. I thought of all the money that had gone into uniforms, training, guns, other weapons and transportation systems. That money could have been spent on food, clothing, and shelter for the less fortunate. Public transportation systems. Art and music. There were so many other uses for that money that made so much more sense than ways to kill enemy troops. How many of these troops knew what they were fighting for? Any of them? What was their motivation for fighting? Fight or be ostracized? Executed? I could only imagine meeting any of the opposing pilots I had faced in the air over France in some neutral setting, as in no war. Take a break from my latest canvas masterpiece for coffee and a baguette. So much bread, why not share with that man sitting alone. His name, Heinrich, matters not. Perhaps he is also a painter. Or a musician. Or house builder. Did it matter, his nationality or trade? We could find something to discuss regardless. But because of the war Heinrich is shooting at me with his Albatross scout and I at him with my SE. Or Camel. For king and country? If our king has a grudge with the leader of another nation, could he not hand off his crown and robe to his second and just step into the boxing ring to do his own personal battle with that leader? Perhaps steeplechase. Or pistols at dawn. There is a romantic notion, eh? Two leaders, two pistols, a spectacular sunrise, and the matter is settled with two lead balls. Perhaps a casket. Or a hospital stay. But the "war" is over in a few minutes. Hundreds of thousands of innocent citizens go about their daily lives and business and go home to sup with their families instead of dying on some godforsaken muddy battlefield. Maybe we pilots still have our powered box kites instead of the powerful, streamlined machines the war has given us. But it would be worth it. Thinking of myself, the war had lead me to meet Clara and Pauline, two wonderful women I otherwise would not have encountered, much less befriended. But life would have lead me to someone, perhaps any number of someones. There is the balance. I meet two wonderful women and some great chaps at the expense of untold thousands killed, maimed, or missing. Was it worth it?

"Lef-tenant?" It was Clara. "The cakes are ready. Shall we finish our tea and go then?"

"Oh. Of course. Sorry. I guess I drifted off."

"I don't blame you. I am not much company this moment."

"You are wonderful company. I so enjoy being with you. And I am sorry I have put you in this funk. But you need to process this new information as you see fit. Right. For the moment, let's go brighten somebody's day with fresh cakes, shall we?"

I paid for the cakes, refusing Clara's attempt to do so, and the proprietor and I loaded the boxes into the motor-car. A hearty handshake and slap on the back, and away we went. We had quite a few cakes, but I knew just where to take them.

"Where are you going?"

"I am making a stop that could help you move on with your life. Let's sweeten the deal with cakes."

"Where are you going?"

"We are stopping at a certain hat shop."

"No."

"Yes. We will do what it takes to get you what you want. You can be a doctor and a surgeon, and we are going to make it happen, however we need to. The image of you bringing a box of cakes to the owner will go a long way."

"Okay. I suppose. Let's."

It couldn't hurt. We walked in with a box apiece. The owner noticed us right away and came to greet us.

"Well, this is a surprise! A pleasant one, I must add. Good morning, madam, and good morning, Lef-tenant! Dare I ask what you have?"

"We had these cakes this morning and wanted to take more back to the nursing school, but the cafe had run out. The proprietor offered to bake another batch for us, and I bought the entire batch. We thought you and your staff would enjoy some."

"Why, certainly we would. Where are they from?"

"It's a little cafe just off the square. The owner served in the Royal Navy, aboard the HMS Dreadnaught."

"Ahh, yes. I have met him. Splendid chap. My wife sometimes goes there. She could be meeting someone for all I know—but who would have her? It's a pleasant enough cafe, though."

"As I haven't had the pleasure in some time, how is your lovely wife?"

"She's a bit under the weather, I'm afraid. She has a cough. It's been with her for a while now and it seems to be getting worse."

"Shame. Delightful woman. I hope she sees it through. She is getting medical attention, isn't she?"

"I don't believe she is. She says it will go away."

Clara spoke up. "She really ought to have it looked at. It could be any number of things, possibly tuberculosis, which could kill her. I have read of a breakout of influenza. That could also be deadly. I'll be happy to visit her, if you wish."

"You?"

"Why, yes. To be blunt, I know what doctors know. I can treat what doctors treat. I only lack the certification. I can visit with, test, and diagnose what is ailing your wife. Again, without certification I cannot prescribe medications, but I will know what she needs. I can see her today. Or I can be reached at the nursing school. I would be delighted to visit her and offer help. She is a perfectly delightful woman, and I would enjoy seeing her again."

"You do make it awfully convenient. She has not been overseeing the staff much of late and things are beginning to slide a bit about the house. Allow me to telephone her to be sure she will be home.

Lef-tenant, does this cause you any inconvenience? I would hate to put you out."

"Why no, sir, not at all. I am merely awaiting the departure ceremony for the current class of pilots, then I am off to the front for a visit. In fact, you may recall, it will be Jeremy's squadron."

"Ahh, yes! I do recall that. I'm sure you are anxious to get back there."

"It will be a change of pace, to be sure. I look forward to visiting with Jeremy and Major Campbell—and getting a few shots in at the Huns, of course. But I am free today. I would only have to know where Clara needs to go. Once we drop off the cakes at the school, we could go directly to her."

"Please excuse me for a moment while I telephone the house."

As he turned to go to his office I felt a jab in the rib cage.

"You are so manipulative!"

"Me? How could you say that? It's for you and for Pauline. She is ill. You can help. And by helping her you show what an asset you are to the community as a doctor. It's a splendid plan, if I do say so."

"I do not disagree. And I didn't say manipulative was bad. Sometimes it is merely necessary, a means to an end, as it were."

"In aerial combat, one does not always get to dive directly out of the sun at one's foe. Sometimes one must stalk one's prey roundabout and wait for the chance to attack."

"I see you have adapted such behavior for your exploits on the ground. Clever. I like the way you think, Lef-tenant."

"Thank you."

While I was sure Clara was not over the shock of losing her fiancé, all this other activity was helpful. I could see she was a woman with a strong constitution who could focus on the matter at hand. Oh, I was positive she would have her moments, but they would be when she was alone, or at least out of the public eye. I resolved to be available to her as long as I was still near. She helped me through a far worse crisis. It was the least I could do for her.

"My wife will be available all day, as she has no plans. You may go visit any time. Here is the address. I appreciate your thoughtfulness. It will be good to have her better and on top of things at the house."

"I'm sure it will, sir. We will drop the cakes off at the school and thence visit your wife."

And so it went. A short while later we arrived at the address and parked in front. It felt odd, having never approached the house from the front. Clara reached past me and knocked on the door. A matronly woman greeted us and showed us in. After closing the door she showed us to Pauline. We entered the dark room and the woman brushed behind us to open the curtains and allow some light in. There lay Pauline, asleep and looking thin and gaunt. "Lack of eating breakfast out", I thought but dared not say, for I knew it was a more serious matter. There was a deep rattle of a cough. Pauline stirred a bit, and the woman touched a shoulder.

"Madam, you have visitors."

Pauline awoke with a start.

"Visitors. Visitors? Who is here?"

"A Lef-tenant and a woman with what appears to be a doctor's bag."

"It's Clara. I am here to see what is ailing you."

Pauline was incoherent.

"Lef-tenant, could you kindly leave the room and close the door so that I may examine my patient? I will come for you when we are finished."

I backed through the door, pulling it shut, and then found a bench in the hallway.

The examination did not take long. I was just settling in after shifting position slightly when Clara came looking for me.

"That didn't take long at all."

"No, once I saw her I didn't think it would."

"What is the matter?"

"I am not completely sure. I will need more testing to ascertain just what it is, but she needs more attention than languishing here in her bed will provide. She is decidedly not well."

"What do we do, then?"

"To begin with, we need to get her to hospital. She cannot receive proper care at home. She needs more fluids right now. We need to consult with her husband and get him to initiate the care she needs."

"Fair enough. Please do instruct the staff on what they need to do for her. Then we can go back to the millinery and have a word with her husband."

I left to be ready to crank the motor-car to life when Clara joined me, which she did presently. Back to the millinery we went. The clerk who greeted us informed us the owner was indisposed, away for the balance of the day. After consulting a moment, we left word for him to telephone Clara as soon as he could for the matter was urgent.

That settled, we returned to the house to ask the staff to urge Pauline's husband to telephone Clara. Back in the motor-car, I asked Clara where she wished to go next.

"Lef-tenant, it has been a most trying day. I have no pressing needs at the school, so I should like to go home. Could you possibly . . ."

"Of course. You need only direct me and I shall take you there."

"You are most kind, Lef-tenant."

"Not at all. I am forever in your debt, remember?"

"Nonsense. Working on you in that field hospital taught me a lot. I would call us even."

"Never. I am eternally grateful."

Clara directed me out of town and into a, well, neglected area. Well, slightly. But after a short drive through that, she had me turn onto a pleasant curved road, but a short road it was. After a few hundred yards Clara announced that we had arrived.

"Where?"

"Directly in front of you, Lef-tenant, at the end of the road. That is my cottage. Well, rented, but mine all the same."

"Quite charming! Very nice indeed."

"Oh, it is cozy. The actual owner lives back at that last corner, so he takes pretty decent care of it for me. Care for some tea?"

"Yes, that is a splendid idea."

"Come, Lief-enant, and I shall take care of it."

We entered the cottage and Clara put more wood on the fire before I could ask. In no time, the cottage was warm. It was indeed cozy. But what more did she need? She spent her waking hours at the school. The cottage was for eating, reading and sleeping. I was just glancing around at the spartan furnishings and lack of decorations when she called me to the small table with fresh hot tea steeping.

"Sugar, Lef-tenant?"

"Yes, please."

We bobbed our tea balls in the water a bit, and she took a sip before I did. I preferred my tea just a little stronger to go with the sweet of the sugar. The quiet was refreshing. It had been a long and trying day at that. It was good to hear nothing for a moment. I elected not to break the reverie. The warmth and crackle of the fire were working us almost into a trance. I looked across the table at Clara, her face blank and nearly without emotion save one tear trailing down her cheek. I knew where she was and I would allow her come back when she was ready. I looked at her in the afternoon sun, filtering in from the opposite side of the cottage, illuminating one side of her face, her nose, and the "apple" of the opposite cheek. The light played in her pale eyes, then welling up in tears. Her hair was strawberry blonde, just red of true blonde. I could not help but think of the popular song about a "Casey" dancing with a strawberry blonde, "and the band played on . . . ." She could be in that song, and I would not mind being "Casey". Not at all. As was my taste in women, she was a bit north of tiny. Her curves took my eyes on a welcome and somewhat familiar tour, dare I say. I really hadn't taken the time to look at her so closely, and I was sorry I had not done so before. But we had always had other matters to discuss. And I knew how Pauline had felt about my showing any interest in her at all, even polite, noncommittal social courtesies.

"Lef-tenant?"

"Yes, Clara?"

"I should like to lie down, at least for a moment. Do you mind?"

"Not at all. I'll just tidy up and—"

"You will do nothing of the sort."

"But I really should—"

"Lef-tenant, I can clean the table later, thank you. I should like you to—"

"Sure, I'll just lea—"

"If you're quite done . . . . I should like you to join me. If you don't mind."

"But, you . . ."

"But I what?"

"You don't think . . ."

"Lef-tenant, we are grown adults. I should think we could do as we please. After the day I have had, I really would prefer not to be alone. I would like to share the company of a man I know I can trust, and you are that man. Would you please stay with me, if only for a short while? You need not say or do anything. Leave your outer wear and jacket here, as well as your boots, please. I shall be happy to help you lace them later."

"That won't be necessary."

"Fine. I'll be waiting."

Predictably enough, my hands comprised ten thumbs when attempting to unlace the boots. I did manage to loose them without the aid of my teeth, however, and I entered the bedroom where she sat on the edge of the bed in considerably fewer layers than she wore but moments before. Her curves were far more enticing with fewer obstructions. She motioned for me to lie toward one side of her bed. As I settled in and made myself comfortable on my back, she lay alongside me, placing her arm across my abdomen and her head on the front of my left shoulder.

"Oh, pardon me, Lef-tenant. I hope I am not hurting your bad arm."

"No, of course not. It is much better, thank you. You really should see it."

"Excellent idea. Let's have a look, shall we?" With that, she took off my tie and began to undo my shirt buttons.

"Here. Let me."

"No!" She lightly slapped my hands out of her way. "I can do this."

And do—well, undo—she did. She rolled me away a little and removed the shirt from my left arm. Tucking the shirt under my back, she pulled me toward her and pulled the shirt off my right arm and dropped it behind her on the floor.

"Lef-tenant, you have healed remarkably well. Yes, you have the predictable scarring, but you appear to be perfectly capable."

"Capable? Of what?" My trousers were feeling a little more snug by now.

"Of anything a normal left arm can do, of course."

"Oh. Yes, it feels pretty good most of the time. I get little pangs now and then, and cold, damp weather is not so kind to me, but overall I feel very good, considering I should be dead."

"Nonsense. I knew you would be okay."

"I'm pleased you did. It seems you held the minority opinion."

"But I won."

"No, I won."

"Yes, I suppose you did."

"Thanks to you, of course."

"You always talk about thanking me. Well, I wish you would get around to it."

With that, Clara swung a leg over me and pulled herself up to a position straddling me at the waist. She undid a bow beneath her neck and slowly removed a floral frock, holding it off to her right and dropping it at the edge of the bed. It caught a little atop the bed but fell, cascading toward my shirt. This left a white camisole that was plainly struggling to hide what was beneath. It did not struggle for long. Clara reached over her shoulder and behind to pull a ribbon and undo the camisole. She held her hands toward mine as if offering them. I took her hands, and she shook her shoulders to allow the liberated camisole to slide down her arms toward me. When it got to her hands, she let go of mine and gently placed the camisole over my face.

"This is thanking you?"

"No, but be patient. You will. Trust me, you will."

"While I am thanking you, will I get to see you?"

"Of course. Just not right away."

"Oh. Alright, then."

"Don't sound so dejected, Lef-tenant!" She reached for my hands, which I had dropped to my chest. She drew them toward her. Specifically, toward her chest. She lightly drew my hands across her shoulders, neck, torso, and breasts. Any time I tried to manipulate my own hands, she would push them off her skin and hold them away.

"Patience, Lef-tenant. You must learn patience."

"I am not always good about being patient."

She wiggled her bum a little. "Yes, I can feel that. Relax. You don't always get to dive on the enemy straightaway, do you?"

"Well, no."

"There you are, then. Sometimes you must stalk for a while before you get an opportunity."

"Yes."

"Patience." With that she placed my hands full on her breasts and held them there. She pulled them in toward her, into the soft but firm flesh. She relieved some of the pressure, then repositioned my hands and placed her nipples between my thumbs and index fingers and squeezed them a little. I now knew not to assist. She was clearly leading the mission. She increased the pressure on her nipples and squeezed my hands as if to knead her breasts.

"There. Do that." Who was I to disobey? She edged her bottom a little further down my body and began to rock in place. A particular place.

"I can—"

"No. Just do what I told you. I'm going solo." Her voice was less controlled than I had ever heard. Her breathing was increasing as her gyrations did the same. I squeezed and I kneaded and squeezed and kneaded some more. She started to heave her breaths as she rocked herself harder, then reached up and pulled my hands tighter against her. She inhaled audibly and moaned when she exhaled, all in rhythm, the pulse quickening as she went. Suddenly she pulled the camisole from my eyes to reveal my hands seemingly holding down a voluptuous bright pink woman who was trying to escape. She was a vivid reddish pink down to her breasts and all the way out her arms. The remaining visible skin was nearly ivory in color, not at all surprising in a woman so fair.

"Harder. Squeeze harder!" I didn't think I could squeeze much harder, but I tried. Her pink went to red, first in the face, then neck, chest, and breasts. Just as her face was going toward crimson, she started.

"Oh! Oh! Oh! Oh! Oh! Oh! Yes! Yes! Yeah-eh-eh-eh-eh-eh-eh-yay-YES! YES! YES!" And with that she collapsed full forward onto me, heaving. I could feel tears on my shoulders, or so I thought. The heaving continued, though lessening, and the color seemingly evaporated from her ivory-toned skin.

"This is something I could live with", I remember thinking. Clara looked spectacular and had a mind of her own which she did not hesitate to express. She was intelligent and inquisitive and seemingly had no limits as to what she could do. I resolved to do whatever it took to help her achieve her goals.

The position, while very intimate, must have looked a sight. Her head and shoulders were on my chest and her bum was in the air as she straddled me with her legs. A short while later she adjusted, allowing her right leg to slide down as her left leg came to rest between mine. That was how we fell asleep.

* * * * *

CHAPTER 71

German

It was near sunset when the train arrived at the station. I asked the conductor if he knew where the airfield was. He held up a finger and shouted over my shoulder. Someone responded and the conductor gestured at me.

"*Mein Herr*, that tender at the end of the platform is taking soldiers there now. You can share the ride, I'm sure. Will you be learning to be an observer also?"

"No, sir, I am a new instructor there. I will be taking them on their first flights." I thanked him and turned to walk to the tender.

Upon arrival I was shown my quarters and the mess. I settled in for the night, looking forward to the next day's flying.

Flying observers around was certainly not exciting work. Up, around, down. Up, around, down. Nothing to it, really. But it was still flying. I took advantage of the opportunity to hone my flying skills. I made every effort to make each flight like the last, as smooth as possible despite the varying conditions. I found many men were apprehensive about the first time going aloft. They were jittery in anticipation of leaving the ground for the first time in their lives. Occasionally I got one who was so afraid I swore the whole airframe was shaking. Most took the new experience well. After fifteen minutes of looking around at the ground, the clouds, and the horizon, they were generally cheerful and looking forward to going up again. Of course, there were the exceptions. I could almost always pick them out even before I started the engine. Pale, stiff, very quiet, awkward movements, I knew I would be setting down as soon as possible after takeoff. We are not all cut from the same cloth. Flying might have appeared a viable alternative to slogging through mud and being shot at constantly, but actually leaving the ground with someone else in control of one's destiny was more than some could handle. No harm done. It was better to find out right away in a relatively safe rear area. There were other duties to perform in the service of *der Kaiser*.

When not in the air I could mostly be found in the maintenance areas. I would assist the men working on the aeroplanes in an effort to further my mechanical knowledge. I learned new things and they had a little help performing their tasks. Sometimes I would just lie down in my quarters and think of Käti and Elsa. It was a wonderful, if unusual, relationship. Then I would think of getting back to Jakob's *Staffel*. I had the itch to fly the smaller *Albatros*. Flying the old D.II type was just a tease. I longed to make it routine. While I understood the *Abteilungführer's* point about the effectiveness of the various roles in the air, I still had a lust to kill the enemy directly. After all, one did not *teach* a war. One *fought* a war. No one has ever had romantic and patriotic notions of going off to teach *für das Vaterland*. Yet someone has to do it. Not every combatant is well versed in his role in the conflict. So dash the romantic stirrings and do the job at hand. As was pointed out to me, nobody is shooting at me and my odds of surviving the war were that much better.

And so it passed. I spent two weeks flying observers around the aerodrome and surrounding territory. I never brought a crate back needing the wings patched.

One day, after a morning of aerial chauffeur work, I received a message that Jakob had telephoned. I was to break away from the observer school when I could and report to him. I was to receive aerobatic instruction from Willi and Swiss, and *Leutnant* Strasser wanted to meet me. I made the necessary arrangements and was permitted to borrow an old Roland *Walfisch* to make the flight.

I was excited to fly the *Walfisch*. True, I had been in one before. True, it was an out of date design. But I had an appreciation for the type and for Jakob, who obviously thought in terms beyond having the right tool for the job. Jakob used his to fly personal flights behind the lines. No other pilot would fly it unless ordered, as I had seen. They all preferred to take a Hannover in the event the *Engländers* were feeling restless.

The aging Roland did not disappoint me at all. I found the machine to be smooth, stable, almost stately in the way it taxied and lifted off. Climb was adequate for general flying purposes, though I could easily understand Jure and other pilots' preference for flying a more up to date machine. I recalled the day Jakob had Jure fly me around in the Roland and we were unable to have any effect on the *Albatros* being pursued by the English. Perhaps a Hannover would have made a difference. Not knowing just how old the airframe was, I did not experiment in any way which might push its limits. Up, over, and down were plenty enough. The *Walfisch* was, again, a stable machine and perfect for the job at hand. I could understand why Jakob had a soft spot for his.

The flight was uneventful, just a wonderful winter day in the air. The landing was pleasant as well. I ran into a little turbulence, though, when I was greeted on the flight line by Jure.

"Oh, no! Jakob has *you* flying *eine alte frau?* Are we regressing as a fighting force?"

"I thought I smelled something while bringing her in! Jure, you old bullet-stopper, how are you?"

"Bullet-stopper? You have room to talk! I must protest my treatment, however. I spent time in a military hospital or two, receiving but one visit from *mein liebchen.* You, on the other hand, get sent to see your *fräulein* and then learn to fly! Just who do you know?"

"Let me tell you who I know! Jakob was responsible for my learning to fly. Who else do I know? Willi and Swiss will be teaching me aerobatics so that I may fly an *Albatros.*"

"*Ja,* so I have heard. I understand when they modify your *Albatros* they are going to paint your gas mask on the sides. Then we will all know it's you!"

"Ha! I could care if they painted *you* on the sides of my 'plane! As long as I have one! I have a war to win, if only one Englishman at a time!"

"Gustav, I am happy for you. Just don't forget the part where you save me from the English Sopwiths!"

"You know you will be my only priority in the air! Your safety is assured. I will protect you."

"I feel safer already. I will feel more so when you get your machine! Welcome back, Gustav!"

By now Jakob was at Jure's side. "Gustav, I see you have moved up in the world. A *Walfisch?*

Very nice!"

"She is wonderful, Jakob! Now I better understand your love for her, having flown her. She is out of date, but she will never be out of style."

"Agreed. Gustav, *Leutnant* Strasser would like to meet you. He is curious as to why he is to modify an *Albatros* for a pilot who doesn't know how to fly aerobatics. I have told him about your idea for this combined unit, which he appreciates. But he still wants to be sure there is an understanding. Specifically, the *Albatros* is conditional upon your learning what Willi and Swiss teach you."

"Completely understandable, *mein Herr*—uh, Jakob! Sorry, I have been in another unit where they—"

"I understand. Using *'mein Herr'* will of course put you in good standing with *Leutnant* Strasser. He is a true officer, if you—"

"Again, understood. *Danke schön.*"

I found *Leutnant* Strasser's office and introduced myself to his adjutant… The adjutant opened Strasser's door and paused. I could hear a muffled voice, slightly agitated, and then a telephone receiver being firmly placed on its stand. After a brief exchange, the adjutant introduced me and I entered. The door closed quietly behind me. I stood at my best exaggerated attention, saluted, and intoned, "*Vicefeldwebel* Gustav Model reporting, *Herr Leutnant.*"

"*Ja,* all this reorganization done at the behest of a *Vicefeldwebel.* Remarkable. I never would have believed it. Why have they not promoted you, Model?"

"I don't know, *Herr Leutnant.* I have not asked."

"Perhaps they are waiting to see if your ideas do the war effort any good. Having studied your proposals, I cannot disagree. We improve the D.III *Albatros* if they cannot be bothered to do it themselves. Sensible enough, if unusual. And creating a *Staffel* and a half? That simplifies communication and coordination. Improved efficiency. I like it. But why you? All the brilliant military minds we have in Germany, and they rename the air service. Wait. That was last year. This year saw *der Luftstreitkräfte* shooting the RFC out of the sky with our superior aeroplanes and pilots. *Wunderbar.* After April, *nichts.* And now this. Model, I hope you are proud."

"I am only trying to help, *mein Herr.*"

"I see you are from a small village in farm country."

"I am, *mein Herr.*"

"Ah, simple and basic people living off the land and marrying among themselves, keeping the Aryan race pure. Are there Jews in your village, Model?"

"I do not recall any, *mein Herr.*"

"Just a simple lad from a farm village. Like me. Model, we should get along well."

"*Danke, mein Herr.* I hope we do."

"Your flying record is impressive, I see. No aerobatics, however."

"*Nein, mein Herr.* I have not needed aerobatics in my assignments so far. I hope to—"

"Learn here. Again, unusual, but I see you have no lack of men willing to work with you."

"I was told—"

"Maier and Engblom. *Ja.* But every one of the men has said they would help."

"I am touched, *mein Herr.*"

"*Maskotte.*"

"*Maskotte, Herr Leutnant?*"

"*Ja.* You are *die maskotte von Jagdstaffel.*" "*Maskotte?*"

"You seem to be a genuinely good man whom everybody likes. They all want you to do well, and they are all willing to help you. You are the key to this *Staffel* and its success. This is excellent. Model, we are going to get along well. You pay attention to what your instructors tell you and you will soon have your own *Albatros,* rounded nose, new *unterflügel,* big engine."

"*Javohl, Herr Leutnant!*"

"One more thing, Model. Do you still carry *eine gasmaske* everywhere you go?"

"I do. *Mein Herr,* have you ever been gassed?"

"*Nein.*"

"I have. I hope you never share the experience, *mein Herr.* I wanted to die."

"Once again, this is unusual, but it causes no harm. In fact, it is a running joke with the men, laughing about you and *die gasmaske.* You are good for the *Staffel.*"

"*Danke schön, Herr Leutnant.*"

I was dismissed with a wave.

As I stepped out of the office I was joined by Sopwith and Jure. "Gustav—you still have your head!"

"*Javohl!* Where else would it be?"

"After meeting with *Leutnant* Strasser, one never knows. He must have four walls around his bed. He always gets up on the wrong side. He is never happy."

"I thought it went well. He sees me as a nice guy who grew up near where he grew up. He says I am unusual, but he seems to like me. He says I am *die maskotte von Jagdstaffel.*"

"Every *Staffel* needs one, I always say. Anyway, Jakob has detailed me to go to town for supplies. Would you care to have a beer? I mean, uh, load the tender?"

"*Javohl!* we could catch up and compare wounds and scars."

"*Ja,* just what I had in mind."

"Or bring Sopwith and we can meet some *fräuleinen* for no good reason."

"Better yet! Though I don't know what I would do if we did."

"Like me, you would enjoy some pleasant conversation and return to base before it got too late."

* * * * *

Chapter 72

German

I was up well before sunrise and in the maintenance area, helping to prepare the aeroplanes for first patrol. There were two Hannas slated to go up and strafe while six *Albatrosen* would already be up to watch for English scouts with ill intent. One of the 'planes was Jure's. When he entered the area I could not resist teasing him.

"Just who is 'Karolin'? I thought the crate looked much better with 'Käti'."

"I'm sure you did. But since my new back-seater couldn't find your Käti and sweep her off her feet, he settled for another. He kept the 'K', though, if that helps."

"Both sides?"

"*Ja,* the painter is resourceful that way."

"I cannot wait to put him to work painting my *Albatros.*"

"You are not to know, but your *Albatros* will be presented to you already painted."

"That takes a lot off my mind, then. As long as it flies and shoots, I don't care."

"You will need to arrange for the names of your many *fräuleinen* to be painted on it, if you wish. Well, your five favorites, at any rate."

"*Zwei.*"

"*Zwei?* Honestly? You don't think that will bring you bad luck?"

"*Nein.* Both are wonderful."

". . . who do not know one another."

"Best friends."

"They share their toy?"

"*Maskotte.*"

"*Maskotte!* Gustav, you are too much!"

I helped Jure up the ladder and into his 'office'. Around us the sound of engines starting made further talk difficult, so I tugged his belt tight, slapped him on the chest, and blew him a kiss. He swiped at me with a gloved hand, but I was down the ladder already. After placing the ladder against the building, I helped the men swing the buses downwind so they could taxi out for takeoff. Once all were away, I went in for more coffee. Jakob was already there.

"So, Gustav, you will begin *jäger* training after this patrol. As I understand, you will use Swiss'

Albatros and follow Willi."

"*Ja.* I am looking forward to it. Next time I will follow Swiss in Willi's *Albatros.* At least until I get my own. That would make things convenient."

"You will have your own, assuming all goes well. As long as the other pilots all have their modified *Albatrosen.* You do understand. But all the men except *Lieutenant* Strasser have said you are welcome to use theirs while waiting for yours."

"They are a fine group of men."

"You are well liked and deservedly so. But you had better learn and learn quickly or *Leutnant* Strasser will transfer you out like so much moldy pumpernickel. Regardless of what else can be said of him, he demands results. Look at your fellow pilots, all solid flyers with a steady victory count. Your performance will be measured against theirs."

"*Javohl.* I will do my best. And Jakob?"

"*Ja?*"

"I appreciate what you have done for me, setting up the shared arrangement and training here.

Danke schön. I will make it worth your while."

"I hope so."

I went to my quarters and donned most of my flying gear. I knew the men would want to warm themselves before going back up into the winter air, but I wanted to be ready when they were. I was ready and on the field to help receive the aeroplanes as they rolled toward the sheds.

Every pilot returned. One *Albatros* was trailing smoke. That one and another also needed holes patched in the wings. None of the pilots were wounded. Just cold. The Hannas had strafed English trenches and the

Albatrosen had protected the Hannas. No enemy machines were seen to go down.

Seeing Jure had enough help exiting his Hanna, I greeted Willi and Swiss as they walked away from their *Albatrosen*.

"Aha, Swiss, here is our anxious student! Ready to learn from the masters, are you?"

"But I am, O Great Blue Baron!"

"I like the sound of that."

"What would you call me?"

"Swiss." We laughed. "When you are teaching, you will be the Tangerine Baron!"

"I will keep 'Swiss', *danke schön*."

"Are you sure?" Another good laugh.

The three of us sat in the mess over hot coffee and discussed what I was to learn. We reviewed the controls and how they affected the flight of the aeroplane. Willi told me about rolls and loops, especially how to approach a loop in the *Albatros*. We agreed on hand signals and just what to look into for the first day.

Swiss followed me to his *Albatros* and helped me into his "office". Willi and I started the *Albatrosen* and took off. I watched Willi turn, then signal. I did the same. He turned the other way, as did I. Willi pulled into a very tight left turn, wings nearly vertical. Then to the right. As I leveled off he went into a shallow dive, then pulled the stick back and started into a climb. The 'plane slowed as it went inverted, then sped up again as it descended out of the loop. I dived slightly, then pulled up like Willi had done. I reached vertical and lost all airspeed. The *Albatros* froze in the air, shuddered a little, started to slide backward, then dropped its nose almost vertically. I was a little startled, but I collected myself, righted the 'plane, and climbed to join Willi. He clapped his hands together in applause, then waved his finger at me, as if to say, "No- no!". He patted the left side of the fuselage, held up one finger, and with the other hand pushed the finger forward. I got the reminder, "Push the throttle!", and clapped my head. He swept his hand forward, "Go again," and I repeated the setup dive, pushed the throttle forward, and looped. Well, it was not smooth and pretty, but it was my first. Willi showed his approval and drew out a loop in the air, more rounded than mine, which had been like a cursive handwriting loop; up, stall over the top, down. I tried again and seemed to spend more time upside down. Willi sketched my loop in the air, then sketched a more rounded version. I looped again and received a tentative upraised thumb for my effort. Then he showed me he was cold and wanted to go back to the airfield.

Swiss greeted me and helped me out of the 'plane. "That was a beautiful stall, Gustav—but I didn't think that was on today's agenda."

"I'm so happy you approve of my failed loop."

"A-ha! Well, let's keep a positive note. You can manipulate how the aeroplane departs a stalled attitude. We can discuss it. But yours looked very good. You stall, the enemy flies by, and you drop down onto his tail. See?"

"*Ja,* that makes sense."

"And you improved your loop with each attempt. Nice. There are times in combat where you need to vary your loop as well, so the first attempts were not necessarily 'wrong'. Were those —"

"My first loops? *Ja.*"

"You show promise. You will soon join us as a *jäger.* Your turns were nice also. You had a good first lesson. Soon we will be dogfighting. Just remember who has saved *deinen hintern* from the ruthless Englishmen! Shoot *them,* not Willi or me!"

"I can tell you apart, no need to worry."

"Gustav! Wonderful stall!" It was Willi.

"*Danke!* You taught me well!"

"Ha! I assume Swiss has discussed your flight?"

"He has. Some good, some not so good. Can we call it a decent start?"

"A *good* start, Gustav. You will catch on in no time. Flying *einsitzers* demands a more aggressive style of flying, but it is still flying. You are merely learning an extension of what you already know. And let me tell you, the ideas you worked out for the D.III *Albatros* are *wunderbar!* My machine can now dive like a wet rock and I have no fear of pulling out. Soon Swiss will love you like I do—once they update his 'plane."

"I only thought about the situation and made suggestions. Thank Jakob and his friend for the bigger engines and arranging for *unterflügel* construction. They made my thoughts into actions."

"You have made up for the disappointment our aeroplane industry has provided us. Mediocrity with newer designations. D.V? D.Va? D.III Pfalz—and D.IIIa? Our old D.III *Albatrosen* were already better. Thanks to your dreams and Jakob's actions, we once again have competitive aeroplanes. Rumor has it Richthofen wants to fly one."

"Why would Richthofen bother?"

"Gustav, he is a soldier *für der Kaiser* and an advocate for flyers like us. He is bitterly disappointed in our aviation industry and he is not afraid to voice his discontent."

"But he loves Fokker's little triplanes."

"*Ja*, he did. Until they started falling apart in the air. Only now are they fixing that problem. The cheap little Dutch bastard cut corners and our airmen paid for it with their lives. I knew Gontermann . . . ."

"They say Fokker is working on a new design."

"What—the DR.I*a?*"

"No, a traditional biplane. Whatever it is, I hope it comes to us soon. And I hope he learned his lesson with the triplane."

"*Ja,* let us hope so. I would trust *you* over that dodgy Dutchman. Richthofen likes the triplane because it is *not* the same old junk the others are building. Who knows—if he likes your modifications, he could advocate updating all *Albatrosen.* Fixing the wing problem on the D.V and D.Va would be a start. The SPAD and SE type Sopwith pilots simply dive away from us since they know the *Albatros* cannot dive with them. I can't wait to drop my blue 'wet rock' on them. Imagine their surprise!"

"I look forward to joining you—in an *Albatros* of my own!"

"We are looking forward to your *jäger* also. We have instructed our artist on just how it is to be painted."

"I don't care what it looks like, as long as the guns work. Do what you will."

"*Javohl!* We will."

That was the tone of my instruction. Talk about maneuvers, then follow the leader in the sky. I made mistakes, but learned from them. When I was not flying I was helping around the airfield, mostly in maintenance and the modification hangar. A little over a week later *Leutnant* Strasser sent for me. After I reported he told me he had talked with Willi and Swiss about my progress.

"Tomorrow morning I want you to go up with the combined patrol. You will replace Walzer and use his *Albatros*. Unless Maier tells you differently, you will be in the rear of the formation. As you likely know, you will climb above the area where the Hannas will strafe the Englanders and you will protect them from any attacking scouts. Are there any questions?"

"*Nein, mein Herr.*"

"If any come up, ask Maier. Dismissed."

I checked with Willi and met the others for the patrol. Though he was not flying, Walzer was there to show me how clean his aeroplane was. "I expect you to return it looking like this, Gustav. Stop somewhere and wipe it down if you have to." He threw a rag at me. I just smiled.

The *Albatrosen* took off first so we could climb to a greater height. I could not help but notice how well Walzer's modified machine performed. Like Willi's, it was noticeably faster and more powerful than Swiss' standard machine had been. I was able to climb at a better rate than I ever had previously in any machine.

It was a bright, cold, and windy day. It was good that Willi did not require a tight formation, for that would have been quite dangerous in the high wind. I kept watch on the two Hannas as they crossed over the void of No Man's Land and lined up to strafe Englishmen. Knowing they were where they needed to be, I swept the sky looking for English scouts. We were in the despised "Hun in the sun" position, but I still blocked the sun with my thumb and looked for visitors. Nothing. I continued to scan the sky.

Then I spied company. The Limeys were charging at ground level from behind their own lines! Here we were thousands of feet in the air, and they were just off the ground with the wind at their backs. As I shoved the stick and throttle forward, I fired a green flare out in front of the others. Willi quickly saw them and held up four fingers, indicating he wanted the four modified *Albatrosen* to dive on the ambushing English while the other two stayed above and kept watch. I tried best I could to gauge my speed and anticipate the paths of the scouts before me, but I ended up following Willi. I would catch on with experience. But the matter at hand was protecting Jure and the other three crewmen aboard the Hannas. I let Willi and the other two pilots continue toward the Sopwiths. I elected to get between the Hannas and the scouts if I could, adding a little protective firepower. I flew about five hundred feet over the English trenches and found a Sopwith coming toward me, apparently unmolested. I hoped to change that. I aimed my dive ahead of him and pushed over to go get him. I watched as he raised the gun on his wing and caused it to "wink" at me, but I held my fire a little longer. I wanted close range, where I stood a better chance of hitting him. A few seconds later I aimed at the gun and fired fifty or sixty rounds. The results were immediate; both right wings folded vertically up and the Sopwith executed a sudden roll to the right it would never recover from. It hit just behind the first English trenches and showered the soldiers with all kinds of dirt, muck, and aeroplane parts. *Guten morgen, jungens!*

Behind the English lines I could see the others fighting near the ground. One *Albatros* flew head on at a Sopwith, both firing as they approached. At the last moment the *Engländer* did a fast roll to avoid a collision and nearly did so. His wing tip brushed that of the *Albatros* and the machine appeared to trip over the wing and tumble in, crashing on a road. The struck *Albatros* swung its tail to the right, nearly flying sideways. Then the pilot corrected and dove at the ground. However unlikely, it worked. Though the left wingtip was damaged, the aeroplane held together. The pilot gently pulled it into a climb and headed toward the airfield. Behind him men ran toward the crashed scout, which was beginning to smoke. Two motorcycles and several tenders approached and had to stop for all the commotion.

Willi and the other pilot formed with the damaged *Albatros* and dashed over the lines as quickly as they could. I could see the rudder of the stricken 'plane compensating for the drag caused by the out-of-shape wingtip. I remained above the formation, looking for additional trouble, and followed them in. As the others set up to land, I circled above. I saw two dots approaching from the southwest. I began to climb for altitude while I checked the field. Jure and the other pilot had landed their Hannas, so the khaki spots growing larger by the second were likely English Sopwiths. They stayed low to the ground, attracting fire from many rifles and machine guns in our trenches. I recognized the wings and distinctive noses of SE types. They apparently had it in mind to strafe the airfield. I knew I was low on ammunition, so I loaded a flare into my pistol and stowed it under my arm, just in case. I elected to use my height to advantage and dove ahead of them. Adjusting my angle of descent as I advanced on them, I attacked from above and behind them to the left, raking the closer scout from the nose back to the cockpit, causing it to trail greyish smoke, and moving on to the farther 'plane with no telling effect. I wasn't sure if I had shot my last rounds or if I had a scant few more. As I overflew the second scout I pulled out the flare pistol and shot down toward where the wing crossed over the fuselage. The flare hit just outboard of the fuselage and started a small fire on the right wing leading edge. While the smoking scout returned to its lines, the second one pulled up and started to chase me. I remember thinking this was going to open his eyes. I accepted the challenge and climbed up and away from my airfield. The *Engländer* attached himself to my tail and fired short bursts in my general direction. "You can do better," I thought, and continued to climb. Then I got an idea. I was not that far from an observation balloon which was scheduled to go aloft around supper time. I lined myself up to fly roughly lengthwise over the emplacement and fired a red flare ahead, hoping they would see it and understand. It was beautiful. While several fired rifles at me in the *Albatros,* the rest of the balloon defenders waited for the English scout. The poor Limey never stood a chance. His SE type nearly stopped in the air as it got hit with innumerable rounds from rifles and machine guns. What was left dropped into the bare tree branches. I did a climbing turn and flew over the unit wagging my wings and waving at all the upturned faces. Two bullets zipped by. Some simply don't pay attention.

When I slowed onto the flight line I was greeted by several pilots, a number of ground crew, and *Leutnant* Strasser. Once I was on the ground everyone yielded to Strasser.

"Model, just what the hell was that?"

"*Mein Herr,* I was following orders."

"What did you score just now? *Drei?*"

"*Ein, mein Herr.*"

"Willi told me you got a scout behind the lines."

"*Ja. Ein.*"

"And the others? Coming toward the airfield?"

"I damaged one and he turned for home. The other I set fire to, then led him over the *drachen* emplacement where they shot him until he fell into the trees, *mein Herr.*"

"So, Model, you claim one down and one damaged."

"*Ja, mein Herr.*"

"We will see, Model. I will look over the reports and decide. But you have one definite and you will wear *das Eiserne Kreuz 1. Danke.*" He shook my hand.

"*Danke schön, Herr Leutnant!*" I don't think he heard. There was a lot of cheering and everyone closed in on me. It felt pretty good after the flight in the cold air.

Walzer caught up to me a little later in the mess, where I was having coffee. "Gustav, you got my pretty *fräulein* all shot up! What am I to do?"

"I apologize, Walzer. It was not personal, I assure you. If you will allow me to finish my coffee, I will help them patch her. I do feel bad."

"Don't. It belongs to *der Kaiser.* They will fix it or he will send me another. You made good use of her, and I am proud of you both."

"When they modify one for me, you may use it if you wish."

"I can only fly one at a time. You fly yours, I'll fly mine."

"Can we count on you for school tomorrow?" It was Swiss and Willi.

"You think I need more school?"

"*Nein.* But as long as we have our orders, *Herr EK1.*"

"I am but a promising student. I have excellent instructors, highly skilled at their craft."

"You left out 'good looking', Gustav!"

"*Ja.* I did."

I continued flying with Willi and Swiss. It would be foolish not to. It was time in the air, for one thing, time to work over maneuvers that could save my life. It was also good to benefit from the experience of the two veteran pilots, each with respectable scores of their own. I had a good day when I shot down the one and damaged another two, but I could not count on all encounters ending in my favor. One had to work at one's chosen craft in order to become proficient.

I was assigned other patrols, each time using another pilot's *Albatros*. I had scraps with other Sopwiths and claimed one or two as damaged, but added nothing to my tally. I enabled other pilots to score as Sopwiths fled or chased me. They were happy to have me along, needless to say. I knew I would have to score if I wanted to stay in the unit. *Leutnant* Strasser had a reputation for sending away those who did not produce results.

Returning from a routine patrol, I was met by Jakob. He informed me I would be needed at the observer school. I was to return later that day in the "borrowed" *Walfisch*.

"Jakob, do I need to fly directly to the school?"

"It is standard practice. What did you have in mind?"

"Do you remember where we met?"

"Ah! I do. Say no more. Come with me, we will make arrangements now."

* * * * *

CHAPTER 73

German

As I approached the "S" in the road, I saw everything was in order. Though there was little traffic normally, the army made sure I had my landing strip. And there was a black saloon near one end, Käti and the tavern owner, Ernst, standing by. I set down on the road and climbed down into Käti's arms. I peeled her away and shook hands with Ernst, thanking him for bringing Käti over to meet me. He assured me he was happy to do so. I moved the ladder to the rear cockpit, put an arm around Käti, and asked her to get in.

"Get in, Gustav? Get *in?*"

"*Ja!* Climb the ladder, get in, sit down. There is a heavy coat you may use, and goggles to protect your eyes."

"But I have never—"

"Exactly. I will share with you what I love. Don't worry. This is my job, taking people up for the first time. I will bring you back, I promise."

Though she was reluctant and felt uncomfortable in her long skirt, I got her up the ladder by promising none of the men would be watching. She didn't believe me for a moment, but it worked. I swear she pulled her skirt away from one calf just to make sure. She stood in the rear cockpit and managed her way into the oversized flying coat. I had her sit down and look out the window. I told her she could stand up and look around once I signaled her it was safe to do so.

"*Stand up?* You are crazy!"

"Men do it all day, every day. You will love it."

"You will remember you are flying with me, not practicing your air stunts?"

"I think I will remember. This is not an *Albatros.* And how could I forget having *mein liebchen* so close?"

"Oh, Gustav, this is crazy! I don't have any training."

I waved the front clear and started the engine. *"What? I cannot hear you!"*

Käti shook her fist at me as I turned forward to manage the areoplane. I gunned the engine and kicked the tail around. I heard something of a squeal behind me. I rolled downwind and kicked the tail around again. Throttling back to idle, I hollered at Käti to stay seated. I remember seeing big, pretty brown eyes and white knuckles holding the edges of the cockpit.

I pushed the throttle forward and we picked up speed. I raised the tail, then pulled us off the ground, causing the rumbling to stop. I dared not look back while climbing, but I could feel all was still. Probably a good sign. I leveled off at two thousand feet and turned to tell Käti it was okay to stand. She was already on her feet. She was a wide-eyed child in a candy shop, looking around in every direction. She pointed at the black saloon and waved at Ernst. I flew her over the village. She never admitted to it, but I know I heard squeals of delight. I heard repeated high pitch bursts of her voice, "Oh!", "Look!", and other things. After maybe twenty minutes I circled around the makeshift landing strip and put us down. Käti had the good sense to sit down before I did. I wondered if she knew how to fire a *Parabellum* gun.

Rolling to a stop with the help of a few soldiers, all I could hear above the engine was, "Oh, Gustav!" Käti was very happy. She may not have needed the ladder to exit the aeroplane, but I had them place one there just in case. I climbed out and onto my ladder, then stepped over to hers in order to help her out of the heavy coat. Stepping out, she managed to catch the hem of her skirt in her hand on the cockpit edge, so the men had a bit of a show until she noticed. She could care less, so taken was she by her first time in the air.

"Oh, Gustav! Oh, Gustav!" she exclaimed over and over as she nearly hugged the breath out of me. "Now I understand! I think I have caught what you have! When can we go again?"

"We will, *liebchen,* we will."

"Elsa is going to be very upset."

"I will find a way to make it up to her."

"I have no doubt."

"I meant I would take her flying another time."

"Then I may become upset."

"There comes a time when a man takes his chances and hopes for the best."

"I could never stay upset with you."

"There. Things are looking better already."

I offered Ernst a ride but he declined. He was happy on the ground, *danke*. He did have me go to the rear of his saloon and pull out a case of schnapps for the soldiers who had assisted. I offered to compensate him, but he said I already had. "I have never seen Käti so happy before you, and never so excited before this. Gustav, you are good for her." We shook hands.

I offered my thanks to the officer in charge of the detail that had helped me down and back up again. Bottle in hand, he told me he would be more than willing to help again. He presented me his calling card with telephone number added by hand. One last, long hug from Käti and I took my leave.

* * * *

CHAPTER 74

German

I brought the old *Walfisch* down onto the airfield on a Sunday afternoon. I had spent the prior two weeks flying would be observers about as per our agreement. Overall the time was pleasant enough. One candidate discovered he was simply not cut out for work in the air. I felt bad for him, to be sure, but I felt worse for the ground crewmen who had to clean up after him. Beyond that it was just sightseeing in the cold air over Germany.

As I descended from the cockpit I was told to go to *Leutnant* Strasser's office. I entered to find no adjutant. Strasser called out, "Model? Is that you?"

"Ja, Herr Leutnant." He told me to come in. I left my heavy flight items in the anteroom and entered.

"Model, I have compared the reports on the flight where you shot the wings off that English scout. The scout you caused to smoke near here crashed in No Man's Land, and the English shelled the wreckage when some of our soldiers attempted to reach the pilot. You damaged it, it's yours. The head of the *drachen* unit thought it was brilliant to lead an enemy scout over his boys. He says they were happy to share in the destruction of an enemy aircraft. Again, you damaged it. And you were resourceful enough to know how to finish it off with no ammunition left. You had fewer than ten rounds per gun remaining according to the armorer report, by the way. This means you have three confirmed victories for the flight. Very well done!

"Danke schön, mein Herr!"

I have put in for a promotion. The paperwork was approved. You are now a *Feldwebel*.

"Danke, Herr Leutnant!"

"I have recommended you for *das Eisernes Kreuz 1,* but I have no word on the approval. I'm afraid we will have to wait and see. I apologize that I do not have confirmation."

"There is a war going on, *mein Herr.* That could slow things."

"So true, so true. But I do have something you will probably appreciate more than a medal. Care to walk with me, *Feldwebel* Model?"

"Javohl, mein Herr!"

I followed Strasser back across the aerodrome to the maintenance hangar. When he reached the door, he gave it three sharp raps before opening it for me. There stood most of the unit personnel with champagne. Jure handed me a glass and clapped me on the upper arm. Someone shouted, "To *Feldwebel* Model!" The rest cheered and we all sipped from our glasses. Before I could react any further, *Leutnant* Strasser waved his arms as if to part the men, which it did.

"Feldwebel Model, this is yours."

There stood a freshly modified D.III type *Albatros.* The rounded nose was a putrid green-yellow color, not unlike that I remember from my gas attack. Instead of a solid line delineating colors, it had the appearance of gas vapors over a black background. The black fin and rudder took up the green "mist effect" again. The tailplane was in the unit colors of red, white, and black. Upper and lower wings were both covered in the preprinted fabric but the upper colors were muted somewhat with a brownish wash. And, on each flat fuselage side, the *Staffel* artist had outdone himself, painting my gas mask and an infantry helmet. I could not help but laugh.

Jure asked me, "Well, Gustav, what do you think? Do you like her?"

Overwhelmed, I asked, "Do the guns work?"

"Javohl! Willi sighted them this morning and Swiss checked them afterward."

"She is an object of beauty! I don't know what to say! *Danke euch alles!"*

Jure asked, "Would you like three English 'dartboards' painted on the engine cowl?"

"Nein! If Richthofen decides to fly it, he will laugh at me! He has what, fifty? *Nein danke.* But I would like to speak to the artist, if I may, about painting a name."

The shout came from across the hangar, *"Herr Feldwebel,* I am at your service!"

"Danke! Tomorrow, or when we have time."

Many of the men finished their champagne and left the hangar to go about their tasks. Our war had only paused; the war was still being waged around us. Several of the men I knew did stay a little longer, mostly other pilots.

Swiss spoke up, "So Gustav, now you have a bird to call your own. She is certainly unique."

Willi added, "She looks a lot like you, but you are generally less green."

"Ah, so you think I'm yellow . . . " The group laughed. "I am concerned, however. Did all of the other pilots have their *Albatrosen* modified? I thought it would take longer than that."

"Gustav, please don't worry. Modifications have been completed for every other pilot . . . who scored three dead Englanders in one flight. My friend, you have raised the bar, so to speak. If you continue to perform at that level, we could all be shipped out. We would miss you!"

"I merely followed my instincts."

"Some instincts. You shot one cold, then watched over the rest of us and protected our airfield. Richthofen himself could have done no better, all things being equal."

"Richthofen? No, please."

"Everybody starts somewhere. You had a very good start. You are more than *die maskotte.*"

"I will do what I can. I want this damned war over with."

"Why? What will you do?"

"I'm not certain, but I will not be killing people every day. Were truth to be told, I would rather be flying *with* the English rather than *against* them. I shoot at them why? Because of their uniform. I say that if we met our current foes outside this stupid war, we would buy each other drinks, laugh, talk, and then go fly together. Don't misunderstand me. I am German. I am loyal to and fight *für der Kaiser und das Vaterland.* I just think there is something better and more productive we could be doing with all this effort. But on the morrow I will be in the air with you, fighting *für der Kaiser. Für das Vaterland!"*

Everyone still present responded, *"Für das Vaterland!"* and downed what champagne they had left.

* * * * *

CHAPTER 75

German

I arose with the sun the next morning. I put on most of my flying gear and went to the mess for some coffee and a quick bite before going up in my newly reworked *Albatros*. The other pilots scheduled to go up were either there already or arrived shortly after I did. Swiss was to lead the flight that day. He held a very brief meeting, essentially showing where the Hannas would be that morning. We knew the rest. Climb above the targeted trenches and watch for English scouts. In light of recent events, one *Albatros* would stay at about two thousand feet and watch behind the English trenches for activity while the other five would hide in the sun.

I walked out to the flight line. There sat my newest *fräulein,* the sun rising enough to shed some light on her. While I didn't care about her appearance, I thought she was the most beautiful one on the line. I shuddered at the color and the memories it dredged up. I laughed at *die gasmaske* painted on the sides, the boys' way of poking fun at me and my petty insecurity. Once again, being the butt of jokes was good for *Staffel* morale. Our artist had done a very nice job, painting a fine rendition of the mask and a typical infantry helmet. I could not complain—it looked good. I could not wait to start my new beauty and feel her in the air. I felt excitement with the anticipation, almost like a first date.

As was my custom, I mounted the ladder, dropped my heavy boots on the seat, and sat on the fuselage to pull them on before stepping into the "office" and strapping in for the flight. I looked around at the other men in various stages of preparation. There was no sense of urgency, just another day at the front, another day of killing Englishmen in hopes of ending the war. I wondered just how many English were left to be killed. And the French. The French had taken a beating worse even than the English. True, Germany had lost her share of men, but nothing compared to the slaughter of Frenchmen and Englishmen. Word was that many of the "Red Pants" soldiers were now school children or old men. Would they really fight to the last man? At what point would they insert women into the trenches? Certainly they were nearing a critical point as a nation and would soon sue for peace. Russia was now in a revolution and had ceased fighting on the eastern front. More German troops were assigned to the west. The only hope France and England had was for fresh troops from the United States, which had finally enjoined in April, if only in word. It would take time to amass an army, clothe it, equip it, and train it to fight. Then it had to send its forces across the Atlantic and figure out where to put them. There certainly was a sense of urgency among *der pickelhauben*. They had to find a way to finish off the Entente before American forces could make any kind of difference. Doings and stirrings from above had been quiet as of late, but it was winter. With the fourth Christmas of the war about to come and go, there was no real end in sight.

"*Herr Feldwebel?* Would you care to come hunting with us? I hear the *Engländers* are running this morning and I, for one, would like a fresh kill to toast later!" It was Swiss, today's leader.

"*Javohl!* With apologies, I was a little lost in thought."

"*Fräuleins*, I hope?"

"*Ja*. This *fräulein*." I spanked the plywood fuselage.

"Ahh, the first encounter with a new *fräulein* . . . the anticipation mounts. I understand! Let us away, Gustav. The English are waiting!"

While Swiss returned to his orange-yellow nosed mount, I called for the ground crewmen to pull the prop through and draw *benzin* into the cylinders. I then cleared them away with, "Switch is on" and cranked the magneto to start the engine. Other *jägern* were taxiing downwind. I waited for Swiss to pass me and I fell in behind him, last in line.

The takeoff was routine. Five of us began our climb to altitude while one *Albatros* seemingly remained behind. I looked down at the sun shining off the bright red nose of the new pilot's standard D.III type and chuckled, remembering the conversation he had had with Willi about his color. He wanted a red nose. Willi suggested another color, citing, "Red? Bah! It's been done!"

But the young man would not settle for any other color, seeing he idolized Richthofen. Willi had been a little cold with him. "Same color, same results? Let's hope so." But he had his red. Good for him, if that's what he wanted. I silently wished him luck.

We circled while we climbed, watching the Hannas take off and head toward their assigned area. They only climbed briefly, as they would be strafing from low level. The red nosed *Albatros* rose above and behind them.

Our reverie was broken by a lot of "zip-zip" "zip-zip-pock". Machine gun fire. Swiss was right. The damned English had been waiting for us. I heard an explosion above me and to the left. I followed the sound to find Swiss' orange-yellow nosed *Albatros* starting to tumble, smoking, wing structure collapsed. *"Scheisse,"* I thought, "he will not get out of that." But I was wrong. Just as I spied a lick of flame in the middle of the mass, I watched the figure of a man seemingly pop out of the tumbling 'plane, bounce off the rudder, and drop toward the ground below. I was sick in the pit of my stomach. But that would have to wait while I tended to my own business. I pushed my nose down and throttle forward in order to gather some speed. My precious new *fräulein* had taken some hits in the wing and I would not stand for her taking any further abuse. The pull of the engine took me by surprise. I had never felt anything like it. It seemed to get to maneuvering speed in almost no time. I managed a half loop, half roll and found myself looking at an SE type Sopwith. It was better than I could have hoped. I pushed the triggers and greeted the Limey with machine gun fire. I saw no more English above him, so I pushed the stick and nosed into a dive. I was at the end of a curious train, a mix of English and German aeroplanes held together by a web of tracer fire, all passing the burning, tumbling wreckage of Swiss' *Albatros*. I could smell the gunpowder, the engine exhaust, and burning wood. I looked around to see that I was not on fire. It could have been another in the "train" below me or it could have been Swiss' 'plane. I put bullets in two or three Sopwiths with no telling effect. They continued to dive, one trailing a little wispy smoke. An *Albatros* fell out of line below and ahead of me, a Sopwith in tow. I adjusted my dive and fired several short bursts into the English crate, which slowed up and then pulled its nose up into a stall. From there it slid briefly backward until the nose fell. A spin was its final maneuver. I followed it with my eyes, watching it hit the ground near our first line trench.

By this time the "train" had broken up. I looked for someone else to "play with", but it seemed everyone had gone home. I looked above me and into the sun. Nothing. I looked for the Hannas below. Nothing. It was time to return home.

I was the last to land. As I rolled toward an empty spot on the line I could just feel the pall. Obviously the news of Swiss' demise had arrived and spread among the men. There were heavy hearts and knotted stomachs. Swiss and Willi had been the backbone of the *staffel* almost since its creation. I had my personal connections with them, obviously, but mine were not the only ones. Swiss had left his mark on everyone there, even Strasser.

I went to the mess for some more coffee. There was talk of grounding Willi, but he would have no part of it.

"Just what would you have me do? Cook? Pour coffee? Make your beds? I am a *man*, not a *frau!* I will fly and I will fight! Swiss knew this could happen. We all know. It seems the world leaders are holding a war. We are all expected to attend and participate. And kill. And die, if need be. *Ich bin der dummkopf hier.* I have a stupid question: If the leaders have the problem, why don't the leaders fight it out themselves? I always liked the idea of 'pistols at dawn'. Quick, easy, final. But it doesn't work like that. No, they send *us* out to settle *their* differences. *We* must *die* on their behalf. Somebody *please* tell me how that makes any sense!"

"Maier, to your quarters! One more word, I will have you arrested for insubordination." It was Strasser.

"Bu—"

"*Schluss jetzt!* Not another word!"

Willi picked up his headgear and stomped out of the room, looking as angry as he could in the bulky, awkward flight clothing. The problem was that he was right. Everyone in the room knew he was right. Strasser knew he was right. Every man present wanted to take Willi's side but no one did. Strasser was merely doing his job as *Staffelführer.* We had to respect that.

There was an exception. The new pilot, Jodl, with the red-nosed *Albatros,* spoke up. "Why would anyone say such things? Like Richthofen, we must all go forth and—"

"Just what do you know about Richthofen, Jodl?" It was Strasser. "How many kills he has? What else do you know about him?"

Jodl looked surprised. "But, but, I . . ."

"Do you know why Richthofen is so good? I will tell you. From his earliest days he was a hunter. He would go into the woods with his rifle and return with game for dinner. He is still a hunter. When he takes time away he goes hunting in the woods. He is an excellent marksman. He merely translates that skill to suit the war. Richthofen is not a great flyer and he knows it. He stalks his prey and watches for circumstances that favor his abilities and his marksmanship. Have you ever hunted, Jodl? Are you a good shot?"

"*Mein Herr,* when I joined the army, I—"

"No, Jodl, you are not a hunter. Here is what I see. You worship Richthofen as some kind of hero. He is a good man, *ja.* But he is well qualified to do what he does. Painting your crate the same color as Richthofen's crates does not make you Richthofen. Have you sighted your guns, Jodl? Have you checked your ammunition, Jodl? Have you studied *"Dicta Bölcke"?* Until you do these things and start killing enemies yourself, you are merely the next poor bastard to be caught unaware. Or, if you are lucky, the next pilot transferred out of my *Staffel* for not scoring enough kills. I believe that if you took the time to learn about Richthofen, you would find he is no happier with the war than the rest of us. My money says he would be far happier in the woods with his hunting rifle. Please tell me if you learn anything different."

"*Javohl, mein Herr!*" Jodl bolted to attention.

"Bah! Get out of my sight. Think about what I just told you. Learn about Richthofen and Bölcke. Sight your guns. Fly like your life depends on what you do and how you do it. Because it does. You might talk to Model. Model has three confirmed enemy aeroplanes to his credit. He shot down another just moments ago. He has not completed aerobatics training. You were not happy he received a modified *Albatros* before you did. But he shot down three English in one flight, defended our aerodrome from attack, and watched over the rest of the *Staffel* while they landed. I think you will find Model's success is more than good mechanical abilities. Model has good instincts. He flies well, shoots well, and has a sense of what is going on around him at all times. Jodl, you fly well. But you have a long way to go. Now leave."

With head hanging and tail between his legs, Jodl left the mess to go lick his wounds. He took a pretty good tongue lashing. I could not help but feel bad for him, but Strasser was right. A red nose does not a Richthofen make. I hoped he realized that. I didn't know him, but I still did not wish him ill. He needed experience to learn.

Later that afternoon I surprised *Leutnant* Strasser by requesting to patrol the lines. Well, it wasn't much of a surprise. He knew his boy had a new toy to play with and granted permission without hesitation. He did suggest I mention to the others that I was going. If anyone went along, I was designated as flight leader.

I visited the mess and found no interest unless they needed to intercept something blown over our way. I went to the maintenance hangar and found Jodl loading his ammunition. I asked if he would like to go up and look around and he readily agreed. He started asking me questions about how I did it. I told him that when I flew patrol I could have nothing else on my mind, only my aeroplane and what was happening around me. The minute I think of something else could be the last minute of my life. I told him I constantly watched the sky and ground around me so I knew exactly what was happening in my area. I showed him how to block the sun with his finger so no one surprised him from the sun's glare. I told him I almost never looked at the gauges in the cockpit unless something didn't seem right, and by then it could be too late. My concentration was always on my surroundings. I watched others in the patrol, as they watched me, mutual protection. I swear, if he had to take notes, he couldn't keep up. He looked like most of what I told him was in another language. I asked him what they taught him in *Jastaschule,* because he was missing the basics of survival in the air, never mind shooting down enemies.

I proposed that we go up together, only I was going to watch him and what he did. I would tell him later what I thought he could do to improve his performance. I defined the patrol area, pending enemy activity, if any, and we helped ready our machines. I let him take off first and I took up a position above and behind him.

I was irritated by the time we reached altitude. I didn't know what was so interesting in his cockpit, but he spent little time looking around and never checked above or below or cleared the sun. It was a wonder he was still alive. After going back and forth a couple times, I fired a red flare to get him back to the field.

Once we were out and our machines stowed, I asked Jodl about the flight. He told me we were alone in the sky. I asked him how he knew that and he looked at me quizzically. I told him he spent entirely too much time looking straight ahead and almost zero time checking the sky around him. He mumbled something about his neck and I told him how disappointed I was. He asked if I was going to say anything to Strasser. I told him it was my duty to report on the flight. As a *Jagdstaffel* we had to fly as a unit and watch for one another. He had not once looked at me in the air, much less check the air around me. I could not depend on him to watch out for his fellow *Staffel* members, which put us all in danger. He was not happy with me in the least. But ours was a dangerous business. I was not about to get killed because of a lazy pilot who couldn't be bothered to watch out for himself. I had a mind to recommend the red be overpainted on his machine—if indeed he was allowed to fly it again. The *Staffelführer* needed to know about this one.

The adjutant saw me in to Strasser's office. I mostly skipped the pleasantries and got to the point. *"Herr Leutnant,* I have just returned from a flight with Jodl."

"Good. Did my lecture make a difference?"

"None. I answered his questions, told him how to look around and be aware. Once we were in the air, he almost never looked anywhere but straight ahead. I cannot tell you, *Herr Leutnant,* how to do your job. But I can tell you I don't want to fly with him again. All he does is fly. He cannot fight what he cannot see, and he makes no effort to look. A hound named Moritz couldn't help him. He is a danger to himself and to anyone in his patrol."

"I value your opinion. I will talk with Willi. *Danke.*"

Jodl was in the mess for dinner that night. It was the last I saw of him.

* * * * *

CHAPTER 76

German

The following morning mine was the *Albatros* "left behind" to watch for any low flying English scouts that might interfere with the strafing Hannas. I climbed to about fifteen hundred feet and stayed about a mile away, keeping close watch over the trenches and beyond. I saw movement behind the lines which quickly took the form of two SE type Sopwiths racing toward the Hannas at low level. I climbed and flew around so I would be behind them and above for my attack. So intent were they on the strafers that they somehow did not notice me. I pushed over at them and opened fire. One of the Sopwiths pulled up short and turned around in a cloud of steam. I counted him as out of the fight and pressed toward the other. My first burst holed his left wings but he continued on, opening fire on one of the Hannas. His shots had no visible effect, and I again fired on him. That time he pulled into a loop, but I was ready. I anticipated his loop and aimed at the top of it, but he was not there. He instead stalled, fell off, and dove under me and pulled into a half loop and roll. Before he came out of the roll he was shooting at me. I countered with a half loop of my own and around we went for at least the next ten minutes. I kept aiming next to the "W" on his wing but he seemingly dodged every bullet. Realizing he was being blown gently over our trenches and was thus the target of anyone who could hold up a rifle, he looked for his escape. The sight of three more *Albatrosen* hurtling down at him was enough. He put a few rounds through my wings, then dove for the ground, throttle wide open as he ran for his lines. I waved at the others as they joined me and we all went back to the field. I circled above while the others landed, then put mine down.

There was activity around one of the Hannas. After I had exited my *Albatros* I learned that a gunner had been shot. He had been pulled out of the 'plane and set on the ground. As I neared the group around the scene, activity ceased. The gunner's wounds were too many and too severe. There was nothing to be done to stop the bleeding and he died there on the ground. I wondered aloud whether the pilot was alright.

"I will be okay, Gustav, once they take this bullet out of my arm."

"Jure, why aren't you getting attention now?"

"I will, now that they are done with Hans. He needed the attention more, the dear boy."

"Damn. I saw them coming and—"

"*Ja,* I watched you. You flew well and shot them both. But this happens in war. You cannot stop every bullet."

"I'm sorry, Jure."

"Oh, don't worry, Gustav. This damned war has turned us into an assembly line like where the Americans build their Fords. *Der Kaiser* will send another gunner and we will continue like before."

"Jure, get that arm fixed. I am certain you can turn that into a few days with your Gwendolyn."

"Oh? Not just a military hospital?"

"I would pull a few strings for you. Home, not hospital."

"You have strings to pull? And you still lower yourself to talk to me? Gustav, I am touched."

"Actually, Jure, you have been shot. Hey! Could I get someone to look at my friend here? He has an English bullet in his arm. Somebody please remove the bullet and dress his wounds before he feels he needs teatime! What he needs is a train home to see his Gwendolyn !"

Two medics took Jure to their room for attention. I called after them, "Schnapps. He needs schnapps!"

Jure got his schnapps. He had his bullet removed. His son got Sopwith, his new dog. Jure got to see Gwendolyn for a week. He got in trouble for staying away too long. I took his place in the Hannover. It was no *Albatros,* but it was a very good machine. I probably should have said something to the gunner before I rolled it over the trenches, but he got a story to tell his grandchildren. I will never forget him screaming the whole way around in frantic falsetto, *"Du bist verdammt verrückt, und ich hasse dich!"* He swore he would never fly with me again, and when Jure returned, he hugged him.

I found time with the *staffel* artist and asked him to add just a little more to my 'plane's finish. He readily agreed. I showed him the left side, just under the cockpit opening, and asked him to paint 'Käti' in black on a white band.

"Would you like her name on both sides?"

"No. On the other side I would like "ELSA"."

"Whichever one visits, she can only see her side of the crate?"

"They would be together, if they visit at all. It's alright."

"*Javohl!* As you wish. You could be crazy, but then again you go up in this crate and trade machine gun fire with the English and French. I'm quite content here on the ground."

* * * * *

CHAPTER 77

British

I thought I heard voices, or at least one voice. A female voice. Female? I opened my eyes to find myself in an unfamiliar environment. But the voice was very familiar. Yes. It was Clara. She was conversing but I heard only her voice. She was talking about a hospital and a patient. Looking about, I found her. What a vision. She was sans clothing from the waist up, an alabaster vision topped with that strawberry blonde hair, a bit out of place. She was pacing back and forth, limited by the cord of the telephone. I watched as the cord rose, pulled taut, and then sagged as she reversed her direction. Of course I watched the late afternoon light playing in her hair as she nodded and turned. There were tiny highlights playing throughout. The way she was pacing and turning I only caught fleeting and partial glances of her breasts, which I still had not really seen. It was almost as if she were teasing me with a peep show, but I knew that at that moment she was oblivious to my presence. She was quite obviously at work. However, I was not at work. So I lay there and enjoyed the "show". I thought of my old friend Knees and his stories about watching the mademoiselles dancing in the French nightclubs. "I'd wager they looked nothing like this treasure before me", I thought. And it appeared I had no one to run from. So I could just relax until Clara was finished with the business at hand, at which point she would likely rejoin me. And when she did, ... I closed my eyes and envisioned what could come next.

"Get dressed!" "Dressed?"

"Yes! We need to leave. I'll change, then I'll help you lace your boots."

"I don't need—"

"Fine. No matter. Hurry please, we must go. Now!"

"What is the matter?"

"Get dressed. I'll tell you in the 'car."

I picked up my shirt and put it on, tucking it in haphazardly since it would be beneath my uniform jacket and overcoat. Clara appeared quickly, looking like she had before we, uh, slept.

"Come on, then!"

I met her by the table, where I sat down and began to work with one boot. As promised, she shooed away my hands so she could lace the boot. Then she handed the other boot to me.

"Get working on this one."

"Yes, ma'am."

In a moment she was out to the car and getting in before I could get to her door.

"Please start the motor-car so we can proceed."

I turned the crank a few times and the engine sputtered to life. Climbing in, I asked Clara, "Just where are we going in such the hurry?"

"To the hospital. It's Pauline. She is there. As I suspected, she did need more fluids. Now I need to diagnose the problem and divine a treatment."

"But won't one of the doctors—"

"You are not helping, Lef-tenant. We must hurry to her so that I may take over her case."

"You can do that?"

"Of course. I will be under a doctor's supervision, of course, since I am only a nurse. But some of the doctors there know me and know I want to become a doctor. They are willing to work with me to help me along, as it were. I have helped several of them when they could not properly diagnose a case and they feel they are in my debt."

"I know how they feel."

"Perhaps. But they don't know how you feel. Or will feel."

"Will feel?"

"Not now. Hurry. Shall I push? Are we there yet?"

Clara meant business. All business. No distractions. I pushed the throttle forward. I could see conversation was pointless unless she initiated it. So I drove as fast as I dared. Clara guided me to the proper entrance and told me I could come in if I wished or return to the airfield.

"Is there anything I can do to be of assistance?"

"Frankly, no. She cannot have a visitor now, and if she could it would likely be her husband."

"Not likely, but . . . ."

"But not you. Here. You may telephone me at any time until you reach me and I will give you a report on my patient. Thank you most kindly for bringing me. Thank you for today . . . thank you."

"When can—"

"Not now. I'm sorry. You will. I need to go." With that she hugged me from the side, not quite long enough for me to react in kind, kissed my cheek, and seemingly bounded out of the motor- car toward the entrance without looking back. She had shown a crack in her all business countenance. For me. I could not be upset over that. She was, after all, rushing to help a close friend in distress.

* * * * *

CHAPTER 78

British

I drove back to the airfield, arriving in the middle of some kind of excitement. I returned the motor-car and stopped by the CO's office. Only his adjutant was there.

"Where is the major?"

"You don't know?!"

"If I knew, I would not ask, would I?"

"Oh. No, sir. I apologize, sir." He snapped to attention and saluted.

"No, no, none of that, it's okay. It's been a long day, that's all. Is something the matter?"

"Someone took a Camel out and crashed, sir—but not yours!"

"Dear me, no. Do you know what happened?"

"Best information is that he was stunting over the athletic fields and lost control. Some say his nose flipped up and over and he went into an inverted spin. Never recovered. I was in here and didn't see it. The major is at the crash site. That's all I know, sir. Again, sir, I apol—"

"Nonsense. Forget it. Thank you."

The Camel was tricky to fly, such were the forces of the spinning engine over that concentrated weight in the nose. One could not relax in it. Ever. One had to fly it with deep suspicions until one was acquainted with its quirks. Never, never trust one until you knew what to expect of it. And even then it could rear up and bite. This one had.

I borrowed the 'car and drove to the athletic fields in case I could be of use. Spotting the CO, I pulled the car up to him and asked how I could help.

"There is not much to do here, Lef-tenant. The lad spun in upside down. He is in very bad shape. I doubt he sees the morning. He seems to be broken and bleeding everywhere. I don't see how he can be saved."

"Can he be transported, sir?"

"Frankly, I don't think he would survive being driven back to the airfield. But if he's expected to die anyway, I don't see the harm. Where would you take him?"

"To the hospital in town, sir."

"Why?"

"Will you trust me, sir? Can he fit in the back of this car with a medic?"

"No. Take that lorry. I'll get the car back. What makes you think that hospital can save him?"

"Have I told you about the nurse who saved my eyesight, my arm, and indeed my life?"

"Yes, you have."

"She is at that hospital this very moment. If anybody can save the lad,—"

"Let's get you set to go—now!"

The CO called to several men and moments later I was on the way to the hospital with the pilot and two medics along. I had the CO call the hospital and leave word for Clara that we were on the way.

After what seemed like an endless drive we arrived at the entrance Clara had used. She had been watching from inside the door. When we arrived she and several orderlies met the lorry and the orderlies and medics took him inside. Clara asked me what had happened, and I told her.

"Oh, dear, it's a wonder he is alive at all."

"They don't expect him to live the night. But I knew that if he had any chance, you were the one to see him."

"You are sweet and altogether too kind. I will do what I can for the lad, of course. You may telephone me at any time if you wish."

"You may also telephone the airfield to leave word on the pilot if you wish. Someone will be near the telephone, even if it's me."

"I need to go." She had been holding my hand in both of hers. She squeezed it and then let go as she turned to leave. I had things I wanted to say, but I knew it would have to wait for another time.

A short while later the medics returned. As I started toward the airfield, I suddenly had an idea and took a short detour past the cafe.

Excusing myself, I went in to visit with my ex-navy friend. I asked what he had left in cakes of any kind. He showed me and I bought them all to take back to the airfield. I handed a small box to the medics, who were surprised and grateful. They now had something to occupy themselves on the ride back. The rest would be distributed, first to the men who recovered the pilot and Camel, and then to whomever got to them. I thought it might break up the routine, if only a little.

All I wanted was a decent meal in the mess. I had not had anything substantial most of the day. One could not continue without fuel for the body.

After several hours I attempted to telephone Clara, but she did not answer. I did not think she would. She was undoubtedly still tending to the young pilot I had delivered to her. I thought about God. If there was a God, perhaps He—or She—would look after the lad. On the other hand, where had God been when the lad lost control of the Camel? No doubt he had prayed to be delivered from his misfortune. For that matter, if there was a God, a loving God, why had untold millions been killed in this damned war? Had God been on holiday? None of this killing nonsense seemed to line up with what we had been told in Sunday school or church. Was God the vindictive sort? Cynical? After all, both sides of the war were sure they had God on their side. Was this some kind of exercise in ego worship? If I kept thinking along these lines, I would never get to sleep, so I tried to think of something else. It didn't take long. I had material for some very pleasant dreams.

I awoke to hard raps on my door. I stumbled out of bed and opened the door to find the CO standing there in a nightshirt, cap, and service issue boots.

"Yes, sir? What can I do for you?"

"May I enter?"

"Of course. Please do."

"Lef-tenant, I want to tell you about your friend the nurse."

"Sir?"

"I just received a call from the hospital. They said our lad had died. Twice."

"That cannot be!"

"And yet he is alive!"

"Cannot be, sir!"

"The doctor said it was the most amazing thing he had ever seen. The lad's heart stopped beating, and your nurse friend pounded and pushed on his chest until it started beating again. It stopped again, but she jumped on the table, straddled the lad, and pushed his chest with all her might. She directed someone to hold his head back and push a hose into his throat and blow into it. His heart started beating again! And he nearly woke up with a half dozen people working on his various wounds! Your friend can indeed work miracles!"

"I knew she would try her hardest. Look what she did for me. I was left for dead, but here I am."

"No need to tell me more. I believe you!"

"How is he, sir?"

"Oh, to be sure, he has a long recovery to look forward to. It will not be easy, but it is better than the alternative."

"So he fared better than the Camel?"

"He did. They might be able to reuse some of the fuselage bracing wires and brackets, but not much more. He did a thorough job on the machine."

"That can happen with a Camel, sir. I approach mine like she's a woman and therefore unpredictable."

"Wise of you. Well, I thought you might want to know about your friend and what she had done for the poor lad. Please forgive me for intruding."

"Not at all, sir. Anytime."

With that the CO left. I knew not to telephone Clara, as she would likely spend the night at the hospital between Pauline and the lad I took her. I could leave word for her at the school the next day. She would either love me or hate me for the additional patient. But I knew she had the best chance of saving the lad. I also knew it would help show her zeal, skills, and abilities as a medical professional. I was better off waiting for her to contact me, once her patients were on the mend and she was able to rest. I had a feeling she was not done with me and I couldn't wait to see what she would do next.

* * * * *

CHAPTER 79

British

The next morning dawned, if one could call it that. Intermittent rain, heavy cloud cover, simply dismal weather on top of the winter cold. It was a perfect day for an inquiry into what had happened the day before, even if the pilot was not available for questioning. I sat in with the CO and other instructors and learned that a crowd had been growing beneath the aerobatic spectacle that was the pilot's flight. He was wringing the Camel for all it was worth and presumably learning to understand the quirks it possessed. And the story they told was remarkably consistent. He had done a magnificent job of stirring up the sky until the nose abruptly lifted and the Camel went inverted and began to spin. I knew that was a very difficult situation for one to extract oneself from, for I had been in that position. What was the difference? I had anticipated problems and had climbed for more altitude before attempting anything approaching that level of difficulty. More altitude represented increased distance to the ground and lengthened time for reaction and recovery. I was over ten thousand feet, whereas he had been flying at about three thousand feet or so. He simply did not have the time to find his way out of that first-time situation. Poor bugger. There was no word from the hospital as to his condition or even if he were alive at all. Everyone expected the worst. Everyone except myself.

The inquiry aside, I was itching to do something. I had nothing to do except wait on the ceremony, still days away. I had no packing to do. I could not even steal away and meet with my friend in town as she was in hospital. I doubted she would be much for conversation in her condition. My Camel was ready save final fueling and arming. Nothing to be done there. I saw no real point to the cornet unless I was actually going to sit in with the orchestra for the ceremony and reception. I suppose I could, other than my participation in the instructors' flyovers.

In my restless state, I decided to go into town, if for no other reason than to get away. I could always pass the time with my naval friend at the cafe. And his coffee and cakes were better than the breakfast fare in the mess. Breakfast in town it would be. I went to borrow a motor-car. As I passed his office the CO called me to come in a moment.

"Yes, sir"

"Your nurse friend called."

"Yes?"

"The student is still alive, however his fate is anything but assured."

"That is good news, sir. Did she say anything else?"

"No. She told me he is still alive and didn't even go into details. She sounded completely worn out, but she said she felt obligated to keep me abreast of things. Remarkable woman, quite thorough."

"Aye, sir, that she is."

"I didn't mean to keep you, Lef-tenant."

"No worries, sir. I am at a loss for something to do until I leave for the front, so I thought I would go to the cafe in town. Would you care for any—"

"Anything you bring would be welcome, thanks. Now away with you!"

"Aye, sir."

I found the cafe predictably slow. I sat at the counter and the proprietor set some coffee in front of me right away.

"Care for anything else? Fresh cakes?"

"Yes, please. And I should like a few to take back to the airfield if you have any."

"Oh, I have cakes. Tell me what you want and I'll box them for you."

He wasted no time getting to the latest news. "I understand there was some excitement out at the old athletic fields yesterday?"

"Aye, there was indeed some excitement. Poor lad managed to work a Camel into an inverted spin and ran out of sky before he could right it."

"Inverted spin . . ."

I showed him upright, then inverted, and twisted my hand somewhat and then he understood.

"So he was upside down and the thing was twirling like a top."

"Essentially, yes. He had never been in that attitude before, and he did not know how to right his machine. He hit the ground like that."

"Good God, no . . . ."

"Aye, he did."

"I am so sorry for the loss of another fine lad."

"He is not dead."

"No? How could that be?"

"I knew Clara—my blonde nurse friend—was at the hospital, so I arranged to take him directly to her."

"And she fixed him?"

"No. She brought him back from dead. Twice."

"Dead? *Twice?*"

"Twice."

"Good Lord! How did she manage that?"

"His heart stopped and she was able to make it beat again."

"I had no idea it could be done!"

"That, good sir, is Clara. She has dedicated her life to medicine and healing."

"Apparently so. And she is only a nurse?"

"She is a nursing instructor, but she wants to be a doctor—a surgeon."

"With her abilities, why isn't she a doctor?"

"Because she is a woman."

"That's all? She's a woman?"

"Aye."

"Just what difference does that make? If she knows her craft so well, she should be what she wants to be."

"If only it were so easy."

"It can be. I know some people. They can help."

"You do?"

"Aye, I do. As a merchant in town I meet regularly with other merchants and such. I can spread the word on your lass Clara. If the right ears get the word, things can happen."

"Do tell."

"I shall. There is a meeting later this week, but I will place a few telephone calls before then. There is no sense keeping someone with her abilities from her goals. I will see to it."

"You needn't put yourself out."

"Oh, no. This is special. The lad should be dead, right?"

"Yes, he should be."

"But your Clara intervened and he is alive."

"For now, yes, but there are no assurances."

"Didn't you say she helped you?"

"Aye, she did, about two and a half years ago. I was left for dead in a field hospital, but she saw to it I was treated and then cleaned my wounds constantly and saw to it that I got proper treatment."

"Yes, yes, I remember now. She is indeed remarkable, isn't she?"

"I should say, yes."

"That settles it, then. Please excuse me, Lieutenant, while I serve those folks coming in. Then I'll box your cakes. Would you like more coffee?"

"I would, when you get to it. There is no hurry."

He poured three coffees for his new customers and greeted them at their table. I was most pleased I had another ally for Clara. I couldn't wait to tell her, whenever that would be. I was sure I would hear from her, but she was all of a sudden quite busy with work, thanks to me. I couldn't feel too bad, however, as it was her chosen calling. She would get to me when she could.

The conversation took a slightly lighter tone upon the owner's return with fresh coffee. Coming out of a bitter cold snap and heading for the fourth Christmas of the war, we wondered when the fighting would end. He reminded me we were approaching the birthday of Jesus, and Jesus' message was one of love. How could God side with anyone who was responsible for so much killing and destruction? I reminded him that I was responsible for some of that death and destruction. He reminded me that I was doing what His Majesty had ordered me to do. I was not to be held responsible for what I had done in service of king and country. I was doing my job. I could not disagree with him. I told him my motive was very much vengeance. The Germans had nearly killed me, more than once, and they had indeed killed two very dear friends, at least, and I wanted to do all I could to end the war. I intended to see to it that Germany lost the war in no uncertain terms.

"Ripping, lad! That's the spirit!"

"We all have our motivations, don't we? I miss my mates. I may never get the men who ended their lives, but I feel the more Germans I do kill, the better my chances."

"Did you lose a mate in the RFC? It wouldn't be surprising."

"Oh? I have lost a number of mates, of course. But mates? Why do you ask?"

"Well, lad, let's say I am onto you."

"Onto me? How so?"

"I have friends and we talk. I have it on good authority that you were a front line scout pilot, but I forget how many German buses you have shot down."

I was stunned.

"And I would guess you don't know how many either."

"Why is that?"

"You don't care. It doesn't matter to you. You want to kill them all. So as long as there are Germans to shoot back, you aren't happy. Am I right?"

"Very much so, I'm afraid."

"The way you act, I am reminded of the incident I read about some months ago. It seems the Germans shot up one of our two-seat aeroplanes and killed the pilot. The observer beat all odds, climbing into the pilot's cockpit, throwing the dead pilot out, and bringing the damaged aeroplane back to his field."

I sat in stunned silence. After a moment I heard myself respond, "That . . . was me."

"That was what?"

"That was me. I was the observer. That observer. My pilot, mentor, and dear friend had been shot badly. I watched him die. Yet I was not ready to die with him. I climbed my way into his cockpit and I tried to push him into the front cockpit. But he slipped over the side and I could not hold him, much less lift him into the aeroplane. He was very heavy with all the layers of clothing to stave off the cold at altitude. The last thing he did was give me this."

I showed him the bladder of scotch.

"I carry it most everywhere. Of all the mementos I could have, this is the only one I do have. Or want. He had shown me how the controls worked and had me taxi the aeroplane."

"You knew how to fly then."

"Well, I knew about the instruments and controls. I never actually flew before that day."

"Yet you managed to bring your ship back to your field and land?"

"Well, I got it back to the field, yes. Land? That depends on what you consider a landing. I put it on the ground and it didn't kill me. But they stripped what they could from the airframe for spare parts and left it where I put it. They were very happy that I didn't put it down in the middle of the field. Truth told, I do not remember putting it down. I remember avoiding another aeroplane landing. I woke up on a table in the mess."

"That was you . . . ."

"Aye, 'twas. They sent me for pilot training. The joke was that I could fly, but my landings needed work. Eventually I ended up in a scout squadron in France. I shot at a lot of German crates. Some of them went down and crashed, caught fire or exploded. I don't know how many. You are correct. I don't care. However, I'm no Ball or McCudden."

"May I ask what brings you here?"

"I am a flight instructor. I take eligible cadet pilots and wring them out on scout aeroplanes to see if they have what it takes to fly, fight, and survive at the front."

"But if you were successful at the front . . . ?"

"Once one becomes successful, as you call it, the brass hats want to preserve him and what he knows. They had wanted to ship me back here to teach, but they didn't know how to make it palatable to me. Then I had an incident. I technically disobeyed orders to strafe German trenches. A fresh replacement pilot saw me and followed me, only to be shot down into "No Man's Land" and killed. They used that to send me here as "punishment", even though they all knew I would never have let that lad over the lines so soon. I merely had not seen him following."

"So you have been misleading me, have you?"

"I am afraid so, sir. I hope you are not terribly upset."

"No, not in the least. I meet a lot of people here, people of all kinds and many and varied temperaments. I do not judge. We all have our reasons, ways, and motivations for what we do. You have never been disrespectful. You merely do not want to blow your own horn, as it were. I can understand and respect that."

"Thank you, you are very kind."

"Think nothing of it. I can probably guess which instructor you are."

"Can you, then?"

"Yes. You are the one who drew the bosom in the air at the last ceremony."

"I call it a 'lazy eight'."

"Lazy eight me arse! You call it what you want, lad, but I know what I saw traced across the sky! Good show!"

We shared a good laugh over my aerobatic signature, of sorts. Then he retrieved several boxes of cakes for me to take back to the airfield and refused any money for them or my coffee.

"Just tell 'em where you 'bought' 'em, Lef-tenant."

I managed to get the boxes into the motor-car intact and departed for the airfield. Our conversation was a little alarming once I thought about it. No, not the part about me and how I had been holding out on him, so to speak. But the part that remained unspoken. If he knew people and talked with them, then he undoubtedly knew who Pauline was. He likely knew her husband, and it was a fair guess that he had an idea about my relationship with Pauline. That could be trouble. Then again, if he had said nothing thus far, he likely wouldn't. Certainly he knew how Pauline's husband felt about her. All the same, I would have to be mindful that he could know. I was probably reading too much into it. He and I had been building our own relationship through our service to king and country. I would have to ask him more about his time on HMS Dreadnought and learn more about him and his service.

And I would find a way to win him completely over. I did have an idea what would do it.

Back at the airfield, I dropped the cakes by the CO's office. His adjutant, while untying a box, informed me I had received a message by telephone.

"Someone named Claire left word that you were to telephone her. If she does not answer, she would appreciate a visit."

"That was all, Corporal?"

"Yes, sir, nothing further."

"Okay. Thank you, Corporal. May I use the telephone?"

"Of course, sir."

I placed a call to Clara. She did not answer. I informed the corporal I needed to borrow the motor-car again and he waved me away.

"Save a box for the CO. And thanks!"

He waved me away more vigorously, shoving more cake into this mouth. Then he saluted.

* * * * *

Chapter 80

British

Once underway in the motor-car, I decided to force myself to take my time getting to Clara's. If she hadn't answered, she was sound asleep. I found my heart was racing at the thought of seeing her again, but I kept the throttle set for a relaxed drive. The air, the sunlight, the clouds, the rural scenery, the lack of any other vehicles on the road, all combined for a beautiful drive. At last I turned onto her lane, then parked near her cottage. I don't know why I walked so quietly toward the door, as I was about to awaken her anyway, but I did. I stood there a moment, collecting myself, then I knocked. And knocked. I knocked a little harder. And again. Nothing. Okay, one last knock. Still nothing. I quietly (?) retraced my steps toward the motor- car. Something stirred behind me. It was the door.

"Lef-tenant . . . ?"

I froze. That voice. The voice brought a flood of memories and feelings, horrible and wonderful and pleasant and urgent, all at once.

"Lef-tenant? Won't you please come in?"

I snapped back into the moment, a little dazed.

"Yes. Why, yes, of course. Forgive me."

I approached the door. She, dressed in the same housecoat I remembered from before, backed against one door frame, allowing not quite enough room for me to pass by. I had to squeeze between her and the opposing door frame to get in, something that caused a large smile to spread across her face. Once I was by, she executed a very deft combination of moves, closing the door, hooking my elbow with her hand, spinning me toward her, then steadying me with both arms around me and her mouth on mine. I remember wondering how much lipstick was left after what she had just been through. "Lef-tenant! I'm surprised you're here!"

"You left a message—"

"Yes, but that didn't mean you would respond."

"Well, I considered leaving you to get your rest."

"See?"

"I know what you have been through. At least I have an idea of the long day you were going through. I had decided to leave it for you to contact me so I did not disturb you."

"As you see, I did contact you. And I'm pleased you have responded."

"Why, thank you. You did have a—"

"I did. That is not yours to worry about, but I appreciate your consideration."

"Then, my dear Clara, what can I do for you? Did you want to talk?"

"Yes, I do want to talk. But later." She reached for my overcoat. "At the moment, I wish to settle a debt. And maybe incur another."

She removed my overcoat and dropped it at a chair. She missed. I reached for it but was pulled away and attacked. A dozen Boche coming out of the morning sun could not have been more thorough.

After I returned the motor-car, the CO intercepted me as I passed by his office.

"Lef-tenant?", he called through a mouthful of cake.

"Sir? Yes, sir?"

"Lef-tenant, have you any word on our flyer?"

"I do. He sustained multiple—"

"With apologies, I do not need a list. Will he live?"

"To the point, sir, yes, he should. But I doubt he will have the opportunity to stunt a Camel any time soon."

"Thank you, Lef-tenant. That bit of news changes the tenor of the letter to his parents. It surprises me that he is still alive. I know what I saw, a lad on the verge of death. Your friend is quite the dogged professional. It would have been far easier for her to let him die."

"Exactly my point, sir. Clara is dedicated to her craft of healing people."

"You do not need to convince me, lad. I just saw it for myself. Good show."

"Indeed, sir."

"These cakes. Are they from the cafe you always go to?"

"Yes, sir, they are."

"One morning we must go together for breakfast. My treat."

"Sir, that would be wonderful. The proprietor served on HMS Dreadnought."

"Dreadnought, eh? I should enjoy meeting him."

"Splendid chap."

As long as he didn't want breakfast the next day. I was to pick up Clara and have breakfast with her. After our "meeting", she had become very tired. While I learned about the pilot, she had said very little about Pauline. She promised to tell me more over breakfast. I was left with the impression the news was not particularly good.

I continued working up my chops on the cornet. I thought I would sit in with the orchestra since I had nothing better to do other than the flyover at the ceremony. I just hope my "lazy eight"

would not be a memorial. I should have more information in the morning.

The morning finally arrived. I borrowed a motor-car and drove briskly over to Clara's cottage. Gingerly I approached the door, and as I was about to knock, it opened to reveal Clara in that same housecoat that was becoming so familiar. Again she stood in the doorway, forcing me to squeeze past her. She closed the door and giggled a little as she hugged and kissed me aggressively. Her housecoat came undone and she made no move to cover up. Instead she unfastened and removed my coat, throwing it at the chair like last time. Unlike last time, it hit the chair, knocking it over, and again the coat was on the floor. She pulled me by the arm, removing my hat. The hat landed on another chair, while I was pushed back on the bed. After making a few "adjustments" she climbed on the bed and straddled me.

"You must like it up there."

"Yes, I do. Are you complaining?"

"Certainly not!"

"Well, grab ahold, flyboy—you are about to hit some turbulence!"

I did as suggested and rode it out. When it was over, she collapsed onto me and kissed me endlessly.

"What's that I feel?"

"Your kissing apparently has regenerative powers, I'm afraid."

"Don't be afraid. I'll take care of it."

And take care of it she did, but with less turbulence. Far less.

"Would you care for more kissing?"

"Later. Definitely later."

"Are you hungry? I am, for certain."

"I was hungry when I arrived. Now I am famished."

"Great. Let me find something to do with my hair and then we can go."

While Clara fussed with her hair and got dressed, I reassembled myself, donned my coat, and righted the chair. I felt something of a conflict. It was an enjoyable conflict, but it was nonetheless a conflict. I had not seen Pauline in hospital for obvious reasons, but she and I had built up a relationship. Clara had become part of the relationship as our "cause". But Clara quickly advanced beyond being a cause for me, though I still believe she had not squarely faced the reality of the death of her fiancé. I was happy to help, if help was what I was providing. It appeared Clara would be the better choice, being single and available, but I was not the sort to walk away from the relationship I had built with Pauline. Pauline would continue to be unavailable unless or until her husband passed away. She was not about to leave him, and no one would blame her. She lacked nothing material. Then there was Jeremy, a fine young chap who was currently in France taking up my cause of killing Germans. A spectacular flyer and good shot, he was more than just a former student. We had the potential for a fine working relationship with our mutual love of flying. But I couldn't help but wonder how he would be affected should he learn of the intimate relationship with his . . .

"Are you ready? Hey! Remember me? You didn't pass out on me, did you?"

"Oh! Sorry. I was thinking of a matter back at the airfield. So very sorry."

"Problems? Do you need to hear it out loud? I can listen."

"Oh, no, no. Thanks, but I shan't trouble you. Let us away to the cafe."

"'Let us away to the cafe'? Are you sure you're not writing a song? It's kinda catchy." With that she started to bounce a little on the balls of her feet with her hands held vertically in front of her, left, left, right, right, chanting, "Let us away . . . to the cafe . . ."

"My, aren't you the proper medical professional!"

"Come on! It's catchy and fun. It has a good beat and I can dance to it!"

"That's right, oh, that's right! We formally met on the dance floor, didn't we? Say, if you enjoy dancing, perhaps we could . . ."

"Yes! I would love to go dancing! It would be great to get out and loosen up from time to time. I love medicine, to be sure, but it certainly can swallow one up some days. The recreation would be good for me and probably wouldn't harm you at all. Besides, . . . " She sidled up to me, face to face, gently grasping my hand. " . . . think of it as a forward, leading to the next chapter of recreational activity. Are you in, flyboy? Or do you need a flow chart?" Her free hand went to the small of my back, pulling me close as she seemed to swallow me in a heavy bout of kissing. Once again, it had its regenerative powers. I reached around her and pulled her even closer.

My hat loosed itself and fell onto the chair I had just risen from.

"Stop that." I said onto her moving lips, "or we shall both starve."

"Can you think of a better way to go?"

"Certainly not. But we have many things to accomplish before we consider going at all. Allow me to help you into your coat."

"You're no fun! Wait. I take that back. You're ripping fun—but you're right. I need food."

With that we departed.

* * * * *

CHAPTER 81

British

"Ah, Lef-tenant! I see you have brought your lovely nurse friend with you! After what I have heard about her, I will give her breakfast on the house. But you must buy yours!"

"Fair enough, Skipper!"

"'Skipper'?"

"Sure, you old sea dog, why not?"

"Fine, then. But unless you need privacy, I want you two right here at the counter. I want to hear more about saving that lad who landed upside down. He should be dead but for you, young lady! How did you do that?"

"Well, my life has been devoted to the study of the human body and how it works. I had an idea and this pilot presented the perfect opportunity to put my idea to work. He was dead—how much worse could I make it?"

"Right. Good point. May I ask what your idea was—is?"

"Yes. There are no secrets when it comes to saving a life. His heart stopped. The heart squeezes and causes blood to flow through the body. I pushed at the heart best I could—it lies behind the ribs—and kept some blood flowing. While doing that, I shocked the area with harder blows in an effort to restart the heart. In his case it worked. But I feel the idea needs development, as it was rather crude the way I performed it."

"Nonetheless, congratulations are in order."

"Thank you. But I was only doing my job. I hope I can advance treatment of such emergencies based on what I did. Or perhaps someone will find a better way."

That said, the exchange went to more mundane conversation about the weather and the war. I told him I was completely bored, just waiting for the word to go to France. Clara kicked my lower leg without changing expression. Just a few more days and I could visit my old squadron and a former student. I was looking forward to killing a few more Germans. Maybe enough to force the kaiser to surrender. That brought a bit of a chuckle from anyone in the vicinity, as Iwas not speaking in hushed tones. Several about the room intoned, "Hear, hear!" One stepped up and asked the proprietor to put my breakfast on his tab, as well as Clara's. I started to protest, but he insisted. "You are risking your life for His Majesty and the rest of us. I can afford to buy a meal or two to show my appreciation!" The rest of the room cheered his gesture and I had no more to say but thanks. I inquired about his business, and he told me he was a partner at the local mortuary. "We have far too much business because of this damned war. Don't you add to it. I never want to see your face in our place of business. Is that a deal?"

"I shall certainly do my best, good sir! Thank you once again."

He clapped me on the shoulder and walked out the door.

"Good man, that one. He served on a destroyer some time back, don't recall which one. We met in a bar in Dunkirk. He is active in the business community."

"You said you knew people."

"Aye. I do. And now he knows about Clara here first hand. That can't hurt."

"Hurt what?" asked Clara.

"Your desire to become a doctor. The skipper here is a member of the local business community. He is well aware of the push to get you what you desire and what you deserve. Your intense study and fine work ethic are becoming common knowledge. All these things increase the chances for you to succeed. It's more than talk. It's seeing you in action, applying your knowledge."

"I had no idea the ripples were spreading this far out over the pond. I'm flattered. You are wonderful."

"I have not acted alone. Remember, Pauline has been working from the inside, as it were. She deserves much credit for spreading the word into the right ears. Speaking of Pauline, are you at liberty to tell me of her condition?"

"No. I cannot. I'm very sorry."

"Is it —"

"I can't say. Please don't ask."

"Uh, . . . okay. Of course. I apologize for persisting."

"No, no, it's perfectly understandable."

"Well, have you had enough? Shall I take you to the school?"

"No. I should like some more coffee if you have the time. Then I shall ask you to take me home, if you would."

"Certainly. It will be my pleasure." I began to feel the slightest pressure against my leg. I could see Clara's ploy of looking deep in thought was merely for appearances. I was a bit relieved I had not upset her very badly, but I was curious as to why she would not say anything about Pauline. I would find out in good time.

We said our goodbyes and thanks and got back into the motor-car for the ride into the country. I had decided not to ask again about Pauline, so the conversation again went to the weather and how it was looking for my planned flight across the channel. Fair enough, I could talk weather.

It was part of my stock in trade to understand it best I could. When we arrived I of course got out and opened Clara's door. Then I escorted her to the front door.

"I suppose I should leave you then."

"Why is that? Is there any hurry?"

"Well, no, but I thought you . . ."

"Wanted more kissing? Correct. And since you're right here, it might as well be you. *In,* flyboy!"

I started to salute but thought better of it and removed my hat instead. Clara again partially obstructed the doorway but I persisted in passing her, eliciting a naughty little laugh from her. She removed my coat and threw it nowhere near the chair, landing it yet again on the floor. She grabbed the front of my shirt and pulled me to her bed, where she lay back, pulling me on top of her.

"Kiss me, flyboy, kiss me." I obliged, again feeling like she was going to swallow me. I started to say something but she clamped her lips over mine. Instantly she replaced them with her finger, saying, "Don't talk, flyboy. Just kiss. Just . . . kiss. Nod slowly if you understand."

I nodded, slowly. Clara's lips replaced her finger, seemingly engulfing me. If I thought I could escape her lips, I knew there was no getting out of her embrace. But why would I want to? I could not think of a better place or predicament than where I was that moment. I had never felt so "as one" with anyone. The concept had never dawned on me before that moment. This woman had succeeded in making me forget about the war, the killing, even the flying. I remember thinking that if the moment simply lingered without interruption I would be very happy. Soft, happy, buoyant colors were flooding my consciousness as if taking positions on a vast canvas and adjusting, realigning, recombining, intermingling, looking like too many tropical fish in an aquarium. I took it all in, never showing a preference or choosing a color or combination, merely allowing it to happen. I was vaguely aware of my body, parts of it chilly, other parts intensely warm, moist with sweat, and the chilled and heated parts changing locations not unlike the colors. Those lips were never far from mine. I was certain they had left mine from time to time but I could never swear to it. Her lips were some kind of portal to pleasure such as I had never anticipated, much less experienced. Warm, pastel, soft, caress, cool, shifting, commingling, wet, sighing, yielding, blending, revisiting, calm, embrace, pause, plunge, trace, kiss, intermix, lips, dripping, tongues, flesh, more kissing, always those lips, ...

* * * * *

CHAPTER 82

British

We awoke hours later, shivering beneath the covers despite our complete embrace. The covers were very moist and the fire had nearly burned itself out. I slipped out of her grasp to tend to the fire. As it began to consume additional wood it cast off more heat and more light. I found Clara's housecoat and wrapped it around her for the moment. She directed me to where she kept a few spare blankets. I pulled one out and wrapped it around the both of us.

"Now this is cozy."

"Well, Clara, we cannot risk you being in a draught and catching something."

"Silly . . . one cannot catch something merely by being cold. Being cold distracts the body from fighting any contagions which may be present. And no, as infectious as you are, you're not a contagion."

"Well, I have caused more than a few Germans to catch a little something."

Clara laughed. "Well, okay, I suppose you have. But you're still not a contagion."

"I shall accept that as your esteemed medical opinion."

"Yes, do. And as long as you're accepting my medical opinion, I feel we should be closer together in order to share our body heat, at least until the fire is back up." With that she drew the blanket—and me— into her grasp and beset me with those wonderfully sensual lips.

As I gasped for air, I asked, "How does the fire look?"

"Don't know. Can't see it."

"Then how can you—"

"Don't talk. Kiss." She started to engulf me yet again.

"Do you ever tire of this?"

"You're still talking." She drew a breath and came at me.

"But really . . ."

"Would you rather play chess?" She framed my face with her hands, her thumbs keeping my jaw from opening. I shook my head. "Do you have anywhere you need to be?" Again I shook my head. "I return to the school next week." My eyes grew large. I grasped her fingers in my hands and pulled my face free. "The motor-car." Clara shrugged, "What of it?" I puzzled a moment, gently lay her back, pinning her hands on either side of her head. "I suppose they have others." I offered my lips to hers and her lips accepted. I increased my weight on her, just in case she tried to escape. She did not.

* * * * *

CHAPTER 83

British

Finally climbing out of the bed, I risked asking, "Is this how you view intimacy, dear Clara?"

She paused. "I don't know how I view intimacy. But I like it."

"Like it? You have a gift for the understatement."

"Okay, I like it. I really like it. A lot. I feel I cannot get enough of it. It's new, it's fresh, it's exciting, and it's . . ."

"Exciting, certainly. But new? Fresh?"

"Well, . . . yes. Very new. You are my first."

"Your first . . . what?"

"You are the first with whom I have shared myself completely."

I was stunned. "But you were . . ."

"Engaged to be wed. Yes, I know. He was a wonderful man. While it is a shame he is gone, I have shed my tears for him."

"Undoubtedly you have. But I see you have . . ."

"Moved along? I have. I tend to be pragmatic. He is gone. No amount of pining will bring him back. I cannot explain it beyond that. I can say that time spent with you has just felt right. I always look forward to more time with you. When I am not with you, I am thinking of you."

"I am flattered, to be sure. You have been very upfront about your feelings and desires."

"Have I been too much for you, dear?"

"Too much? I should say not, but such behavior is the exception, as opposed to the rule. Everyone is always so coy, putting on a front, disingenuous. I find you most refreshing."

"That has always been my nature. If I see something I want, I take it. My intended marriage was arranged. While he was truly wonderful, he was not my choice. He treated me well, but I was with him more to please the families. With you, . . . I can't explain it, but I want to be with you. And, frankly, you being a pilot, I want to get all the time I can with you while . . . you . . ."

"While I am still alive?"

"Well, yes. I know you are about to go back to France, if only for a short while. But the possibility exists that you will not return."

"You needn't worry. I—"

"One bullet or shell fragment. That's all it takes. Whether intended or just happenstance. Or a failed engine. Or any of a number of circumstances. A lot can go wrong."

"Would you prefer I quit the whole match and follow my painting, maybe my music?"

"I would never dictate how you live your life. What you do is part of who you are. I should love to see your paintings, however."

"I would as well. They are in here." I pointed to my head.

"I see. But you have painted others."

"They are in the family home. I hope. It has been a while since I've been there. But I look forward to the next painting, after the war. In the meantime, I play my cornet. I will likely sit in with the orchestra for this ceremony. If you would like to attend . . ."

"If I can get away, I should love to."

"That would be ripping of you. I'm sure I could slip away for a dance."

"I hope so. Why else would I attend?"

"So you have a penchant for musicians?"

"I have a penchant for this musician." She moved closer, those lips leading the way.

"Musicians can be unstable, moody, undependable . . ."

"I have a stable career. People will always fall ill and need care. You needn't worry. Be with me. Paint. Make music. You make me happy." Her voice was becoming more hushed.

"You mean to say, . . ." Her lips were upon me.

"Not another word." Her lips once again engulfed mine, silenced the conversation, and initiated yet another encounter. What was a man to do?

* * * * *

CHAPTER 84

British

The morning of the ceremony I looked out my window to discover
a familiar friend, the fog,

The morning of the ceremony I looked out my window to discover a
familiar friend, the fog, plying its way around my little garden and beyond.
The fog was not very thick, but it still comprised the commingling trails
of vapor and particles that I was so enthralled with. Since I had to warm
up the cornet a bit in order to sit in with the orchestra later, I pulled it
out and buzzed a few easy notes. Letting my vision blur a little, I sensed
the motion of the mists and the subtly increasing light. My easy notes
came to resemble something by Debussy, meandering around with
sections of whole tone scales and soft arpeggios, increasing slightly with
the movement of the bright mists, then a gradual diminuendo as the
mists allowed themselves to disappear into the day's bright light. It was
going to be a beautiful day, likely with puffs of cloud for a backdrop to
the flying demonstration.

Thinking on to the flying, I thought perhaps I should reacquaint
myself with my Camel. It might not remember me. The more I thought
about the idea, the more I liked it, so I pulled on some flying clothes
and went to ask the ground crew to prep my aerial partner. We got
her started, and I sat in her while she warmed up, thinking about
the past several days spent with Clara. She had taken me over like
a storm, engulfing me completely, and not solely with her lips. She
was supremely intelligent and knowledgeable on so many topics and
concepts, yet able to let go completely and love with abandon. She
was quite adept at switching gears in her mind, darting from medical
expertise to romance or finance or anything else with no visible effort
or outward preparation. Getting to know her more and more, I found
her completely delightful to be with. And there was no sneaking about
needed, no excuses or happenstance to concoct. Then Pauline came to

mind. Completely different woman, but not to be discounted. She had introduced a few ideas of her own, and she was completely along with helping Clara achieve her goals and advancing the plight of women in general. However, she was the one topic Clara had demurred, refusing to discuss at all. Why was this, I wondered. Was Pauline's situation that dire? Did Clara not wish to distress me with bad news? Was Pauline's condition steadily improving, but Clara did not want anything to get in the way on her drive for my heart? I could hardly just walk into the hospital and ask to visit, for that would be wholly inappropriate and possibly opening suspicion as to what could be going on between us. People had a way of talking about such things. We needed none of that. As I had no business at the hat shop, I could only query Clara and hope she responded.

The Clerget had come up to temperature, so I waved off the wheel chocks and rolled her out. Taxi and takeoff being as per the norm, I climbed to several thousand feet before attempting any maneuvers. Though it had been a number of days, we fell in synch like it had been a few hours. Even with her quirks, she was a sheer delight to dance with across the skies and puffs of cloud I had envisioned earlier. Climbs, dives, zooms, rolls, loops, reversals, spirals and spins, all fell nicely into place. I went through my signature maneuver a few times, again without trouble, then took her down. It had been a perfectly wonderful flight, and I was excited to be performing later that day, possibly for Clara.

I walked by the CO's office to check with him about the situation in France and asked for any updates. He ribbed me about finally coming back to the airfield, suggesting he was about to call the local authorities and initiate a search. Of course I teased that if he had any use for me, he needed to say so before I absconded with another motor-car.

"Lef-tenant, I suggest you take the motor-car once our ceremony is over with. The weather over the Channel and northern France is currently miserable, but expected to be clear in a couple of days. You may wish to use those days to put your affairs in order as you see fit. The next clear day will find you on your way to your old squadron."

"Great news, sir—indeed, ripping!"

There it was. I would soon be on my way to the front, my old squadron—such as it was. How many of the old lads would still be there? And Jeremy. I wonder if he had that triplane working just yet. Jeremy could be my avenue to news about Pauline. After all, her son would want to know about his mum. I stopped by the mess for coffee and something light to eat, then washed off the morning's castor oil and soot from the Camel flight. I had to look presentable for the orchestra, after all. Beyond that, I was not going to worry about anything. If Clara could make the ceremony, I would know it, likely by her hat. There wasn't another one like it, after all. If she did not attend, I could still have a wonderful day of music and flying. After that I could assemble my meager bag for the flight over the Channel. I could not see taking a lot, especially for a brief visit. There was very little room in the cockpit for anything beyond a heavily bundled pilot and a flare pistol, so my bag could end up atop the upper wing. We would see. But not to worry about it at this point.

I checked back with the CO and learned that I was to fly the fifth and tenth passes in the aerial demonstration. With the tenth I would end the show. He assured me my Camel would be in place and full of fuel when I came out to it. That taken care of, I went to my quarters to change and get my cornet.

That was one of the nice things about being in the service. Clothing is provided. One has his combat uniform and his dress uniform. No decisions to be made regarding style, color, or anything else. If it was a formal affair, the dress uniform was the choice. Talk about keeping things simple. While I appreciated my colors, the simplicity was satisfying on another level. Nothing to think about, there is only one answer. I could occupy my mind with other thoughts.

Dress uniform on, cornet case in hand, I took a bag of flight clothes to my Camel and tossed it into the cockpit. It was just a coverup to keep the dress uniform looking good. I would not be up long enough to be bothered by the cold. From there I went to the hall and found the orchestra conductor. We went over a few details and I sat down with the others. We would be playing before long. I would be watching for that certain unique hat.

The conductor got all to sit, agree on a tune, and, like pulling a propeller, brought down his baton to start the music. People arrived and I saw many wonderful hats perched atop many lovely women. Pleasant enough, to be sure, but not what I was looking for. I wasn't worried. She never promised she would be there. So I just played the cornet, pitching in where I could. We had very few written arrangements. Mostly the leader would call a tune and a key, wait for any protests, then count us off. I always skirted the melody unless I heard someone else playing it, in which case I would play rhythmic counterpoint or a countermelody. Filling in various aspects of a tune kept me on my toes. I found it very enjoyable, if not always easy. It pleased me to be a part of an artistic organization, creating on the spot. If Clara wanted something to dance to, the orchestra would satisfy that demand. But I was happy to pass the time playing my riffs and solos and watching the dancers. Some were just clogging along, barely keeping to the beat, but every once in a while a pair of real dancers took the floor. That was a delight to watch, looking as though they were rehearsed and choreographed. Good dancers would actually influence what I played, as I felt I was egging them on to do more. When they did strive a bit harder I felt almost like we were in communication, and in a way I suppose we were. Music can be so powerful, what with the effect it can have on people and their moods and their own abilities to perform. I never understood it, but if I were tapping my fingers, I could do it faster and more rhythmically with music playing. It was like becoming part of the music or vice versa.

With no sight of Clara, the music stopped, or at least paused for a while. The ceremony began, my cue to put the cornet in its box and get ready to fly. As I was slipping off toward the exit, I heard a familiar voice.

"Lef-tenant? Lef-tenant! Could we please talk?"

It was Mr Trafford. "Good day to you, sir! Yes, I would be delighted to talk—but I need to go fly in the aerial demonstration. I hate to ask, but if you could wait for a short while, I will be all yours."

"Certainly. I'm just relieved I was able to find you. It's important, but it can wait a short while longer. I'm sorry I've detained you. I shall watch for you."

"Each instructor will fly two passes. I am last. I can see you right out of the 'plane or I can change again."

"Don't bother for me. I will meet you after you've come down. Again, sorry I've—"

"No, not at all! You can buy me a scotch later."

"Bottle or case? Name it, it's yours."

"Either would be ripping—but I meant a glass."

"Done. Go now."

That was curious. I could not help but wonder what he wanted to discuss. While my mind raced to Pauline, it could easily have been something about Jeremy. Perhaps he received a letter with a request. It would have to wait for the moment. I had to concentrate on what I was to do in the Camel. Like playing music, one had to keep one's mind on what one was doing lest something go awry.

I went into the hangar where my Camel was kept to pull on and fasten the coverall. Even if I was not in France, the winter weather was still cold—and even more so at altitude. No sense freezing over a twenty minute or so flight. Once the extra layer was in place I went out to my Camel, which had just been started. Two of the lads assisted me into the cockpit and made sure the lap belt was tight. I then had only to wait until the other instructors taxied away and I fell in behind them. I had something I wanted to try, so while the others reached their desired starting altitudes I climbed further aloft. By the time I reached my beginning height, the fourth instructor was beginning his routine. I watched as he did a loop and a couple of rolling passes before tracing a horizontal figure eight directly over the airfield. As he flew away for the last time he wagged his wings to signal me to begin. I fired a red flare in the air, then a blue flare. I turned tightly to the left three times, to the right three times, then dove slightly to build momentum to begin a loop. At the top of the loop I cut my engine and set up for inverted flight. Almost immediately I kicked hard right rudder. As I knew it would, the Camel went into an inverted spin. I adjusted the ailerons a bit and rode her down. At about twenty-five hundred feet I straightened her out, pulled back on the stick to "finish the loop", then dove hard toward the middle of the flight line and into a large, grand loop. I finished by flying over the CO's office, wagging my wings for the second round of flights to begin. I climbed back to twenty-five hundred feet and watched the first two instructors fly their combinations of maneuvers. The third and fourth instructors put on a mock dogfight with some very close appearing passes on one another. When they flew away in opposite directions wagging their wings, I went into my "signature" maneuver, the "Lazy Eight". After that, I did a pass rolling the Camel, but pausing the roll at forty-five, ninety, one-thirty-five degrees, inverted, and so on, at each eighth of the roll around. Later we called it an "eight point roll", a variation on a theme.

We each then flew low over the flight line, waving at the assembled throng, and landed in order. As promised, Jeremy's father was waiting near where I taxied the Camel in. Once the lads helped me to the ground and I had my headgear and gloves off he handed me a glass. The aroma was unmistakeable. Twelve year old scotch. He held another glass in front of his face.

"Cheers, Lef-tenant! Good show!"

I drew in about half the scotch and allowed it to mill about my mouth, filling every last bit with an almost indescribably smooth sensation. I closed my eyes, tilted my head back, and was briefly transported. The taste was very familiar, and part of me hoped I would open my eyes and find my old mate and mentor, Knees, standing with me before a line of FE2bs. It was a pleasant notion, and I kept my eyes closed a little longer to hold that thought. I knew it was not to be, no matter how badly I wanted it. As I opened my eyes I felt a tear seeking its way down my cheek.

"This is wonderful, sir. Thank you."

"You almost looked like you left me here for a moment. I was afraid . . ."

"I did, sir. A very dear friend used to drink a scotch quite similar to this. Thanks to the damned Boche he is no more—uh, forgive my indiscretion, sir."

"Understood. I will send you a case."

"Most kind of you, sir, but I am about to leave."

"Leave?"

"Yes, sir. As soon as the weather clears over the Channel I am flying back to my old squadron."

"To visit with Jeremy? Splendid."

"Well, yes, sir, in part. I am sure I will be flying with him as part of a refresher of sorts. I need to keep abreast of the latest tactics at the front so I have the latest information to pass along to my next class of student pilots."

"I see. But you will get to see him. I am sure you will give him my warmest regards. Does he know about his mother?"

"I don't know. What about his mother?"

"You don't know? She has been in hospital."

"I knew she had gone there. But she is still there?"

"She is, yes. I visit her regularly, but she does not respond to anything. She just lies there and moans quietly from time to time. Looks terrible. Damned people cannot or will not tell me what is the matter. Is it influenza? Tuberculosis? Cancer? They don't tell me. I had hoped perhaps you knew something."

"How would I know anything?"

"Well, I know you have seen her socially. She has met you at the one cafe for breakfast. More than once."

How did he know that? "Well, yes, sir, she happened in one day while I was having coffee. She offered to buy me breakfast and we talked for a while. She is such a bright, witty, intelligent and thoughtful woman . . ."

"Yes, yes, I suppose. And you two have been promoting the nursing instructor who wants to be a doctor. Clara—right?"

"Aye, sir, we have."

"I heard some remarkable stories about her recently. Seems she kept a pilot who crashed his aeroplane from dying. The hospital staff could not believe what she did—but it worked. Damnedest thing I've ever heard of. Something about starting his heart after it stopped. I don't know—but the lad is still alive!"

"That much I know of, sir. The lad will not be flying any time soon, but he has a great story to tell, thanks to Clara. I do not know anything about your wife. Clara has said nothing, no doubt out of respect for her and your privacy."

"Well, it was worth asking. Do tell me when you return and I will send that scotch."

"No need, sir, but tha—"

"Nonsense. After what you have done for my son? You will get a case a month if you want."

"Thank you, sir, but really—I'll tell you what. I expect to see Clara later today. If you don't mind, I will ask about your wife. If I learn anything, I shall . . ."

"Good man. Thank you. I hope to hear from you."

With that he was away.

"'Lazy Eight' me arse, lad! Those—that—was beautiful! And spinning upside-down? You are out of your mind! I'm a little surprised your departing friend didn't recognize the image you traced."

"I'm not . . . " I looked around to see the cafe proprietor, who shook my hand and clapped me on the shoulder. "Well, good day, Skipper! It's good to see you where I work for a change."

"I told you, Lef-tenant, I try to attend these functions. I simply love to watch the aerial demonstrations. And, as an added treat, I got to hear your hot little cornet with the band. Very nice work! You are just a master at whatever you do."

"If I enjoy it, it's worth the effort. I feel my true calling is as a painter, but I will wait until after the war to continue that pursuit."

"Painter! I must say I'm a bit surprised. I had you to be a more active sort. Well. Do you paint portraits?"

"I have done still life, landscapes, and light studies. Until recently I have not been inspired to paint portraits other than perhaps abstracts."

"Ah. Monet?"

"He is an influence, yes. You are familiar, I see."

"Yes. I enjoy the arts. Could you do a seascape? We should talk. I would like to have a nice seascape for my home, perhaps with HMS Dreadnought. I hope you would consider a commission work."

"Sight unseen? You are the trusting one."

"Let's say I have faith in you. I like the way you work, and I think it would appear in your paintings as well as your music and flying. It appears you have at least one other patron, from what I have seen."

"You haven't talked about what you have seen, I trust. That was—"

"I know who it was. I know who you eat breakfast with. Or did. She has not been in for a bit. But I would never betray anything like that other than an urgent legal matter. Your secrets are safe with me."

"I—we—appreciate that. She is currently in hospital. Her husband says she is unresponsive but the staff tell him nothing. I am not family so I cannot visit without raising suspicion. He was just asking if maybe Clara had said something about her condition, which she has not. As you might suppose, I have been quite concerned about her myself. She has inspired me to paint portraits, at least of her."

"I'm not surprised. She has obviously inspired you in other pursuits. She is a fine woman. I look forward to seeing her at the cafe when she is better. Speaking of which, I need to get back there. Will I see you soon?"

"Yes, sir, you will. I will likely be in tomorrow morning. I am currently waiting out the weather over the Channel so I can visit my old squadron in France."

"Being reassigned?"

"It's only for a week or so, to stay current. But I'll be back soon, so don't close down the shop just yet."

"Hardly. We can chat more in the morning then. Good show, lad. Well done. 'Lazy Eight' . . . ."

He chuckled as he walked away. I went back to the hangar to change and clean up a little. Then back to the orchestra, which was stomping right along with a nearly full dance floor. When it came time to serve dinner, we throttled back a bit. I played a few more numbers, then grabbed a quick bite back at the mess. I returned to my quarters, washed up, and put on a fresh uniform. I borrowed a motor-car from the pool and drove over to Clara's cottage. Though I did not see her 'car, I stopped and knocked at the door. There was no answer, of course, so I began my drive back into town. As luck would have it, I spotted her driving home in her 'car about halfway to town. With no other traffic on the road, I merely turned around and followed. I was nearly on her bumper turning onto her lane, and by the time she had gathered her things I opened her door and helped her down. Despite being burdened with handfuls of bag handles and such, she allowed herself to fall into my waiting arms. There she lingered just a bit.

"I am so happy to see you!" she cooed in my ear. I took what I could of her things and walked to the door. She unlocked, I opened, and we went in. We put her things down and I helped her off with her coat.

"How was your day? The ceremony? Did all go well?"

"Yes, all went as planned. I played with the orchestra, flew my routines, played a little more, then left. No harm done."

"I am so sorry I could not get away to see you. Busy day at the hospital."

"Care to talk about anything? I am happy to listen if you want to vent a little."

"Okay, but could we talk over food? I am hungry."

"We could probably still get to the cafe."

"Perhaps so. But I brought some things home to cook."

"How about I cook while you wash up a bit. I assume you wanted to freshen a bit."

"I will use that as an excuse to allow you to cook. Food tastes so much better when somebody else cooks it!"

"Understood. What do you have? Wait. No need to show me. Do I have free range of the pantry?"

"Oh, of course! Cook it all!"

"Well, hardly. But I will come up with something. You have some time to unwind a bit. Do you need a glass of wine? Hit of scotch? Brandy?"

"Brandy. Good idea. You know where I keep it. Have some if you like. I will try not to be long."

"Take all the time you need. I have cooking to do."

And so it went. She departed for her bedroom and pulled the door almost closed. I heard water running from time to time and little else. I busied myself with a decent meal using a piece of beef, some vegetables, and rice. By the time she returned, wearing that familiar housecoat, I was almost ready to serve.

"Dare I ask about your day?"

"I would rather ask about yours. Were there many people there for the ceremony?"

"Yes, one fewer than I had hoped and a few more than I had expected."

"How does that work?"

"Well, a certain someone was too busy with work, so the hats there were nice but not as nice as I have seen."

"Shame."

"Indeed. And I had a couple of visitors."

"Oh?"

"Yes. Mr Trafford stopped by to ask me about his wife. It seems she is unresponsive when he visits, which he says is regularly. He tells me she is restless, but never wakes up, and that she moans from time to time. As I am about to visit their son in France, is there anything I should know? I understand you may be bound to protect their privacy, but can you tell me anything about her condition?"

"Well, I would rather not. But it is only fair you should know. It appears the two of you are in league over me, if nothing else. She is not doing well. She appears to have influenza, the 'Spanish flu'. I had been limited in what I could do for her, but once she lost her baby, and I was able to—"

"Lost her what?!"

"Her baby. Wait—you didn't know? She was maybe three months into her term. When she fell ill, her body was not able to support both her and her child. I suppose it was the instinct to preserve the self, I don't know. But the fetus simply stopped one night. Her condition is still too precarious to remove its remains. But she must expel that matter to avoid further complications."

"I had no idea. She never said anything to me—not that it was any of my business. As you know, she is a married woman. But she never said she was looking forward to any more children. I don't know."

"Well, that is her situation. I suppose you can deliver that news to her son."

"What about her husband? He obviously doesn't know."

"Tell him if you wish. Or tell him to ask for me and I will tell him. I have not seen him there any time I have stopped by, but I also have other duties to attend to. I easily could have missed him. I cannot speak for the hospital staff."

"No, of course not."

"Okay. Where is my brandy? I'm sorry if I appear a little cross. I have had a long day, and tomorrow does not look to be much better. If it is not too much trouble, I should like to have a brandy and maybe another, and relax. Please say something relaxing or interesting that will not involve much thinking on my part."

"First, I apologize. Here is your brandy. I will be nearby to pour you another. As many as you like. As for interesting, I did have another visitor today at the airfield."

"Here we go . . . and who was that?"

"Our friend from the cafe, the proprietor."

"Oh! Skipper?"

"One in the same. He is fascinated by our flying demonstrations. So he broke away and came out to see us fly. While he was waiting he listened to the orchestra and very much enjoyed that. He of course spoke highly of you and sent his kind regards. You have another friend in the man, one with connections who may be helpful in getting you along to your goal."

"How sweet."

"You are remarkable. And the word is getting out."

"Thank you. You do understand, do you not, that if I achieve my goals, it will entail long days on a regular basis. You might not see a lot of me some days. Would that be troubling?"

"Certainly not. It would be great to see you get what you want. I don't understand."

"Well, Flyboy, I didn't think I would have to draw up a battle plan for you. Perhaps I was wrong. It goes something like this: You and I are spending a lot of time together of late. I very much enjoy your company. I feel so alive when I am with you. You are very good for me. You give me something to look forward to while I am at work. I hope you have similar feelings for me. Now, can you draw a line from dot to dot and see the direction where this could be headed? Or do I need to explain it further?"

"Well, I think you have made your point. I have very similar feelings toward you, Clara. I am afraid, however, to promise anything to you due to the war and the very real possibility of my going back to serve on the front lines—actually over the front lines and beyond, over enemy territory. So many things can go wrong and result in my death or capture. I feel that could be a problem."

"Point taken. But with you I am more than willing to take that chance. It is risky, true, but so is my quest to be a surgeon. Actually," she approached me with her empty glass, "I was hoping you needed further explanation, which I would be more than happy to supply."

"Well, okay, I could use a little more tutelage. Ripping idea, actually. But I recall someone being hungry. I'll pour you more brandy. And tea. And I shall set two plates. Can the explanation wait until after we have eaten?"

"Why, yes, it can. See? You are good for me. I'll have the tea with dinner. Brandy after."

* * * * *

CHAPTER 85

British

The next morning I telephoned the CO's office and asked to speak with him. The adjutant said he had not been in yet, so I asked the adjutant about the weather over the Channel. He wished me a good day, for there would be no flying over the Channel. I thanked him and promised I would stop by with cakes "for the CO". He chuckled and assured me the CO would get some of the cakes.

Knowing that the day was mine, I slipped back in bed with Clara. "Would you care for some breakfast at the cafe?"

"That would be very nice, thanks. I need to stop by the school this morning for a short while, and I need to check on my patients at the hospital. If you don't mind a little waiting, perhaps you could drive me."

"I would be happy to, since I will not be hopping the Channel today. But I thought you had a busy day today."

"I apologize. I was tired and confused my days. Today is light, so you are stuck with me. No flying? Too bad. We had better get started. Wait right here for a moment, and then we will work up an appetite for breakfast." She pulled on her housecoat, put more wood on the fire, spent a moment in the bathroom, and returned to me. Dropping her housecoat on the foot of the bed, she pushed me onto my back. "I feel like driving."

"But you just asked me to—"

"Stop talking," she said as she straddled me. "I'll drive now, you take us into town. Will that meet with your approval?"

"A most satisfactory arrangement. I'm sorry I questioned you."

"You're still talking? Maybe one of these will stop that . . . ."

Clara was indeed a pragmatic woman who utilized simple methods and what was on hand, so to speak, to solve basic problems. I could but admire her practical nature.

* * * * *

CHAPTER 86

British

When we arrived at the cafe I was ravenous, even though Clara had done most all the work. Again our friend greeted us with coffee and insisted we sit at the counter. He enjoyed showing off Clara to other customers. Other customers with influence. Though he had an idea of the answer, he made it a point to ask about the student pilot who crashed his Sopwith. Clara gave him a brief and general update and he again asked about how she had saved his life the night of the crash. He was a splendid advocate, getting Clara to tell the story in her own words so she could be overheard by another customer, presumably a gentleman with influence. Then we got to order our breakfast and I asked him to make up a few boxes of cakes to take by the airfield.

After a big breakfast and some interesting conversation, not to mention a little "Clara on display", I took Clara to the nursing school and dropped her off. I decided to take the cakes back to the airfield while she was tending to business. When I walked into the CO's office to leave said cakes and tease the adjutant, he spoke first.

"Ah, splendid, Lef-tenant, sir! I was just about to go look for something to have with my coffee. Thank you for saving me the walk. I'll see that the old man gets some." Opening one box, "My, I see you have outdone yourself this time. So fresh, so moist, so appealing! Have one with me? Sir?"

"Heavens, no—but thank you. I've just had a substantial breakfast. Not to be rude, but unless you have something . . ."

"Actually, I do. Just came in a few minutes ago. A man telephoned for you. He did not leave his name but asked that you stop by the hat shop at your convenience. He will be there all day. Does that mean anything to you, sir?"

"It does, yes—thank you. I will take care of that. Kindly give my regards to the—"

"Old man? Good morning, Lef-tenant. I see what brought you, so I won't ask. Well done."

"Good morning, sir. I hope you enjoy . . ."

"In a rush? Do you have a moment?"

"Certainly, sir." I followed him into his office and he pulled the door to.

"It's your former squadron, old bean. It seems they had a scrap with *der Fritzen* and came out on the losing end. Lost two pilots and one SE with others taking some damage. Several minor wounds. A few of the boys filed 'out of control' claims, but none have been substantiated."

"Good Lord, sir. Was Jeremy—"

"He was involved, yes. Filed one of the claims. His SE took a few through the wings and one through a water line. Cooked his engine, but he got it home. He is okay other than his pride."

"What were they flying?"

"That is the odd part. Our lads said they were flying older Albatross scouts. D.IIIs. But they flew better than any D.IIIs they had seen. The SEs were barely a match. The Boche dove like stones and zoomed hard, not what we have been accustomed to. They have always been careful in a dive, the lower wing structure weak. Curious."

"Curious indeed. Doesn't make sense. What was Jeremy's report about them?"

"You know the lad. He thinks he is the greatest thing since cracked ice. But, gifted as he is, he couldn't get a good shot at any of them. They were six to our five, one of the infernal Hispano gear boxes acting up just as the show got started. The lad had to put down behind the lines and was captured. I hope the bastards copy the damned gear box!"

"Bloody shame. I hope I have the chance to meet them."

"Hard to say. They seem to be quite the nomadic lot. They go where needed."

"I suppose Jeremy and I will have to create a need. Killing Germans seems to be the quickest way to end the damned war. So if we kill a lot of them that should get the attention of *der Fritzen* and bring them back."

"It's worth a try. If you're killing Germans anyway, you are not going out of your way just for them. Good show then. I did hear that you checked in this morning. Good of you."

"I must stay in touch, sir. Communication is key."

"Right. Well, carry on then. I shall look forward to being rid of you for a bit."

"Thanks."

* * * * *

CHAPTER 87

British

I picked up Clara at the school. Before I restarted the motor-car I mentioned the telephone message I had received. She asked how I wanted to proceed.

"I would just as soon meet it head on, if you don't mind. We could stop in together and see what is on his mind."

"That would be best. And while I am technically not the physician in charge, his wife is my patient. Yes, let's go visit him together. But first I need to stop by the hospital and see the latest entries on her chart. That way I will have current information for him. While I am there I can also check on the pilot and I will be done. Will that be satisfactory?"

"It will." I cranked the motor-car and to the hospital we went. I waited in the lobby while she tended to business. I windmilled through newspapers of the past couple days. News of the war. Speculation on the war. Criticism of the war effort by Crimean War veterans and others. Sports. Weather. Channel possibly clear in the next day or two. Hmm. Sports. Local news. Photographs of several people I know I had seen. Ah! Customers at the cafe. So my naval friend did move in upper social circles. Upcoming meeting for board of directors at local nursing school. Controversy over female nominee to head the school. What's this? I was not aware of any other female qualified for the position. It could only be . . .

"Are you ready to go?"

"Oh! Yes, let's!"

"I apologize it took so long."

"Problems with the pilot?"

"Problems keeping him in bed. The lad thinks he is ready to fly to France and take on the Germans. He isn't. But his attitude is wonderful, even if his body is still a little behind. He will be perfectly normal in no time."

"So the problem—"

"Is Pauline. Yes. Her influenza has progressed and she is very weak. I cannot do anything unless or until her body increases its resistance to the viral infection. We can feed her body, but it is up to her to improve. I'm afraid I have no good news for her husband."

"Well, let's go see him and get this over with."

"Agreed. I would like to go home and think of other things. Or nothing."

I helped her into the motor-car and cranked it to life. Getting in, I mentioned the interesting item I had seen about the nursing school. "It seems they want to nominate a female to head the nursing school. Is this anyone I know?"

"Why yes it is. You know her intimately and will soon know her again in such a manner."

"Now there is something to look forward to . . . . Anyway, you have not mentioned this appointment."

"No. It's not news, really. It's a logical progression for me. It's an honor and I appreciate it. But it's not what I want. However, until I can advance toward what I do want, this will be nice. I do not see any problem getting the position. It's just a matter of some board members thinking women are somehow inferior and less equipped for the requirements of the job. The opposite is the truth, really. Women have a better capacity for such a position, especially in such a compassionate field as healthcare."

"You will get no argument from me. I appreciate women and their capacities and abilities. While you are delightful to look at, you have so much more to offer. I see it as a relatively untapped resource—women in general and you in particular."

"Ahh, flattery . . . do you expect that to get you somewhere?"

"Can't hurt. I am certainly getting my hopes up."

"I hope that's not all."

"What?"

"No, nothing. Look-we're here."

I took Clara's hand as she stepped down from the motor-car and opened the shop door for her. As the door closed Mr. Trafford stepped out of the back to greet us.

"Ah! Lef-tenant. Good of you to stop my. And what a pleasure to see you again, Miss . . ." "Clara. Please call me Clara. It is good to see you again, Mr Trafford." She curtsied and he lightly took her hand and offered a slight bow.

"Well, Clara. It seems you are the subject of some controversy. I have a board meeting to attend, the major point on the agenda being your appointment to head the nursing school. So you know, you have my support. I have seen your work in various capacities, and your dedication to your chosen field has won me over. You should be a wonderful headmistress."

"I appreciate your confidence. I only hope the news I bear will not shake that confidence."

"What news is that?"

I spoke up. "I assume, sir, that you called me here to talk about your wife, specifically her condition."

"You are correct. I had hoped you had talked with Miss—uh, Clara, here. But you have outdone yourself and brought her here for me to talk to. How thoughtful. Clara, if I may, how is she?"

"I will be honest, sir, in that her condition is not good. She is suffering from effects of the influenza virus, the so-called 'Spanish flu'. She is weak and has a secondary source of infection I cannot treat until her body shows increased resistance and resilience. All we can do right now is give her nutrition and fluids and wait. I'm sorry I cannot give you better news."

"What secondary infection is that?"

"It is a delicate matter, sir, uh . . ."

"I can step outside if you need privacy."

"No, Lef-tenant, that will not be necessary. I have the gist of the news and do not need every detail. That's a shame. She has done a wonderful job of running the household. Now this. What a shame. Now, what can I do?"

"Well, Mr Trafford, not a lot. Pray for her if you are a believer in prayer."

"Of course."

"Visit. Talk to her. I cannot prove that it works, but having your support cannot hurt."

"Even if she does not respond?"

"Even if she does not respond. Her mind could still possibly sense your presence and process that information."

"It would be good to have her back in the house. She did such a good job . . . . Thank you, Clara, for the information. Thank you, Leftenant, for bringing her by. Mighty thoughtful of you. My, the two of you make such a handsome couple. Best wishes to you both. I'll get back to work now so I can stop by the hospital later. Thank you both once again."

With that he reentered the back room and we departed. I suggested we stop by a market and pick up a few things so I could cook dinner later.

"Isn't it a woman's job to cook?"

"It is—if she wants it to be. But a man can cook as well."

"That depends on the man. You are man enough to cook, but not all are."

"Call it another art form. I can create. Call it control. I decide what goes into my body."

"Now that idea I like."

"Oh? Art?"

"Well, yes, art, but deciding what goes into my body."

"You do mean food . . ."

"Well, . . , yes, . . . food as well." Clara pouted just a little, then smiled. I could see an enjoyable day—and evening—ahead.

* * * * *

CHAPTER 88

British

As the light began to build the next morning, I could see nothing but low clouds. I telephoned the CO's office and he picked up. I asked him about the weather forecast.

"There is a low ceiling currently, but it is expected to clear later this morning. You should have time for breakfast and any farewells before you enjoy a beautiful view of the Channel. Are you up to it, lad?"

"Indeed, sir. I have been waiting for this. I shall see you soon."

"Good show. And remember . . ."

"Cakes for you and the staff. Of course."

I returned to the bedroom where Clara was just starting to prepare for her day. Her housecoat was on but open as she selected a pair of stockings.

"How does the Channel look?"

"Socked in."

"Shame."

"But it should clear in a few hours. Today I leave for France."

Clara placed the stockings on the dresser and turned to face me. "You have been anxious to go. I understand. But I had better give you something so you remember me. After all, I want you back." She placed her arms on my shoulders, locked her fingers behind my neck, and pulled me close to kiss me. Then she sat me on the bed, opened my robe, and pushed me back. While it did not take a lot of time, her performance was indeed memorable. If I was not very hungry before, I was indeed hungry after.

We dressed and went to the cafe for breakfast. On the way I cautioned Clara not to mention I was going to France. I was sure it was not vital and sensitive military information, but just the same I assumed the RFC would prefer it not be broadcast.

I had a hearty breakfast and bought cakes for the lads at the airfield, then returned Clara to her cottage. She clung to me, telling me to be careful, look around, and everything short of how to lace my boots. It was a little melodramatic for me, but I understood. She had already lost someone special to the war and she seemed rather attached to me, which I appreciated. All I could really tell her was to take care of herself and her business. I would be back before she knew it. My mission had changed, after all. My primary job was not killing Germans. It was to teach others how to survive at the front while killing Germans. My visit to France was mostly to stay in touch with German tactics and how they may have evolved since I was last there. I would spend little time before enemy gunfire. As much as I wanted to do some of the killing myself, I had found other things which were more important. I found myself accepting the role given me to train others to do what I had done. Meeting my angel of mercy and falling in love were certainly incentives as well. I found I was willing to do whatever I needed to do in order to prosecute the war, win the war, and move on to whatever awaited me beyond. Things were looking good for me. Too good, possibly, but I was willing to accept that.

I reminded Clara of the meeting she was to attend that morning. That brought her back to reality. She put in a few more kisses and held me entirely too tight before wishing me well and changing her clothes for the meeting. As much as I wanted to watch her just a little longer, I had to get back to the airfield so I could take advantage of the break in the weather.

* * * * *

CHAPTER 89

British

Arriving back at the airfield, I delivered the cakes to the adjutant and asked to see the CO. As he selected a cake for immediate consumption, he jerked his thumb in the direction of the CO's office door. I looked around the jamb to find him elbow deep in paperwork.

"Ah! You're here. I know you are more than ready to get cracking. What else is on your mind?"

"Well, sir, you likely know our inverted spin pilot is on the mend. Nothing new to report other than his health is improving, which is remarkable for someone who should be dead and buried. The staff are having problems keeping him still. He's always popping out of his bed, it seems."

"Aye, the lad owes a large debt to your nurse friend. I sincerely hope she gets what she is aspiring to. She has my vote."

"Thank you, sir. She is about to take over running the nursing school. It's not what she wants, but it is another step forward in and of itself. But I'm sure you don't want to discuss her."

"Actually, I would prefer to discuss your friend. However, we are here to proceed with winning a war. I don't really have anything more to add to our prior discussions. Go over, give my regards to the squadron commander, do a bit of poking about, and get back. If you hear anything more about *der Fritzen*, that would be good as well. Is there anything else?"

"No, sir. Well, there are some cakes out here for you. But you had better move now, while there are still some left. One would think they were Germans, the way this bloke is killing them!" "Yes, I smelled them, thank you. We are going to miss your deliveries while you are away."

"You know where I get them, sir. Send your hungry adjutant into town for some. Just order an extra box so some of them make it back here to you."

"Good idea. Well, then, carry on. I shall look forward to hearing from you. Leave a few Germans for the rest of His Majesty's forces to deal with."

"Aye, sir. I shall try to restrain myself."

In moments I was on the flight line with my Camel. I checked it over and found everything to be in order. I placed my bag on the upper wing center section. It was not much, really, but there was simply no room in the cockpit for even a modest packet. I borrowed a ladder and lashed the bag to the front cabane struts and tied it to the center wing rib through the open "window" of the wing. I donned the rest of my flight clothing and a couple of the lads helped me up and into the Camel. One swung the prop, then they saluted. I returned the salute, then the salutes turned to waves as I taxied away.

Takeoff was routine, but it felt very good to get up again and feel the freedom of the open sky. Though there were some heavy clouds in the distance, there were but small, light clouds above me. Typically, it was cold as I climbed over the old athletic fields. I don't know why, but I felt a bit sentimental while looking at them and thinking of the events that had occurred on and over them. Silly, I thought, because I will be back in a week or so. Then I thought of Clara. Hard not to. On a whim I flew in the direction of her cottage. I flew along the road we used, looking for any traffic. Sure enough, there she was, motoring into town on her way to the nursing school. I nosed the Camel down in her direction, nearly head-on with her motor-car but to the side of the road. I waved at her, though I doubt she saw it. There was an open area ahead of her, so I circled around and did a roll while crossing her path. She stopped the vehicle, stepped out on the running board. Hanging on with one hand, she waved wildly with the other. Then she stepped down and wrapped her arms around herself as if hugging. She twisted her body a little, side to side, then gave a big wave as she stepped back into her 'car. I think she knew.

With that bit of romance out of the way, it was back to business. I climbed to altitude and flew toward Dover and then out over the English Channel. There were several patrol aeroplanes in sight, as well as naval traffic on the surface. Then something moved in the distance.

I lost sight of it for a moment, but then it moved again or somehow set itself out from the endless sea to the northeast. I kept it in sight this time. It was an aircraft. I saw no "dartboards" on the wings, so it was German. Flying toward it, I realized it was a seaplane, possibly a Brandenburg, and it was lining up a strafing run on one of His Majesty's ships. I decided to attempt to dissuade it and lined up a dive to intercept it before it was in a good firing range. I was not quite diving out of the sun, but I did have the sun behind me somewhat, masking my assault. As I drew to within three hundred yards or so, the rear gunner spotted me. He hit his pilot on the shoulder, then fired a short burst at me. I observed the sun shining off the goggles of the pilot, and then I watched the strangest occurrence. Flying barely above the water, when the pilot twisted his body to see me he apparently moved the stick to port. His port wing dipped just enough to catch the water, and set the whole aircraft to somersaulting across the waves. It came to rest on the surface, inverted. One of the crew popped to the surface a moment later, then disappeared again, likely trying to get the other man out of his cockpit. I continued toward the vessel, a destroyer, did a roll, and waved as I crossed their bow. Hell, I thought, a Boche in the water without firing a shot. That will go into the flight report.

I again went to several thousand feet and flew the rest of the way to my old squadron. Conveniently, they were still using the aerodrome I had flown from. I set down and was caught by several fitters who guided the Camel into position along the sheds and helped me onto the ground. One of the first to have a look at the visiting Camel was Major Campbell, who reached me as I pulled off my leather cap and goggles. I saluted and he waved me off.

"Ah, Noble-Brown! But for the Camel, yours is a face from the past! It's been so long, how are you?"

"I am well, sir, thank you. You look good. Are those a few grey hairs I see?"

"They are. Consequences of command, I'm afraid."

"I suppose. Well, sir, I am training you a number of hungry pilots. Hopefully they come over and kill lots of Germans and soon we can all go home."

"That's the spirit, lad! You seem to be adapting to your new role. I had hoped you would."

"Yes, sir. I have seen the light. I have adjusted well to life at HE. I have a routine to put the lads through. I have a good rapport with the CO there and I have a few friends in town. One formerly served on the Dreadnought."

"Dreadnought? Well, impressive ship. Good show, lad. Speaking of impressive, I will assume you have captivated the female population."

"Well, no, sir, but let's say I am happy. Damnedest thing, too."

"Do tell."

Do you remember when I went looking for the nurse who saved my life and then my arm in the field hospital?"

"I do. Never found a trace, as I recall."

"Right. Well, it turns out her brother was a student scout pilot. She was there when her brother and Jeremy left to enter the pilot pool. I heard her voice and met her. She is taking over directing the nursing school in town."

"And you two are an item?"

"You could say, yes."

"Well done, lad. No wonder you are content to stay there and instruct. I cannot blame you."

"Well, sir, there are good and bad to everything. How is Jeremy?"

"I will let you ask him. He should be back from patrol before long. It has picked up a bit, but still not much going on."

"Any word on *der Fritzen?*'

"Nothing."

"Too bad."

"Itching for a fight, are we? Been too long, eh?"

"I put one down in the Channel of the way over."

"No."

"Yessir, it was about to strafe one of our destroyers. I dove on it, it caught a wingtip in the water and cartwheeled. One crewman survived, maybe both. I didn't linger. The destroyer probably picked up any survivors. I will file a report and claim."

"You do not waste any time, I see."

"I just want to go home, sir."

"Hear, hear. Come file your report, then."

"What about Jeremy's triplane?"

"You can see that when he returns. I shall let him show you himself."

"Good enough."

We had drifted to Campbell's office by then so we sat down and caught up on things. We had very similar views on the prosecution of the war. Things were not going so well for the Allies, at least not as was being reported in the newspapers. The propaganda department was issuing releases that did not line up with the reality. In simple terms, Great Britain, France, and Italy pushed at the line held by Germany and Austria/Hungary but could not move it. In the east Russia was facing increasing internal turmoil. If the United States did not send assistance soon, in the form of men and materiel, Germany could well win the war. We saw Russia's revolution as justification for Germany to send troops to the west and tip the balance in their favor. We saw the role of the RFC as increased bombing of rear areas and munitions factories, as well as strafing and troop harassment on the front lines and immediate rear areas. The increased activity over German territory could only lead to higher casualties.

"I'm afraid you had the right idea all along, looking for more ways to harass the Germans on the ground. It appears strategy has caught up to your tactical view. Have you been talking to the War Department?"

"Nobody of any consequence, sir. You know how they are, they wouldn't recognize common sense if it hit fell on them."

"Right you are."

"Excuse me . . . but is this a private conversation? Or do you welcome any and all to join?"

"Jeremy—good to see you!" I stood up to shake his hand, but had to return his salute first.

"And you, sir. You've gone rotary, I see. A Camel? I thought you preferred the SE."

"Have you flown a Camel? It is quite the animal, wholly different in feel from the SE."

"Having flown my Fokker, I would believe that. Does it want to turn right?"

"It seems that's all it wants."

"Ahh, like the Fokker . . ."

"What is your most difficult maneuver in the triplane?"

"Straight and level. I swear, it cannot be done. It has the attention span of a puppy."

"Good training for the Camel, I see."

"Would you like to see it, sir?"

"I would. Is there anything else, Major?"

"Nothing that cannot wait. We can catch up later. Carry on."

Jeremy and I each opened a door to the hangar that housed "his" Fokker. He hoisted the little triplane onto a shoulder and backed it out into the daylight.

"Jeremy, I have never seen anything like it. This is fabulous."

"Do you think any fellow Brits will shoot at her?"

"Not if there is any light on her. Absolutely not."

There was not a straight line painted anywhere on the thing. He had made good use of the resources on hand. The entire airframe was painted RFC roundel blue. The rudder had the suggestion of a roundel on each side. There were roundels painted in the standard six positions, set off by a thin white surround. The face of the engine cowl was white with a red center dot. On the underside there was an exaggerated roundel suggested by a large red dot under the lower wing trailing edge surrounded by white, and a further thin white outline suggesting a roundel too large to fit.

"I take it you approve, sir?"

"Looks absolutely ripping! How does she fly?"

"She is unbelievable. I'm relieved the Heinies don't all have Clergets in theirs! She flits about like a bluebottle avoiding a swat. Oh, she cannot outrun an SE, but I knew that at the outset. I have been flying her whenever I could, but we have yet to try my tactic."

"Yes, I heard about that. Perhaps I can be along when you do."

"That's good of you, sir. I know Major Campbell will approve."

"Care to show her off?"

"Perhaps. I would like to eat something, however. Care to join me?"

"Certainly. I hope there are a few more familiar faces about."

"Perhaps a few, sir. There is quite the turnover in personnel, between transfers, promotions, HE, and, well, the hazards of combat flying."

"Of course. Wait. Do you have a fitter who is obsessed with women?"

"All of them, sir."

"Right. Huh. No, this one, well, it's hard to explain. When I was here he carried with him a paper photograph of some lass with her ankle and a bit of calf visible. Scandalous material."

"You mean Paper Doll!"

"Paper Doll?"

"Yes! We all watch for him to pull out and stare at that tattered photo clipped out of some old penny dreadful from 1900, or so it appears."

"Okay, so one thing has not changed. I will have to visit him. I kept him busy working on patching my 'plane. He would not dare touch that clipping, what with all the dope on his hands! If I were near, he would glare at me! Like I went up intending to get shot at—Sorry, mate!"

"He does keep largely to himself However, there is one thing that will bring him out into the sunlight—"

"Visiting women."

"Yes! He is night and day different! He seems to set up the angle and keep close watch—"

"In the event a heavy skirt will suddenly up and fly away—or be blown in a breeze or prop wash or something."

"He is a queer duck, that one."

"I suppose. But he is just acting out the way most of us blokes feel, being a bit more obvious about it. I'm sorry I have not made photographs of the woman I am seeing back in Blighty. Then again, I don't know if I want him leering at her the way he does."

"Oh, I don't know, sir. That could be a source of pride, having something everyone else wants."

"That is the other side of it, yes, I suppose. But I am happy with her, she seems to appreciate me, and I am only interested in showing off her professional abilities."

"What does she do, sir?"

"She is a nurse. Or was. She saved my life when I was in the infantry, saved my arm which was very nearly amputated, all in a field hospital. I lost track of her—never actually saw her due to eye injuries. We became reacquainted at the dance the night you finished up pilot training."

"The blonde woman, pale green eyes? I know her brother. You danced with her until Mum bumped into you or something. I don't know what was going on, but it looked funny. I laughed. I recall Father being rather put out over it."

"I don't understand that myself. Anyway, Clara—the blonde woman—is about to take over the nursing school in town. Nice, I suppose, but she wants to be a doctor, a surgeon. We are trying to muster forces to help that happen."

"Perhaps you should talk to my father. He is on the board of directors of the school."

"Yes, thank you, we have. I think he approves of her and her aspirations. At least we hope so."

"Speaking of doctors, have you heard about Mum? She is in hospital. Or was."

"Yes, she is, I'm afraid. Spanish flu. She is not doing well, sorry to say. I have not seen her. Clara is tending to her and gives me periodic updates. I hope you do not mind the intrusion into your privacy."

"Heavens, no! Not after what you did for me! Mum simply adores you. You can do no wrong by her. She brings you up often in letters. Apparently you and she have met for breakfast and you have shown her about. I think that is wonderful. Father has never paid her much attention, though I don't know why. She is quite an attractive woman, for her age."

"Aye, she is that. And her personality positively sparkles. Your father is one lucky man, to be sure."

"If only he knew. He has always treated her like mundane hired help. She deserves far better."

"Well, mate, have you had enough to eat? Don't want to overtax that engine!"

"Right. Let's go. Care to come up with me?"

"No, not now. I would like to see you shake her out a bit. Then, if you are up to it, maybe we can go look for some fun."

"Yessir! That's the spirit, sir!"

In no time Jeremy was in the cockpit, engine running, ready to taxi out. I called for Major Campbell to come out, which he did without hesitation.

"You are going to like this, Lef-tenant. This lad can fly! He seems instinctive, like the machine is part of him. Doesn't matter, SE or Fokker, he just feels what to do."

"Voss."

"Yes! He is a lot like Voss. I swear he could fly that triplane backwards if he felt the need."

Just then the little blue triplane took off low over the sheds, a gloved hand waving to the port side of the cockpit. I was relieved he didn't try to roll it right off the ground, though I knew he could. Maybe I was getting old. Mature. Hell, cautious. And I was not much older than he.

"Jeremy must have heard us talking. He had circled around and come back into the wind, low over the aerodrome. Suddenly he began kicking his rudder side to side without moving the ailerons. As a result, the Fokker did a flat turn on its vertical axis to the right, then left, then right, than left again—while not altering the direction of flight—before getting to the line of sheds we were standing in front of. I had heard of Voss using that maneuver against 56 Squadron the evening he died, fending off multiple attackers at once. Had Jeremy asked around about Voss?

His next pass was with the wind, performing a roll to the left. Then he flew the opposite way again, rolling to the right. Then he dove a little and zoomed into a loop. At the top he let his airspeed drop so the little bugger stalled. He immediately applied full power and kicked the tail up and forward, with the result that he was flying in his original direction but about two hundred feet higher. Next he made it look like it was completely out of control, like a leaf falling out of a tree. Just past the point of no return, at least from our perspective, he snapped it to and flew out of it. I could not help but think of his flying on a level with my painting. It was art.

Jeremy brought the little blue devil down to ground level at the far end of the field, moving much too fast to land. But a repeat of the flat turns slowed his airspeed to the point where he could just pull it into a mild stall and settle delicately on the grass. When he taxied into the waiting arms of the ground crew, I could only think to thump my closed right fist onto my heart a few times. That had been an exciting display.

Being who I am, I was not able to let that challenge go unanswered. I asked the lads to fuel up my Sopwith, then I retrieved my bag from the center section and left it with Major Campbell. He looked at me quizzically and asked what I intended to do.

"I am going to fly his routine. Mostly. And I have a wrinkle to throw in at the end. He's good, but I can find my way around as well."

"You have never been one to sit back and conform. Give it a go, then."

Before Jeremy was out of his "office", I was rolling out and kicking it around for takeoff. I started from the far end of the field. Checking my temp gauge, I knew what the first move was going to be. I gave the Clerget full power and she fairly leapt off the ground. I immediately threw the stick to the side and adjusted with the rudder, resulting in a perfect snap roll, coming back level over the Major's head. Next time around I attempted the flat turns. I thought they were not too bad for first attempt. Then I fairly duplicated his demonstration until the end. Picking up a little more altitude, I then dove and pulled a half loop and roll, another dive, half loop and roll, then set her down to land.

As I rolled up, Jeremy aped my thumping fist over the heart, then stood upright and saluted.

When I walked back to see Jeremy and the Major, they were both a little confused.

"Just what was that last maneuver, my boy? I know what it looked like!"

"Some people call it the 'Lazy Eight'."

"Oh, no, sir. It was no eight. But I know what it was and its inspiration."

"I'm not sure I follow."

"It was a bosom, sir. A particular bosom. I've seen the shape many times."

I held my breath for a brief moment.

"Goos show, sir! It was magnificent!"

"So you approve."

"Indeed, sir! I approve wholeheartedly! Well done."

"Thank you, Jeremy. I appreciate that, coming from you."

"I am just happy you found such inspiration. I wish only the best for both of you—*them!*—Both of them!"

"Thank you. I think."

"Hungry, sir? Catch a bite before we go Heinie hunting?"

"Something light after our flights would be welcome. After you."

Jeremy and I entered the mess hoping to get a little something so we could go up again, but that did not look likely. It seemed everyone but the fitters working on our aeroplanes wanted to talk about our little demonstration. Since there was sporadic air activity, that was the most exciting thing to happen in a while. We nibbled a little while answering questions and responding to comments. When our fitters came in we knew our aircraft were ready to fly, so we got up to leave. We had no shortage of followers, so we put a few of them to work turning around our 'planes, chocking the wheels, pulling the props, and so on. One man managed to catch a propeller blade on a finger, but he was lucky. It just hurt like hell for a day or two.

Taxi and takeoff went well, and the odd formation of Fokker and Sopwith lifted away from the airfield and flew toward the lines. I instantly recalled the surrounding terrain and features. They looked mostly the same except everything was brown and grey instead of brown and green. Winter had made its mark on the region. Everything simply looked bleak. It appeared we had the sky to ourselves. There was the occasional corps aircraft with escort, going to or returning from art/obs or photographic missions. I spied a Hannover harassing our front line trenches, so I wagged my wings to alert Jeremy. He wagged his wings and pointed his gloved hand at his own chest. He wanted it. I gave him a sweeping "after you" motion with my arm, then prepared to follow him down.

We could not have asked for a better scenario. Jeremy positioned himself between the Hannover and the sun, then dove ahead of it, anticipating its speed. He pulled to within a hundred yards before sending a fifty round burst into the Hannover's fuselage. The rear gunner never fired, apparently being lulled by the familiar triplane silhouette. I will never know if he thought the Sopwith was stalking the triplane or what. The Hannover immediately poured white smoke behind it and the pilot delicately lifted his machine to fly over his own trenches and set down in the nearest pasture or road or anywhere he could mostly fit it. We dared not fly over the spot where the Hannover went down lest every Boche in sight fired their guns at us or maybe threw stones. We moved on to look for other opportunities.

There were a few brightly colored Albatros scouts high above us but they declined to pursue us. They must have been somehow confused, for they outnumbered us. No matter. We would find something else to do.

We patrolled the squadron's regular sector and found none too much going on. I did notice that the bright colored Albatros scouts shadowed our activity up and down the lines. But we stayed on our side of the lines and they stayed on theirs. I feigned a strafing run on a German trench line but the scouts just circled above. They were interested but they were not ready to commit.

I thought it unwise to prosecute any more offensive actions, what with our attending foes above and our petrol supply dwindling. I wagged my wings and pointed away from the lines. Jeremy wagged his and initiated the turn toward the aerodrome. A short while later, with the aerodrome in sight, Jeremy, out in front a little, wagged his wings, dove a little, then looped. He came out of the loop on my tail and pushed his throttle a bit more open as he dove at my tail. I pulled the stick into my lap, the sudden climb causing the Camel to stall and fall back on its tail. Recovering, I found myself on Jeremy's tail but a bit behind him. Then I watched him attempt his "Voss" maneuver. But it was different. The triplane rotated on its vertical axis but turned beyond the usual ninety degrees or so to its direction of flight. That was where the little bugger lost its form. The tail dropped, as did the right wings, and the machine simply tumbled. There was nothing I could have done to help, leaving me simply an observer to the event. Though we were not very high above the ground, Jeremy managed to wrangle the tripe back to flying form. He came out lower than my altitude, turned back in the direction of the aerodrome, wagged his wings to show me he was alright, then continued on. I was relieved. I made a mental note to tell Major Campbell that Jeremy could not fly the Fokker backwards. Yet.

Moments later he touched down on the aerodrome. I was not far behind. I rolled the Camel up next to his Fokker just as he reached the ground. As the lads chocked the wheels and began to undo the harness, I yelled, "Just what in Hell was that!"

"Well, sir, I had to try it . . ."

"That much I understand. But you really should have had a lot more sky between you and the ground. You very nearly plowed her in."

"No, 'Mum', it wasn't that close at all."

"You were lucky!"

"Obviously you have never flown one of these crates."

"Your point?"

"All I had to do was get the nose pointed in the direction of flight—or, in this case, fall, and the massive lift of the wings restores control. It's a little tricky, due to the inherently unstable nature of the little bugger, but I'm getting the hang of it. It's a wonderful machine. No speed to speak of—with all the drag, it even falls slowly!—but simply a wonder to fly. Hell, I'd love to take this one back home and keep it for after the war!

"Okay, you had an idea and tried it. But it was still risky, endangering the life of one of His Majesty's RFC pilots. A well trained one, at that."

"You're giving yourself a lot of credit, aren't you."

"Sure, why not?"

"Blowing your own horn, as it were."

"No, actually I'm blowing your horn. Or one of them."

"Do explain."

"I used to play cornet. When your mother learned that little bit she gave me one of your cornets. She said you had lost interest."

"Well, I used to enjoy it. Arban was always a challenge. But I just grew away from it. As far as I'm concerned, sir, you may have the other two. If the interest is rekindled, I shall look you up."

"Thanks, but I can only play one at a time. But I'll tell you what— when your mum is feeling better, I'll pass that on to her."

"Yes, please do. As long as there is at least one there, she will bother me about playing it. Please. Take them. It was fun, but I have other things to do."

"Understood. Flying seems to have taken its place for now."

"Yes, sir, I simply love to fly. Killing Germans is actually secondary to flying. I know, sir, it should be the other way around, flying as an expedient to kill, but it's the flying that I like. Oh, the competition is keen, I must say. I like the idea of 'Us *versus* Them', a very high stakes game. It's a shame that the loser dies or is injured, but that is the nature of war, I suppose, kill or be killed. It's a concentrated lesson on life, in a way. At any rate, I try not to make it personal. My goal is to put the machine down. If it kills the pilot, I cannot be too concerned. Were the situation reversed, I'm sure Heinie Heinrich is not too worried over how I turn out."

"Are you thinking of flying after the war?"

"No, sir. I am thinking of surviving the war. If that works out, then yeah, maybe flying would be a good job to consider. How about you, sir?"

"Well, to be honest, I want to paint."

"Houses?"

"Art. I want to paint canvases. Still life, portraits, commissions. I am fascinated by light and how it constantly changes."

"Monet."

"Yes! You know about Monet?"

"Well, no, but Mum mentioned it in a letter, probably the first letter in which she mentioned you."

"That was our first d—uh, excursion. I drove her to the arboretum to show her how light affected the appearance of flowers."

"That's right. Yes, sir, you have made quite the impression on my parents. In fact, Father would set you up in your own studio."

"Why would he do that? That's nonsense."

"No, sir. Father is very taken with you. He would see to it you have whatever you need. Studio? It's yours. Need pigments? Brushes? Canvas? Just ask. Want a motor-car? Yours. He would probably give you Mum if you showed an interest. God knows he shows none."

"Forgive my disbelief. I cannot imagine anything of the sort."

"What is the one thing my parents have other than that mortuary of a house? Their son. You saved their son. Sir, they would give you anything you ask for. I am extremely grateful as well, more than I could tell you in words. But I haven't the means to repay you."

"There is no repay—"

"But there is. You say your nurse friend—Clara?—wants to be a doctor. Have you proposed it to Father? Because he will see to it, hands down. If you want her to be a doctor—and she is qualified—he will see that it happens. I can say a lot of things about him, but when he puts his mind to something, it gets done. Bank on it. Tea, sir?"

"Uh, what?"

"Tea. I'm cold from the flight. Let's call it tea time."

"Oh. Of course. Let's."

Well that took me aback. It was a lot to digest. There were some concepts bouncing around there that I was not accustomed to. Was it the difference in class? I had the distinct impression Jeremy knew of my dalliances with his mother and approved. It was no secret that his father had no interest in his mother, just as she had said. As if that were not enough, to find his father was ready to back whatever venture I wished to embark upon was somewhat beyond comprehension. He would even see that Clara became a doctor? I was reeling at that point.

". . . those Albatrosses above. Sir?" Jeremy was talking to me and I had not been listening.

"I'm sorry. My mind wandered. Please forgive me."

"'Course, sir. I asked you about those Albatrosses that were above us and across the lines. They followed us but did not attack. Do you think they were *der Fritzen?*"

"Good question, lad. From what I've heard, I would say not. They would have attacked."

"But they had just seen an unusual sight, sir. One of their own, a Fokker, shot down another of their own. Maybe they were a little confused."

"I know how they feel—I mean yes, you are probably correct. I did see them watching us and nothing more. If they were *der Fritzen*, then they believe in collecting information. That makes sense to me. Know your enemy."

We heard aeroplanes overhead, and looked out a window to watch three SEs land and coast to a stop near their sheds. The pilots appeared quite animated, so I went to see what the matter was. Jeremy was close behind.

". . . probably dead already. Never pulled out of it."

"What 'appened, mate?"

"Aww, Jer, it was bloody awful. The new chap took one in the head or somethin'. Dropped a wing, dove, never recovered. No smoke, nothin', 'e just flew 'er in. Then three of the ruddy pastel bastards ran 'Gun' into the ground. Shot 'im up bloody good, 'e hadta put 'er down in Kaiserland."

"Pastel?" I asked, but Jeremy touched my arm to quiet me.

"Bugger, mate. Did you get any of them?"

"We'd just run in at least two of their Hannoveraners that were peppering our lads in the trenches. The pastel swine dove on us. We'd left the new guy above, but they got 'im on the way down to us."

"Right bastardly of them. Pastel? Albatrosses? Pretty noses, black rear, white and red on the tails?"

"The same. Right. Fritzes. Murderous buggers!"

Jeremy got the information I wanted. So the Albatrosses we observed were indeed *der Fritzen*. This was an important discovery.

"Well, lad, care to go back up and see if any of 'em still want to play?"

"Precisely my thoughts, sir. I'll have them top off my SE and your Camel."

* * * * *

CHAPTER 90

British

In ten minutes' time we were climbing for altitude. My intent was to be above everything and look for activity. Altitude means advantage. These buses of ours dove better than they climbed, so it made sense to be above one's foe. One could even shut off the engine and dive in near silence, using one's machine guns to announce their arrival . Aye, the perfect gift for the Hun in your life. There was no such thing as climbing in silence. Those engines made a horrendous racket when clawing the air for height.

We reached twelve thousand feet, leveled off, and looked around. There was the usual selection of corps aircraft going about their mundane but vitally important work of directing artillery fire and crossing into German territory to gather information about and photographs of army activity behind the trenches. Off to our northwest we caught a sudden flash of flame as a German sausage caught fire and settled to the ground. While our attention was being held we saw another brief flare. It traveled horizontally but dropped to the ground and continued to burn. The poor bugger who had bagged the balloon ended up paying for it. Shooting at balloons was very hazardous business. Those charged with protecting the balloon knew the situation and were thoroughly prepared to do harm. They knew the height of the tethered balloon, and they knew there were limited ways to attack one. The level attack, firing incendiary rounds in hopes of igniting the volatile hydrogen gas, was easy to defend. Simply fire antiaircraft shells timed to explode at the height of the balloon. The diving approach was more difficult to defend against from the ground, but often there was a detail of scouts patrolling around the balloon specifically watching for attacking aeroplanes. Again, they knew where the attacker had to go. With all the defensive measures in place, one might be skilled and/or lucky enough to get through and put some shots into the balloon, but they stood a fair chance of being killed in the attempt. I knew. I had seen it. Major Campbell had seen it as well, closer than any of us wanted to experience.

I observed that the surrounding terrain had not much changed. There was no green. It was in part due to the season. But the land had absorbed an astounding amount of munitions. Each blast took away whatever greenery there had been and replaced it with dirt. Some explosions added rubble and debris to the mix. The result was largely brown with a little remaining snow adding a little white but mostly greys. But the snow tended to be in low light areas, so it appeared greyish blue in the shadows. I had learned to watch for aeroplanes against this backdrop, sensing motion rather than picking out individual aircraft. Once I sensed motion, I could focus on it to see if it had a French or British "dartboard" on the wings. If not, it was a Hun. The black crosses on Hun aeroplanes often did not stand out against the ground, making their camouflage efforts a little better than ours. Then the individual German pilots countered that by painting their aeroplanes like circus wagons, making them easy to spot as they stood out from the usual browns of the ground below. These colors were what I was looking for. And look I did. For about an hour we both looked for something to stand out and draw our attention. We saw nothing.

The last thing a British flyer wanted to do was get caught deep in enemy territory running low on petrol. The prevailing winds tended to push aerial activity east, as we all knew, which could be troublesome if one were not mindful. So after an hour at height with no results I fired a red flare in front of Jeremy. Let's go home.

About half an hour later we climbed out of our cockpits feeling like we had accomplished nothing. We were cold. And we were hungry. After stopping for tea in the mess, we exchanged our cold flight gear for fresher, warmer clothing, and returned to the mess to eat. Major Campbell asked to join us and we discussed the day's activities. Then we planned patrols for the next day. Short two pilots and aeroplanes, the major expected replacements to arrive in the next few days. Once the major had gone, Jeremy mentioned he had received a letter from home.

"Father is getting on well, though he loathes having to deal with household matters."

"He misses your mum, then."

"As much as he is going to, I imagine. He mentioned you and Clara."

"He did?"

"Yes. He adores the two of you. You make a wonderful couple. He is completely in favor of her in charge of the nursing school. He is open to her being a doctor, but says he will have to wait for an opportunity to advance her cause. Her work saving a pilot who crashed impressed him greatly, but he is concerned about Mum and her influenza. He says there are complications but does not elaborate. What do you know?"

"First, I'm pleased he likes Clara. She is very good at what she does and she is very confident of her abilities. But I don't know much about your mother. I do not pry into what is not my business."

"Don't blame you there. But if you learn anything . . ."

"Of course."

* * * * *

CHAPTER 91

British

The next morning dawned while I was climbing for altitude on my own side of the lines. It had been a while since I had taken off in the dark and watched the day catch up with me. It was a fond memory revived, witnessing the sunlight coming gradually over the horizon, throwing ahead of it long shadows and then slowly withdrawing the shadows and replacing them with light. And the change of colors from murky dark green brown to deep purple and blue to dirty brown with black details and the occasional puff of cloud. The odd artillery shell burst below with a red-orange spark followed by a black puff, which threw a longish but brief shadow. As the light intensified the brown became a little lighter. with deep lines of black and grey denoting waterways, roads, and railway lines.

Jeremy and I were trying to be above anything else in the air that morning. The scheduled patrol had left about a half hour after we did. We were again looking for *der Fritzen* in hopes of bringing at least one down and possibly talking with the pilot in order to learn what we could about this supposed elite unit. We were watching in hopes they would be up and want to harass the early patrol. We were not disappointed. Off to the east I spotted a half dozen silhouettes against the horizon, diving at the patrol below. I rocked my wings, then pulled up a wing, and nosed over after them. Jeremy was close behind. Our wires screamed in the wind as we allowed our 'planes to dive on what turned out to be a flight of Albatrosses. We could dive faster than they could, but they started earlier than we did and were lower. They reached our fellow squadron members before we reached them. I knew what they were doing. Each man had picked out a target and was intent on doing said target great harm. There was nothing we could do but dive and hope to catch them.

There was no fight to speak of. Each Albatross fired a long burst at his target SE and kept diving past, banking toward their own back area. Two of the SEs gave chase but to no avail. Jeremy and I dropped past them but could not get a good shot at any of the brightly colored Hun scouts. Once we decided they were too far ahead of us, we turned to assess what damage had been done. The two chasing pilots joined us as we recrossed the lines, and there were three SEs near patrol altitude. One SE was missing, but we spotted it below, trailing what appeared to be a grey plume behind it. Whatever had been hit, the pilot was in control and presumably looking for a place to put her down. We were bitterly cold and overdue another cup of hot coffee or cocoa or anything in hopes of regaining feeling in our faces, hands, and feet. Not even the hot—well, warm exhaust pipe could help with the cold at altitude. And my Camel didn't even have that, exhaust gases mostly venting below the fuselage.

I set down last, making sure everyone save the one pilot was down safely. Jeremy was there to offer a hand as I stepped off the ladder to the ground in my ungainly flying gear. We went directly to the mess and stood by the fire as the others picked out something to eat with their coffee or tea.

"Damn. Sir."

"Aye. We got up ahead of 'em, but they got the drop on us. Well played, I must admit."

"What do we need to do? Find their aerodrome and ambush them?"

"Not a bad idea. I suppose we should have followed them, except we were low on petrol. And I was so very cold!" "Yes, sir, it was cold!"

"I will keep your idea in the back of my mind, though. It's a good one."

We had no need to stalk *der Fritzen*. Our next patrol was to escort a flight of Bristol F.2b two- seat fighters as they strafed the German trenches. While they busied themselves shooting up the front trench line and machine gun emplacements, and so on, we circled several thousand feet above in and around some nearby clouds. While I thought I had seen the dots first, Jeremy was already diving into a half loop and rollout for additional altitude. There were four or five dots roughly aligned with the high sun of the day, and they were steadily growing larger. Albatrosses. Five of them. Various bright colors in front, black rear fuselages, they looked great next to our drab SEs and my Camel. And they were formidable opponents. Four of them dropped in the direction of the Biffs while one peeled away to fire at Jeremy, likely the only SE they had seen. Jeremy pulled up and over into his "falling leaf" maneuver, but the Albatross had already fired. Jeremy immediately began to leak white vapor, and soon trailed grey behind his apparently uncontrolled flight path. I timed my machine gun burst to rake the bright green-nosed Albatross as he dove past, then I nosed the Camel over onto his tail. I sent him a few dozen more reminders from behind. The enemy caught fire and his dive went vertical. Just after his lower wings sheared off to flutter in different directions, the flaming Albatross crashed a few yards in front of the German trench. The resulting explosion knocked a Biff off course a little, but no Harm was done. The Bristols were finishing their work and leaving for their aerodrome with two of them trailing smoke. I saw no further trace of the Albatrosses as I climbed again to look for Jeremy. The other SEs followed the Biffs as I searched. Nothing. No SE. No smoke trail. Fortunately, no other burning crash site. I had to assume he had found someplace to set it down. The squadron would likely have word by the time I returned. One last look around revealed only a few other British aeroplanes up in the vicinity, so I banked and headed home.

Upon arrival I was congratulated for my latest, the green and black Albatross, but I shrugged it off. I was more concerned with Jeremy and the Biffs which were trailing smoke. Both Biffs had landed. One rear gunner was dead. The pilot and gunner of the other aeroplane had minor wounds. No word about Jeremy.

I picked up some hot tea in the mess and visited Major Campbell. His telephone jangled as I walked in and he uttered a few one syllable responses and a thank you. Putting the handset down, he looked up at me and smiled. "Not to worry, old bean, your former student put her down on another aerodrome, a different Biff squadron. Radiator shot up, other minor damage. His SE will be brought here tomorrow by lorry. They were not so clear on him. He was hit, not badly, should be just fine. We will have a better idea whenever he returns. That could be today, could be with his SE tomorrow. Not altogether bad news, all things considered."

"No, sir, it could indeed be a lot worse."

"So you brought down another Boche. Well done."

"Thank you, sir. I doubt he survived. He hit just after his crate broke up and expanded the trench in that vicinity. Scared the hell out of a Biff crew, blowing them off course."

"Don't you worry about them, they're young, they're tough."

"I just wish I could have brought down that Fritz alive so we could talk to him. Next time."

The major splashed a little brandy in the bottoms of two tumblers. "Well, then, to next time!" We picked up and clinked our glasses together, then tossed down their contents.

"Aye, sir, next time."

"How many Boche have you downed now?"

"Don't know, don't care. Sir. The one that interests me is the next one."

"Good show, lad."

As I turned to leave the telephone jangled and the Major picked up the handset. With a lax salute/wave I left him to get back to work.

"Lef-tenant! Come here, Lef-tenant!" I returned to the doorway.

"It's the Trafford lad. He has passed out. He does not respond to anything."

"He's not—"

"No, his heart is beating and he is breathing. Just no response. They want to take him to a field hospital."

"Was he hit in the head?"

"Yes, a bullet glanced off his head somewhere."

"He needs more than a field hospital. Permission to take him to HE, sir—I know just who can help him."

"Just how do you propose—"

"The Biff squadron—they're nearby. Have them remove the rear gun and everything nonessential from one of their 'planes, fill it with petrol and load the front gun."

"And you're going to take him, just like that?"

"Head wound, sir. Serious. I'll take him fast and low."

"We don't know the weather."

"Find out and forward the information to that aerodrome. Doesn't matter, though, it has to be done. Have them bundle him into the back seat. Could you also alert the flying school to have a lorry ready? Sir?"

"I suppose we have nothing to lose. Well, than, . . ."

"Thank you, sir!"

I ran to my Camel and had the lads splash a little petrol into the main tank, and I was away. The flight was short and I set her down hot. I could see the fitters were swarmed around one Biff, and I rolled up nearby. Jeremy was being strapped in, wrapped in several layers of blankets.

An officer approached and introduced himself. I saluted and returned the greeting. "And you have a mate in HE who can care for this lad?"

"You could say that, sir. She will give him the best care he can get."

"She?"

"Yes, sir. 'She' runs a nursing school and seeks to be a surgeon. She saved my life and that of a student pilot who pancaked a Camel in an inverted spin. Brought him back from dead— twice."

"A woman?"

"Yes, sir. Permission to take off?"

"Yes, yes, dismissed. Carry on. And our Bristol . . ."

"I will return it, sir. Or you can get another."

I fairly leapt into the cockpit. While they strapped me in, I familiarized myself with the gauges, throttles, and hand pumps. A little like the SE. Close enough for jass, anyway. It would get us there. Several of the lads pointed me downwind and I departed the line. Takeoff was fast as I got acquainted with the new machine. The big strong engine in front gave me great confidence. It flew like a fighter, but bigger. I kept her low so the diminished pressure and oxygen at normal altitude would not be factors to Jeremy's condition. I stayed behind our lines in hopes that no one would fire on us, but they later found bullet holes in the wings. Some blokes would fire at anything in the air.

Breaking out over the Channel I found much going on. There were surface ships with escorts. There were British patrols above. There were German seaplanes near my altitude, no doubt plotting strafing runs on British shipping. I made it a point to stay away from them. It was not my mission to interfere, especially if there were British patrols above. I also did not want to be part of the fight when the Brits dove on the seaplanes. Another time, another time.

I had been told to expect more clouds as I approached the English coast, and I found them. But I had flown through worse. Though it felt like forever, the flight was fairly fast. I circled once and set down. While the ground crew unwrapped Jeremy and transferred him to the lorry I barged into the CO's office and used the telephone to find Clara. She was surprised to hear from me.

"Oh, my darling! Such a pleasure to—"

"Can you get to the hospital right away?"

"I do have a meeting to attend, but—"

"It's Jeremy Trafford. Head wound, bullet, glancing blow. He passed out and remains unresponsive."

"I will be waiting there for him."

"No time to talk. On my way." With another half salute I ran out of the office to the lorry. A few fitters rode along to keep Jeremy from rolling about. Once again the drive was short but interminable. At last I slowed to the hospital entrance. The fitters pulled him to the rear of the lorry where Clara and I got our first look. Jeremy's face was pale but part of an eye was completely red.

"Hemorrhage. Get him to room three." Clara grasped my hand, squeezed it hard, and quickly left. She had far more important things to do. I returned the lorry and the lads to the airfield. Since I would not be returning to France until the next morning I borrowed a motor-car and went into town to have a bite at the cafe.

"Lef-tenant! What a pleasant surprise. I thought you were in France killing huns."

"Well, 'Skipper', I splashed one in the Channel on the way over. And I bagged another one this morning over the trenches, if that is any help."

"Well done, me lad! Good show. What will you have? It's on the house."

I suddenly realized just how hungry I was. I ordered a decent meal and my host was more than willing to serve it. My, but it was good. He insisted I have some pie. I refused, but to no avail. When that disappeared quickly, he offered more, but I asked what he had left from the morning's cakes. I wanted to take some back to the airfield. Without hesitation he boxed some for me.

"Now that you've eaten, Lef-tenant, may I inquire what brings you back so soon? Unless you'd rather not say, of course."

"I don't mind. You recall the Traffords."

"Yes, of course I do."

"Their son was wounded over the lines this morning. At first everything looked minor and routine, but he lost consciousness and would not respond to anything. Knowing he was hit in the head, I suspected it was serious and I flew him over here for Clara to see. I felt seeing her gave him a better chance than a field hospital. I had just left him at the hospital shortly before I arrived here."

"I'm sorry, mate. But we both know he is in the best of hands. I'll keep him in me prayers."

"Damn! What is the matter with me?"

"What is it?"

"His father! I need to tell Mr Trafford about Jeremy. How could I have forgotten that?"

"Easy, mate, you've been busy today between shooting at Germans and delivering a seriously wounded pilot to the best chance he has of survival. Telling the old man would not have made anything any better. And you had to eat at some point. You can go now. He will be happy to see you, I am confident."

"You're probably right. Thanks."

The chaps back at the airfield would have to wait for their cakes. I drove to the hat shop and inquired whether I could see Mr Trafford. I was told he was predisposed and could not be disturbed. I pressed the urgency of the matter.

"Please, you must interrupt him, as this is a most urgent matter involving his son. Tell him it's Lef-tenant—"

"Noble-Brown! It's good to see you, my lad. Do tell, what is this urgent matter?"

"Good day, sir. I'm sorry to report that your son has been wounded in combat."

"You came all the way here to tell me that?"

"Indeed. I just flew Jeremy in from France."

"You flew him?"

"Mr Trafford, he and I were over the lines this morning and encountered German aeroplanes. During the fight his 'plane was hit and he put it down on another squadron's aerodrome. They found he had been hit also, but his wounds were considered minor. Later he passed out and would not respond to anything. As soon as I learned he had a head wound, I insisted on bringing him here so Clara could work on him. He has been there only a short while."

"Will he be all right?"

"I wish I could say. I don't know. But I thought it important that you know."

"I must get to the hospital."

"I can drive you."

"No, no, I will go. You have done more than enough already. Thank you for now. I will talk with you later, but I must go."

"Yes, sir. I'm sorry I couldn't deliver better news."

"As far as I am concerned, you delivered something far more important. I will be in touch."

With that, Mr Trafford was away.

* * * * *

CHAPTER 92

German

December passed into January. We were not home by the war's fourth Christmas. There was not a lot of flying to be done. I managed to down two more Englishmen. One was obvious, an explosion in the air and parts scattering over several acres on the ground. The other one was trailing smoke when I last saw it, but I was busy with visiting Englishmen and could not follow its progress. *Leutnant* Strasser checked other reports of the fight and found it had crashed just behind the English trenches and started a fire.

I saw very little of Käti and even less of Elsa, but that was part of the hardship of war. I had had it pretty good from time to time, and things didn't always go as I would have wanted. It was just another reason to want to end the damned war and get on with life, however that went. I continued my stints flying first time observer candidates. *Leutnant* Strasser went along with the program since we were not flying much at the front anyway. He was agreeable with the original logic of observers enabling more damage to be done to the enemy. However, he did express his concern should we become more active, especially if there was an offensive. "If" there was an offensive. Looking back on the prior two springs, it was not a matter of "if": It was a matter of when and where. The spring of 1918 would be crucial to Germany. Throughout the winter American troops had been arriving in greater numbers. Rumor had it the "Yanks" were taking over southeastern England and the French were not ready for such numbers—even though the French were desperate for men of fighting age. According to other rumors there was a squabble over just how to use the fresh, "green" troops. General Pershing apparently wanted to keep the Americans together in American units and have them fight in unit strength on their own sector of the front. But the British and French wanted the American soldiers used as replacements in British and French units. We laughed over the latter notion. If true, it was obviously a matter of bruised egos. The British and French armies had been beaten about almost on schedule over the prior three years, but they refused to accept the appearance of America coming to their rescue and making them look somehow weak or inefficient. We wondered whether Pershing would simply take his troops and go home. We thought that a great idea. Think of the fun we would have teaching the French to speak German. Especially the *mademoiselles*—that is, *Frauen*.

The lack of flying of course allowed boredom to set in. There was only so much to do to an aeroplane when it was not being flown. Once my *fräulein* was taken care of it was a matter of small talk or letters. I had correspondence with my family, Käti, and Elsa. I would read a letter and write a response. I found myself wondering why Käti and Elsa didn't send theirs together. It's not like there were any secrets. One wasn't going behind the other's back. Oh, well, it was nice to know they were thinking of me.

I was in the habit of flying my modified *Albatros* between the observer school and the *staffel*. On one flight, however, the engine "felt funny". When I got to my aerodrome I mentioned it and the mechanic sent me to see Jakob. Jakob invited me to sit and asked what was the matter. I told him and he frowned.

"Is there a problem?"

"Well, there could be. Your engine is an experimental Daimler Mercedes my salvage friend was able to get for me for front line evaluation. It has been an excellent engine, hasn't it?"

"It has been the best engine I have sat behind."

"The problem is that if there are any concerns about the engine, Daimler Mercedes technicians must work with it so they can accumulate any applicable data. I will call and see what we can work out for it. But for now the airframe cannot be moved nor the engine started. The machine is grounded."

"I don't suppose this can be worked into any kind of leave, can it?"

"It's perfectly sensible to me. In fairness, however, you must win *Leutnant* Strasser's approval since you report directly to him. I doubt you have any trouble getting leave, but you must take the steps."

"Fair enough. If I should manage leave, do you have an extra Hanna parked somewhere I could use?"

"I do, and you are welcome to use it. However, we must be able to reach you in the event the Hanna is needed."

"Perfectly understandable. I will go see if I can have a word with *Leutnant* Strasser."

Strasser was available to talk with me, and I explained the trouble with the engine.

"I told that damned Jew lover this would be a problem."

*"Mein Herr, h*ave you flown with the engine? It is the most powerful engine I have worked with. Unless you have another one here, my *Albatros* is certainly the best one on the line. This is only a teething problem, so to speak."

"Why do you say that?"

"It flies well. I can only sense something is amiss. If I had to, I would use it to intercept a raid right now. I was only thinking of the maintenance crew. It's easier to fix something minor than to rebuild an engine."

"Okay. So the machine has been grounded?"

"Javohl."

"I should send you on leave or something. It would be better than having you around here doing nothing."

"I'm pleased you brought that up."

"Ja, go."

"Danke schön, Herr Leutnant!"

Returning to Jakob's office, I made the arrangements for the Hanna. I called the tavern looking for Käti, but Elsa picked up the receiver. "Elsa, how are you?"

"Gustav! *Mein* Gustav! It's good to hear from you! Are you coming to visit?"

"I am."

"Wunderbar! I will tell Käti. But this time you will take *me* flying!"

"That's fair—I would love to."

"I can't wait!"

"I will be there tomorrow. You will fly with me. Now, is Ernst near you? I would like to ask a few questions." Elsa put me on with Ernst and I made arrangements to land on his acreage at the edge of town. I did not see the sense of taking the army away from its duty and neither did Ernst. I thanked him and told him I would be there in the morning.

The next day was miserable. Cold, overcast, windy, everything about it said, "Don't fly." I didn't care. I flew. It was not far to fly, and the reward was more than worth the risk. The flight was just as I had suspected it would be. While normally it was just a routine hop, look around, then land, this one demanded full attention the entire time in the air. Wind speed and direction were variable. Taxiing was less than a joy. I was happy I had the more stable Hannover, especially with the ballast in the rear to compensate for the lack of a gunner. When I landed I had plenty of room for the aeroplane to slow on its own. I saw Ernst's black saloon parked near where I was taxiing to. One of the doors opened and Elsa burst out, running in my direction. I frantically waved her away from the Hanna. She looked a little crestfallen, but she was still in one piece. She brought me a ladder and climbed to greet me. When the kissing paused I asked her to help undo the harness, which she did.

"Gustav, aren't you going to take me flying?"

"No, Elsa, not today. It's too dangerous. The air is too rough. I want your first time to be gentle."

"It was," she sighed.

"First time *in the air,* Elsa."

"Oh! Okay," she sighed.

I left my flying gear in the cockpit, grabbed my little travel bag, and joined Ernst and Elsa in the saloon. Elsa curled up like a kitten and just lay against my chest. It was sweet.

Käti greeted us as we stopped outside the tavern. It was wonderful to see her. Ernst sent the saloon home and we all entered the tavern to have lunch.

* * * * *

CHAPTER 93

German

The next day dawned bright and calm. The sky beckoned, throwing in a few puffy clouds as a tease. I rolled out of bed and made coffee. As I sat by the window with a cup, Elsa sat up and looked around. Moments later she sidled up to me. "My back was cold."

"Sorry, but look at the wonderful day forming. Would you like to go up?"

"You think it would be okay? I want to go, *javohl!*"

"It will be cold up there. I have a heavy flying coat for you, but more clothing is better."

"You would know, my flying hero."

"Elsa, please. I just want to end the war so our lives can move to more pleasant things."

"Pleasant things? Such as . . . ?"

"Get dressed, Elsa."

Käti awoke and poured herself some coffee. Joining me, she asked if Elsa would be at work that morning or flying.

"Elsa will join you at the tavern a little later, if that is suitable. How many drink in the morning?"

"Some mornings might surprise you, Gustav. This will help settle Elsa. She has been incensed that I got to fly. With you. She is jealous."

"While I love Elsa, you, *liebchen,* matter even more."

"I know. You are wonderful to allow Elsa into our relationship."

"*Ja,* some days it is truly a chore to have two beautiful women to cater to, but I think I'll manage." That got me a slap on the arm.

Elsa rejoined us, dressed to stay warm. Or so she thought. Käti and I dressed and the three of us walked to the tavern and met Ernst, who was opening the business. Käti helped with a few things and then told Ernst to go so Elsa could be back before things got too busy. Elsa was getting excited about going up. Where the day before she was a cuddling kitten, that morning she was like a puppy on its first ride in a motor-car. I almost had to hold her still.

Arriving at the Hannover, I put a ladder against the side and helped Elsa into the cockpit, telling her to put on the flying coat and helmet. I offered to strap her in, and she held her hands together in front of her. "Never mind," I told her. "Just sit down when I take off and land. When we are level, you may stand if you wish." Then I accessed the front cockpit, put on my coat, boots, and helmet, and strapped myself in before donning my gloves.

Ernst's driver was kind enough to pull the propeller through. I checked Elsa once more, noting her eyes were as big as I had ever seen them. I cranked the magneto and the engine started. As the temperatures came up I taxied to the end of the open area, kicked the tail around—much to Elsa's delight, and pushed the throttle forward. The prop pulled us along and in no time we were in the air, climbing toward the puffy clouds. At about two thousand feet I felt the 'plane shift a little. I looked back and found my puppy standing up, protruding above me, looking excitedly around. She kept repeating, *"Wunderbar, Gustav! Oh, wunderbar!"* I flew around the village, Elsa squealed, touched my shoulder, and pointed. "Oh, Gustav, can we fly higher? Will it go higher?" I responded with a gentle climb and she marveled at how small the village was becoming.

A few minutes later she touched my shoulder and asked, "Can we fly to them so I can wave?" I looked where she was pointing and did not like what I saw. Coming toward us from the west was a large formation. My guess was that they were coming to bomb the rail junction where I had been wounded and introduced to Käti. They were flying above ten thousand feet. I counted at least three types of English crates, though I could not discern quite what they were. I did notice, however, that we had been detected, as several scouts were coming down to have a look at the lone Hannover.

I certainly did *not* like my odds. I was alone in the sky with a civilian where the gunner should have been. I could not count on Elsa being any help. In fact, I feared for her safety. The English bastards didn't care if I had a woman on board. How would they know? She looked like most any gunner that moment. I decided the best I could do was take them on as a large fighter with one gun in front.

"Elsa, sit down. They are English. Fasten the strap if you can, and hold on!" I climbed for more altitude. Altitude was everything in combat, and today was no exception. I looked at Elsa. She was sitting quietly and looking around. She looked remarkably calm.

There were five scouts coming to look in on us, SE type Sopwiths. They circled above, two peeling away to dive on us. I began to dive. As soon as they began shooting I pulled the Hanna into a tight roll. Elsa squealed. Surprisingly I came out behind the two SE types and immediately opened fire on one, then the other. It was my day with a machine gun. One Sopwith immediately caught fire and the other began to smoke. Both turned west and I turned my attention to the other three. I found two. The third had found me and was putting rounds through my left wings. I of course dove and briefly spiraled before straightening out and climbing into a half loop, half roll. Elsa squealed and laughed out loud. I was happy someone was having fun. I certainly was not. I put a few rounds into the *Engländer's* tail, then pulled into a tight left turn. Elsa laughed. There were more bullets raining on us from above. I felt an impact and sudden burning sensation in my left upper arm.

"*Scheisse!*"

"Gustav! What?"

"I'm hit!"

"Hit? They *shot mein* Gustav?"

"*Ja!*"

Then I got the surprise of my life. Gunfire. Very close. In a shallow dive, I looked over my shoulder to find Elsa taking aim and squeezing off five round bursts at the closest SE. It began to smoke heavily and pulled up short. I gathered my wits and turned away from the others, dove and pulled into a loop. Rolling at the top, I found another SE in front of me and fired a few rounds at it. Behind me I heard a fifteen round burst or so, then another maybe a little longer. I looked at her target to find it was beginning to tumble out of control.

At that point I welcomed company in the form of six *Albatrosen* with candy cane stripes on their fuselages. They dove into the melee along with several other Sopwiths. We would be okay. But Elsa was not done. She put a hand on my shoulder and pointed at an SE a few hundred feet away and slightly above. Her other hand was on the Parabellum handle. She shouted in my ear, "That one is the *schwein* who shot my Gustav!" There was no arguing with a woman holding a machine gun. I dove and pulled into a zooming turn toward my assailant. As soon as she could get an angle on my English assailant, Elsa began to fire in ten to twenty round bursts. I watched the crate "stutter" briefly, then turn west. Elsa put one more short burst into him, then I had him lined up with my gun. I held up my hand and we quietly watched while he continued straight and level. Elsa squeezed my shoulder. "Let me finish him!"

"Elsa, he is *kaput*. He is not flying the 'plane."

I flew alongside the Sopwith and confirmed my hunch. The pilot's head had nodded over onto his chest. I pointed. Elsa shook her fist and screamed, *"Schweinhund!"* I held up my hand. "He cannot hear." Still enraged, she continued to shake her fist anyway.

I looked around. I needed attention for the bullet in my arm. I was in no danger of dying, but it did burn like hell. The terrain was familiar, and I knew just where to go. In a few moments, I circled the airfield, saw no activity, and landed. I taxied up to the line of sheds and let it coast to a stop. The first face to look upon us was a familiar one. Jakob approached, bringing a ladder. Elsa saw him and shouted, "He is hurt! *Mein* Gustav is hurt!"

The female voice got the attention of everyone. Soon we were anything but alone. The morning strafing mission had left not long before we arrived, which explained the relative quiet. I was assisted out of the "front office" and taken to the nearest hangar for attention to my wound. Elsa removed her borrowed flying coat and helmet and practically leapt to the ground, standing at my side and holding my hand. As I suspected, the wound was minor, but still I had been shot. I had to be wary of infection and I was going to hurt. Getting shot, after all, was not like cutting oneself shaving.

Obviously, the question came up about how I managed to get shot with a civilian—a woman—in the Hannover. And while the question could have, and did, come from everyone at the airfield, the pertinent questioner was *Leutnant* Strasser. He encouraged us to join him in his office. Upon sitting down, Elsa finally realized how cold she was after having been up in the winter sky and Strasser had coffee brought for the three of us.

"*Feldwebel* Model, this is most interesting. You arrive at my airfield flying one of my Hannovers with a civilian *fräulein* aboard, and you have obviously been in combat. I understand you have been hurt, but would you care to enlighten me as to how this occurred? 'Unusual' does not begin to cover this."

The only thing I could do was tell him the truth. The joyride, the approaching English formation, the ensuing action. Strasser was incredulous. I told him that once the Sopwiths dropped out of formation, I had only one choice. Had I not enjoined combat, they would have chased us down anyway.

"*Fräulein*, I must apologize for *Feldwebel* Model's complete lack of judgement. He had no business taking you into harm's way. I am relieved you were not harmed. You are well, are you not?"

"*Herr Leutnant*—Strasser, is it? I am cold but otherwise well. You need not apologize for Gustav—*Feldwebel* Model. He is a superb man, the finest I have known. He did not just take me into combat. I asked him to take me flying and the English *schweinen* happened to arrive. Gustav meant no harm other than to the English. I only wish we had killed more of them—they were shooting at *mein* Gustav!"

"More of them?"

"*Ja*. There were still some left when other *jägern* arrived to help."

"How many did you get?"

"Five, *Herr Leutnant*. Four down, one damaged."

"Five, Model? With one gun? That is remarkable!"

"*Mein Herr*, I got one and damaged another. Elsa got three definite kills."

"*Drei?*"

"*Javohl, mein Herr.*"

"Where did she learn to shoot like that?"

"I wanted to ask her that myself. I feel I owe her my life."

"*Nein, mein* Gustav, you flew the aeroplane beautifully! I have never had a better, more exciting time in my life! And you were hurt! I don't know how you endured that and shot the English too!"

"Now if I understand this, you, Model, took our *fräulein* up in a Hannover on a joyride well behind the lines to see her village when a formation of Englishmen arrived. The English saw you and shot at you and you shot back."

"*Ja, mein Herr.* I believe they meant to bomb the rail junction on the outside of the village. It has been bombed before."

"Gustav was very caring and careful. I rode in the back until they shot Gustav. That upset me and I shot back."

"I could not believe it, *mein Herr.* She sent one straight down smoking and on fire. One tumbled down out of control. The third pilot was shot in the head and his Sopwith was flying west. She wanted to shoot more, but I showed her. *Kaput.*"

"How on earth do I write the report on this?"

"I don't know, *mein Herr.* My report will contain the truth, as I have told you here."

"*Drei kaput* because of an untrained civilian . . . *fräulein?*"

"*Ja.* Unconventional but true."

"Unconventional? I was protecting *mein* Gustav!"

"Why have you not married this *fräulein*, Model?"

"I have a war to fight, *mein Herr*, but I do love her."

"I understand. She's not a Jew . . ."

"I am of Irish and German heritage, not Jewish."

"This is the one, Model."

"She is remarkable, *mein Herr. Danke schön, mein* Elsa."

* * * * *

CHAPTER 94

German

I was not punished for our improbable exploit, no doubt because we managed to destroy at least four English crates. We were free to go, but it was recommended that I stay for a while under observation due to being shot in combat. The Hannover needed patching, so that was agreeable enough. We ate in the mess and Elsa was the center of attention. She fended off several advances by telling them, "I am for Gustav and Gustav only."

After we ate I took her to the maintenance hangar to see my *Albatros.*

"Gustav! Why the terrible color?"

"It's the color of the poison gas that nearly killed me when I was in the infantry. The color was chosen by my *staffel* mates."

"Why would they choose that—oh, look! *Die gasmaske!*"

"That's why."

"They make fun of you for it?"

"*Ja,* but it's okay. I'm used to it and it gives them something to laugh about."

"Look! My name! Wouldn't Käti be upset?"

"*Nein.* Look at the other side."

"Oh, Gustav! You do love us both!"

"*Javohl!*"

"Oh, and we love you!"

From there we went to visit Jakob.

"I just heard from Strasser about your exploits. *Fräulein* Elsa, you may ride behind my pilots any day!"

"*Nein.* Only for Gustav!"

"I can arrange that."

"Have you heard from the factory mechanics about my engine?"

"Only that they will get here when they can. You chose an excellent time to get shot."

"You think Gustav wanted to get shot?"

"Gustav is a different kind of man. One never knows."

"Elsa, he is teasing with me."

"I know—but who *wants* to be shot?"

"Agreed."

"Are you two leaving soon? Or do you want to go on the afternoon strafing run?"

"I think we will get Elsa home, now that she has a story to tell."

"What's funny is that her victories will probably be confirmed. By the way, please fill out a combat report before you leave. I need it for official purposes. You know, nothing is over until the paperwork is finished and filed."

"Of course. Do you think Elsa could use the telephone to contact the tavern where she works? She is late for work."

"As long as she saves the details for later. I need the line open."

As luck would have it, Käti picked up the telephone. I thought I heard some kind of excited static. Elsa was brief. "We are well, but Gustav was shot. *Ja,* again. But I killed the *schwein. Javohl*—and two more. But they were shooting at Gustav! We are leaving. We will be there soon. I need to go. Gustav's boss needs the telephone. *Danke*—I love you, too!"

"Well, Gustav, you'd better get your friend to work. Elsa, it has been a great pleasure to meet you! I do hope we meet again."

"The pleasure would be mine, *Herr Huaptmann.* I wish you continued recovery."

"Please—it's Jakob. *Und danke schön!*"

"Jakob, if you happen through my little village, do stop in and say hello. Your first drink is on me. Gustav speaks well of you, and I am happy we have met."

"Gustav, I know my wife loves me, but I don't know if she would shoot down half of the RFC to protect me. Take care of this *fräulein!*"

"*Javohl,* Jakob, I will."

I was able to get into the cockpit, but I could not quite get my boots on. Elsa kept them with her. She asked if the Parabellum was loaded. Somebody assured her it was. She thanked them and looked very content. After the propeller was pulled through, I had to crank the magneto with my right hand. But the engine started and we made it into the air. After a brief and unmolested flight, we set down on Ernst's property. Ernst's driver had been watching for us, and he helped me to the ground. Elsa was beside herself after her morning and seemed to float to the ground. The driver held the door while we got in back of the saloon, and Elsa once again became a kitten. She cuddled against me until we arrived at the tavern. When we arrived she sprang out of the saloon, hugged Käti, gave Ernst a peck on the cheek, and excused herself to freshen up and change clothes. Käti looked bewildered.

"What the hell happened? It was only a brief look around the village—wait—they bombed the railroad again. You don't mean . . ."

"*Ja,* English *jägern* from that formation of *Engländern* dove on us. I had no choice but to fight them."

"Elsa must have been scared witless!"

"*Nein.* Elsa squealed like she was riding on white water. She had a great time. Then I got shot. She was upset and started shooting."

"Elsa was shooting?"

"*Ja.* Damn good shooting. She killed three Englishmen. She handled the Parabellum like she had been shooting one her entire life."

"The what?"

"Machine gun."

"Elsa flew for the first time and killed three enemy flyers. With a machine gun. *Our* Elsa?"

"*Ja.* Our Elsa. She saved my life—both our lives."

Käti shook her head. "You must need a beer. I know I do."

We went inside and had our beer. Ernst sat down with us, then a refreshed Elsa joined us. "Elsa, are you alright after this morning's adventure?"

"*Ja!* I want to go up again, but I know Gustav is hurt. I will wait."

"You would go up again? You could have been killed!"

"Käti, you have been up there. It's beautiful!"

"Beautiful, *ja,* except for the Englishmen who wanted to kill you!"

"That was exciting. Did you know Gustav can fly upside down? And twist through the air?"

"Twisting and upside down? Gustav, you didn't!"

"I had to in order to avoid the English bullets. I think that was Elsa's favorite part. Then I was shot and Elsa used the machine gun. Maybe that was Elsa's favorite part. I don't know."

"They shot our Gustav—*mein* Gustav! That upset me!"

"It seems our Elsa is a natural with a machine gun. Jakob, *mein Staffelführer,* says she is always welcome to fly for him."

"Käti, I saw Gustav's aeroplane. Black, ugly yellow-green, m*it die gasmaske,* and it has our names on it."

"Our names?"

"*Javohl!* One name on each side of my 'office'. The two of you bring me luck."

"Isn't he wonderful, Käti?"

Of course, being wounded kept me from anything military for a while. I did not miss much at the front, what with winter holding court. The Daimler mechanics eventually arrived to observe and work on the engine in my *Albatros.* The problem was minimal but contributed to improvements in the design and manufacturing procedures. I offered to fly the first time observer candidates but was turned down due to my wound. "Next time," they told me. I kept in touch with Jakob, who teased me about needing my "hot" gunner at the front. I reminded him she would only fly with me and he told me to hold off while my arm healed. Maybe then we could talk. Jakob did ask me to bring back the Hannover in exchange for my Albatros. I told him it would upset Elsa if I flew it without her. He said any man in the *Staffel* would be happy to fly her home, but Elsa would have no part of it. She was a "one pilot gunner". I made the exchange and Käti was able to see my hot little machine with both names on the sides. She marveled that I had designed the aeroplane, but I corrected her, pointing out my suggestions, the stronger lower wing and rounded nose. The testing pilots had decided against the enlarged elevator, saying it made little difference in the handling.

Käti was ready to act on her idea of expanding her cottage so the three of us could live there, but I reminded her of the war and the possibility that I might not survive. She thought I was being negative.

I agreed, but it was a possibility. After all, I had been gassed, bombed, and shot more than once. I reminded her of the air battle with Elsa on board. She agreed with me that she should save her money for the time being. I was touched. It was an interesting relationship.

* * * *

CHAPTER 95

British

I dropped off the motor-car and stopped by the CO's office with the cakes. The adjutant was more than happy to relieve me of my burden. While untying a box he jerked his head toward the door. "He's in there." I rescued a box to take to the CO and entered his office.

"Ah, you're back. Any word?"

"No, sir, nothing. I'm sure Clara will call here with any news. She was waiting when we arrived and took him inside right away. I stopped by the hat shop and told his father what had happened. By now he is by Jeremy's side, or at least as close as he can be."

"I see by the boxes you have eaten. You have had quite the day. Go rest a while if you like. Or go back into town. The fitters have patched the Biff. Why were you flying over the lines anyway?"

"I wasn't, sir. I don't understand it. They can't paint the dartboards under the wings any larger, yet some dullards still shoot at their own aeroplanes."

"One would think they would test for basic intelligence as well as physical fitness while screening applicants for the military. Then again, they just want sheep who shoot. I think that is why they won't issue parachutes to the RFC. It gives the men something to think about. It distracts from the mission."

"Hear, hear, sir. We've lost a number of good men because they did not have the parachute as an option. Pity, really."

"We call them 'brass hats' for a reason."

I took my leave and went to my quarters. Even after a nip or two from the bladder, I was simply too restless to sleep. I needed something to do. I took the CO up on his offer and drove a motor-car into town. The cafe still had some folks in it, so I stopped to see my naval friend. He hailed me as I entered, beckoned, and poured me a cup of coffee.

"What's the matter, Lef-tenant? I'm surprised you're back."

"Too much going on, I guess. Unusually for me, I could not just drop off to sleep. I thought I would stop in and see what you have baked since I was here last."

"I pulled out some pies after you went to visit the lad's father. They're over there."

Surprise me. You know what I like."

"I know what he likes—may I pick for him?"

It was the most unmistakable voice of my life. "What brings you here?"

"I have had a long day and I need something to eat."

"So how is—"

"No. Talk about anything else. Anything. I need a break and I am taking it. I will be telephone the aerodrome after I have eaten. You are welcome to come with me and hear for yourself. That will have to do. I'm sorry."

"Very well, then. Pick something for me and order yourself something—unless you prefer I order for you."

"Now that is an idea. Go on, order me, uh, something. I want to see what you think I like. I will, however, reserve the right to change the order if it is not to my liking."

"Okay. Skipper, if I may, the lady will have bangers and mash with onion gravy—" Clara drew a breath as she lifted a finger—"on the side." Clara smiled and lowered her finger—and hand—to her side.

"Very nicely done, Lef-tenant! You do pay attention."

"I have an eye for detail. And I find you endlessly fascinating. I may not always do well by you, but I will always try."

"Noted, Lef-tenant. Thus far, no complaints. None."

That set the tone for the meal, light and flirtatious conversation. When she had eaten enough, I suggested I follow her home. The drive alone would give her a little more separation. It appeared she needed it. Once we arrived at her home, I borrowed a trick from her book. She unlocked the door and I opened it for her, standing in the doorway and forcing her to push past me. While she was flustered at first that I was in her way, she quickly caught on and enjoyed the role reversal, such as it was.

"Once again, Lef-tenant, you have been paying attention. You are not unlike a puppy, clamoring for more play. Is that what you need?"

"Well, as they say, it takes one to know one. We can be like a pair of puppies, can't we?"

"More like rabbits!"

"Yes, I suppose. Sometimes."

"Care to play like rabbits?"

"No objections from me. But didn't you need to place some telephone calls?"

"Yes, yes, thank you, but just the one. I spoke to Mr Trafford at the hospital. By the way, he had much glowing praise for you. Your cross-Channel dash made quite the impression."

"Not my intent. It was simply the best thing to do for Jeremy at that moment."

"You are a good man."

"Thanks to you, I am still here to try."

"Flattery not needed, you are already there. As soon as I use the telephone."

"Please do."

Clara placed her call to the aerodrome and waited for a moment to speak to the CO. After the usual pleasantries, she went to the heart of the matter. "Corporal Trafford is resting and will be well very soon. Yes, yes, it was a serious matter, swelling of the brain tissue due to the concussion of the bullet that hit his skull. Yes. Well, it sounds fantastic, but the procedure was quite simple. I merely relieved the pressure. Yes, isn't it. The corporal responded to physical stimuli, and I expect he will respond to conversation by tomorrow. Yes, of course. I shall keep you posted. You are very welcome. What? Why, yes, I saw him at the cafe when I stopped for dinner. Yes, splendid indeed. Yes, yes. Of course. I shall talk to you on the morrow. Good night."

"Well very soon?"

"You cannot take him back to France just yet, but he will return soon. He will need several days, perhaps a week, before he tries to fly again."

"Once again, thanks to you."

"More correctly, thanks to *us*. You are very perceptive. Bringing him here was infinitely better than bouncing him off to a field hospital. They may have come up with the right diagnosis and treatment, but I realized it right away. And I was working under much better circumstances. I do not mean to belittle those in the field hospitals, but they work under very different conditions and pressures. There are very good people to be found in those units."

"No need to convince me. I already know. I am living proof. Thanks to you. Now . . . come sit down and take the rest of the night off."

"Sit down? Hold on. The only things I want to take off are these clothes. Give me your coat."

Clara took my coat and hat and threw them at the chair. And missed. A few other items landed nearby. I supposed we would pick them up later. Already on the floor, they weren't likely to fall again. Clara obviously had things other than housekeeping on her mind.

* * * * *

CHAPTER 96

British

When I woke up I realized I had overslept. At first I was upset, but a quick glance out my window showed there was no need to hurry. I could barely see past my garden, such was the fog. I would not be returning the Biff until later in the day, if then. I took my time getting cleaned up and stopped by the CO's office to check on the weather.

"I thought you would be in town by now!"

I only just woke up, sir."

"Yes, I saw it was a late night for you."

"You saw?"

"I don't always sleep well. I happened to notice the motor-car parking in the pool area. Don't worry. As I understand it, you may have saved Corporal Trafford's life. Well done. After what you did I will not begrudge you a little, uh, recreation."

"Yes, sir, thank you, sir."

"Well, are you off to town to pick us up some of those fine cakes?"

"Why, yes I am. Funny you should know."

"If you keep bringing us cakes, you may be picking up a larger uniform for your CO."

"I could do that sir. Or I could stop bringing the cakes."

"See here, Lef-tenant—I was not complaining. I appreciate what you do for us."

"Happy to, sir!"

"Very well. Off with you. Go so you can get back."

"Sir? Uh, yes, sir!"

Arriving in town, I entered the cafe and I found a fresh cup of coffee being poured for me at the counter.

"'allo, Lef-tenant! How's the Trafford lad coming along?"

"Well, sir. He may not fly right away, but he will fly again and soon."

"Another fine job by our Clara?"

"Aye. Remarkable woman, that one."

"Say, how's Mrs Trafford? I have not heard anything on her in some time?"

"Apparently no significant change. Clara has not brought her up in conversation."

"Shame, really. She has long been a good customer. And it is pleasant to see the two of you talking. I can tell you get on very well."

"Aye, we do. Or did. She is also quite the remarkable woman, very much under-appreciated."

"I have never understood what her husband did not see in her. She is beautiful, and once she realizes one appreciates women as equals, there is no turning off her charm."

"Agreed. She is very bright and catches on quickly."

"And she loves to be tie—uh, tidy. Around the house. Very tidy woman, that one."

"Yes, apparently she is. She has had me into her parlor to play music. The parlor is always spotless. I am in her debt, as she lent me Jeremy's cornet so I could get the lip back in shape."

"She has mentioned that, yes. I'm happy she did. You're a fine player."

"Why, thank you!"

Was it something about the "elite" class? My naval friend, in his little slip of the tongue, had just spilled the beans about his relationship with Pauline. I imagined there were any number of questions to be asked, but none really mattered at the moment. Funny, though, in that he appeared not to mind another man with "his" woman. Or were they casual about their relationship? Did I mean as much to Pauline as she led me to believe? And he no doubt knew whom Mr Trafford was seeing. Wait—none of this matters. The word was out. I still felt for Pauline and hoped she recovered from the "Spanish flu" or whatever malady had her in its grip.

I suppose that my relationship with Clara was timely and ultimately better for me. The world sure could hold a lot of confusion within its folds.

I let the conversation move along to the inevitable, the war and the weather. Yes, I would be returning to France as soon as the weather permitted. No, Corporal Trafford would not accompany me. Yes, that Biff was quite an aeroplane. I was happy to have had the opportunity to fly one. I wish Knees would have had that same opportunity.

I bought most of the inventory of cakes to take back to the aerodrome, and the proprietor gave me the rest. Mighty fine of him. Yes, I would certainly tell everyone where I got them. I took my leave and drove back to the airfield. I decided I would leave all the cakes with the adjutant just to see how many he would eat. He then directed me to the CO's office and the CO so I could get a weather update.

"Well, Lef-tenant, you're in luck. The weather is lifting and the Channel will be clear by the time you reach it. You should have a pretty good flight, even if it's not sunny. The Biff is fueled, armed, and ready to go."

"Thank you, sir."

"No, thank *you,* Lef-tenant. You may have saved a life."

"That was what I had in mind, sir." I saluted and the CO dismissed me. I stopped by my quarters in order to don my flight gear, then went to the flight line and the Biff. I could not help but notice how much larger it was than the Camel or SE I was used to. But it sure could fly. Perhaps if my Art/Obs unit had had these, Knees would still be among the living. But I could not change what had happened. No sense dwelling on the tragedy. I was better served remembering the man, so once I was strapped in I removed the bladder from under my great coat and toasted the man.

The Biff's big Rolls Royce engine once again pulled me effortlessly off the ground and toward Dover, en route to France. I did not allow potential targets to lure me away from my mission of delivering the Biff to its squadron. There wasn't much to tempt me. Other units, mostly British, were tending to matters and did not need any assistance from a Bristol on a ferry flight. On into France we went. I found the aerodrome, circled the field once, then set it down smoothly and rolled out toward the flight line, where ground crewmen caught me and turned me around. As I climbed out of the cockpit the unit CO approached me.

"It's about time you brought our Biff back. We were beginning to believe you had seen the light and would never return it. We appreciate your change of heart, Lef-tenant."

"It's almost like flying an SE. *And* a Camel. But it flies well for something so large.

"We like to think so. Your itty-bitty bird will be rolled out and prepared while you warm up and have something to eat. Our treat. How's the Trammel lad coming along?"

"Sir, Corporal Trafford is well, thank you. My aspiring surgeon friend knew just what to do. She performed the operation and now the lad responds to stimuli. He speaks when he is spoken to. She expects him to be in the air within a month, probably sooner."

"After what I saw, your friend must be a bloody miracle worker. I did not expect the lad to survive the flight. Bloody brilliant. Well done. Come, let's eat."

The Biff CO was a good egg. He asked more about Clara and her aspirations and kept doing a low whistle as I mentioned highlights from her resume, notably myself. He told me he had a relative in His Majesty's government who dealt with the healthcare system, such as it was. He intended to tell him about Clara and her aspirations. "Couldn't hurt," I thought.

We continued our pleasant conversation until I had eaten quite enough. I took my leave and walked back to the flight line to look over my Camel. Everything looked to be shipshape. A couple of lads pulled the prop through and then pulled the engine to life. Seconds later I was back in the skies over France, headed for my former "home".

* * * * *

CHAPTER 97

British

I brought my Camel in for a landing on my old squadron's aerodrome. A number of people were there to greet me as I began to climb out of the cockpit. Major Campbell had joined the throng. He stepped to the bottom of the ladder and asked if Jeremy would be landing at any moment.

"Sir, I am not a miracle worker. I merely transported him to one. He will be fine. He could be flying again within the week. If everything checks out, he will return here—if you will have him, sir.

"Of course I will have him back. Who the hell else is going to fly that gaudy damned triplane?"

"Oh, I don't know, sir. I know someone who could be tempted."

"Without a doubt. Just not today. Get some rest. The little blue bugger will be here tomorrow."

The "little blue bugger" was indeed there the next day. Major Campbell arranged for me to do tasks on the ground while the morning patrols went out. He played me like a fiddle, in fact, telling me I could take the triplane up at about the time the rest of the squadron would be taking lunch. He knew how badly I wanted to fly the thing, and he provided maximum audience for my performance. He did not order me to go up. He didn't have to, and he knew it.

That is how it played out. As the first of the late morning flyers started touching down, Major Campbell had the Fokker rolled out so I could check it over and have fuel, castor oil, and some ammunition loaded on board. Then he had the engine started so it could warm up a little. When the last pilot rolled up to the sheds, he gave me a big "thumbs up" and I taxied downwind, kicking the rudder as I went. I wanted some idea of how sensitive the controls would be. The best I could figure, the lads were going to have quite the spectacle to look at while they ate and unwound a little.

Obviously the major had more of a plan than I had. I knew I was going to taxi and then take off. Beyond that was anyone's guess. I would improvise it as I went.

I managed not to ground loop the "little blue bugger", even if the machine was a little more nonchalant about the possibilities. I faced the wind, mostly, and let go of the "blip switch". I had full throttle almost immediately and the takeoff roll encouraged my first move. Almost immediately after leaving the ground, I pushed the stick to port and corrected with the rudder into a sweeping roll. I kept pushing the stick to port and the roll tightened as I climbed until it snapped back to right-side up over a hundred fifty feet above the sheds. Of course I couldn't hear anything past the Clerget engine, but I could see a lot of hand clapping and arm waving as I circled the field. What a nimble little 'plane! It did not take me long to realize how a gifted pilot like Jeremy would be able to tumble the bugger across the skies. I would have my hands full facing him in this monkey. I wondered if clipping the wings shorter on the Camel would make any difference. Then I decided to dash all those thoughts and stay with the project of the moment. I went down and back up the line rolling without effort. Then I started looking into left turns.

Suddenly I caught some movement out of the corner of my eye. I looked and could not believe what I saw—a flight of Albatrosses coming upwind toward the airfield! Flying low, they either didn't notice me above them or they thought I was one of their own. No matter, they left me with a near ideal situation. They looked like a necklace of sorts, flying nose to tail, a mix of colors, most with the mosaic-looking wings, several with green and purple-brown wings, and one with silvery wings. Fuselages of various colors, the tails were all red and white. Starting at the far end of the airfield from them, I merely dove at the leader, raking him with my twin Vickers guns, and continued with the next 'plane and the next. I managed to put the attack into disarray, though I did not see how many, if indeed any, actually went down. I knew that if there were any SEs on the ground with petrol and ammunition already on board, they would be trying to take off and fight off the raiders. Maybe my run would give them some open air to fly into.

In the meantime, I had a problem. Well, two problems. One was an Albatross of the newer type, the other, mostly silver, possibly a Pfalz. They were both on my tail and I knew I had little ammunition left, having lifted off with but a partial load. But, recalling the surrounding terrain and features, I quickly came up with a plan. I did a snap roll, hoping to come out behind them, and it worked. Well, somewhat. The Albatross had begun a climb, but the Pfalz was still flying straight and mostly level. I managed to hole his wings with about twenty rounds or so. When I next pressed the triggers nothing happened. Out of ammunition, I needed another plan. Right after I located the climbing Albatross. Ah, there he was. I knew I could outfly them both, but I needed to know where they were in order to do so.

With one near me in one direction and the other a little farther out in another direction, I set off in a third direction. There was a railway trestle over a ravine that had always tempted me when I had been assigned to Major Campbell's squadron. The problem was that I was not sure my SE would fit between the pilings. It looked so close, but I was not willing to chance it. Now, flying the smaller Fokker, my memory of the trestle told me it should fit. The other problem with the terrain there was that the ravine "closed up" just above the trestle, becoming reduced in both depth and width. I would have to fly under the trestle and begin to climb while passing beneath the structure. It would be tricky at best. But I had two pilots behind me with a whole lot more ammunition between them than I.

I set off toward the trestle, about five miles distant. My Hun companions were quick to follow. I found the little blue bugger was fairly fast, considering all the drag of the three wings plus the sub-wing between the wheels. But they were at least as fast. The Pfalz continued to fly mostly straight at me, while the Albatross jinked around, looking for firing angles on me. I had a constant chorus of zip-crack and zip-pop as bullets whizzed past my head, occasionally striking a wing. I dared not fly straight away from them lest they zero in on me. About two thousand feet up, I approached the trestle and initiated a broad turn to starboard. Both Huns started into tighter turns, hoping to out-turn me, a silly notion in and of itself. Anyway, the feign worked. I snap rolled onto my back and dove out toward port and the trestle. As I drew near, I could see I would clear the trestle itself. The terrain beyond was another matter. But I was running a little short on options. Looking over my shoulder, I got an eyeful of Albatross, and the straight-ahead Pfalz was not far behind him. I planned my perigee to be just before the trestle. From there I would climb and go to starboard.

I wanted to close my eyes. I was a little afraid. But it was too late for that. No excuses. Now or never. Stiff upper lip, all that. Eyes wide open, watching the terrain beyond, I bottomed out immediately ahead of the trestle, pulled the stick back and slightly to the right, and just afterward nudged the rudder. I was in. I was under. Blood beginning to drain from my head, I was out. There was a bang, but I continued into my climbing turn to starboard. Looking over my right shoulder, all I could see was the Albatross and it's frightened pilot. He had elected to fly just over the trestle, and a few of his bullets struck my tailplane. I got out of the way just in time, as he flew head-on into the ground. The straight-ahead Pfalz remained true to form and flew under the trestle. That was some blunder. His wingspan was even greater than the SE. He hit both pilings, collapsing his wing structure, and continued into the ground just below his mate in the Albatross.

I continued my circle to starboard as I climbed away. I watched for any sign of life on the ground. I saw none at that moment. Both crashes were smoking, I could see a little flame in the Pfalz's debris field. There was a short train approaching the ravine, about a mile distant. I flew in that direction and fired a red flare just in case the trainman didn't see the smoke. Then I flew back toward the airfield, relieved the little blue bugger was still in the air.

I approached the field wagging my wings as if to say, "Don't shoot, it's only me." I circled once in order to assess any damage. I saw men swarmed around three of the SEs and a few pointing at a couple of the sheds, but that was all. One, then another, and then more men spotted me and began to wave. I flew downwind, turned, and set down on the surprisingly clear landing strip. About a half dozen lads caught the wings and guided me to the flight line, where Major Campbell set up and climbed a ladder. He hugged my head, beat me about the shoulders, and began to undo my harness.

"Noble-Brown, that was the god-damnedest bit of flying I have ever seen! You must have felt like you were knocking down tin ducks at a festival! I counted four down, two Boche pilots dead, two taken away for treatment. There could be more. But where have you been?"

"Well, sir, I shot at the line of Huns and kept going because two of them decided to follow me. Out of ammo, I flew under that trestle I used to tell you about."

"You did? Under? The one on the face of the hill, over a ravine? Good gravy! And the Huns?"

"I will give them credit for trying. The one, anyway. He flew under but left his wings on the downhill face of the pilings. His Heinie mate flew over the bridge. They both landed rather suddenly."

"Landed?"

"Well, their flights ended rather abruptly. They won't be at mess for supper."

"Six then. You got six? In one flight? My God!"

"Yes, sir, if you say so. Was anyone hurt here? I don't see much damage. Did anyone get up to chase them off?"

"Two or three received minor wounds. A few SEs were hit, mostly bullet patching to be done, and a few bullets hit some of the sheds, mostly ricochets. No one went up. No need. The Huns tucked tails and went home. Those who could. You singlehandedly sent them packing!"

"I'm glad no one was hurt badly, sir. I was worried."

"Don't you realize, lad? You just shot down six Hun bastards! Unbelievable!"

"It's not like they're worth anything. I'm happy I could help."

"What did you think of that little *schnitzel-wagen?*"

"Could you ask me over some food, sir?"

"Of course."

Moments later, in the mess, "Sir, that little Fokker is quite the machine. It's compact and tight and will do about anything I ask of it. I'm not surprised Jeremy tried to fly the little shit backwards. At this point I'm convinced it could. I sure as hell don't want to go up against him in the little thing. Not in a Camel! Same engine as mine, the bugger will fly rings around me and knot the bow when I'm finished."

"It seems you're sold on the thing."

"It's definitely the most fun I've had while strapped into a seat! Take it up! See for yourself!"

"Perhaps I shall. Can't let you and Trafford have all the fun!"

"That's the spirit, sir!"

It turned out that five Albatrosses had gone down near the airfield that day. Nobody else claimed any, so I was given credit for all five in addition to the two on the hillside by the trestle. The bang I heard while going under the trestle was likely a wheel hitting the ground, a rock, or something. The ground crew pulled out a branch of some kind tangled up in the landing gear. It was apparently a very tight fit. When they patched the bullet holes, they painted the white disc with black Iron Cross over each patch. I smirked as I wondered if the little blue bugger was the only German aeroplane with Iron Crosses on the patches instead of Allied roundels . . . .

* * * * *

CHAPTER 98

British

My time at the front was winding down, as a new group of pilots was due soon back in HE. I talked with the men and Major Campbell about conditions, our aeroplanes, those of the Germans, and the quality of pilot flying the hun crates. I was searching for more information on *der Fritzen* but it seemed none was available. Even though they were to fly when and where needed, they could not have simply disappeared. I flew whenever I could get up, hoping to find something.

There was one surprise that brightened my time in France. The Yank, Wellington, returned to the unit after a lengthy convalescence. Though he was still anxious to go at the Germans with everything he had, he was somewhat humbled by his experience of having been shot down on takeoff during the raid on our aerodrome. The first thing he did upon arrival was seek out Major Campbell and thank him for crediting him with the downed Albatross the morning of the raid.

"You and I both know I didn't get off a shot. In no way did I harm that Boche bastard, sir."

"Corporal Wellington, I have your armorer report that says you likely fired two or three bursts—

easily enough to down a Hun. I defy you to prove otherwise. You were the only one to get off the ground that morning. You showed courage bordering on foolhardiness. That courage deserves a reward. Congratulations, Corporal, on your victory. It's good to have you back. Now go get some more of the Hun bastards, would you?"

"Yes, sir! Try and hold me back—I have a score to settle. Oh, and one more thing? Sir?"

"What is it?"

"If it's not too much to ask, might I have a 'W' painted on my SE? I want them to know who is out to kill them."

"Fair enough. We just received three SEs from the repair depot. Fly them, take your pick, and I will have your 'W' painted on for you."

"Welly!" I walked in on the conversation. "How are you, Yank? It's great to see you back!"

"Thank you, sir!" he said, snapping to attention.

"I'll have none of that. It's just me. Say, could you use some company looking over the SEs?"

"Why, yes—I could."

"You've got to see this project a former student of mine has concocted."

"Student?"

"Yes, I'm only here temporarily. I am an instructor in HE. One of my lads came here, fell in love with Fokker's little triplane. I'd be happy to have you try and keep up with us while you look over your choices."

"You're on, Lieutenant! Major?"

"Dismissed. You two play nice now. Save it for the Heinies!"

Wellington saluted, I waved, and we left the office.

It was a fun and spirited afternoon as Wellington chose his new SE. My lusty old friend, Geoff, said he would paint it up with "W"s right away. I thanked him, but he wasn't quite done.

"Excuse me, Lef-tenant? I've been meaning to ask you about the decoration on your upper wing."

"Oh. The 'Lazy Eight'?"

"Bullshit—sir!"

"No 'sir' needed, Geoff, it's only me."

"Well, if that is an 'eight', you need a new painter. We both know what that is. I'm just curious whose it is. Have we been naughty?"

"Now, Geoff . . . a gentleman never tells. But I will say—one look at her and you would tear up that old paper clipping you carry about."

"Aye, sir. I'm sure she's a fine lady."

"Geoff, you need to keep in touch. After the war I intend to paint her."

"What color? Will she mind? Sorry, 'sir', just teasing!"

"You will appreciate it, I assure you. Let's just say she has all the right pieces in all the right places."

"I will look forward to it. For now, however, I will get busy painting not-so-lazy 'W's."

"Aye—thank you, mate!" I clapped Geoff on the shoulder and took my leave.

Later that afternoon I took Wellington to see his new mount with "W"s applied. Needless to say, he was pleased with the results.

"That's not a little, uh, brash for the RFC?"

"If anyone objects, you may tell them I ordered the painting done. You merely fly the aeroplane. One never knows—yours could be the model for new squadron markings!"

"Forgive me if I do *not* hold my breath on that count."

"Well, it was a thought . . . ." We had a brief laugh. Stiff upper lip and all, cheerio, all that. I continued, "Welly, old mate, I brought you here for another reason."

"What's that?"

"I merely want to share how I managed to survive so long at the front."

"Survive? How many have you shot down again?"

"Don't know. Honestly, don't care. I've no doubt killed far more on the ground, strafing and bombing. In my narrow field of view, it's the only way to win the war—kill the enemy. Now I train other pilots to come kill on my behalf, if you will."

"To me it's just not the same. Wouldn't you rather be here, flying and fighting and killing the bastards yourself?"

"Part of me craves just that. I am happy to be back here, going up against the bloody Boche again. But another part of me looks at the big picture. I take a group of pilots, shake them up, and sort them out. Some stay with me to fly scouts. Others, for various reasons, are better suited to other duties. They are not lesser men, certainly, but they have skills better suited to other tasks. In effect, I help make up His Majesty's armed forces and keep the war machine operating. Just how many victories or kills do my students go on to achieve?"

"It is a bit of a shame though. Watching you fly that little blue Fokker fills me with envy. And I see you now fly a Camel? I never saw you as the aerobatic type."

"Never was. Until I flew a Camel. The bugger begs to be stunted. You could fly mine if you wish, if only for the experience. It's merely a different tool as opposed to the SE. The SE is faster and more stable. The Camel is always trying to turn right. The SE almost flies itself, but the Camel demands constant attention. But back to survival . . . . Welly, you must get in the habit of looking over your own aeroplane. The riggers and fitters do a good job overall, but they must work on all squadron aeroplanes. You need to follow after them and make sure yours is in top form. Check the wires, check the play in the controls, pay attention to the engine, the ammunition, anything that affects your performance in the air. I know you want to kill every Fritz that pulls his wheels off the ground, so make sure your weapon is in the best shape possible."

"Honestly, I always felt that was drudgery. Tugging at wires, checking HT leads, fitting ammunition. Dull. But look at you, well on your way to being the next Ball or Mannock. The little extra you do makes sense, even if it lacks excitement."

"Surviving the war—does that excite you? It does me. I yearn to put this killing behind me. I want to set up my paint studio and create works of art. I want to pursue my music. I want to remove these accursed guns and fly for the love of flying. Have you ever just looked about while in the air? Not looking for the enemy, but just looking at all the beauty around you? Flying is phenomenal!"

"Uh, I believe the current term is 'ripping'?"

"Ripping it is, Yank! And I have found a special someone. She is at least as exciting as flying. I want to be with her and possibly start a family. And all that comes from making sure my aeroplane, my mount, my weapon, is in the best shape it can be in when I take it aloft to find the Boche and do battle."

"That makes sense to me."

"Great. What do you say we meet after mess and work over our machines. Tomorrow I would like to take you over the lines. Maybe we can flush out a few Huns to shoot at?"

"Ripping, sir. I would be delighted."

That, then, was the evening. My Camel was already to my liking. I just had to check the ammunition and load it. I showed Wellington my routine. He seemed eager to learn. Well, interested. He was right. It was drudgery. But it was also time well spent if one hoped to see the war through. I became better acquainted with Wellington. He had left school in the American state of Missouri, left home, made his way into Canada, and lied about his age to get into the RFC. He had been bitter about President Wilson's isolationist stance on the war in Europe and was anxious to get into the fight against Germany. He took to flying rather well, and suddenly found himself at the front. He was poised to make good his claims about shooting down all the Germans, and on the morning of the raid on our aerodrome he foolishly ordered his 'plane started. Being shot down on takeoff did more than nearly kill him. It pounded some sense into him, as it were. He had been face to face with death. Rather than ruin his desire to win the war singlehandedly, the crash and subsequent recovery had tempered his resolve. The experience was a large dose of reality, a lesson in perspective, a step toward being a soldier, a man. While he was still a youth in flux, I liked what I saw. When he first arrived, he had eschewed the same advice. Now he saw it as a helpful step toward his goal, something sensible to follow. He would probably never like the routine, but he would learn to love it for the value it returned.

* * * * *

CHAPTER 99

British

Wellington went up with the early patrol the next morning. As was the norm of late, no Germans were to be found in the air locally save the Rumplers crossing the lines fifteen thousand feet or so above—completely out of range in terms of climb time. The lads had made a few perfunctory passes over the trenches, serving rounds of .303 to go with the Huns' coffee. Needless to say, Wellington was disappointed. I found him in the mess, hunched over a steaming cup of coffee. I clapped him on the back with a cheery greeting, nearly pushing his face into the cup.

"Yeah, top o' the mornin' to *you*. I hate this damned coffee—but it is probably the hottest liquid in the building and the best way to begin to feel warmth. Or my fingers."

"Oh, so you don't want to go back up and kill off a few Fritzes? I'm sorry I—"

"What Fritzes? We saw nothing."

"You would have, had you gone farther behind their lines. They are rather like bees defending their hive. They know the wind blows us over toward them. They don't need to come looking for us. If they wait, we will appear over their neck o' the woods, their hive. Then they will come out and play. So what do you say? Care to go poke 'em with a stick?"

"But the major—"

"Approves. I already told him. So unless you need a nap, . . ."

"Shit. Naps are for babies and old men. Let's go fuel and arm my SE. Wanna see some flying?"

"I shall look forward to the lesson. Let's go."

Welly's SE was being fueled. He insisted on sorting his own ammunition, a good sign, and we were ready to go up before long. We took off, his "W" followed by my "Lazy Eight", and circled the field a few times as we climbed. I wagged my wings to get his attention, then signaled for Welly to look around. Just look at all the beauty. The sun was coming into its own for the day, illuminating what cumulous clouds there were that morning, as well as filling in the shadows and allowing the browns and grays to come into their own, such as that went. Well, at any rate, the sky was beautiful. The ground was an unnecessary reminder that we were participants in a war.

Arriving at about nine thousand feet, we turned toward the lines. From about our altitude down, we saw plenty of Allied aerial activity. The British were mostly to the northwest of our location, and a little to the southeast we saw French patrols underway. Welly wagged his wings and pointed down at our trenches, where two Hannoveraners were strafing. I gave an exaggerated nod, waved my hand as if to erase a chalkboard, and pointed up and toward the sun. Welly nodded back, having seen them as well. There were about a half dozen Albatrosses a thousand feet or so above us. We began to climb toward them. Getting them out from between us and the sun, I thought they looked like so many paint brushes, each dipped in a different color. Brightly colored noses, black rear fuselages, and the usual assortment of wing treatments, they were largely works of art themselves. Unfortunately, they each carried two machine guns and a pilot bent on killing us or destroying our aircraft.

While we were watching them and climbing to meet them, four peeled off and dove away from us. I projected their path, toward the Hannoveraners, which were being badgered by British scouts. That left a more manageable two Albatrosses at altitude. Still above us, I watched as the white-nosed Hun tipped into a dive toward me, followed soon after by a green-nosed Hun. I made doubly sure Wellington was aware we were about to be attacked, which he was. He started into a shallow dive while I held altitude for the moment. The Albatrosses kept coming. I started into a dive, waiting for them to start shooting. As they fired, I snapped a roll and came out behind them, firing. The white Hun kept his course toward Welly, but the green one seemed to hesitate just a little before pulling into a left turn. Wellington cut his engine and unlocked his Lewis gun. Somehow the white Albatross managed just to hole Welly's wings a bit before diving past him. As he passed above, Welly opened fire into his belly, or at least in that direction. The white

Albatross began to trail, appropriately enough, white steam, likely from a damaged radiator. He continued to dive away and Welly, having restarted his engine, pulled into a half loop and half roll in order to look in on my green-nosed friend and me.

I was mostly toying with my Hun. I would let him get a bead on me, then I'd pull into a hard right turn and elude him. I would relax a bit while he found his way onto my tail again, then turn left, and so on. I kept him concentrated on me while Wellington flew away, climbed, and then dove on the Albatross with both guns firing. I half looped and watched the Boche stagger a bit in the air. He stalled briefly, then fell off on one wing and into a dive, trailing black smoke. Fortunately Welly noticed what I had seen, the other four Albatrosses climbing back up to help their comrades. I fired a red flare in front of Wellington and we went back to our field.

I let him land first, then set down myself. As I pulled alongside, I could see he was pounding the air above with both fists and shouting. I climbed out of my Camel and went to greet him. I got to him right behind Major Campbell. Wellington was yelling, "Got one! I got one!"

The major could not help himself. "What—only one?"

"Major, sir, the other one wised up and left with a hole in his radiator, or perhaps . . . "

"Well, okay then. Is that two?"

"I'd say the green-nosed one was a probable. He was trailing a lot of black smoke, but we had to leave due to increased enemy activity. It was about to get pretty warm for us—so to speak."

"Very nice, Lef-tenant, one out of control and the other damaged. That was Wellington. What were you doing, if I may ask?"

"Well, sir, seeing how Wellington had the situation in hand, I put my feet up and puffed on a cigar. Sir. But I did alert him that more were on the way."

"Lit the flare with your cigar, did you?"

"Yes, sir, but I would not advise it. Ya gotta be quick."

The major smiled. "Well done." We filed our flight reports. Eventually Welly received confirmation for his out of control green-nosed Hun. By that time, he had shot down three more, two of them in flames. He was on his way to conquering everything the kaiser could put up against him.

That afternoon, in the mess, however, Wellington looked a little confused. "Why didn't you finish off that green bastard? He was obviously no match."

"Oh, I wouldn't put him down. He was a fine flyer. He was flying an old 'plane, that's all."

"But still, he was easy meat, yet you wouldn't take a shot at him."

"I wanted you to have him."

"So you let me have a kill that should have been yours?"

"No. I knew he was going down one way or another. But the whole system of victories means more to you than it does to me. I just kept him busy while you got into position. You, mate, did all the work. It's your kill. Congratulations."

"Well, okay, but I don't need any—"

"No, of course you don't need the help. Consider it as 'priming the cylinders' before they fire on their own. He's yours, and I am confident that there will be many more."

"At least let me buy you a beer then!"

"Great—you're on!"

There was another patrol scheduled for the afternoon and then Wellington was permitted to join me—and, by then, several other pilots and a few fitters—and go into town. To be sure, some of the lads got rowdy, but I managed to keep them mostly in line. We never did uncover who somehow stretched a brassiere across the windscreen of the lorry, but there was a woman somewhere in town, uh, "lacking support". As the *gendarme* did not come looking the next morning, I had to assume it was somehow a consensual matter.

That about wrapped up my visit to Major Campbell's squadron. It was great to catch up with the remaining mates. It was amazing to fly Jeremy's reworked Fokker. It was a shame Jeremy had to leave early, as it were, but he should be alright in time. And the return of Corporal Wellington. What an unexpected turn of events. Though somewhat tempered, he still had the fire, the enthusiasm, the impatience to shoot down all the Boche he could see. I could only hope the time I spent with him would improve his odds of survival. It was easy to lose sight of basic things like maintenance when things were going well. I hoped he would keep after his machine.

It appeared we had no further word on *der Fritzen*, but it was not for a lack of trying. The "flying paintbrushes" appeared to be a spirited bunch, but I saw nothing particularly noteworthy to report. It was a bit odd they were flying older model Albatrosses, but my understanding was that the newer models, as well as the machine from the Pfalz firm, were dud. If they preferred the older models, for whatever reason, so be it. I certainly wasn't worried how new the crate was, as long as it trailed smoke and perhaps caught fire as it hurtled out of control toward the ground below.

* * * * *

CHAPTER 100

German

About the second week of March Jakob telephoned and requested that I return to the aerodrome. He told me I was needed but would not elaborate over the telephone. I said my goodbyes and flew back. At a *Staffel* meeting I learned of Operation Michael, to begin on 21 March. As a small part of the offensive, Jakob and Strasser decided we were to be known as *der Fritzen.* Each aeroplane received a letter 'F' on the fuselage spine, and the pilots were free to add the letter 'F' anywhere else they wanted. If the enemy wanted to call us "Fritz" we would show them "Fritz" was still full of fight. Our orders were to remain on standby while the offensive opened. Once the shooting began, the British Third and Fifth Armies faltered and our troops advanced. At that point we were sent to fly cover over the Peronne area. Jakob procured some Halberstadt CL types to strafe alongside our Hannas. He offered to have one painted any way Elsa wanted if she would come join the unit with her hot trigger finger. I laughed at the notion. "Would you have us share a room? Or a tent?" He quickly agreed that it simply would not look proper. Overhearing the conversation, *Leutnant* Strasser weighed in.

"I could care less where she sleeps. She is a delightful woman. More important, she is an excellent shot. Most important, she is not a goddamned Jew!"

I watched Jakob go red in the face as he grabbed the table instead of Strasser's neck. I responded, *"Danke, Herr Leutnant.* I will keep that in mind." Satisfied he had done his damage, Strasser walked away.

"Gustav, I swear, I could kill that man. He is completely rude and uncaring. People of his ilk . . ."

"I understand. Let it pass, Jakob. You don't want him to know he is getting to you."

"Oh, it's no secret. I tolerate him because he is very good at leading *der Jagdstaffel*. Man for man, his Staffel is better than Richthofen's. I merely have no use for him as a person. One of these days, . . ."

"I don't hear a word of this, Jakob."

"Danke. You are a kind man."

Strafing the English continued as they retreated. With the strongest *Albatros* in the *Staffel*, I typically flew highest and kept watch for English scouts. By the original standards, I was now a *kanone*. But as flying equipment changed and scoring frequency increased, the qualifications for the *Pour le Merite* also increased. I would have to kill more English and/or French in order to wear one at my throat. Frankly, while it would have been nice, I could really care less about the medal. I wanted the war to be over. If I were to be awarded with one in the course of winning the war, that would be one thing. But winning the war was more important. My award would be the rest of my life.

* * * * *

CHAPTER 101

German

Come early April, we learned we no longer had the Royal Flying Corps to face over No Man's Land. The English equivalent to our *pickelhauben* combined the RFC with the Royal Naval Air Service to form the Royal Air Force. I rolled my eyes at the news. Changing the name would help win the war? Just how? Reorganizing the pecking order would at least give the Limey paper pushers something to do while their troops retreated toward home. Progress.

About a week later Jakob summoned me to join him. He showed me into the rear seat of a Hannover and flew us to our usual aerodrome. There was a new machine nearly alone on the flight line. It had a finish like Fokker's triplanes, streaky on upper surfaces, but was significantly larger and but a biplane. There was a radiator mounted in the nose, immediately behind the propeller. I remarked, "Jakob, this is one big crate. It smacks of Fokker's work, but what is it?"

"Essentially, Gustav, it's a gift. Technically, this is a Fokker prototype brought up to the standards of the new Fokker D.VII. The production D.VII is about to go to Richthofen's *Jagdgeschwader*. This one, however, has an experimental engine by BMW, out of Bavaria. Since you were so helpful with your redesign of the D.III *Albatros, IdFlieg and* Fokker want to know what you think of this machine. It seems your name is getting around in the technical community. Who knows? You could find yourself working with Fokker and his man Platz. There are worse things."

"Indeed, Jakob. I assume this is approved by *Leutnant* Strasser."

"I don't care what that narrow minded *schwein* thinks. I am in charge. And IdFlieg had this sent in for you specifically. You may take her up when you are ready. There is no hurry. You will of course be expected to report on your perceptions of the airframe and the engine.

How does it compare to your redesign of the *Albatros?* How would you improve it? Are there any glaring problems?"

"Was this design flown by our top aces in the recent gathering at Adlershof?"

"*Javohl.* It was a favorite. But at *IdFlieg* they remember what you did. Even if you are not a leading ace, your opinion matters. So fly it. See what you think."

"*Danke schön, mein Herr!*"

"You're welcome, but I am merely the messenger. I would suggest you fly it here first and get to know its characteristics. I am staying here for now, so you may visit with your report or write it in my office. Then you may take your gift to the *Staffel* if you like."

"You will let it out of your sight? Even without my letter 'F', putrid green, or *die gasmaske?*"

"The artist is here. You may have him paint it any way you want. The crate is yours."

"You know me, Jakob. As long as it works, I don't care what it looks like."

"Well, if you're ready, I'd like to see what it looks like in the air."

"*Javohl!*"

I mounted the ladder, dropped my heavy boots onto the seat, pulled them on while sitting on the fuselage, then clambered into my new "office". The controls were typical and I again found myself looking out over two machine guns and an inline engine. I noticed the wings were of a thicker airfoil. I also noticed no bracing wires for the wing structure. I would have to ask about that. Strapped in, gloves on, I had the propeller pulled through, then announced, "Switch is on!" to clear the area around the prop. I cranked the magneto and the engine sputtered to life. Taxiing downwind, I realized the new Fokker was about the size of my *Albatros,* but it looked a little bigger. Maybe it was the squared fuselage and wingtips. No matter. I wanted to feel it in the air. I began with throttle response, pushing the lever forward and adjusting the mixture. The Bavarian engine pulled right away. The tail came off soon, and the scuffle of wheels against the ground disappeared very soon afterward. Similar to what I had heard about Fokker's triplane, the thick airfoil had plenty of lift. Climbing out was effortless. The machine felt faster and "more free", possibly due to the lack of wires and the drag they caused, yet the wing cellule was strong. I varied my path slightly as I felt the response of the controls. I could see where this would be a wonderful partner in the air.

Once I had a few thousand feet between myself and the ground, I began to poke and prod the Fokker. It seemed more than happy to oblige. Dives, climb, rolls, snap rolls, turns, all were effortless. Loops were also no problem. Half loop, half roll, anything I wanted to do. Then I bumped up the power a little and pulled it to vertical. It climbed readily and slowly faded to a stop. But it was reluctant to stall. It would just hang there in what must have looked like a trance. If I wanted a true stall, I had to cut power. I found it was not difficult to manipulate the stall into whatever direction I desired.

I don't remember just when it started, but I found myself with a happy grin plastered on my face. Flying this Fokker was *wunderbar*. How would the English call it—*ripping!* It would dive like a wet brick and pull out without effort. I tried everything I could think of looking for a bad characteristic. I found but one. It only held so much *benzin*. At some point I would have to set down and get more When I finally did, Jakob was waiting.

"Well, Gustav, what do you think?"

"As far as I can tell, she has no faults, though I did watch the temperature gauge climb a bit. Maybe venting the engine compartment will keep that in check. Beyond that she is like a body part. I almost don't have to think about what I'm doing. She seems to know. I could not make her stumble at all. Fighting in this should be a dream. Have you flown her?"

"Absolutely not. She is yours."

"I will share her with you. Get into your gear and take her up while I write my report."

"You will not have to ask me again." With that Jakob pulled on his flying clothing which he had pulled off while watching me. I helped turn the Fokker around and added *benzin*. Jakob climbed the ladder into the cockpit and I helped him strap in. "Any advice for me?"

"Ja, enjoy yourself. This girl may make you forget about your beloved *Walfisch."*

"I will try, Gustav, I will try."

Jakob taxied downwind and turned to take off. Without hesitation he pushed the throttle and the Fokker did just as she had done for me. Jakob waved as he flew her over, and I went to his office to start my report. Reliving the flight, I couldn't help but smile. I pictured parts of the flight as combat maneuvers and how I thought the Fokker would treat the SE and rotary type Sopwiths. I didn't see how they had a chance unless they caught me completely by surprise. The only concern I could think of was close combat with the rotary Sopwith, which could turn right like nothing else save Fokker's little triplane. I wrote and I daydreamed and I considered and soon Jakob joined me with a smile similar to mine.

"Wunderbar, Gustav! *Wunderbar!"*

"Uh, *ripping?"*

"Ja, ripping! What a machine! And the engine! Gustav, this machine will get you your *Pour le Merite!"*

"Perhaps. As long as it helps Germany win the war. You say Richthofen is getting these?"

"Ja, in the next week or two. Fokker is building them as we speak. Now, do you want to hear a good one? *IdFlieg* has ordered *Albatros* to build Fokker's D.VII in both their main factory and their *Ostdeutsch* factory. How is that for revenge?"

"Revenge? For their uninspired work on their D.V and D.Va types?"

"As you know, those lumbering barges are just that next to this Fokker. Gustav, *IdFlieg* has given you a gift indeed. And if you don't have any ideas for painting your wonderful Fokker, I am just going to have the painter express himself on it. Last chance, my friend."

"It flies beautifully and that is all I care about other than having Käti and Elsa painted along the cockpit. Ugly mist, *mein gasmaske,* Strasser's 'F', I don't care."

"Shall we go tell him then? Perhaps he can start while we eat."

Lunch was a quiet affair, most of the personnel being away with the aeroplanes for the offensive. Jakob and I caught up. His wife was well, even if she missed him. Jakob asked if I had plans to get married. I told him that I honestly didn't know. My relationship was beyond the norm, to say the least. Both women were beautiful people in their own way and neither seemed to mind the odd aspect of our arrangement. I told Jakob I would just ride things out and see where they went. As long as we were all happy, I didn't see any problem.

Jakob opened up somewhat about how Strasser's derogatory remarks about Jews in general and his wife in particular were getting under his skin. Neither he nor I understood why the differences meant so much to people like Strasser. There were Jews fighting for Germany, as well as Jews fighting against Germany. They were people, largely like anyone else. We didn't see why they should be regarded differently, but obviously Strasser did.

"Gustav, it's bad enough listening to Strasser rail on about Aryans and Jews. But when he makes it a personal crusade against my chosen partner in life, I get hot. Very hot. I work hard to get along with him in order to run the *Staffel*. And I keep my distance, avoiding any other contact. But when our paths do cross, he is unbearable. One day, Gustav, one day . . ."

"Jakob, I cannot add to what you have said. You must stay your course. Unfortunately, I don't see Strasser changing his ways. He accepts me since I am from farming country, much like he is. But I stop short of his views on racial purity. People are people and should be able to coexist. I say this in the midst of a horrible war over what? People who are upset that we are not all alike, using an assassination as tinder to light this whole conflagration. Nice, isn't it?"

"*Ja*, I'll say."

"You have heard me say it before. I would rather be socializing with our so-called enemies than exchanging gunfire with them. I understand, us versus them, but the whole idea sickens me when I'm not flying missions. If they stopped this nonsense today, six months from now you and I could be having lunch with Frenchmen or Englishmen and enjoying ourselves. And for what it's worth, I would be delighted to meet your *frau*. I'm certain she is a wonderful woman. Besides, you have already met my '*frau*'—well, one of them!"

"I have, Gustav. She is a lovely woman—when she isn't behind a machine gun!"

After lunch we went back to the hangar where the painter was at work. We found the door locked with a note attached, "Fokker ready tomorrow morning". We returned to Jakob's office so he could check on a few things, then we flew back to the *Staffel*. I was in time to go up on yet another strafing run. I traded shots with a few Sopwiths but observed no serious damage. Several of the two seaters returned shot up pretty badly. The joke was that one Halberstadt had more patches on it than original fabric. The English were on retreat, but they were not without fight. Much to our surprise, the Limeys were not ready to pack up and go home.

Early the next morning I escorted Jakob in my *Albatros*. He was taking one of the Halberstadts back to our aerodrome for repairs. I flew quite a bit higher than he, just in case he attracted attention, which he did. From my lofty position I watched as two SE type Sopwiths set up to surprise Jakob out of the sun, or what there was of it. I was already in the sun from their perspective. As they were about to attack, I cut my engine and nosed over toward them. Falling rapidly, I decided to shoot first at the one of the right, then switch to the other. My first bursts "tickled" the *benzin* tank, causing it to explode. An exploding aeroplane made for an easy confirmation, which made me smile. Anything that reduces paperwork makes me smile. I then shot at the other with no result. A moment later I realized the result, as it never pulled out of its dive.

By that time I was alongside Jakob and waved. He held up two fingers, then his thumb. I motioned for him to move it along as best he could. I climbed above him, but we saw no further action. I circled the aerodrome while Jakob landed, then I set down near him. What stirred my curiosity was what I did not see. The Fokker was nowhere in sight. As soon as I reached the ground I called for Jakob to come with me to see if it was in the hangar. I had to laugh as I approached the door. Instead of a sign denying entry, there was a brief sign, "Enter", and e*in gasmaske* hanging from a handle. I pulled open a door and we entered.

The *Staffel* painter was preparing for work on the Halberstadt Jakob had just brought. He heard us and joined us by the Fokker. He was happy with his work and so was I. It was similar to the *Albatros,* which I had assumed would be the case. He left most of the streaked finish intact, except for the tail unit, which was overpainted in the unit colors of red, white, and black bands, perpendicular to the line of flight. He also left the "patee" crosses in place, black iron crosses on more or less square white fields. The nose panels were repainted black except the panel just ahead of the cockpit, which was still a utilitarian light grey-green. Under the radiator was solid in a yellow-green similar to that on my *Albatros.* The same "gaseous" effect was applied lightly over the streaked finish, this time misting a little onto the lower wings. "Käti" and "Elsa" were along either side of the cockpit. Aft of the cockpit was my familiar motif, *die gasmaske.* Atop the rear fuselage was the specified letter "F" for *der Fritzen.* "Do you like it, *Herr Feldwebel?*"

"*Javohl!* Very nice work! Jakob, pay the man." Jakob tossed a bottle of schnapps which had been part of the ballast Jakob had carried in lieu of a gunner. "If that is not enough, I will get you more."

"This is *wunderbar,* but I always welcome further incentive and inspiration. *Danke schön!*"

"Has it been cleared for flight?"

"*Javohl!*" Just be careful—I will never be able to match Fokker's streaking."

"Colors, colors. All it has to do is fly and shoot—but I appreciate your work."

Jakob joined in, "*Your* work this morning was wonderful, Gustav. *Zwei bastarde!*"

"I couldn't let them hurt you! Or the schnapps!"

"At least you put me before the schnapps."

"This time."

"Well, let's get this Fokker outside so you may return to *der Jagdstaffel.*"

I helped push my new crate outside and bring the Halberstadt into the hangar for repairs. Then I took off to rejoin the rest of *der Fritzen.* Several miles from the temporary aerodrome I suspected something was amiss. It appeared a large formation of aeroplanes was above the airfield. As I approached I realized I was coming up on a bombing raid, so I climbed as quickly as I could in order to attack. I did see several *Albatrosen* in the air, but they were badly outnumbered. A flight of triplanes joined the fight against the English bombers and scouts. I determined that the Sopwiths were busy with the Fokkers and *Albatrosen,* so I decided to attack the bombers from behind, trying to get at least some before they were able to deliver their loads.

I nosed over into a shallow dive and came up under the rearmost bomber, off to the right of the rest. I had a full load of ammunition, but my *benzin* was running low. I put a burst into the last bomber, adjusted my course, and shot at the next one up, then the next. I put shots into five of the six bombers, then moved along to the next flight and tried the same tactic. I found I could approach a stall and just hang in the air, shooting upward into the bombers' bellies. Soon I was surrounded by bombers breaking formation. I dove away, climbed, and went for a more typical diving pass. I sent bursts toward a number of bombers without noting any results, then continued through the swirling mass of fighters below. I shot at two SE type Sopwiths that were harassing a triplane, chasing both off its tail. Again, I noticed no immediate results. The triplane pilot left the fight, and since my *benzin* was quite low I followed him away. About ten minutes later the triplane touched down on a rather crude airfield. I circled the field once and then followed it in. The field was in horrible condition, but we both managed to pull up to the line of tents, where we were helped out of our aeroplanes.

"*Danke schön, mein freund!*"

"*Gern geschehen!*"

"Schnapps?"

"Schnapps *und benzin!*"

"We will be happy to supply both!"

"*Danke!*"

"You will have to meet Herr Rittmeister. He will be pleased with what you have done."

It was then I noticed the red noses and struts of most of the aeroplanes. My host continued, "I am *Leutnant* Hans Weiss, *führer* of *Jagdstaffel 11.*"

"Herr Leutnant, I am *Feldwebel* Gustav Model, of *der Fritzen."* I saluted.

Weiss returned the salute. "So you are Model. I have heard of you. *Herr Rittmeister* has mentioned you. He has flown your modified *Albatros.* Suffice to say his next meeting with the folks at *Albatros* was not a happy one for them. How did he say it, 'A backseat gunner has managed to accomplish what your entire design team could not do?' He is also watching the progress of your mixed unit. While it is a step backward, mixing aeroplane classes, it consolidates communications within one *Staffel."*

"I am humbled, *Herr Leutnant.* I was being critical one day, and my *Schlastaführer* organized the ideas into a more formal proposal. I am pleased it has worked thus far."

"You have Richthofen to thank for your new Fokker. It was marked for him, but he felt you would appreciate it after what you did to shame *Albatros*—and Pfalz. *Jagdgeschwader I* is to begin receiving the new D.VIIs in another week or so."

"Herr Leutnant, I don't know what to say."

"Then I will say it, *Herr* Model. *Danke schön.* Your ideas are helping Germany's war effort and deserve to be rewarded." I turned around—it was Richthofen. I snapped to attention and saluted. Richthofen returned the salute and continued.

"I flew your modified *Albatros* recently while you were convalescing. It's a wonderful machine. It was a pleasure to dive and recover without worrying about the whole crate coming apart. I never would have believed the difference the rounded, spinner-less nose made. Model, call it genius, call it good research, I don't care, but you are making a difference. I certainly hope Herr Fokker doesn't bung up this new design like he did the triplane. We lost some very good men due to his cutting corners. This new machine could take back control of the air, and you have the first one at the front."

"I am honored to be flying your machine, *Herr Rittmeister."*

"Nonsense. The crate is yours. I will have one soon enough. And speaking of nonsense, I understand you and a *fräulein* had quite an adventure recently!" He smiled.

"Herr Rittmeister, I took a friend up to see her village from the air. While we were in the air an English formation appeared, coming to bomb a nearby rail junction. I know it was dangerous to fight them, but to run would have put me on defense from the beginning."

"I agree with your reasoning."

"Mein Herr, we shot down four English scouts, possibly a fifth."

"Ja, Model, *und drei für die fräulein. Drei!"*

"Ja, once they shot me, I don't think she wasted a bullet!"

"Never upset *eine fräulein* with a machine gun!"

"Javohl, Herr Rittmeister! Javohl!" The three of us laughed.

"Model, I am delighted to have met you. And remember, if you have an idea no one else will listen to, I will be your audience. *Danke."*

I saluted. *"Herr Rittmeister."*

Weiss took me by the arm. "Model, let's go have that schnapps while they look over your Fokker, refuel and rearm it. I know you want to get back to *der Fritzen.* I love that name, by the way! Your idea, I assume?"

"From my friend's work. She works in a tavern where men meet daily and discuss the war and how it *should be* fought. She calls them *der pickelhauben,* but everyone else calls them *der Fritzen.* I just thought that if the English want to call us *Fritz,* we could show them what we are made of."

"It is certainly more interesting than just numbers!"

* * * * *

CHAPTER 102

German

I was delayed at *Jasta* 11's temporary field for a few hours. While I enjoyed schnapps and swapped stories with pilots and others, my *Staffel* had to repair their landing strip enough that they could vacate that field and move to a more serviceable location. The timing was actually good, as *der Fritzen* had been assigned to support the new offensive to the north. I joined them that evening at their new airfield. Needless to say, the then one-of-a-kind Fokker was the center of attention. *Leutnant* Strasser was very jealous and tried to take the machine for himself, but Jakob countered, saying the machine was assigned to me for technical analysis by *IdFlieg* and Richthofen. If Strasser wanted one, he could ask them. Strasser countered with a stream of bile, hatred, and profanity that no one could keep up with. Jakob stood up to answer, but I sat him down while a number of men stood between them.

The next morning we received orders to strafe a section of the English trenches with the usual "escort". Strasser took command of the *jägern*. With the Fokker I was to be the uppermost of the escorts. From my position I watched a most interesting action unfold. As we had hoped, a flight of English Sopwiths approached the lines and dove on the two-seaters strafing the trenches. There had been six of us in the escort. I was highest, another stayed closer to the strafing 'planes, and four were near my altitude waiting to dive on any visiting Limeys. When the Sopwiths appeared, I observed *five Albatrosen* dive on them. There was a modified *Albatros* I had not seen before. I watched the most unlikely shooting I had seen other than Elsa's that one morning over her village. The "new" *Albatros* stayed above Strasser. When Strasser dove on the Sopwiths, the "new" crate stayed behind Strasser. I watched the "new" *Albatros'* tracer fire seemingly go through Strasser and hit a Sopwith. The Sopwith began to smoke and Strasser's machine began to emit steam. Strasser pulled up and around to see where the bullets had come from. Seeing the "new" 'plane, he climbed toward it. The "new" 'plane climbed in turn, leaving Strasser behind. I watched Strasser pound his fists on the front cockpit padding, then fire on the "new" *Albatros* from an unrealistic range and angle. He dove, half looped, and half rolled but could not gain any altitude. The "new" 'plane stayed just out of effective range. I decided to climb to keep an overall view of the odd skirmish and easily stayed above the fray. I will admit I was distracted by the two *Albatrosen* and their game, but I thought no one was above us. That familiar "zip-zip . . . zip-zip-zip" sound demonstrated how wrong I was as bullets whizzed past my head. The thunderous roar of two SE type Sopwiths passed immediately above my head. Both were firing at Strasser, who never saw them coming. He flung his arms out of the cockpit, no doubt involuntarily, and his modified *Albatros* went into a death spiral. From about twelve thousand feet, it spiraled slowly, then more quickly until it resembled a shark diving for the bottom while spinning about its own axis. Faster and faster it dove and spun until it hit in front of a German trench in No Man's Land and seemingly stuck in the mud. While I was shocked at the sudden demise of my *Staffelführer*, I still had to chuckle a bit: The wing cellule never failed. I made a mental note to pass this good news along to my mates.

Though I was somewhat startled by the morning's events, I managed to keep track of the "new" *Albatros*. As suspected, it returned to our new home airfield. I landed just after it did to discover its pilot's identity. I rolled alongside as the pilot reached the ground and pulled off his helmet.

"Jakob! How could you?"

"Gustav, I don't know what you are talking about."

"Strasser. Does that name mean anything to you?"

"*Nein*. It means nothing to me. Not worth my spit."

"You know what happened up there."

"My report will state that *Leutnant* Strasser was shot down by two English scouts. He apparently failed to check his surroundings. It's true what they say, the one you don't see will always get you. And what will *your* report say, Gustav, my friend?"

"You are correct, Jakob, it's the one you don't see. And Strasser never saw them coming."

"*Danke,* Gustav, *danke schön.*"

"Why, Jakob, I don't know what you're talking about. Oh, did you notice?"

"Notice what?"

"The wings," I smiled. "After a spiraling dive from twelve thousand feet they never failed."

"Proud of that, are you, Gustav?"

"Let's just say it's a good thing to know."

"I will pass along the word."

"*Ja,* please do. And Jakob, if I were to look under that fresh black paint on your *Albatros?*"

"Gustav, it's a wonderful machine. I couldn't just let it sit there. After all, I had a small part in its creation. Besides, you have *die gasmaske* on your new Fokker."

"So true. And there is no one I would rather see flying my *Albatros.*"

"Unless your friend Elsa decided to join us." Jakob lightly shoved me, hooked his elbow in mine, and we went to the new mess for coffee before filling out our reports. It took me a little longer to complete mine, thanks to Jakob and his flippant mention of Elsa. My mind wandered off, thinking of Käti and Elsa and how I missed them. Of course I thought of Elsa's morning with the Parabellum, achieving in ten minutes or so what most observer/gunners will never do with her three confirmed kills. With shooting like that, she could fly my backseat any and every day. But flying a *jäger* was an additional challenge. She could undoubtedly fly an aeroplane. After all, several women around the world held pilot certificates. There was no mystery to flying. Well, maybe the various types of clouds and the weather they portend. Stick, rudder bar, throttle, mixture control, a hand pump or two, and a few gauges to look at when things don't feel right. One did not need superhuman strength to operate an aeroplane. She could do it. But would she perform so well day to day? She shot so well that one morning defending me after I was shot. She was channeling her anger, and doing a remarkable job of it. Would she do the same *für der Kaiser und das Vaterland?* I had no answers, but the questions were interesting. I supposed it could happen, but Germany would first have to go through its supply of men of fighting age, then younger and older males. France was then at that stage, utilizing school age boys and older men in some "less aggressive" units. I thought of Marie on her farm without her husband, who was surprisingly in the French army. Germany had many to go through before anyone like Elsa would be considered for military service. The military was, after all, a man's world. Women did not vote. In many places women could not own property. They were considered more as domestic help than people who had professional aspirations or careers. While a selfish part of me would have enjoyed having Elsa in my *Staffel*, it was obviously better and safer for her to do what she was doing.

Once everyone had returned from the morning flight and finished their reports, Jakob brought up the death of *Leutnant* Strasser. Strangely enough, no one mentioned anything unusual about his crash. There were sentiments about losing a good airman and how hard it would be to replace him. Jakob followed up, asking if the men felt there was any need for an observance or ceremony of some sort. No one supported the notion. No one had actually liked Strasser. To a man they thought the time was better spent working on appointing someone to replace him, at least until *IdFlieg* made a decision. Someone brought up Willi, and before he could react, everyone seconded the motion. Willi was our new *Staffelführer,* at least for the time.

Willi stood up and thanked everyone for their confidence in his abilities, Strasser's shoes would be difficult to fill, and so on. He suggested we all concentrate on our next flight that afternoon. True, it would be much like the morning flight, but one had to be prepared.

"Say, Gustav", shouted Willi, "We have had a gunner wounded. It's not bad, but I don't want him flying again today. Does your *fräulein* live near here? What was she, Ilse?"

"Elsa. Her name is Elsa. She lives about a forty-five minute flight from here. I would be glad to go get her. I'll be back first thing next week!"

"Gustav, you would be kind to return that soon! I don't know that I would have such dedication!"

"Also, I don't know that she would fly with just anyone. When she downed the three Limeys, she was upset I had been shot."

"Well, go get her. When you return, I'll have someone shoot you! Any other problems?"

"Other than the heavy flight clothing not being at all complimentary, none I can think of. But I have to say, being shot is getting a little old."

Jakob spoke up. "This is all very amusing, but it does nothing to prepare for the next flight. Willi, I will take the place of the injured gunner if need be. Let's get ready."

There was a gunner to fill in for the mission. It was typical for what we did. The two-seaters strafed, the *jägern* watched for and fought against English Sopwiths. Two of our newer pilots shot down an Englishman apiece. I remained above everyone else and mostly watched. My sense of hope was somewhat buoyed. This offensive looked a lot like the prior offensive in that our ground forces simply had their way with the English troops. The English were in retreat and being driven closer to the channel. The French, to the south, were trying to stop the flow of our troops. I hoped *der pickelhauben* had a sense of what they held that moment. The French were, on a practical level, all but beaten. The English were not much better off. The Yanks were beginning to arrive, and it was but a matter of time before all those fresh, if untested, men found their way to the front lines. It was imperative to exploit the advantage of these two offensives while that was still possible.

* * * * *

CHAPTER 103

German

After a month of heavy fighting up and down the newly altered front lines, our *Staffel* was sent back to our home aerodrome for rest and repairs to our aeroplanes. Jakob had flown in earlier that day to help the maintenance crews prepare for the coming workload. As we air personnel arrived, he made us aware of the news: Richthofen had failed to return from a mission earlier that day. He was last seen chasing an English Sopwith along and over the Somme River, deeper into Allied territory. Eventually the news grew worse. His triplane had crashed and he had died from his wounds. Every German airmen felt the sense of loss. We had all marveled at his mounting list of victories and his seeming invulnerability, even after he was shot the prior summer— likely by one of his own men. While I hadn't seen anything unusual in my brief encounter, many said he was a changed man after having suffered a head wound at that time. On the surface it wasn't much, but how much damage had been done emotionally or internally? His *Jagdgeschwader* received Fokker's new D.VII model shortly after *der Rittmeister's* passing, but he never flew one in combat. I thought of my wonderful Fokker and a deep chill ran through me. It was supposed to go to him, but he deferred. Would it have made a difference in what turned out to be his last aerial combat? I shook off the chill. Thinking like that would change nothing. Like the rest of us, he knew the possible consequences of what we did. He made his decisions and lived by them, whether shepherding new pilots or passing on a new aeroplane. Even so, I was humbled that he thought enough of me to give me such a gift.

I approached Jakob with a question about the observer school I had flown for. With a week or so for rest and repairs, should I see about putting in some time there? He laughed out loud.

"Gustav, you aren't much of a liar, are you? I know you don't much care for the observers."

"That's not true! Remember, the observers are arguably more important than *jägern*. A properly trained observer can . . ."

"Please, Gustav! Your real concern lies between here and the observer school! Can't you simply ask to go visit your *fräuleinen*?"

"*Ja,* I could. But it would be unfair to the other men. We can't have our flyers cavorting all over the country just to see their *frauen.*"

"And there, *mein freund,* is your answer. I'm sorry, Gustav, but you are too important here to allow to leave. The school has other pilots. You will just have to wait to see your *fräuleinen.*"

"What if I brought Elsa back?"

"We would enjoy that, though not so much as you, but *nein.* We have others who can shoot machine guns at the English."

"Can you hate me for—"

"Certainly not. I expected it. How about a consolation prize? Care to come into town with me for a drink?"

"You, not Jure?"

"See if Jure would like to go for supplies. That would be nice. Good idea, Gustav!"

* * * * *

CHAPTER 104

German

After about a week we resumed our tasks, moving up and down the front. Some missions were the familiar strafing of English or French trenches. Some were higher altitude patrols to deny Allied observation aircraft access to our rear areas. My new Fokker, with its BMW engine, was clearly superior at 20,000 feet and above. Only my former *Albatros* came close to the Fokker's high altitude performance. Though we had some injuries, surprisingly there were no deaths in the *Staffel*.

I began to notice an anomaly. Flying above everyone else, I was able to take in the overall scenario of each flight. Admittedly, most of our missions were similar in nature, baiting the British and/or French with our strafing machines, then diving on any who attacked them. At this point I will say all English Sopwiths looked alike. Whether they were the rotary type or the SE type, they were largely snot green in color, more or less, other than national markings and maybe a few discreet markings mostly in white. But I noticed the same Englanders time and again. There was a rotary type Sopwith with a saggy figure eight on the top wing, an SE type Sopwith with prominent "W"s painted on the wings and fuselage, and—strangely enough—a blue Fokker triplane with British "dartboard" markings. There were usually others, but these crates stood out. At first they kept their distance, as if they were observing. Then they began to attack, though cautiously. Their antics were interesting and effective. The "W" SE type began to take away our two-seaters with the pilot's aggressive tactics, as well as two of our newer *Albatros* pilots. The rotary Sopwith managed to shoot down another *Albatros* after some expert maneuvering. The biggest problem, however, was the blue Fokker. Nothing could stay with it. We all knew the little triplane, but this one had more energy than any I had seen. As far as I could tell, none of our pilots had so much as put a bullet into it, much less do any damage. Anyone who attempted to attack it soon found it on their tail with a trail of bullet holes forming, usually approaching the cockpit.

Something had to be done. Willi and I devised a plan. We would watch for the blue Fokker and attempt to engage it. As soon as things started, Willi would dive on it. Knowing the reflexive style of the pilot, I would dive on it immediately afterward. The thought was that if Willi didn't take care of him, maybe he could distract him while I set up my diving pass.

Soon enough we had our chance. Our mission started with the strafing two-seaters. Sure enough, the blue Fokker was down low waiting for them. The pilot went after a Halberstadt and two *Albatrosen* dove to intercept him. Willi followed in short order, possibly putting a few rounds through the blue wings. Willi was engaged immediately by the rotary Sopwith I had observed. This was an excellent pilot in a wonderful machine. Willi had his hands full, so my dive was on the rotary Sopwith type. The Sopwith immediately turned right out of my path, so I had no clean shots at it. However, I lined up with the captured blue Fokker. I had the latest Fokker model, so I decided to see how it compared. That was a mistake on my part. While I noticed a few rounds striking the blue Fokker, I did no damage. On the other hand, he was able to outturn me and start walking bullet holes up my wing. I stalled, hoping he would fly over me, but he was too quick, diving beneath me and speeding off to the southwest. Another time.

One day I returned from a mission to find I had a message from Rudolf Berthold, *führer* of *Jagdgeschwader II*. He had flown a newly introduced aeroplane, the Siemens-Schuckert D.III counter-rotary engine *jäger*. He very much liked the machine and passed along his support for it, recommending I find a way to fly one. He was confident I would share his enthusiasm. While I could not imagine anything better than my Fokker, I felt it was worth looking into if Berthold had gone out of his way to tell me about it. I brought up the idea with Jakob, who joked that the name was bigger than the airframe. He said he would bring up the suggestion to *IdFlieg*.

A day or two later I found myself in a similar situation with my *Staffel* and the group of *Engländern* who seemed to be following us up and down the front. Again Willi engaged the rotary Sopwith and I dove to help. In and among the swirl of aeroplanes I saw an opening to put some rounds into the Sopwith, and I pulled back on the stick. This induced the "hanging stall", from which I fired a few short bursts into the center section of the Sopwith. What I managed to miss was the blue triplane, which maneuvered into a position to fire at me. One burst did the trick for him. He shot at my underside and placed a very hot round into my left thigh. *Scheisse!*

It is never a joy to be shot. A bullet in the body is a distinctly painful experience under any circumstances. In this case, however, I was maneuvering my Fokker, trying to keep the Sopwith in front of my guns. My legs were flexing as they pushed the rudder bar, and suddenly my left hamstrings were injected with molten metal, or so it felt. My legs froze for a moment and my Fokker fell off it's stall. It began to tumble at low altitude, so I had to react quickly. It bothered me to leave my *Staffel* mates, but I would be of no use to them with one leg out of commission. I regained control, dove out, and sped to our aerodrome, recently captured from the English. I needed extra help to get out of the Fokker, and I was carried to a tent hangar for attention to my leg. Jakob was at my side in short order.

"You really could have used Elsa and her Parabellum today!"

"Javohl! She would have been most useful. *So ist der krieg."*

"Ah, but you have found your way to visit her as well as Käti!"

"I would have asked for time away."

"And I would have turned you down. You devil, you!"

"If you tell me you know how I feel, I will see to it that you do."

"Point taken. Assuming no complications, you may leave tomorrow. If you wish to."

"Danke."

As it turned out, my wound was a fairly serious one. I was able to fly out the next morning, but it was quite painful. As per arrangements, I flew to Ernst's estate and set down, where I was assisted by Käti and Ernst's driver. Käti kept watch on my leg wound. Elsa kept watch on everything else, or so it seemed.

After about a week or so I contacted the observer school and offered to fly for them as before. I explained the nature of my wound. I was not fit for combat flying, but I could handle the light duty of introducing observer candidates to flight. I truly enjoyed being with Käti and Elsa, but I felt I needed to do something to help the war effort. Germany had, after all, made some advances, and I wanted to help sustain the momentum any way I could. I cleared everything through Jakob and began right away, flying four days a week.

The first day back I of course saw Elsa and Käti at the tavern. As always, Käti and I ate and Elsa kept our steins full. When Käti and I hugged Elsa and prepared to leave, Elsa promised to be over later. "I'll bring chocolate cake . . . !" She did. There was not much sleeping done that night.

One morning during a routine introductory flight I had a thought. Between flights I looked up the *führer* and asked if the school had any dual control aeroplanes.

"*Ja*, there are a few, but we rarely use them, as you understand."

"*Javohl, mein Herr.* Would you permit me to use one to teach a civilian friend to fly? Of course I would do so when I am not required to fly observers."

"Your request is unusual, but in light of things I see no point denying you. How will you get your friend here, unless he lives nearby."

"No, she lives a short distance from here. I would need the two-seater to retrieve her."

"She? This *is* unusual."

"*Mein Herr*, while I am engaged with the two-seater, my new Fokker crate will be sitting on the flight line. If by chance you had a desire to fly the newest combat machine at the front . . ."

"Why Model, I thought you would never ask! We have no use for dual control aeroplanes here. Whatever you do with one, I will look the other way. Now, about that Fokker . . ."

"*Mein Herr*, you know where it is. Let me know if you need assistance getting strapped in."

"*Danke schön, Herr* Model!"

It was that easy. My next flight to Ernst's estate was in an old *Albatros* B type. As I climbed down Käti asked about my fancy painted aeroplane.

"I borrowed this one, *liebchen,* so I could take you up for a look around."

"Nein! I know what happened when you took Elsa up!"

"I could telephone the English and inquire as to their bombing schedule . . ."

"Funny. *Nein.*"

"Perhaps Elsa would be interested."

"With you, probably. If she is crazy enough, let her. I will wait until the shooting is over with. Then I can fly."

Käti snuggled against me in the back of the saloon. When she and I entered the tavern Elsa was immediately at my side. At the first chance she wrapped herself around me and whispered how happy she was to see me. I asked if she wanted to go up and look around again.

"Javohl! When can we go?"

"You do remember the last time . . . "

"I do. And your point is . . . ?"

"No point. Whenever you have the time we will go."

Elsa squeezed me tight. "I can't wait!"

It was my turn to whisper. "I have a surprise for you when we do go up."

"What surprise?"

"You will see. I know you will like it."

"I'll have to surprise you in return."

All I could do was smile.

The next day Ernst was gracious enough to allow Elsa some time, if needed, in order to go up with me. He had his driver wait and take us to the *Albatros.* I retrieved the flying clothing I had left in the cockpits and offered a set to Elsa, who protested. "But Gustav, it's May. Don't you feel how warm it is?"

"I do, *ja.* But do you remember how cold it was when you went up before?"

"It was cold—before I used the gun. But it was winter."

"It will be almost as cold today. Put on the flying gear and leave it open if you wish. You will close it once you get up there. Trust me."

Elsa pouted. "All right. I will. I trust *mein* Gustav."

With clothing on but not closed, Elsa climbed into the rear cockpit. "Gustav, there is something different here. This looks just like your area in front. What is all of this?"

"Elsa, those are the controls that make the aeroplane fly. The instruments tell what the aeroplane and engine are doing."

"Why is all this in my area?"

"I thought you would like to learn how to fly."

"Fly? Me? I can learn how to fly?"

"Javohl!"

"But I am a woman!"

"Other women have learned to fly. Some have flown in their country's military. Would you like to learn?"

"Javohl! This is your surprise?"

"Ja."

"This *is* a surprise! How exciting! I love *mein* Gustav!"

I showed Elsa the controls, how they affected the aeroplane, and told her to watch the controls move and how the aeroplane reacted. Then Ernst's driver and I pushed the *Albatros* around, I climbed in and started the engine. I taxied, turned, and took off. I climbed to about two thousand feet, circled the town, circled in the opposite direction, rocked the wings, and so on while holding my arm up to demonstrate what I was about to do with the stick and using my hands to show how I would use the rudder bar. I heard the occasional squeal from Elsa, who was clearly having a wonderful time..

I flew straight and level, then turned to Elsa. "Now very lightly touch the controls and *feel* them while I fly. Don't move them yourself." Elsa nodded. I mostly repeated what I had flown. Again I looked at Elsa. "Did you feel it?" She nodded. I told her, "Now you try. Circle the town to the left. Gently." Her face lit up as she nodded.

The *Albatros* felt a little tentative, but it flew mostly the way I had flown it. I turned around. *"Gut?" "Gut!"* she replied. I drew as I talked, "Now circle the other way." She did, with a little more confidence.

"Gut?" "Gut!" "Touch the controls very lightly and I will land." Elsa pouted. I told her, "You need to work. We will fly again tomorrow." She smiled and nodded.

The landing went well, and I turned the *Albatros* around. The driver brought a ladder and we exited the aeroplane and took off the heavy flying gear. I put the clothing in the rear cockpit and we were driven into town. Elsa appeared to be flying still, she was so animated.

"Oh, Gustav! I got to fly!"

"Ja, and we live to tell about it!"

"Gustav!"

"I tease. You flew well for first time and no instruction. I can't wait to show you more tomorrow."

Elsa melted into me as Ernst's driver took us to the tavern. She was very content with her day to that point. Upon arrival she kissed my cheek and sprang out of the motorcar as if shocked and hugged Käti, who was coming out to meet us. "Käti! I got to fly!"

"Ja, I knew Gustav was taking you up again."

"Nein, Käti—I got to fly the aeroplane! I made it turn!"

"And nobody died?"

"Nein! Gustav is teaching me how to fly!"

"Do you trade seats? How?"

I tried to clarify. "Both seats have controls. I show her what to do, then have her do it. Typically, she is a little tentative, but she will learn. Would you like to learn?"

"Danke. But *nein,* not until the shooting is over. You must be hungry, *liebchen.* Come in and eat."

I was hungry, to be sure, but I had to get by Elsa, who was again showing her appreciation. I hugged her in return and suggested she get ready to work. We would have time later.

Käti and Ernst were very kind to allow Elsa to fly with me the next two mornings. Elsa took to flying quite naturally. She understood from the beginning the importance of smooth transitions from one mode to another. As she grew accustomed to the characteristics of the old *Albatros'* controls her turns were beautiful. It seemed she could make *die alte dame* dance across the sky. I was content for the moment to have Elsa fly level, turn, and gently dive and climb. Once she was used to that, I planned on working on takeoffs and landings, probably the following week. And if I thought Elsa was firmly attached to me before, I felt our bond growing even stronger. Sometimes she wanted to talk about flying and aeroplanes. Other times she just wanted to hold me and be held in turn. I can't say I had a preference.

* * * * *

CHAPTER 105

German

About two weeks later I returned to the observer school to find a message waiting for me.

When I finished that week I was to return to the "home" aerodrome for *der Fritzen*. I telephoned the tavern and Ernst promised he would deliver my "duty calls" message. Käti would take it in stride, but that's Käti. Elsa was more emotional and would take it hard that she couldn't fly with her Gustav.

I arrived at the airfield to be greeted by Jakob. "Ah, Gustav! Do you want to hear the bad news first or see the good news."

"What's the bad news?"

"Willi. He is missing."

"Willi?"

"*Ja*. They found his 'plane, crashed near the front lines, but no sign of Willi. There is a crazy story that he was taken by a Sopwith."

"Shot down?"

"No. Taken. Someone at the front said they saw an English Sopwith carrying a man on its wing. Of course we all think he was too deep in his schnapps. It doesn't make sense."

"Who is leading *der Staffel?*"

"I am, for now, but the men selected you."

"To follow Willi is an honor, but . . . ."

"Are you able to fly combat?"

"I am still quite sore, but I can try some aggressive flying and see how the leg feels."

"I had hoped you would say that. It leads me to the good news. Follow me."

Jakob took me to the hangar where my Fokker had been painted. As he reached for the door handle, he told me a present from IdFlieg and Berthold had been delivered by Berthold himself. "Berthold wished you a speedy recovery, but nudged me as he said he hoped you did not rush back to the war until you were ready."

"So Willi is gone and I missed Berthold's visit. How very unfortunate."

"This should make you feel somewhat better." Jakob opened the door and turned on some lights to reveal a smallish aeroplane with an aggressive stance and short, stubby fuselage. I could tell it had been here for at least a few days. It had been painted to resemble other aeroplanes, dark fuselage with putrid green "gas" and *die gasmaske*."

"Would you like to take her up, Gustav?"

"I would. But could we get some food and something warm to drink? To fly at any kind of altitude is to revisit winter."

"Javohl, Gustav. I will have her pushed outside and readied for you."

Over warm food and hot coffee Jakob told me the aeroplane was a Siemens-Schuckert SSW D.III. It had a powerful counter-rotary engine which yielded a slow propeller speed, necessitating a large four blade propeller. While *IdFlieg* and most pilots were enthusiastic about the Fokker D.VII, which was arriving in *Jagdstaffeln,* Berthold was more excited over the SSW. He hoped that I would share his enthusiasm and influence IdFlieg to order more of them.

"Well, the very least I can do is fly Berthold's darling. It looks interesting enough, and if Berthold has again gone out of his way to put me in one, there must be something about it. I am intrigued."

"I have been tempted, to be honest, but Berthold brought it for you."

"Jakob, you could have flown it! You, of all people. Would you like to fly her? Go ahead."

"No, Gustav, now that you are here it's yours. I would love to take her up after you, though, if you don't mind."

"Javohl! Let's see if she is ready."

She was indeed ready. She looked magnificent in the midday sun, the dark stained wood fuselage, the horrid green, the tricolor tailplane, and the curious preprinted fabric. And her stance. She was ready to conquer the air. Who was I to keep her waiting?

The small headrest fairing did get in the way of my ritual of pulling on my boots while sitting just behind the cockpit. That might have to be removed, I thought. But it was smaller than the monstrosity Albatros had initially mounted on their D.V—which most pilots had removed, as it obscured the rearward vision and created a blindspot.

Boots on, I slid down onto the seat and was strapped in. The engine already primed, I called "Switch is on", and the prop was pulled. The large engine sputtered, coughed, belched smoke, and finally caught, the sputter turning to a steady drone. I waved and the chocks were pulled away. The visibility from the cockpit while taxiing was terrible, such was the angle of the fuselage, due to the tall landing gear necessary to clear the large prop. I kicked the rudder side to side a little and looked around the nose since I could not see over it.

At the end of the field I kicked the rudder and turned into the wind. The field clear, I didn't hesitate to push the throttle open. Right away, I knew what Berthold liked about this machine. Her aggressive stance was more than a promise. It was an assurance. We were off the ground and climbing almost before I knew it. I was so confident in this machine I did something I had never done: I rolled her as I climbed over the tents and hangars at the end of the airstrip. This was going to be fun!

And so it went. The SSW "climbed like a monkey," to borrow from Richthofen's description of the Fokker DR.I. I was five thousand feet in the air in no time. With that cushion of altitude, I went through a somewhat abbreviated test ritual. She was magnificent in every way. She was fast, she was maneuverable, and she was *fun!* Turns, climbs, dives, rolls, loops, she had no limits. This was a solid airframe with a wonderful engine.

While alone in the air, I thought of Willi. His disappearance had baffled everyone. It was perhaps the worst part of a very bad day for *der Fritzen*. The *Engländern* had arrived in force just after sunrise and simply had their way over our airfield. I was told Willi was the only one to get off the ground and return the fight. Anyone else who tried was shot down immediately. The English even had one of Fokker's triplanes, the all blue one I had traded shots with, that almost hovered over the field looking for any comers. In the wake of the attack we had several dead and a number of wounded, not to mention a heavy loss of aeroplanes and equipment. As a result, the replacement aeroplanes were a mix of *Albatrosen* D.V and D.Va and a few Pfalz D.IIIa types. This was what was available, cast aside by other *Jagdstaffeln* as they received their new Fokker D.VIIs. Jakob demanded some of the new Fokkers, or at least some *Albatros* D.IIIs to rebuild, but *IdFlieg* countered that he had no one to fly them.

I acted on an impulse. I knew the *Jagdstaffel* was out, such as it was, on a strafing mission. I decided to look in on them with my new SSW. After a brief search I found them, occupied with a number of English Sopwiths. Not waiting for my turn at all, I just dove in and helped myself. I don't know the right word for the SSW. Agile? Nimble? Effective? Devastating? She would do anything I wanted, almost on impulse. Control response was immediate and precise. I looked for anything with blue/white/red on it and opened fire, as if they all had conspired to do in my friend Willi. I shot SE type Sopwiths off the tails of our replacement pilots. I greeted several rotary type Sopwiths with telling bursts from my guns. I was certain of one that crashed directly after I shot it, and there were two or three others that may have. I was most pleased that my SSW and I had ruined the day for a number of the tea-sipping bastards.

The others gathered and flew back to the airfield. I climbed to watch over them, but no English followed. After everyone else was down, I brought the little SSW down to join them. Jakob was there to help me out of the cockpit, with another man standing next to the ladder.

"Well, Gustav, what do you think?"

"Do I have to tell you? Have you ever seen me do a roll on takeoff? I swear this little thing was tailored for me. I think it, it does it. I flew over to join the mission. I must have put bullets into every English crate involved. One crashed right away, and there could be two or three others. I was having too much fun to keep track of them. When do you want to try her?" I stepped to the ground.

"I will. *Feldwebel* Gustav Model, meet Anthony Fokker."

"*Herr* Fokker, it is indeed a pleasure. I hope I didn't offend you."

"No, of course not. I am a pilot myself. I flew one of these at Adlershof. It is a magnificent machine. Your assessment is correct. I wonder about the engine, however. It is a marvel, but perhaps a bit complicated for wartime flying? It's new. We shall see."

"I understand three factories are building your wonderful D.VII. I suppose that is enough, isn't it?"

"Oh, no! I would be delighted if Siemens-Schuckert Werke were building mine as well! Their royalty payments spend like anyone else's. Speaking of mine, I see you are flying a what I consider a special machine. Yours was a prototype, flown by many at Adlershof. It was instrumental in getting me all the government contracts. Of course it has been updated and fitted with an experimental engine. How is it treating you, *Herr* Model?"

"It's a wonderful machine, *Herr* Fokker! It is not as immediate as the SSW, but it is an excellent partner in the air. Again, it's an impulsive flyer, requiring little effort to do as I wish. At the same time, one need not fly the D.VII all the time. It is well mannered where the SSW can be a little unruly if left unattended."

"Excellent, *Herr* Model! You are as good as I have heard. I have been watching you since you redesigned the Albatros D.III. That was very thoughtful work on your part."

"It was nothing special. I just learned that the Austrians were flying the D.III with none of the problems we were having. I discovered the difference, as well as their improvements, and suggested we do the same. If *Albatros* wasn't going to—"

"Precisely. You are a man of action."

"I just want to put this war behind me. I'm not sure what I will do, but anything is better than trading bullets. Frankly, I'm tired of getting shot. There has to be something better."

"I could use you on my staff."

"I am honored, *Herr* Fokker, but I have no technical training other than working in my father's blacksmith shop and stable."

"Neither have I, or at least nothing to speak of. But you have a pilot's intuition and a good sense of what makes a great aeroplane. I have Platz and his staff for the technical drudgery. But you would be a good addition. Besides, Model, it would get you away from the shooting. And I plan on building aeroplanes beyond the end of the war. The market will change, but I will adapt and build what the market wants. What do you think?

"Jakob?"

"Don't ask me. You are a fine combat pilot, and I could use you here. But you have become a friend as well. I would not criticize a friend for making a decision that improves his life. If any of your claims are confirmed today, you will qualify for the *Pour le Merite*. *Der Kaiser* has nothing higher to give you. I think you should go. And if ever you need an assistant on your staff, . . ."

"To file reports? I will know where to find you." I extended my hand.

"Just leave the bottom drawers empty!" Jakob took my hand and shook it with both of his.

Funny. I had been given two aeroplanes by *IdFlieg*. Jakob insisted I take both with me. Fokker had travelled by train, so he offered to help me. He flew his D.VII, "for sentimental reasons". I followed him to Schwerin, where he introduced me to his staff. Then he showed me to my modest quarters. I could have expected that from Fokker—it was spartan. I explained that I needed a few personal items, and he gave me three days to take care of that. "But I insist you take the D.VII. You are, after all, a 'Fokker man' now!"

"But what about the—"

"Keep it! It's a wonderful machine! I will rent you hangar space . . . okay, no rent for the hangar space. I just don't want it visible on my airfield unless you are flying it. You understand."

"Javohl, Herr Fokker!" I telephoned the tavern to let them know I was on my way.

* * * * *

CHAPTER 106

British

The next morning dawned bright, clear, and cold. I saw no delays getting into the air and headed back to HE, at least due to the weather. I walked over to the maintenance area and helped Geoff patch a few holes in wings from the day before.

"Do you want white discs and black crosses on these?"

"Bugger off, Lef-tenant. Bugger off! Do they still do that?"

"I hope they did it on the little blue bugger! Think of it! Iron Cross patches on a German crate!"

"Ya know, I like it. If they didn't, I will detail someone to do it. Great idea—thanks!"

"Just don't tell him I got the little thing all shot up. He will never forgive me."

"What's it worth to you, Lef-tenant, to keep me silent?"

"I will make a photograph of my current companion and deliver it to you personally."

"Oh? Really? The one who inspired the, uh, 'Lazy Eight'?"

"Now then, Geoff. A gentleman doesn't tell. I shall leave that for you to decide. If you can take your eyes off her legs, that is."

"You wouldn't."

"But I would. And more importantly, so would she."

"She wouldn't."

"Ah, but she would. If I asked."

"That is one obedient woman."

"Not at all. She is just spirited and adventurous. And she enjoys pleasing me."

"She doesn't have a sister, does she? A cousin? 'ow's 'er mum, then?"

"I'll ask. No promises beyond, mate! Wait—she has a brother! Fine looking lad."

"Sorry, mate, I don't play on that team! But thanks, all the same . . . ."

With that I left and visited with Major Campbell. I thanked him for putting up with me and allowing me to have a go at the little blue bugger.

"No, Lef-tenant, I'm glad you took her up, though I doubt the Boche share my opinion. She'll be lonely without you or Trafford to pay her any attention."

"I disagree, sir. You should take a while and treat yourself. She is a wonderful dance partner, once you are comfortable with her wild side. What did Trafford say, oh yes, she has the attention span of a puppy. You might want to borrow a Camel as a transition from the SE. Just a thought."

"You are probably right. I will simply make the time and have a go. I deserve a little fun now and then."

"Aye, sir. You do."

"Well, thanks for adding to the squadron's score. Took you long enough. And you haven't been much bother. I'm sure Geoff enjoyed the company. No one pays him any attention unless they need something."

"Simply human nature, sir. He's a good bloke. A little iffy around the edges, but we're all a bit dodgy in places. Some just hide it better than others."

"I am certainly glad you are not so charitable when summing up the Boche bastards!"

"Frankly, sir, I'm sure they are mostly good eggs as well. Unfortunately, we are at war or I should love to drop in on them with a bottle of schnapps. Maybe when this damned silliness is over with and behind us."

"I'm with you there. I'd be happy to choose a French cafe, watch the people go by, and perhaps offer a drink to any pilot who happened along. Unless a lovely *mademoiselle* took my offer first."

"Well, sir, I'd better get in the air before Old Man Winter plays any more tricks."

"Yes, do. Please give my regards to Trafford."

"I shall, as soon as I can get to him."

"And send me more like him!"

"Aye that!"

* * * * *

CHAPTER 107

British

After a cold but otherwise beautiful flight I set down on my assigned airfield and rolled up to the flightline. I exited my Camel and stopped in to visit the CO. He was out for the day, but his adjutant greeted me.

"I almost didn't recognize you with no boxes of sweets! Welcome back! I understand you had quite a day over there."

"Your new uniform looks quite nice. Fits a lot better than the old one."

"Uh, thank you, sir. I think."

"Yes, I had quite the good time over there, other than Trafford being wounded. Any word on him?"

"He has been improving steadily. Your girlfriend is quite the doctor!"

"Or will be. We are working on that."

"I don't see the problem. Apparently the other doctors there are scratching their heads over her. Everyone she touches gets better. Isn't that what doctors are supposed to do?"

"Yes, my lad, that is the whole point. If she does the job, give her the title and position."

"Makes sense to me, sir. Oh, didn't you shoot down ten Huns that one day? I heard you were flying a Boche crate when you did it."

"Seven. They tell me I got seven. Five over the aerodrome and two more who chased me."

"Seven! Still, sir, I don't know if that has ever been done!"

"Don't know. I'm just happy I was able to show them the way, as it were. Seven closer to war's end as far as I'm concerned."

"What were you flying, sir?"

"Trafford had modified a little Fokker crate. Three wings. He put a Clerget engine in it and Vickers guns. Climbs and stunts like a chimpanzee on cocaine. I was stunting over the field when the Heinies decided to raid us. They lined up coming one way, I flew the other, shooting as I went. Fish in a barrel, all that."

"But seven? I'll bet McCudden and Mannock are shaking their heads."

"I doubt that. They are seasoned flyers, very good at what they do. I'm just a bloke with a vendetta. They have shot down more Hun crates than I, but I have probably killed far more men than they have, strafing and bombing the trenches. I'm not out to challenge them: I am out to win the war."

"Yes, sir."

"And unless the new students are arriving first thing, I will have you more cakes tomorrow. We need to plan your next uniform, lad."

"Uh, well, . . ."

"May I use the telephone?"

"Of course. Use his." He gestured toward the office.

I called the nursing school and was put through to the head administrator, possessor of the most recognizable voice in my life.

"Clara, are you free for dinner tonight?"

"I am now! You're back? How exciting!"

"I could cook for you if you like. I just need a key to get in."

"I know where you could obtain a key. But it's going to cost you."

"I hope so! I will be by soon."

"Look for a chubby blonde woman in a pink coat. She will have it."

"Nice of her, but I was hoping to see you."

"You are silly—but don't change!"

"I need to. I just flew the Channel."

"You're too much. See you soon!"

A short while later I arrived just as Clara came out the door. I was able to park very near, so she jumped in and left all of her lipstick on my face. I asked her what she wanted.

"Do you mean dinner? Or later?"

"I mean dinner. As for later, surprise me."

"I doubt it will surprise you, but hopefully you like it. I don't care about dinner. Anything will be wonderful if I have you with me."

"How is Jeremy?"

"He is driving everyone crazy. We want to release him just to get him out of the building! But we are afraid he will think it's just a scratch and go on to do something stupid. I mean unintentionally cause harm to himself."

"How is Pauline?"

"We'll talk later. Honest. I promise."

"That bad . . ."

"You are quite perceptive. Sorry, that was uncalled for."

"Don't worry."

"I really do need to get back to work." She planted a kiss on my lips, and about a minute later she allowed me to come up for air. And with a wave she was gone. Wow.

I stopped at a market and managed to buy a piece of steak just off the lorry. Beautiful cut of meat. It was a bit dear, but I could be dead the following week. I picked up some vegetables and spices for garnish.

I heard her motor-car just after dark and went to greet her. Some things never change and some things never get old. Clara managed to wedge herself into the doorway with me, causing that awkward kiss and squeeze maneuver we had done so many times. Once I peeled her away I explained that dinner would be just a few minutes while I cooked the steak.

"Perfect. I can get undressed. I mean changed."

The steak began to sizzle in the pan. "Either would do. It's not like you are frying steak." A moment later I was wrapped in naked woman, trying to hold the side of the steak on the pan while being kissed on the side of my face. Then she squealed and jumped away.

"Damn! I get your point! The sizzle is more than just sound!"

"And the sizzle is about done. You could dish out the sides if you like."

Pulling on her housecoat, she obliged while I set the steak aside. I would cut it at the table. In the meantime I opened a bottle of wine and we sat at the table.

Clara began the conversation. "I promised we would talk, so let's start there. I'm afraid Mrs Trafford will not be getting better. While you were away, she delivered, with much assistance, a dead fetus. I thought

I might be able to help her after that event, but she has remained unresponsive. Unless something changes dramatically, I fear it is just a matter of time until she expires."

It took a moment to let that sink in and process. I knew Clara was a dedicated medical professional. If she could not help Pauline, Pauline likely could not be helped. I supposed that was the way things worked. Not everything went how one wanted.

"Dare I ask how Mr Trafford is taking it?"

"He is quite stoic about it. He is completely understanding and has not asked many questions. Just details."

"Details?"

"Procedures, mostly. Disposition, legal matters."

"He's given up and moved on."

"I will not speculate on their personal relationship. I shall stick to the medical matters and leave it at that. It's safer that way."

"And Jeremy is making you crazy in the opposite way?"

"Oh, you don't know! He wants to go to France, fly, and kill! He has no regard for his condition.

'Turn me loose—let me at those Boche bastards!' He reminds me of someone I know." "Anyone I know?"

"Sometimes. I hope you know who cooked this steak! This is wonderful!"

"I know he would be happy to cook for you every night. At least once the war is over, whenever that will be. Four Christmases now. Will it ever end? I just want to put this madness behind me and paint. And please you."

"Don't worry, flyboy. This meal is excellent. And I'm sure you will soon please me again and again."

"Oh, but I hope so . . . ."

* * * * *

Chapter 108

British

My life settled back into its routine. A new class of pilots needed training and sorting out. There was the usual bell curve of talent. There were those better suited for other pursuits. There was far less carnage than the prior class, for which I was very happy. I was able to arrange for Jeremy to spend some time with my class before he was released to return to France. Clara appreciated the idea. Jeremy could fly and monitor his condition while in the air but no one was shooting at him. Even he thought it an effective compromise. And I enjoyed his company and help with the student pilots.

Jeremy used his free time to grow closer to his father. Oh, to be sure, Mr Trafford still had visions of his son taking over the family business. Jeremy continued to resist, but I asked Jeremy to keep an open mind. Sure, there were many possibilities before him once the war was over. But I tried to show him the magnitude of what his father was offering him. And I pointed out that the business could be run in a much less hands-on manner. He could promote someone from within or hire someone new to run the business day to day. Jeremy could keep watch over operations and finances and still be free for other things. He could even do as his mother had insisted and bring women into the business in a design capacity. He liked my ideas and promised he would consider them.

Sadly, his mother never recovered. She remained in a vegetative state until one night she simply ceased living. Someone somewhere pointed the finger at me as being the father of her stillborn child. I could but deny the accusation with no substantial evidence until Clara stood by me. Breaking the conventional norms, she announced that we were engaged to be wed and had been for quite some time. This surprised me in more ways than one. Then she pounded her point home. As a "liberated" woman and a relative pillar in the medical community, she intimated that she and I had been "having relations" for some time with no effort at contraception yet she was without child. That's right, she pronounced me as sterile and offered to prove it should anyone challenge her assertions. Once I was over Clara's revelations, I had a pretty good idea who the father was. I chose not to breathe a word of it. I treasured the friendship I had with him and only wanted to continue as friends. And, at that point, it made no difference. Pauline's child, like Pauline, was no more. Raking up the muck made no sense. Let those without lives of their own worry about it.

My relationship with Pauline had been unlikely but wonderful. I had a window on this vibrant, intelligent, talented, and funny woman that few had. Her husband somehow passed on all she had to offer for reasons I never did learn. While he seemed a reasonable chap toward me, he never showed her any regard as anything beyond a socially necessary accessory. He seemed to make something of an exception when she pitched Clara before him, and that was the end of what I saw as his involvement with women. He sold them hats. Hats designed by men. But what he missed in Pauline I reveled in. She had a love of music and the arts not unlike mine. She was inquisitive and quirky. And, of course, she had been my "rite of passage" into one aspect of manhood. I carried nothing but the fondest memories of Pauline and our brief time together. And hearing even a snippet of "Alexander's Ragtime Band" still pastes a furtive smile on my face that is difficult to remove.

The relationship with Clara was simply ripping. I couldn't imagine things going any better. True, her position with the nursing school and aspirations toward being a doctor took up large tracts of her time. She continued to oversee the school, put in time at the hospital "under physician's supervision", and travel to conferences. But if I were available, she would telephone me just to say hello and hear my voice. She would tease and flirt with me like she wanted to pick me up in a bar. Of course, my ego and I did not mind at all. She knew how to attract and then hold a man's interest. I was extremely fortunate she had found favor with me.

One day I received a message at the airfield requesting that I stop by the millinery. It had not been long since Pauline's funeral, and I wondered what Mr Trafford had in mind. Since I was leaving to pick up Clara, I decided to stop in after we had eaten breakfast. He always liked to see Clara, and we could sweeten the visit with some fresh cakes for him and his staff. When we arrived, Mr Trafford met us at the door and relieved Clara of the boxes she was carrying.

"I am delighted you could get here so soon, Lef-tenant. And Clara, what a pleasant surprise! It's good to see you as well. Would you care for another hat?"

"Oh, no, I couldn't."

"But you could. Just tell me what you want and it's yours."

"You are too kind."

"Mr Trafford, your message only said you wanted me to stop by. Is everything all right? What can I do for you, sir?"

"Everything is fine, Lef-tenant. I cannot tell you how wonderful it is having Jeremy at home. You both have been exemplary and beyond. I could ask nothing more of you. In fact, well, could you follow me, please?"

Mr Trafford led us through a door, down a corridor, and into a warehouse. He stopped by a large object which was under a fabric cover.

"Lef-tenant, you have been borrowing motor-cars from the airfield to get around." "Aye, sir, I have."

"Well, my lad, I thought you could use a motor-car of your own. This, then, is yours."

Mr Trafford pulled away the cloth to reveal a bright red roadster. I stepped back, wide-eyed, shaking my head.

"Mr Trafford, I couldn't."

"But at my insistence you shall. I looked at any number of motor-cars, and this one is perfect. It's an American Ford, a "T" model. Not only does it fit the image of a dashing scout pilot, but it is a very reliable marque. Built on an assembly line, it uses common parts, readily available. This vehicle will serve you well."

"But sir—"

"No further discussion, my lad. After all you have done for my son, you will find no end to my gratitude. You meant a great deal to my late wife as well. Anything you need or merely want, you simply come to me. I will see that you have it. Now, if you will forgive me, I have other business to tend to. I'll have someone open the door so you may take your 'car and go about your day. I'll be in touch."

Mr Trafford reached for my far shoulder, pulled me against him, let go, firmly shook my hand, and disappeared back down the corridor. I heard him call, "Thank you for the cakes!", then a door closed.

I just stood there. Clara stepped in, so to speak.

"You get in over here. I will take you to the other 'car, then follow you to the airfield. Hello? Are you in there, Flyboy?"

"I'm sorry. I'm a little shocked right this moment, that's all."

"I understand. But we can't stand here all day. C'mon, get in."

Just then there was a clatter as the warehouse door was opened. I got in.

* * * * *

CHAPTER 109

British

As spring approached the rumor mill seemed to peak regarding a German offensive. It stood to reason, for the fierce cold was loosing its grip on France, yielding to temperatures more conducive to men sacrificing themselves on the altar of war. Or so I viewed it, having seen it up close. Our reconnaissance missions brought back proof of activity in the German rear areas. There was a continual effort to move men and materiel into and toward occupied France. Of course bombing missions were sent to impede progress any way they could, as well as daylight strafing and ground attack raids. I monitored the situation as best I could through the CO at my training airfield in HE. My interest was in the unit known, at least in the rumor mill, as the Fritzes. Rumors said they existed, but facts did not back up the rumors.

The Germans launched Operation Michael on 21 March, 1918, with great success. Our troops fled before the German advance. Distressing as this news was, I finally got word confirming the existence of the Fritzes. A pilot was brought down behind our lines in one of those curious looking Albatross scouts. From the description, I knew I had seen and flown against the unit. Brightly painted noses, black rear fuselage, red/white/black tailplane, and the letter "F" on the wing and fuselage. Other crates from his unit were similar save the nose colors. To close the deal, so to speak, when asked his unit, the pilot replied, "Der Fritzen". Proof!

Right away I lobbied my CO to release Jeremy and myself to join Major Campbell's squadron in order to seek out these Fritzes. As my class of pilots was winding down, I was excused from participating in any ceremonies. He required Jeremy to be cleared for combat with a medical waiver, which Clara supplied. It was a matter of clear weather for our passage to France. Presently the day dawned which allowed us to make our flight, and we arrived with nary a problem. Major Campbell supplied his latest information and the two of us flew to look for our quarry the next day. We stayed high over the lines and eventually found them, but we did not engage them. We observed their tactics, setting us up with the strafing two-seaters while their scouts loitered above to dive on any of our lads going for the bait. There was nothing new going on other than the fact that the two-seaters were painted in a similar manner to the Albatrosses. That told me they were flying as a single unit. The strafing aircraft certainly did damage to troops and morale, and it seemed a bonus that they could snare our scouts as they tried to defend our mates in the trenches. If nothing else, it distracted some scouts from intercepting other aeroplanes on observation or bombing missions.

When Jeremy and I returned to the aerodrome we talked with Major Campbell. I had some ideas I wanted to hear out loud, possibly with feedback from the major. The blue triplane was still on hand, so I suggested we do what was needed to put Jeremy in it. He could stay down low where the Fokker was most useful. I wanted at least another pilot to join me higher up. I suggested Wellington, the rambunctious Yank. More would be better, and I left that to Major Campbell's discretion. The plan was a loose one, to be sure. The higher pilots could watch for the Albatrosses and distract them while Jeremy flew against the two-seaters down low. And just like my jass music, I would have to play fast and loose, ready to improvise as needed. I knew Jeremy could outfly about anything in his little blue bugger. I would work with him in my Camel to be sure he was ready for the strain of combat. Wellington, who had scored additional victories since returning to the squadron, was a straight-in attacker. He was a master at the diving attack, shooting on the way down, diving past, then zooming away in order to climb and set up another dive. He was maturing nicely. Oh, he still wanted to score more than Richthofen or anyone else, but he had tempered his approach. A little. My thought was to have some promising pilots come along and do pretty much what Wellington did. My, but it would have been difficult to think in such terms when I first encountered Wellington, he had been that rash. But here he was, a seasoned scout pilot and model for others to emulate. I was quite proud of his progress. His work with me could set him up to be a flight leader.

Major Campbell had not said much. He listened, lit up a pipe, drew on it a bit, and considered what I was saying. Finally I asked him what he thought.

"Lef-tenant, it seems to me you have it worked out. I am a little wary of keeping Trafford down low alone, but as you point out, nothing in the air can stay with him in close combat at that altitude. As long as he keeps watch, he should be okay. Just don't be afraid to send him some help. Taking Wellington along is a good idea. I might want to rotate him between your flights and patrolling for Boche reconnaissance crates. Maybe the occasional balloon run. All in the interest of rounding him out as a scout pilot. You do understand."

"Yes, of course. These *Fritzen* won't last forever, after all. I should think we would go on squadron strafing missions in an effort to demoralize the Boche. They have had it too easy on this offensive of theirs. And our lads would appreciate the support. Any hope of counterattacking any time soon?"

"I have my doubts. Our troops seem to be gathering to the north, toward the Channel. The French are trying to counter the Germans with boys and old men. Frankly, the Americans are our best hope to do anything as it stands. Our brass hats will not agree. According to them, everything is fine. I'd really like to know what gas they're sniffing to be so out of touch. It does not look good."

The Germans obviously smelled blood, for they opened another offensive to the north of Operation Michael. From Lille they broke through to the west. The army's situation was ever more dire with our troops being forced toward the Channel with no help in sight from the brass hats. Campbell's squadron was assigned to join other units strafing the advancing Germans. Jeremy noticed something interesting. The Boche, of course, fired back at the strafing Brits. But most stopped and pointed at the triplane, apparently thinking it one of their own. Until Jeremy opened fire with his Vickers guns. His runs were somehow more effective than others'.

Needless to say, our actions attracted the attention of the Fritzes. We soon noticed short-nosed Albatrosses diving on us from above. Wellington and I were high up, watching for just that opportunity.

I had to give them credit for a lot of nerve. They had the expected Albatrosses diving down on our strafing scouts, which Welly and I promptly dove after in turn. But, in addition, there were Albatrosses down low, escorting their own strafing two-seaters. In the midst of an attack, they mounted an attack of their own. This had the benefit of drawing away our scouts in an effort to defend our own lads who were already in retreat.

There soon developed two adjacent storms swirling with climbing, diving, twisting aeroplanes. I caught a glimpse of Wellington, likely having the time of his life. He was bolting and twisting amongst a virtual smorgasbord of German scouts, injecting Vickers rounds every which-way. He wanted them all. It was plainly obvious. He fully intended to down them all, then likely join the other fracas and do the same. It was wonderful to watch him in his "W" bedecked SE, firing one gun, the other, both, as he saw fit, into what looked like an artist's palette of colored Albatrosses. I saw an explosion occur on board one Albatross, followed by flames. I wish I could describe more of his efforts, but I was involved in that same swirl of colorful Fritz scouts, exchanging hot lead with any and all I encountered. The Albatrosses were faster than my Camel, but the Camel was more agile. I had to swivel my head constantly in order to avoid being caught by surprise. I took hits in the wings and had a few bullets just miss my left arm due to having both hands on the stick that moment.

Of course other units joined the storms, which were generally merging into one huge go-around. There were less colorful Albatrosses and similar Pfalzes, most less colorful than *der Fritzen*, but with unit colors here and there. There were more SEs and Camels, of course, and eventually there were a few French cockades in the mix as SPADs looked in. Everything was held together in a web of tracer trails. Here and there a combatant would fall to the ground, often trailing a brackish smoke to mark briefly their path of descent. Others would fall out of the "cloud" in a spin, recover, and race—or limp—toward their aerodrome.

This whole aerial circus lasted perhaps twenty to thirty minutes. I can't be sure, as I left after about twenty-five minutes, out of ammunition. While I had shot at a lot of Huns, I couldn't lay a solid claim to any going down from my efforts. I saw Wellington's probable, but no others I could assign to a specific pilot. Rather than take the time and effort to spin, I simply dove out of the fray and went home on the deck. I landed in a mix of activity, some desperate, some celebratory. A few of our lads had been shot and managed to bring their SEs home. They were being worked on while their aeroplanes were assessed for damage and necessary repairs. Another was elated, running among the others yelling, "Two! I got two of the Hun buggers!"

Then there was Jeremy. I rolled up next to his little blue Fokker. He was being unstrapped but appeared to be in no hurry to exit the 'plane. He turned toward me and smiled. I was helped out of my Camel and checked over. I pointed out what I knew of the damage, then waddled around the tail of Jeremy's Fokker.

"What are you so happy about?"

"Well, I made it back."

"I knew you would. Probably not a lot of damage to your little blue bugger, either."

"Yeah, some."

"What, then?"

"That was some ripping great shit, wasn't it? That was the most fun I have had in my life! Everywhere I look, dirty Huns to shoot at! Hell, I stayed ten minutes after I ran out of ammunition!"

"Why would you do that?"

"I picked one, outflew it, then dove right at it. I just wanted to scare the shit out of them. Then I picked another and tried to land on its wing."

"You likely did scare the shit out of someone. From personal experience, . . ."

"Yes, I've heard. Sorry, sir, but you were my inspiration—no offense."

"None taken, though one would think you could draw upon your own experience."

"Ouch! Fair enough . . . ."

"So how many did you get?"

"No bloody idea. But without guns I got at least two! Scared one bastard so bad he jerked the stick and flew into his mate. They locked up, then broke up, and they hit the ground together on an artillery gun—then the fiery crash started cooking off the shells! They have one hell of a mess to clean up over there!"

"Yeah, you are clearly broken up over that one."

"Does it show?" Jeremy threw his head back and laughed. "When can we go back?"

"Let's see who made it back and assess damage. The Huns will be there. Or here, if we can't stop the hemorrhaging. We need to get back out there and bomb and strafe some more. It's a shame we can't hang a few bombs on your blue bugger."

"Have any grenades?"

"I like how you think. I'll look."

Major Campbell insisted we hold off on further flying for the day. We had several wounded pilots and a lot of mostly minor damage to repair. I got Jeremy to come with me while I worked on my Camel, then other SEs, patching bullet holes and being useful to the fitters. I liked looking after my own 'plane and they appreciated the help. As I had supposed, the little blue bugger had very few holes to patch. All the same, Jeremy got a chuckle when he saw the patches from my epic day aloft, complete with black crosses. Oh, the irony!

Early the next morning I led my ad hoc assemblage into he air. I could not help but watch as the sun arose over war torn France. I had grown accustomed to the forlorn nature of the mostly brown landscape, but my inner soul lamented the almost complete lack of green. It was, after all, spring. Spring is when the world experiences new growth. The browns of winter yield to the greens of spring along with some early flowers. But not in 1918. Attaining our desired altitude, the countryside below was a mash of browns with an ugly black double scar in the near distance. The scar was the trench line recently overrun by the Germans. We hoped to do our small part in putting them back behind their trenches and then further to the east as we eventually ended this senseless slaughter and won the war.

Jeremy and another pilot stayed behind to allow us time to climb to fifteen thousand feet. They then took off and stayed low. The plan was to watch for and then engage the Fritzes. It was a certainty they would be up again.

We had not long to wait. I spotted the specks in the distance and watched them grow into variously colored Albatrosses. I knew Jeremy and the other pilot would have two-seaters to keep them busy soon. In fact, his blue Fokker stood out against the torn brown landscape. I watched it maneuver and could tell he was attacking. I knew what came next. It was like listening to a recording on the squadron gramophone. As if on cue, the Fritzes began to dive on the action below. Wellington, six other SEs, and I began to dive in turn. I noticed a blue nosed Albatross seemingly hesitate before diving, so I also stayed high to keep an eye on him. At least five hundred yards apart, we slowly circled to the left, just watching. I looked down on the action below and heard an engine revving. The blue Albatros was rolling in an effort to attack me. I countered with a loop to go above him. After a brief scuffle, no shots fired, we settled back into the counterclockwise circle. The Albatross tried again to roll across the divide. I countered with a very tight right turn, hoping to catch him before he was ready to fire. I almost got him, but he was not . . . quite . . . in my sights. Bugger. I dove and turned, hoping to loop up again, but he somehow got a bead on me and walked a double line of bullet holes through my port wings, just outboard of the fuselage. Whew! I pulled the sharpest right turn I could and found him. He was diving away. I got on his tail, but he was at least one hundred fifty yards ahead. Giving my Clerget everything I could, I still could not catch him. I marveled at how fast he was diving his Albatross—they were notorious for coming apart in such a dive. I followed, hoping to watch his wings separate, but they never did. First he, then I dove into the melee below, not unlike the one the day before. While I did fire a number of bursts at targets of opportunity, I never found my blue-nosed foe in front of me. I did see him fire a burst at Jeremy, but I was too busy to see if it had any effect. A few moments later I was about to fire on a Hun two-seater when I was startled by that familiar "zip-pock" sound as bullets struck behind me and then my port wings. It was "Blue Nose". He had company, though, as two SEs were converging on him, so I broke off to the right. As I traded the speed for a loop to get altitude, I heard a kind of muffled clang out in front. My power dropped precipitously and I nearly stalled. I didn't know what had just happened, but I knew I had to get away and put her down quickly. I dropped out and headed west with the "zip—zip—zip" of bullets all around me. I turned my head in time to watch Jeremy come seemingly out of nowhere and put a solid close range burst into an Albatross, which spiraled into the ground next to a road. Jeremy stayed above me while I nursed my wounded Camel. With no further attention from the Boche I managed to get back to our airfield.

* * * * *

CHAPTER 110

British

"Well *that* is a problem." The mechanic pulled his head out of the fuselage behind the engine.

"What's *that?*"

"You were lucky to get back, sir. Both magnetos were damaged."

"I tried all kinds of things up there, including the magneto selector. It wasn't as bad on both magnetos."

"That is why you made it back. Good guess, sir."

"You can fix it. Right?"

"Yes, sir. Eventually."

"Eventually?"

"When we get the right magnetos to replace these. We don't have 'em. We're an SE squadron. Look around. Sir."

"Good point, lad. Sorry if I sound testy."

"Forget it, sir. It was nothing. I'll see if I can scare up a pair."

"Thanks, lad. Can I get you anything from the mess? Coffee?"

"Coffee, sir. Yes, sir, always coffee."

A Camel pilot in an SE squadron. A stranger in a strange land. Stranded. Jeremy came to look in on me. "Can't fix it?"

"Not until they can get the right magnetos. Wait. Doesn't your little blue bugger—"

"Don't even think about it. You can have my whole damned SE, I don't care. But don't even look at my tripe."

"Well. Consider the question withdrawn. But I will take the SE."

"Sure. Go ahead. You can even paint Mum's—uh, . . . 'lazy eight' on the wing. If you want."

"Thanks, but the regulation SE will be sufficient. I'll look 'er over so we can get back after those Fritz buggers. You didn't see which one shot out my magnetos, did you?" "I did. Albatross. Blue nose."

"He's going to be one *kaput* Fritz when I get to him."

"Getting a little personal, are we?"

"Yeah, I suppose. He and I scrapped before he dove into the swirl below. My Camel simply could not stay with him in that dive. I didn't think the Albatross could dive like that and keep its wings. Damnedest thing . . . ."

"You've seen the shortened nose. I would not be surprised if they strengthened the wing as well. Did you notice all their lower wings were the same, regardless of the upper wing finishes? They are faster than I remember them, too. Sir, I'm quite content to stay down low and outfly them among the treetops. Speed is meaningless once the maneuvering begins, and that little Fokker can elude anything in the air—especially with that Clerget!"

"Oh, trust me—I know!"

"Yeah, I've heard. I missed a helluva show. How many did you get that day?"

"Hell, I don't remember . . . seven, was it?"

"They're still talking about it. They couldn't wait to tell me what you had done in the thing!" "It's quite the crate. I understand why you tried to fly it backwards. It's that good."

I worked over Jeremy's SE to my satisfaction. Not that it was in bad shape. It just had not been used much. As I was loading the guns one of the fitters offered to paint the SE if I wanted, but I declined. At this point, I just wanted it to fly and shoot. Bloody nice of him to offer, though. I wished I could drive into town and get boxes of cakes for the fitters and mechanics. Good chaps, all of them. Even Geoff, in his own way.

I took the SE up to shake it out in the sky and get reacquainted with the stationary engine. It didn't take long. Soon I was flying many of the maneuvers I had done in the Camel. The SE just felt heavy compared to the Camel. But one did the best one could with what was on hand. I was ready to go chase down the Fritzes. A quick check with Major Campbell showed me he, too, was ready for me to go chase down Fritzes. I found Jeremy and Wellington and they picked up a few more who were itching for a fight.

We soon took off to climb to fifteen thousand feet, unless we found something before we reached that altitude. Jeremy and Wellington stayed behind while we climbed, taking off twenty minutes later and staying low. I will give the Fritzes credit for not disappointing us. We were at about ten thousand feet when they spotted us and dove from above. I was fixated on the color blue, but I took on the first one I could get anything like a clean shot at. It had a red nose and proved to be an easy victim, spewing smoke after my first burst. It spun down and may have returned to its airfield. I did not take the time to follow him down or check on him. I moved on to another Albatross while looking for my blue-nosed adversary. He was not along on this flight. Could he have been damaged or wounded earlier? No matter. A Hun is a Hun. I will not discriminate among colors. They all look pretty good with smoke and/or flames added. I shot at whatever crossed in front of me, then went down to check on Jeremy and Welly. I watched a Boche two-seater do an impromptu landing, quickly shedding its landing gear and wings. I don't know who downed it, but it was certainly down. I would note it in my report and let the major sort it out. A moment later I watched Jeremy put several bursts into another Albatross which broke off and headed east. Incensed about the lack of the blue-nosed Albatross, I followed. I wanted to see where these Fritzes were keeping themselves, and following a potentially wounded or damaged crate was a good way to find out.

He led me directly to their airfield. They apparently shared the field with another squadron, as some of the Albatrosses were varnished natural wood. I also saw a new type of scout, a little larger than the Albatross with more squared lines and a frontal radiator. As long as I was looking around, I decided I could be shooting, so shoot I did. I flew a low pass over the flight line of the black-tailed Fritzes, locating the one with the blue nose. That one received some special attention. A man ran out onto the middle of the field and shook his fist at me. I turnedaround, gave him some dancing lessons to the tune of my overhead Lewis gun, showed him the sign of the archer, then sped home. I immediately planned the next morning's flight.

* * * * *

CHAPTER III

British

The plan was for every available pilot to take off with whatever bombs they could carry and follow me to the Fritzes' aerodrome. I marked it on a map so they knew where to find it in the event I didn't make it there. I suggested staggered altitudes while crossing the lines, then under one thousand feet while sprinting to the target. Once there, the directions were simple: bomb, strafe, and repeat. Jeremy would bring up the rear in his Fokker in case any of the Fritzes tried to take off.

The flight started as planned. Predictably, one of the geared Hisso SEs acted up and the pilot dropped out. The rest of us continued on. Jeremy stayed at treetop level and could not resist tossing a couple grenades into the trenches. I led the procession over the Fritzes' field. It was about a quarter hour after sunrise and the ground appeared to be striped from the long shadows. The squadron's Albatrosses were lined up with predictable German precision. I could not help but give the two finger archer "salute" with one hand while flying and shooting with the other. I dropped my bombs near fuel carts, hoping for maximum damage, and fired bursts at the 'planes with their engines running. I watched what appeared to be the same man shaking his fist at me as he ran to the blue-nosed Albatros. He leapt into the cockpit and seemed to roll away entirely too soon. He was looney if he expected to fly combat without being strapped in. Wellington saw the attempted takeoff and dove on the Albatross to put some Vickers rounds through its tail. The pilot never looked back, such was his fixation on me. Jeremy tried to engage him but he simply flew away from the slower triplane.

Meanwhile I had climbed to circle the field and go in again. I found another Albatross trying to taxi away and take off, but I dispelled any heroic illusions by ruining the radiator and possibly hitting the pilot. The 'plane rolled left of center and lost momentum, stopping just out of the way of further takeoffs. Another valiant soul got off the ground but was in no position to deal with a triplane already in the air. Jeremy made short work of putting him back on the ground just past the airfield's boundary. I watched the pilot do a ground loop as he avoided a pair of horses in their pasture.

After another go-around, I fired a red flare above the middle of the field, beckoning the lads to come home. We climbed out, Wellington lingering just a moment to assess damage for the report. After Welly did not join us flying west, I circled back to see if I could find him. Find him I did. He was being engaged by the blue-nosed Albatross. I dove in on the pair and walked a line of holes up the Hun's port wings. The sun reflected off his goggles as he looked up at me. They weren't even over the pilot's eyes. I shot another burst toward him as Welly made a break to get away. After the slightest hesitation the Hun gave chase. In a minute he was on Welly's tail, firing quick bursts. I picked up a little altitude and did a shallow dive, but as I fired the Hun turned away to port. After a few maneuvers we ended up looking at one another across the familiar circle. It seemed his modified Albatros was faster than my SE, but the SE was a little more agile. The agility was the key, as he had not been strapped in. If I could keep him maneuvering I could keep him unsteady in the seat. So I did a half-loop, half-roll. He added power and did a climbing turn. I dove under his path, loosing a few rounds from my Lewis gun, then pulled up into a full loop. As I finished I found him on my tail, so I looped again. This time he started up after me, but cut power and stalled. As I came down I found him in front of me, so I fired a burst from both guns. He pulled up and seemed to "hop" over the bullets' path. I saw him stay up as the Albatross settled. He was indeed not buckled in. I pulled up into another half-loop, half-roll and he climbed toward me. Another loop. He got on my tail and began to fire. Another loop. This time he followed me, up and over. I went to full throttle and did a large loop, nearly stalling at the top. He followed me yet again, and then I found myself looking at the most unbelievable sight. Over my shoulder I saw the Albatross flying inverted with the pilot hanging out of the 'plane.

I don't consider myself a cruel person by nature. Live and let live. Respect others, all that. At the same time I wanted to win this damned war and move along with what appeared to be a fairly promising life. Finding Clara, the nurse who had saved me, literally life and limb, and falling madly in love with her had made me supremely happy. Learning I was to be a beneficiary of the Trafford fortune out of gratitude for helping their son had stunned me, but I got used to the idea that I could soon be in my own painting studio. Jeremy was a fine chap in his own right, and I looked forward to dealings with him after the war, perhaps involving our common passion, flying. One more dead Boche would bring me one step closer to ending the war, at least in my mind. I watched as his arms were still in the cockpit and I realized he was clinging to the control stick. I had to admire the sturdy construction. Then he began to move. I watched an arm drop, then stab out at the cockpit rim. He caught the rim with one hand, just above his seat, then transferred the other hand. I circled and watched the drama play out. What else could I do? Shoot him and end the struggle? I suppose watching could be considered cruel, but I was understandably curious.

The Hun, facing rearward, began to swing his legs. His movement caused the tail to come down, come down, come down a little more, until he managed to wrap his legs about the rear fuselage. The fuselage was approaching vertical, but the 'plane appeared to hang in the air. I saw a chance for the poor bugger and decided I could not just let him die. If not for the uniform, we could be friends. It was possible. He was also a flyer. I approached the curious aerial ornament, slowing as I did, my tail starting to droop beneath me. He stared, incredulous, wide-eyed. I waved, pointed at my port wingtip, and held my left hand level. Then grabbed the stick with the left hand and showed him the right hand with two fingers where the left hand had been. Still wide eyed, he nodded. I slipped the SE's port lower wing tip toward him. Closer, closer I drew. I placed the tip beneath him. Holding onto the cockpit, he reached out a leg and made contact. He closed his eyes tight for an instant, then opened them and reached for a strut. I pushed the stick to starboard to compensate for the weight. He managed to grab the front port strut and follow with his other hand, letting go of his Albatross. My left wing dropped somewhat, but increased pressure to starboard brought me close to level. I opened the throttle and pushed the SE into a shallow dive in order to get out from under the now pilotless Albatross, which stalled and fell off toward me, as if trying to retrieve its pilot. It was close, but we were now free as it fell away. I pointed at the rigging wires and pantomimed grabbing them, then patted the side of the fuselage. Still wide-eyed and incredulous, he gave me an exaggerated nod. He transferred his weight inside the strut and began to walk on the rear wing spar while holding the rigging wires until he encountered the propeller slipstream. Losing his leather helmet, he backed out of the turbulence, looked at me, and nodded. I gave him a thumbs-up and proceeded over the lines. I set down at the closest airfield I could find and did so as gently as I could. My new Boche best friend held on tight and kept his position on my wing. When someone slapped a ladder against the side of the SE he leapt from the wing to the ladder, climbed it, grabbed my head and kissed me repeatedly. *"Freund, mein freund! Danke schön, mein kamerad! Danke schön!"*

Two men grabbed the Hun and threw him to the ground. One yelled, "Who the hell are you?"

"Wait, wait! Go easy—he's had a rough start to his day already!"

"Alright, mate, then who the hell are *you?*"

"Lef-tenant Noble-Brown—on temporary assignment to Major Campbell's squadron."

"Oh, with the blue triplane?"

"Aye. This chap is in no condition to give you any trouble. We interrupted his morning coffee by shooting up his aerodrome. He hopped into his crate, an Albatross with a pretty cobalt blue nose, and took off to defend his field."

"Okay, but how did you end up with him?"

"Well, he is brave but a bit foolish. He didn't have anyone buckle him in. He just took off, shot at my mate, then got into it with me. I saw he wasn't strapped in and got him to do a slow loop. He started to fall out of his 'plane, but held onto the stick. I slowed to watch, and he was trying so hard I couldn't just let him die. It was too much like being on fire. I slowed to about stall and offered him my wingtip—and here he is."

"But sir, he could have taken you with him!"

"Aye, but he didn't. Call me soft, but he went from Hun to fellow flyer in a very bad situation."

"I'll say. *Jesus*—Kent, do you smell this poor devil?"

"Smells like shit to me!" Another sniff. "Schnitzel?"

"Mein kamerad! Danke schön! Danke!"

I had to laugh. "Lads, I've been there!"

All the commotion caught the attention of the squadron CO, who came out to look things over. Iintroduced myself and explained the situation.

"Lef-tenant, I think you are crazier than the Hun. You took a real risk up there. I just heard from a balloon unit. They described what you did. That's confirmation for your kill. Congratulations."

"Thanks, I suppose, but let's call it a victory. I didn't kill anyone."

"Fair enough. We'll take him from here."

"Sir, I beg to differ. Could we clean him up and take him to Campbell's airfield? I would like him to meet the chaps. He is one of the Fritzes. We have spent a lot of time and effort to hunt them down. And now I have one of them."

The Hun, my new best friend, stuck his thumb in his chest and proclaimed, *"Ja, der Fritzen. Ich bin der führer."* Then he extended his hand toward me. *"Danke, mein freund!"*

"Fair enough, Lef-tenant. But I am sending guards with you. He will be a valuable asset."

"Aye. We will start the interrogation with some scotch whiskey."

"Javohl! Whiskey!"

"Clean this dirty Boche and get a lorry ready. Lef-tenant, we will donate the first bottle of the interrogation. Well done."

Word of my aerial rescue spread quickly. It helped that someone on board the balloon had a motion picture camera on board and managed to film the incident—even if the images were so grainy one could barely make out what was happening. My new friend was a hit with Major Campbell's squadron. He tied on a good one and was fairly helpful in and among his repeated shouts to thank me. It seemed he would not let me out of his sight. When the time came for him to leave, I told him directly and through an interpreter to look me up after the war.

Not having a permanent address, I told him, "Trafford Hats", put my hand on my head like a skull cap, and repeated, "Trafford Hats. *Ich bin* Noble-Brown." He hugged me, kissed both cheeks, and mussed up my hair. *"Kamerad!"* He was led off to sober up and face more interrogation before being placed in a POW camp. Perhaps I would hear from *Herr* Wilhelm Maier after the war.

* * * * *

CHAPTER 112

British

"Lef-tenant!" "Aye?"

"You missed the early patrol."

"I didn't feel like flapping my arms—and I don't have an aeroplane. And do you have to shout?"

"Major Campbell would like to see you—if that will fit into your schedule. And you still owe me that photograph you promised."

"Geoff, I didn't forget your damned photograph. Sorry, mate, there's a war on. My word is good, don't worry. Thanks for the word about the major."

A short while later, I think, I pushed my swollen head through the major's door. "You wanted to see me, sir?"

"Yes. Please, sit down. Tea?"

"That would be wonderful, sir."

"The pot, cups, and tea are over there. Help yourself."

"Aye, sir. Thanks."

"Lef-tenant, you are going back to HE."

"Not without magnetos I'm not."

"You may wait for the magnetos. Then off you go. For the moment, you will be assigned to the school you left to come here. But you are on indefinite leave."

"Leave, sir? Am I being punished?"

"Quite the opposite. You are to make appearances at War Bond rallies. Fly your Camel or your SE. Do some stunts. Talk to the people about the war effort and encourage them to buy bonds."

"That possibility had been mentioned. But just me?"

"Did anyone help you rescue that Boche bloke?"

"Willi? No, sir."

"There you are, then."

"You miss my point, sir. They might turn out to see some bloke toss his crate around, sure. But what if we added some drama?"

"And just what 'drama' would you add?"

"Jeremy. And his triplane. Think of it. Put crosses on it, like it was, and we chase each other around the sky for a while, both flying stunts. Unfortunately, he would always have to lose."

"That part won't sit well with him, I know. But it's a good idea. I would hate to lose a flyer like that, though."

"Understood, sir. But there are others. Wellington, for one."

"Yes, he has progressed farther than I ever thought he would. Funny, he has his sights set on you—scoring more victories, you know."

"However many that is, I don't know."

"You added your 'kamerad' recently. That could have been Wellington's."

"Aye. But I'm so happy I was able to do what I did. I have a friend—for life."

"I have no doubt you will see him again once the war is behind us. Whenever that will be."

"Aye. Whenever indeed. The bloody Huns are cleaning our clocks. But they no longer have the Fritzes to help them. They would be hard pressed to assemble a flight after what we did that morning."

"I'm still sorting out the reports to see who shot what. I get the impression you wrought some measure of havoc on them. Well done."

* * * * *

CHAPTER 113

British

So it looked like I was out of the war. Or at least the shooting part. I was to participate in the public relations and fundraising necessary to pay for the war. Play nice for the home crowd and hope they lend the government their hard-earned money. Funny. I thought I would go out in some blaze of glory. I suppose I did, what with the aerial rescue and all. I would have to create that blaze of glory if they released Jeremy and his blue Fokker. I suppose they would have to get him a spiked helmet and maybe an exaggerated stage mustache so he "looked German". Huh. I would be the fair-haired lad, fighting for king and country .

In the mean time I would be able to see Clara, the love of my life. I really missed everything about her, from her comforting voice to her smile to her flirtatious ways. Even her scent. I was ready to go find and install those magnetos myself if it would get me close to Clara just a little sooner. Yes, I was more than ready to leave the killing behind. I certainly hoped I did see Willi after the war. I had said I would rather be sharing a cafe table with an "enemy" pilot than shooting at one. I would likely have my chance.

I decided to return Geoff's visit. He had been around awhile and likely knew where to scrounge the magnetos I needed. "Geoff! I'm sorry if I was perhaps a little short earlier. I was—"

"What do you want? Sir. I'm still patching the shot up buses from yesterday."

"I would be glad to help."

"Uh-huh. What do you want? Sir."

"Magnetos. You probably know where to find them. I can get a lorry and we can go procure what we need."

"What *you* need. Magnetos don't patch bullet holes."

"No, but I do. I'll help patch now and we go get magnetos later. I promise I won't ask about putting little black crosses on the patches."

"Well, good morning, sir! I couldn't be happier that you stopped by. Why, yes, I would be happy to go galavanting about the war-torn countryside looking for magnetos. You may start on the 'W' SE. I think the bastard flew through every tracer trail he could find just to give me something to do. Bugger! I think I liked him more when he got shot down."

"Now, Geoff, he has matured into a wonderfully talented flyer and a crack shot."

"Thanks to *me!* I have patched every surface on his bloody crate, most of them more than a few times. What does he do? Take it out and get it shot up again. Don't they teach the Germans to *shoot?*"

"I see I shall have to up the ante after the war. A photograph of my Clara *and* a painting of an old acquaintance I shall never forget."

"The painting doesn't sound too promising."

"I'll show you why I'll never forget her, if you understand my meaning. Visualize, Geoff, visualize."

"Oh. *Oh!* Right, mate! You're on! Sir! I'll be right there to help with 'W'."

"No hurry, Geoff."

"Ya know, sir, those magnetos are a bugger to get to."

"You help get them, I will do the swap. I understand the workload you have."

"You're a swell guy, Lef-tenant. You must really want to get in front of Boche guns again."

"Quite the opposite, I'm afraid. My war is over—at least the part where every Fritz and Heinrich has a shot at me. That's what the major wanted to see me about. I am to participate in the War Bond drive. Toss the Camel around a bit, say 'allo, and ask them to buy bonds."

"Congratulations on the promotion, sir! We will miss you here. But I will find you after the war." "I sincerely hope you do. I'll make it easy and write down where to contact me. Don't lose it. Keep it with that tattered old clipping you carry around. Speaking of after the war, what will you do?"

"I don't know. I could work on motor-cars or aeroplanes, I suppose, but I would like to become a photographer."

"Have you worked with cameras?"

"I've had some training through the RFC—well, now the RAF. It's a start. I have money put away. Perhaps I can afford the equipment to expose frames and develop the images. I will need to learn more, but that is something of a dream, I guess."

"It's good you have a way to sustain yourself while you investigate your options in any case."

I had Major Campbell telephoning other squadrons in search of magnetos. He managed to find an aerodrome with four of them on hand and no need for them. I borrowed a lorry and obtained them myself so Geoff would have more time to patch bullet holes. The magnetos were tricky to get to, going into the fuselage behind the firewall, but the changeover was straightforward. I checked my work and put things back together. I was ready to go up and see how I did.

Geoff took a moment to roll the Camel onto the flight line. He chocked the wheels while I fueled her, waited while I pulled the prop through, then pulled it when I activated the magnetos. She fired right away and sounded great. I waited a few moments for the temperature to start coming up, then waved the clocks away. As the Germans almost never came behind our lines I didn't bother with ammunition. I decided that since my shooting war was over I would put on a demonstration for all who cared to notice. Back and forth I went, into and away from the wind, doing various maneuvers and combinations. A crowd formed on the airfield below, and others stopped what they were doing to watch a fool go out of his mind relieving boredom. It was incredibly fun after several days without my Camel. I just did what came to mind and threw the thing across the sky.

Wouldn't you know I picked the exceptional day. By exceptional I meant that I was joined by two German scouts, an Albatross and a Pfalz. The problem was that they were shooting at me and I could not shoot back. I thought they were from *der Fritzen* because the Albatross had a shortened nose. It had a black fuselage and tricolor tailplane. The Pfalz was mostly grey-silver, typical of the type. The Albatross was fast, but neither could keep with me in a turn. So I kept turning. I set up the usual circle with the Albatros, watching how the pilot dealt with the circumstances. I kept an eye on the Pfalz, as it kept trying to sneak up on me. I thought I could use their various tactics against them, and soon enough the Albatross tried to power up and across the circle, diving at me and trying to lead me with his guns. At about the same time the Pfalz dove on me from above. I made a quick calculation and shoved the stick to port and forward. I dove away to the left, causing both Huns to correct their paths in order to put shots into me. They apparently forgot about each other, though, as I was later told it looked like the Albatross almost landed on the Pfalz' top wing. A wheel struck the wing where the struts attached outboard, and the Pfalz went inverted and dove into the ground. The Albatross was last seen flying rapidly to the east.

The Pfalz pilot was dead when someone got to him. No information to be gained there. There was, however, an "F" on the rear fuselage. Between that and the short nose on the Albatross, I knew I had dealt with the Fritzes. The pilots' quality had fallen off dramatically. If these lads were typical, the Fritzes were no longer a threat. At best they were a shadow of what they had been.

Major Campbell met me on the ground. "Geoff told me you had no ammunition with you, yet you still managed to bring one down, nearly both. How on Earth . . . ."

"I studied their tactics and used them to organize a get-together."

"Good thinking—but you were lucky!"

"Aye."

Well, if I could outfly two Hun scouts and bring one down without ammunition, I imagined my Camel was ready to hop the Channel. If the next morning's weather cooperated, I would be leaving France for the last time until after the war. Though I had heard any number of wonderful things about France, I couldn't say I was going to miss her. My prospects looked far better back in HE.

* * * * *

CHAPTER 114

German

It was May of 1918 and my war appeared to be over. I say "appeared to be" for one never knows. The only predictable thing is unpredictability, for circumstances could change at any time and negate whatever had happened to that point. Militarily, things looked pretty good for Germany. The army had opened offenses on several sections of the Western Front with great success. The English were being pushed back to the Channel. The French were conscripting old men and children. Both had leaders that seemed to be living in a fantasy world, insisting all was well when they had their backs to the wall. One wonders how they would define catastrophe.

Käti and Elsa were elated that I was no longer being shot at. They talked about looking for work in Schwerin, but I told them not to get too far ahead of things. If events took a turn I could be back up trading bullets with the English, French, and/or Americans. I was allowed to work with Fokker through the good graces of *der Kaiser*. I would continue to love them and see them whenever I could. I told them I was in a good position with Fokker. I would never be wealthy working for him, but he had his ear to the ground about how the war was going, as well as how the German government was reacting to it. If there was a time to get out, he would be among the first to know. After all, a failing government couldn't pay its contractors. Fokker was not a German patriot; he was a Dutch businessman.

My duties turned out to be those of a test pilot and advisor to Platz and his team of engineers. True, I was not versed in engineering lingo, but they were accustomed to interpreting "pilot talk" after working with Fokker, himself a gifted pilot. As I understood it, Fokker mostly had the ideas and Platz designed the structure to support Fokker's ideas, adjusting as needed to make them functional.

At the end of May our army launched a new offensive across the *Chemin des Dames,* to the south of where the March offensive had originated. A complete surprise, it backed the French all the way to the Marne River. Of course *der Fritzen* were part of the action, whether strafing the fleeing French troops or battling the *escadrilles* in the skies above. I kept in touch with Jakob, who lamented the lack of trained pilots and gunners. He missed Willi. He missed me. Hell, he even missed Strasser, bastard though he was. Jure was no longer with the *Staffel,* having sustained yet another serious wound. After time in hospital, Jure was permitted to rehabilitate at home with his wife and son. He would be recalled if and when he had recovered fully.

Then things began to change. Our offensive to the south was stalled and then turned. What was the difference? Americans. Army and Marine units attacked our troops on three hills, not unlike the French had tried and failed at for four years. Our commanders knew there were Americans attacking them and decided the Americans had to be beaten and shown they were no match for Germany's armed forces. Despite the German resolve the Americans forced them off the hills and refused to allow them on again. The Germans had been outfought. Another German offensive, building on the success of Operation Michael, was turned back by American troops with French assistance. The German army began a strategic withdrawal to more defensible positions, but in some quarters panic began to build. Rumor had it that one general wanted to withdraw to a stronger position and immediately sue for peace. From this point on it began to look more and more like a matter of time before Germany faced defeat. I was more than willing to continue the fight *für das Vaterland,* but at the same time I began to look for what was best for Käti, Elsa, and myself. Fokker fought the military to keep me, for which I was grateful. I had to look hard at the situation. What would a defeated Germany look like? I assumed there would be occupying forces. What about war reparations? Dividing territory among the victors? Living conditions for the German people? The state of the German economy? Many, many questions, very few answers. The only certainty was uncertainty. I was not at all happy about our prospects.

One morning Fokker asked me about money. Did I have any? I told him I had been putting away most of my pay since *der Kaiser* provided what I needed day to day. He advised me to start pulling money and contacting the German embassy in the United States, looking for investment opportunities. War bonds, other stocks and bonds dealing with day to day life. Nothing military in nature, since the war's end would create a glut of anything dealing with weaponry, ammunition, and so on. He would help me arrange wire transfers of funds.

"Model, look around you. Since the Americans have joined the British and French, things have gone poorly for Germany. To be blunt, Germany will lose the war. No ifs about it. There are too many American troops. They have managed to fight primarily as American units rather than be pissed away like the French and British have done with their own men for the last four years. Unlike their allies, the Americans have a firm grasp on reality. Germany has nothing left that can stop them. Hell, the blockade has even taken away our castor oil. Anything powered by a rotary engine, my pet triplane, your SSW, they're now useless. As you know, I've taken a promising rotary parasol design and put its wing on a D.VII. It's making a big impression with the pilots, thanks to your suggestions, and should get orders. Well, it would if the Germans had a chance. Like Germany, the design is going nowhere."

"I agree, *Herr* Fokker. What do you plan to do?"

"I am sure you have noticed my absences from time to time. I am setting up a factory in the Netherlands where I will continue building aeroplanes after the war. You are welcome to join me, if you wish. I don't see Germany as a desirable place to be by war's end. There will likely be chaos and fighting among factions and a total lack of reason. Every faction will blame another faction for the defeat. If you have anyone dear to you, you may want to advise them to get out now. I will see to it your loved one is able to stay with you—I assume you have a special woman?"

"Two."

"Two? Two women? Well!"

"It's a long story."

"But with a happy ending! Or at least a happy story thus far . . . . No matter. Bring them. Have them invest their money outside Germany also. There is no way of knowing how long the instability will last."

"*Danke schön, Herr* Fokker, I shall tell them of your generous offer of assistance."

"There is not much for you to do for the next few days. Why don't you go tell them all about my generosity. Everyone else says I'm cheap. I could use the good word."

"Are you sure?"

"I am. Go. And remember, take the Fokker!" He smiled. "Leave your beer barrel in the hangar."

"*Javohl—und danke!*"

* * * * *

CHAPTER 115

German

I sat down with Käti, Elsa, and Ernst at the tavern just after closing. Elsa had placed steins of cold beer for each of us. In hushed tones we discussed the war, its direction, how it would affect Germany, and what we would do about it. Ernst, a businessman, had opinions not unlike Fokker's. With the influx of fresh, well trained American soldiers, Germany could not win the war. There was unrest in the military, some wanting to sue for peace and others wanting to fight to the last man. It was a picture of futility. Germany's social structure would also collapse into warring factions. Ernst was already investing abroad and looking into options for his land and business holdings in Germany. He clearly was not happy about the changes coming into his life, but he was preparing to meet the challenges and move on.

I knew Käti had been putting money away. She still had the idea of adding to her cottage so the three of us could live together. I hated to break it to her, but I told her she might be better advised to sell it and move abroad. Ernst backed my opinion, suggesting the Netherlands or Great Britain—or the United States. Käti could see this all coming, but it was still unsettling.

Elsa was taken aback by all of this talk. While we all held her in high esteem, she was the least financially able of us. She listened to us discussing plans and occasionally wiped a tear from her eye. I asked what was wrong. "Gustav, what am I going to do? I can't say I have nothing, but I don't have much. I am not equipped to make these changes like all of you are."

"Elsa, you are very important to us. We will not allow you to fail. I will not allow you to fail. We love you. Listen—*Herr* Fokker is moving his operations to the Netherlands as the war is coming to a close. He has offered me continuing employment. And he said he will help provide housing for you and Käti. It likely will not be much, but you have a place to go."

"But I will be a burden. I am merely a barmaid."

"No, Elsa, you currently work as a barmaid. That is not who you are. You are no more a barmaid than I am a soldier."

"Airman," Käti quipped, breaking the tension.

"*Ja*, airman." I fought a smile and lost.

"My point is, when the war is over I will no longer wear a military uniform. I will work as a pilot and advisor for Fokker and my life will move on. I—we—will support you, Elsa, and make sure you are able to move on to what you want to be or do. Think about it. What do you want to do?"

"Fly," Elsa answered, almost under her breath.

"Fly? Did you say fly?"

"*Ja*. I want to fly." Her voice crescendoed. "Like you, Gustav, I want to fly!"

"Then I will see to it that you fly. I should be able to get *Herr* Fokker's help. Anything to put his name in the public eye."

"You *will?*"

"*Javohl!* There is no reason for you not to fly. Ernst, how soon could you spare Elsa?"

"Give me a few days, Gustav. What do you have in mind?"

"I want Elsa to join me in Schwerin. We will find something for her to do for *Herr* Fokker. And I will arrange to teach her to fly." "Consider it done. What about Käti?"

"Käti, *liebchen*, do you mind?"

"Of course not. I will stay here to help Ernst and do something with my cottage. I can always join you there, can't I?"

"*Javohl, liebchen!*"

"Then we need to move."

Elsa smiled. "We need to move, *ja*, but first we need to celebrate. Drinks, anyone?"

Ernst spoke up. "No more for me. It's late and I need to go home and rest."

Käti agreed. "Let's go home. Elsa, you are welcome, of course."

"I'll bring the chocolate cake!"

And she did.

Herr Fokker had said to take a few days, so I did. He knew to telephone the tavern to reach me. It was wonderful to spend time with Elsa and Käti. The deteriorating conditions due to four years of war and the Allied blockade were topics of conversation, as were possible avenues of escape. There was some handwringing, there was some drinking, and there was time together. Ernst gave Elsa a final work date, so she and I walked to the railway depot and I purchased her ticket to Schwerin. She fussed a little about it, but I insisted, telling her to hold her money while she could. With the war ending, the world would be cast into a period of uncertainty which would likely cause inflation and other difficulties while things worked to some level of moderation.

This left Käti in a cloud of doubt. I had no question about her feelings for me, but change was upon us and some people are simply resistant to change. They fall into a routine and hate anything to disrupt the routine. People are creatures of habit. Käti was content to stay in her village and work in Ernst's tavern. She loved her little cottage, a short walking distance from work. Maybe she did not love quite everything about working at the tavern, but it was her routine. I could see she was going to hang onto her routine to the end. Her cottage was and probably would remain perfectly habitable. But Ernst was investigating a move abroad, which would likely necessitate selling the tavern. Unrest and inflation, along with a new owner at the tavern, were likely to uproot Käti's world. Alcohol sales would likely continue, though the restaurant end could well take a dive since eating out, away from home, was a luxury, a discretionary decision. It was hard to tell. Käti was a very reasonable woman, but the approaching instability was getting to her. She was unwilling to commit just then, but she did agree to cancel plans to expand her cottage. She was trying to imagine moving to the Netherlands to be with me while I worked for Fokker. Different language, different money, no routine to follow, nearly no familiar faces, it was all very unsettling to her. Should she keep her cottage, just in case? Perhaps she could rent it. Should she sell it and have the money so she could . . . could what? She wanted to be with Elsa and me, but was that enough for her? Would she forsake that love for the hope of keeping her routine?

Käti sent Elsa to the cottage one morning with a message that *Herr* Fokker had telephoned. It took her easily a half hour to deliver the actual message, waiting until I untied her wrists and massaged them.

"Wait—where are you going? Aren't you going to continue up my arms, then massage my shoulders, back, and, well, you know . . . ."

"*Nein, mein schöne gefangen.* I must telephone *Herr* Fokker and see what he wants. He would not disturb me if it were not important. Are you coming along?"

"The tavern is not at all busy. Käti said there was no hurry."

"I could tell her you got tied up with something."

Still prone on the bed, she crossed her wrists behind her. "*Ja*, I wish you would . . . ."

I bound her hand and foot and she closed her eyes and smiled. I surprised her with a gag, which she initially fought. As I walked toward the door I slapped her bottom sharply. She became a little more animated when I suggested leaving the door unlocked. Such pretty eyes.

It turned out that *Herr* Fokker's call was not so important. He wanted to go over some fine points on the monoplane prototypes we had both flown. Then he asked if I was about ready to leave my little love nest and come back to work. I offered to fly back the next morning, first thing. "Make it the day after, Model. It is unlikely the Germans are going to buy anything but the rotary parasol. They have any number of the little rotary engines in warehouses. They simply have no castor oil to keep them running. But it's not my job to tell the customer what they want. I'll just build what they order and hope they can pay for it. There is no hurry coming back other than to continue development of the V-8 and inline engined parasols. Those have potential, whether for Germany's war or for anyone else once the war ends."

"I will see you soon, then, *mein Herr*."

"*Wiedersehen.*"

Käti asked me if I wanted to stay for lunch. I told her I was in the middle of something at the cottage.

"I'm sure of that. Well, come back when you tie things up. We can have lunch together. And if you play your cards right, you could be in the middle of something this afternoon."

"I may hold you to that, *liebchen*. In fact, let me hold you." We hugged. "I'll be back soon."

"Bring Elsa. She can cover for me while you and I eat."

* * * * *

Chapter 116

German

Fokker was annoyed. His V-8 parasol prototype looked fabulous. The old adage was, "If it looks right, it will fly right." This number should have been tearing up the skies, but it just didn't climb. The inline engined parasol was a better flyer overall, especially with the BMW engine. Fokker hated to invest in a project and come away empty, so he thought about what to do with the V-8 parasol. He got the idea of enclosing the pilot and engine in armor, perhaps making it a dedicated trench strafer. It didn't climb well anyway, so why not give it a job that did not require climbing? That was life at Fokker's shop. He came up with ideas and Platz took them off the paper and brought them to life, so to speak. Fokker and I would fly Platz' work and talk about it, then make suggestions for improvements. Fokker and Platz would discuss ideas and Platz would act on them. There was rarely a slow day. Well, sometimes the rainy days were a little short, at least for me. I would stay in case Fokker needed something. He would find me, ask me what I was doing there on such a poor flying day, and send me back to my quarters. Elsa grew to love rainy days.

I would have Elsa dress well so she and I could walk around town and keep an eye open for work for her. The uncertainty of the war situation was at work on the local economy. There was nothing of interest for Elsa. I took her back to Fokker's office one not so fine day. He, of course, was delighted to see her. He asked what he could do for her.

I answered for her. "*Herr* Fokker, if you have any work Elsa could do for you, she would be delighted to do it for you."

"I don't have much to offer, but I can look around. What would she like to do?"

"You may talk to me, *Herr* Fokker. I could help with clerical tasks and filing. Light duty cleaning. But what I would *like* to do is fly."

"Fly?"

"Ja, like Gustav. He has taught me on an old *Albatros,* but only basic skills."

"This is true, Model?"

"Javohl. She flies well for someone with so little experience. If you have anything we could use to continue her training, she would work for you as needed in turn."

"I am not working on any dual control aeroplanes. But I can easily get one for you to use. I'll tell you what: if you can teach her to fly such that she can do demonstrations of my products, I will absorb any expenses of her training. I know there are and have been female pilots, but they are still a relative rarity. It would be one more thing to keep people talking about Fokker and his products. I like the idea. So please excuse me while I track down a dual control machine for you two." He started to walk away, then halted and turned around. "Wait. Is this the *fräulein* with three confirmed kills?"

"Javohl!" we answered together. To this day I know I saw gilder signs in his eyes. In Elsa he suddenly saw money.

It didn't take Fokker long to find what we needed and get it to Schwerin. Lessons continued whenever I had nothing pressing to do. Elsa caught on quickly and showed great intuition. If I did something to throw her off, she recovered almost as quickly as I would have. I began to fly aerobatics, with Elsa on board. She loved it. She would squeal with joy. I had to scold her to pay attention to the controls and how I manipulated them to get the desired results. *"Ja, ja,"* she would say, then she would pout. Just a little. But she understood. I knew she would fly solo very soon. Then she and I would fly to a second, then third airfield so she could learn about and practice navigation. We already discussed the sky, clouds, wind and weather. It was all common sense to her. She was turning into a fine pilot.

Elsa'a solo came and went. It was anticlimactic. She climbed into the cockpit and I climbed the ladder to be beside her and strap her in. "What are you going to do, Gustav?" She batted her eyes at me and held her hands in front, wrists crossed.

"I am going to fasten and tighten your safety harness. We don't want you falling out of the 'plane onto some unsuspecting person, do we?"

"It depends on the person, I suppose . . . " Elsa was incorrigible. I liked that.

She started the engine, taxied, took off, flew the prescribed number of circuits, and landed. It could have been me. Or any competent pilot. That is not to demean Elsa in any way: Rather, she fit right in as a pilot. It was another step toward doing what she wanted to do. In fact, when she set *die alte frau* down and I helped her out of the cockpit, she gestured toward my D.VII. "What about yours?"

"What?"

"I want to fly it."

"So fly it."

"Really?"

"I will only tell you it does not fly like *die alte frau*."

"I believe you. When may I go?"

"Take it now. After all, you are dressed for the occasion."

I didn't have to ask her twice. She bounded out of one aeroplane and practically into the other. I helped her with the harness once again and she responded. *"Danke.* Move away."

She taxied, kicked the tail around, and pushed the throttle forward. Like *die alte frau* had moments before, my D.VII bounded into the air as if chasing Englishmen. Her circuits were faster, her turns tighter and with more bank. Seeing me drifting toward the center of the airfield, she completely surprised me by buzzing me. Very closely. I didn't think she would hit me, but pulling out of a dive so low to the ground, I was not going to stand there and chance it. I dove like an American baseball player trying to beat a throw back to first base. By now everyone was out to see the spectacle. But Elsa was not finished. While I stood up and sputtered grass out of my mouth, she went past the end of the field, turned around, and flew over again, this time performing two rolls. Fokker watched, shading his eyes with his hand, then clapped his hands together in applause. I walked over to join him. He was clearly pleased.

"Model, you have taught her well!"

"I never taught her that. I merely demonstrated with her in the other seat. She would squeal."

"Squeal while paying close attention. For first rolls, those were well done."

Elsa flew over again, this time in a gentle climb. She turned once more and approached us in a shallow dive. I shook my head, but she pulled the stick back and started into a loop. But she had not advanced the throttle far enough and the machine slowed to a halt at an awkward angle. *"Scheisse,"* I said almost under my breath. Just then, she cut the throttle, let the machine begin to slide, then she kicked the rudder to control the fall, and let it get vertical. With no extra room for error, she corrected her direction with the ailerons, and seemingly dove at the spot where she had buzzed me. That dive would have hit me, but she managed to avoid contact with the ground. She regained some altitude in another circuit of the field, then landed.

I was incredulous. I thought I heard Fokker squeal. I ran toward the taxiing D.VII.

"Have you lost your mind?"

"Of course not. I paid close attention to you when you performed your stunts. I merely did not use enough throttle for the loop I wanted. But I found my way out of it. This is a very nice machine, by the way. I can see why you like it. When can I—"

"You are completely beautiful! Climb down out of that thing while I catch my breath so I can hug you!"

"What?"

"You could easily have died just now, but you are poring over your actions so you can correct them next time up. I am shocked, horrified, stunned, amazed, wondrous, and madly in love!"

"And all I get is a hug?"

* * * * *

CHAPTER 117

German

Elsa's learning curve was such that I feared *der Kaiser* would want her to fly with a *Jagdstaffel*. I imagined all she had to do was fly protection for me and the Allies would feel the loss of aeroplanes. My, but she was protective. In the meantime it was a matter of follow the leader. I flew either Fokker's BMW powered parasol or my Siemens "beer barrel". Elsa was in my D.VII prototype. I would lead, she would follow. Whatever I did, she did. She would duplicate—or improve on—anything I did in the air. She was magnificent.

I quickly found that having Elsa follow me around was no longer effective. What else could I show her? We moved on to the next step, simulated combat. We would rotate between the D.VII, the "beer barrel", and the BMW parasol, all fine aeroplanes. Fokker had "found" some castor oil for my Siemens' rotary engine. I didn't question him about it, I merely said thanks and kept flying. Elsa and I consistently pushed each other to our limits. I wondered how the airframes held together through all the abuse. One day, in the parasol, I executed a half loop and violent half roll at the top, only to hear a "crack". I immediately throttled back, waved my arm over my head to get Elsa's attention, checked the field for traffic, and set down. Fokker, having heard the noise, met me on the flight line with one of his inspectors. The determination was that part of a plywood panel on the wing had popped out of place due to being overstressed. Fokker ordered the wing removed, disassembled, and analyzed for any further damage. There was none. Fokker was relieved.

"Model, it seems that if there is a problem, you or your friend will find it. The two of you are wonderful in the air. It could be worked into a routine. People would pay money to watch you. I would pay to watch you, and I can get around up there myself. You may have found something to do after the war, hopefully flying my products while still under my employment.

"*Danke schön, Herr Fokker.* Perhaps you should put Elsa on the payroll."

"My thoughts exactly. Elsa is a wonderful talent and she is becoming well versed in aeroplanes and how they operate. While she lacks the technical terminology, she is very expressive so we can determine any problem she spots. She will acquire the terminology as she spends time with it."

"Elsa needs an aeroplane of her own. People recognize my 'plane with *die gasmaske.* She is every bit the flyer I am, so she deserves recognition as well."

"Good point. I will get a production D.VII and have a BMW engine installed in it for her."

"Why not get a D.VII F with the BMW already installed?"

"Appearances, dear Model. Pilots covet the D.VII F. Imagine them learning I have held one back from combat so a civilian woman could fly it. They would storm the factory with torches and pitchforks. I'll get a Daimler Mercedes powered unit and make the switch here."

"I understand. Morale is bad enough in *der Jagdstaffeln.*"

"Do you think the mechanic who painted yours could paint hers? He does nice work."

"If he is still there it should be no problem. He is quite creative and talented enough to express what he comes up with. If you wish, I could telephone Jakob and ask."

"Please do. Come with me as I request the D.VII, then talk to Jakob. We will get the wheels turning."

Fokker was not one to wait around. He pounced on the idea, ordering a D.VII brought over from the factory. Learning there was one with an apparent bad engine, he proclaimed it to be perfect. That day the D.VII was brought over to the airfield and mechanics performed the engine swap, leaving the Daimler Mercedes engine for the Daimler engineers to pore over. The exchange complete, the wings were attached and Elsa's D.VII was ready for her to fly.

I telephoned and found Jakob in his office doing the never-ending paperwork and filing. We caught up a bit and he assured me the artist would be thrilled to paint Elsa's new D.VII. "He is busy right this moment, as we have not had the best of times lately. If only we could get thoroughly trained pilots. The replacements don't seem to know much more than basics. They come back all shot up. If they come back at all. Gustav, just make sure you have a full load of ammunition when you fly here. You will need it. I only hope we are still at this aerodrome when you arrive."

"*Danke schön*, Jakob. Perhaps we will shoot a few out of your way when we come."

"That would be a pleasant turn of events."

I replaced the receiver and Fokker reached for it again, summoning Elsa to his office. She arrived promptly and Fokker addressed her. "Elsa, you have made stellar progress learning to fly. Model—your Gustav—suggested that you should have your own aeroplane to continue with. I agreed. It is waiting for you outside."

Elsa's eyes grew wide and she began to tremble. "*Nein!* My own Fokker? Gustav! My own Fokker!" I placed a hand on her shoulder and guided her toward the door. We stepped outside and her D.VII was parked almost wingtip to wingtip with mine. Being from the latest production run, hers differed from mine. It was covered completely in the preprinted camouflage fabric with dark green metal panels in front. There were numerous louvers in the nose panels to vent excess engine heat. Elsa was beside herself. "When may I fly it?"

"Now. Or whenever you can get into your flying gear."

Elsa carried a nearby ladder to the side of her 'plane, placed it, and climbed in, skirt and all, calling, "Gustav! Come help fasten me in!"

I obliged, grabbing a nearby pair of goggles. "Here—at least protect your eyes."

"*Danke.* Now move."

She cranked the magneto, the BMW came to life, and a moment later Elsa taxied away. At the end of the field she kicked her tail around and pushed the throttle forward at the same time. Without hesitation the Fokker accelerated, picked up its tail and lifted off the ground. I smiled as Elsa passed by, her braided red hair trailing in the slipstream. "There," I thought, "is what the artist can paint on her aeroplane." I made a note of it. It was perfect. Elsa almost always kept her long red hair in a loose braid.

The demonstration was brief. She made her first pass doing two completely flawless rolls. After a brief stretch of straight and level, she snapped a third roll. Her next two passes were climbing as she waved at us below. Then she did a shallow dive into a huge, beautifully executed loop. On her return pass she surprised everyone, passing overhead at about forty miles per hour, barely sustaining flight. It was as if she were hanging on the propeller and could fall at any moment. At the end of the field she pushed the throttle forward, regained normal flying attitude, turned around and landed. I met her with the ladder and climbed to help her with the harness. As soon as she was free, she stood, hugged me, and practically swung on my neck, sliding down to the ladder. As I stepped off the ladder she grasped my arm with both hers. "Gustav, are you busy now?" she asked in a stage whisper.

"*Nein . . .*"

"Then come with me."

"Are you—"

"*Ja!* Come with me! I cannot wait!"

With my hand in hers, she marched off the airfield, pausing long enough to kiss *Herr* Fokker on the cheek and say, "*Danke schön!*" She pulled me along to my quarters, closed and locked the door behind us, hugged me tight, and kissed me all over my face. "You are the most wonderful man *ever.*" We were busy for a while.

* * * * *

CHAPTER 118

German

When I got the chance, I asked *Herr* Fokker when we could have Elsa's D.VII painted. He listed a few days' worth of projects he needed my input on, then said once these were resolved we were free to take a few days and go. We could even stop by and visit with Ernst and Käti if the painting did not take too long.

After my tasks were completed, Elsa and I prepared to leave. She looked perplexed.

"What is the matter?"

"How am I to take anything with me? There is no room!"

"There is a little room behind the seat, but you must be careful not to foul the control wires."

"How many outfits is that?"

"I don't normally measure things in 'outfits', but I would guess maybe one or two."

"I could stuff a few things into my flying coat."

"*Ja*, but you need to be able to maneuver the 'plane."

"That is not much."

"Elsa, it's a warplane. It carries you, fuel, and ammunition, just as it was designed to do. But *Herr* Fokker has shown me what he intends to build after the war. He feels flying will become an important mode of transportation, like the railway. When people travel, they take things with them. So Fokker's traveling aeroplanes will have dedicated areas for things people take along—a cargo hold. But that does not solve your current dilemma."

"You are correct, Gustav, we are at war. There are sacrifices to be made. Hmph." With that she assembled a small bag with a carry strap to hang over the seat and a smaller one to tuck into her flying coat. "We can go now." I picked up my one minimal bag and we walked to our aeroplanes.

"You know where we are going," I said as she pulled on her boots.

"*Ja.* I follow *mein* Gustav." She smiled.

"Watch the sky in every direction. Never stop looking. We are flying into a combat area. There could be English Sopwiths."

"Don't worry. I will protect *mein* Gustav."

"You know how—"

"—to *shoot? Javohl!*" There was something sinister in her expression. I felt a measure of reassurance. And a chill.

Elsa climbed into her D.VII. I climbed up to fasten her harness. As I reached in front of her she pulled my face toward hers and kissed me, holding me there for a few long seconds. The ground personnel howled. As she released me, she whispered, *"Ich liebe dich, mein* Gustav."

Without hesitation I responded, *"Ich liebe dich, mein* Elsa." She kissed me again. Fortunately she was wearing no lipstick. "Let us *fly, mein* Gustav!"

I was strapped in presently and we departed. Once we reached seven thousand feet or so she rocked her wings at me and I responded in kind. We flew on side by side, enjoying a splendid summer day. As we approached the front I waved, touched my head, and made a circling motion over my head, then swiveled my head up, down, and around. Elsa circled her hand over her head and mimicked my head motion. Oddly, she gained a little altitude and drifted to a position behind me and to the side, just the position I was going to take relative to her. No matter, as long as we were both watching the sky.

About fifteen minutes later a red flare arced out in front of me and to the side. I looked over my shoulder. Elsa held up three fingers and pointed up. Straining my eyes, I saw nothing. I heard Elsa's engine rev harder and watched her climb away. I pushed my throttle, dove briefly, then zoomed up to follow her, still seeing nothing. Elsa continued to climb and point toward the sun. At around ten thousand feet I finally saw what she was pointing at, three specks. As the specks approached they took the form of SE type Sopwiths. They were not meeting us for tea. At one point I watched as Elsa dropped her tail and turned about ninety degrees to the left. She fired her guns and I shook my head at the overanxious shooting. Until one of the Sopwiths grew a light trail of smoke and turned away to the west. Then the menacing specks numbered two. I shook my head again, this time in amazement. She could not possibly be so good.

I decided to take charge and meet the *Engländern* straight on. I had to protect Elsa . . . who, like me, was climbing toward the Sopwiths at full throttle. Soon enough we were exchanging lead greetings and weaving a web of tracer trails. We passed one another in close proximity. Elsa cut her throttle way back, kicked her rudder, pushed the throttle forward again, and gave chase to the slightly closer enemy. I pulled my stick back and watched as she shot the pilot in the head and shoulder. His SE no longer maneuvered. It just dropped to the ground, nearly two miles below. After following it down with my eyes and shaking my head in amazement, I started toward the other SE type. I was just in time for the show. The Sopwith pulled a rather sudden climbing turn. Almost anticipating the turn, Elsa cut her throttle, pulled on the stick, and fired her guns ahead of the Englishman, who obligingly flew through her stream of bullets. A small explosion erupted, leaving the English bus ablaze. I watched as the pilot rolled his SE upside down and seemed to spring out of the burning cockpit. He had quickly chosen to escape the horror of the flames. But then, face down, he held his arms near his sides and drifted toward a wingtip, which he grabbed. Oddly, he was apparently going to ride his flaming aeroplane to the ground. His odds were better than tumbling through space, though I doubt they were much better. Interesting.

Elsa was by my side. She rocked her wings, waved, and made a forward scooping motion with her palm up as if to say, "After you." I rocked my wings in turn, waved, and turned toward my old aerodrome.

Upon arrival I got out of my Fokker and ran over to Elsa. "That was some show!"

"What?"

"You dispatched three Englanders in what, ten minutes?"

"Closer to five."

"You could have been killed."

"*Ja,* not unlike you. But if I had done nothing, then what? And please don't tell me about your experience. The bullets don't know or care."

"You have me there. But the first one? I would never fire at such a distance."

"I understand. But I had to try."

"You were lucky."

"*Ja,* perhaps . . . ."

"So, Gustav," It was Jakob. "Two more down with one damaged? I received a telephone message from someone in the rear area who recognized the *jasta* tail stripes."

"*Nein.* I shot at a couple SE type Sopwiths, that's all."

"Well, the observer saw—"

"Saw Elsa in action."

"Elsa?"

"*Javohl.* All Elsa."

"They could have hurt *mein* Gustav!"

"My friend, you have one incredible *fräulein!*"

"I agree. Could I fill out my report in the mess over something warm?"

"Of course. I will be with you as soon as I have your artist friend look over your Fokkers and plan what to paint on hers."

"What would you like, Elsa?"

"I don't know. I am simply thrilled to have it."

"I have an idea." I held up Elsa's hair, typically in a loose braid. How about painting her braided hair along the deck behind the cockpit?"

"Gustav—I love it!"

"And four upright hashes, crossed by a fifth, to show her five victories."

"I like that, Gustav. Elsa?"

"If you wish. That would be okay."

"What else would you like? Favorite color or number?"

"Names. I want 'Käti' under the cockpit on the right. And under the left I want '*mein* Gustav'."

"'Käti' and 'Gustav'."

"Nein. 'Käti' und 'mein Gustav'. 'Mein Gustav'."

"Javohl. I'm sorry I mistook you."

"Oh! 'Mila'. I want 'Mila' somewhere I can always see when I am flying."

"'Mila'?," Jakob asked.

"Meine tochter."

"I didn't know you—"

"She doesn't, Jakob. Not any more." Elsa wiped away a tear and I gave Jakob a look intended to say, "Drop it". He understood.

"I will meet you two in the mess as soon as I give the artist the information. I'll have someone paint the English dartboard on any patches."

"Only Elsa's, if she wants them."

"Ja! How cute! I want them!"

"There you are, Jakob my friend."

Elsa and I walked into the mess and everyone stood up. Someone called, "Two more for *Herr* Model!"

"Nein, nein! Two more for *Elsa!* Plus one damaged."

Silence.

The same person then responded, "Two for Elsa!"

Everyone else cheered. I had to add, "Two *more* for Elsa!"

Someone asked, "Two *more?*"

"Ja! Now she has *five!*"

"Three—no, *five* cheers for Elsa!" The mess erupted in cheers. Elsa blushed.

Another asked, "How did you do it, Elsa?"

"They could have hurt *mein* Gustav!"

I had to say it. "Never argue with a woman holding a machine gun!"

More cheers.

* * * * *

CHAPTER 119

German

Elsa took advantage of the down time and lay down for a nap. I took advantage of Elsa's nap. I visited with the mechanic who was to paint the new Fokker. He was very happy with the assignment.

"Mein Herr, I almost wish there were more bullet holes to patch. She likes the idea of the English dartboards? Almost no one wants them here."

"Make up a few extra 'patches' if you want. She will never know."

"Good idea!"

"Have you seen Elsa? Do you know what her hair looks like?"

"Don't worry. I have seen her, *mein Herr.* I will capture her hair. And the names. 'Käti' by the cockpit on the right, and '*mein* Gustav' on the left? '*Mein Gustav'?"*

'That's what she wants. She calls me that all the time."

"And 'Mila' somewhere she can see it while flying? How about the center of the top wing trailing edge, around the cutout?"

"Perfect! Directly in front of her eyes. She will love it. When do you think it will be ready?"

"Tomorrow, midday, *mein Herr."*

I pulled out of my bag a bottle of schnapps. "Will this be sufficient?"

"Javohl! I would do it for nothing, but *danke schön!"*

"For nothing? Nonsense. You deserve to be compensated for your talent. I cannot wait to see what you do after the war."

"With any luck, *mein Herr . . ."*

"Keep in touch with me. I will be working for Fokker after the war. You can reach me through his factory. I will do what I can, even if it is only doing what you do now, fix aeroplanes."

"Something is better than nothing. Will he be in Schwerin?"

"For now. I will leave it at that. But find him and you will find me."

"*Danke, Herr* Model." He shook my hand. "Or should I say '*mein* Gustav'?"

"Please don't. Gustav will be fine."

"Call me Art. Art Kunst." We shook hands. "I will see you and Elsa tomorrow."

The next morning a well rested Elsa was anxious. "Is it ready yet?"

"*Nein*. Midday."

"I have to wait?"

"We have no choice. Art is a busy man with things to do. He is making time for you. He's doing the best he can while doing a good job. You have seen his work. He is very talented."

Elsa pouted, possibly the cutest thing I have ever seen. "I know, I know. I just can't wait to see it."

"We could find something to do while we wait."

"You don't mean—"

"*Ja*, borrow a *Hanna* and see the front."

"Oh. I thought you meant . . ."

"Oh . . . *nein*. Too much noise."

"But you know how to take care of that . . . ."

"Elsa, you are incorrigible. And impossi—" Elsa stifled me with her lips, a very effective technique. She—and her lips—were very persuasive. She got her way. Apparently only one person heard a thump and asked through the door if I was okay. I assured them I was and thanked them for asking. Elsa laughed. Or tried to.

Still having time to pass, I asked Jakob if he needed an extra Hanna on a strafing run. While he was never going to turn down experienced help, he was concerned about Elsa. I assured him there was no need for the concern. Elsa would love it and take to the challenge. He sighed and assented. I retrieved Elsa and our flying gear and met Jakob by the Hanna. He had two ladders placed by the two cockpits. He was surprised to see Elsa climb into the front cockpit. I heard him say under his breath, "My dear, this will be a challenge." But he climbed the ladder and helped strap her in. Meanwhile, I sat on the rear deck to pull on my bulky flying boots, then slid into the rear cockpit. I checked for grenades and ammunition, then patted Elsa on the shoulder. She went through the starting sequence, taxied, and took off. We followed two other two-seaters toward the front. Elsa did what they did, but closer to the ground, firing short bursts into the trenches. I did the same from the rear and tossed grenades as well.

To make things more interesting, I saw three SE type Sopwiths joining us from the direction of the sun. I touched Elsa's shoulder and shouted, *"Drei!"* Without hesitation she pushed the throttle all the way forward and climbed out of the trenches to meet and greet our company.

She was very good. The other two aeroplanes of our patrol were also climbing. Shots were exchanged and swirling about commenced. One of our aeroplanes developed a smoke trail and broke away to run for the aerodrome. An SE type followed after it. Elsa saw that and broke away from her fight to give chase. The SE she had been fighting also followed us. He quickly got on our tail and went underneath, where I could not shoot at him. I hit Elsa's shoulder and swung my arm down as I shouted, "Ein!" She understood and threw the stick to the right until the wings were nearly vertical. I had the perfect shot and pulled the trigger. She swung the stick the other way and the Hanna swung like a pendulum until the wings were nearly vertical again, giving me another shot. Another swing, another shot, and the SE pilot crashed into his own trench line.

Elsa reacquired the other SE type and resumed the chase, but it was too late for the other two- seater, which performed a crash-landing, wiping away its landing gear and ending up in a *kopfstand*. Elsa and I both fired at the SE type as it turned toward its own lines, but all I saw was a small trail of steam behind it. We later learned the two in the crashed aeroplane were banged around a little but otherwise alright.

Elsa took us back to the aerodrome and executed another perfect landing. Taxiing to a stop, she turned to me. "Now? May I see it *now?*"

"Never argue with a woman holding a machine gun" came to mind. *"Ja, mein liebchen.* You may see it now."

We exited the Hanna. "Take me to it, Gustav!" With one arm around my flying boots and the other around Elsa, I took her to the hangar door. The artist had painted a sign and hung it from the doorknob. "Mila awaits." I put down my boots and pulled open the door. Elsa stood still and gasped. "Oh, Gustav, she is beautiful!"

The Fokker had every element the artist had been asked to do. And more. The metal nose panels were painted a cupric orange. The same color was on the top center of the upper wing and both surfaces of the elevator. The exposed printed fabric portion of the fin was overpainted in a yellow-green color.

Elsa was elated. "How did you know to use these colors? This is perfect!"

"I used the stone you wear at your throat to get the colors. It's a pretty stone. It compliments your features."

"Mein Gustav gave me the stone. It's my favorite!" Elsa placed her hands on the artist's shoulders and kissed his cheek. *"Danke. Danke schön."* He closed his eyes. "Better than schnapps . . . ."

Jakob allowed me to telephone Fokker, who asked me to be back the next day sometime so we could get back to work. I assured him we would be back with tales to tell and I thanked him for the time away. I then telephoned the tavern, handing the receiver to Elsa before anyone picked up. She was delightful, telling Käti we would be there very soon. She asked if there would be any chocolate cake. I had to laugh. Jakob looked at me questioningly. He did not understand.

After exchanging goodbyes with Jakob and Art, Elsa and I took off to go visit Käti and Ernst. Coming to altitude, Elsa pointed toward the front. I waved her off and pointed the other way. I pictured the pout in my mind, for I could not tell if she did one under all that flying gear. But knowing *mein* Elsa, ...

It was good visiting with Käti and Ernst, even if it was brief. They were in good spirits, though Käti seemed a bit preoccupied. I knew she had a lot on her mind. She was, like many, resistant to change and part of her held onto hope that maybe things would blow over without much happening. She had her job, she had her cottage. Things could work out, just wait and see.

Ernst, on the other hand, was doing what he could to prepare for the inevitable. He was moving money out of Germany and preparing to sell the tavern. If all else failed, he would have Käti run it for him. She refused to listen to his warnings. She wanted no part of it. He knew he would have an honest, hard working manager, come what may. And if he sold, he could recommend Käti to the new owner.

Suffice to say Käti didn't have chocolate cake on her mind. It was a quiet evening, talking over wine. We all turned in early. Käti had the tavern to tend to, Elsa and I had to fly to Schwerin.

Ernst and Käti were along to see us off early in the morning. Käti loved Elsa's D.VII and the way it was painted. She asked that we make photographs of our aeroplanes, us standing with our aeroplanes, and so on. They would look good hanging in the tavern. I assured her that would be easy to arrange, as *Herr* Fokker loved to fuss with his cameras. If we asked him, he would no doubt film us flying. "That would be something to see," I thought.

There were rainclouds coming in from the west, so Elsa and I wanted to get into the air ahead of the turbulence. There were hugs all around. I told Käti once again that I would love to see her come to Schwerin, but she just smiled. I wanted to leave everything positive, so I let the idea drop. She knew that I cared for her. That was enough. We did not need to agree on everything.

I turned the Fokker around. Elsa checked that the switches were off so I could pull the propellers. We donned our flight gear, took our places in our "offices", cranked our BMWs to life, and lifted off. Before our small audience could get into the saloon to leave, Elsa rolled her Fokker. I followed her, rolling in the opposite direction. She looped, I looped. After a few more passes, we flew low over our friends and waved. Käti had on her most beautiful smile. Then it was on toward Schwerin. I thought I saw something ominous over the western horizon, but two little Fokkers were not likely to turn away a bombing formation. If indeed that was what I had seen. If Elsa had seen it, she did not let on. Knowing Elsa as I do, I'd say she didn't see it. It seemed she was not one to turn tail in the air. Then again, perhaps her increasing knowledge of flying—and fighting—had given her a sense of perspective.

* * * * *

CHAPTER 120

German

Anthony Fokker himself greeted us after we set down at Schwerin. He very much approved of Elsa's painted D.VII. "Model, wouldn't you like to have a new D.VII like Elsa's?"

"Oh, it would be nice, I'm sure, but there is nothing wrong with the one I have. What is the sense of fixing something that is not broken? *Danke,* but I prefer the one I have. Besides, I would look silly with a braid."

"Ha! That you would. But I would still appreciate your pragmatic nature. I am pleased you are both back. Apparently you met with the English at some point?"

"*Ja,* we did. Elsa defended us, beginning with damaging an SE type Sopwith from at least 350 yards. Damnedest shot I've seen. The bloke went home trailing smoke. The other two crashed below us."

"So our civilian colleague has what, five confirmed kills now? Most remarkable."

"*Ja,* that she is. You will see the five hash marks on her 'plane."

"*Ja,* nice touch! I like the patches on the wings, too. I must make photographs of it. Of both of them! If you don't mind, I can do it now and you can stand by your respective aeroplanes."

"That would be perfect, *mein Herr,* as long as we can drink something warm while you set up your camera. It may be summer here, but it's still winter at ten thousand feet."

"Of course! Meet here in fifteen minutes or so? Let's say twenty minutes and I will set up my motion picture camera. I can film you taking off and flying passes overhead."

"Good idea! We will wear our formal headgear."

"Your what? Oh, never mind. Formal headgear . . . ." He shook his head.

I would imagine most would see what happened next as completely silly. Mostly thawed, Elsa and I, minus our heavy boots and headgear, clowned for the camera with our Fokker D.VIIs as backdrop. We bowed and curtsied to one another, shook hands, stood arm in arm and smiled and waved. I helped Elsa into her boots and fastened her harness before performing my ritual of dropping my boots onto the seat, sitting on the turtledeck pulling on my boots, then sliding down onto the seat. While someone else operated the camera, Fokker himself secured my harness. Elsa took off, I took off. Elsa rolled, I rolled. Elsa looped, I looped. We flew side by side and waved at the camera below, then we landed. Fokker was beside himself.

"If all this film develops, it will be marketing gold! If only it would show the colors . . . ."

Fokker asked me to stop by his office to discuss projects once I had changed. He was still working on monoplanes and a two seat version of the D.VII. We went over a list of items to check on for each one. Then he asked about Elsa and her flying. "She is simply a natural, isn't she? And aggressive! Two more Englishmen down in what, ten minutes?"

"Five. She is remarkable. She flies completely by intuition, as if the 'plane becomes an extension of her being. And I have never seen such a sense of anticipation. It's like she reads her opponents' minds and counters their movements before they happen. She lives to fly, and she loves her new D.VII. And her only motivation for shooting is to keep me from harm. She is very protective."

"I don't mean to meddle in personal affairs, but didn't you say you have two *fräuleinen?* That seems unlikely if she is so protective."

"I don't mind. Yours is a fair and valid point. But Käti at one point saved Elsa's life and helped her to recover from a tragic personal situation. The two of them have a very strong bond between them and it happens they both like me for whatever reason."

"So the three of you all get along, as well as any two of you. Remarkable."

"I don't completely understand, but they are each remarkable women in their own right. Both attracted to me? I must be dreaming."

"But why will Käti not come here? Certainly she sees what is happening with the war and what will almost definitely happen once Germany loses. She must get out now."

"We have all told her, including the owner of the tavern she manages. She knows, but she refuses to believe it. Part of her thinks everything will simply continue as it is and always has been. The tavern, her cottage, everything. I refuse to fight with her or force her to do something she is not wont to do on her own. Her feelings deserve my respect whether I agree or not. She knows we both care for her and would love to have her along with us. That has to be enough. I can only hope she changes her mind and joins us."

"Too bad, Model. Why doesn't she fly?"

"Because of what happened when I took Elsa up in the Hannover. We went from seeing the view from three thousand feet to fighting for our lives. Käti wanted no part of that."

"Can't blame her. That was when Elsa shot three Englishmen, wasn't it?"

"*Ja.* Käti said she would fly when the shooting was over with. Sensible, that one."

"I hope she can. Let me know how I can help."

"*Danke, mein Herr,* but it's all up to Käti."

* * * * *

CHAPTER 121

German

And so it went. I continued working for Fokker as he prepared to vacate Schwerin in favor of his native Netherlands. Elsa and I would take a train over in order to look for somewhere to live.

We thought it odd we had not heard from Käti or Ernst, but we knew they were busy putting things in order. Or at least we hoped. In either case we would hear from them when it was convenient to them. We did not want to distract them from their efforts, as there was no telling when the end would come.

Occasionally I would hear from Jakob. Things were not well in his combined *Staffel*. Though they were beginning to receive Fokker's D.VIIs, there was no one experienced enough to help make a difference. Jakob was certain they were pulling students from schools, the new pilots looked so very young. He said it wasn't so much that they flew; they just managed not to crash. Much. The only painting Art was doing was applying dope to bullet patches. The Staffel was moving almost daily, such was the onslaught of Allied forces. The sky was full of British and American aeroplanes with a few French here and there. Jakob reported that Jure and Gwendolyn had fled from advancing Allied ground forces and were on the road somewhere looking for a place to live. His son did not understand and his *frau* was carrying another child. I knew well that Fokker could not employ the entire *Luftstreitkräfte,* but I suggested Jure look him up in Schwerin. Jakob responded by asking if Fokker could use someone experienced in paperwork and filing. His world was coming apart. After four years of fighting the enemy, he said it was closer to fighting to stay alive. He was unsure if the lack of communication from *IdFlieg* was failure on *IdFlieg's* part or breakdown of the communication network, but he suspected both were to blame. He was considering taking a new D.VII and flying it into Switzerland or the Netherlands, whichever was closer at any given time. Internment had to be better than retreat. He saw no chance of Germany winning the war short of divine intervention, and he was not holding his breath waiting for that. Understandably enough, Jakob sounded desperate.

* * * * *

CHAPTER 122

British

Since my first appearance at a War Bond rally was not exactly distant, I awoke Clara the next morning and made breakfast. Then she left for the nursing school and I left for the aerodrome to pick up my Camel and fly to the site of the rally. Upon arrival there were plenty of folks to point where I should leave my Camel. Mostly they wanted it in plain sight, but such that I would not blow away women and small children with prop wash when we started her up for the aerial demonstration.

I have to say it: I was bored. Speech after speech, trying to stay awake, waiting for my cue to get into the Camel. Well, first I was to be introduced to the crowd, walk back and forth across the stage and remind the audience that there were many like me still in France with the RAF, as well as any number of men—and women—around the world in other branches of service, not to mention field medical personnel. We were all fighting for king and country and protecting our citizens no matter where they traveled. "Please be generous with your War Bond purchases." Then someone else took over to talk about me while I pulled on a little extra clothing for my flight. I climbed the ladder to the cockpit, stepped in, sat down, received assistance with the lap strap, then donned my flight helmet and the damned white silk scarf they had given me "for appearances". Stage drama done with, we went through starting the engine, after which I took off and performed a five minute or so routine featuring rolls, loops, turns, dives, all the usual tricks. Though I had been cautioned and advised not to, I performed my signature "Lazy Eight" to finish the flight.

That was about it. I stayed afterward to sign pictures of me that were made available to any who were interested. It was fun, but it was also the first time and I saw where it would likely get old. No matter. King and country, stiff upper lip—at least no one was shooting at me.

I was back in time to start supper for Clara. She entered, took in the aroma, and sighed, "I think I am going to enjoy this new assignment." "No promises, my dear, but I will try."

"Oh, I know. But I can still cook, so don't worry about me." She patted her middle. "Missing a meal here and there would not be the worst thing, would it?"

"It's not worry, it's caring for someone I love deeply. And don't miss too many meals—I enjoy you as someone to have and to hold."

"Well, that's different then. Care away. I will get changed while you continue caring." She managed to recreate her front door routine in the kitchen, rubbing herself past me. "We need more room."

"Hardly," I smiled.

And so it went. There was the occasional overnight stay, but mostly I attended events in major population centers. More people to attend, more people reached, more effective expenditure of funds. It was routine, to be sure, but only for those of us putting on the rallies. I kept it firmly in mind that it was a unique experience for the people attending the rallies. While I had met many people, I tried to make everyone I greeted at the rallies feel somehow special. These people were footing the bill for the war. Many of them had lost loved ones in France, the Middle East, or anywhere around the world. They certainly deserved the respect of some RAF flyboy whose way they were also paying. There were similar speeches around the country, similar flying demonstrations, lots of handshaking and signing my name. It was indeed my duty to these people. And no one was shooting at me.

Until one day. I was flying a more or less standard aerial demonstration. Coming out of a roll, I was startled by the sound of machine guns behind me. I cursed out loud and looked over my shoulder to find a Fokker triplane hard on my tail. I knew immediately that it was Jeremy. I did a hard diving turn to port and threw him off as he was expecting the Camel's strongpoint of a turn to starboard. I was lucky to elude him and I knew it. The "fight" continued for several minutes before we broke things off and landed. I was so happy to see him that I gave him a big hug and then nearly pulled his arm off shaking his hand.

"Why didn't you tell me?"

"Would it have been as much fun?"

"No, I suppose not . . . but still!"

"Well, here I am. Now there are the two of us. Maybe we need to load you with blank rounds and organize a routine."

"And get you an oversized mustache and *pickelhaub* helmet."

"Playing to stereotypes?"

"It was a thought. Perhaps too theatrical?"

"Perhaps. However, if I am ordered . . . ."

"The order will not come from me. This silly white scarf is not my idea."

"How are things, sir? Still with Clara, I trust?"

"Yes, yes, of course. Let's meet the people and then we will catch up."

"Yes, sir. We could fly home and meet at the cafe if you like."

"Ripping, lad. We can take the motor-car your father bought for me."

"Yes, I've heard. Good for you—and there will be more."

"Hardly appropriate. I'm not his son, after all."

"Weren't. You weren't his son. Now it's a different story. Relax. We have been over this. We'll talk later."

"Aye, lad. Let's go meet the people who are paying for the war, one way or another."

Jeremy was a welcome addition. We got along famously, even if he always lost our encounters in the air. We both knew he was the better stunt pilot. Like me, however, Jeremy appreciated that no one was shooting at him. He got me caught up on what was happening at the front. The Fritzes were no more, or at least no longer worthy of note. Germany was hitting hard with their offenses, but some sensed desperation. There were many rumors circulating, more than normal. What would war be—or life, for that matter—without rumors? Like the weather, it gave people something to talk about, whether productive or no.

One of the many rumors heard around this time was that an American intelligence officer, a young captain, had looked over the intelligence data before him and predicted an offensive at the end of May to the south, across the *Chemin des Dames*. Virtually everyone scoffed at his prediction, thinking he, like the Americans in general, were new, green, and ridiculously out of touch. Everyone, that is, except the Germans. On 27 May they did exactly what the Yank captain had said they would do, attack over the ridge of the *Chemin des Dames* and by 5 June they had advanced about thirty miles to the Marne River and in the direction of Paris. So much for conventional thinking.

That was, however, the Germans' last hurrah. On 6 June American Army and Marine forces entered the war and simply outfought the Germans. Another German breakout to the north of that one was quelled by American and French troops. The tide was turning. The unleashing of fresh American forces, about a half million of them, was more than even the seasoned Germans could handle. Maybe, maybe, we would all be home by this Christmas. I was more than ready to take off and walk away from my uniform.

It appeared that the war was finally going the way we had been told for more than four years. Four years of mindless wholesale slaughter, feeding men and boys to the German aggressors and their modern weapons, and the War Department kept telling us everything was fine. From what we had gleaned from contacts and friends we had served with, it appeared they were finally correct.

Our Yank friend Wellington continued to add to his victory list. Scouts, two-seaters, observation balloons, bombers, high altitude observation aeroplanes, it made no difference to him. If it could be shot down, he shot it down. To his tangible victory list, add the intangible low level strafing and bombing. Intangible, that is, except to those on the receiving end. Though wounded several times, he made flight commander in another squadron. He was being considered for commander of a new Sopwith Snipe squadron, but the war ended before that could happen. He did very well for himself, considering his inauspicious beginnings. He dropped by my "home" aerodrome one day in a Snipe and we got caught up. He was now a remarkable young man, even a little humble. I asked if I could fly his Snipe, but he countered. "Take your Camel up and see what it will do with this!" I saw no reason not to, so I had the Camel prepped. Now I was no slouch in the Camel, but Welly cleaned my clock. At times I swore there were two of him.

The Snipe was not as agile as the Camel, but it excelled in every other way. Ahh, the march of progress in the quest to kill one's enemies. I then flew the Snipe and loved it, but the Camel was better suited for the job at hand. Its light weight and agility made it better over a small area. I asked what he was going to do once the war ended. He said he would transfer to the United States Army Signal Corps, of which the Air Service was a branch. He wanted to help form and expand the new unit and wanted it to be a separate branch of the military. He had high hopes of continuing the expansion of the Air Service and bringing American manufacturers on as suppliers of aeroplanes and equipment. He often mentioned an American officer he had befriended, a Billy Mitchell. He wholly subscribed to Mitchell's theories and shared his enthusiasm for flying and an American air arm.

The war was indeed winding down. The Germans had no choice but to sue for peace. They eventually chose to negotiate with the American president, Woodrow Wilson. His vision of the postwar world was more in line with what Germany hoped for, as opposed to the British and French visions which essentially dismantled Germany and made the country responsible for war reparations. The British and French were incensed, to say the least, that the Germans had bypassed them. The way the war was ended essentially planted the seeds for a much larger conflagration. Said seeds sprouted and bore fruit, so to speak, a generation later.

Back at Home Establishment, the War Bond rallies continued. Some of the things Jeremy had mentioned began to happen. His father requested that I visit and bring Clara with me. He told us he had been looking into real estate and wanted to buy us a house. He had several in mind, but we were free to look about and possibly find something on our own. He offered to buy the cottage Clara had been living in and help with anything needed to make it into a rental property. He suggested we take something on the edge of town or out in the country, the better for my pursuit of art and painting. He insisted I bring him receipts for any art supplies I purchased. I told him that was not at all necessary, but he insisted. "My lad, you will need the supplies in order to complete the commission for me."

"You want me to do a painting for you, Mr Trafford?"

"Of course. I will supply some photographs and newspaper photographs, whatever I can find for you, and I would like you to paint a portrait of my late wife. I want a traditional portrait, none of this cubist trash they are doing. Can you do that? Pauline simply loved you after what you did for our Jeremy. She talked of you almost constantly. I will of course reward you handsomely for your first commission. Oh. Flowers. Could your painting include flowers? She loved them."

I could not believe my ears. My first commission would be something I had wanted to do anyway? I knew just what to paint, Pauline in her dark green skirt and yellow floral blouse. I needed no photographs, but I would take every scrap Mr Trafford offered.

"Yes, Mr Trafford. I would be honored to paint your wife for you. She was a beautiful woman, quick, witty, and very intelligent. I will look forward to materials from you, and at the same time I will prepare some sketches for your approval. Thank you, sir."

"Clara, I have not forgotten you and your desire to advance in the medical field. I have been talking with others in the community on your behalf. There is still ample resistance, but I feel I am making headway. I hope you can work in your current capacity for the moment while I continue my efforts."

"Thank you, Mr Trafford. Of course, let me know if I may be of assistance."

"Oh, and you both may be interested to know that I am honoring a suggestion made by my late wife. I am bringing on two women to work in the design department. They will apprentice for now, and soon they will take the places of two men who will retire. Pauline used to pester me about women designing hats for women. In light of what you, Clara, are doing, I will be hiring more women in general. Times change, and I must change with them to remain relevant and competitive."

Clara responded, "That is wonderful, sir." I nodded my assent.

"Thank you both for coming over. Please look at the houses I have suggested. And others. Let me do this for you. It means a lot to me after how you have helped our son."

We thanked Mr Trafford for his generosity and offers, shook his hand, and departed, more than a little overwhelmed.

Clara and I looked over the properties Mr Trafford recommended, as well as quite a few others. We were in no hurry as Clara had her rented cottage. I moved into the cottage the following spring, after I finally left the RAF. I would have been out sooner, but Jeremy and I had such a wonderful time together flying for the War Bond rallies that I stayed past the end of the war. I finally left once Jeremy took another assignment which prevented his flying the rallies.

I lost track of the properties we considered. In the end, we purchased a plot of land outside town and had a house built. We did not intend for Mr Trafford to pay for any part of the venture, but he never flinched, paying for the plot and the structure, as well as anything dealing with my art studio and supplies. It happened that the plot we bought bordered a smallish airfield. I had a large hangar erected on the grounds. It was there that I stored several surplus SE5as, Camels, and two Fokker Triplanes, including the one Jeremy had modified in France. I had in mind a plan of sorts for after the war, and the surplus aeroplanes were to be central players.

Mr Trafford played a further role in our real estate ventures, buying the cottage Clara rented and selling it to her for ten pounds. She and I lived there until our house was completed and the cottage then became a rental property.

Jeremy stayed in the RAF a while longer, but finally left when he felt there were more and better opportunities for him in civilian life. He returned to the home where he was raised and took over running the household, which pleased his father to no end, not to mention the staff. He learned about his father's millinery, gradually taking over the business and allowing his father to relax somewhat. He knew his father had a "friend", but he never could divine her identity. Ah, well, good for them. After much consideration, Jeremy took up studying business, eventually earning a degree or two. He diversified into related clothing businesses, and landed some key government contracts. He had trusted management and paid them well, so his involvement was less than what his father had done. This allowed him to frequent my aeroplane collection and help maintain same.

On occasion, Jeremy and I would organize something of an aerobatics exhibition and ask a minimal charge to see it. Each exhibition drew more spectators, which planted a seed in our imaginations. There was something attractive about the notion of getting paid for what we enjoyed doing. And though our proceeds were meager at the time, we saw that it was possible. It fueled many a discussion while tending to our "fleet".

I still enjoyed blowing jass on the cornet, and I found a few outlets where I could play. There was a dance band in town not unlike the squadron orchestra I had sat in with. And there were a few rhythm sections in need of a soloist. I loved my music, still considering it painting for the ears. Jeremy became a fan, often dropping by to hear me play gigs and enjoying drinks and a few laughs. He made it a point of bringing me the other two cornets his mother had bought him. He liked to listen, but he didn't care to join me playing the "wretched things", as he called them.

I took Mr Trafford a number of sketches of Pauline, most of them after he lent me his promised materials. I truly did not need the materials, and the sketches were mostly done before I obtained them. He chose what he liked most, then used a few others to tweak the image to his liking. I put together a final sketch, which he approved. I painted what I have to say was—and is—a stunning likeness of a woman I loved and enjoyed immensely. Mr Trafford actually teared up when I delivered the final product, showing more emotion for the painting than I ever saw him show for the woman. I still shake my head over what he apparently failed to see in his wife. To wit, I did not have the entire story, so I cannot judge. They had both been more than wonderful to me, so I never criticized either of them. I had nothing but the kindest things to say about them.

Mr Trafford continued his work on Clara's behalf. He hired more women to work in his millinery. And, to show his dedication to Clara, he had her care for him when his person physician passed away. This was unheard of at that time, but by then he did not care. He had seen some of the things she had done in the medical field, starting with me. That mattered more to him than public opinion. In the meantime Clara continued as head of the nursing school. She worked to improve the quality of education to be had there and hired more female instructors. Along with her duties she took Pauline's case, did intensive research on various aspects, and published her findings in a noted medical journal. It upset her that she could not save Pauline, but she hoped her findings would lead to more information and possibly prevent another death.

I was in my top floor studio one day, working on sketches for the cafe proprietor's painting of the HMS Dreadnought, when I heard a motor-car stop outside the house, then drive away. No harm done, I thought, and I returned to my sketching. Then I heard someone at the door. As I started down the steps I heard a man's voice. His English was somewhat halting. Approaching the door, I heard him ask, "Misster Noble Brown? Hallo? *Achtung! Herr Leutnant?*" Was the voice somewhat familiar? I hesitated, then opened the door to receive a grand surprise, one I had hoped for but never expected. I was thrilled and elated at my good fortune. This was going to be good!

GERMAN TRANSLATIONS:

Scheisse—shit

Kampfflieger—military pilot

Jagdstaffel—fighter squadron

Pickelhauben—slang for the highest German military strategists, referring to the German WWI helmet with spike on top. Similar to Allied "brass hats".

Gitterschwanz—"lattice tail", referring to Allied pusher designs and how the tail control surfaces were connected to the rest of the aeroplane

Huaptmann—military (army) captain

Fliegertruppe—German air fighting unit early in the war. This name was changed in 1916.

Eiserne Kreuz—Iron Cross

Mein Herr—sir, as in military respect

Javohl—certainly, yes, of course—a term of ascent

Gasmaske—gas mask

Auf wiedersehen—goodbye

Fräulein—unmarried woman

Kinder—children

EK II—military award, Iron Cross second class

Kaput—finished, done for, dead

Oberleutnant—First Lieutenant

Schweinhund—swine, bastard, son of a bitch, etc.

Gott im Himmel!—heavens above!

Guten tag—(greeting) good day

Lieber—dear

Walfisch—whale

Vizefeldwebel—military (army) rank similar to corporal

Schlactstaffel—battle squadron, attack squadron

Nicht mit der mein Herr scheisse!—roughly, "None of this 'sir' shit!"

Benzin—gasoline

Alte (frau)—old (woman)

Leutnant—lieutenant
Schöne (maid)—fair, beautiful, lovely (maiden)
Kamerad—comrade, friend
Jäger—fighter
Unseren Dank—our thanks
Walzer König—waltz king
Unseren arsch—our butts
Liebchen—sweetheart
Das kind—the child
Jastaführer—fighter squadron commander
Schlastführer—attack squadron commander
Jägern—fighters
Einsitzer—single seater (fighter aircraft)
Jagdfliegern—fighter pilots
Scheisskopf—shithead
Tot—dead
IdFlieg—German inspectorate of air power
Oberst—(army) colonel
Abteilung—unit, section, department, squadron
Flugzeug—aeroplane
Moment mal!—Just a minute!
Nichts—nothing more
Unterflügel—lower wing
Maskotte—mascot
Deinen hintern—your backsides (bottoms, butts, hides)
Guten morgen, jungens!—Good morning, boys!
Euch alles—you all
Schluss Jetzt!—That's enough!
Ich bin der dummkopf hier.—I am the stupid one here.
Du bist verdammt verrückt, und ich hasse dich!—You are fucking crazy
and I hate you!
Freund—friend
Gern geschehen—you're welcome, my pleasure
Feldwebel—sergeant
Zwei Bastarde—two bastards

So ist der krieg—such is war
Gefangen—captive, prisoner
Ich liebe dich—I love you
Tochter—daughter
Kunst—art
Kopfstand—headstand

CPSIA information can be obtained
at www.ICGtesting.com
Printed in the USA
BVHW031617020419
544230BV00049B/5/P

9 781796 020694